WELCOME  WORLDS OF
!

D0782837

TAKE A TOUR of the hot spots of Venus with guide Audee Walthers, in the very first Heechee story, "The Merchants of Venus."

FIND OUT WHAT HAPPENS when the world's greatest mentalist gets a little too good at fooling his public in "The Things That Happen."

EXPLORE A FUTURISTIC NEW YORK CITY, where new technology and old vices vie for control of radical urban re-engineering in "The Greening of Bed-Stuy."

SHARE THE EXCITEMENT of an alternate history in which aging pilot Johnny Williamson is rejected by NASA's astronaut program, until his act of heroism on a fateful day in Dallas gives him the chance to play a pivotal role in the Apollo program in "The Mayor of Mare Tranq."

GET A PEEK into the world of Marchese Boccanegra in "Saucery," when the discovery of real Martians makes it hell for honest frauds to make a living.

EXPERIENCE A SPINE-CHILLING VIEW of nuclear holocaust, where the best luck is to just survive, in the chilling, poignant Hugo Award–winning "Fermi and Frost."

GO ALONG FOR AN INCREDIBLE RIDE to a far star, in a mind-bending trip with a crew bound for a payoff beyond human comprehension, in the stunning novella "The Gold at the Starbow's End."

"These carefully selected tales really are platinum Pohl,
so there's not a foot misplaced in all the thirty stories."
—Gahan Wilson, *Realms of Fantasy*

ALSO BY FREDERIK POHL

*denotes a Tor Book

PLATINUM POHL

THE COLLECTED BEST STORIES

FREDERIK POHL

ORB

A TOM DOHERTY ASSOCIATES BOOK

NEW YORK

This is a work of fiction. All the characters, organizations, and events portrayed in these stories are either products of the author's imagination or are used fictitiously.

PLATINUM POHL: THE COLLECTED BEST STORIES

First publication and copyright information for reprinted material appears on pages 461 through 463, which constitute a continuation of this copyright page.

Edited by James Frenkel

An Orb Book
Published by Tom Doherty Associates, LLC
175 Fifth Avenue
New York, NY 10010

www.tor.com

Library of Congress Cataloging-in-Publication Data

Pohl, Frederik,
    Platinum Pohl : the collected best stories / Frederik Pohl.
       p. cm.
    "A Tom Doherty Associates book."
    ISBN-13: 978-0-765-30145-1
    ISBN-10: 0-765-30145-8
    1. Science fiction, American. I. Title.

PS3566.O36A6 2005
813'.54—dc22

                                            2005043965

Printed in the United States of America

For my great-granddaughter,
ALEXANDRA EMŐKE VIOLET ANN POHL-WEARY
(better known as Sasha),
and for all who come after

CONTENTS

INTRODUCTION

·   ·

FREDERIK POHL HAS DONE just about everything that one can do in the field of science fiction. When he was still a teenager he began to edit science fiction magazines; he started getting his stories published when he was even younger. He has won all the major awards—the Hugo, Nebula, and Campbell for best novel; he has been lauded as a Grand Master by the Science Fiction Writers of America; he's written an enormous number of very good short stories; and he has collaborated on both short stories and novels, both with great success.

If this weren't enough, he has also edited anthologies, including the groundbreaking Star Science Fiction anthologies of original stories. In addition, he's edited lines of SF books for Bantam and Ace, at different times. He has been an agent; he has been president of the SFWA.

He has achieved other notable feats in the field as well, but I think you can get an idea. This man is one of the giants in the field.

Editing this volume of his collected best stories was both a joy and a nightmare. In the course of his career so far, he has written hundreds of stories. Some were originally published under pseudonyms, others were collaborations with other authors. (Still others were pseudonymous collaborations!) When you count up the stories and the total wordage, he has produced more than a million words of short fiction—this in addition to his many novels.

The thirty stories that follow represent fiction from as early as the 1940s and as recent as just a few years ago. Our goal in this collection is to present the best short stories, novelettes, and novellas of Frederik Pohl's career to date. He's still writing, of course, but we had to stop somewhere . . . though we reserve the right to include new stories in a subsequent edition of this book. There are some exclusions. Some of Pohl's short stories have been incorporated into his novels, and we have not included stories that he later used in creating longer works. Nonetheless, we have included stories from two books that could easily be considered novels: *The Day the Martians Came* and *The Years of the City*. In both these books, the stories are identifiable as discrete stories, but also exist as elements in a longer narrative.

Frederik Pohl started writing science fiction when he was very young, when the field itself was pretty young, too. In many of the stories reprinted here one can clearly see what many call the "sense of wonder" that inspired Pohl and his young contemporaries—authors such as Isaac Asimov, Damon Knight, Richard Wilson, Donald A. Wollheim, and others—when they were starting to write and publish stories in the 1930s, and that still inspires science fiction writers—and editors and readers—today.

Many young people have that sense of wonder—a curiosity about what lies outside the bounds of our world or in the future. However, most people lose that curiosity—the need to explore, to play in realms outside their experience—as they get older. One of the many pleasures of this collection is seeing the persistence of Pohl's sense of wonder in stories penned over more than a half century.

In a very real way, these stories are twentieth-century fiction, marked by the events and reflecting sociopolitical currents of the century. Yet like any really good literature, they also transcend their time, because of their profound humanity, the universality of their themes, and overarching concerns.

We've included some stories that put the reader in a specific place and time that Pohl captures with unerring accuracy—in some cases the time of the story's creation, in others a time or a scenario perhaps yet to come. Pohl is gifted with a very sharp eye for human behavior and with a great ear for dialogue, and these talents hold him in very good stead when he is evoking the *now*—whether in a contemporary setting or an entirely alien one.

He also has a fine grasp of politics and for the workings of legislative bodies, the courts, and other human institutions. To be sure, his models tend to be United States institutions, but he does excellent research, and when he's writing about someplace other than the United States, you can depend on his observations of those places being accurate; like many auhors, Pohl has traveled widely, and he brings to stories set overseas his careful first-person observations.

Readers who did not experience much of the twentieth century will find among these stories a considerable amount of cultural and social history expertly masked in the guise of necessary background, for Pohl, like generations of savvy observers, has always made society a big part of the story. Sociopolitical issues such as the threat of global nuclear war, overpopulation, pollution, and dependence on fossil fuels, to name but a few, are key elements in some of the stories. So are issues of social justice, about which Pohl is passionate.

Yet the issues that run through many of these stories never overwhelm the stories themselves. Pohl's characters just won't let them. Those characters are a varied and fascinating bunch—young and old, male and female, nasty and nice—they're all people who engage your interest, whether or not you agree with what they say and do. That, perhaps, is Pohl's greatest achievement. Creating characters that come to seem vividly alive and real may not sound very difficult, but there are many writers who fail to create such characters despite possessing other formidable skills. And his stories *move*. No matter what the tale, there is invariably something intriguing going on, something that engages your interest and won't let you stop reading.

Some of these stories are very serious, while others are just fun. Long hours were spent by this editor trying to decide which stories to keep and which to exclude, and there were dozens of very entertaining stories that had to be left out, because this book could not be a thousand pages long.

When all was said and done, we ended up with stories that showcase the enormous range of tone and texture, concepts and themes, plots and characters that Frederik Pohl has brought to life in his fiction. Early in this introduction I wrote it had been a joy and a nightmare to edit this collection, but that's not really true. Though deciding what should stay and what must go was terribly difficult, it was also an enormous amount of fun, because it gave me a chance to experience the richness of the stories.

May you enjoy these choices as much as I have.

—James Frenkel
Madison, Wisconsin
March 1, 2005

PLATINUM POHL

THE MERCHANTS OF VENUS

Frederik Pohl has probably heard from too many readers about the pun in the title of this suspenseful novella. The answer to your question is: No. This has nothing much to do with Shakespeare's play. It has a lot to do with Venus, with people living on the edge, with the spirit of exploration, and the reasons people have for doing dangerous and otherwise risky business.

"The Merchants of Venus," first published in 1972, was also the first story Pohl wrote about the presence of mysterious alien Heechee in the solar system. Since then, he has written a *lot* about the Heechee, and readers have been much the better for his interest in the artifacts and other leavings of that race. *Gateway* (1976), his first novel about our discovery of the Heechee, won the triple crown of science fiction—the Hugo, Nebula, and John W. Campbell Memorial Awards for best novel—and that was just the beginning of a memorable series of books.

Before *Gateway* came "The Merchants of Venus."

1

My Name, Audee Walthers. My job, airbody driver. My home, on Venus, in a Heechee hut most of the time; wherever I happen to be when I feel sleepy otherwise.

Until I was twenty-five I lived on Earth, in Amarillo Central mostly. My father, a deputy governor of Texas. He died when I was still in college, but he left me enough dependency benefits to finish school, get a master's in business administration, and pass the journeyman examination for clerk-typist. So I was set up for life.

But, after I tried it for a few years, I discovered I didn't like the life I was set up for. Not so much for the conventional reasons; I don't mind smog suits, can get along with neighbors even when there are eight hundred of them to the square mile, tolerate noise, can defend myself against the hood kids. It wasn't Earth itself I didn't like, it was what I was doing on Earth I didn't like, and so I sold my UOPWA journeyman's card, mortgaged my pension accrual, and bought a one-way ticket to Venus. Nothing strange about that. What every kid tells himself he's going to do, really. But I did it.

I suppose it would have been all different if I'd had a chance at Real Money. If my father had been full governor instead of a civil-service client. If the dependency benefits had included Unlimited Medicare. If I'd been at the top instead of in the middle, squeezed both ways. It didn't happen that way, so I opted out by the pioneer route and wound up hunting Terry marks at the Spindle.

Everybody has seen pictures of the Spindle, the Colosseum and Niagara Falls. Like everything worth looking at on Venus, the Spindle was a Heechee leftover. Nobody had ever figured out what the Heechee wanted with an underground chamber three hundred meters long and spindle-shaped, but it was there, so we used it; it was the closest thing Venus had to a Times Square or a Champs Elysées. All Terry tourists head for it first. That's where we fleece them.

My airbody-rental business is reasonably legitimate—not counting the fact that there really isn't much worth seeing on Venus that wasn't left there, below the surface, by the Heechee. The other tourist traps in the Spindle are reasonably crooked. Terries don't mind, although they must know they're being taken; they all load up on Heechee prayer fans and doll-heads, and those paperweights of transparent plastic in which a contoured globe of Venus swims in a kind of orange-brown snowstorm of make-believe fly ash, blood-diamonds, and fire-pearls. None of them are worth the price of their mass-charge back to Earth, but to a tourist who can get up the price of passage in the first place I don't suppose that matters.

To people like me, who can't get the price of anything, the tourist traps matter a lot. We live on them. I don't mean we draw our disposable income from them; I mean that they are how we get the price of what to eat and where to sleep, and if we don't have the price we die. There aren't too many ways of earning money on Venus. The ones that might produce Real Money—oh, winning a lottery; striking it rich in the Heechee diggings; blundering into a well-paying job; that kind of thing—are all real long-shots. For bread and butter everybody on Venus depends on Terry tourists, and if we don't milk them dry we've had it.

Of course, there are tourists and tourists. They come in three varieties. The difference between them is celestial mechanics.

There's the quick-and-dirty kind. On Earth, they're just well-to-do; they come every twenty-six months at Hohmann-orbit time, riding the minimum-energy circuit from Earth. Because of the critical times of a Hohmann orbit, they never can stay more than three weeks on Venus. So they come on the guided tours, determined to get the most out of the quarter-million-dollar minimum cabin fare their rich grandparents had given them for a graduation present, or they'd saved up for a second honeymoon, or whatever. The bad thing about them is that they don't have much money, since they'd spent it all on fares. The nice thing about them is that there are a lot of them. While they're on Venus, all the rental rooms are filled. Sometimes they'd have six couples sharing a single partitioned cubicle, two pairs at a time, hot-bedding eight-hour shifts around the clock. Then people like me would hold up in Heechee huts on the surface and rent out our own belowground rooms, and maybe make enough money to live a few months.

But you couldn't make enough money to live until the next Hohmann-orbit time, so when the Class II tourists came along we cut each other's throats over them.

They were medium-rich. What you might call the poor millionaires: the ones whose annual income was barely in seven figures. They could afford to come in powered orbits, taking a hundred days or so for the run, instead of the long, slow Hohmann drift. The price ran a million dollars and up, so there weren't nearly as many of them; but they came every month or so at the times of reasonably favorable orbital conjunctions. They also had more money to spend. So did the other medium-rich ones who hit us four or five times in a decade, when the ballistics of the planets had sorted themselves out into a low-energy configuration that allowed three planets to come into an orbit that didn't have much higher energy cost than the straight Earth-Venus run. They'd hit us first, if we were lucky, then go on to Mars. If it was the other way around, we got the leavings. The leavings were never very much.

But the very rich—ah, the very rich! They came as they liked, in orbital season or out.

When my tipper on the landing pad reported the *Yuri Gagarin,* under private charter, my money nose began to quiver. It was out of season for everybody except the very rich; the only question on my mind was how many of my competitors would be trying to cut my throat for its passengers while I was cutting theirs.

Airbody rental takes a lot more capital than opening a prayer-fan booth. I'd been lucky in buying my airbody cheap when the fellow I worked for died; I didn't have too many competitors, and a couple of them were U/S for repairs, a couple more had kited off on Heechee diggings of their own.

So, actually, I had the *Gagarin's* passengers, whoever they were, pretty much to myself. Assuming they could be interested in taking a trip outside the Heechee tunnels.

I had to assume they would be interested, because I needed the money very much. I had this little liver condition, you see. It was getting pretty close to total failure. The way the doctors explained it to me, I had like three choices: I could go back to Earth and linger a while on external prostheses; or I could get up the money for a transplant. Or I could die.

2

The name of the fellow who had chartered the *Gagarin* was Boyce Cochenour. Age, apparently forty. Height, two meters. Ancestry, Irish-American-French.

He was the kind of fellow who was used to command. I watched him come into the Spindle as though it belonged to him and he was getting ready to sell it. He sat down in Sub Vastra's imitation Paris Boulevard-Heechee sidewalk cafe. "Scotch," he said, and Vastra hurried to pour John Begg over super-cooled ice and hand it to him, all crackling with cold and numbing to the lips. "Smoke," he said, and the girl who was traveling with him instantly lit a cigarette and passed it to him. "Crummy-looking joint," he said, and Vastra fell all over himself to agree.

I sat down next to them—well, not at the same table, I mean; I didn't even look at them. But I could hear what they said. Vastra didn't look at me, either, but of course he had seen me come in and knew I had my eye on them. But I had to let his number-three wife take my order, because Vastra wasn't going to waste any time on me when he had a charter-ship Terry at his table. "The usual," I said to her, meaning straighttalk in a tumbler of soft drink. "And a copy of your briefing," I added, more softly. Her eyes twinkled at me over her flirtation veil. Cute little vixen. I patted her hand in a friendly way, and left a rolled-up bill in it; then she left.

The Terry was inspecting his surroundings, including me. I looked back at him, polite but distant, and he gave me a sort of quarter-nod and turned back to Subhash Vastra. "Since I'm here," he said, "I might as well go along with whatever action there is. What's to do here?"

Sub grinned widely, like a tall, skinny frog. "Ah, whatever you wish, sah! Entertainment? In our private rooms we have the finest artists of three planets, nautch dancers, music, fine comedians—"

"We've got plenty of that in Cincinnati. I didn't come to Venus for a nightclub act." He wouldn't have known it, of course, but that was a good move; Sub's private rooms were way down the list of night spots on Venus, and the top of the list wasn't much.

"Of course, sah! Then perhaps you would like to consider a tour?"

"Aw." Cochenour shook his head. "What's the point? Does any of it look any different than the space pad we came in on, right over our heads?"

Vastra hesitated; I could see him calculating second-order consequences in his head, measuring the chance of the Terry going for a surface tour against what he might get from me as commission. He didn't look my way. Honesty won out—that is, honesty reinforced by a quick appraisal of Cochenour's gullibility. "Not much different, no, sah," he admitted. "All pretty hot and dry on the surface, at least for the next thousand kilometers. But I wasn't thinking of the surface."

"What then?"

"Ah, the Heechee warrens, sah! There are many miles just below this settlement. A guide could be found—"

"Not interested," Cochenour growled. "Not in anything that close."

"Sah?"

"If a guide can lead us through them," Cochenour explained, "that means they've all been explored. Which means they've been looted. What's the fun of that?"

"Of course," said Vastra immediately. "I see what you're driving at, sah." He looked noticeably happier, and I could feel his radar reaching out to make sure I was listening, though he didn't look in my direction at all. "To be sure," he said, "there is always the chance of finding new digs, sah, provided one knows where to look. Am I correct in assuming that this would interest you?"

The third of Vastra's house brought me my drink and a thin powder-faxed slip of paper. "Thirty percent," I whispered to her. "Tell Sub. Only no bargaining, no getting anybody else to bid—" She nodded and winked; she'd been listening too, and she was as sure as I that this Terry was firmly on the hook. It had been my intention to nurse the drink as long as I could, but prosperity loomed before me; I was ready to celebrate; I took a long happy swallow.

But the hook didn't have a barb. Unaccountably the Terry shrugged. "Waste of time, I bet," he grumbled. "I mean, really. If you knew where to look, why wouldn't you have looked there already, right?"

"Ah, mister," cried Subhash Vastra, "but there are hundreds of tunnels not explored! Thousands! And in them, who knows, treasures beyond price!"

Cochenour shook his head. "Skip it," he said. "Bring us another drink. And see if you can't get the ice *cold* this time."

Somewhat shaken, I put down my drink, half-turned away to hide my hand from the Terries, and looked at the facsimile copy of Sub's report on them to see if it could tell me why Cochenour had lost interest.

It couldn't. It did tell me a lot, though. The girl with Cochenour was named Dorotha Keefer. She had been traveling with him for a couple of years now, this being their first time off Earth; there was no indication of any marriage, or any intention of it, at least on his part. She was in her early twenties—real age, not simulated by drugs and trans-plants. Cochenour himself was well over ninety.

He did not, of course, look anywhere near that. I'd watched him come over to the table, and he moved lightly and easily, for a big man. His money came from land and petro-foods; according to the synoptic on him, he had been one of the first oil million-aires to switch over from selling oil as fuel for cars and heating plants to food produc-tion, growing algae in the crude that came out of his wells and selling the algae in processed form for human consumption. So he'd stopped being a mere millionaire and turned into something much bigger.

And that accounted for the way he looked. He'd been on Full Medical, with extras. The report said his heart was titanium and plastic. His lungs had been transplanted from a twenty-year-old killed in a copter crash. His skin, muscles and fats—not to mention his various glandular systems—were sustained by hormones and cell-builders at what had to be a cost of well over a thousand dollars a day. To judge by the way he stroked the girl sitting next to him, he was getting his money's worth. He looked and acted no more than forty, at most—except perhaps for the look of his pale-blue, diamond-bright, weary and disillusioned eyes.

What a lovely mark! I swallowed the rest of my drink, and nodded to the third for another. There had to be a way to get him to charter my airbody.

All I had to do was find it.

Outside the rail of Vastra's cafe, of course, half the Spindle was thinking exactly the same thoughts. This was the worst of the low season, the Hohmann crowd were still three months in the future; all of us were beginning to run low on money. My liver transplant was just a little extra incentive; of the hundred maze-runners I could see out of the corner of my eye, ninety-nine needed to cut in on this rich tourist's money as much as I did, just for the sake of staying alive.

We couldn't all do it. Two of us, three, maybe even half a dozen could score enough to make a real difference. No more than that. And I had to be one of these few.

I took a deep swallow of my second drink, tipped Vastra's third lavishly—and conspicuously—and turned idly around until I was facing the Terries dead-on.

The girl was talking with a knot of souvenir vendors, looking interested and uncer-tain. "Boyce?" she said over her shoulder.

"Yeah?"

"What's this thing for?"

He bent over the rail and peered. "Looks like a fan," he said.

"Heechee prayer fan, right," cried the dealer; I knew him, Booker Allemang, an old-timer in the Spindle. "Found it myself, miss! It'll grant your every wish, letters every day from people reporting miraculous results—"

"Sucker bait," grumbled Cochenour. "Buy it if you want."

"But what does it do?"

He laughed raucously. "What any fan does. It cools you down." And he looked at me, grinning.

I finished my drink, nodded, stood up and walked over to the table. "Welcome to Venus," I said. "May I help you?"

The girl looked at Cochenour for approval before she said, "I thought this was very pretty."

"Very pretty," I agreed. "Are you familiar with the story of the Heechees?"

Cochenour pointed to a chair. I sat and went on. "They built these tunnels about a quarter of a million years ago. They lived here for a couple of centuries, give or take a lot. Then they went away again. They left a lot of junk behind, and some things that weren't junk; among other things they left a lot of these fans. Some local con man like BeeGee here got the idea of calling them 'prayer fans' and selling them to tourists to make wishes with."

Allemang had been hanging on my every word trying to guess where I was going. "You know it's right," he said.

"But you two are too smart for that kind of come-on," I added. "Still, look at the things. They're pretty enough to be worth having even without the story."

"Absolutely!" cried Allemang. "See how this one sparkles, miss! And the black and gray crystal, how nice it looks with your fair hair!"

The girl unfurled the crystalline one. It came rolled like a diploma, only cone-shaped. It took just the slightest pressure of the thumb to keep it open, and it really was very pretty as she waved it gently. Like all the Heechee fans, it weighed only about ten grams, and its crystalline lattice caught the lights from the luminous Heechee walls, as well as the fluorescents and gas tubes we maze-runners had installed, and tossed them all back in iridescent sparks.

"This fellow's name is Booker Garey Allemang," I said. "He'll sell you the same goods as any of the others, but he won't cheat you as much as most of them."

Cochenour looked at me dourly, then beckoned Sub Vastra for another round of drinks. "All right," he said. "If we buy, we'll buy from you, Booker Garey Allemang. But not now."

He turned to me. "And what do you want to sell me?"

"Myself and my airbody, if you want to go looking for new tunnels. We're both as good as you can get."

"How much?"

"One million dollars," I said immediately. "All found."

He didn't answer at once, though it gave me some pleasure to notice that the price didn't seem to scare him. He looked as pleasant, or anyway as unangrily bored, as ever. "Drink up," he said, as Vastra and his third served us, and gestured with his glass to the Spindle. "Know what this was for?" he asked.

"You mean why the Heechees built it? No. They were pretty small, so it wasn't for headroom. And it was entirely empty when it was found."

He gazed tolerantly at the busy scene, balconies cut into the sloping sides of the Spindle with eating and drinking places like Vastra's, rows of souvenir booths, most of them empty at this idle season. But there were still a couple of hundred maze rats around, and the number had been quietly growing all the time Cochenour and the girl had been sitting there.

He said, "It's not much to see, is it? A hole in the ground, and a lot of people trying to take my money away from me."

I shrugged.

He grinned again. "So why did I come, eh? Well, that's a good question, but since you didn't ask it I don't have to answer it. You want a million dollars. Let's see. A hundred K to charter an airbody. A hundred and eighty or so to rent equipment, per week. Ten days minimum, three weeks a safer guess. Food, supplies, permits, another fifty K. So we're up to close to seven hundred thousand, not counting your own salary and what you give our host here as his cut for not throwing you off the premises. Right, Walthers?"

I had a little difficulty in swallowing the drink I had been holding to my mouth, but I managed to say, "Close enough, Mr. Cochenour." I didn't see any point in telling him that I already owned the equipment, as well as the airbody, although I wouldn't have been surprised to find out that he knew that too.

"You've got a deal, then. And I want to leave as soon as possible, which should be, um, about this time tomorrow."

"Fair enough," I said, and got up, avoiding Sub Vastra's thunderstricken expression. I had some work to do, and a little thinking. He'd caught me off base, which is a bad place to be when you can't afford to make a mistake. I knew he hadn't missed my calling him by name. That was all right; he'd known that I had checked him out immediately. But it was a little surprising that he had known mine.

3

The first thing I had to do was double-check my equipment; the second was go to the local, validate a contract, and settle up with Sub Vastra; the third was see my doctor. The liver hadn't been giving me much trouble for a while, but then I hadn't been drinking grain alcohol for a while.

It took about an hour to make sure that everything we would need for the expedition was i.s., with all the spare parts I might reasonably fear needing. The Quackery was on my way to the union office, so I stopped in there first. It didn't take long. The news was no worse than I had been ready for; Dr. Morius studied the readout from his instruments carefully. It turned out to be a hundred and fifty dollars' worth of carefully, and expressed the guarded hope that I would survive three weeks away from his office, provided I took all the stuff he gave me and wandered no more than usual from his dietary restrictions. "And when I get back?" I asked.

"About the same, Audee," he said cheerily. "Total collapse in, ah, oh, maybe ninety more days."

He patted his fingertips. "I hear you've got a live one," he added. "Want me to book you for a transplant?"

"How live did you hear he was?" I asked.

"Oh, the price is the same in any case," he told me good-humoredly. "Two hundred K, plus the hospital, anesthesiologist, preop psychiatrist, pharmaceuticals—you've already got the figures."

I did, and I knew that with what I might make from Cochenour, plus what I had put away, plus a small loan on the airbody, I could just about meet it. Leaving me broke when it was over but, of course, alive.

"Go ahead," I said. "Three weeks from tomorrow." And I left him looking mildly pleased, like a Burmese hydro-rice man watching another crop being harvested. Dear daddy. Why hadn't he sent me through medical school instead of giving me an education?

It would have been nice if the Heechee had been the same size as human beings, instead of being about 40 percent shorter. In the smaller tunnels, like the one that led to the Local 88 office, I had to half-crouch all the way.

The deputy organizer was waiting for me. He had one of the few good jobs that didn't depend on the tourists, or at least not directly. He said, "Subhash Vastra's been on the line. He says you agreed to thirty percent, and besides you forgot to pay your bar bill to the third of his house."

"Admitted, both ways."

"And you owe me a little too, Audee. Three hundred for a powderfax copy of my report on your pigeon. A hundred for validating your contract with Vastra. And if you want guide's papers, sixteen hundred for that."

I gave him my credit card and he checked the total out of my account into the local's. Then I signed and card-stamped the contract he'd drawn up. Vastra's 30 percent would not be on the whole million-dollar gross, but on my net; even so, he might make as much out of it as I would, at least in liquid cash, because I'd have to pay off all the outstanding balances on equipment and loans. The factors would carry a man until he scored, but then they wanted to get paid. They knew how long it might be until he scored again.

"Thanks, Audee," said the deputy, nodding over the signed contract. "Anything else I can do for you?"

"Not at your prices," I told him.

"Ah, you're putting me on. 'Boyce Cochenour and Dorotha Keefer, Earth-Ohio, traveling *S. V. Yuri Gagarin,* Odessa registry, chartered. No other passengers.' No other passengers," he repeated, quoting from the synoptic report he'd furnished. "Why, you'll be a rich man, Audee, if you work this pigeon right."

"That's more than I ask," I told him. "All I want is to be a living one."

But it wasn't entirely true. I did have some little hope—not much, not enough to talk about, and in fact I'd never said a word about it to anyone—that I might be coming out of this rather better than merely alive.

There was, however, a problem.

See, in the standard guide's contract and airbody leasing terms, I get my money and that's all I get. If we take a mark like Cochenour on a hunt for new Heechee tunnels and he finds something valuable—marks have, you know; not often, but enough to keep them hopeful—then it's his. We just work for him.

On the other hand, I could have gone out by myself any time and prospected; and then anything I found would be all mine.

Obviously anybody with any sense would go by himself if he thought he was really going to find anything. But in my case, that wasn't such a good idea. If I staked myself to a trip and lost, I hadn't just wasted time and maybe fifty K in supplies and wear and tear. If I lost, I was dead.

I needed what I would make out of Cochenour to stay alive. Whether we found anything interesting or not, my fee would take care of that.

Unfortunately for my peace of mind, I had a notion that I knew where something very interesting might be found; and my problem was that, as long as I had an all-rights contract with Cochenour. I couldn't afford to find it.

The last stop I made was in my sleeping room. Under the bed, keystoned into the rock, was a guaranteed break-proof safe that held some papers I wanted to have in my pocket from then on.

When I came down on to Venus for the first time, it wasn't scenery that interested me. I wanted to make my fortune.

I didn't see much of the surface of Venus then, or for nearly two years after that. You don't see much in the kind of spacecraft that can land on Venus; a twenty-thousand-millibar surface pressure means you need something a little more rugged than the bubble-ships that go to the Moon or Mars or farther out, and there's not much tolerance in the design for putting unnecessary windows into the hull. It didn't matter much, because anywhere except near the poles there's not much you can see. Everything worth seeing on Venus is *in* Venus, and all of it once belonged to the Heechees.

Not that we know much about the Heechees. We don't even rightly know their name—"heechee" is how somebody once wrote down the sound that a fire-pearl makes when you stroke it, and as that's the only sound anybody knows that's connected with them, it got to be a name.

The hesperologists don't know where the Heechees came from, although there are some markings on scraps of stuff that the Heechees used for paper that seem to be a star chart—faded, incomplete, pretty much unrecognizable; if we know the exact position of every star in the galaxy two hundred fifty thousand years ago, we might be able to locate them from that, I suppose. Assuming they came from this galaxy. There are no traces of them anywhere else in the solar system, except maybe in Phobos; the experts still fight about whether the honeycomb cells inside the Martian moon are natural or artifacts, and if they're artifacts they're no doubt Heechee. But they don't look much like ours.

I wonder sometimes what they wanted. Escaping a dying planet? Political refugees? Tourists that had a breakdown between somewhere and somewhere, and hung around just long enough to make whatever they had to make to get themselves going again? I used to think that they'd maybe come by to watch human beings evolving on Earth, sort of stepfathers beaming over the growing young race; but we couldn't have been much to watch at that time, halfway between the Australopithecines and the Cro-Magnards.

But, though they packed up nearly everything when they left, leaving behind only empty tunnels and chambers, there were a few scraps here and there that either weren't worth taking along or were overlooked: all those "prayer fans," enough empty containers of one kind or another to look like a picnic ground at the end of a hard summer, some trinkets and trifles. I guess the best known of the "trifles" is the anisokinetic punch, the carbon crystal that transmits a blow at a ninety-degree angle; that made somebody a few billion just by being lucky enough to find one, and smart enough to analyze and duplicate it. But all we've ever found is junk. There must have been good stuff worth a million times as much as those sweepings.

Did they take all the good stuff with them?

Nobody knew. I didn't know, either, but I thought I knew something that had a bearing on it.

I thought I knew where the last Heechee ship had taken off from; and it wasn't near any of the explored diggings.

I didn't kid myself. I knew that wasn't a guarantee of anything.

But it was something to go on. *Maybe* when that last ship left they were getting impatient, and maybe not as thorough in cleaning up behind themselves.

And that was what being on Venus was all about. What other possible reason was there for being there? The life of a maze rat was marginal at best. It took fifty thousand a year to stay alive. If you had less than that you couldn't pay air tax, capitation tax, water assessment, or even a subsistence-level bill for food. If you wanted to eat meat more than once a week, and demanded a cubicle of your own to sleep in, it cost more than that.

Guide's papers cost a week's life; when any of us bought them, we were gambling that week's cost of living against the chance of a big enough strike, either from the Terry tourists or from what we might find, to make it possible to get back to Earth—where no one starved, no one died for lack of air, no one was thrust out into the high-pressure incinerator that was Venus's atmosphere. Not *just* to get back to Earth. To get back in the style every maze rat had set himself as a goal when he headed sunward in the first place: with money enough to live the full life of a human being on Full Medical.

That was what I wanted. The big score.

4

Not by accident, the last thing I did that night was to visit the Hall of Discoveries.

The third of Vastra's house winked at me over her flirtation veil and turned to her companion, who looked around and nodded.

I joined them. "Hello, Mr. Walthers," she said.

"I thought I might find you here," I said, which was no more than the truth, since Vastra's third had promised to guide her this way. I didn't know what to call her. "Miss Keefer" was accurate, "Mrs. Cochenour" was diplomatic; I got around it by saying, "Since we'll be seeing a lot of each other, how about getting on to first names?"

"Audee, is it?"

I gave her a twelve-tooth smile. "Swede on my mother's side, old Texan on my father's. Name's been in his family a long time, I guess."

The Hall of Discoveries is meant to get Terry prospects hotted up, there's a little of everything in it, from charts of the worked diggings and a full-scale Mercator map of Venus to samples of all the principal finds. I showed her the copy of the anisokinetic punch, and the original solid-state piezophone that had made its discoverer almost as permanently rich as the guy who found the punch. There were about a dozen fire-pearls, quarter-inch jobbies, behind armor glass, on cushions, blazing away with their cold milky light.

"They're pretty," she said. "But why all the protection? I saw bigger ones lying on a counter in the Spindle without anybody even watching them."

"That's a little different, Dorotha," I told her. "These are real."

She laughed out loud. It was a very nice laugh. No girl looks beautiful when she's laughing hard, and girls who worry about looking beautiful don't do it. Dorotha Keefer looked like a healthy, pretty girl having a good time, which when you come down to it is about the best way for a girl to look.

She did not, however, look good enough to come between me and a new liver, so I took my mind off that aspect of her and put it on business. "The little red marbles over there are blood-diamonds," I told her. "They're radioactive and stay warm. Which is one way you can tell the real one from a fake: Anything over about three centimeters is a fake. A real one that big generates too much heat—square-cube law, you know—and melts."

"So the ones your friend was trying to sell me—"

"—are fakes. Right."

She nodded, still smiling. "What about what you were trying to sell us, Audee? Real or fake?"

The third of Vastra's house had discreetly vanished, and there was nobody else in the Hall of Discoveries but me and the girl. I took a deep breath and told her the truth. Not the whole truth, maybe; but nothing but the truth.

"All this stuff," I said, "is what came out of a hundred years of digging. And it's not much. The punch, the piezophone, and two or three other gadgets that we can make work; a few busted pieces of things that they're still studying; and some trinkets. That's all."

She said, "That's the way I heard it. And one more thing. None of the discovery dates on these things is less than fifty years old."

She was smart and better informed than I had expected. "And the conclusion," I agreed, "is that the planet has been mined dry. You're right, on the evidence. The first diggers found everything there was to be found . . . so far."

"You think there's more?"

"I *hope* there's more. Look. Item. The tunnels. You see they're all alike—the blue walls, perfectly smooth; the light coming from them that never varies; the hardness. How do you suppose they were made?"

"Why, I don't know—"

"Neither do I. Or anybody else. But every Heechee tunnel is the same, and if you dig into them from the outside you find the basic substrate rock, then a boundary layer that's sort of half wall-stuff and half substrate, then the wall. Conclusion: The Heechees didn't dig the tunnels and then line them, they had something that crawled around underground like an earthworm, leaving these tunnels behind. And one other thing: They overdug. That's to say they dug tunnels they didn't need, lots of them, going nowhere, never used for anything. Does that suggest anything to you?"

"It must have been cheap and easy?" she guessed.

I nodded. "So it was probably a machine, and there really ought to be at least one of them, somewhere on this planet, to find. Next item. The air: They breathed oxygen like we do, and they must have got it from somewhere. Where?"

"Why, there's oxygen in the atmosphere—"

"Sure. About a half of one percent. And better than 95 percent carbon dioxide; and somehow they managed to get that half of one percent out of the mixture, cheaply and easily—remember those extra tunnels they filled!—along with enough nitrogen or some other inert gas—and they're present in only trace amounts—to make a breathing mixture. How? Why, I don't know, but if there's a machine that did it, I'd like to find that machine. Next item: Aircraft. The Heechee flew around the surface of Venus at will."

"So do you, Audee! Aren't you a pilot?"

"Sure, but look at what it takes. Surface temperature of two-seventy C. and not enough oxygen to keep a cigarette going. So my airbody has two fuel tanks, one for hydrocarbons, one for oxidants. And—did you ever hear of a fellow named Carnot?"

"Old-time scientist, was he? The Carnot cycle?"

"Right again." That was the third time she'd surprised me, I noted cautiously. "The Carnot efficiency of an engine is expressed by its maximum temperature—the heat of combustion, let's say—over the temperature of its exhaust. Well, but the temperature of the exhaust can't be less than the temperature of what it flows into—otherwise you're not running an engine, you're running a refrigerator. And you've got that two-seventy ambient air temperature; so you have basically a lousy engine. *Any* heat engine on Venus is lousy. Did you ever wonder why there are so few airbodies around? I don't mind; it helps to have something close to a monopoly. But the reason is they're so damn expensive to run."

"And the Heechees did it better?"

"I *think* they did."

She laughed again, unexpectedly and once more very attractively. "Why, you poor fellow," she said in good humor, "you're hooked on the stuff you sell, aren't you? You think that some day you're going to find the mother tunnel and pick up all this stuff."

Well, I wasn't too pleased with the way things were going; I'd arranged with Vastra's third to bring the girl here, away from her boyfriend, so I could pick her brains in private. It hadn't worked out that way. The way it was working out, she was making me aware of her as a person, which was a bad development in itself, and worse than that, making me take a good look at myself.

I said after a minute, "You may be right. But I'm sure going to give it a good try."

"You're angry, aren't you?"

"No," I said, lying, "but maybe a little tired. And we've got a long trip tomorrow, so I'd better take you home, Miss Keefer."

5

My airbody lay by the spacepad and was reached the same way the spacepad was reached. Elevator to the surface lock, a tractor-cab to carry us across the dry, tortured surface of Venus, peeling under the three-hundred-kilometer-an-hour wind. Normally I kept it under a foam housing, of course. You don't leave anything free and exposed on the surface of Venus if you want to keep it intact, not even if it's made of chrome steel. I'd had the foam stripped free when I checked it out and loaded supplies that morning. Now it was ready. I could see it from the bull's-eye ports of the crawler, through the green-yellow murk outside. Cochenour and the girl could have seen it too, if they'd known where to look, but they might not have recognized it.

Cochenour screamed in my ear, "You and Dorrie have a fight?"

"No fight," I screamed back.

"Don't care if you did. You don't have to like each other, just do what I want you to do." He was silent a moment, resting his throat. "Jesus. What a wind."

"Zephyr," I told him. I didn't say any more, he would find out for himself. The area around the spacepad is a sort of natural calm area, by Venusian standards. Orographic lift throws the meanest winds up over the pad and all we get is a sort of confused back eddy. The good part is that taking off and landing are relatively easy. The bad part is that some of the heavy metal compounds in the atmosphere settle out on the pad. What passes for air on Venus has layers of red mercuric sulfide and mercurous chloride in the lower reaches, and when you get above them to those pretty fluffy clouds you find some of them are hydrochloric and hydrofluoric acid.

But there are tricks to that, too. Navigation over Venus is 3-D. It's easy enough to proceed from point to point; your transponders will link you to the radio range and map your position continuously on to the charts. What's hard is to find the right altitude, and that's why my airbody and I were worth a million dollars to Cochenour.

We were at the airbody, and the telescoping snout from the crawler was poking out to its lock. Cochenour was staring out the bull's eye. "No wings!" he shouted, as though I was cheating him.

"No sails or snow chains, either," I shouted back. "Get aboard if you want to talk! It's easier in the airbody."

We climbed through the little snout, I unlocked the entrance, and we got aboard without much trouble.

We didn't even have the kind of trouble that I might have made myself. You see, an airbody is a big thing on Venus. I was damn lucky to have been able to acquire it and, well, I won't beat around the bush, you could say I loved it. Mine could have held ten people, without equipment. With what Sub Vastra's purchasing department had sold us and Local 88 had certified as essential aboard, it was crowded with just the three of us. I was prepared for sarcasm, at least. But Cochenour merely looked around long enough to find the best bunk, strode over to it and declared it his. The girl was a good sport, and there I was, left with my glands all charged up for an argument and no argument.

It was a lot quieter inside the airbody. You could hear the noise of the wind right enough, but it was only annoying. I passed out earplugs, and with them in place the noise was hardly even annoying.

"Sit down and strap up," I ordered, and when they were stowed away I took off.

At twenty thousand millibars wings aren't just useless, they're poison. My airbody had all the lift it needed built into the seashell-shaped hull. I fed the double fuels into the thermojets, we bounced across the reasonably flat ground around the spacepad (it was bulldozed once a week, which is how come it stayed reasonably flat) and we were zooming off into the wild yellow-green yonder, a moment later the wild brown-gray yonder, after a run of no more than fifty meters.

Cochenour had fastened his harness loosely for comfort. I enjoyed hearing him yell as he was thrown about. It didn't last. At the thousand-meter level I found Venus's semi-permanent atmospheric inversion, and the turbulence dropped to where I could take off my belt and stand.

I took the plugs out of my ears and motioned to Cochenour and the girl to do the same.

He was rubbing his head where he'd bounced into an overhead chart rack, but grinning a little. "Pretty exciting," he admitted, fumbling in his pocket. Then he remembered to ask. "Is it all right if I smoke?"

"They're your lungs."

He grinned more widely. "They are now," he agreed, and lit up. "Say. Why didn't you give us those plugs while we were in the tractor?"

There is, as you might say, a tide in the affairs of guides, where you either let them flood you with questions and spend the whole time explaining what that funny little dial means or you go on to do your work and make your fortune. What it came down to was, was I going to come out of this liking Cochenour and his girlfriend or not?

If I was, I should try to be civil to them. More than civil. Living, the three of us, for three weeks in a space about as big as an apartment kitchenette meant everybody would have to work real hard at being nice to everybody else, and as I was the one who was being paid to be nice, I should be the one to set an example. On the other hand, the Cochenours of the worlds are sometimes just not likeable. If that was going to be the case, the less talk the better; I should slide questions like that off with something like "I forgot."

But he hadn't actually been unpleasant, and the girlfriend had actually tried to be friendly. I said, "Well, that's an interesting thing. You see, you hear by differences in pressure. While we were taking off the plugs filtered out part of the sound—the pressure waves—but when I yelled at you to belt up, the plugs passed the overpressure of my voice, and you understood it. However, there's a limit. Past about a hundred and twenty decibels—that's a unit of sound—"

Cochenour growled, "I know what a decibel is."

"Right. Past a hundred and twenty the eardrum just doesn't respond anymore. So in the crawler it was too loud; with the plugs, you wouldn't have heard anything."

Dorotha had been listening while she repaired her eye makeup. "What was to hear?"

"Oh," I said, "nothing, really. Except, well—" Then I voted to think of them as friends, at least for the time being. "Except in the case of an accident. If we'd had a gust, you know, that crawler could have flipped right over. Or sometimes solid objects come flying over the hills and into you before you know it. Or—"

She was shaking her head. "I understand. Lovely place we're visiting, Boyce."

"Yeah. Look," he said. "Who's flying this thing?"

I got up and activated the virtual globe. "That's what I was just coming to. Right now it's on autopilot, heading in the general direction of this quadrant down here. We have to pick out a specific destination."

"That's Venus?" the girl asked. "It doesn't look like much."

"Those lines are just radio range markers; you won't see them looking out of the window. Venus doesn't have any oceans, and it isn't cut up into nations, so making a map of it isn't quite like what you'd expect on Earth. That bright spot is us. Now look." I overlaid the radio-range grid and the contour colors with mascon markings. "Those blobby circles are mascons. You know what a mascon is?"

"A concentration of mass. A lump of heavy stuff," offered the girl.

"Fine. Now look at the known Heechee digs." I phased them in as golden patterns.

"They're all in the mascons," Dorotha said at once. Cochenour gave her a look of tolerant approval.

"Not all. Look over here; this little one isn't, and this one. But damn near all. Why? I don't know. Nobody knows. The mass concentrations are mostly older, denser rock—basalt and so on—and maybe the Heechee found it easier to dig in. Or maybe they just liked it." In my correspondence with Professor Hegramet back on Earth, in the days when I didn't have a dying liver in my gut and took an interest in abstract knowledge, we had kicked around the possibility that the Heechee digging machines would only work in dense rock, or rock of a certain chemical composition. But I wasn't prepared to discuss that with them.

"See over here, where we are now"—I rotated the virtual globe slightly by turning a dial—"that's the big digging we just came out of. You can see the shape of the Spindle. It's a common shape, by the way. You can see it in some of the others if you look, and there are digs where it doesn't show on these tracings but it's there if you're on the spot.

That particular mascon where the Spindle is is called Serendip; it was discovered by accident by a hesperological—"

"Hesperological?"

"—a geological team operating on Venus, which makes it a hesperological team. They were drilling out core samples and hit the Heechee digs. Now these other digs in the northern high-latitudes you see are all in one bunch of associated mascons. They connect through interventions of less dense rock, but only where absolutely necessary."

Cochenour said sharply, "They're north and we're going south. Why?"

It was interesting that he could read the navigation instruments, but I didn't say so. I only said, "They're no good. They've been probed."

"They look even bigger than the Spindle."

"Hell of a lot bigger, right. But there's nothing much in them, or anyway not much chance that anything in them is in good enough shape to bother with. Subsurface fluids filled them up a hundred thousand years ago, maybe more. A lot of good men have gone broke trying to pump and excavate them, without finding anything. Ask me. I was one of them."

"I didn't know there was any liquid water on Venus or under it," Cochenour objected.

"I didn't say water, did I? But as a matter of fact some of it was, or anyway a sort of oozy mud. Apparently water cooks out of the rocks and has a transit time to the surface of some thousands of years before it seeps out, boils off, and cracks to hydrogen and oxygen and gets lost. In case you didn't know it, there's some under the Spindle. It's what you were drinking, and what you were breathing."

The girl said, "Boyce, this is all very interesting, but I'm hot and dirty. Can I change the subject for a minute?"

Cochenour barked; it wasn't really a laugh. "Subliminal prompting, Walthers, you agree? And a little old-fashioned prudery, too, I expect. What she really wants to do is go to the bathroom."

Given a little encouragement from the girl, I would have been mildly embarrassed for her, but she only said, "If we're going to live in this thing for three weeks, I'd like to know what it offers."

I said, "Certainly, Miss Keefer."

"Dorotha. Dorrie, if you like it better."

"Sure, Dorrie. Well, you see what we've got. Five bunks; they partition to sleep ten if wanted, but we don't want. Two shower stalls. They don't look big enough to soap yourself in, but they are if you work at it. Three chemical toilets. Kitchen over there—well. Pick the bunk you like, Dorrie. There's a screen arrangement that comes down when you want it for changing clothes and so on, or just if you don't want to look at the rest of us for a while."

Cochenour said, "Go on, Dorrie, do what you want to do. I want Walthers to show me how to fly this thing anyway."

It wasn't a bad start. I've had some real traumatic times, parties that came aboard drunk and steadily got drunker, couples that fought every waking minute and got together only to hassle me. This one didn't look bad at all, apart from the fact that it was going to save my life for me.

There's not much to flying an airbody, at least as far as making it move the way you want it to is concerned. In Venus's atmosphere there's lift to spare. You don't worry about things like stalling out; and anyway the autonomic controls do most of your thinking for you.

Cochenour learned fast. It turned out he had flown everything that moved on Earth and operated one-man submersibles as well. He understood as soon as I mentioned it to him that the hard part of pilotage was selecting the right flying level and anticipating when you'd have to change it, but he also understood that he wasn't going to learn that in one day. Or even in three weeks. "What the hell, Walthers," he said cheerfully enough. "At least I can make it go where I have to, in case you get caught in a tunnel or shot by a jealous husband."

I gave him the smile his pleasantry was worth, which wasn't much. "The other thing I can do," he said, "is cook. Unless you're really good at it? No, I thought not. Well, I paid too much for this stomach to fill it with hash, so I'll make the meals. That's a little skill Dorrie never got around to learning. Same with her grandmother. Most beautiful woman in the world, but had the idea that was all there was to it."

I put that aside to sort out later; he was full of little unexpected things, this ninety years old young athlete. He said, "All right, now while Dorrie's using up all the water in the shower—"

"Not to worry; it all recycles."

"Anyway. While she's cleaning up, finish your little lecture on where we're going."

"Right." I spun the virtual globe a little. The bright spot that was us had moved a dozen degrees already. "See that cluster where our track intersects those grid marks?"

"Yeah. Five big mascons close together, and no diggings indicated. Is that where we're going?"

"In a general sense, yes."

"Why in a general sense?"

"Well," I said, "there's one little thing I didn't tell you. I'm assuming you won't jump salty over it, because then I'll have to get salty too and tell you you should have taken the trouble to learn more about Venus before you decided to explore it."

He studied me appraisingly for a moment. Dorrie came quietly out of the shower in a long robe, her hair in a towel, and stood near him, watching. "It depends on what you didn't tell me," he said.

"There's a no-trespassing sign on most of those mascons," I said. I activated the pilotage chart overlay, and bright cherry-red warning lines sprang up all around the cluster.

"That's the south polar security area," I said. "That's where the Defense boys keep the missile range and the biggest part of their weapons development areas. And we're not allowed to enter."

He said harshly, "But there's only a little piece of one mascon that isn't off-limits."

"And that's where we're going," I said.

6

For a man more than ninety years old, Boyce Cochenour was spry. I don't mean just healthy looking. Full Medical will do that for you, because you just replace whatever wears out or begins to look shopworn and tatty. You cannot, however, very well replace the brain, so what you usually see in the very rich old ones is a bronzed, strong body that shakes and hesitates and drops things and stumbles. About that Cochenour had been very lucky.

He was going to be wearing company for three weeks. He'd insisted I show him how to pilot the airbody. When I decided to use a little flight time to give the cooling system a somewhat premature thousand-hour check, he helped me pull the covers, check the refrigerant levels and clean the filters. Then he decided to cook us lunch.

The girl took over as my helper while I restowed some of the supplies to get the autosonic probes out. At the steady noise level of the inside of an airbody our normal conversational voices wouldn't carry to Cochenour, less than three meters away, and I thought of pumping her about him. I decided against it. What I didn't know was just curiosity. I knew he was paying me the price of a new liver already. I didn't need to know what he and the girl thought about when they thought about each other.

So our conversation was along the lines of how the probes would fire charges and time the echoes, and what the chances were of finding something really good ("Well, what are the chances of winning a sweepstake? Bad for any individual who buys a ticket—but there's always one winner somewhere!"), and what had made me come to Venus in the first place. I mentioned my father's name, but she'd never heard of him. Too young, for one thing, no doubt. And she was born and bred in Southern Ohio, where Cochenour had worked as a kid and to which he'd returned as a billionaire. He'd been building a new processing center there and it had been a lot of headaches— trouble with the unions, trouble with the banks, trouble, bad trouble, with the government—so he'd decided to take a few months off and loaf. I looked over to where he was stirring up a sauce and said, "He loafs harder than anybody else I ever saw."

"He's a work addict. I imagine that's how he got rich in the first place." The airbody lurched, and I dropped everything to jump for the controls. I heard Cochenour howl behind me, but I was busy locating the right transit level. By the time I had climbed a thousand meters and reset the autopilot, he was rubbing his wrist and glowering at me.

"Sorry," I said.

He said dourly, "I don't mind your scalding the skin off my arm, I can always buy more skin, but you nearly made me spill the gravy."

I checked the virtual globe. The bright marker was two-thirds of the way to our destination. "Is it about ready?" I asked. "We'll be there in an hour."

For the first time he looked startled. "So soon? I thought you said this thing was subsonic."

"I did. You're on Venus, Mr. Cochenour. At this level the speed of sound is maybe five thousand kilometers an hour."

He looked thoughtful, but all he said was, "Well, we can eat any minute." Later he said, while we were finishing up, "I think maybe I don't know as much about this planet as I might. If you want to give us the usual guide's lecture, we'll listen."

I said, "Well, you pretty much know the outlines. Say, you're a great cook, Mr. Cochenour. I packed all these provisions, but I don't even know what this is I'm eating."

"If you come to my office in Cincinnati," he said, "you can ask for Mr. Cochenour, but while we're living in each other's armpits you might as well call me Boyce. And if you like it, why aren't you eating it?"

The answer was, because it might kill me, but I didn't want to get into a discussion that might lead to why I needed his fee so badly. I said, "Doctor's orders, have to lay off the fats pretty much for a while. I think he thinks I'm putting on too much weight."

Cochenour looked at me appraisingly, but only said, "The lecture?"

"Well, let's start with the most important part," I said, carefully pouring coffee. "While we're in the airbody you can do what you like, walk around, eat, drink, smoke if you got 'em, whatever. The cooling system is built for more than three times as many people, plus their cooking and appliance loads, with a safety factor of two. Air and water, more than we'd need for two months. Fuel, enough for three round-trips and some maneuvering. If anything went wrong we'd yell for help and somebody would come and get us in a couple of hours at most—probably it would be the Defense boys, and they have *super*sonic bodies. The worst thing would be if the hull breached and the whole Venusian atmosphere tried to come in. If it happened fast we'd be dead. It never happens fast, though. We'd have time to get in the suits, and we can live in them for thirty hours. Long before that we'd be picked up."

"Assuming, of course, that nothing went wrong with the radio at the same time," said Cochenour.

"Right. You can get killed anywhere, if enough accidents happen at once."

He poured himself another cup of coffee, tipped a little brandy into it and said, "Go on."

"Well, outside the airbody it's a little more tricky. You've only got the suit, and its useful life, as I say, is only thirty hours. It's a question of refrigeration. You can carry all the air and water you want, and you don't have to worry about food, but it takes a lot of compact energy to get rid of the diffuse energy all around you. It takes fuel for the cooling systems, and when that's gone you better be back in the airbody. Heat isn't the worst way to die. You pass out before you begin to hurt. But the end result is you're dead.

"The other thing is, you want to check your suit every time you put it on. Pressure it up and watch the gauge for leaks. I'll check it too, but *don't rely on me*. It's your life. And the faceplates are pretty strong; you can drive nails with them without breaking them, but they can be broken if hit hard enough against a hard enough surface. That way you're dead too."

Dorrie said quietly, "One question. Have you ever lost a tourist?"

"No." But then I added, "Others have. Five or six get killed every year."

"I don't mind odds like that," said Cochenour. "Actually, that wasn't the lecture I was asking for, Audee. I mean, I certainly want to hear how to stay alive, but I assume you would have told us all this before we left the ship anyway. What I really wanted to know was how come you picked this particular mascon to prospect."

This old geezer with the muscle-beach body was beginning to bother me. He had a disturbing habit of asking the questions I didn't want to answer. There was a reason why I had picked this site; it had to do with about five years of study, a lot of digging, and about a quarter of a million dollars' worth of correspondence, at space-mail rates, with people like Professor Hegramet back on Earth.

But I didn't want to tell him all of my reasons. There were about a dozen sites that I really wanted to explore. If this happened to be one of the payoff places, he would come out of it richer than I would—that's what the contracts you sign say: 40 percent to the charterer, 25 percent to the guide, the rest to the government—and that should be enough for him. If it happened not to pay off, I didn't want him taking some other guide to one of the others I'd marked.

So I only said, "Call it an informed guess. I promised you a good shot at a tunnel that's never been opened, and I hope to keep my promise. And now let's get the food put away; we're within ten minutes of where we're going."

With everything strapped down and ourselves belted up, we dropped out of the relatively calm layers into the big winds again.

We were over the big south-central massif, about the same elevation as the lands surrounding the Spindle. That's the elevation where most of the action is on Venus. Down in the lowlands and the deep rift valleys the pressures run fifty thousand millibars and up. My airbody wouldn't take any of that for very long, and neither would anybody else's, except for a few of the special research and military types. Fortunately, the Heechee didn't care for the lowlands either. Nothing of theirs has ever been located much below twenty-bar. Doesn't mean it isn't there, of course.

Anyway, I verified our position on the virtual globe and on the detail charts, and deployed the autosonic probes. The winds threw them all over the place as soon as they dropped free. It doesn't much matter where they go, within broad limits, which is a good thing. They dropped like javelins at first, then flew around like straws until the little rockets cut in and the ground-seeking controls fired them to the ground.

Every one embedded itself properly. You aren't always that lucky, so it was a good start.

I verified their position on the detail charts; it was close enough to an equilateral triangle, which is about how you want them. Then I opened the scanning range and began circling around.

"Now what?" bellowed Cochenour. I noticed the girl had put the earplugs back, but he wasn't willing to miss a thing.

"Now we wait for the probes to feel around for Heechee tunnels. It'll take a couple of hours." While I was talking I brought the airbody down through the surface layers. Now we were being thrown around. The buffeting got pretty bad, and so did the noise.

But I found what I was looking for, a surface formation like a blind arroyo, and tucked us into it with only one or two bad moments. Cochenour was watching very carefully, and I grinned to myself. That was where pilotage counted, not en route or at the prepared pads around the Spindle. When he could do that he could get along without somebody like me.

Our position looked all right, so I fired four hold-downs, tethered stakes with explosive heads that opened out in the ground. I winched them tight and all of them held.

That was also a good sign. Reasonably pleased with myself, I opened the belt catches and stood up. "We're here for at least a day or two," I said. "More if we're lucky. How did you like the ride?"

The girl was taking the earplugs out, now that the protecting walls of the arroyo had cut the thundering down to a mere constant scream. "I'm glad I don't get airsick," she said.

Cochenour was thinking, not talking. He was studying the control board while he lit another cigarette.

Dorotha said, "One question, Audee. Why couldn't we stay up where it's quieter?"

"Fuel. I carry about thirty hours, full thrust, but that's it. Is the noise bothering you?" She made a face.

"You'll get used to it. It's like living next to a spaceport. At first you wonder how anybody stands the noise for a single hour. After you've been there a week you miss it if it stops."

She moved over to the bull's-eye and gazed pensively out at the landscape. We'd crossed into the night portion, and there wasn't much to see but dust and small objects whirling through our external light beams. "It's that first week that I'm worried about," she said.

I flicked on the probe readout. The little percussive heads were firing their slap-charges and measuring each other's sounds, but it was too early to see anything. The screen was barely beginning to build up a shadowy pattern, more holes than detail.

Cochenour finally spoke. "How long until you can make some sense out of that?" he demanded. Another point: He didn't ask what it was.

"Depends on how close and how big anything is. You can make a guess in an hour or so, but I like all the data I can get. Six or eight hours. I'd say. There's no hurry."

He growled, "*I'm* in a hurry, Walthers. Keep that in mind."

The girl cut in. "What should we do, Audee? Play three-handed bridge?"

"Whatever you want, but I'd advise some sleep. I've got pills if you want them. If we do find anything—and remember, if we hit on the first try it's just hundred-to-one luck—we'll want to be wide awake for a while."

"All right," said Dorotha, reaching out for the spansules, but Cochenour demanded: "What about you?"

"Pretty soon. I'm waiting for something." He didn't ask what. Probably, I thought, because he already knew. I decided that when I did hit my bunk I wouldn't take a sleeping pill right away. This Cochenour was not only the richest tourist I had ever guided, he was one of the best informed, and I wanted to think about that for a while.

What I was waiting for took almost an hour to come. The boys were getting a little sloppy; they should have been after us before this.

The radio buzzed and then blared: "Unidentified vessel at one three five, zero seven, four eight and seven two, five one, five four! Please identify yourself and state your purpose!"

Cochenour looked up inquiringly from his gin game with the girl. I smiled reassuringly. "As long as they're saying 'please' there's no problem," I told him, and opened the transmitter.

"This is Pilot Audee Walthers, airbody Poppa Tare Nine One, out of the Spindle. We are licensed and have filed approved flight plans. I have two Terry tourists aboard, purpose recreational exploration."

"Acknowledge. Please wait," blared the radio. The military always broadcasts at maximum gain. Hangover from drill-sergeant days, no doubt.

I turned off the microphone and told my passengers, "They're checking our flight plan. Not to worry about."

In a moment the Defense communicator came back, loud as ever. "You are eleven point four kilometers bearing one eight three degrees from terminator of a restricted area. Proceed with caution. Under Military Regulations One Seven and One Eight, Sections—"

I cut in, "I know the drill. I have my guide's license and have explained the restrictions to the passengers."

"Acknowledged," blared the radio. "We will keep you under surveillance. If you observe vessels or parties on the surface, they are our perimeter teams. Do not interfere with them in any way. Respond at once to any request for identification or information." The carrier buzz cut off.

Cochenour said, "They act nervous."

"No. They're used to seeing us around. They've got nothing else to do, that's all."

Dorrie said hesitantly, "Audee, you told them you'd explained the restrictions to us. I don't remember that part."

"Oh, I explained them all right. We stay out of the restricted area, because if we don't they'll start shooting. That is the Whole of the Law."

7

I set a wake-up for four hours, and the others heard me moving around and got up too. Dorrie fetched us coffee from the warmer, and we stood drinking it and looking at the patterns the computer had traced.

I took several minutes to study them, although it was clear enough at first look. There were eight major anomalies that could have been Heechee warrens. One was almost right outside our door. We wouldn't even have to move the airbody to dig for it.

I showed them the anomalies, one by one. Cochenour just looked at them thoughtfully. Dorotha asked after a moment, "You mean all of these are unexplored tunnels?"

"No. Wish they were. But, one: Any or all of them could have been explored by someone who didn't go to the trouble of recording it. Two: They don't have to be tunnels. They might be fracture faults, or dikes, or little rivers of some kind of molten material that ran out of somewhere and hardened and got covered over a billion years ago. The only thing we know for sure so far is that there probably aren't any unexplored tunnels in this area *except* in those eight places."

"So what do we do?"

"We dig. And then we see what we've got."

Cochenour said, "Where do we dig?"

I pointed right next to the bright delta of our airbody. "Right here."

"Because it's the best bet?"

"Well, not necessarily." I considered what to tell him, and decided the truth was the best. "There are three that look like better bets than the others—here, I'll mark them." I keyed the chart controls, and the best looking traces immediately displayed letters: A, B and C. "A runs right under the arroyo here, so we'll dig it first."

"Those three because they're the brightest?"

I nodded, somewhat annoyed at his quickness, although it was obvious enough.

"But C over here is the brightest of the lot. Why don't we dig that first?"

I chose my words carefully. "Because we'd have to move the airbody. And because it's on the outside perimeter of the survey area; that means the results aren't as reliable as they are for this one right under us. But those aren't the most important reasons. The most important reason is that C is on the edge of the line our itchy-fingered friends are telling us to stay away from."

Cochenour laughed incredulously. "You mean you're telling me that if you find a real untouched Heechee tunnel you'll stay out of it just because some soldier tells you it's a no-no?"

I said, "The problem doesn't arise just yet; we have seven anomalies to look at that are legal. Also, the military will be checking us from time to time, particularly in the next day or two."

Cochenour insisted, "All right, suppose we check them and find nothing. What do we do then?"

I shook my head. "I never borrow trouble. Let's check the legal ones."

"But suppose."

"Damn it, Boyce! How do I know?"

He gave it up then, but winked at Dorrie and chuckled. "What did I tell you, honey? He's a bigger bandit than I am."

For the next couple of hours we didn't have much time to talk about theoretical possibilities, because we were too busy with concrete facts.

The biggest fact was an awful lot of hot high-speed gas that we had to keep from killing us. My own hot-suit was custom made, of course, and only needed the fittings and tanks to be checked. Boyce and the girl had rental units. They'd paid top dollar for them, and they were good, but good isn't perfect. I had them in and out of them a dozen times, checking the fit and varying tensions until they were as right as I could get them. There's a lot of heat and pressure to keep out when you go about the surface of Venus. The suits were laminated twelve-ply, with nine degrees of freedom at the essential joints. They wouldn't fail; that wasn't what I was worried about. What I was worried about was comfort, because a very small itch or rub can get serious when there's no way to stop it.

But finally they were good enough for a first trial, and we all huddled in the lock and exited on to the surface of Venus.

We were still darkside, but there's so much scatter from the sun that it doesn't get really dark more than a quarter of the time. I let them practice walking around the airbody, leaning into the wind, bracing themselves against the hold-downs and the side of the ship, while I got ready to dig.

I hauled out our first instant igloo, dragged it into position, and ignited it. As it smoldered it puffed up like the children's toy that used to be called a Pharaoh's Serpent, producing a light, tough ash that grew up around the digging site and joined in a seamless dome at the top. I'd already emplaced the digging torch and the crawl-through lock; as the ash grew I manhandled the lock to get a close union, and got a perfect join first time.

Dorrie and Cochenour stayed out of the way when they caught sight of my waving arm, but hung together, watching through their triple-vision plugs. I keyed on the radio. "You want to come in and watch me start it up?" I shouted.

Inside the helmets, they both nodded their heads. "Come on, then," I yelled, and wiggled through the crawl lock. I signed for them to leave it open as they followed me in.

With the three of us and the digging equipment in it, the igloo was even more crowded than the airbody. They backed away as far as they could get, bent against the arc of the igloo wall, while I started up the augers, checked they were vertical, and watched the first castings spiral out.

The foam igloo absorbs more sound than it reflects. Even so, the din inside the igloo was a lot worse than in the howling winds outside. When I thought they'd seen enough to satisfy them for the moment, I waved them out of the crawl-through, followed, sealed it behind us, and led them back into the airbody.

"So far, so good," I said, twisting off the helmet and loosening the suit. "We've got about forty meters to go, I think. Might as well wait in here as out there."

"How long is that?"

"Maybe an hour. You can do what you like; what I'm going to do is take a shower. Then we'll see how far we've got."

That was one of the nice things about having only three people aboard: We didn't have to worry about water discipline very much. It's astonishing how a quick wet-down revives you after coming out of a hotsuit. When I'd finished mine I felt ready for anything.

I was even prepared to eat some of Boyce Cochenour's gourmet cookery, but fortunately it wasn't necessary. The girl had taken over the kitchen, and what she laid out was simple, light, and reasonably nontoxic. On cooking like hers I might be able to survive long enough to collect my charter fee. It crossed my mind for a moment to wonder what made her do it; and then I thought, of course, she'd had a lot of practice. With all the spare parts in Cochenour, no doubt he had dietary problems far worse than mine.

Well, not "worse," exactly, in the sense that I didn't think he was quite as likely to die of them.

According to the autosonic probes, the highest point of the tunnel I had marked "A," or of whatever it was that had seemed like tunnels to their shock waves, was close to the little blind valley in which I'd tied down.

That was very lucky. It meant that we might very possibly be right over the Heechee's own entrance.

The reason that was lucky was not that we would be able to use it the way the Heechee had used it. There wasn't much chance that its mechanisms would have survived a quarter of a million years, much of it exposed to surface wind, ablation, and chemical corrosion. The good part was that if the tunnel had surfaced here it would be relatively easy to bore down to it. Even a quarter of a million years doesn't produce really hard rock, especially without surface water to dissolve out solids and produce compact sediments.

Up to a point, it turned out pretty much the way I had hoped. What was on the surface was little more than ashy sand, and the augers chewed it out very rapidly. Too rapidly; when I went back into the igloo it was filled almost solid with castings, and I had a devil of a job getting to the machines to switch the auger over to pumping the castings out through the crawl lock.

It was a dull, dirty part of the job, but it didn't take long.

I didn't bother to go back into the airbody. I reported what was happening over the radio to Boyce and the girl, staring out of the ports at me. I told them I thought we were getting close.

But I didn't tell them exactly how close. Actually, we were only a meter or two from the indicated depth of the anomaly, so close that I didn't bother to pump out all of the castings. I just made enough room to maneuver around, then redirected the augers; and in five minutes the castings were beginning to come up with the pale blue glimmer that was the sign of a Heechee tunnel.

8

About ten minutes after that I keyed on my helmet transmitter and shouted: "Boyce! Dorrie! We've hit a tunnel!"

Either they were sitting around in their suits or they dressed faster than any maze rat. I unsealed the crawl-through and wiggled out to help them, and they were already coming out of the airbody, staggering against the wind over to me.

They were both yelling questions and congratulations, but I stopped them. "Inside," I ordered. "See for yourself." As a matter of fact, they didn't have to go that far. They could see the color as soon as they knelt to enter the crawl-through.

I followed, and sealed the lock behind me. The reason for that is simple enough. As long as the tunnel isn't breached, it doesn't matter what you do. But the interior of a Heechee tunnel that has remained inviolate is at a pressure only slightly above Earth-normal. Without the sealed dome, the minute you crack the casing you let the whole twenty-thousand-millibar atmosphere of Venus pour in, heat and ablation and all. If the tunnel is empty, or if what's in it is simple, sturdy stuff, there might not be any harm. But if you hit the jackpot you can destroy in half a second what has waited for a quarter of a million years.

We gathered around the shaft and I pointed down. The augers had left a clean shaft, about seventy centimeters by a little over a hundred, with rounded ends. At the bottom you could see the cold blue glow of the outside of the tunnel, only pocked and blotched by the loose castings I hadn't bothered to get out.

"Now what?" demanded Boyce. His voice was hoarse with excitement, which was, I guessed, natural enough.

"Now we burn our way in."

I backed my clients away as far as they could get, pressed against the remaining heap of castings, and unlimbered the fire-jets. I'd already hung sheer-legs over the shaft, and they went right down on their cable with no trouble until they were a few centimeters above the round of the tunnel. Then I fired them up.

You wouldn't think that anything a human being might do would change the temperature of the surface of Venus, but those fire-drills were something special. In the small space of the igloo the heat flamed up and around us, and our hotsuit cooling systems were overloaded in seconds.

Dorrie gasped, "Oh! I—I think I'm going to—"

Cochenour grabbed her. "Faint if you want to," he said fiercely, "but don't get sick. Walthers! How long does this go on?"

It was as hard for me as it was for them; practice doesn't get you used to something like standing in front of a blast furnace with the doors off the hinges. "Maybe a minute," I gasped. "Hold on—it's all right."

It actually took a little more than that, maybe ninety seconds; my suit telltales were shouting alarm for more than half of the time. But they were built for these overloads, and as long as we didn't cook, the suits wouldn't take any permanent harm.

Then we were through. A half-meter circular section sagged, fell at one side and hung there.

I turned off the firejets, and we all breathed hard for a couple of minutes, while the suit coolers gradually caught up with the load.

"Wow," said Dorotha. "That was pretty rough."

I looked at Cochenour. In the light that splashed up out of the shaft I could see he was frowning. I didn't say anything. I just gave the jets another five-second burn to cut away the rest of the circular section, and it fell free into the tunnel. We could hear it clatter against the floor.

Then I turned on my helmet radio. "There's no pressure differential," I said.

The frown didn't change, nor did he speak.

"Which means this one has been breached," I went on. "Let's go back to the airbody and take a break before we do anything else."

Dorotha shrieked, "Audee! What's the matter with you? I want to go down there and see what's inside!"

Cochenour said bitterly, "Shut up, Dorrie. Don't you hear what he's saying? This one's a dud."

Well, there's always the chance that a breached tunnel opened up to a seismological invasion, not a maze rat with a cutting torch, and if so, there might be something worthwhile in it anyway. And I didn't have the heart to kill all Dorotha's enthusiasm with one blow.

So we did swing down the cable, one by one, into the Heechee dig, and look around.

It was wholly bare, as most of them are, as far as we could see. That wasn't actually very far, for the other thing wrong with a breached tunnel is that you need pretty good equipment to explore it. With the overloads they'd already had, our suits were all right for a couple of hours but not much more than that, and when we tramped about half a mile down the tunnel without finding a thing, they were both willing to tramp back and return to the airbody.

We cleaned up and made ourselves something to drink. Even squandering more of the water reserves on showers didn't do much for our spirits.

We had to eat, but Cochenour didn't bother with his gourmet exhibition. Silently, Dorotha threw tabs into the radar oven, and we fed gloomily on emergency rations.

"Well, that's only the first one," she said at last, determined to be sunny about it. "And it's only our second day."

Cochenour said, "Shut up, Dorrie; the one thing I'm not is a good loser." He was staring at the probe trace. "Walthers, how many tunnels are unmarked but empty, like this one?"

"How can I answer a question like that? If they're unmarked, there's no record of them."

"So those traces don't mean anything. We might dig one a day for the next three weeks and find every one a dud."

I nodded. "We surely might, Boyce."

He looked at me alertly. "And?"

"And that's not the worst part of it. I've taken parties out to dig who would've gone mad with joy to open even a breached tunnel. It's perfectly possible to dig every day for weeks and never hit a real Heechee tunnel at all. Don't knock it; at least you got some action for your money."

"I told you, Walthers, I'm not a good loser. Second place is no good." He thought for a minute, then barked: "You picked this spot. Did you know what you were doing?"

Did I? The only way to answer that question would be to find a live one, of course. I could have told him about the months of studying records from the first landings on. I could have mentioned how much trouble I went to, and how many regulations I broke, to get the military survey reports, or how far I'd traveled to talk to the Defense crews who'd been on those early digs. I might have let him know how hard it had been to locate old Jorolemon Hegramet, now teaching exotic archeology back in Tennessee, and how many times we'd corresponded; but all I said was, "The fact that we found one tunnel shows I knew my business as a guide. That's all you paid for. It's up to you if we keep looking or not."

He looked at his thumbnail, considering.

The girl said cheerfully, "Buck up, Boyce. Look at all the other chances we've got—and even if we miss, it'll still be fun telling everybody about it back in Cincinnati."

He didn't even look at her, just said, "Isn't there any way to tell whether a tunnel has been breached or not without going inside?"

"Sure," I said. "You can tell by tapping the outside shell. You can hear the difference in the sound."

"But you have to dig down to it first?"

"Right."

We left it at that, and I got back into my hotsuit to strip away the now useless igloo so that we could move the drills.

I didn't really want to discuss it anymore, because I didn't want him to ask a question that I might want to lie about. I try the best I can to tell the truth, because it's easier to remember what you've said that way.

On the other hand, I'm not fanatic about it, and I don't see that it's any of my business to correct a mistaken impression. For instance, obviously Cochenour and the girl had the impression that I hadn't bothered to sound the tunnel casing because we'd already dug down to it and it was just as easy to cut in.

But, of course, I had tested it. That was the first thing I did as soon as the drill got down that far. And when I heard the high-pressure *thunk* it broke my heart. I had to wait a couple of minutes before I could call them to tell them that we'd reached the outer casing.

At that time, I had not quite faced up to the question of just what I would have done if it had turned out that the tunnel had not been breached.

9

Cochenour and Dorrie Keefer were maybe the fiftieth or sixtieth party I'd taken on a Heechee dig, and I wasn't surprised that they were willing to work like coolies. I don't care how lazy and bored they start out, by the time they actually come close to finding something that belonged to an almost completely unknown alien race, left there when the closest thing to a human being on Earth was a slope-browed furry little beast killing other beasts with antelope bones, they begin to burn with exploration fever.

So they worked hard, and drove me hard, and I was as eager as they. Maybe more so, as the days went past and I found myself rubbing my right side, just under the short ribs, more and more of the time.

The military boys overflew us half a dozen times in the first few days. They didn't say much, just formal requests for identification, which they already well knew, then away. Regulations say if you find anything you're supposed to report it right away. Over Cochenour's objections, I reported finding that first breached tunnel, which surprised them a little, I think.

And that's all we had to report.

Site B was a pegmatite dike. The other two fairly bright ones, that I called D and E, showed nothing at all when we dug, meaning that the sound reflections had probably been caused by nothing more than invisible interfaces in layers of rock or ash or gravel. I vetoed trying to dig C, the best looking of the bunch. Cochenour gave me a hell of an argument about it, but I held out. The military were still looking in on us every now and then, and I didn't want to get any closer to their perimeter than we already were. I half-promised that, if we didn't have any luck elsewhere in the mascons, we'd sneak back to C for a quick dig before returning to the Spindle, and we left it at that.

We lifted the airbody, moved to a new position, and set out a new pattern of probes.

By the end of the second week we had dug nine times and come up empty every time. We were getting low on igloos and probes. We'd run out of tolerance for each other completely.

Cochenour had turned sullen and savage. I hadn't planned on liking the man much when I first met him, but I hadn't expected him to be as bad as that. Considering that it had to be only a game with him—with all his money, the extra fortune he might pick up by discovering some new Heechee artifacts couldn't have meant anything but extra points on a score pad—he was playing for blood.

I wasn't particularly graceful myself, for that matter. The plain fact was that the pills from the Quackery weren't helping as much as they should. My mouth tasted like rats had nested in it, I was getting headaches, and I was beginning to knock things over. See, the thing about the liver is that it sort of regulates your internal diet. It filters out poisons, it converts some of the carbohydrates into other carbohydrates that you can use, it patches together amino acids into proteins. If it isn't working, you die. The doctor had been all over it with me, and I could visualize what was going on inside me, the mahogany-red cells dying and being replaced by clusters of fat and yellowish matter. It was an ugly kind of picture. The ugliest part was that there wasn't anything I could do about it. Only go on taking pills, and they wouldn't work past a matter of a few days more. Liver, bye-bye; hepatic failure, hello.

So we were a bad bunch. Cochenour was a bastard because it was his nature to be a bastard, and I was a bastard because I was sick and desperate. The only decent human being aboard was the girl.

She did her best, she really did. She was sometimes sweet and often even pretty, and she was always ready to meet the power people, Cochenour and me, more than halfway. It was clearly tough on her. She was only a kid. No matter how grown up she acted, she just hadn't been alive long enough to grow a defense against concentrated meanness. Add in the fact that we were all beginning to hate the sight and sound and smell of each other (and in an airbody you get to know a lot about how people smell). There wasn't much joy on Venus for Dorrie Keefer.

Or for any of us, especially after I broke the news that we were down to our last igloo.

Cochenour cleared his throat. He sounded like a fighter-plane jockey blowing the covers off his guns in preparation for combat, and Dorrie attempted to head him off with a diversion. "Audee," she said brightly, "you know what I think we could do? We could go back to that site that looked good near the military reservation."

It was the wrong diversion. I shook my head. "No."

"What the hell do you mean, 'No'?" rumbled Cochenour, revving up for battle.

"What I said. No. That's a desperation trick, and I'm not that desperate."

"Walthers," he snarled, "you'll be desperate when I tell you to be desperate. I can still stop payment on that check."

"No, you can't. The union won't let you. The regulations are very clear about that. You pay up unless I disobey a lawful directive; you can't make me do anything against the law, and going inside the military reservation is extremely against the law."

He shifted over to cold war. "No," he said softly, "you're wrong about that. It's only against the law if a court says it is, after we do it. You're only right if your lawyers are smarter than my lawyers. Honestly, Walthers, I pay my lawyers to be the smartest there are."

The difficult part was that he was even more right than he knew he was, because my liver was on his side. I couldn't spare time for arbitration because without his money and my transplant I wouldn't live that long.

Dorrie, listening with her birdlike look of friendly interest, got between us again. "Well, then, how about this? We just put down here. Why don't we wait and see what the probes show? Maybe we'll hit something even better than that Trace C—"

"There isn't going to be anything good here," he said without looking at her.

"Why, Boyce, how do you know that? We haven't even finished the soundings."

He said, "Look, Dorotha, listen close one time and then shut up. Walthers is playing games. You see where we are now?"

He brushed past me and tapped out the program for a full map display, which somewhat surprised me because I didn't know he knew how. The charts sprang up with virtual images of our position, the shafts we'd already cut, the great irregular edge of the military reservation overlaid on the plot of mascons and navigation aids.

"You see? We're not even in the high-density mass areas now. Is that true, Walthers? We've tried all the good locations and come up dry?"

I said, "You're partly right, Mr. Cochenour, but I'm not playing games. This site is a good possibility. You can see it on the map. We're not over any mascon, that's true, but we're right between two of them that are located pretty close together. Sometimes you find a dig that connects two complexes, and it has happened that the connecting passage was closer to the surface than any other part of the system. I can't guarantee we'll hit anything here, but it's not impossible."

"Just damn unlikely?"

"Well, no more unlikely than anywhere else. I told you a week ago, you got your money's worth the first day just finding any Heechee tunnel at all, even a spoiled one. There are maze rats in the Spindle who went five years without seeing that much." I thought for a minute. "I'll make a deal with you," I said.

"I'm listening."

"We're down here, and there's at least a chance we can hit something. Let's try. We'll deploy the probes and see what they turn up. If we get a good trace we'll dig it. If we don't—then I'll think about going back to Trace C."

"*Think* about it!" he roared.

"Don't push me, Cochenour. You don't know what you're getting into. The military reservation is not to be fooled with. Those boys shoot first and ask questions later, and there aren't any policemen or courts on Venus to even ask them questions."

"I don't know," he said after a moment.

"No," I said, "you don't, Mr. Cochenour, and that's what you're paying me for. I do know."

"Yes," he agreed, "you probably do, but whether you're telling me the truth about what you know is another question. Hegramet never said anything about digging between mascons."

And then he looked at me with a completely opaque expression, waiting to see whether I would catch him up on what he had just said.

I didn't respond. I gave him an opaque look back. I didn't say a word; I only waited to see what would come next. I was pretty sure that it would not be any sort of explanation of how he happened to know Hegramet's name, or what dealings he had had with the greatest Earthside authority on Heechee diggings, and it wasn't.

"Put out your probes and we'll try it your way one more time," he said at last.

I plopped the probes out, got good penetration on all of them, started firing the noise-makers. I sat watching the first buildup of lines on the scan as though I expected them to carry useful information. They couldn't, of course, but it was a good excuse to think privately for a moment.

Cochenour needed to be thought about. He hadn't come to Venus just for the ride, that was clear. He had known he was going to be sinking shafts after Heechee digs before he ever left Earth. He had briefed himself on the whole bit, even to handling the instruments on the airbody. My sales talk about Heechee treasures had been wasted on a customer whose mind had been made up to buy at least half a year earlier and tens of millions of miles away.

All that I understood, but the more I understood the more I saw that I didn't understand. What I really wanted was to give Cochenour a quarter and send him to the movies for a while so I could talk privately to the girl. Unfortunately, there was nowhere to send him. I managed to force a yawn, complain about the boredom of waiting for the probe traces to build up, and suggest a nap. Not that I would have been real confident he wasn't lying there with his ears flapping, listening to us. It didn't matter. Nobody acted sleepy but me. All I got out of it was an offer from Dorrie to watch the screen and wake me if anything interesting turned up.

So I said the hell with it and went to sleep myself.

It was not a good sleep, because lying there waiting for it gave me time to notice how truly lousy I felt, and in how many ways. There was a sort of permanent taste of bile in the back of my mouth not so much as though I wanted to throw up as it was as though I just had. My head ached, and I was beginning to see ghost images wandering fuzzily around my field of vision. When I took my pills I didn't count the ones that were left. I didn't want to know.

I'd set my private alarm for three hours, thinking maybe that would give Cochenour time to get sleepy and turn in, leaving the girl up and about and perhaps conversational.

But when I woke up there was Cochenour, cooking himself a herb omelette with the last of our sterile eggs. "You were right, Walthers," he grinned, "I was sleepy. Had a nice little nap. Ready for anything now. Want some eggs?"

Actually I did want them; but of course I didn't dare eat them, so I glumly swallowed what the Quackery had allowed me to have and watched him stuff himself. It was unfair that a man of ninety could be so healthy that he didn't have to think about digestion, while I was—well, there wasn't any profit in that kind of thinking, so I offered to play some music, and Dorrie picked *Swan Lake*, and I started it up.

And then I had an idea and headed for the tool lockers. They needed checking. The auger heads were about due for replacement, and I knew we were low on spares; and the other thing about the tool lockers was that they were as far from the galley as you could get and stay inside the airbody, and I hoped Dorrie would follow me. And she did.

"Need any help, Audee?"

"Glad to have it," I said. "Here, hold these for me. Don't get the grease on your clothes." I didn't expect her to ask me why they had to be held. She didn't. She only laughed.

"Grease? I don't think I'd even notice it, dirty as I am. I guess we're all about ready to get back to civilization."

Cochenour was frowning over the probe trace and paying us no attention. I said, "Meaning which kind of civilization, the Spindle or Earth?"

What I had in mind was to start her talking about Earth, but she went the other way. "Oh, the Spindle, Audee. I thought it was fascinating, and we really didn't get to see much of it. And the people. Like that Indian fellow who ran the cafe. The cashier was his wife, wasn't she?"

"One of them. She's the number-one wife; the waitress was number three, and he has another one at home with the kids. There are five of them, all three wives involved." But I wanted to go in the other direction, so I said, "It's pretty much the same as on Earth. Vastra would be running a tourist trap in Benares if he wasn't running one here, and he wouldn't be here if he hadn't shipped out with the military and terminated here. I'd be guiding in Texas, I suppose. If there's any open country left to guide in, maybe up along the Canadian River. How about you?"

All the time I was picking up the same four or five tools, studying the serial numbers and putting them back. She didn't notice.

"How do you mean?"

"Well, what did you do before you came here?"

"Oh, I worked in Boyce's office for a while."

That was encouraging; maybe she'd remember something about his connection with Professor Hegramet. "What were you, a secretary?"

"Something like that. Boyce let me handle—oh, what's that?"

That was an incoming call on the radio, that was what that was.

"So go answer," snarled Cochenour from across the airbody.

I took it on the earjack, since that is my nature; there isn't any privacy to speak of in an airbody, and I want what little crumbs of it I can find. It was the base calling, a comm sergeant I knew named Littleknees. I signed in irritably, regretting the lost chance to pump Dorotha about her boss.

"A private word for you, Audee," said Sergeant Littleknees. "Got your sahib around?"

Littleknees and I had exchanged radio chatter for a long time, and there was something about the cheerfulness of the tone that bothered me. I didn't look at Cochenour, but I knew he was listening—only to my side, of course, because of the earjack. "In sight but not receiving," I said. "What have you got for me?"

"Just a little news bulletin," the sergeant purred. "It came over the synsat net a couple of minutes ago. Information only. That means we don't have to do anything about it, but maybe you do, honey."

"Standing by," I said, studying the plastic housing of the radio.

The sergeant chuckled. "Your sahib's charter captain would like to have a word with him when found. It's kind of urgent, 'cause the captain is righteously kissed off."

"Yes, base," I said. "Your signals received, strength ten."

The sergeant made an amused noise again, but this time it wasn't a chuckle, it was a downright giggle. "The thing is," she said, "his check for the charter fee bounced. Want to know what the bank said? You'd never guess. 'Insufficient funds,' that's what they said."

The pain under my right lower ribs was permanent, but right then it seemed to get a lot worse. I gritted my teeth. "Ah, Sergeant Littleknees," I croaked, "can you, ah, verify that estimate?"

"Sorry, honey," she buzzed sympathetically in my ear, "but there's no doubt in the world. Captain got a credit report on him and it turned up n.g. When your customer gets back to the Spindle there'll be a make-good warrant waiting for him."

"Thank you for the synoptic report," I said hollowly. "I will verify departure time before we take off."

And I turned off the radio and gazed at my rich billionaire client.

"What the hell's the matter with you, Walthers?" he growled.

But I wasn't hearing his voice. I was hearing what the happy fellow at the Quackery had told me. The equations were unforgettable. Cash = new liver + happy survival. No cash = total hepatic failure + death. And my cash supply had just dried up.

10

When you get a really big piece of news you have to let it trickle through your system and get thoroughly absorbed before you do anything about it. It isn't a matter of seeing the implications. I saw them right away, you bet. It's a matter of letting the system reach an equilibrium state. So I puttered for a minute. I listened to Tchaikovsky. I made sure the radio switch was off so as not to waste power. I checked the synoptic plot. It would have been nice if there had been something to show, but, the way things were going, there wouldn't be, of course, and there wasn't. A few pale echoes were building up. But nothing with the shape of a Heechee dig, and nothing very bright. The data were still coming in, but there was no way for those feeble plots to turn into the mother lode that could save us all, even broke bastard Cochenour. I even looked out at as much of the sky as I could to see how the weather was. It didn't matter, but some of the high white calomel clouds were scudding among the purples and yellows of the other mercury halides. It was beautiful and I hated it.

Cochenour had forgotten about his omelette and was watching me thoughtfully. So was Dorrie, still holding the augers in their grease-paper wrap. I grinned at her. "Pretty," I said, referring to the music. The Auckland Philharmonic was just getting to the part where the little swans come out arm in arm and do a fast, bouncy *pas de quatre* across the stage. It has always been one of my favorite parts of *Swan Lake*. "We'll listen to the rest of it later," I said, and snapped it off.

"All right," snarled Cochenour, "what's going on?"

I sat down on an igloo pack and lit a cigarette, because one of the adjustments my internal system had made was to calculate that we didn't have to worry much about coddling our oxygen supply anymore. I said, "There's a question that's bothering me, Cochenour. How did you get on to Professor Hegramet?"

He grinned and relaxed. "Is that all that's on your mind? I checked the place out before I came. Why not?"

"No reason, except that you let me think you didn't know a thing."

He shrugged. "If you had any brains you'd know I didn't get rich by being stupid. You think I'd come umpty-million miles without knowing what I was coming to?"

"No, you wouldn't, but you did your best to make me think you would. No matter. So you dug up somebody who could point you to whatever was worth stealing on Venus, and somebody steered you to Hegramet. Then what? Did he tell you I was dumb enough to be your boy?"

Cochenour wasn't quite as relaxed, but he wasn't aggressive either. He said, "Hegramet told me you were the right guide to find a virgin tunnel. That's all—except briefing on the Heechee and so on. If you hadn't come to us I would have come to you; you just saved me the trouble."

I said, a little surprised, "You know, I think you're telling me the truth. Except you left out one thing: It wasn't the fun of making more money that you were after, it was just money, right? Money that you needed." I turned to Dorotha, standing frozen with the augers in her hand. "How about it, Dorrie? Did you know the old man was broke?"

Putting it that way was not too smart. I saw what she was about to do just before she did it, and jumped off the igloo. I was a little too late. She dropped the augers before I could get them from her, but fortunately they landed flat and the blades weren't chipped. I picked them up and put them away.

She had answered the question well enough.

I said, "I see you didn't know. Tough on you, doll. His check to the captain of the *Gagarin* is still bouncing, and I would imagine the one he gave me isn't going to be much better. I hope you got it in furs and jewels, and my advice to you is to hide them before the creditors want them back."

She didn't even look at me. She was only looking at Cochenour, whose expression was all the confirmation she needed.

I don't know what I expected from her, rage or reproaches or tears. What she did was whisper, "Oh, Boyce, I'm so sorry," and she went over and put her arm around him.

I turned my back on them, because I didn't like looking at him. The strapping ninety years old buck in Full Medical had turned into a defeated old man. For the first time, he looked all of his age and maybe a little more: the mouth half open, trembling; the straight back stooped; the bright blue eyes watering. She stroked him and crooned to him.

I looked at the synoptic web again, for lack of anything better to do. It was about as clear as it was going to get, and it was empty. We had nearly a 50 percent overlap from our previous soundings, so I could tell that the interesting-looking scratches at one edge were nothing to get excited about. We'd checked them out already. They were only ghosts.

There was no rescue there.

Curiously, I felt kind of relaxed. There is something tranquillizing about the realization that you have nothing much left to lose. It puts things in a different perspective. I don't mean to say that I had given up completely. There were still things I could do. They might not have anything to do with prolonging my life, but the taste in my mouth and the pain in my gut weren't letting me enjoy life very much anyway. I could, for instance, write Audee Walthers off; since only a miracle could keep me from dying in a matter of days, I could accept the fact that I wasn't going to be alive a week from now and use what time I had for something else. What else? Well, Dorrie was a nice kid. I could fly the airbody back to the Spindle, turn Cochenour over to the gendarmes, and spend my last day or so introducing her around. Vastra or BeeGee would help her get organized. She might not even have to go into prostitution or the rackets. The high season wasn't that far off, and she would do well with a little booth of prayer fans and Heechee lucky pieces for the Terry tourists. Maybe that wasn't much, even from her point of view, but it was something.

Or I could fling myself on the mercy of the Quackery. They might let me have the new liver on credit. The only reason I had for thinking they wouldn't was that they never had.

Or I could open the two-fuel valves and let them mix for ten minutes or so before hitting the igniter. The explosion wouldn't leave much of the airbody or us, and nothing at all of our problems.

Or—

"Oh, hell." I said. "Buck up, Cochenour. We're not dead yet."

He looked at me for a minute. He patted Dorrie's shoulder and pushed her away, gently enough. He said, "I will be, soon enough. I'm sorry about all this, Dorotha. And I'm sorry about your check, Walthers; I expect you needed the money."

"You have no idea."

He said with difficulty, "Do you want me to explain?"

"I don't see that it makes any difference, but, yes, out of curiosity I do."

I let him tell me, and he did it steadily and succinctly. I could have guessed. A man his age is either very, very rich or dead. He was only quite rich. He'd kept his industries going on what was left after he siphoned off the costs of transplant and treatment, calciphylaxis and prosthesis, protein regeneration here, cholesterol flushing there, a million for this, a hundred grand a week for that . . . oh, it went, I could see that. "You just don't know," he said, "what it takes to keep a hundred-year-old man alive until you try it."

I corrected him automatically. "Ninety, you mean."

"No, not ninety, and not even a hundred. I think it's at least a hundred and ten, and it could be more than that. Who counts? You pay the doctors and they patch you up for a month or two. You wouldn't know."

Oh, wouldn't I just, I said, but not out loud. I let him go on, telling about how the federal inspectors were closing in and he skipped Earth to make his fortune all over again on Venus.

But I wasn't listening anymore; I was writing on the back of a navigation form. When I was finished, I passed it over to Cochenour. "Sign it," I said.

"What is it?"

"Does it matter? You don't have any choice, do you? But it's a release from the all-rights section of our charter agreement; you acknowledge you have no claim, that your check's rubber, and that you voluntarily waive your ownership of anything we find in my favor."

He frowned. "What's this bit at the end?"

"That's where I give you ten percent of anything we do find, *if* we do find anything."

"That's charity," he said, but he was signing. "I don't mind charity, especially since, as you point out, I don't have any choice. But I can read that web as well as you can, Walthers, and there's nothing on it to find."

"No," I said, folding the paper and putting it in my pocket. "But we're not going to dig here. That trace is bare as your bank account. What we're going to do is dig Trace C."

I lit another cigarette and thought for a minute. I was wondering how much to tell them of what I had spent five years finding out and figuring out, schooling myself not even to hint at it to anyone else. I was sure in my mind that nothing I said would make a difference, but the words didn't want to say themselves anyway.

I made myself say:

"You remember Subhash Vastra, the fellow who ran the trap where I met you. He came to Venus with the military. He was a weapons specialist. There's no civilian career for a weapons specialist so he went into the cafe business when they terminated him, but he was pretty big at it in the service."

Dorrie said, "Do you mean there are Heechee weapons on the reservation?"

"No. Nobody has ever found a Heechee weapon. But they found targets."

It was actually physically difficult for me to speak the next part, but I got it out. "Anyway, Sub Vastra says they were targets. The higher brass wasn't sure, and I think the matter has been pigeonholed on the reservation by now. But what they found was triangular pieces of Heechee wall material—that blue, light-emitting stuff they lined the tunnels with. There were dozens of them, and they all had a pattern of radiating lines; Sub said they looked like targets to him. And they had been drilled through, by something that left the holes chalky as talc. Do you know anything that would do that to Heechee wall material?"

Dorrie was about to say she didn't, but Cochenour interrupted her. "That's impossible," he said flatly.

"Right, that's what the brass said. They decided it had to be done in the process of fabrication, for some Heechee purpose we'll never know. But Vastra says not. He says they looked exactly like the paper targets from the firing range under the reservation. The holes weren't all in the same place; the lines looked like scoring markers. That's evidence he's right. Not proof. But evidence."

"And you think you can find the gun that made those holes where we marked Trace C?"

I hesitated. "I wouldn't put it that strongly. Call it a hope. But there is one more thing.

"These targets were turned up by a prospector nearly forty years ago. He turned them in, reported his find, went out looking for more and got killed. That happened a lot in those days. No one paid much attention until some military types got a look at them; and that's how come the reservation is where it is. They spotted the site where he'd reported finding them, staked out everything for a thousand kilometers around and labeled it all off limits. And they dug and dug, turned up about a dozen Heechee tunnels, but most of them bare and the rest cracked and spoiled."

"Then there's nothing there," growled Cochenour, looking perplexed.

"There's nothing they found," I corrected him. "But in those days prospectors lied a lot. He reported the wrong location for the find. At the time, he was shacked up with a young lady who later married a man named Allemang, and her son is a friend of mine. He had a map. The right location, as near as I can figure—the navigation marks weren't what they are now—is right about where we are now, give or take some. I saw digging marks a couple of times and I think they were his." I slipped the little private magneto-fiche out of my pocket and put it into the virtual map display; it showed a single mark, an orange X. "That's where I think we might find the weapon, somewhere near that X. And as you can see, the only undug indication there is good old Trace C."

Silence for a minute. I listened to the distant outside howl of the winds, waiting for them to say something.

Dorrie was looking troubled. "I don't know if I like trying to find a new weapon," she said. "It's—it's like bringing back the bad old days again."

I shrugged. Cochenour, beginning to look more like himself again, said, "The point isn't whether we really want to find a weapon, is it? The point is that we want to find an untapped Heechee dig for whatever is in it—but the soldiers think there *might* be a weapon somewhere around, so they aren't going to let us dig, right? They'll shoot us first and ask questions later. Wasn't that what you said?"

"That's what I said."

"So how do you propose to get around that little problem?" he asked.

If I were a truthful man I would have said I wasn't sure I could. Looked at honestly, the odds were we would get caught and very likely shot; but we had so little to lose, Cochenour and I, that I didn't think that important enough to mention. I said:

"We try to fool them. We send the airbody off, and you and I stay behind to do the digging. If they think we're gone, they won't be keeping us under surveillance, and all we have to worry about is being picked up on a routine perimeter search."

"Audee!" cried the girl. "If you and Boyce stay here—But that means I have to take the airbody, and *I* can't fly this thing."

"No, you can't. But you can let it fly itself." I rushed on: "Oh, you'll waste fuel and you'll get bounced around a lot. But you'll get there on autopilot. It'll even land you at the Spindle." Not necessarily easily or well; I closed my mind to the thought of what an automatic landing might do to my one and only airbody. She would survive it, though, ninety-nine chances out of a hundred.

"Then what?" Cochenour demanded.

There were big holes in the plan at this point, but I closed my mind to them, too. "Dorrie looks up my friend BeeGee Allemang. I'll give you a note to give him with all the coordinates and so on, and he'll come and pick us up. With extra tanks, we'll have air and power for maybe forty-eight hours after you leave. That's plenty of time for you to get there, find BeeGee and give him the message, and for him to get back. If he's late, of course, we're in trouble. If we don't find anything, we've wasted our time. But if we do—"

I shrugged. "I didn't say it was a guarantee," I added, "I only said it gave us a chance."

Dorrie was quite a nice person, considering her age and her circumstances, but one of the things she lacked was self-confidence. She had not been trained to it; she had been getting it as a prosthesis, from Cochenour most recently, I suppose before that from whoever preceded Cochenour in her life—at her age, maybe her father.

That was the biggest problem, persuading Dorrie she could do her part. "It won't work," she kept saying. "I'm sorry. It isn't that I don't want to help. I do, but I can't. It just won't work."

Well, it would have.

Or at least I think it would have.

In the event, we never got to try it. Between us, Cochenour and I did get Dorrie to agree to give it a try. We packed up what little gear we'd put outside, flew back to the ravine, landed and began to set up for the dig. But I was feeling poorly, thick, headachy, clumsy, and I suppose Cochenour had his own problems. Between the two of us we managed to catch the casing of the drill in the exit port while we were off-loading it, and while I was jockeying it one way from above, Cochenour pulled the other way from beneath and the whole thing came down on top of him. It didn't kill him. But it gouged his suit and broke his leg, and that took care of my idea of digging Trace C with him.

11

The suit leg had been ruptured through eight or ten plies, but there was enough left to keep the air out, if not the pressure.

The first thing I did was check the drill to make sure it wasn't damaged. It wasn't. The second thing was to fight Cochenour back into the lock. That took about everything I had, with the combined weight of our suits and bodies, getting the drill out of the way, and my general physical condition. But I managed it.

Dorrie was great. No hysterics, no foolish questions. We got him out of his suit and looked him over. He was unconscious. The leg was compounded, with bone showing through; he was bleeding from the mouth and nose, and he had vomited inside his helmet. All in all he was about the worst-looking hundred-and-some-year-old man you'll ever see—live one, anyway. But he hadn't taken enough heat to cook his brain, his heart was still going—well, whoever's heart it had been in the first place, I mean; it was a good investment, because it pumped right along. The bleeding stopped by itself, except from the nasty business on the leg.

Dorrie called the military reservation for me, got Eve Littleknees, was put right through to the Base Surgeon. He told me what to do. At first he wanted me to pack up and bring Cochenour right over, but I vetoed that—said I wasn't in shape to fly and it would be too rough a ride. Then he gave me step-by-steps and I followed it easily enough: reduced the fracture, packed the gash, closed the wound with surgical Velcro and meat glue, sprayed a bandage all around and poured on a cast. It took about an hour, and Cochenour would have come to while we were doing it except I gave him a sleepy needle.

So then it was just a matter of taking pulse and respiration and blood-pressure readings to satisfy the surgeon, and promising to get him back to the Spindle shortly. When the surgeon was through, still annoyed at me for not bringing Cochenour over, Sergeant

Littleknees came back on. I could tell what was on her mind. "Uh, honey? How did it happen?"

"A great big Heechee came up out of the ground and bit him," I said. "I know what you're thinking and you've got an evil mind. It was just an accident."

"Sure," she said. "Okay. I just wanted you to know I don't blame you a bit." And she signed off.

Dorrie was cleaning Cochenour up as best she could—pretty profligate with the water reserves, I thought. I left her to it while I made myself some coffee, lit a cigarette, and sat and thought.

By the time Dorrie had done what she could for Cochenour, then cleaned up the worst of the mess and begun to do such important tasks as repairing her eye makeup, I had thought up a dandy.

I gave Cochenour a wake-up needle, and Dorrie patted him and talked to him while he got his bearings. She was not a girl who carried a grudge. I did, a little. I got him up to try out his muscles faster than he really wanted to. His expression told me that they all ached. They worked all right, though.

He was able to grin. "Old bones," he said. "I knew I should have gone for the recalciphylaxis. That's what happens when you try to save a buck."

He sat down heavily, the leg stuck out in front of him. He wrinkled his nose. "Sorry to have messed up your nice clean airbody," he added.

"You want to clean yourself up?"

He looked surprised. "Well, I think I'd better, pretty soon—"

"Do it now. I want to talk to you both."

He didn't argue, just held out his hand, and Dorrie took it. He stumped, half-hopped toward the cleanup. Actually Dorrie had done the worst of it, but he splashed a little water on his face and swished some around in his mouth. He was pretty well recovered when he turned around to look at me.

"All right, what is it? Are we giving up?"

I said. "No. We'll do it a different way."

Dorrie cried, "He can't, Audee! Look at him. And the condition his suit's in, he couldn't last outside an hour, much less help you dig."

"I know that, so we'll have to change the plan. I'll dig by myself. The two of you will slope off in the airbody."

"Oh, brave man," said Cochenour flatly. "Who are you kidding? It's a two-man job."

I hesitated. "Not necessarily. Lone prospectors have done it before, although the problems were a little different. I admit it'll be a tough forty-eight for me, but we'll have to try it. One reason. We don't have any alternative."

"Wrong," said Cochenour. He patted Dorrie's rump. "Solid muscle, that girl. She isn't big, but she's healthy. Takes after her grandmother. Don't argue, Walthers. Just think a little bit. It's as safe for Dorrie as it is for you; and with the two of you, there's a chance we might luck in. By yourself, no chance at all."

For some reason, his attitude put me in a bad temper. "You talk as though she didn't have anything to say about it."

"Well," said Dorrie, sweetly enough, "come to that, so do you. I appreciate your wanting to make things easy for me, Audee, but, honestly, I think I could help. I've learned a lot. And if you want the truth, you look a lot worse than I do."

I said with all the sneer I could get into my voice, "Forget it. You can both help me for an hour or so, while I get set up. Then we'll do it my way. No arguments. Let's get going."

That made two mistakes. The first was that we didn't get set up in an hour; it took more than two, and I was sweating sick oily sweat before we finished. I really felt bad. I was past hurting or worrying about it; I just thought it a little surprising every time my heart beat. Dorrie did more muscle work than I did, strong and willing as promised, and Cochenour checked over the instruments, and asked a couple of questions when he had to to make sure he could handle his part of the job, flying the airbody. I took two cups of coffee heavily laced with my private supply of gin and smoked my last cigarette for a while, meanwhile checking out with the military reservation. Eve Littleknees was flirtatious but a little puzzled.

Then Dorrie and I tumbled out of the lock and closed it behind us, leaving Cochenour strapped in the pilot's seat.

Dorrie stood there for a moment, looking forlorn; but then she grabbed my hand and the two of us lumbered to the shelter of the igloo we'd already ignited. I had impressed on her the importance of being out of the wash of the twin-fuel jets. She was good about it; flung herself flat and didn't move.

I was less cautious. As soon as I could judge from the flare that the jets were angled away from us, I stuck my head up and watched Cochenour take off in a sleet of heavy-metal ash. It wasn't a bad take-off. In circumstances like that I define "bad" as total demolition of the airbody and the death or maiming of one or more persons. He avoided that, but the airbody skittered and slid wildly as the gusts caught it. It would be a rough ride for him, going just the few hundred kilometers north that would take him out of detection range.

I touched Dorrie with my toe and she struggled up. I slipped the talk cord into the jack on her helmet—radio was out, because of possible perimeter patrols that we wouldn't be able to see.

"Change your mind yet?" I asked.

It was a fairly obnoxious question, but she took it nicely. She giggled. I could tell that because we were faceplate to faceplate and I could see her face shadowed inside the helmet. But I couldn't hear what she was saying until she remembered to nudge the voice switch, and then what I heard was:

"—romantic, just the two of us."

Well, we didn't have time for that kind of chitchat. I said irritably, "Let's quit wasting time. Remember what I told you. We have air, water and power for forty-eight hours. Don't count on any margin. One or two of them might hold out a little longer, but you need all three to stay alive. Try not to work too hard; the less you metabolize, the less your waste system has to handle. If we find a tunnel and get in, maybe we can eat some of those emergency rations over there—provided it's unbreached and hasn't heated up too much in a quarter of a million years. Otherwise don't even think about food. As for sleeping, forget—"

"Now who's wasting time? You told me all this before." But she was still cheery.

So we climbed into the igloo and started work.

The first thing we had to do was clear out some of the tailings that had already begun to accumulate where we left the drill going. The usual way, of course, is to reverse and redirect the augers. We couldn't do that. It would have meant taking them away from cutting the shaft. We had to do it the hard way, namely manually.

It was hard, all right. Hotsuits are uncomfortable to begin with. When you have to work in them, they're miserable. When the work is both very hard physically and complicated by the cramped space inside an igloo that already contains two people and a working drill, it's next to impossible.

We did it anyhow, having no choice.

Cochenour hadn't lied; Dorrie was as good as a man. The question was whether that was going to be good enough. The other question, which was bothering me more and more every minute, was whether I was as good as a man. The headache was really pounding at me, and I found myself blacking out when I moved suddenly. The Quackery had promised me three weeks before acute hepatic failure, but that hadn't been meant to include this kind of work. I had to figure I was on plus time already. That is a disconcerting way to figure.

Especially when ten hours went by and I realized that we were down lower than the soundings had shown the tunnel to be, and no luminous blue tailings were in sight.

We were drilling a dry hole.

Now, if we had had the airbody close by, this would have been an annoyance. Maybe a big annoyance, but not a disaster. What I would have done was get back in the airbody, clean up, get a good night's sleep, eat a meal, and recheck the trace. We were digging in the wrong place. All right, next step is to dig in the right place. Study the terrain, pick a spot, ignite another igloo, start up the drills and try, try again.

That's what we *would* have done. But we didn't have any of those advantages. We didn't have the airbody. We had no chance for sleep or food. We were out of igloos. We didn't have the trace to look at. And I was feeling lousier every minute.

I crawled out of the igloo, sat down in the next thing there was to the lee of the wind, and stared at the scudding yellow green sky.

There ought to be something to do, if I could only think of it. I ordered myself to think.

Well, let's see. Could I maybe uproot the igloo and move it to another spot?

No. I could break it loose all right with the augers, but the minute it was free the winds would catch it and it would be good-bye, Charlie. I'd never see that igloo again. Plus there would be no way to make it gastight anyway.

Well, then, how about drilling without an igloo?

Possible, I judged. Pointless, though. Suppose we did hit lucky and hole in? Without an igloo to lock out those twenty thousand millibars of hot gas, we'd destroy the contents anyway.

I felt a nudge on my shoulder, and discovered that Dorrie was sitting next to me. She didn't ask any questions, didn't try to say anything at all. I guess it was all clear enough without talking about it.

By my suit chronometer fifteen hours were gone. That left thirty-some before Cochenour would come back and get us. I didn't see any point in spending it all sitting there, but on the other hand I didn't see any point in doing anything else.

Of course, I thought, I could always go to sleep for a while . . . and then I woke up and realized that that was what I had been doing.

Dorrie was asleep beside me.

You may wonder how a person can sleep in the teeth of a south polar thermal gale. It isn't all that hard. All it takes is that you be wholly worn out, and wholly despairing. Sleeping isn't just to knit the ravelled sleeve, it is a good way to shut the world off when the world is too lousy to face. As ours was.

But Venus is the last refuge of the Puritan ethic. Crazy. I knew I was as good as dead, but I felt I had to be doing something. I eased away from Dorrie, made sure her suit was belted to the hold-tight ring at the base of the igloo, and stood up. It took a great deal of concentration for me to be able to stand up, which was almost as good at keeping care out as sleep.

It occurred to me that there still might be eight or ten live Heechees in the tunnel, and maybe they'd heard us knocking and opened up the bottom of the shaft for us. So I crawled into the igloo to see.

I peered down the shaft to make sure. No. They hadn't. It was still just a blind hole that disappeared into dirty dark invisibility at the end of the light from my head lamp. I swore at the Heechees who hadn't helped us out, and kicked some tailings down the shaft on their nonexistent heads.

The Puritan ethic was itching me, and I wondered what I ought to do. Die? Well, yes, but I was doing that fast enough. Something constructive?

I remembered that you always ought to leave a place the way you found it, so I hauled up the drills on the eight-to-one winch and stowed them neatly. I kicked some more tailings down the useless hole to make a place to sit, and I sat down and thought.

I mused about what we had done wrong, as you might think about a chess puzzle.

I could still see the trace in my mind. It was bright and clear, so there was definitely something there. It was just tough that we'd lucked out and missed it.

How had we missed it?

After some time, I thought I knew the answer to that.

People like Dorrie and Cochenour have an idea that a seismic trace is like one of those underground maps of downtown Dallas, with all the sewers and utility conduits and water pipes marked, so you just dig where it says and you find what you want.

It isn't exactly like that. The trace comes out as a sort of hazy approximation. It is built up, hour by hour, by measuring the echoes from the pinger. It looks like a band of spiderweb shadows, much wider than an actual tunnel and very fuzzy at the edges. When you look at it you know that somewhere in the shadows there's something that makes them. Maybe it's a rock interface or a pocket of gravel. Hopefully it's a Heechee dig. Whatever it is, it's there somewhere, but you don't know just where, exactly. If a tunnel is twenty meters wide, which is a fair average for a Heechee connecting link, the shadow trace is sure to look like fifty, and may be a hundred.

So where do you dig?

That's where the art of prospecting comes in. You have to make an informed guess.

Maybe you dig in the exact geometrical center—as far as it is given you to see where the center is. That's the easiest way. Maybe you dig where the shadows are densest, which is the way the half-smart prospectors do, and that works almost half the time. Or maybe you do what I did, and try to think like a Heechee. You look at the trace as a whole and try to see what points they might have been trying to connect. Then you plot an imaginary course between them, where you would have put the tunnel if you had been the Heechee engineer in charge, and you dig somewhere along there.

That's what I had done, but evidently I had done wrong.

In a fuzzy-brained sort of way, I began to think I saw what I'd done.

I visualized the trace. The right place to dig was where I had set the airbody down, but of course I couldn't set up the igloo there because the airbody was in the way. So I'd set up about ten yards upslope.

I was convinced that ten yards was what made us miss.

I was pleased with myself for figuring it out, although I couldn't see that it made a lot of practical difference. If I'd had another igloo I would have been glad to try again, assuming I could hold out that long. But that didn't mean much, because I didn't have another igloo.

So I sat on the edge of the dark shaft, nodding sagaciously over the way I had solved the problem, dangling my legs and now and then sweeping tailings in. I think that was part of a kind of death wish, because I know I thought, now and then, that the nicest thing to do would be to jump in and pull the tailings down over me.

But the Puritan ethic didn't want me to do that. Anyway, it would have solved only my own personal problem. It wouldn't have done anything for old Dorrie Keefer, snoring away outside in the thermal hurricane.

I then began to wonder why I was worrying about Dorrie. It was a pleasant enough subject to be thinking about, but sort of sad.

I went back to thinking about the tunnel.

The bottom of the shaft couldn't be more than a few yards away from where we had bottomed out empty. I thought of jumping down and scraping away with my bare gloves. It seemed like a good idea. I'm not sure how much was whimsy and how much the fantasy of a sick man, but I kept thinking how nice it would be if there were Heechees still in there, and when I scratched into the blue wall material I could just knock politely and they'd open up and let me in. I even had a picture of what they looked like: sort of friendly and godlike. It would have been very pleasant to meet a Heechee, a live one that could speak English. "Heechee, what did you really use those things we call prayer fans for?" I could ask him. Or, "Heechee, have you got anything that will keep me from dying in your medicine chest?" Or, "Heechee, I'm sorry we messed up your front yard and I'll try to clean it up for you."

I pushed more of the tailings back into the shaft. I had nothing better to do, and who could tell, maybe they'd appreciate it. After a while I had it half full and I'd run out of tailings, except for the ones that were pushed outside the igloo, and I didn't have the strength to go after them. I looked for something else to do. I reset the augers, replaced the dull blades with the last sharp ones we had, pointed them in the general direction of a twenty-degree offset angle downslope, and turned them on.

It wasn't until I noticed that Dorrie was standing next to me, helping me steady the augers for the first yards of cut, that I realized I had made a plan.

Why not try an offset cut? Did we have any better chance?

We did not. We cut.

When the drills stopped bucking and settled down to chew into the rock and we could leave them, I cleared a space at the side of the igloo and shoved tailings out for a while; then we just sat there and watched the drills spit rock chips into the old shaft. It was filling up nicely. We didn't speak. Presently I fell asleep again.

I didn't wake up until Dorrie pounded on my head. We were buried in tailings, but they weren't just rock. They glowed blue, so bright they almost hurt my eyes.

The augers must have been scratching at the Heechee wall liner for hours. They had actually worn pits into it.

We looked down, and we could see the round bright blue eye of the tunnel wall staring up at us. She was a beauty, all ours.

Even then we didn't speak.

Somehow I managed to kick and wriggle my way through the drift to the crawl-through. I got the lock closed and sealed, after kicking a couple of cubic meters of rock outside. Then I began fumbling through the pile of refuse for the flame drills. Ultimately I found them. Somehow. Ultimately I managed to get them shipped and primed. I fired them, and watched the bright spot of light that bounced out of the shaft and made a pattern on the igloo roof.

Then there was a sudden short scream of gas, and a clatter as the loose fragments at the bottom of the shaft dropped free.

We had cut into the Heechee tunnel. It was unbreached and waiting for us. Our beauty was a virgin. We took her maidenhead with all love and reverence and entered into her.

12

I must have blacked out again, and when I realized where I was I was on the floor of the tunnel. My helmet was open. So were the side-zips of my hotsuit. I was breathing stale, foul air that had to be a quarter of a million years old and smelled every minute of it. But it was air. It was denser than Earth normal and a lot more humid; but the partial pressure of oxygen was about the same. It was enough to live on, in any case. I was proving that by breathing it and not dying.

Next to me was Dorrie Keefer.

The blue Heechee wall light didn't flatter her complexion. At first I wasn't sure she was breathing. But in spite of the way she looked her pulse was going, her lungs were functioning, and when she felt me poking at her she opened her eyes.

"We made it," she said.

We sat there grinning foolishly at each other, like Hallowe'en masks in the blue Heechee glow.

To do anything more than that, just then, was quite impossible. I had my hands full just comprehending the fact that I was alive. I didn't want to endanger that odds-against precarious fact by moving around. But I wasn't comfortable, and after a moment I realized that I was very hot. I closed up my helmet to shut out some of the heat, but the smell inside was so bad that I opened it up, figuring the heat was better.

Then it occurred to me to wonder why the heat was only unpleasant, instead of instantly fatal. Energy transport through a Heechee wall-material surface is very slow, but not a quarter of a million years slow. My sad old brain ruminated that thought around for awhile and came up with a conclusion: At least until quite recently, some centuries or thousands of years, maybe, this tunnel had been kept cool. Automatic machinery, of course, I thought sagely. Wow, that by itself was worth finding. Broken down or not, it would be worth a lot of fortunes. . . .

And that made me remember why we were there in the first place, and I looked up the corridor and down, to see what treasures were waiting there for us.

When I was a school kid in Amarillo Central my favorite teacher was a crippled lady named Miss Stevenson, and she used to tell us stories out of Bulfinch and Homer. She spoiled a whole weekend for me with the story of one Greek fellow who wanted to be a god. He was king of a little place in Lydia, but he wanted more, and the gods let him come to Olympus, and he had it made until he fouled up. I forget how; it had something to do with a dog, and some nasty business about tricking the gods into eating his own son. Whatever it was, they gave him solitary confinement for eternity, standing neck deep in a cool lake in hell and unable to drink. The fellow's name was Tantalus, and in that Heechee tunnel I had a lot in common with him. The treasure trove was there all right, but we couldn't reach it. We hadn't hit the main tunnel but a sort of angled, Thielly-tube detour in it, and it was blocked at both ends. We could peer past half-closed gates into the main shaft. We could see Heechee machines and irregular mounds of things that might once have been containers, now rotted, with their contents on the floor. But we hadn't the strength to get at them.

It was the suits that made us so clumsy. With them off we might have been able to slip through, but then would we have the strength to put them back on again in time to meet Cochenour? I doubted it. I stood there with my helmet pressed to the gate, feeling like Alice peering into her garden without the bottle of drink-me, and then I thought about Cochenour again and checked the time.

It was forty-six hours and some odd minutes since he had left us. He was due back any time.

And if he came back while we were here, and opened the crawl-through to look for us and was careless about the seal at both ends, twenty thousand millibars of poison gas would hammer in on us. It would kill us, of course, but besides that it would damage the virgin tunnel. The corrosive scouring of that implosion of gas might wreck everything.

"We have to go back," I told Dorrie, showing her the time. She smiled.

"Temporarily," she said, and turned and led the way.

After the cheerful blue glow of the Heechee tunnel the igloo was cramped and miserable, and what was worse was that we couldn't even stay inside it. Cochenour probably would remember to lock in and out of both ends of the crawl-through. But he might not. I couldn't take that chance. I tried to think of a way of plugging the shaft, maybe by pushing all the tailings back in again, but although my brain wasn't working very well, I could see that was stupid.

So we had to wait outside in the breezy Venusian weather, and not too much later, either. The little watch dial next to my life-support meters, all running well into the red now, showed that Cochenour should in fact have arrived by now.

I pushed Dorrie into the crawl-through, squeezed in with her, locked us both through, and we waited.

We waited a long time, Dorrie bent over the crawl-through and me leaning beside her, holding on to her and the tie-down clips. We could have talked, but I thought she was either unconscious or asleep from the way she didn't move, and anyway it seemed like an awful lot of work to plug in the phone jack.

We waited longer than that, and still Cochenour didn't come.

I tried to think things through.

There could have been a number of reasons for his being late. He could have crashed. He could have been challenged by the military. He could have got lost.

But there was another possibility that made more sense than all of them. The time dial told me he was nearly five hours late now, and the life-support meters told me we were right up against the upper maximum for power, near it for air, well past it for water. If it hadn't been for breathing the Heechee gases for a while, we would have been dead by then, and Cochenour didn't know about that.

He had said he was a bad loser. He had worked out an end-game maneuver so he wouldn't have to lose. I could see him as clearly as though I were in the airbody with him, watching his own clocks, cooking himself a light lunch and playing music while he waited for us to die.

That was no frightening thought; I was close enough to it for the difference to be pretty much a technicality, and tired enough of being trapped in that foul hotsuit to be willing to accept almost any deliverance. But the girl was involved, and the one tiny little rational thought that stayed in my half-poisoned brain was that it was unfair for Cochenour to kill us both. Me, yes. Her, no. I beat on her suit until she moved a little, and after some time managed to make her move back into the crawl-through.

There were two things Cochenour didn't know. He didn't know we'd found breathable air, and he didn't know we could tap the drill batteries for additional power.

In all the freaked-out fury of my head, I was still capable of that much consecutive thought. We could surprise him, if he didn't wait much longer. We could stay alive for a few hours yet, and then when he came to find us dead and see what prize we had won for him, he would find me waiting.

And so he did.

It must have been a terrible shock to him when he entered the igloo with the monkey wrench in his hand and leaned over me, and found that I was still alive and able to move, where he had expected only a well-done roast of meat. The drill caught him right in the chest. I couldn't see his face, but I guess at his expression.

Then it was only a matter of doing four or five impossible things. Things like getting Dorrie up out of the tunnel and into the airbody. Like getting myself in after her, and sealing up, and setting a course. All these impossible things, and one other, that was harder than all of them, but very important to me.

I totalled the airbody when we landed, but we were strapped in and suited up, and when the ground crews came to investigate, Dorrie and I were still alive.

13

They had to patch me and rehydrate me for three days before they could even think about putting my new liver in. In the old days they would have kept me sedated the whole time, but, of course, they kept waking me up every couple of hours for some feedback training on monitoring my hepatic flows. I hated it, because it was all sickness and pain and nagging from Dr. Morius and the nurses and I could have wished for the old days back again, except, of course, that in the old days I would have died.

But by the fourth day I hardly hurt at all, except when I moved, and they were letting me take my fluids by mouth instead of the other way.

I realized I was going to be alive for a while, and looked upon my surroundings, and found them good.

There's no such thing as a season in the Spindle, but the Quackery is all sentimental about tradition and ties with the Mother Planet. They were playing scenes of fleecy white clouds on the wall panels, and the air from the ventilator ducts smelled of green leaves and lilac.

"Happy spring," I said to Dr. Morius.

"Shut up," he said, shifting a couple of the needles that pincushioned my abdomen and watching the tell-tales. "Um." He pursed his lips, pulled out a couple of needles, and said:

"Well, let's see, Walthers. We've taken out the splenovenal shunt. Your new liver is functioning well, although you're not flushing wastes through as fast as you ought to. We've got your ion levels back up to something like a human being, and most of your tissues have a little moisture in them again. Altogether," he scratched his head, "yes, in general, I would say you're alive, so presumably the operation was a success."

"Don't be a funny doctor," I said. "When do I get out of here?"

"Like right now?" he asked thoughtfully. "We could use the bed. Got a lot of paying patients coming in."

Now, one of the advantages of having blood in my brain instead of the poison soup it had been living on was that I could think reasonably clearly. So I knew right away that he was kidding me; I wouldn't have been there if I hadn't been a paying patient, one way or another, and though I couldn't imagine how, I was willing to wait a while to find out.

Anyway, I was more interested in getting out. They packed me up in wetsheets and rolled me through the Spindle to Sub Vastra's place. Dorrie was there before me, and the third of Vastra's house fussed over us both, lamb broth and that flat hard bread they like, before tucking us in for a good long rest. There was only the one bed, but Dorrie didn't seem to mind, and anyway at that point the question was academic. Later on, not so academic. After a couple of days of that I was up and as good as I ever was.

By then I had found out who paid my bill at the Quackery. For about a minute I had hoped it was me, quickly filthy rich from the spoils of our tunnel, but I knew that was impossible. We could have made money only on the sly, and we were both too near dead when we got back to the Spindle to conceal anything.

So the military had moved in and taken everything, but they had shown they had a heart. Atrophied and flinty, but a heart. They'd gone into the dig while I was still getting glucose enemas in my sleep, and had been pleased enough with what they'd found. I even tried to get Sergeant Littleknees a finder's fee. Not much, to be sure. But enough to save my life. It turned out to be enough to pay off the loosely secured checks I'd written to finance the expedition, and surgical fee and hospital costs, and just about enough left over to put a down payment on a Heechee hut of our own.

For a while it bothered me that they wouldn't tell me what they'd found. I even tried to get Sergeant Littleknees drunk when she was in the Spindle on furlough. But Dorrie was right there, and how drunk can you get one girl when another girl is right there watching you? Probably Eve Littleknees didn't know anyhow. Probably no one did except a few weapons specialists. But it had to be something, because of the cash award, and most of all because they didn't prosecute for trespass on the military reservation. And so we get along, the two of us. Or three of us.

Dorrie turned out to be good at selling fire pearls to the Terry tourists, especially when her pregnancy began to show. She kept us in eating money until the high season started, and by then I found I was a sort of celebrity, which I parlayed into a bank loan and a new airbody, and so we're doing well enough. I've promised that I'll marry her if our kid turns out to be a boy, but as a matter of fact I'm going to do it anyway. She was a great help, especially with my own private project back there at the dig. She couldn't have known what I wanted to bring back Cochenour's body for, but she didn't argue, and sick and wretched as she was, she helped me get it into the airbody lock.

Actually, I wanted it very much.

It's not actually a *new* liver, of course. Probably it's not even secondhand. Heaven knows where Cochenour bought it, but I'm sure it wasn't original equipment with him. But it works. And bastard though he was, I kind of liked him in a way, and I don't mind at all the fact that I've got a part of him with me always.

THE THINGS THAT HAPPEN

In his long career, Frederik Pohl has been interviewed a number of times, especially on radio. In the course of his public career he has met both those who do magic and those who debunk it. He has written stories in which someone is fooled or tricked for some reason, and some in which a trickster is himself tricked.

The protagonist of "The Things That Happen" is a mentalist and a very, very good one. There are always those, however, who doubt the truth of such powers. When such antagonists meet, interesting things are bound to happen, as they do in this subtly twisted tale from 1985.

When I do a college date all I promise is to give a forty-minute talk with half an hour additional for "discussion." That's in the contract. There isn't a word about bending any spoons, or reading minds, or saying what somebody has in his pocket. I never say I'll do anything at all, outside of talk for a while. Sometimes I don't. I've got my memorized BAPS, or Basic All-Purpose Speech, which tells them how I don't understand my gifts, and how sometimes they work and sometimes they don't, and how maybe (I make a joke out of it) there's some truth to what somebody told me, that superior beings from the planet Clarion keep interfering with my gifts. Then I tell them a bunch of funny little stories about Johnny Carson and Merv Griffin and various celebrities I've appeared with . . . and then, after I've said thank-you-very-much to let them know it's time to applaud, when some of them start yelling out, "Stop my watch for me, Hans!" I'll just shake my head. "Not tonight, please," I say. "I just don't feel a thing, please." And I let them hiss.

Fritzl didn't like that. He said if they hissed too often there wouldn't be any more college dates, but then I got really tired of what Fritzl said. Besides, there hadn't been that many college lecture dates lately anyway.

In fact, the whole paranormal powers business had been really slow for me lately, which was why I let Fritzl talk me into this enterprise. I didn't want to. But he kept on saying, "Fifty. Thousand. Dollars." the way he did, and I couldn't hold out.

We did it carefully. First he staked the office out for a couple of days, and then I turned up cold one early afternoon. The guy and the woman were out to lunch, and the bookkeeper was filling in for the usual receptionist while she had her lunch. Perfect timing. I walked in the door, big grin, a little apologetic. "I'd like to see Dr. Smith or Miss Baker, please. My name is Hans Geissen. Oh, they're not? Well, I'll just wait, if you don't mind." And I didn't give the woman much of a chance to mind, because I was off rubbernecking around the walls before she answered. I was careful not to give her any reason to worry about me. There was a railing that divided Them from Us, and I stayed on the unprivileged side. But I didn't sit down. I walked around the waiting room, looking at the scrolls and the certificates and the portraits. There was a Doctor of Divinity sheepskin made out to the Reverend Samuel Shipperton Smith, from some denominational college in Hobart, Tasmania. There was a portrait of a skinny woman in Grecian robes, with a Grecian hairdo and holding a Grecian kind of lyre or harp or whatever they are. The Honorable Miss Gwendoline Stella Baker was the name on the gold plate on the frame.

There's always plenty of interesting stuff in a waiting room, if you know how to look for it. What you don't want is for anyone to see you looking at it, so as I passed the coffee table by the orange plastic-covered couch I picked up a copy of *People* and paged it slowly as I wandered. I didn't overdo it. When I thought I'd done enough I sat down with the magazine in my lap and read it assiduously, looking up not at all, until the changing of the guard. When the real receptionist came back from her Burger King hold-the-lettuce Whopper and the two of them whispered over me I didn't raise my head. The bookkeeper scuttled away. The receptionist took her seat and immediately began a whispery phone conversation. Time passed. I let it pass. When, half an hour later, she disappeared into a private office in response to a faint murmur, I was when she came out just where she had left me when she went in. "Mr. Geissen?" she said.

I looked up, blinking a couple of times as though trying to remember what I was doing there.

"Dr. Smith and Miss Baker will see you in just a few minutes in the conference room."

"Oh, thank you," I said. "I'll be ready." But the fact was that I already was.

"You got by the people at S.R.I.," Fritzl said, "you got by the people at M.I.T., you got by Carson and 'Good Morning America' and the 'Today' show. You can handle these two people."

"Naturally I can handle them," I said. "It isn't a question of *handling* them. It's a question of what you can go to jail for."

"You just don't make any claims, stupid," he said. The way he talked to me!

"Of course I don't make any claims." I never did. I always said these things weren't under my control. I didn't promise a thing. I stayed on the move, sure, and if I got a chance to get away with it I'd turn your watch back or unzip your fly, and when your ballpoint pen breaks I'm just as surprised as you are. But if I don't get any chances, well, then I just give you the shamefaced grin that says some days are like that. "Get me a drink," I said, and got up and went over to the window. We were staying in the Plaza. A suite. Not a very big suite, but do you know how much even the little ones cost? But you can't be at the Y.M.C.A. when you want to do the "Today" show.

He brought me my Campari and black cherry soda, and along with it a bracelet. I always wear a lot of jewelry; this one was intertwined snakes, and it fit right in, but I hadn't asked for it. "What now?" I asked.

He said, "Try to bend it." I couldn't. "Stainless steel, silver-plated," he said. "You want to bend a ten-penny spike, just stick it in there and push hard. It'll bend."

"Maybe," I said. I don't like to bend anything stronger than spoons, because it's hard to do it without grunting and straining.

"No maybe. And it's magnetic, for in case you want to do a compass . . ." Hell, I had six different ways of doing the compass effect already, all of them good. The best is this little plastic marble with a magnet inside that I hold in my mouth. You've seen me do the compass on television? I just lean over it, concentrating, and the needle spins all around the card? Mostly I use the marble, and if I think some wise guy is going to look in my mouth afterward all I have to do is swallow it. Only they cost thirty bucks each, and it's kind of undignified to have to look for them afterward. ". . . when you go to see this guy Smith and his *schatzi*," he explained, but I'd already figured out what he was up to.

"I didn't say I'd do that," I said.

"No, stupid, you didn't say that," he mimicked me, "but you don't got no choice, believe me."

"We're not doing so bad," I said.

"We are doing *schrecklich*," he said. "Go see these two *shtunkers*. Let them tell you what a great psychic you are. Let them give you that fifty thousand dollar prize, then come back here and we split it up and head for some other country. Australia, maybe. We ain't ever done Australia."

"And what if I don't like Australia?"

"*Machts nicht,* kiddo. This place we used up. Only when you see them don't screw it up, okay?"

I said huffily, "I never screw it up! I've been doing this a long time, Fritzl." And he looked at me with those big, brown, hostile Kraut eyes.

"That's what bothers me, stupid. You're getting sloppy."

But I wasn't sloppy with the Reverend, or with the Honorable Miss either. She wasn't wearing her Grecian robes. She was wearing a three-piece gray wool pantsuit that looked like she'd bought it by mail order and forgotten her size. I told them my name, bashful and polite, and the Honorable Miss sniffed and said, "Oh, yes, Geissen. You're the show-business one. We've heard of you. I suppose you've come about the prize."

I have to say Fritzl had had a good idea about that. I was not surprised to hear that they'd heard of me—hell, crazies watch television, too—and I was ready with surprise and indignation. "Prize? I'm not looking for anything from you. I came because—" I pulled the clipping out of my pocket—"somebody sent me this classified ad." FREE TEST was the headline, and then it went on to say that anyone who thought he might have ESP or clairvoyance or any other paranormal experience could come to this office to be tested.

"And you want to be tested?" asked the Reverend Doctor. His voice was hostile. So was his body stance; he was sitting, tightly clutching his belly, erect on the far side of the conference table.

I shrugged. "I don't know if I'm a fake or not," I said.

Looks passed between them. I waited. "Get the file," said Smith, and the Honorable Miss rose to pluck a folder out of a cabinet. She pawed through it, extracted a sheet and handed it to him. He looked it over, nodded and passed it to me.

I had seen it before. It was a report that I knew well.

From *Preliminary Notes on H.G.,* by Gerard T. K. Shapman, *Journ. Amer. Parapsych.,* Vol. VIII No. 3 Pg. 262:

I first encountered the subject H.G. as an undergraduate in August, 1970. A number of incidents suggested latent noumetic talents but, in the absence of rigorous controls and a statistical base for analyses, I was unable to make a satisfactory assessment. However, three incidents from that era are worthy of recording.

1. H.G.'s early ability to manipulate objects at a distance ("telekinesis"[1]) was displayed in a laboratory experiment in which I was present at all times. Nevertheless, six connections in a transformer system were displaced.[2] I had set up and tested the connections myself. The room was locked and empty until H.G. entered it in my company. He was under my constant observation until I discovered the displaced connections. There was only one door, which was secured by a deadfall bolt lock. The windows were barred. There was no possibility, or evidence, of any intrusion.[3] Significantly, the telekinetic effects were exerted in a manner which seriously and adversely affected H.G.'s laboratory credits; causing him to fail the course. (Similar observations have been made by others. Cf., Renfrew,[4] Bayreuth,[5] and others.)

2. In the second instance, H.G. was able to describe the contents of a closed box[6] to which he had no possibility of previous access. There were no visual, auditory, olfactory or tactile clues. Although his description was not exact in detail it was inarguably correct in principle.

3. In the third instance, from a distance of more than 3,000 miles (4800 km.) he referred to my new wife by her personal nickname in a letter mailed to me from Germany after our marriage. He had never met her. The letter was in response to a notice in the alumni magazine, *Tech Times*,[7] which gave only her actual name, not in the least like the "pet name," by which I called her, which he had never heard.

All of these, and other, incidents were suggestive but, of course, by no means conclusive. However, when in the following year H.G. was discharged from the United States Army and returned to the Cambridge area I asked him to participate in a series of rigorous tests which established conclusively that he possessed paranormal powers to a previously unknown degree.

"Ah, yes. The M.I.T. tests," I said. "I was working as a French Fry Man in the McDonald's at Harvard Square when Dr. Shapman came in for a Big Mac and vanilla shake."

"Tests have been faked," said suspicious old Sam Smith, looking skinny and mean.

I threw myself abjectly on the ground and licked his shoes—I don't mean literally. "I know that," I said. "I don't blame you if you don't believe them."

"What about believing you, Geissen?" asked the old lady. "Do you think you're a trustworthy witness?"

"Not at all," I said, and squeezed out a tear—I do mean literally. I've always been able to cry whenever I wanted to. "I don't even know what happens, Miss Baker. No. I shouldn't have come here. I'll go—"

Smith let me get as far as standing up, crossing the room, putting my hand on the doorknob. Then he said, voice like a rusty oven door, "We don't go by belief, Geissen. We go by evidence."

"And it's true," said Miss Baker judgmatically, "that this Dr. Shapman was not as big a fool as most."

But about that I couldn't agree with her.

I'd known Shapman a long time, since I was a sophomore at M.I.T., the year before I dropped out. He was my physics prof. He was also into psychic phenomena, though he didn't bring it into his classes, and some of the other guys tried to ass-kiss him by bragging about the dreams they'd had that foretold when their fathers would run off the road coming home from a party, stuff like that. I didn't bother. I listened to the gossip, mostly about how he was being given a hard time by those other faculty types Minsky and Lettvin and so on. Shapman got cut up by them, but he had tenure. And nobody could say he was crooked. He and his mother were in it together, I guess she turned him on to it. They'd been members of the Society for Psychical Research, fooled around with Rhine cards, all that stuff. Never got far until they got me, and then you never saw such happy people.

They didn't show it to me much. Old lady Baker was right, Shapman wasn't as big a fool as most, and when he got down to rigorous testing, after I got back from my eighteen months in the army and he found me in the McDonald's, he was suspicious as hell. He had me doing my stuff inside a Faraday cage, a room completely enclosed in a dielectric, and he was always going over the copper screen with capacitance detectors, looking for leaks. He never found any. Who needed leaks by then? By then I had had eighteen months with Fritzl.

He did, though, start me in the business, when I was still his student.

I was squeezing out a "D," right on the narrow edge of flunking the course and being kicked out of the whole school. What was wrong with that was that the draft was still going, and there was the Army hot for my bod the minute the Institute bounced me. So I was hungry to pass.

So, this day in October, Shapman told me I was getting an F for a lab demonstration and I squeezed out my tear and he gave me permission to redo the experiment. I forget exactly what it was, but I was supposed to do something with a laser and I couldn't make it lase. I got there early, checked over the equipment, screwed it up. I began to pump, but I wasn't watching the voltages. We blew a fuse. I replaced the fuse, and then the whole damned thing wouldn't work.

Hell with it. I turned everything off, locked the door and went out into the yard to smoke a joint. The late warm Massachusetts October sunlight was precious. The dope was good. I sat there, reading a book on spiders. I don't get all choked up about spiders, but one of the guys was telling me how spiders make love, and it sounded dirty enough to tell girls in bars, so I was looking it up. And I forgot the time. And when I thought of going back in the hall Shapman was there already, unlocking the door, balancing a four-inch cardboard box with holes in it. "Ah," he said, watching me bounce trippily toward him, "I see you're in a good mood, Mr. Geissen."

"Sorry I'm late, sir." I squinted at the box. "What've you got there, sir, a black widow?"

"What?" He stopped with the door half open, staring suspiciously.

"I said I thought maybe you had a black widow spider in there, sir," I said, courteous, alert, reverent.

He didn't say anything for a moment. Then he said, "Come on in, Geissen." He held the door for me to pass, then came in after me and set the box down. He was in a brown study. "How did you know that?" he asked.

"Know what, sir?" He glared at me. "You mean it really is a black widow spider?"

"No, it isn't. It's a banded argiope, but it's a spider all right."

I didn't push it. "I don't know, Professor Shapman," I said, all open and honest. "It just, I don't know, it *felt* all crawly and leggy, like. Maybe it was seeing the holes in the box."

"Yeah." Still frowning to himself, he turned on the lights and sat down next to his spider. I could see that it had a little tag attached to it, you know, the kind you put on presents. "Get on with the experiment," he said. "I have to meet somebody."

"Yes, sir." I wasn't about to tell him that I'd screwed the equipment up. I was feeling nice and warm and comfortable from the good dope, and I went through the motions with him frowning at me every second.

"You're not getting enough voltage," he said sharply.

"I know that, Professor Shapman,"—*lawdy, massah, I'se doin' the bestest I kin*—"there seems to be something wrong."

"Impossible," he said sharply, put down the spider, came over to the rig. After a minute of fooling around he went over to the bench with the transformer. "That's very funny," he complained.

"What's that, Professor Shapman?" I dripped humility.

"The wiring is wrong." He looked up at me, sharp suspicion. "Did you fool around with this part?"

"Me, Professor Shapman?" Injured innocence this time; and he shook his head.

"No, you couldn't have, could you? You weren't even in this part of the room." Suspicion was fading, but he was still staring at me. And me, I was feeling pretty mellow.

"That's the way it goes sometimes, Professor," I said, meaning nothing in particular by it.

Unfortunately, he asked me, "What do you mean by that?"

He was chilling my nice warm marijuana glow, and I didn't want him to. I improvised. "Oh, well," I said, "I mean . . . well, it's hard to put into words, but things happen."

"Things *happen?*"

"Different kinds of things. Like fuses blow. Clocks stop. Wires come loose from distributor caps. Things like that, Professor, I don't know why they happen but they do." I was just winging it. The dope was talking, more than me.

It made him look thoughtful, but that's as far as it went. He fiddled with the power source and I fiddled with the argon tube and we finally got a good stream of coherent light. But we didn't talk much after that, and the son of a bitch failed me for the course anyway.

So the army got my bod, I wound up in Wiesbaden, and in the Amerika Haus there I met Fritzl. He was stealing books out of the library to improve his English. Dumb-looking little Kraut, he looked about fourteen, was actually two years older than I was—in some ways, oh, *much* older. He was going to be a famous conjuror. We used to meet in the back of the magic shop where he worked in Frankfurt and he told me how he would go on the stage in America and make his fortune.

Then he got the better idea.

Have I mentioned that the Honorable Miss Gwendoline Stella Baker looked a lot like a snake? Not one of your friendly little garter snakes, I mean, not even a rattler. What she looked like was a cobra, with her hair spread out like the cobra's hood and her long neck wavering as though getting ready to strike. She struck. "I am surprised, Mr. Geissen," she hissed, "that a man who is as much of a television star as you hasn't been here before."

"To see if you can fool us out of the fifty thousand dollars," The Reverend Dr. Samuel Shipperton Smith chimed in.

I nodded to show that I was trying to see their point of view. "I don't blame you for being suspicious," I said. "I would be too. I guess you get a lot of phonies coming in here for that money."

"You must think we're very stupid, Geissen," she went on, still sounding snaky. It was a hiss, all right, but it was more than that, it was a kind of false-teeth whistle. Looking at her closely her teeth did look funny. Probably china choppers; probably the bustline was falsies; she didn't seem to fit the figure she displayed. And Smith himself was obviously wearing a toupee and, I was pretty sure, some kind of suntan makeup on his face. He added his two cents' worth:

"You probably think everybody is stupid. Do you expect anyone to believe that there are people on the planet Clarion who make your tricks fail most of the time?"

"I don't do tricks, Mr. Smith," I said politely. "Do you want me to go away?"

Pause while they looked at each other. Then, "We didn't tell you to come," said Smith. "Go if you want to."

He didn't sound as if he really meant it, so all I did was open the door to the outside office. I stood there for a minute, while the receptionist looked up to see what I was doing. I took a quick look at my wristwatch, then turned back to the freaks. I looked as though I were making up my mind to say something to them. I didn't think I would really have to, because the secretary had seen me look at my watch, and naturally that made her look at the clock, and her gasp came later than I expected it but it came. "Reverend Smith!" she called. "The clock's stopped."

I looked embarrassed.

Smith looked sarcastic. That skinny face didn't look handsome the best day of its life, and when it was looking sarcastic it looked particularly weasely. "Used your time in the waiting room profitably, did you?" he asked me.

"My time?" I blinked. "In the waiting room? Oh, you mean I could have done something to the clock?" I allowed myself to look hangdog. "If you think that, Mr. Smith, I guess I should stop wasting your time."

"No, do stay," said the Honorable Miss Baker, looking as poisonous as he but in her own snaky, rather than weasely, way. "What other little surprises did you set up for us?"

"Things just happen," I said miserably. "I'm sorry! I always tell them I'm sorry!"

"And do you tell them you're a fake, Geissen?" she demanded.

"That, too! Yes! I tell them I think it is all a fake, this whole thing—only I don't know who is faking it!"

Because, you see, that's really what I did tell them, because that's what Fritzl told me to do. It always worked. The more you say you don't do anything, the more they prove to you that you do. And of course, after all those hours of practicing with Fritzl in the back room of the magic shop in Frankfurt, there was plenty I *could* do.

Only at first I only did it for fun. Like when Professor Shapman showed up at the McDonald's. He was just in for a Big Mac and a shake, but when he saw me there he turned purple. "Geissen! When did you get out of the army? Listen, I want to talk to you."

The manager was giving me looks. "I'm busy, Professor," I said, which was true.

"A minute of your time," he begged. "You, are you the manager? This man is a former student and it's important that I talk to him, all right?" And then, when we were in a booth at the back of the store, he said, "I've been thinking about you. Would you be interested in, ah, performing a series of tests?"

"What kind of tests?" I asked, watching him spill shredded lettuce and secret-formula sauce on his shirt front. I took a napkin and reached across the table to wipe up the worst of it.

"Paranormal studies, Hans. Just a few hours of that sort of thing, the cards, the sealed envelopes, you know."

"I don't know what you're talking about," I declared. "What kind of money are we talking?"

He looked baffled, mouth ajar to spill some more of his Big Mac. "Money?"

"I get my two-thirty-five an hour here, Professor Shapman. I need it to live on."

"If it's a question of money—"

"That's what it's a question of."

"—maybe something could be worked out," he finished, beginning to chew again. "Why don't you think about it? Give me a call?"

I sighed and wiped up another dollop of sauce from his tie. "I'll think," I said, "but honestly, Professor Shapman, I don't know how many favors I want to do you. You flunked me out, you know. And I've got to get back to work."

And I did, without looking back at him, but out of the corner of my eye I saw him watching me as he finished his sandwich. I kept busy. When he got up to leave he paused to dump his tray in the trash container and then headed back toward me. I thought he was going to tell me that he'd noticed his slide-rule tie clip was bent double, but he hadn't noticed that. All he wanted was to say, "By the way, the Spider Lady sends her regards."

So that night I told Fritzl about it and he gave me hell. "Stupid! You got a pigeon and you let him get away! What's this 'Spider Lady' dreck?"

I shrugged. "I saw in *Tech Times* that he got married so I sent him a get-well card. I wrote on it 'Best wishes to you and the Spider Lady.' He'd got this spider for her, see—and I'd been drinking—"

"Drinking! Yah, I know about you and drinking back in Wiesbaden. You don't start that again!"

I said reasonably, "You don't give me orders, Fritzl. I don't mind sharing a room with you till you get your career started, but—"

"Career! You don't know what's career!" he yelled, getting excited. "Now you listen and I tell you what to do. You call up this Herr Professor and tell him you changed your mind. Then we start career."

I was getting sore. He was always a pretty bossy guy, Fritzl, but the deal we'd made in Germany was that I'd be his manager if I helped him get to America. Nobody said anything about his being mine. There was a bar in Lexington that said they might take him on for a tryout if we got somebody with a guitar to back him up, so I began, "What about—"

"What about everything," he said grimly, "is that in one hour you are going to call this Herr Professor and tell him you come over. Then I tell you what to do. But first you spend the next hour practicing with the cards!"

The good part of it was that the Spider Lady was a nice-looking woman. Her real name was Lillian, and she had that good woman smell that's part perfume and part sex, and when she let me in and sat me down to wait for her husband she didn't mind touching a little bit while she took my coat. There were possibilities there. "We're just going to eat, Hans," she said, "and you look like you could use a home-cooked meal."

So I let myself be persuaded. A good cook she was not; steak and salad and baked potato, but the steak was gray all the way through and the potato still hard; but while we were eating our knees touched a couple times under the table. Then she cleared away and old Shapman brought out the Rhine cards.

You know what they are. There are twenty-five cards in the pack, five each of five different symbols. There's a cross, a star, wavy lines, all that stuff. I took a brandy from him. It was cheap New York State brand-X, not what I'm used to these days, but at the time it tasted pretty good to me, and I let Shapman run through the cards three times. The first time I got seven right. The second four. The third time six. "Hum," he said, disappointed. "Well, it's a *little* over chance, but—"

"I didn't feel anything," I said apologetically.

He looked thoughtful. "What do you mean, feel anything?"

I shrugged. "Sometimes I feel like I can do it, sometimes I don't. It doesn't mean anything, I guess, I mean, I don't think I really have any of this crazy psi stuff—"

He looked indignant, and the Spider Lady grinned. "I wonder if what you need is another brandy, Hans?" she offered, and while she was getting up to get it Shapman said:

"I want to show you something." And so he went out of the room to get something and she was over at the sideboard, and there was I with the deck of cards right in front of me. By the time she turned back with my drink I was standing up, looking out the window. She handed me the glass and reached past me, to a sort of desk at the window, to pick up a deck of ordinary playing cards.

"Hey, we going to do some tests with them?" I asked.

She laughed. "I'm just tidying up, Hans. I play a lot of solitaire, with Jerry away so much—he's running the M.I.T. chapter of the Psychic Research Society, you know." I didn't know. "He's pretty hopeful about you," she went on. "According to him, you do all kinds of things."

"All kinds," I agreed, looking at her. Nice legs, if a little plump, and she was wearing a really short skirt to make sure they were noticed. She was a lot closer to my age than to Shapman's. "I mean," I said, "I don't know about this ESP stuff."

"Really?"

"It's just that funny things happen. I guess the professor told you about that laser test rig that got scr—that got messed up. And then"—I chuckled—"well, there was a funny one in Germany. I had some, you know, dope in my locker, and they pulled a surprise inspection. I was scared out of my head. I wished the grass would go away. Then, just as the captain was coming to me, I heard this noise, and there was the pouch and the hash pipe rolling on the floor."

Shapman had come up behind me. "Teleportation?" he asked eagerly.

"I don't know what you call it. It wasn't what I was wishing. I was wishing the damn stuff was in China! The captain couldn't miss it, it was right in front of him. But it worked out all right. He couldn't prove it was mine, so I just got restricted to base instead of a D.D."

Shapman sighed and changed the subject. He held his open palm out to me. "Do you know what this is?"

Of course I did. "It's one of those M.I.T. tie clips. How'd you break it?"

"I was going to ask you that," he barked.

I said apologetically, "I don't think I ever saw it before, Professor. If I stepped on it or something I'm really sorry."

He sighed. He turned the bent clip over in his hand a couple of times, then put it carefully in his pocket. "Why are the best talents so erratic?" he asked the world.

I said, "I don't think I'm much of a talent. Oh, yes, things happen. Things get broken—pencils, keys, wristwatches. Glasses. Sometimes I put my sunglasses down when I come home, and I don't know if they're going to be in one piece or not when I go to get them again."

He took his pipe out of his pocket. "Want to try to break this?" he challenged, and his wife squealed.

"Jerry! I paid thirty-four dollars for—"

"Don't worry, Mrs. Shapman," I laughed. "I wouldn't know how. Only"—I hesitated, then shrugged—"only, I have to admit, sometimes I *feel* as though I could do anything. Really confident."

He fumbled in his pocket for a notebook, began to jot things down in it. "How were you feeling when we were running the cards?"

"Not too confident, no."

"Want to try it again?" He started back to the table and I stopped him.

"Wait a minute," I said. "Sometimes—Look, just put your hand on the top card, okay?"

He looked suspicious, but he did. I thought for a while. "Maybe—Maybe if you just peeked at it, I mean don't let me see it or anything. . . ."

He started to do that, then paused and took his glasses off. No chance of me playing any tricks by seeing a reflection, no sir! He cupped the top card, staring at it, then glancing eagerly at me.

I disappointed him. I gave it a good long wait, then I shook my head. "Let me try touching," I said, and reached out and touched his other skinny hand. I made a face. "Square?" I said doubtfully. It was the wavy lines.

He said sadly, "It's the wavy lines."

"I just don't get anything from you," I apologized. "Maybe if Mrs. Shapman—"

"Absolutely. Come on, Lil! Here, just put your hand on top here—"

She wasn't reluctant at all. Smiling, she picked up the top card and gave me her hand to hold.

I said triumphantly: "Square!"

It was. She picked up the next one.

"Star! . . . Square again. . . . Wavy lines. . . ." And I went through about twenty cards, and then I stopped.

"I don't want to do any more," I said.

"What do you mean, you don't want to do any more?" Shapman demanded. "Go ahead, Geissen! There are only a few more in the deck—"

"I'm really sorry," I said, swallowing, "but that brandy—maybe I shouldn't have—"

"Now, *please*, Geissen! You got seventeen out of twenty! Just finish the run!"

"Leave the boy alone," his wife ordered, looking at me sharply. "Are you all right, Hans?"

"Not really," I said faintly. "Could I have a glass of water? Or—" And I stood up, looking very unwell indeed, and the Spider Lady understood at once and pointed me toward the little toilet off the foyer. I vomited noisily and a lot. It was a terrible waste of a not very good dinner and some fair brandy, and all I had to do was to stick my finger a little bit down my throat. While I was rinsing the taste out of my mouth there was a knock on the door. Shapman. He didn't wait to be invited in. He pushed the door open and stood there.

"Sev. En. Teen," he said.

I spat the water out into the bowl and took another mouthful.

"Please, Hans," he begged. "Just one more run!"

I said faintly, "I really want to go home. Could you call me a cab?"

"I'll drive you. Or you could stay here, and we'll try again in the morning—Lily! Let's make up the spare—"

"No," I said definitely. "Home."

I could see that he was wavering between firm and cherishing. He came down on cherishing because, I knew, he wanted to keep me sweet for the next time; only I didn't think there was going to be a next time. Not with him. With Lily Shapman, though, that was something else, because all the time I was running the deck I'd felt her little hot finger wriggling against my little hot palm. And as we were getting into the car he paused, took out the notebook again and said, "I just want to write down the date and get your signature and—*Jesus!*"

Lillian Shapman, helping me into the rear seat, called irritably, "What is it now, Jerry?"

"Look at my pen!" It was a Bic ballpoint, snapped clean in half. "And I *swear* nobody touched it after I put it in my pocket!"

And when Fritzl asked how it went I told him it had gone fine indeed. "I got the pen when he helped me on with my coat," I said. "No sweat. And the cards were a breeze." Seventeen out of twenty! I could have done all twenty—standing on my head, drinking a glass of water, once he went out of the room and left me with them.

"That was good," said Fritzl, uttering an unwilling compliment. "Now you don't see him a while."

"How about his wife?" I asked, half joking, but Fritzl took me seriously.

"Why not? Then if he says later you're a fake you have got there a very good reason why he is jealous. No. Good all the way. Now we just wait till he writes it up."

"Okay, I yawned, getting ready to go to bed. But before I sacked in I pulled the phone plug out. I didn't want Shapman calling me up when he got home and found that his pipe was broken too.

That's the secret, you see. Never promise to do anything in particular. But if you ask me to read a secret message inside an envelope I'll stop your watch or tell you your dead aunt-by-marriage's maiden name or, what the hell, tie a knot in your garters. I've got these really nice specialties, like one where I give you a box of Crayolas and let you touch the back of my neck and then I tell you what color it is. Only if you ask me to do that I probably won't deliver . . . but while I'm failing, watch your ballpoint pens.

The way it turned out I did go back to Shapman. I let him put me in the Faraday cage, and I made his compass spin, and I bollixed up his pocket calculator—and all the while, the evenings he was out at the Society, the cage I was in was the Spider Lady's, and I claim I bollixed her up to where she was spinning like a top, and at that one I never failed at all.

"Oh," grumbled the Reverend Doctor, "sit down, Geissen. Do you want the fifty thousand or not?"

Along about then my instincts began to taste something sour. If he was going to throw me out, he should have thrown me out. If he wasn't, he should have been a little friendlier. . . . But he wasn't unfriendly, exactly, when he pushed past me to talk to the receptionist. I sat down, snaky Miss Baker watching me silently and carefully, while Smith muttered at the girl outside and she whispered back. He came back in and closed the door.

"All the red pens have black caps now and all the black ones have red. A very stupid trick, Geissen. Also her electric pencil sharpener doesn't work."

Snaky hiss from the Honorable Miss. "You'd think he'd show some imagination," she said. I shrugged. They both watched me silently for a moment.

Then Smith said, "There are one or two things."

I looked up, trying not to look as though I cared one way or another. "I don't know what you mean, sir," I said politely.

Grunt. "We have tapes of some of your television appearances, Geissen." That wasn't news to me, of course. It was very unlikely they would have missed any, given what they were supposed to be looking for. "Do you remember the one with that talk-show man in Palo Alto?"

I made believe to have to search my memory, but actually I remembered it very well. It was one of my better gigs. It was thinking on my feet, and that was what I was a lot better than Fritzl at.

"I think so," I said cautiously. "I think I got there late." Actually, that was just lying to stay in practice. I hadn't got there late, I got there in plenty of time, and I sat in the green room reading a magazine, where everybody could watch me so they'd know I wasn't doing anything tricky. I didn't bother with makeup. Why would a nice, clean, eager-to-please young fellow like me put something artificial on his face? I didn't move until they called me to go out front.

Then it didn't go well at all.

They sat me down, and I saw my host run off to the wings during the commercial; his girlfriend handed him something, and I couldn't see what; then the commercial was over and he was standing in front of his desk. "All right, Hans," he beamed, "I've got something in my closed fist. Can you tell me what it is?"

The son of a bitch. I knew everything on his desk or in his pockets, of course. I didn't know what his girl might have handed him. I winged it. "I'm getting an image— I don't know—All I can see, it's kind of round?" No response on his face. What would the bitch have handed him, a kind of powder-puff maybe? "I get a feeling of softness— It's something kind of, I don't know—" I tried to look blushy. "Sort of personal, I think."

Polite smile. "Can you say what color it is?"

"Uh. . . . Not really. Kind of light?"

He grinned and opened his hand and it was, for Christ's sake, an *ice cube*. Jesus! Why hadn't I seen the water dripping? It had begun to melt a little, and so the corners were a little rounded off from melting. But that wasn't good enough.

I tried a save. "I guess Clarion must have moved into the constellation of Sagittarius," I said, grinning.

He all but laughed in my face. "The *what?*"

I was stalling, waiting for inspiration. "The planet Clarion. I don't know if it's real. Only somebody told me I'd never be able to do anything when they were in a bad sign."

"Sure," he said, openly winking at the audience. "You want to tell us about these flying-saucer people that mess you up?"

"They don't come in flying saucers, as far as I know. It's just a theory, you know? Like the square root of minus one."

"Oh, yeah," said wise-ass, nodding hard, "the square root of minus one."

"Exactly," I said eagerly, cudgeling my memory—what had Fritzl told me about the stuff in his desk drawer? Or his wallet? "It's imaginary, maybe, but it works. Like they're afraid of us, see, and if they find anybody who really does have psi powers they wreck it for him, so Earthlings won't ever be a threat. . . ." Diner's Club card, AmEx gold card, two fifty-dollar bills, one of them folded into the driver's license—"Oh, I'm getting something!" I cried.

"The boot?" he grinned, and the audience chortled.

"No, no really! Soft, round, pale-colored—yes, that's it." I leaned over and whispered in his ear. "The Trojan in your wallet." He jumped back, staring at me. "Only," I said bashfully, "I wouldn't, you know, count on that one, because it has a hole in it." And I didn't have to say any more, because his face said it for me, and as the audience caught on I got about the biggest laugh—the biggest one on my side, anyway—of my career.

But I never got invited back on that show. . . .

"So how did you know he had a condom in his wallet?" asked Smith.

I shrugged. "Lots of guys carry them," I said.

"In this age of the pill?" he demanded.

"Like," I said, blushing, "if he's afraid somebody might have kind of a disease? *I* don't know, Mr. Smith."

"No," said Smith thoughtfully. He looked at the woman. She looked out of her lidless, shiny eyes at him. He made up his mind. "Come in my private office," he ordered abruptly, stood up, led the way, opened the door, turned on the light switch.

The light didn't light. Instead, his TV set burped and buzzed and turned itself on. It was daytime television, a rerun of "My Favorite Martian."

"You sit still," ordered Smith, and his eyes were furious. I expected a reaction. I didn't expect it to be that big. I sat. Miss Baker was poking around in his desk, and she squawked and grabbed him, muttering in his ear, holding up a sheet of paper. It had a caricature of her on it, and it had been locked inside the desk. He muttered back, and waved to the bookcase; she began investigating that while he methodically emptied everything in his desk.

I just sat, waiting. Feeling good. Admiring the office. It had everything, including a wet bar with a sink and a refrigerator and a little gas range and a Dispos-All and a Cuisinart. There was a handsome leather couch along one wall, about twenty-five hundred dollars better looking than the raggedy old thing in the reception room; the desk itself was teak, and the chair behind it was one of those electric things that fits any position. When he sat down in it and pushed a button absentmindedly it lurched and nearly threw him across the room. He yelled out in anger. I didn't understand what he said, but Miss Baker did. She jumped to the window, pointing out at the fire escape. Smith jumped after her, then shook his head, snarling something, and pointed to the joints in the window. They had been painted shut long before. Nobody had needed to open that window, with the air conditioner mounted right below it; and certainly nobody had come in through it lately. He turned away; then, with a sudden thought, turned back. He looked at the air conditioner, then at me.

Then he shook his head. Certainly a big fellow like me could never have squeezed through that space, even if he had been able to get the air conditioner out from outside. And indeed I couldn't.

But skinny little Fritzl could. By now he was back in the apartment, resting up. But he'd done the job.

I don't know what-all they found. Fritzl was an ingenious man, and he'd had more than half an hour while we were talking in the other office. I don't even know if they found everything. What I know is that after a while Smith stopped looking, and sat back on the desk, looking at me. He said something to Miss Baker that I couldn't understand.

"I'm sorry, Mr. Smith," I said politely. "What did you say?"

"I said we cannot, after all, take chances," he told me, and she nodded, the eyes fixed on me in a way I didn't like.

He went to the wall, where a picture of the Coliseum had been replaced with a full-length color photograph of me holding a bent spoon. He ripped the picture off and felt the wall behind it. There was nothing to see there, but he dug his fingernails into a crack in the paneling. A square of the wall came away. There was a safe behind it. I watched with admiration; not even Fritzl had found that! He opened it and took out something that looked, to my surprise, like a weapon.

It was.

It was not any kind of gun I had ever seen before, and it didn't make a gunshot noise. All it did was kind of poop out a quick purplish glow.

But that purplish glow was pretty powerful stuff, because all at once I was all limp. It was like novocaine suddenly hit every nerve and muscle. Nothing felt attached to me anymore. I fell over. None of my limbs responded to anything I asked of them. My mouth wouldn't speak. Only my eyes stayed open.

For a moment Smith and Baker were almost as still as I. I could hear them whispering faintly to each other, but they watched me without moving. Then Smith pointed to the sink. Baker slithered over to it, turned on the water, touched the switch for the Dispos-All.

It didn't work.

She snapped something at Smith, who came over and looked into my eyes. "You affected that, too?" he asked. "Ah, a really powerful talent. Well, I will just get my tools and fix it."

Miss Baker didn't respond, or even look at him as he went out, closing the door after him. She was busy with something else. From a cabinet under the sink she took out a plastic sheet and spread it on the floor. From another, a selection of knives, cleavers, a butchers' bone saw. She arranged them carefully on the plastic, working fast. Her hair fell in her eyes; she pulled the wig off and her bald skull looked more snakelike than ever.

And she didn't speak, and I couldn't.

I couldn't to her, and I couldn't to Smith when he came back and patiently, methodically began disassembling the Dispos-All. Nor did he speak to me. Not while he was getting comfortable by removing his own wig, and the false nose that covered the ugly pit in the middle of his face he breathed through; not while he was putting the disposer back together; not even while he was helping Miss Smith into the white coverall that would keep her other clothes from unwanted stains. Only then did he come over to look down at me.

"One thing you might like to know," he said. "The name of the planet isn't Clarion." And then he leaned down to take my shoulders, while skinny Miss Baker easily lifted my legs and they carried me over to the plastic sheeting with the knives, the saw, and the cleaver.

THE HIGH TEST

One of the great dreams of science fiction is going into space. Of course, it's not good enough just to go—the fun is in going places you haven't been before. And to do that, you need to be able to pilot a spaceship. Frederik Pohl has this dream. In an introduction to the first publication of "The High Test," he said, "When I was about ten or eleven years old I used to daydream . . . about flying a great big marvelous interstellar spaceship across the universe, something like the *Skylark of Space*. . . . "

It goes without saying that someone has to teach people how to fly spaceships, just as there are people to teach people how to drive cars. "The High Test," first published in 1983, is about a young man who teaches spaceship piloting. It's safe to say that worse things can happen in this line of work than happen to your average driving instructor. In the case of James Paul Madigan, there are some things that *nobody* could have prepared him for.

2213 12 22 1900ugt

Dear Mom:

As they say, there's good news and there's bad news here on Cassiopeia 43-G. The bad news is that there aren't any openings for people with degrees in quantum-mechanical astrophysics. The good news is that I've got a job. I started yesterday. I work for a driving school, and I'm an instructor.

I know you'll say that's not much of a career for a twenty-six-year-old man with a doctorate, but it pays the rent. Also it's a lot better than I'd have if I'd stayed on Earth. Is it true that the unemployment rate in Chicago is up to eighty percent? Wow! As soon as I get a few megabucks ahead I'm going to invite you all to come out here and visit me in the sticks so you can see how we live here—you may not want to go back!

Now, I don't want you to worry when I tell you that I get hazardous duty pay. That's just a technicality. We driving instructors have it in our contracts, but we don't really earn it. At least, usually we don't—although there are times like yesterday. The first student I had was this young girl, right from Earth. Spoiled rotten! You know the kind, rich, and I guess you'd say beautiful, and really used to having her own way. Her name's Tonda Aguilar—you've heard of the Evanston Aguilars? In the recombinant foodstuff business? They're really rich, I guess. This one had her own speedster, and she was really sulked that she couldn't drive it on an Earth license. See, they have this suppressor field; as soon as any vehicle comes into the system, zap, it's off, and it just floats until some licensed pilot comes out to fly it in. So I took her up, and right away she started giving me ablation. "Not so much takeoff boost! You'll burn out the tubes!" and "Don't ride the reverter in hyperdrive!" and "Get out of low orbit—you want to rack us up?"

Well, I can take just so much of that. An instructor is almost like the captain of a ship, you know. He's the boss! So I explained to her that my name wasn't "Chowderhead" or "Dullwit!" but James Paul Madigan, and it was the instructors who were supposed to yell at the students, not the other way around. Well, it was her own speedster, and a really neat one at that. Maybe I couldn't blame her for being nervous about somebody else driving it. So I decided to give her a real easy lesson. Practicing parking orbits—if you can't do that you don't deserve a license! And she was really rotten at it. It looks easy, but there's an art to cutting the hyperdrive with just the right residual velocity, so you slide right into your assigned coordinates. The more she tried the farther off she got. Finally she demanded that I take her back to the spaceport. She said I was making her nervous. She said she'd get a different instructor for tomorrow or she'd just move on to some other system where they didn't have benefacted chimpanzees giving driving lessons.

I just let her rave. Then the next student I had was a Fomalhautian. You know that species: they've got two heads and scales and forked tails, and they're always making a nuisance of themselves in the United Systems? If you believe what they say on the vidcom, they're bad news—in fact, the reason Cassiopeia installed the suppressor field was because they had a suspicion the Fomalhautians were thinking about invading and taking over 43-G. But this one was nice as pie! Followed every instruction. Never gave me any argument. Apologized when he made a mistake and got us too close to one of the miniblack holes near the primary. He said that was because he was unfamiliar with the school ship, and said he'd prefer to use his own space yacht for the next lesson. He made the whole day better, after that silly, spoiled rich brat!

I was glad to have a little cheering up, to tell you the truth. I was feeling a little lonesome and depressed. Probably it's because it's so close to the holidays. It's hard to believe that back in Chicago it's only three days until Christmas, and all the store windows will be full of holodecorations and there'll be that big tree in Grant Park and I bet it's snowing . . . and here on Cassiopeia 43-G it's sort of like a steam bath with interludes of Niagara Falls.

I do wish you a Merry Christmas, Mom! Hope my gifts got there all right.

Love,
Jim Paul

2213 12 25 late

Dear Mom:

Well, Christmas Day is just about over. Not that it's any different from any other day here on 43-G, where the human colonists were mostly Buddhist or Moslem and the others were—well! You've seen the types that hang around the United Systems building in Palatine—smelled them, too, right? Especially those Arcturans. I don't know whether those people have any religious holidays or not, and I'm pretty sure I don't *want* to know.

Considering that I had to work all day, it hasn't been such a bad Christmas at that. When I mentioned to Torklemiggen—he's the Fomalhautian I told you about—that today was a big holiday for us he sort of laughed and said that mammals had really quaint customs. And when he found out that part of the custom was to exchange gifts he thought for a minute. (The way Fomalhautians think to themselves is that their heads whisper in each other's ear—really grotesque!) Then he said that he had been informed it was against the law for a student to give anything to his driving instructor, but if I wanted to fly his space yacht myself for a while he'd let me do it. And he would let it go down on the books of the school as instruction time, so I'd get paid for it. Well, you bet I wanted to! He has some swell yacht. It's long and tapered, sort of shark-shape, like the TU-Lockheed 4400 series, with radar-glyph vision screens and a cruising range of nearly 1800 l.y. I don't know what its top speed is—after all, we had to stay in our own system!

We were using his own ship, you see, and of course it's Fomalhautian made. Not easy for a human being to fly! Even though I'm supposed to be the instructor and Torklemiggen the student, I was baffled at first. I couldn't even get it off the ground until he explained the controls to me and showed me how to read the instruments. There's still plenty I don't know, but after a few minutes I could handle it well enough not to kill us out of hand. Torklemiggen kept daring me to circle the black holes. I told him we couldn't do that, and he got this kind of sneer on one of his faces, and the two heads sort of whispered together for a while. I knew he was thinking of something cute, but I didn't know what at first.

Then I found out!

You know that CAS 43, our primary, is a red giant star with an immense photosphere. Torklemiggen bragged that we could fly right through the photosphere! Well, of course I hardly believed him, but he was so insistent that I tried it out. He was right! We just greased right through that thirty-thousand-degree plasma, like nothing at all! The hull began to turn red, then yellow, then straw-colored—you could see it on the edges of the radar-glyph screen—and yet the inside temperature stayed right on the button of 40° Celsius. That's 43-G normal, by the way. Hot, if you're used to Chicago, but nothing like it was outside! And when we burst out into vacuum again there was no thermal shock, no power surge, no instrument fog. Just beautiful! It's hard to believe that any individual can afford a ship like this just for his private cruising. I guess Fomalhaut must have some pretty rich planets!

Then when we landed, more than an hour late, there was the Aguilar woman waiting for me. She found out that the school wouldn't let her change instructors once assigned. I could have told her that; it's policy. So she had to cool her heels until I got back. But I guess she had a little Christmas spirit somewhere in her ornery frame, because she was quite polite about it. As a matter of fact, when we had her doing parking orbits she was much improved over the last time. Shows what a first-class instructor can do for you!

Well, I see by the old chronometer on the wall that it's the day after Christmas now, at least by Universal-Greenwich Time it is, though I guess you've still got a couple of hours to go in Chicago. One thing, Mom. The Christmas packages you sent didn't get here yet. I thought about lying to you and saying they'd come and how much I liked them, but you raised me always to tell the truth. (Besides, I didn't know what to thank you for!) Anyway, Merry Christmas one more time from—

Jim Paul

2213 12 30 0200ugt

Dear Mom:

Another day, another kilobuck. My first student today was a sixteen-year-old kid. One of those smart-alecky ones, if you know what I mean. (But you probably don't, because you certainly never had any kids like that!) His father was a combat pilot in the Cassiopeian navy, and the kid drove that way, too. That wasn't the worst of it. He'd heard about Torklemiggen. When I tried to explain to him that he had to learn how to go slow before he could go fast, he really let me have it. Didn't I know his father said the Fomalhautians were treacherous enemies of the Cassiopeian way of life? Didn't I know his father said they were just waiting their chance to invade? Didn't I know—

Well, I could take just so much of this fresh kid telling me what I didn't know. So I told him he wasn't as lucky as Torklemiggen. He only had one brain, and if he didn't use all of it to fly this ship I was going to wash him out. That shut him up pretty quick.

But it didn't get much better, because later on I had this fat lady student who just oughtn't to get a license for anything above a skateboard. Forty-six years old, and she's never driven before—but her husband's got a job asteroid-mining, and she wants to be able to bring him a hot lunch every day. I hope she's a better cook than a pilot! Anyway I was trying to put her at ease, so she wouldn't pile us up into a comet nucleus or something, so I was telling her about the kid. She listened, all sympathy—you know, how teenage kids were getting fresher every year—until I mentioned that what we were arguing about was my Fomalhautian student. Well, you should have heard her then! I swear, Mom, I think these Cassiopeians are psychotic on the subject. I wish Torklemiggen were here so I could talk to him about it—somebody said the reason CAS 43-G put the suppressor system in in the first place was to keep them from invading, if you can imagine that! But he had to go home for a few days. Business, he said. Said he'd be back next week to finish his lessons.

Tonda Aguilar is almost finished, too. She'll solo in a couple of days. She was my last student today—I mean yesterday, actually, because it's way after midnight now. I had her practicing zero-G approaches to low-mass asteroids, and I happened to mention that I was feeling a little lonesome. It turned out she was, too, so I surprised myself by asking her if she was doing anything tomorrow night, and she surprised me by agreeing to a date. It's not romance, Mom, so don't get your hopes up. It's just that she and I seem to be the only beings in this whole system who know that tomorrow is New Year's Eve!

Love,
Jim Paul

2214 01 02 2330ugt

Dear Mom:

I got your letter this morning, and I'm glad that your leg is better. Maybe next time you'll listen to Dad and me! Remember, we both begged you to go for a brand-new factory job when you got it, but you kept insisting a rebuilt would be just as good. Now you see. It never pays to try to save money on your health!

I'm sorry if I told you about my clients without giving you any idea of what they looked like. For Tonda, that's easy enough to fix. I enclose a holo of the two of us which we took this afternoon, celebrating the end of her lessons. She solos tomorrow. As you can see, she is a really good-looking woman and I was wrong about her being spoiled. She came out here on her own to make her career as a dermatologist. She wouldn't take any of her old man Aguilar's money, so all she had when she got here was her speedster and her degree and the clothes on her back. I really admire her. She connected right away with one of the best body-shops in town, and she's making more money than I am.

As to Torklemiggen, that's harder. I tried to make a holopic of him, but he got really upset—you might even say nasty. He said inferior orders have no right to worship a Fomalhautian's image, if you can believe it! I tried to explain that we didn't have that in mind at all, but he just laughed. He has a mean laugh. In fact, he's a lot different since he came back from Fomalhaut on that business trip. Meaner. I don't mean that he's different physically. Physically he's about a head taller than I am, except that he has two of them. Two heads, I mean. The head on his left is for talking and breathing, the one on his right for eating and showing expression. It's pretty weird to see him telling a joke. His jokes are pretty weird all by themselves, for that matter. I'll give you an example. This afternoon he said, "What's the difference between a mammal and a roasted hagensbiffik with murgry sauce?" And when I said I didn't even know what those things were, much less what the difference was, he laughed himself foolish and said, "No difference!" What a spectacle. There was his left-hand head talking and sort of yapping that silly laugh of his, dead-pan, while the right-hand head was all creased up with giggle lines. Some sense of humor. I should have told you that Torklemiggen's left-hand head looks kind of like a chimpanzee's, and the right one is a little bit like a fox's. Or maybe an alligator's, because of the scales. Not pretty, you understand. But you can't say that about his ship! It's as sweet a job as I've ever driven. I guess he had some extra accessories put on it while he was home, because I noticed there were five or six new readouts and some extra hand controls. When I asked him what they were for he said they had nothing to do with piloting and I would find out what they were for soon enough. I guess that's another Fomalhautian joke of some kind.

Well, I'd write more but I have to get up early in the morning. I'm having breakfast with Tonda to give her some last-minute run throughs before she solos. I think she'll pass all right. She surely has a lot of smarts for somebody who was a former Miss Illinois!

Love,
Jim Paul

2214 01 03 late

Dear Mom:

Your Christmas package got here today, and it was really nice. I loved the socks. They'll come in real handy in case I come back to Chicago for a visit before it gets warm. But the cookies were pretty crumbled, I'm afraid—delicious, though! Tonda said she could tell that they were better than anything she could bake, before they went through the CAS 43-G customs, I mean.

Torklemiggen is just about ready to solo. To tell you the truth, I'll be glad to see the last of him. The closer he gets to his license the harder he is to get along with. This morning he began acting crazy as soon as we got into high orbit. We were doing satellite-matching curves. You know, when you come in on an asymptotic tractrix curve, just whistling through the upper atmosphere of the satellite and then back into space. Nobody ever does that when they're actually driving, because what is there on a satellite in this system that anybody would want to visit? But they won't pass you for a license if you don't know how.

The trouble was, Torklemiggen thought he already did know how, better than I did.

So I took the controls away to show him how, and that really blew his cool. "I could shoot better curves than you in my fourth instar!" he snarled out of his left head, while his right head was looking at me like a rattlesnake getting ready to strike. I mean, mean. Then when I let him have the controls back he began shooting curves at one of the mini-black holes. Well, that's about the biggest no-no there is. "Stop that right now," I ordered. "We can't go within a hundred thousand miles of one of those things! How'd you pass your written test without knowing that?"

"Do not exceed your life-station, mammal!" he snapped, and dived in toward the hole again, his fore hands on the thrust and roll controls while his hind hands reached out to fondle the buttons for the new equipment. And all the time his left-hand head was chuckling and giggling like some fiend out of a monster movie.

"If you don't obey instructions," I warned him, "I will not approve you for your solo." Well, that fixed him. At least he calmed down. But he sulked for the rest of the lesson. Since I didn't like the way he was behaving, I took the controls for the landing. Out of curiosity I reached to see what the new buttons were. "Severely handicapped mammalian species!" his left head screeched, while his right head was turning practically pale pink with terror. "Do you want to destroy this planet?"

I was getting pretty suspicious by then, so I asked him straight out: "What is this stuff, some kind of weapon?"

That made him all quiet. His two heads whispered to each other for a minute, then he said, very stiff and formal, "Do you speak to me of weapons when you mammals have these black holes in orbit? Have you considered their potential for weaponry? Can you imagine what one of them would do, directed toward an inhabited planet?" He paused for a minute, then he said something that really started me thinking. "Why," he asked, "do you suppose my people have any wish to bring culture to this system, except to demonstrate the utility of these objects?"

We didn't talk much after that, but it was really on my mind.

After work, when Tonda and I were sitting in the park, feeding the flying crabs and listening to the singing trees, I told her all about it. She was silent for a moment. Then she looked up at me and said seriously, "Jim Paul, it's a rotten thing to say about any being, but it almost sounds as though Torklemiggen has some idea about conquering this system."

"Now, who would want to do something like that?" I asked.

She shrugged. "It was just a thought," she apologized. But we both kept thinking about it all day long, in spite of our being so busy getting our gene tests and all—but I'll tell you about that later!

Love,
Jim Paul

2214 01 05 2200ugt

Dear Mom:

Take a *good look* at this date, the 5th of January, because you're going to need to remember it for a while! There's big news from CAS 43-G tonight . . . but first, as they say on the tube, a few other news items.

Let me tell you about that bird Torklemiggen. He soloed this morning. I went along as check pilot, in a school ship, flying matching orbits with him while he went through the whole test in his own yacht. I have to admit that he was really nearly as good as he thought he was. He slid in and out of hyperdrive without any power surge you could detect. He kicked his ship into a corkscrew curve and killed all the drives, so he was tumbling and rolling and pitching all at once, and he got out of it into a clean orbit using only the side thrusters. He matched parking orbits—he ran the whole course without a flaw. I was still sore at him, but there just wasn't any doubt that he'd shown all the skills he needed to get a license. So I called him on the private TBS frequency and said, "You've passed, Torklemiggen. Do you want a formal written report when we land, or shall I call in to have your license granted now?"

"Now this instant, mammal!" he yelled back, and added something in his own language. I didn't understand it, of course. Nobody else could hear it, either, because the talk-between-ships circuits don't carry very far. So I guess I'll never know just what it is he said, but, honestly, Mom, it surely didn't sound at all friendly. All the same, he'd passed.

So I ordered him to null his controls, and then I called in his test scores to the master computer on 43-G. About two seconds later he started screeching over the TBS, "Vile mammal! What have you done? My green light's out, my controls won't respond. Is this some treacherous warm-blood trick?"

He sure had a way of getting under your skin. "Take it easy, Torklemiggen," I told him, not very friendlily—he was beginning to hurt my feelings. "The computer is readjusting your status. They've removed the temporary license for your solo, so they can lift the suppressor field permanently. As soon as the light goes on again you'll be fully licensed, and able to fly anywhere in this system without supervision."

"Hah," he grumbled, and then for a moment I could hear his heads whispering together. Then—well, Mom, I was going to say he laughed out loud over the TBS. But it was more than a laugh. It was mean, and gloating. "Depraved retarded mammal," he shouted, "my light is on—and now all of Cassiopeia is mine!"

I was really disgusted with him. You expect that kind of thing, maybe, from some spacehappy sixteen-year-old who's just got his first license. Not from an eighteen-hundred-year-old alien who has flown all over the Galaxy. It sounded sick! And sort of worrisome, too. I wasn't sure just how to take him. "Don't do anything silly, Torklemiggen," I warned him over the TBS.

He shouted back: "Silly? I do nothing silly, mammal! Observe how little silly I am!" And the next thing you know he was whirling and diving into hyperspace—no signal, nothing! I had all I could do to follow him, six alphas deep and going fast. For all I knew we could have been on our way back to Fomalhaut. But he only stayed there for a minute. He pulled out right in the middle of one of the asteroid belts, and as I followed up from the alphas I saw that lean, green yacht of his diving down on a chunk of rock about the size of an office building.

I had noticed, when he came back from his trip, that one of the new things about the yacht was a circle of ruby-colored studs around the nose of the ship. Now they began to glow, brighter and brighter. In a moment a dozen streams of ruby light reached out from them, ahead toward the asteroid—and there was a bright flare of light, and the asteroid wasn't there anymore!

Naturally, that got me upset. I yelled at him over the TBS: "Listen, Torklemiggen, you're about to get yourself in real deep trouble! I don't know how they do things back on Fomalhaut, but around here that's grounds for an action to suspend your license! Not to mention they could make you pay for that asteroid!"

"Pay?" he screeched. "It is not I who will pay, functionally inadequate live-bearer, it is you and yours! You will pay most dreadfully, for now we have the black holes!" And he was off again, back down into hyperspace, and one more time it was about all I could do to try to keep up with him.

There's no sense trying to transmit in hyperspace, of course. I had to wait until we were up out of the alphas to answer him, and by that time, I don't mind telling you, I was *peeved*. I never would have found him on visual, but the radar-glyph picked him up zeroing in on one of the black holes. What a moron! "Listen, Torklemiggen," I said, keeping my voice level and hard, "I'll give you one piece of advice. Go back to base. Land your ship. Tell the police you were just carried away, celebrating passing your test. Maybe they won't be too hard on you. Otherwise, I warn you, you're looking at a thirty-day suspension plus you could get a civil suit for damages from the asteroid company." He just screeched that mean laughter. I added, "And I told you, keep away from the black holes!"

He laughed some more, and said, "Oh, lower than a smiggs-troffle, what delightfully impudent pets you mammals will make now that we have these holes for weapons—and what joy it will give me to train you!" He was sort of singing to himself, more than to me, I guess. "First reduce this planet! Then the suppressor field is gone, and our forces come in to prepare the black holes! Then we launch one on every inhabited planet until we have destroyed your military power. And then—"

He didn't finish that sentence, just more of that chuckling, cackling, *mean* laugh.

I felt uneasy. It was beginning to look as though Torklemiggen was up to something more than just high jinks and deviltry. He was easing up on the black hole and kind of crooning to himself, mostly in that foreign language of his but now and then in English: "Oh, my darling little assault vessel, what destruction you will wreak! Ah, charming black hole, how catastrophic you will be! How foolish these mammals who think they can forbid me to come near you—"

Then, as they say, light dawned. "Torklemiggen," I shouted, "you've got the wrong idea! It's not just a traffic regulation that we have to stay away from black holes! It's a lot more serious than that!"

But I was too late. He was inside the Roche limit before I could finish.

They don't have black holes around Fomalhaut, it seems. Of course, if he'd stopped to think for a minute he'd have realized what would happen—but then, if Fomalhautians ever stopped to think they wouldn't be Fomalhautians.

I almost hate to tell you what happened next. It was pretty gross. The tidal forces seized his ship, and they stretched it.

I heard one caterwauling astonished yowl over the TBS. Then his transmitter failed. The ship ripped apart, and the pieces began to rain down into the Schwarzschild boundary and plasmaed. There was a quick, blinding flash of fall-in energy from the black hole, and that was all Torklemiggen would ever say or do or know.

I got out of there as fast as I could. I wasn't really feeling very sorry for him, either. The way he was talking there toward the end, he sounded as though he had some pretty dangerous ideas.

When I landed it was sundown at the field, and people were staring and pointing toward the place in the sky where Torklemiggen had smeared himself into the black hole. All bright purplish and orangey plasma clouds—it made a really beautiful sunset, I'll say that much for the guy! I didn't have time to admire it, though, because Tonda was waiting, and we just had minutes to get to the Deputy Census Director, Division of Reclassification, before it closed.

But we made it.

Well, I said I had big news, didn't I? And that's it, because now your loving son is

Yours truly,
James Paul Aguilar-Madigan,
the newlywed!

MY LADY GREEN SLEEVES

Prisons have provided the setting for a number of memorable works of fiction—in particular, there have been some terrific films set in prisons. Not a lot of science fiction has been set in prisons, though. Frederik Pohl, however, has never been one to shy away from something that hasn't been done before.

The definition of "science fiction" is something endlessly debated among readers, fans, and academics interested in the genre. The debate will not be decided within these pages, but the limits of what may be called "science fiction" will perhaps be stretched in these stories.

One sort of SF is that in which it isn't technology, but rather social institutions that are different from those we know in the real world. In "My Lady Green Sleeves," first published in 1957, things are different. Prison life will seem familiar to readers who have read or seen prison tales, but the class system of the world of this story is one that one doesn't see in everyday life. However, a warning: If you think this is an idle speculation, you underestimate the author.

1

His name was Liam O'Leary and there was something stinking in his nostrils. It was the smell of trouble. He hadn't found what the trouble was yet, but he would. That was his business. He was a captain of guards in Estates-General Correctional Institution— better known to its inmates as the Jug—and if he hadn't been able to detect the scent of trouble brewing a cell block away he would never have survived to reach his captaincy.

And her name, he saw, was Sue-Ann Bradley, Detainee No. WFA-656R.

He frowned at the rap sheet, trying to figure out what got a girl like her into a place like this. And, what was more important, why she couldn't adjust herself to it, now that she was in.

He demanded, "Why wouldn't you mop out your cell?"

The girl lifted her head angrily and took a step forward. The block guard, Sodaro, growled warningly, "Watch it, auntie!"

O'Leary shook his head. "Let her talk, Sodaro." It said in the *Civil Service Guide to Prison Administration:* "Detainees will be permitted to speak in their own behalf in disciplinary proceedings." And O'Leary was a man who lived by the book.

She burst out, "I never got a chance! That old witch Mathias never told me I was supposed to mop up. She banged on the door and said, 'Slush up, sister!' And then ten minutes later she called the guards and told them I refused to mop."

The block guard guffawed. "Wipe talk! That's what she was telling you to do. Cap'n, you know what's funny about this? This Bradley is—"

"Shut up, Sodaro." Captain O'Leary put down his pencil and looked at the girl. She was attractive and young—not beyond hope, surely. Maybe she had got off to a wrong start, but the question was, would putting her in the disciplinary block help straighten her out? He rubbed his ear and looked past her at the line of prisoners on the rap detail, waiting for him to judge their cases. He said patiently, "Bradley, the rules are you have to mop out your cell. If you didn't understand what Mathias was talking about you should have asked her. Now, I'm warning you, the next time—"

"Hey, Cap'n, wait!" Sodaro was looking alarmed. "This isn't a first offense. Look at the rap sheet—yesterday she pulled the same thing in the mess hall." He shook his head reprovingly at the prisoner. "The block guard had to break up a fight between her and another wench, and she claimed the same business—said she didn't understand when the other one asked her to move along." He said virtuously, "The guard warned her then that next time she'd get the Green Sleeves for sure."

Inmate Bradley seemed to be on the verge of tears. She said tautly, "I don't care. I don't care!"

O'Leary stopped her. "That's enough! Three days in Block O," he snapped, and waved her away. It was the only thing to do—for her own sake as much as for his. He had managed, by strength of will, not to hear that she had omitted to say "sir" every time she spoke to him; but he couldn't keep it up forever, and he certainly couldn't overlook hysteria. And hysteria was clearly the next step for her.

All the same, he stared after her as she left. He handed the rap sheet to Sodaro and said absently, "Too bad a kid like her has to be here. What's she in for?"

"You didn't know, Cap'n?" Sodaro leered. "She's in for conspiracy to violate the Categoried Class laws. Don't waste your time with her, Cap'n—she's a figger-lover!"

Captain O'Leary took a long drink of water from the fountain marked "Civil Service." But it didn't wash the taste out of his mouth.

What got into a girl to get her mixed up with that kind of dirty business? He checked out of the cell blocks and walked across the yard, wondering about her. She'd had every advantage—decent Civil Service parents, a good education, everything a girl could wish for. If anything, she had had a better environment than O'Leary himself, and look what she had made of it.

"Evening, Cap'n." A bleary old inmate orderly stood up straight and touched his cap as O'Leary passed by.

"Evening." O'Leary noted, with the part of his mind that always noted those things, that the orderly had been leaning on his broom until he'd noticed the captain coming by. Of course, there wasn't much to sweep—the spray machines and sweeperdozers had been over the cobblestones of the yard twice already that day. But it was an inmate's job to keep busy. And it was a guard captain's job to notice when they didn't.

There wasn't anything wrong with that job, he told himself. It was a perfectly good civil-service position—better than post-office clerk, not as good as congressman, but a job you could be proud to hold. He *was* proud of it. It was *right* that he should be proud of it. He was civil-service born and bred, and naturally he was proud and content to do a good, clean civil-service job. If he had happened to be born a fig—a *clerk*, he told himself; if he had happened to be born a clerk, why, he would have been proud of that too. There wasn't anything wrong with being a clerk—or a mechanic or a soldier, or even a laborer for that matter. Good laborers were the salt of the earth! They weren't smart, maybe, but they had a—well, a sort of natural, relaxed joy of living. O'Leary was a broadminded man, and many times he had thought almost with a touch of envy how *comfortable* it must be to be a wipe—a *laborer*, he corrected himself. No responsibilities. No worries. Just an easy, slow routine of work and loaf, work and loaf.

Of course, he wouldn't *really* want that kind of life, because he was Civil Service, and not the kind to try to cross over class barriers that weren't *meant* to be—

"Evening, Cap'n."

He nodded to the mechanic inmate who was, theoretically, in charge of maintaining the prison's car pool, just inside the gate. "Evening, Conan," he said. Conan, now—he was a big buck greaser, and he would be there for the next hour, languidly poking a piece of fluff out of the air filter on the prison jeep. Lazy, sure. Undependable, certainly. But he kept the cars going—and, O'Leary thought approvingly, when his sentence was up in another year or so, he would go back to his life with his status restored, a mechanic on the outside as he had been inside, and he certainly would never risk coming back to the Jug by trying to pass as Civil Service or anything else. He knew his place.

So why didn't this girl, this Sue-Ann Bradley, know hers?

2

Every prison has its Green Sleeves—sometimes they are called by different names. Old Marquette called it "the canary"; Louisiana State called it "the red hats"; elsewhere it was called "the hole," "the snake pit," "the Klondike." When you're in it you don't much care what it is called; it is a place for punishment.

And punishment is what you get.

Block O in Estates-General Correctional Institution was the disciplinary block, and because of the green straitjackets its inhabitants wore it was called the Green Sleeves. It was a community of its own, an enclave within the larger city-state that was the Jug. And like any other community, it had its leading citizens . . . two of them. Their names were Sauer and Flock.

Sue-Ann Bradley heard them before she reached the Green Sleeves. She was in a detachment of three unfortunates like herself, convoyed by an irritable guard, climbing the steel steps toward Block O from the floor below, when she heard the yelling.

"Owoo-o-o," screamed Sauer from one end of the cell block; and "Yow-w-w!" shrieked Flock at the other.

The inside deck guard of Block O looked nervously at the outside deck guard. The outside guard looked impassively back—after all, he was on the outside. The inside guard muttered, "Wipe rats! They're getting on my nerves."

The outside guard shrugged.

"Detail, *halt!*" The two guards turned to see what was coming in as the three new candidates for the Green Sleeves slumped to a stop at the head of the stairs. "Here they are," Sodaro told them. "Take good care of 'em, will you? Especially the lady—she's going to like it here, because there's plenty of wipes and greasers and figgers to keep her company." He laughed coarsely and abandoned his charges to the Block O guards.

The outside guard said sourly, "A woman, for God's sake. Now, O'Leary knows I hate it when there's a woman in here. It gets the others all riled up."

"Let them in," the inside guard told him. "The others are riled up already."

Sue-Ann Bradley looked carefully at the floor and paid them no attention. The outside guard pulled the switch that turned on the tanglefoot electronic fields that swamped the floor of the block corridor and of each individual cell. While the fields were on, you could ignore the prisoners—they simply could not move fast enough, against the electronic drag of the field, to do any harm. But it was a rule that even in Block O you didn't leave the tangler fields on all the time—only when the cell doors had to be opened or a prisoner's restraining garment removed.

Sue-Ann walked bravely forward through the opened gate—and fell flat on her face. It was like walking through molasses; it was her first experience of a tanglefoot field.

The guard guffawed and lifted her up by one shoulder. "Take it easy, auntie. Come on, get in your cell." He steered her in the right direction and pointed to a green-sleeved straitjacket on the cell cot. "Put that on. Being as you're a lady, we won't tie it up—but the rules say you got to wear it, and the rules—Hey! She's crying!" He shook his head, marveling. It was the first time he had ever seen a prisoner cry in the Green Sleeves.

However, he was wrong. Sue-Ann shoulders were shaking, but not from tears. Sue-Ann Bradley had got a good look at Sauer and at Flock as she passed them by, and she was fighting off an almost uncontrollable urge to retch.

Sauer and Flock were what are called prison wolves. They were laborers—"wipes," for short—or at any rate they had been once; they had spent so much time in prisons that it was sometimes hard even for them to remember what they really were, outside. Sauer was a big, grinning redhead with eyes like a water moccasin. Flock was a lithe five-footer, with the build of a water moccasin—and the sad, stupid eyes of a calf.

Sauer stopped yelling for a moment. "Hey, Flock," he cried.

"What do you want, Sauer?" called Flock from his own cell.

"Didn't you see, Flock?" bellowed Sauer. "We got a lady with us! Maybe we ought to cut out this yelling so as not to disturb the lady!" He screeched with howling, maniacal laughter. "Anyway, if we don't cut this out, they'll get us in trouble, Flock!"

"Oh, you think so?" shrieked Flock. "Jeez, I wish you hadn't said that, Sauer. You got me scared! I'm so scared I'm gonna have to yell!"

The howling started all over again.

The inside guard finished putting the new prisoners away and turned off the tangler field once more. He licked his lips. "Say, you want to take a turn in here for a while?"

"Uh-uh," said the outside guard.

"You're yellow," the inside guard said moodily. "Ah, I don't know why I don't quit this lousy job. Hey, you! Pipe down or I'll come in and beat your head off!"

"Ee-ee-ee!" shrieked Sauer. "I'm scared!" Then he grinned at the guard, all but his water-moccasin eyes. "Don't you know you can't hurt a wipe by hitting him on the head, boss?"

"Shut *up!*" yelled the inside guard. . . .

Sue-Ann Bradley's weeping now was genuine. She simply could not help it. The crazy yowling of the hard-timers, Sauer and Flock, was getting under her skin. They weren't even—even *human,* she told herself miserably, trying to weep silently so as not to give the guards the satisfaction of hearing her. They were animals!

Resentment and anger she could understand—she told herself doggedly that resentment and anger were *natural* and *right.* They were perfectly normal expressions of the freedom-loving citizen's rebellion against the vile and stifling system of Categoried Classes. It was *good* that Sauer and Flock still had enough spirit to struggle against the vicious system—

But did they have to scream so?

The senseless yelling was driving her crazy. She abandoned herself to weeping, and she didn't even care who heard her any more. Senseless!

It never occurred to Sue-Ann Bradley that it might not be senseless, because noise hides noise. But then, she hadn't been a prisoner very long.

3

"I smell trouble," said O'Leary to the warden.

"Trouble, trouble?" Warden Schluckebier clutched his throat and his little round eyes looked terrified—as perhaps they should have. Warden Godfrey Schluckebier was the almighty Caesar of ten thousand inmates in the Jug, but privately he was a fussy old man trying to hold onto the last decent job he would have in his life. "Trouble? *What* trouble?"

O'Leary shrugged. "Different things. You know Lafon, from Block A? This afternoon he was playing ball with the laundry orderlies in the yard."

The warden, faintly relieved, faintly annoyed, scolded:

"O'Leary, what did you want to worry me for? There's nothing wrong with playing ball in the yard. That's what recreation periods are for!"

"No. You don't see what I mean, warden. Lafon was a professional on the outside— an architect. Those laundry cons were laborers. Pros and wipes don't mix, it isn't natural. And there are other things." O'Leary hesitated, frowning. How could you explain to the warden that it didn't *smell* right? "For instance— Well, there's Aunt Mathias in the women's block. She's a pretty good old girl—that's why she's the block orderly, she's a lifer, she's got no place to go, she gets along with the other women. But today she put a woman named Bradley on report. Why? Because she told Bradley to mop up in wipe talk and Bradley didn't understand. Now, Mathias wouldn't—"

The warden raised his hand. "Please, O'Leary," he begged. "Don't bother me about that kind of stuff." He sighed heavily and rubbed his eyes. He poured himself a cup of steaming black coffee from a brewpot, reached in a desk drawer for something, hesitated, glanced at O'Leary, then dropped a pale blue tablet into the cup. He drank it down eagerly, ignoring its temperature.

He leaned back, looking suddenly happier and more assured.

"O'Leary," he said, "you're a guard captain, right? And I'm your warden. You have your job, keeping the inmates in line, and I have mine. Now, your job is just as important as my job," he said piously, staring gravely at O'Leary. "*Everybody's* job is just as important as everybody else's, right? But we have to stick to our own jobs. We don't want to try to *pass.*"

O'Leary snapped erect, abruptly angry. Pass! What the devil way was that for the warden to talk to him.

"Excuse the expression, O'Leary," the warden said anxiously. "I mean, after all, 'Specialization is the goal of civilization,' right?" He was a great man for platitudes, was Warden Schluckebier. "*You* know, you don't want to worry about my end of running the prison. And I don't want to worry about yours. You see?" And he folded his hands and smiled like a civil-service Buddha.

O'Leary choked back his temper. "Warden, I'm telling you that there's trouble coming up. I smell the signs."

"Handle it, then!" snapped the warden, irritated at last.

"But suppose it's too big to handle? Suppose—"

"It isn't," the warden said positively. "Don't borrow trouble with all your supposing, O'Leary." He sipped the remains of his coffee, made a wry face, poured a fresh cup and, with an elaborate show of not noticing what he himself was doing, dropped three of the pale blue tablets into it this time.

He sat beaming into space, waiting for the jolt to take effect.

"Well, then," he said at last. "You just remember what I've told you tonight, O'Leary, and we'll get along fine. 'Specialization is the—' Oh, curse the thing."

His phone was ringing. The warden picked it up irritably—that was the trouble with those pale blue tablets, thought O'Leary; they gave you a lift, but they put you on edge. "Hello," barked the warden, not even glancing at the viewscreen. "What the devil do you want? Don't you know I'm— What? You did *what?* You're going to WHAT?"

He looked at the viewscreen at last with a look of pure horror.

Whatever he saw on it, it did not reassure him. His eyes opened like clamshells in a steamer.

"O'Leary," he said faintly, "my mistake."

And he hung up—more or less by accident; the handset dropped from his fingers.

The person on the other end of the phone was calling from Cell Block O.

Five minutes before he hadn't been anywhere near the phone, and it didn't look as if his chances of ever getting near it were very good. Because five minutes before he was in his cell, with the rest of the hard-timers of the Green Sleeves.

His name was Flock.

He was still yelling. Sue-Ann Bradley, in the cell across from him, thought that maybe, after all, the man was really in pain. Maybe the crazy screams were screams of agony, because certainly his face was the face of an agonized man.

The outside guard bellowed: "Okay, okay. Take ten!"

Sue-Ann froze, waiting to see what would happen. What actually did happen was that the guard reached up and closed the switch that actuated the tangler fields on the floors of the cells. The prison rules were humanitarian, even for the dregs that inhabited the Green Sleeves. Ten minutes out of every two hours, even the worst case had to be allowed to take his hands out of the restraining garment. "Rest period" it was called—in the rule book; the inmates had a less lovely term for it.

At the guard's yell, the inmates jumped to their feet.

Bradley was a little slow getting off the edge of the steel-slat bed—nobody had warned her that the eddy currents in the tangler fields had a way of making metal smoke-hot. She gasped, but didn't cry out. Score one more painful lesson in her new language course. She rubbed the backs of her thighs gingerly—and slowly, slowly. The eddy currents did not permit you to move fast. It was like pushing against rubber; the faster you tried to move, the greater the resistance.

The guard peered genially into her cell. "You're okay, auntie." She proudly ignored him as he slogged deliberately away on his rounds. At least he didn't have to untie her, and practically stand over her while she attended to various personal matters, as he did with the male prisoners. It was not much to be grateful for, but Sue-Ann Bradley was grateful. At least, she didn't have to live *quite* like a fig—like an underprivileged clerk, she told herself, conscience-stricken.

Across the hall, the guard was saying irritably, "What the hell's the matter with you?" He opened the door of the cell with an asbestos-handled key held in a canvas glove.

Flock was in that cell, and he was doubled over.

The guard looked at him doubtfully. It could be a trick, maybe. Couldn't it? But he could see Flock's face, and the agony in it was real enough. And Flock was gasping, through real tears: "Cramps. I—I—"

"Ah, you wipes always got a pain in the gut." The guard lumbered around Flock to the drawstrings at the back of the jacket. Funny smell in here, he told himself—not for the first time. And imagine, some people didn't believe that wipes had a smell of their own! But this time, he realized cloudily, it was a rather unusual smell. Something burning. Scorching—almost like meat scorching.

It wasn't pleasant. He finished untying Flock and turned away; let the stinking wipe take care of his own troubles. He only had ten minutes to get all the way around Block O, and the inmates complained like crazy if he didn't make sure they all got the most possible free time. He was pretty good at snow-shoeing through the tangler field. He was a little vain about it, even; at times he had been known to boast of his ability to make the rounds in two minutes, every time. . . .

Every time but this.

For Flock moaned behind him, oddly close.

The guard turned, but not quickly enough. There was Flock—astonishing, he was half out of his jacket; his arms hadn't been in the sleeves at all! And in one of the hands, incredibly, there was something that glinted and smoked.

"All right," croaked Flock, tears trickling out of eyes nearly shut with pain.

But it wasn't the tears that held the guard, it was the shining, smoking thing, now poised at his throat. A shiv! It looked as though it had been made out of a bedspring, ripped loose from its frame God knows how, hidden inside the green-sleeved jacket God knows how—filed, filed to sharpness over endless hours. No wonder Flock moaned! For the eddy-currents in the shiv were slowly cooking his hand; and the blister against his abdomen where the shiv had rested during other rest periods felt like raw acid.

"All right," whispered Flock, "just walk out the door, and you won't get hurt. Unless the other screw makes trouble, you won't get hurt—so tell him not to, you hear?" He was nearly fainting with the pain.

But he hadn't let go.

He didn't let go. And he didn't stop.

4

And it was Flock on the phone to the warden—Flock with his eyes still streaming tears, Flock with Sauer standing right behind him, menacing the two bound deck guards.

Sauer shoved Flock out of the way. "Hey, warden!" he said—and the voice was a cheerful bray, though the serpent eyes were cold and hating. "Warden, you got to get a medic in here. My boy Flock, he hurt himself real bad and he needs a doctor." He gestured playfully at the guards with the shiv. "I tell you, warden. I got this knife, and I got your guards here. Enough said? So get a medic in here quick—you hear?"

And he snapped the connection.

O'Leary said, "Warden, I told you I smelled trouble!"

The warden lifted his head, glared, started feebly to speak, hesitated, and picked up the long-distance phone. He said sadly to the prison operator: "Get me the Governor—fast!"

Riot!

The word spread out from the prison on seven-league boots. It snatched the City Governor out of a friendly game of Seniority with his Manager and their wives—and just when he was holding the Porkbarrel Joker concealed in the hole. It broke up the Base Championship Scramble Finals at Hap Arnold Field to the south, as half the contestants had to scramble in earnest to a Red Alert that was real. It reached to police precinct houses and TV newsrooms and highway checkpoints, and from there it filtered into the homes and lives of the nineteen million persons that lived within a few dozen miles of the Jug.

Riot. And yet, fewer than half a dozen men were actually involved.

A handful of men, and the enormous bulk of the city-state quivered in every limb and class. It was like a quarrel of fleas on the hide of a rhino!

But a flea-bite can kill a rhino with the slow agony of communicated disease; and the city-state around the prison leaped in fear. In its ten million homes, in its hundreds of thousands of public places, the city-state's people shook under the impact of the news from the prison.

For the news touched them where their fears lay. Riot! And not merely a street brawl among roistering wipes, or a barroom fight of greasers relaxing from a hard day at the plant—the riot was down among the corrupt sludge that underlay the state itself. Wipes brawled with wipes, and no one cared; but in the Jug all classes were cast together.

Thirty miles to the south, Hap Arnold Field was a blaze of light. The airmen tumbled out of their quarters and dayrooms at the screech of the alert siren, and behind them their wives and children stretched and yawned and worried. An alert! The older kids fussed and complained and their mothers shut them up. No, there wasn't any alert scheduled for tonight; no, they didn't know where Daddy was going; no, the kids couldn't get up yet—it was the middle of the night!

And as soon as they had the kids back in bed, most of the mothers struggled into their own airwac uniforms and headed for the Briefing Area to hear.

They caught the words from a distance—not quite correctly. "Riot!" gasped an aircraftswoman first-class, mother of three. "The wipes! I *told* Charlie they'd get out of hand, and—Alys, we aren't safe. You know how they are about GI women! I'm going right home and get a club and stand right by the door and—"

"Club!" snapped Alys, radarscope-sergeant, with two children querulously awake in her nursery at home. "What in God's name is the use of a club? You can't hurt a wipe hitting him on the head. You'd better come along to Supply with me and draw a gun—you'll need it before this night is out!"

But the airmen themselves heard the briefing loud and clear over the scramble-call speakers, and they knew it was not merely a matter of trouble in the wipe quarters. The Jug! The governor himself had called them out; they were to fly interdicting missions at such-and-such levels on such-and-such flight circuits around the prison. So the rockets took off on fountains of fire; and the jets took off with a whistling roar; and last of all the helicopters took off . . . and they were the ones who might actually accomplish something. They took up their picket posts on the prison perimeter, a pilot and two bombardiers in each copter, stone-faced, staring grimly alert at the prison below.

They were ready for the breakout.

But—there wasn't any breakout.

The rockets went home for fuel. The jets went home for fuel. The helicopters hung on—still ready, still waiting.

The rockets came back and roared harmlessly about, and went away again. They stayed away. The helicopter men never faltered and never relaxed. The prison below them was washed with light—from the guard posts on the walls, from the cell blocks themselves, from the mobile lights of the guard squadrons surrounding the walls. North of the prison, on the long, flat, damp developments of reclaimed land, the matchbox row houses of the clerical neighborhoods showed lights in every window as the figgers stood ready to repel invasion from their undesired neighbors to the east, the wipes. In the crowded tenements of the laborers' quarters, the wipes shouted from window to window; and there were crowds in the bright streets.

"The whole bloody thing's going to blow up!" a helicopter bombardier yelled bitterly to his pilot, above the flutter and roar of the whirling blades. "Look at the mobs in Greaserville! The first break-out from the Jug's going to start a fight like you never saw—and we'll be right in the middle of it!"

He was partly right. He would be right in the middle of it—for every man, woman and child in the city-state would be right in the middle of it; there was no place anywhere that would be spared. *No Mixing.* That was the prescription that kept the city-state alive. There's no harm in a family fight—and aren't all mechanics a family, aren't all laborers a clan, aren't all clerks and office workers related by closer ties than blood or skin? But the declassed cons of the Jug were the dregs of every class; and once they spread the neat compartmentation of society was pierced. The break-out would mean riot on a bigger scale than any prison had ever known. . . .

But he was also partly wrong. Because the breakout wasn't seeming to come.

The Jug itself was coming to a boil.

Honor Block A, relaxed and comfortable at the end of another day, found itself shaken alert by strange goings-on. First there was the whir and roar of the Air Force overhead. *Trouble.* Then there was the sudden arrival of extra guards, doubling the normal complement—day-shift guards, summoned away from their comfortable civil-service homes at some urgent call. *Trouble for sure.*

Honor Block A wasn't used to trouble. A Block was as far from the Green Sleeves of O Block as you could get and still stay in the Jug. Honor Block A belonged to the prison's halfbreeds—the honor prisoners, the trusties who did guards' work because there weren't enough guards to go around. They weren't Apaches or Piutes; they were camp-following Injuns who had sold out for the white man's firewater. The price of their services was privilege—many privileges. Item: TV sets in every cell. Item: Hobby tools, to make gadgets for the visitor trade—the only way an inmate could earn an honest dollar. Item: In consequence, an exact knowledge of everything the outside world knew and put on its TV screens (including the grim, alarming reports of "trouble at Estates-General") and the capacity to convert their "hobby tools" to—other uses.

An honor prisoner named Wilmer Lafon was watching the TV screen with an expression of rage and despair.

Lafon was a credit to the Jug—he was a showpiece for visitors. Prison rules provided for prisoner training—it was a matter of "rehabilitation." Prisoner rehabilitation is a joke, and a centuries-old one at that; but it had its serious uses, and one of them was to keep the prisoners busy. It didn't much matter at what.

Lafon, for instance, was being "rehabilitated" by studying architecture. The guards made a point of bringing inspection delegations to his cell to show him off. There were his walls, covered with pin-ups—but not of women. The pictures were sketches Lafon had drawn himself; they were of buildings, highways, dams and bridges; they were splendidly conceived and immaculately executed. "Looka that!" the guards would rumble to their guests. "There isn't an architect on the outside as good as this boy! What do you say, Wilmer? Tell the gentlemen—how long you been taking these correspondence courses in architecture? Six years! Ever since he came to the Jug."

And Lafon would grin and bob his head, and the delegation would go, with the guard saying something like: "Believe me, that Wilmer could design a whole skyscraper—and it wouldn't fall down, either!"

And they were perfectly, provably right. Not only could Inmate Lafon design a skyscraper, but he had already done so. More than a dozen of them. And none had fallen down.

Of course, that was more than six years back, before he was convicted of a felony and sent to the Jug. He would never design another. Or if he did, it would never be built. For the plain fact of the matter was that the Jug's rehabilitation courses were like rehabilitation in every prison that was ever built since time and punishment began. They kept the inmates busy. They made a show of purpose for an institution that had never had a purpose that made sense. And that was all.

For punishment for a crime is not satisfied by a jail sentence—how does it hurt a man to feed and clothe and house him, with the bills paid by the state? Lafon's punishment was that he, as an architect, was *through*. Savage tribes used to lop off a finger or an ear to punish a criminal. Civilized societies confine their amputations to bits and pieces of the personality. Chop-chop, and a man's reputation comes off; chop again, and his professional standing is gone; chop-chop and he has lost the respect and trust of his fellows. The jail itself isn't the punishment. The jail is only the shaman's hatchet that performs the amputation. If rehabilitation in a jail worked—if it was *meant* to work—it would be the end of jails.

Rehabilitation? Rehabilitation for what?

Wilmer Lafon switched off the television set and silently pounded his fist into the wall.

Never again to return to the Professional class! For naturally, the conviction had cost him his membership in the Architectural Society, and *that* had cost him his Professional standing.

But still—just to be out of the Jug, that would be something! And his whole hope of ever getting out lay not here in Honor Block A, but in the turmoil of the Green Sleeves, a hundred meters and fifty armed guards away.

He was a furious man. He looked into the cell next door, where a con named Garcia was trying to concentrate on a game of Solitaire Splitfee. Once Garcia had been a Professional too; he was the closest thing to a friend Wilmer Lafon had. Maybe he could now help to get Lafon where he wanted—*needed*—to be. . . .

Lafon swore silently and shook his head. Garcia was a spineless milksop, as bad as any clerk—Lafon was nearly sure there was a touch of the inkwell somewhere in his family. Clever enough, like all figgers. But you couldn't rely on him in a pinch.

He would have to do it all himself.

He thought for a second, ignoring the rustle and mumble of the other honor prisoners of Block A. There was no help for it; he would have to dirty his hands with physical activity.

Outside on the deck, the guards were grumbling to each other. Lafon wiped the scowl off his black face, put on a smile, rehearsed what he was going to say, and rattled the door of his cell.

"Shut up down there!" one of the screws bawled. Lafon recognized the voice; it was the guard named Sodaro. That was all to the good. He knew Sodaro, and he had some plans for him.

He rattled the cell door again and called: "Chief, can you come here a minute, please?"

Sodaro yelled, "Didn't you hear me? Shut up!" But in a moment he came wandering by and looked into Lafon's tidy little cell.

"What the devil do you want?" he grumbled.

Lafon said ingratiatingly, "Hey, chief, what's going on?"

"Shut your mouth," Sodaro said absently and yawned. He hefted his shoulder holster comfortably. That O'Leary, what a production he had made of getting the guards back! And here he was, stuck in Block A on the night he had set aside for getting better acquainted with that little blue-eyed statistician from the Census office.

"Aw, chief. The television says there's something going on in the Green Sleeves. What's the score?"

Sodaro had no reason not to answer him; but it was his unvarying practice to make a con wait before doing anything the con wanted. He gave Lafon a ten-second stare before he relented.

"That's right. Sauer and Flock took over Block O. What about it?"

Much, much about it! But Lafon looked away to hide the eagerness in his eyes. Perhaps, after all, it was not too late. . . . He suggested humbly: "You look a little sleepy. Do you want some coffee?"

"Coffee?" Sodaro scratched. "You got a cup for me?"

"Certainly! I've got one put aside—swiped it from the messhall, you know, not the one I use myself."

"Um." Sodaro leaned on the cell door. "You know I could toss *you* in the Green Sleeves for stealing from the messhall."

"Aw, chief!" Lafon grinned.

"You been looking for trouble. O'Leary says you were messing around with the bucks from the laundry detail," Sodaro said half-heartedly. But he didn't really like picking on Lafon, who was, after all, an agreeable inmate to have on occasion. "All right. Where's the coffee?"

They didn't bother with tanglefoot fields in Honor Block A. Sodaro just unlocked the door and walked in, hardly bothering to look at Lafon. He took three steps toward the neat little desk at the back of the cell, where Lafon had rigged up a drawing board and a table, where Lafon kept his little store of luxury goods. Three steps. And then, suddenly aware that Lafon was very close to him, he turned, astonished— A little too late. He saw that Lafon had snatched up a metal chair; he saw Lafon swinging it, his black face maniacal; he saw the chair coming down. He reached for his shoulder holster; but it was very much too late for that.

5

Captain O'Leary dragged the scared little wretch into the warden's office. He shook the con angrily. "Listen to this, warden! The boys just brought this one in from the Shops Building. Do you know what he's been up to?"

The warden wheezed sadly and looked away. He had stopped even answering O'Leary by now, he had stopped talking to Sauer on the interphone when the big convict called, every few minutes, to rave and threaten and demand a doctor. He had almost stopped doing everything except worry and weep. But—still and all, he was the warden. He was the one who gave the orders.

O'Leary barked, "Warden, pay attention! This little greaser has bollixed up the whole tangler circuit for the prison. If the cons get out into the Yard now you won't be able to tangle them. You know what that means? They'll have the freedom of the Yard, and who knows what comes next?"

The warden frowned sympathetically. "Tsk, tsk."

O'Leary shook the con again. "Come on, Hiroko! Tell the warden what you told the guards."

The con shrank away from him. Beads of sweat were glistening on his furrowed yellow forehead. "I—I had to do it, Cap'n!" he babbled. "I shorted the wormcan in the tangler subgrid, but I had to! I got a signal, 'Bollix the grid tonight or *wheep*, someday you'll be in the Yard and they'll static you!' What could I do, Cap'n? I didn't want to—"

O'Leary pressed: "Who did the signal come from?" But the con only shook his head, perspiring the more.

The warden asked faintly, "What's he saying?"

O'Leary rolled his eyes to heaven. And this was the warden—couldn't even understand shoptalk from the mouths of his own inmates!

He translated: "He got orders from the prison underground to short-circuit the electronic units in the tangler circuit. They threatened to kill him if he didn't."

The warden drummed with his fingers on the desk.

"The tangler field, eh? My, yes. That is important. You'd better get it fixed, O'Leary. Right away."

"Fixed? Warden, look—who's going to fix it?" O'Leary demanded. "You know as well as I do that every mechanic in the prison is a con. Even if one of the guards would do a thing like that—and I'd bust him myself if he did!—he wouldn't know where to start. That's mechanic work."

The warden swallowed. He had to admit that O'Leary was right. Naturally nobody but a mechanic—and a specialist electrician from a particular subgroup of the greaser class at that—could fix something like the tangler field generators. That was a fact of life. These days, he thought pathetically, the world was so complex that it took a specialist to do anything at all.

He said absently, "Well, that's true enough. After all, 'Specialization is the goal of civilization,' you know."

O'Leary took a deep breath—he needed it.

He beckoned to the guard at the door. "Take this greaser out of here!" The con shambled out, his head hanging.

O'Leary turned to the warden and spread his hands.

"Warden," he said reasonably, "don't you see how this thing is building up? Let's not just wait for the place to explode in our faces! Let me take a squad into Block O before it's too late."

The warden pursed his lips thoughtfully and cocked his head, as though he were trying to find some trace of merit in an unreasonable request.

He said at last, "No."

O'Leary made a passionate sound that was trying to be bad language; but he was too raging mad to articulate it. He walked stiffly away from the limp, silent warden and stared out the window.

At least, he told himself, *he* hadn't gone to pieces. It was his doing, not the warden's, that all the off-duty guards had been dragged double-time back to the prison, his doing that they were now ringed around the outer walls or scattered on extra-man patrols throughout the prison.

It was something, but O'Leary couldn't believe that it was enough. He'd been in touch with half a dozen of the details inside the prison on the intercom, and all of them had reported the same thing. In all of E–G not a single prisoner was asleep. They were talking back and forth between the cells, and the guards couldn't shut them up; they were listening to concealed radios, and the guards didn't dare make a shakedown to find them; they were working themselves up to something. To what?

O'Leary didn't want ever to find out what. He wanted to go in there with a couple of the best guards he could get his hands on—shoot his way into the Green Sleeves if he had to—and clean up the infection.

But the warden said no.

O'Leary moaned and stared balefully at the hovering helicopters.

The warden was the warden! He was placed in that position through the meticulously careful operations of the Civil Service machinery, maintained in that position year after year through the penetrating annual inquiries of the Reclassification Board. It was *subversive* to think that the Board could have made a mistake!

But O'Leary was absolutely sure that the warden was a scared, ineffectual jerk.

The interphone was ringing again.

The warden picked up the handpiece and held it limply at arm's length, his eyes fixed glassily on the wall. It was Sauer from the Green Sleeves again; O'Leary could hear his maddened bray.

"I warned you, warden!" O'Leary could see the big con's contorted face in miniature, in the viewscreen of the interphone. The grin was broad and jolly; the snake's eyes poisonously cold. "I'm going to give you five minutes, warden, you hear? Five minutes! And if there isn't a medic in here in five minutes to take care of my boy Flock—your guards have had it! I'm going to chop off a hand and throw it out the window, you hear me? And five minutes later another hand! And five minutes later—"

The warden groaned weakly. "I've called for the prison medic, Sauer. Honestly I have! I'm sure he's coming as rapidly as he—"

"Five minutes!" And the ferociously grinning face disappeared.

O'Leary leaned forward. "Warden. Warden, let me take a squad in there!"

The warden stared at him for a blank moment. "Squad? No, O'Leary. What's the use of a squad? It's a medic I have to get in there. I have a responsibility to those guards, and if I don't get a medic—"

A cold, calm voice from the door: "I am here, warden!"

O'Leary and the warden both jumped up. The medic nodded slightly. "You may sit down."

"Oh, doctor! Thank heaven you're here." The warden was falling all over himself, getting a chair for his guest, flustering about.

O'Leary said sharply, "Wait a minute, warden. You can't let the doctor go in alone!"

"He isn't alone!" The doctor's intern came from behind him, scowling belligerently at O'Leary. He was youngish, his beard pale and silky, a long way from his first practice. "I'm with him!"

O'Leary put a strain on his patience. "They'll eat you up in there, Doc! Those are the worst cons in the prison. They've got two hostages already—what's the use of giving them two more?"

The medic fixed him with his eyes. He was a tall man and he wore his beard proudly. "Guard, do you think you can prevent me from healing a sufferer?" He folded his hands over his abdomen and turned to leave.

The intern stepped aside and bowed his head. O'Leary surrendered.

"All right, you can go. But I'm coming with you—with a squad!"

Inmate Sue-Ann Bradley cowered in her cell.

The Green Sleeves was jumping. She had never—no, *never,* she told herself wretchedly—thought that it would be anything like this. She listened unbelieving to the noise the released prisoners were making, smashing the chairs and commodes in their cells, screaming threats at the bound and terrified guards.

They were like—like—*animals!*

She faced the thought, with fear, and with the sorrow of a murdered belief that was worse than fear. It was bad that she was, she knew, in danger of dying right here and now; but what was even worse was that the principles that had brought her to the Jug were dying too.

Wipes were *not* the same as civil-service people!

A bull's roar from the corridor, and a shocking crash of glass; that was Flock, and apparently he had smashed the TV interphone.

"What in the world are they *doing?*" Inmate Bradley sobbed to herself. It was beyond comprehension. They were yelling words that made no sense to her, threatening punishments that she could barely imagine on the guards. Sauer and Flock, they were laborers; some of the other rioting cons were clerks, mechanics—even civil-service or professionals, for all she could tell. But she could hardly understand any of them. Why was the quiet little Chinese clerk in Cell Six setting fire to his bed?

There did seem to be a pattern, of sorts—the laborers were rocketing about, breaking things at random; the mechanics were pleasurably sabotaging the electronic and plumbing installations; the white-collar categories were finding their dubious joys in less direct ways—liking setting fire to a bed. But what a mad pattern!

The more Sue-Ann saw of them, the less she understood.

It wasn't just that they *talked* different—she had spent endless hours studying the various patois of shoptalk, and it had defeated her; but it wasn't just that. It was bad enough when she couldn't understand the words—as when that trusty Mathias had ordered her in wipe shoptalk to mop out her cell.

But what was even worse was not understanding the thought behind the words.

Sue-Ann Bradley had consecrated her young life to the belief that all men were created free, and equal—and alike. Or alike in all the things that mattered, anyhow. Alike in hopes, alike in motives, alike in virtues. She had turned her back on a decent civil-service family and a promising civil-service career to join the banned and despised Association for the Advancement of the Categoried Classes—

Screams from the corridor outside.

Sue-Ann leaped to the door of her cell to see Sauer clutching at one of the guards. The guard's hands were tied but his feet were free; he broke loose from the clumsy clown with the serpent's eyes, almost fell, ran toward Sue-Ann.

There was nowhere else to run. The guard, moaning and gasping, tripped, slid, caught himself and stumbled into her cell. "Please!" he begged. "That crazy Sauer—he's going to cut my hand off! For heaven's sake, ma'am—stop him!"

Sue-Ann stared at him, between terror and tears. Stop Sauer! If only she could stop Sauer. The big redhead was lurching stiffly toward them—raging, but not so angry that the water-moccasin eyes showed heat.

"Come here, you figger scum!" he brayed.

The epithet wasn't even close—the guard was civil-service through and through—but it was like a reviving whip-sting to Sue-Ann Bradley.

"Watch your language, Mr. Sauer!" she snapped, incongruously.

Sauer stopped dead and blinked.

"Don't you dare hurt him!" she warned. "Don't you see, Mr. Sauer, you're playing into their hands? They're trying to divide us. They pit mechanic against clerk, laborer against armed forces. And you're helping them! Brother Sauer, I beg—"

The redhead spat deliberately on the floor.

He licked his lips, and grinned an amiable clown's grin, and said in his cheerful, buffoon bray: "Auntie, go verb your adjective adjective noun."

Sue-Ann Bradley gasped and turned white.

She had known such words existed—but only theoretically. She had never expected to *hear* them. And certainly, she would never have believed she would hear them, applied to her, from the lips of a . . . a *laborer.* At her knees, the guard shrieked and fell to the floor.

"Sauer, Sauer!" A panicky bellow from the corridor; the redheaded giant hesitated. "Sauer, come on out here! There's a million guards coming up the stairs. Looks like trouble!"

Sauer said hoarsely to the unconscious guard, "I'll take care of *you.*" And he looked blankly at the girl, and shook his head, and hurried back to the corridor.

Guards were coming, all right—not a million of them, but half a dozen or more. And leading them all was the medic, calm, bearded face looking straight ahead, hands clasped before him, ready to heal the sick, comfort the aged or bring new life into the world.

"Hold it!" shrieked little Flock, crouched over the agonizing blister on his abdomen, gun in hand, peering insanely down the steps. "Hold it or—"

"Shut up." Sauer called softly to the approaching group: "Let the doc come up. Nobody else!"

The intern faltered; the guards stopped dead; the medic said calmly: "I must have my intern with me." He glanced at the barred gate wonderingly.

Sauer hesitated. "Well—all right. But no guards!"

A few yards away Sue-Ann Bradley was stuffing the syncoped form of the guard into her small washroom.

It was time to take a stand.

No more cowering, she told herself desperately. No more waiting. She closed the door on the guard, still unconscious, and stood grimly before it. Him, at least, she would save if she could. They could get him, but only over her dead body. . . .

Or anyway—she thought with a sudden throbbing in her throat—over her body.

6

After O'Leary and the medic left, the warden tottered to a chair—but not for long. His secretary appeared, eyes bulging. "The governor!" he gasped.

Warden Schluckebier managed to say: "Why, Governor! How good of you to come—"

The governor shook him off and held the door open for the men who had come with him. There were reporters from all the news services, officials from the township governments within the city-state. There was an air GI with the major's leaves on his collar—"Liaison, sir," he explained crisply to the warden, "just in case you have any orders for our men up there." There were nearly a dozen others.

The warden was quite overcome.

The governor rapped out: "Warden, no criticism of you, of course, but I've come to take personal charge. I'm superseding you under Rule Twelve, Para. A, of the Uniform Civil Service Code. Right?"

"Oh, *right!*" cried the warden, incredulous with joy.

"The situation is bad—perhaps worse than you think. I'm seriously concerned about the hostages those men have in there. The guards, the medic—and I had a call from Senator Bradley a short time ago—"

"Senator Bradley?" echoed the warden.

"Senator *Sebastian* Bradley. One of our foremost civil servants," the governor said firmly. "It so happens that his daughter is in Block O, as an inmate."

The warden closed his eyes. He tried to swallow, but the throat muscles were paralyzed.

"There is no question," the governor went on briskly, "about the propriety of her being there—she was duly convicted of a felonious act, namely conspiracy and incitement to riot. But you see the position."

The warden saw. All too well the warden saw.

"Therefore," said the governor, "I intend to go in to Block O myself. Sebastian Bradley is an old and personal friend—as well," he emphasized, "as being a senior member of the Reclassification Board. I understand a medic is going to Block O. I shall go with him."

The warden managed to sit up straight. "He's gone. I mean—they already left, Governor. But I assure you, Miss Brad—Inmate Bradley—that is, the young lady is in no danger. I have already taken precautions," he said, gaining confidence as he listened to himself talk. "I, uh, I was deciding on a course of action as you came in. See, Governor, the guards on the walls are all armed. All they have to do is fire a couple of rounds into the Yard—and then the copters could start dropping tear gas and light fragmentation bombs and—"

The governor was already at the door. "You will *not*," he said; and, "Now, which way did they go?"

O'Leary was in the Yard, and he was smelling trouble, loud and strong.

The first he knew that the rest of the prison had caught the riot fever was when the lights flared on in Cell Block A. "That Sodaro!" he snarled; but there wasn't time to worry about that Sodaro. He grabbed the rest of his guard detail and double-timed it toward the New Building, leaving the medic and a couple of guards walking sedately toward the Old. Block A, on the New Building's lowest tier was already coming to life; a dozen yards, and Blocks B and C lighted up.

And a dozen yards more, and they could hear the yelling; and it wasn't more than a minute before the building doors opened.

The cons had taken over three more blocks. How? O'Leary didn't take time even to guess. The inmates were piling out into the Yard. He took one look at the rushing mob. Crazy! It was Wilmer Lafon leading the rioters, with a guard's gun and a voice screaming threats! But O'Leary didn't take time to worry about an honor prisoner gone bad, either. "Let's get out of here!" he bellowed to the detachment, and they ran. . . .

Just plain ran. Cut and ran, scattering as they went.

"Wait!" screamed O'Leary, but they weren't waiting. Cursing himself for letting them get out of hand, O'Leary salvaged two guards and headed on the run for the Old Building, huge and dark, all but the topmost lights of Block O. They saw the medic and his escort disappearing into the bulk of the Old Building; and they saw something else. There were inmates between them and the Old Building! The Shops Building lay between—with a dozen more cell blocks over the workshops that gave it its name—and there was a milling rush of activity around its entrance, next to the laundry shed—

The laundry shed.

O'Leary stood stock still. Lafon talking to the laundry cons; Lafon leading the breakout from Block A. The little greaser who was a trusty in the Shops Building sabotaging the Yard's tangler circuit. Sauer and Flock taking over the Green Sleeves with a manufactured knife and a lot of guts. Did it fit together? Was it all part of a plan?

That was something to find out—but not just then. "Come on," O'Leary cried to the two guards, and they raced for the temporary safety of the main gates.

The whole prison was up and yelling now.

O'Leary could hear scattered shots from the beat guards on the wall—*Over their heads, over their heads!* he prayed silently. And there were other shots that seemed to come from inside the walls—guards shooting, or convicts with guards' guns, he couldn't tell which. The Yard was full of convicts now, in bunches and clumps; but none near the gate. And they seemed to have lost some of their drive. They were milling around, lit by the searchlights from the wall, yelling and making a lot of noise . . . but going nowhere in particular. Waiting for a leader, O'Leary thought, and wondered briefly what had become of Lafon.

"You Captain O'Leary?" somebody demanded.

O'Leary turned and blinked. Good Lord, the governor! He was coming through the gate, waving aside the gate guards, alone. "You him?" the governor repeated. "All right, glad I found you. I'm going in to Block O with you!"

O'Leary swallowed, and waved at the teeming cons. True, there were none immediately nearby—but there were plenty in the Yard! Riots meant breaking things up; already the inmates had started to break up the machines in the laundry shed and the athletic equipment in the Yard lockers; when they found a couple of choice breakables like O'Leary and the Governor they'd have a ball! "But Governor—"

"But my foot! Can you get me in there or can't you?"

O'Leary gauged their chances. It wasn't more than fifty feet to the main entrance to the Old Building—not at the moment guarded, since all the guards were in hiding or on the walls, and not as yet being invaded by the inmates at large.

He said, "You're the boss! Hold on a minute—" The searchlights were on the bare Yard cobblestones in front of them; in a moment the searchlights danced away.

"Come on!" cried O'Leary, and jumped for the entrance. The governor was with him, and a pair of the guards came stumbling after.

They made it to the Old Building.

Inside the entrance they could hear the noise from outside and the yelling of the inmates who were still in their cells; but around them was nothing but gray steel walls and the stairs going up to Block O. "Up!" panted O'Leary, and they clattered up the steel steps.

They nearly made it.

They would have made it—if it hadn't been for the honor inmate, Wilmer Lafon, who knew what he was after and had headed for the Green Sleeves through the back way. In fact, they did make it—but not the way they planned. "Get out of the way!" yelled O'Leary at Lafon and the half-dozen inmates with him; and "Go to hell!" screamed Lafon, charging; and it was a rough-and-tumble fight, and O'Leary's party lost it, fair and square.

So when they got to Block O it was with the governor marching before a convict-held gun, and with O'Leary cold unconscious, a lump from a gun-butt on the side of his head.

As they came up the stairs, Sauer was howling at the medic: "You got to fix up my boy! He's dying, and all you do is sit there!"

The medic said patiently, "My son, I've dressed his wound. He is under sedation, and I must rest. There will be other casualties."

Sauer raged, and he danced around; but that was as far as it went. Even Sauer wouldn't attack a medic! He would as soon strike an Attorney, or even a Director of Funerals. It wasn't merely that they were professionals—even among the professional class, they were special; not superior, exactly, but *apart*. They certainly were not for the likes of Sauer to fool with, and Sauer knew it.

"Somebody's coming!" cried one of the other freed inmates.

Sauer jumped to the head of the steps, saw that Lafon was leading the group, stepped back, saw who Lafon's helpers were carrying, and leaped forward again. "Cap'n O'Leary!" he roared. "Gimme!"

"Shut up," said Wilmer Lafon, and pushed the big redhead out of the way. Sauer's jaw dropped, and the snake eyes opened wide.

"Wilmer," he protested feebly. But that was all the protest he made, because the snake's eyes had seen that Lafon held a gun. He stood back, the big hands half outstretched toward the unconscious guard captain, O'Leary, and the cold eyes became thoughtful.

And then he saw who else was with the party. "Wilmer!" he roared. "You got the governor there!"

Lafon nodded. "Throw them in a cell," he ordered, and sat down on a guard's stool, breathing hard. It had been a fine fight on the steps, before he and his boys had subdued the governor and the guards; but Wilmer Lafon wasn't used to fighting. Even six years in the Jug hadn't turned an architect into a laborer; physical exertion simply was not his métier.

Sauer said coaxingly, "Wilmer, won't you leave me have O'Leary for a while? If it wasn't for me and Flock you'd still be in A Block, and—"

"Shut up," Lafon said again, gently enough, but he waved the gun muzzle. He drew a deep breath, glanced around him and grinned. "If it wasn't for you and Flock," he mimicked. "If it wasn't for you and Flock! Sauer, you wipe clown, do you think it took *brains* to file down a shiv and start things rolling? If it wasn't for *me*, you and Flock would have beat up a few guards, and had your kicks for half an hour, and then the whole prison would fall in on you! It was me, Wilmer Lafon, that set things up, and you know it!" He was yelling, and suddenly he realized he was yelling. And what was the use, he demanded of himself contemptuously, of trying to argue with a bunch of lousy wipes and greasers? They never understand the long, soul-killing hours of planning and sweat; they wouldn't realize the importance of the careful timing—of arranging that the laundry cons would start a disturbance in the Yard right after the Green Sleeves hard-timers kicked off the riot; of getting the little greaser Hiroko to short-circuit the Yard field so the laundry cons could start their disturbance. It took a *professional* to organize and plan—yes, and to make sure that he himself was out of it until everything was ripe, so that if anything went wrong *he* was all right. It took somebody like Wilmer Lafon—a *professional*, who had spent six years too long in the Jug—

And who would shortly be getting out.

7

Any prison is a ticking bomb. Estates-General was in process of going off.

From the Green Sleeves where the trouble had started, clear out to the trusty farms that ringed the walls, every inmate was up and jumping. Some were still in their cells—the scared ones, the decrepit oldsters, the short-termers who didn't dare risk their early discharge. But for every man in his cell, a dozen were out and yelling.

A torch, licking as high as the hanging helicopters, blazed up from the Yard—that was the laundry shed. Why burn the laundry? The cons couldn't have said. It was burnable, and it was there—burn it!

The Yard lay open to the wrath of the helicopters, but the helicopters made no move. The cobblestones were solidly covered with milling men. The guards were on the walls, sighting down their guns; the helicopter bombardiers had their fingers on the bomb trips. There had been a few rounds fired over the heads of the rioters, at first.

Nothing since.

In the milling mob, the figures clustered in groups. The inmates from Honor Block A huddled under the guards' guns at the angle of the wall. They had clubs, as all the inmates had clubs, but they weren't using them.

Honor Block A—on the outside, civil service and professionals. On the inside, the trusties, the "good" cons.

They weren't the type for clubs.

With all of the inmates, you looked at them and you wondered what twisted devil had got into their heads to land them in the Jug. Oh, perhaps you could understand it—a little bit at least—in the case of the figgers in Blocks B and C, the greasers in the Shop Building—that sort. It was easy enough for some of the Categoried Classes to commit a crime, and thereby land in jail. Who could blame a wipe for trying to "pass," if he thought he could get away with it? But when he didn't get away with it, he wound up in the Jug, and that was logical enough. And greasers liked civil-service women, everyone knew that. There was almost a sort of logic to it—even if it was a sort of inevitable logic that made decent civil-service people see red. You *had* to enforce the laws against rape if, for instance, a greaser should ask an innocent young female postal clerk for a date. But you could understand what drove him to it. The Jug was full of criminals of that sort. And the Jug was the place for them.

But what about Honor Block A?

Why would a Wilmer Lafon—a certified public architect, a Professional by category—draw a portrait in oils and get himself jugged for malpractice? Why would a dental nurse—practically a medic—sneak back into the laboratory at night and cast an upper plate for her mother? Greasers' work was greasers' work; she knew what the penalty was. She must have realized she would be caught.

But she had done it. And she had been caught; and there she was, this wild night, huddled under the helicopters, feebly waving the handle of a floor mop.

It was a club. And she wasn't the type for clubs.

She shivered and turned to the stock convict next to her. "Why don't they break down the gate?" she demanded. "How long are we going to hang around here, waiting for the guards to get organized and pick us off?"

The convict next to her sighed and wiped his glasses with a beefy hand. Once he had been an Income-Tax Accountant, disbarred and convicted on three counts of impersonating an attorney when he took the liberty of making changes in a client's lease. He snorted, "Damn wipes! Do they expect us to do *their* dirty work?"

The two of them glared angrily and fearfully at the other convicts in the Yard.

And the other convicts, huddled greaser with greaser, wipe with wipe, glared ragingly back. It wasn't *their* place to plan the strategy of a prison break.

Captain Liam O'Leary muttered groggily, "They don't want to escape, all they want is to make trouble. I know cons." He came fully awake, sat up and focused his eyes. His head was hammering.

That girl, that Bradley, was leaning over him. She looked scared and sick. "Sit still! Sauer is just plain crazy—listen to them yelling out there!"

O'Leary sat up and looked around, one hand holding his drumming skull.

"They do so want to escape," said Sue-Ann Bradley. "Listen to what they're saying!"

O'Leary discovered that he was in a cell. There was a battle royal going on outside. Men were yelling, but he couldn't see them.

He jumped up, remembering. "The governor!"

Sue-Ann Bradley said, "He's all right. I *think* he is, anyway. He's in the cell right next to us, with a couple guards. I guess they came up with you." She shivered, as the yells in the corridor rose. "Sauer is angry at the medic," she explained. "He wants him to fix Flock up so they can—'crush out,' I think he said. The medic says he can't do it. You see, Flock got burned pretty badly with a knife he made—something about the tangle-foot field—"

"Eddy currents," said O'Leary dizzily.

"I guess so. Anyway, the medic—"

"Never mind the medic. What's Lafon doing?"

"Lafon? The black one?" Sue-Ann Bradley frowned. "I didn't know his name. He started the whole thing, the way it sounds. They're waiting for the mob down in the Yard to break out, and then they're going to make a break—"

"Wait a minute," growled O'Leary. His head was beginning to clear. "What about you? Are you in on this?"

She hung between laughter and tears. Finally: "Do I *look* like I'm in on this?"

O'Leary took stock. Somehow, somewhere, the girl had got a length of metal pipe—from the plumbing, maybe. She was holding it in one hand, supporting him with the other. There were two other guards in the cell, both out cold—one from O'Leary's squad, the other, O'Leary guessed, a deck guard who had been on duty when the trouble started. "I wouldn't let them in," she said wildly. "I told them they'd have to kill me before they could touch that guard."

O'Leary said suspiciously, "What about you? You belonged to that Double-A-C, didn't you? You were pretty anxious to get in the Green Sleeves, disobeying Auntie Mathias' orders. Are you sure you didn't know this was going to—"

It was too much. She dropped the pipe, buried her head in her hands. He couldn't tell if she laughed or wept, but he could tell that it hadn't been like that at all.

"I'm sorry," he said awkwardly, and touched her on the shoulder. He turned and looked out the little barred window, because he couldn't think of any other way to apologize. He heard the wavering beat in the air, and saw them—bobbing a hundred yards up, their wide metal vanes fluttering and hissing from the jets at the tips. The GI copters. Waiting—as everyone seemed to be waiting.

Sue-Ann Bradley demanded shakily, "Is anything the matter?"

O'Leary turned away. It was astonishing, he thought, what a different perspective he had on those helicopter bombers from inside Block O. Once he had cursed the warden for not ordering tear gas, at least, dropped. . . . He said harshly, "Nothing. Just that the copters have the place surrounded."

"Does it make any difference?"

He shrugged. Does it make a difference? The difference between trouble and tragedy, or so it now seemed to Captain O'Leary. The riot was trouble. They could handle it, one way or another—it was his job, any guard's job, to handle *prison* trouble.

But to bring the GIs into it was to invite race riot. Not prison riot—race riot. Even the declassed scum in the Jug would fight back against the GIs. They were used to having the civil-service guards over them—that was what guards were for. Civil-service presidents presided, and civil-service governors governed, and civil-service guards guarded. What else? It was their job—as clerking was a figger's job, and mechanics were a greaser's, and pick-and-shovel strong-arm work was a wipe's. But the armed services— their job was, theoretically, to defend the country against forces outside. *Race* riot. The cons wouldn't stand still under attack from the GIs.

But how could you tell that to a girl like this Bradley? O'Leary glanced at her covertly. She *looked* all right. Rather nice-looking, if anything. But he hadn't forgotten why she was in E-G. Joining a terrorist organization, the Association for the Advancement of the Categoried Classes. Advocating desegregation—actually getting up on a street corner and proposing that greasers' children be allowed to go to school with GIs', that wipes intermarry with civil service. Good Lord, they'd be suggesting that doctors eat with laymen next!

The girl said evenly, "Don't look at me that way. I'm not a monster."

O'Leary coughed. "I, uh, sorry. I didn't know I was staring." She looked at him with cold eyes. "I mean," he said, "you don't *look* like anybody who'd get mixed up in, well, miscegenation."

"Miscegenation! Dirty mind!" she blazed. "You're all alike, you talk about the mission of the Categoried Classes and the rightness of segregation—and it's always just the one thing that's in your minds. Sex! You're—you're trying to turn the clock back," she sobbed. "I'll tell you this for sure, Captain O'Leary! I'd rather marry a decent, hard-working clerk any day than the sort of low-grade civil-service trash I've seen around here!"

O'Leary cringed. He couldn't help it. Funny, he told himself, I thought I was shockproof—but this goes too far!

A bull-roar from the corridor. Sauer. O'Leary spun. The big redhead was yelling: "Bring the governor out here. Lafon wants to talk to him!"

O'Leary went to the door of the cell, fast.

A slim, pale con from Block A was pushing the governor down the hall, toward Sauer and Lafon. The governor was a strong man, but he didn't struggle. His face was as composed and remote as the medic's; if he was afraid, he concealed it extremely well.

Sue-Ann Bradley slipped beside O'Leary. "What's happening?"

He kept his eyes on what was going on. "Lafon is going to try to use the governor as a shield, I think." The voice of Lafon was loud, but the noises outside made it hard to understand. But O'Leary could make out what the dark ex-professional was saying: "—know damn well you did something. But what? *Why don't they crush out?*" Mumble-mumble from the governor; O'Leary couldn't hear the words. But he could see the effect of them in Lafon's face, hear the rage in Lafon's voice. "Don't call me a liar, you civvy punk! You did something. I had it all planned, do you hear me? The laundry boys were going to rush the gate, the Block A bunch would follow—and then I was going to breeze right through. But you loused it up. You must've!" His voice was rising to a scream. O'Leary, watching tautly from the cell, thought: He's going to break. He can't hold it in much longer.

"All *right!*" shouted Lafon, and even Sauer, looming behind him, looked alarmed. "It doesn't matter what you did. I've got you now, and *you* are going to get me out of here. You hear? I've got this gun, and the two of us are going to walk right out, through the gate, and if anybody tries to stop us—"

"Hey," said Sauer, waking up.

"—if anybody tries to stop us, you'll get a bullet right in—"

"Hey!" Sauer was roaring loud as Lafon himself now. "What's this talk about the *two* of you? You aren't going to leave me and Flock!"

"Shut up," Lafon said conversationally, without taking his eyes off the governor.

But Sauer, just then, was not the man to say "shut up" to, and especially he was not a man to take your eyes away from.

"That's torn it," O'Leary said aloud. The girl started to say something.

But he was no longer there to hear.

It looked very much as though Sauer and Lafon were going to tangle. And when they did, it was the end of the line for the governor.

O'Leary hurtled out of the sheltering cell and skidded down the corridor. Lafon's face was a hawk's face, gleaming with triumph; as he saw O'Leary coming toward him, the hawk sneer froze. He brought the gun up, but O'Leary was a fast man.

O'Leary leaped on the lithe black honor prisoner. Lafon screamed, and clutched; and O'Leary's lunging weight drove him back against the wall. Lafon's arm smacked against the steel grating and the gun went flying. The two of them clinched and fell, gouging, to the floor.

O'Leary had the advantage; he hammered the con's head against the deck, hard enough to split a skull. And perhaps it split Lafon's, because the dark face twitched, and froth appeared at the lips; and the body slacked.

One down!

And Sauer was charging. O'Leary wriggled sidewise, and the big redhead blundered crashing into the steel grate. Sauer fell, and O'Leary caught at him. He tried the hammering of the head, he swarmed on top of the huge clown. But Sauer only roared the louder. The bull body surged under O'Leary, and then Sauer was on top and O'Leary wasn't breathing. Not at all.

Everything was choking black dust.

Good-bye, Sue-Ann, O'Leary said silently, without meaning to say anything of the kind; and even then he wondered why he was saying it.

O'Leary heard a gun explode beside his head.

Amazing, he thought, I'm breathing again! The choking hands were gone from his throat.

It took him a moment to realize that it was Sauer who had taken the bullet, not him.

Sauer who now lay dead . . . not O'Leary. But he realized it, when he rolled over, and looked up, and saw the girl with the gun still in her hand, staring at him and weeping.

He sat up. The two guards still able to walk were backing Sue-Ann Bradley up; the governor was looking proud as an eagle, pleased as a mother hen.

The Green Sleeves was back in the hands of law and order.

The medic came toward O'Leary, hands folded. "My son," he said, "if your throat needs—"

O'Leary interrupted him. "I don't need a thing, Doc! I've got everything I want, right now."

8

Inmate Sue-Ann Bradley cried, "They're coming! O'Leary, they're coming!"

The guards who had once been hostages clattered down the steps to meet the party. The cons from the Green Sleeves were back in their cells. The medic, having finished his chores on O'Leary himself, paced meditatively out into the wake of the riot, where there was plenty to keep him busy. A faintly bilious expression tinctured his carven face. He had not liked Lafon or Sauer.

The party of fresh guards appeared, and efficiently began relocking the cells of the Green Sleeves. "Excuse me, Cap'n," said one, taking Sue-Ann Bradley by the arm, "I'll just put this one back—"

"I'll take care of her," said Liam O'Leary. He looked at her sideways as he rubbed the bruises on his face.

The governor tapped him on the shoulder. "Come along," he said, looking so proud of himself, so pleased. "Let's go out in the Yard for a breath of fresh air." He smiled contentedly at Sue-Ann Bradley. "You too," he said.

O'Leary protested instinctively, "But she's an inmate!"

"And I'm a governor. Come along."

They walked out into the Yard. The air was fresh, all right. A handful of cons, double-guarded by sleepy and irritable men from the day shift, were hosing down the rubble on the cobblestones. The Yard was a mess; but it was quiet now. The helicopters were still riding their picket line, glowing softly in the early light that promised sunrise.

"My car," the governor said quietly to a state policeman who appeared from nowhere. The trooper snapped a salute and trotted away.

"I killed a man," said Sue-Ann Bradley, looking abstracted and a little ill.

"You saved a man," corrected the governor. "Don't weep for that Lafon. He was willing to kill a thousand men if he had to, to break out of here."

"But he never did break out," said Sue-Ann.

The governor stretched contentedly. "Of course not. He never had a chance. Lafon spent too much time in the Jug; he forgot what the world was like. Laborers and clerks join together in a breakout? It would never happen. They don't even speak the same language—as my young friend here has discovered."

Sue-Ann blazed: "I still believe in the equality of man!"

"Oh, please do," the Governor said, straight-faced. "There's nothing wrong with that! Your father and I are perfectly willing to admit that men are equal; but we can't admit that all men are the *same*. Use your eyes! What you believe in is your own business—

but," he added, "when your beliefs extend to setting fire to segregated public lavatories as a protest move, which is what got you arrested, you apparently need to be taught a lesson. Well, perhaps you've learned it. You were a help here tonight, and that counts for a lot. . . ."

Captain O'Leary said, face furrowed, "What about the warden, Governor? They say the category system is what makes the world go round, it fits the right man to the right job and keeps him there. But look at Momma Schluckebier! He fell apart at the seams. He—"

"Turn it around, O'Leary."

"Turn—?"

The governor nodded. "You've got it backward. Not the right man for the job—the right job for the man! We've got Schluckebier on our hands, see? He's been born; it's too late to do anything about that. He will go to pieces in an emergency. So where do we put him?"

O'Leary stubbornly clamped his jaw, frowning.

"We put him," the governor went on gently, "where the best thing to *do* in a crisis is to go to pieces! Why, O'Leary, you get some hot-headed man of action in here, and every time an inmate sneezes in E-G you'll have bloodshed! And there's no harm in a prison riot. Let the poor devils work off steam. I wouldn't have bothered to get out of bed for it—except I was worried about the hostages. So I came down to make sure they were protected."

O'Leary's jaw dropped. "But you were—"

The governor nodded. "I was a hostage myself. That's one way to protect them, isn't it? By giving the cons a hostage that's worth more to them."

He yawned, and looked around for his car. "So the world keeps going around," he said. "Everybody is somebody else's outgroup, and maybe it's a bad thing, but did you ever stop to realize that we don't have wars anymore? The categories stick tightly together. Who is to say that that's a bad thing?" He grinned. "Reminds me of a story, if you two will pay attention to me long enough to listen. There was a meeting—this is an old, *old* story—a neighborhood meeting of the leaders of the two biggest women's groups on the block. There were eighteen Irish ladies from the Church Auxiliary and three Jewish ladies from B'nai B'rith. The first thing they did was have an election for a temporary chairwoman. Twenty-one votes were cast. Mrs. Grossinger from B'nai B'rith got three, and Mrs. O'Flaherty from the Auxiliary got eighteen. So when Mrs. Murphy came up to congratulate Mrs. O'Flaherty after the election, she whispered, 'Good for you! But isn't it terrible, the way these Jews stick together?' "

He stood up and waved wildly, as his long official car came poking hesitantly through the gate. "Well," he said professionally, "that's that. As we politicians say, any questions?"

Sue-Ann hesitated. "Well," she said—"yes, I guess I do have a question. What's a Jew?"

Maybe there was an answer. And maybe the question answered itself; and maybe the governor, riding sleepily homeward in the dawn, himself learned something from it which was true: That a race's greatest learning may be in the things it has learned enough to forget.

THE KINDLY ISLE

The protagonist of this story is someone who has lucked out. He used to work for a laboratory that was set up to design biological warfare weapons for use against enemies of the United States. He wasn't a researcher, but he knew what was going on, and we get the feeling that he was glad to work instead for a company that developed commercial properties. Checking out the prospects of a half-built resort on a tropical island is what brings him to the isle of the story's title.

One of the pleasures of 1984's "The Kindly Isle" is watching the plot develop as the characters also develop. Clever and skilled is Pohl in painlessly integrating these elements in a tale that has no big explosions but a few real surprises.

1

The place they called the Starlight Casino was full of people, a tour group by their looks. I had a few minutes before my appointment with Mr. Kavilan, and sometimes you got useful bits of knowledge from people who had just been through the shops, the hotels, the restaurants, the beaches. Not this time, though. They were an incoming group, and ill-tempered. Their calves under the hems of the bright shorts were hairy ivory or bald, and all they wanted to talk about was lost luggage, unsatisfactory rooms, moldy towels and desk clerks who gave them the wrong keys. There were a surly couple of dozen of them clustered around a placatory tour representative in a white skirt and frilly green blouse. She was fine. It was gently, "We'll find it," to this one and sweetly, "I'll talk to the maid myself," to another, and I made a note of the name on her badge. Deirdre. It was worth remembering. Saints are highly valued in the hotel business. Then, when the bell captain came smiling into the room to tell me that Mr. Kavilan was waiting for me—and didn't have his hand out for a tip—I almost asked for his name, too. It was a promising beginning. If the island was really as "kindly" as they claimed, that would be a significant plus on my checklist.

Personnel was not my most urgent concern, though. My present task was only to check out the physical and financial aspects of a specific project. I entered the lobby and looked around for my real-estate agent—and was surprised when the beachcomber type by the breezeway stretched out his hand. "Mr. Wenright? I'm Dick Kavilan."

He was not what I expected. I knew that R. T. Kavilan was supposed to be older than I, and I took my twenty-year retirement from government service eight years ago. This man did not seem that old. His hair was blond and full, and he had an all-around-the-face blond beard that surrounded a pink nose, bronzed cheeks and bright blue eyes. He didn't think of himself as old, either, because all he had on was white ducks and sandals. He wore no shirt at all, and his body was as lean and tanned as his face. I had dressed for the tropics, too, but not in the same way: white shoes and calf-length white socks, pressed white shorts and a maroon T-shirt with the golden insignia of our Maui hotel over the heart. I understood what he meant when he glanced at my shoes and said, "We're informal here—I hope you don't mind." Formal he certainly was not.

He was, however, effortlessly efficient. He pulled his open Saab out of the cramped hotel lot, found a gap in the traffic, greeted two friends along the road and said to me, "It'll be slow going through Port, but once we get outside it's only twenty minutes to Keytown"—all at once.

"I've got all day," I said.

He nodded, taking occasional glances at me to judge what kind of a customer I was going to be. "I thought," he offered, "that you might want to make just a preliminary inspection this morning. Then there's a good restaurant in Keytown. We can have lunch and talk—what's the matter?" I was craning my neck at a couple we had just passed along the road, a woman who looked like a hotel guest and a dark, elderly man. "Did you see somebody you wanted to talk to?"

We took a corner and I straightened up. "Not exactly," I said. Somebody I had once wanted to talk to? No. That wasn't right, either. Somebody I should have wanted to talk to once, but hadn't, really? Especially about such subjects as Retroviridae and the substantia nigra?

"If it was the man in the straw hat," said Kavilan, "that was Professor Michaelis. He the one?"

"I never heard of a Professor Michaelis," I said, wishing it were not a lie.

In the eight years since I took the hotel job I've visited more than my share of the world's beauty spots—Pago-Pago and the Costa Brava, Martinique and Lesbos, Bermuda, Kauai, Barbados, Tahiti. This was not the most breathtaking, but it surely was pretty enough to suit any tourist who ever lived. The beaches were golden and the water crystal. There were thousand-foot forested peaks, and even a halfway decent waterfall just off the road. In a lot of the world's finest places there turns out to be a hidden worm in the mangosteen—bribe-hungry officials, or revolutions simmering off in the bush, or devastating storms. According to Dick Kavilan, the island had none of those. "Then why did the Dutchmen give up?" I asked. It was a key question. A Rotterdam syndicate was supposed to have sunk fourteen million dollars into the hotel project I had come to inspect—and walked away when it was three-quarters built.

"They just ran out of money, Mr. Wenright."

"Call me Jerry, please," I said. That was what the preliminary report had indicated. Probably true. Tropical islands were a bottomless pit for the money of optimistic cold-country investors. If Marge had lived and we had done what we planned, we might have gone bust ourselves in Puerto Rico . . . if she had lived.

"Then, Jerry," he grinned, turning into a rutted dirt road I hadn't even seen, "we're here." He stopped the car and got out to unlock a chainlink gate that had not been unlocked recently. Nor had the road recently been driven. Palm fronds buried most of it and vines had reclaimed large patches.

Kavilan got back in the car, panting—he was not all that youthful, after all—and wiped rust off his hands with a bandanna. "Before we put up that fence," he said, "people would drive in or bring boats up to the beach at night and load them with anything they could carry. Toilets. Furniture. Windows, frames and all. They ripped up the carpets where they found any, and where there wasn't anything portable they broke into the walls for copper piping."

"So there isn't fourteen million dollars left in it," I essayed.

He let the grin broaden. "Look now, bargain later, Jerry. There's plenty left for you to see."

There was, and he left me alone to see it. He was never so far away that I couldn't call a question to him, but he didn't hang himself around my neck, either. I didn't need to ask many questions. It was obvious that what Kavilan (and the finders' reports) had said was true. The place had been looted, all right. It was capricious, with some sections apparently hardly touched. Some were hit hard. Paintings that had been screwed to the wall had been ripped loose—real oils, I saw from one that had been ruined and left. A marble dolphin fountain had been broken off and carted a few steps away—then left shattered on the walk.

I had come prepared with a set of builder's plans, and they showed me that there were to have been four hundred guest rooms, a dozen major function areas, bars and restaurants, an arcade of shops in the basement, a huge wine cellar under even that, two pools, a sauna—those were just the sections where principal construction had gone well along before the Dutchmen walked away. I saw as much of it as I could in two hours. When my watch said eleven-thirty I sat down on an intact stone balustrade overlooking the gentle breakers on the beach and waited for Kavilan to join me. "What about water availability?" I asked.

"A problem, Jerry," he agreed. "You'll need to lay a mile and a quarter of new mains to connect with the highway pipes, and then when you get the water it'll be expensive."

I wrinkled my nose. "What's that smell?"

He laughed. "Those are some of the dear departed of the island, I'm afraid, and that's another problem. Let's move on before we lose our taste for lunch."

Kavilan was as candid as I could have hoped, and a lot more so than I would have been in his place. It was an island custom, he said, to entomb their dead aboveground instead of burying them. Unfortunately the marble boxes were seldom watertight. The seepage I had smelled was a very big minus to the project, but Kavilan shook his head when I said so. He reached into the hip pocket of his jeans, unfolded a sweatproof wallet and took out a typed, three-page list.

I said he was candid. The list included all the things I would have asked him about:

Relocation of cemetery	$ 350,000
New water mains, 1.77 miles	680,000 (10-inch)
	790,000 (12-inch)
Paving access road, 0.8 miles	290,000
But it also included:	
Lien, Windward Isles Const. Co.	1,300,000
(Settlement est.	605,000)
Damage judgment, Sun/Sea Petro.	2,600,000
(Settlement est.	350,000)
Injunction, N.A. Trades Council	
(Est. cost to vacate	18,000)

The total on the three-page list, taking the estimated figures at face value, came to over three million dollars. Half the items on it I hadn't even suspected.

The first course was coming and I didn't want to ruin a good lunch with business, so I looked for permission, then pocketed the paper as the conch salad arrived. Kavilan was right. It was good. The greens were fresh, the chunks of meat chewed easily, the dressing was oil and vinegar but with some unusual additions that made it special. Mustard was easy to pick out, and a brush of garlic, but there were others. I thought of getting this chef's name, too.

And thought it again when I found that the escalope of veal was as good as the conch. The wine was even better, but I handled it sparingly. I didn't know Dick Kavilan well enough to let myself be made gullible by adding a lot of wine to a fine meal, a pretty restaurant and a magnificent view of a sun-drenched bay. We chatted socially until the demitasses came. How long had he been on the island? Only two years, he said, surprising me. When he added that he'd been in real estate in Michigan before that, I connected on the name. "Sellman and Kavilan," I said. "You put together the package on the Upper Peninsula for us." It was a really big, solid firm. Not the kind you take early retirement from.

"That's right," he said. "I liked Michigan. But then I came down here with some friends who had a boat—I'm a widower, my boys are grown—and then I only went back to Michigan long enough to sell out."

"Then there really is a lure of the islands."

"Why, that's what you're here to find out, Jerry," he said, the grin back again. "How about you? Married?"

"I'm a widower too," I said, and touched my buttoned pocket. "Are these costs solid?"

"You'll want to check them out for yourself but, yes, I think so. Some are firm bids. The others are fairly conservative estimates." He waved to the waiter, who produced cigars. Cuban Perfectos. When we were both puffing, he said, "My people will put in writing that if the aggregate costs go more than twenty percent over that list we'll pay one-third of the excess as forfeit." Now, that was an interesting offer! I didn't agree to it, not even a nod, but at that point Kavilan didn't expect me to. "When the Dutchman went bust," he added, "that list added up to better than nine million."

No wonder he went bust! "How come there's a six million dollar difference?"

He waved his cigar. "That was seven years ago. I guess people were meaner then. Or maybe the waiting wore the creditors down. Well. What's your pleasure for this afternoon, Jerry? Another look at the site, or back to Port?"

"Port, I think," I said reluctantly.

The idea of spending an afternoon on the telephone and visiting government offices seemed like a terrible waste of a fine day, but that was what they paid me for.

It kept me busy. As far as I could check, the things Kavilan had told me were all true, and checking was surprisingly easy. The government records clerks were helpful, even when they had to pull out dusty files, and all the people who said they'd return my calls did. It wasn't such a bad day. But then it wasn't the days that were bad.

I put off going to bed as long as I could, with a long, late dinner, choosing carefully between the local lobster and what the headwaiter promised would be first-rate prime rib. He was right; the beef was perfect. Then I put a quarter into every fifth slot machine in the hotel casino as long as my quarters held out; but when the light by my bed was out and my head was on the pillow the pain moved in. There was a soft Caribbean moon in the window and the sound of palms rustling in the breeze. They didn't help. The only question was whether I would cry myself to sleep. I still did that, after eight years, about one night in three, and this was a night I did.

2

I thought if I had an early breakfast I'd have the dining room to myself, so I could do some serious thinking about Val Michaelis. I was wrong. The tour group had a trip in a glass-bottomed boat that morning and the room was crowded; the hostess apologetically seated me with a young woman I had seen before. We'd crossed paths in the casino as we each got rid of our cups of quarters. Hair to her shoulders, no makeup—I'd thought at first she was a young girl, but in the daylight that was revised by a decade or so. She was civil—civilly silent, except for a "Good morning" and now and then a "May I have the marmalade?"—and she didn't blow smoke in my face until we were both onto our second cups of coffee. If the rest of her tour had been as well-schooled as she it would have been a pleasant meal. Some of them were all right, but the table for two next to us was planning a negligence suit over a missing garment bag, and the two tables for four behind us were exchanging loud ironies about the bugs they'd seen, or thought they had seen, in their rooms. When she got up she left with a red-haired man and his wife—one of the more obnoxious couples present, I thought, and felt sorry for her.

Kavilan had given me the gate key, and the bell captain found me a car rental. I drove back to the hotel site. This time I took a notebook, a hammer, a Polaroid and my Swiss Army knife.

Fortunately the wind was the other way this morning and the aromatic reminders of mortality were bothering some other part of the shoreline. Before going in I walked around the fence from the outside, snapping pictures of the unfinished buildings from several angles. Funny thing. Pushing my way through some overgrown vines I found a section of the fence where the links had been carefully severed with bolt cutters. The cuts were not fresh, and the links had been rubbed brighter than the rest of the fence; somebody had been getting through anyway, no doubt to pick up a few souvenirs missed by his predecessors. The vines had not grown back, so it had been used fairly recently. I made a note to have Kavilan fix that right away; I didn't want my inventory made obsolete as soon as I was off the island.

One wing had been barely begun. The foundations were half full of rain water, but tapping with the hammer suggested the cementwork was sound, and a part where pouring had not been finished showed good iron-bar reinforcement. In the finished wing, the vandalism was appalling but fairly superficial in all but a dozen rooms. A quarter of a million dollars would finish it up, plus furnishings. Some of the pool tiles were cracked—deliberately, it seemed—but most of the fountains would be all right once cleaned up. The garden lighting fixtures were a total writeoff.

The main building had been the most complete and also the most looted and trashed. It might take half a million dollars to fix the damage, I thought, adding up the pages in my notebook. But it was much more than a half-million-dollar building. There were no single rooms there, only guest suites, every one with its own balcony overlooking the blue bay. There was a space for a ballroom, a space for a casino, a pretty, trellised balcony for a top-floor bar—the design was faultless. So was what existed of the workmanship. I couldn't find the wine cellar, but the shop level just under the lobby was a pleasant surprise. Some of the shop windows had been broken, but the glass had been swept away and it was the only large area of the hotel without at least one or two piles of human feces. If all the vandals had been as thoughtful as the ones in the shopping corridor, there might have been no need to put up the fence.

About noon I drove down to a little general store—"Li Tsung's Supermarket," it called itself—and got materials for a sandwich lunch. I spent the whole day there, and by the time I was heading back to the hotel I had just about made up my mind: the site was a bargain, taken by itself.

Remained to check out the other factors.

My title in the company is assistant international vice president for finance. I was a financial officer when I worked at the government labs, and money is what I know. You don't really know about money unless you know how to put a dollar value on all the things your money buys, though, so I can't spend all my time with the financial reports and the computer. When I recommend an acquisition I have to know what comes with it.

So, besides checking out the hotel site and the facts that Kavilan had given me, I explored the whole island. I drove the road from the site to the airport three times—once in sunlight, once in rain and once late at night—counting up potholes and difficult turns to make sure it would serve for a courtesy van. Hotel guests don't want to spend all their time in their hotels. They want other things to go to, so I checked out each of the island's fourteen other beaches. They want entertainment at night, so I visited three discos and five other casinos—briefly—and observed, without visiting, the three-story verandahed building demurely set behind high walls and a wrought-iron gate that was the island's officially licensed house of prostitution. I even signed up for the all-island guided bus tour to check for historical curiosities and points of interest and I did not, even once, open the slim, flimsy telephone directory to see if there was a listing for Valdos E. Michaelis, Ph.D.

The young woman from the second morning's breakfast was on the same tour bus and once again she was alone. Or wanted to be alone. Halfway around the island we stopped for complimentary drinks, and when I got back on the bus she was right behind me. "Do you mind if I sit here?" she asked.

"Of course not," I said politely, and didn't ask why. I didn't have to. I'd seen the college kid in the tank top and cutoffs earnestly whispering in her ear for the last hour, and just before we stopped for drinks he gave up whispering and started bullying.

I had decided I didn't like the college kid either, so that was a bond. The fact that we were both loners and not predatory about trying to change that was another. Each time the bus stopped for a photo opportunity we two grabbed quick puffs on our cigarettes instead of snapping pictures—smokers are an endangered species, and that's a special bond these days—so it was pretty natural that when I saw her alone again at breakfast the next morning I asked to join her. And when she looked envious at what I told her I was going to do that day, I invited her along.

Among the many things that Marge's death has made me miss is someone to share adventures with—little adventures, the kind my job keeps requiring of me, like chartering a boat to check out the hotel site from the sea. If Marge had lived to take these trips with me I would be certain I had the very best job in the world. Well, it is the best job in the world, anyway; it's the world that isn't as good anymore.

The *Esmeralda* was a sport-fishing boat that doubled as a way for tourists to get out on the wet part of the world for fun. It was a thirty-footer, with a two-hundred-horse-power outboard motor and a cabin that contained a V-shaped double berth up forward, and a toilet and galley amidships. It also came with a captain named Ildo, who was in fact the whole crew. His name was Spanish, he said he was Dutch, his color was assorted and his accent was broad Islands. When I asked him how business was he said, "Aw, slow, mon, but when it comes January—" he said "Johnerary"—"it'll be *good.*" And he said it grinning to show he believed it, but the grin faded. I knew why. He was looking at my face, and wondering why his charter this day didn't seem to be enjoying himself.

I was trying, though. The *Esmeralda* was a lot too much like the other charter boat, the *Princess Peta,* for me to be at ease, but I really was doing my best to keep that other boat out of my mind. It occurred to me to wonder if, somewhere in my subconscious, I had decided to invite this Edna Buckner along so that I would have company to distract me on the *Esmeralda.* It then occurred to me that, if that was the reason, my subconscious was a pretty big idiot. Being alone on the boat would have been bad. Being with a rather nice-looking woman was worse.

The bay was glassy, but when we passed the headland light we were out in the swell of the ocean. I went back to see how my guest was managing. Even out past shelter the sea was gentle enough, but as we were traveling parallel to the waves there was some roll. It didn't seem to bother Edna Buckner at all. As she turned toward me she looked nineteen years again, and I suddenly realized why. She was enjoying herself. I didn't want to spoil that for her, and so I sat down beside her, as affable and charming as I knew how to be.

She wasn't nineteen. She was forty-one and, she let me know without exactly saying, unmarried, at least at the moment. She wasn't exactly traveling alone; she was the odd corner of a threesome with her sister and brother-in-law. They (she let me know, again without actually saying) had decided on the trip in the hope that it would ease some marital difficulties—and then damaged that project's chance of success by inviting a third party. "They were just sorry for me," said Edna, without explaining.

Going over the tour group in my mind, I realized I knew which couple she was traveling with. "The man with red hair," I guessed, and she nodded.

"And with the disposition to match. You should have heard him in the restaurant last night, complaining because Lucille's lobster was bigger than his." Actually, I had. "I will say," she added, "that he was in a better mood this morning. He even apologized, and he can be a charmer when he chooses. But I wish the trip were over. I've had enough fighting to last me the rest of my life."

She paused and looked at me speculatively for a moment. She was swaying slightly in the roll of the boat, rather nicely as a matter of fact. I started to open my mouth to change the subject but she shook her head. "Do you mind letting your shipmates tell you their troubles, Jerry?"

I happen to be a pretty closed-up person—more so since what happened to Marge. I didn't know whether I minded or not; there were not very many people who had offered to weep on my shoulder in the past eight years. She didn't wait for an answer, but went on with a rush: "I know it's no fun to listen to other people's problems, but I kind of need to say it out loud. Bert was an alcoholic—my husband. Ex-husband. He beat me up about once a week, for ten years. It took me all that time to make up my mind to leave him and so, when you think about it, I seem to be about ten years behind the rest of the world, trying to learn how to be a grown-up woman."

It obviously cost her something to say that. For a moment I thought she was going to cry, but she smiled instead. "So if I'm a little peculiar, that's why," she said, "and thank you for this trip. I can feel myself getting less peculiar every minute!"

Money's my game, not interpersonal relationships, and I didn't have the faintest idea of how to react to this unexpected intimacy. Fortunately, my arm did. I leaned forward and put it around her shoulder for a quick, firm hug. "Maybe we'll both get less peculiar," I said, and just then Ildo called from the wheel:

"Mon? We're comin' up on you-ah bay!"

The hotel site looked even more beautiful from the water than it had from the land. There was a pale half-moon of beach that reached from one hill on the south to another at the northern end, and a white collar of breaking wavelets all its length. The water was crystal. When Ildo dropped anchor I could follow the line all twenty-odd feet to the rippled sand bottom. The only ugliness was the chain-link fence that marched around the building site itself.

The bay was not quite perfect. It was rather shallow from point to point, so that wind-surfing hotel guests who ventured more than a hundred yards out might find themselves abruptly in stronger seas. But that was a minor problem. Very few tourists would be able to stay on the boards long enough to go a hundred yards in any direction at all. The ones who might get out where they would be endangered would have the skills to handle it. And there was plenty of marine life for snorkelers and scuba-divers to look at. Ildo showed us places in under the rocky headlands where lobsters could be caught. "Plenty now," he explained. "Oh, mon, six year ago was *bad*. No lobster never, but they all come back now."

The hotel, I observed, had been intelligently sited. It wasn't dead center in the arc of the bay, but enough around the curve toward the northern end so that every one of the four hundred private balconies would get plenty of sun: extra work for the air-conditioners, but satisfied guests. The buildings were high enough above the water to be safe from any likely storm surf—and anyway, I had already established, storms almost never struck the island from the west. And there was a rocky outcrop on the beach just at the hotel itself. That was where the dock would go, with plenty of water for sport-fishing boats—there were plenty of sailfish, tuna and everything else within half an hour's sail, Ildo said. The dock could even handle a fair-sized private yacht without serious dredging.

While I was putting all this in my notebook, Edna had borrowed mask and flippers from Ildo's adequate supply and was considerately staying out of my way. It wasn't just politeness. She was obviously enjoying herself.

I, on the other hand, was itchily nervous. Ildo assured me there was nothing to be nervous about; she was a strong swimmer, there were no sharks or barracuda likely to bother her, she wasn't so far from the boat that one of us couldn't have jumped in after her at any time. It didn't help. I couldn't focus on the buildings through the finder of the Polaroid for more than a couple of seconds without taking a quick look to make sure she was all right.

Actually there were other reasons for looking at her. She was at home in the water and looked good in it. Edna was not in the least like Marge—tall where Marge had been tiny, hair much darker than Marge's maple-syrup head. And of course a good deal younger than Marge had been even when I let her die.

It struck me as surprising that Edna was the first woman in years I had been able to look at without wishing she were Marge. And even more surprising that I could think of the death of my wife without that quick rush of pain and horror. When Edna noticed that I had put my camera and notebook away she swam back to the boat and let me help her aboard. "God," she said, grinning, "I needed that." And then she waved to the northern headland and said, "I just realized that the other side of that hill must be where my old neighbor lives."

I said, "I didn't know you had friends on the island."

"Just one, Jerry. Not a friend, exactly. Sort of an honorary uncle. He used to live next door to my parents' house in Maryland, and we kept in touch—in fact, he's the one that made me want to come here, in his letters. Val Michaelis."

3

Ildo offered us grilled lobsters for lunch. While he took the skiff and a face mask off to get the raw materials and Edna retreated to the cabin to change, I splashed ashore. He had brought the *Esmeralda* close in, and I could catch a glimpse of Edna's face in the porthole as she smiled out at me, but I wasn't thinking about her. I was thinking about something not attractive at all, called "bacteriological warfare."

Actually the kind of warfare we dealt with at the labs wasn't bacteriological. Bacteria are too easy to kill with broad-spectrum antibiotics. If you want to make a large number of people sick and want them to stay sick long enough to be no further problem, what you want is a virus.

That was the job Val Michaelis had walked away from.

I had walked away from the same place not long after him, and likely for very similar reasons—I didn't like what was happening there. But there was a difference. I'm an orderly person. I had put in for my twenty-year retirement and left with the consent, if not the blessing, of the establishment. Val Michaelis simply left. When he didn't return to the labs from vacation, his assistant went looking for him at his house. When the house turned up empty, others had begun to look. But by then Michaelis had had three weeks to get lost in. The search was pretty thorough, but he was never found. After a few years, no doubt, the steam had gone out of it, as new lines of research outmoded most of what he had been working on. That was a nasty enough business. I wasn't a need-to-knower and all I ever knew of it was an occasional slip. That was more than I wanted, though. Now and then I would spend an hour or two in the public library to make sure I'd got the words right, and try to figure how to put them together, and I think I had at least the right general idea. There are these things called oncoviruses, a whole family of them. One kind seems to cause leukemia. A couple of others don't seem to bother anybody but mice. But another kind, what they called "type D," likes monkeys, apes and human beings; and that was what Michaelis was working on. At first I thought he was trying to produce a weapon that would cause cancer and that didn't seem sensible—cancers take too long to develop to be much help on a battlefield. Then I caught another phrase: "substantia nigra." The library told me that that was a small, dark mass of cells way inside the brain. The substantia nigra's A9 cells control the physical things you learn to do automatically, like touch-typing or riding a bike; and near them are the A10 cells, which do something to control emotions. None of that helped me much, either, until I heard one more word:

Schizophrenia.

I left the library that day convinced that I was helping people develop a virus that would turn normal people into psychotics.

Later on—long after Val had gone AWOL and I'd gone my own way—some of the work was declassified, and the open literature confirmed part, and corrected part. There was still a pretty big question of whether I understood all I was reading, but it seemed that what the oncovirus D might do was to mess up some dopamine cells in and around the substantia nigra, producing a condition that was not psychotic exactly, but angry, tense, irresponsible—the sort of thing you hear about in kids that have burned their brains out with amphetamines. And the virus wouldn't reproduce in any mammals but primates. They couldn't infect any insects at all. Without rats or mice or mosquitoes or lice to carry it, how do you spread that kind of disease? True, they could have looked for a vector among, say, the monotremes or the marsupials—but how are you going to introduce a herd of sick platypuses into the Kremlin?

Later on, I am sure, they found meaner and easier bugs; but that was the one Michaelis and I had run away from. And nobody had seen Val Michaelis again—until I did, from Dick Kavilan's Saab.

Of course, Michaelis had more reason to quit than I did, and far more reason to hide. I only made up the payrolls and audited the bills. He did the molecular biology that turned laboratory cultures into killers.

The lobsters were delicious, split and broiled over a driftwood fire. Ildo had brought salad greens and beer from Port, and plates to eat it all on. China plates, not paper, and that was decent of him—he wasn't going to litter the beauty of the beach.

While we were picking the last of the meat out of the shells Edna was watching me. I was doing my best to do justice to the lunch, but I don't suppose I was succeeding. Strange sensation. I wasn't unhappy. I wasn't unaware of the taste of the lobster, or the pleasure of Edna's company, or the charm of the beach. I was very nearly happy, in a sort of basic, background way, but there were nastinesses just outside that gentle sphere of happiness, and they were nagging at me. I had felt like that before, time and again, in fact; most often when Marge and I were planning what to do with my retirement, and it all seemed rosy except for the constant sting of knowing the job I would have to finish first. The job was part of it now, or Val Michaelis was, and so was the way Marge died, and the two of them were spoiling what should have been perfection. Edna didn't miss what was going on, she simply diagnosed it wrong. "I guess I shouldn't have dumped my troubles on you, Jerry," she said, as Ildo picked up the plates and buried the ashes of the fire.

"Oh, no," I said. "No, it's not that—I'm glad you told me." I was, though I couldn't have said why, exactly; it was not a habit of mine to want that kind of intimacy from another person, because I didn't want to offer them any of mine. I said, "It's Val Michaelis."

She nodded. "He's in some kind of trouble? I thought it was strange that he'd bury himself here."

"Some kind," I agreed. "Or was. Maybe it's all over now." And then I made my decision. "I'd like to go see him."

"Oh," said Edna, "I don't know if he's still on the island."

"Why not?"

"He said he was leaving. He's been planning to for some time—he only stayed on to see us. What's this, Friday? The last time I saw him was Tuesday, and he was packing up then. He may be gone."

And he was. When Ildo deposited us at the Keytown dock and the taxi took us to the apartments where Michaelis had lived, the door of his place was unlocked. The rented furniture was there, but the closets were empty, and so were the bureau drawers, and of an occupant the only sign remaining was an envelope addressed to Edna:

> I thought I'd better leave while Gerald was still wrestling with his conscience. If you see him, thank him for the use of his space—and I hope we'll meet again in a couple of years.

Edna looked up at me in puzzlement. "Do you know what that part about your space means?"

I gave the note back to her and watched her fold it up and put it in her bag. I thought of asking her to burn it, but that would just make it more important to her. I wanted her to forget it. I said, "No," which was somewhat true. I didn't *know*. And I surely didn't want to guess.

By the time we were back on the boat I was able to be cheerful again, at least on the surface. When we docked at our own hotel Edna went on ahead to change, while I sent Ildo happily off with a big tip. He was, Edna had said, a pretty sweet man. He was not alone in that; nearly everyone I'd met on the island was as kindly as the island claimed; and it hurt me to think of Val Michaelis going on with his work in this gentle place.

We had agreed to meet for a drink before dinner—we had taken it for granted that we were going to have dinner together—and when I came to Edna's room to pick her up she invited me in. "That Starlight Casino is pretty noisy, Jerry, and I've got this perfectly beautiful balcony to use up. Can you drink gin and tonic?"

"My very favorite," I said. That wasn't true. I didn't much like the taste of quinine water, or of gin, either, but sitting on a warm sunset balcony with Edna was a lot more attractive than listening to rockabilly music in the bar.

But I wasn't good company. Seeing Edna off by herself in the bay had set off one set of memories, Val Michaelis's note had triggered another. I didn't welcome either train of thought, because they were intruders; I was feeling almost happy, almost at peace—and those two old pains kept coming in to remind me of misery and fear. I did my best. Edna had set out glasses, bottles, a bucket of ice, a plate of things to nibble on, and the descending sun was perfect. "This is really nice, Marge," I said, accepting a refill of my glass . . . and only heard myself when I saw the look on her face.

"I mean Edna," I said.

She touched my hand when she gave the glass back to me. "I think that's a compliment, Jerry," she said sweetly.

I thought that over. "I guess it is," I said. "You know, I've never done that before. Called someone else by my wife's name, I mean. Of course, I haven't often been in the sort of situation where—" I stopped there, because it didn't seem right to define what I thought the present "situation" was.

She started to speak, hesitated, took a tiny sip of her drink, started again, stopped and finally laughed—at herself, I realized. "Jerry," she said, "you can tell me to mind my own business if you want to, because I know I ought to. But you told me your wife died eight years ago. Are you saying you've never had a private drink with a woman since then?"

"Well, no—it has happened now and then," I said, and then added honestly, "but not very often. You see—"

I stopped and swallowed. The expression on her face was changing, the smile softening. She reached out to touch my hand.

And then I found myself telling her the whole thing.

Not the *whole* whole thing. I did not tell her what the surfboard looked like, with the ragged half-moon gap in the side, and I didn't tell her what Marge's body had looked like—what was left of it—when at last they found it near the shore, eight days later. But I told her the rest. Turning in my retirement papers. The trip to California to see her folks. The boat. The surfboard. Marge paddling around in the swell, just before the breakers, while I watched from the boat. "I went down below for just a minute," I said, "and when I came back on deck she was gone. I could still see the surfboard, but she wasn't there. I hadn't heard a thing, although she must have—"

"Oh, Jerry," said Edna.

"It has to do with water temperatures," I explained, "and with the increase in the seal population. The great white shark didn't used to come up that far north along the coast, but the water's a little warmer, and there are more seals. That's what they live on. Seals, and other things. And from a shark's view underwater, you see, a person lying on a surfboard, with his arms and legs paddling over the side, looks a lot like a seal. . . ."

I saw to my surprise that she was weeping. I shouldn't have been surprised. As I reached forward and put my arms around her, I discovered that I was weeping, too.

That was the biggest surprise of all. I'd done a lot of weeping in eight years, but never once in the presence of another human being, not even the shrinks I'd gone to see. And when the weeping stopped and the kissing began I found that it didn't seem wrong at all. It seemed very right, and a long, long time overdue.

4

My remaining business with Dick Kavilan didn't take long. By the time Edna's tour group was scheduled to go home, I was ready, too.

The two of us decided not to wait for the bus to the airport. We went early, by taxi, beating the tours to the check-in desk. By the time the first of them arrived we were already sitting at the tiny bar, sipping farewell pina coladas. Only it was not going to be a farewell, not when I had discovered she lived only a few miles from the house I had kept all these years as home base.

When the tour buses began to arrive I could not resist preening my forethought a little. "That's going to be a really ugly scene, trying to check in all at once," I said wisely.

But really it wasn't. There were all the ingredients for a bad time, more than three hundred tired tourists trying to get seat assignments from a single airline clerk. But they didn't jostle. They didn't snarl, at her or each other. The tiny terminal was steamy with human bodies, but it almost seemed they didn't even sweat. They were singing and smiling—even Edna's sister and brother-in-law. They waved up at us, and it looked like their marriage had a good shot at lasting a while longer, after all.

A sudden gabble from the line of passengers told us what the little callboard confirmed a moment later. Our airplane had arrived from the States. Edna started to collect her bag, her sack of duty-free rum, her boots and fur-collared coat for the landing at Dulles, her little carry-on with the cigarettes and the book to read on the flight, her last-minute souvenir T-shirt . . . "Hold on," I said. "We've got an hour yet. They've got to disembark the arrivals and muck out the plane—you didn't think we'd leave on time, did you?"

So there was time for another pina colada, and while we were drinking them the newcomers began to straggle off the DC-10. The noise level in the terminal jumped fifteen decibels, and most of it was meal complaints, family arguments and clamor over lost luggage. The departing crowd gazed at their fretful replacements good-humoredly.

And all of a sudden that other unpleasant train of thought bit down hard. There was a healing magic on the island, and the thought of Val Michaelis doing the sort of thing he was trained to do here was more than I could bear. I hadn't turned Michaelis in, because I thought he was a decent man. But damaging these kind, gentle people was indecent.

I put down my half-finished drink, stood up and dropped a bill on the table. "Edna," I said, "I just realize there's something I have to do. I'm afraid I'm going to miss this flight. I'll call you in Maryland when I get back—I'm sorry."

And I really was. Very. But that did not stop me from heading for the phone.

The men from the NSA were there the next morning. Evidently they hadn't waited for a straight-through flight. Maybe they'd chartered one, or caught a light flight to a nearby island.

But they hadn't wasted any time.

They could have thanked me for calling them, I thought. They didn't. They invited me out to their car for privacy—it was about as much of an "invitation" as a draft notice is, and as difficult to decline—while I answered their questions. Then they pulled out of the hotel lot and drove those thirty-mile-an-hour island roads at sixty. We managed not to hit any of the cows and people along the way. We did, I think, score one hen. The driver didn't even slow down to look.

I was not in the least surprised. I didn't know the driver, but the other man was Joe Mooney. Now he was a full field investigator, but he had been a junior security officer at the labs when Michaelis walked away. He was a mean little man with a high opinion of himself; he had always thought that the rules he enforced on the people he surveilled didn't have to apply to him. He proved it. He turned around in the front seat, arm across the back, so he could look at me while ostensibly talking to his partner at the wheel: "You know what Michaelis was working on? Some kind of a bug to drive the Russians nuts."

"Mooney, watch it!" his partner snapped.

"Oh, it's all right. Old Jerry knows all about it, and he's cleared—or used to be."

"It wasn't a bug," I said. "It was a virus. It wouldn't drive them crazy. It would work on the brain to make them irritable and nasty—a kind of personality change, like some people get after a stroke. And he didn't just try. He succeeded."

"And then he ran."

"And then he ran, yes."

"Only it didn't work," grinned Mooney, "because they couldn't find a way to spread it. And now what we have to worry about, we have to worry that while he was down here he figured out how to make it work and's looking for a buyer. Like a Russian buyer."

Well, I could have argued all of that. But the only part I answered, as we stopped to unlock the chain-link gate, was the last part. And all I said was, "I don't think so."

Mooney laughed out loud. "You always were a googoo," he said. "You sure Michaelis didn't stick you with some of that stuff in reverse?"

I hadn't been able to find the entrance of the wine cellar, but that pair of NSA men had no trouble at all. They realized at once that there had to be a delivery system to the main dining room—I hadn't thought of that. So that's where they went, and found a small elevator shaft that went two stories down. There wasn't any elevator, but there were ropes and Mooney's partner climbed down while Mooney and I went back to the shopping floor. About two minutes after we got there a painters' scaffold at the end of the hall went over with a crash, and the NSA man pushed his way out of the door it had concealed. Mooney gave me a contemptuous look. "Fire stairs," he explained. "They had to be there. There has to be another entrance, too—outside—so they can deliver the wine by truck."

He was right again. From the inside it was easy to spot, even though we had only flashlights to see what we were doing. When Mooney pushed it open we got a flood of tropical light coming in, and a terrible smell to go with it. For a moment I wondered if the graveyard wind had shifted again, but it was only a pile of garbage—rotted garbage—long-gone lobster shells and sweepings from the mall and trash of all kinds. It wasn't surprising no one had found the entrance from outside; the stink was discouraging.

No matter what else I was, I was still a man paid to do a job by his company. So while the NSA team were prodding and peering and taking flash pictures, I was looking at the cellar. It was large enough to handle all the wines a first-class sommelier might want to store; the walls were solid, and the temperature good. With that outside door kept closed, it would be no problem to keep any vintage safely resting here. The Dutchman shouldn't have given up so easily, just because he was faced with a lot of lawsuits—but maybe, as Dick Kavilan had said, people were meaner then.

I blinked when Joe Mooney poked his flashlight in my face. "What are you daydreaming about?" he demanded.

I pushed his hand away. "Have you seen everything you need?" I asked.

He looked around. There wasn't a whole lot to see, really. Along one wall there were large glass tanks—empty, except for a scummy inch or two of liquid at the bottom of some of them, fishy smelling and unappetizing. There were smaller tanks on the floor, and marks on the rubber tile to show where other things had been that now were gone. "He took everything that matters out," he grumbled. "Son of a bitch! He got clean away."

"We'll find him," his partner said.

"Damn right, but what was he doing here? Trying out his stuff on the natives?" Mooney looked at me searchingly. "What do you think, Wenwright? Have you heard of any cases of epidemic craziness on the island?"

I shrugged. "I did my part when I called you," I said. "Now all I want is to go home."

But it wasn't quite true. There was something else I wanted, and that was to know if there was any chance at all that what I was beginning to suspect might be true.

The next day I was on the home-bound jet, taking a drink from the stew in the first-class section and still trying to convince myself that what I believed was possible. *The people were meaner then.* It wasn't just an offhand remark of Kavilan's; the hotel manager told me as I was checking out that it was true, yes, a few years ago he had a lot of trouble with help, but lately everybody seemed a lot friendlier. *Val Michaelis was a decent man.* I'd always believed that, in the face of the indecencies of his work at the labs . . . having left, would he go on performing indecencies?

Could it be that Michaelis had in fact found a different kind of virus? One that worked on different parts of the brain, for different purposes? That made people happier and more gentle, instead of suspicious, paranoid, and dangerous?

I was neither biologist nor brain anatomist to guess if that could be true. But I had the evidence of my eyes. *Something* had changed the isle from mean, litiginous, grasping—from the normal state of the rest of the world—to what I had seen around me. It had even worked on me. It was not just Edna Buckner's sweet self, sweet though she was, that had let me discharge eight years of guilt and horror in one night. And right here on this plane, the grinning tour groups in the back and even the older, more sedate first-class passengers around me testified that something had happened to them. . . .

Not all the first-class passengers.

Just across the aisle from me one couple was busy berating the stewardess. They didn't like their appetizer.

"Langouste salad, you call it?" snapped the man. "I call it *poison.* Didn't you ever hear of allergy? Jesus, we've been spending the whole week trying to keep them from pushing those damned lobsters on us everywhere we went. . . ."

Lobsters.

Lobsters were neither mammals nor insects. And the particular strains of Retroviridae that wouldn't reproduce in either, I remember, had done just fine in crustaceans.

Like lobsters.

5

The NSA team caught up with me again six months later, in my office. I was just getting ready to leave, to pick Edna up for the drive down to Chesapeake Bay, where the company was considering the acquisition of an elderly and declining hotel. I told them I was in a hurry.

"This is official business," Mooney's partner growled, but Mooney shook his head.

"We won't keep you long, Wenright. Michaelis has been reported in the States. Have you heard anything of him?"

"Where in the States?"

"None of your business," he snapped, and then shrugged. "Maryland."

I said, "That would be pretty foolish of him, wouldn't it?" He didn't respond, just looked at me. "No," I said, "I haven't heard anything at all."

He obviously had not expected anything more. He gave me a routinely nasty look, the whatever-it-is-you're-up-to-you-won't-get-away-with-it kind, and stood up to go. His partner gave me the routinely unpleasant warning: "We'll be watching you," he said.

I laughed. "I'm sure you will. And don't you think Michaelis will figure that out, too?"

That night I told Edna about the interview, though I wasn't supposed to. I didn't care about that, having already told her so much that I wasn't supposed to about Michaelis's work and my suspicions. There were a lot of laws that said I should have kept my mouth shut, and I had broken all of them.

She nibbled at her salad, nodding. We were dining in the hotel's open-air restaurant; it was late spring, and nearly as warm as it had been back on the island. "I hope he gets away," she said.

"I hope more than that. I hope he lives and prospers with his work."

She giggled. "Johnny Happyseed," she said.

I shook my head slightly, because the maitre-d' was approaching and I didn't want him to hear. He was a plump young man with visions of a career at the Plaza, and he knew what I was there for. He was desperately anxious to make my report favorable. The hotel itself was fine. It was the top management that was incompetent, and if we bought it out there would be changes—as he knew. Whether he would be one of the changes I didn't yet know.

So when he asked, "Is everything satisfactory, Mr. Wenright?" he was asking about more than the meal. I hadn't been there long enough to have made up my mind—and certainly wouldn't have told him if I had. I only smiled, and he pressed on: "This is really a delightful old hotel, Mr. Wenright, with all sorts of marvelous historical associations. And it's been kept up very well, as you'll see. Of course, some improvements are always in order—but we get a first-class clientele, especially in the softshell crab season. Congressmen. Senators. Diplomats. Every year we get a series of seminars with Pentagon people—"

Edna dropped her fork.

I didn't, but I was glad to have him distracted by the necessity of clapping his hands so that a busboy could rush up at once with a fresh one. Then I said, "Tell me, isn't it true that the crabbing has been very poor lately? Some sort of disease among the shellfish?"

"Yes, that's true, Mr. Wenright," he admitted, but added eagerly, "I'm sure they'll come back."

I said, "I absolutely guarantee it." He left chuckling, and wondering if he'd missed the point of the joke.

I looked at Edna. She looked at me. We both nodded.

But all either of us said, after quite a while, was Edna's, "I wonder what kind of seafood they eat in Moscow?"

THE MIDDLE OF NOWHERE

When "The Middle of Nowhere" was published in 1955, we knew a lot less about Mars than we know today. We were more than forty years away from flybys, landings, Mars rovers . . . it was still pretty much a Red Planet of mystery. Therefore, science fiction writers could write anything they wanted about Mars, so long as it didn't seem ridiculous.

Frederik Pohl has written a number of stories about Mars, and his Martian stories have changed with the available scientific knowledge. But this story could take place on any planet we don't know a lot about. It's not so much about the planet itself as it is about what might happen to a world—Earth, Mars, or another—where technology outlasts its creators.

It's not a new theme, but Pohl's treatment is full of the excitement and danger of the unknown . . . and its possibilities.

Just ahead of us we saw a cluster of smoke trees suddenly quiver, though there wasn't a whisper of a breeze, and begin to emit their clouds of dense yellow vapor from their branch tips.

"Let's get a move on, Will," said Jack Demaree. His voice was thin and piercing, like the thin air all about us. "It's going to get really hot here in the next twenty minutes."

The steel and glass town of Niobe was in sight, a quarter mile ahead. "Sure," I said, and changed pace. We had been shambling along, as lazily as we could, in the effort-saving walk you learn in your first week on Mars. I stepped it up to the distance-devouring loose run that is only possible on a light-gravity planet like Mars.

It is tough to have to run in a thin atmosphere. Your lungs work too hard; you feel as though every step is going to be your last. Hillary and Tenzing found no harder going on Everest than the friendliest spot on the surface of Mars—except, of course, that by day the temperature is high, and the light gravity lets you stand effort that would otherwise kill you. But we hadn't much choice but to run. The smoke trees had passed their critical point, and the curious gelatinous sulfur compounds that served them for sap had passed into gas with the heat. When that happened, it meant that the sun was nearly overhead; and with only Mars's thin blanket of air to shield you, you do not stay out in the open at high noon.

Not that we needed to see the smoke trees to know it was getting hot. A hundred and twenty in the shade it was, at least. If there had been any shade.

Demaree passed me with a spurt just as we reached the outskirts of Niobe, and I followed him into the pressure chamber of the General Mercantile office. We use helium in our synthetic atmosphere, instead of Earth's nitrogen. So they gave us the pressure in one big ear-popping dose, without any danger of the bends we might have got from nitrogen. I swallowed and rubbed my ears; then we shed our sand-capes and respirators and walked into the anteroom.

Keever looked out of his private office, his lean horse face sagging with curiosity.

"Demaree and Wilson reporting," I said. "No sign of natives. No hostile action. No anything, in fact, except it's hot."

Keever nodded and pulled his head back in. "Make out a slip," his voice floated out. "And you go out again in two hours. Better eat."

Demaree finished shaking the loose sand out of his cape into a refuse shaft and made a face. "Two hours. Oh, lord." But he followed me to the Company cafeteria without argument.

The first thing we both did was make a dash for the drinking fountain. I won, and sopped up my fill while Demaree's dry and covetous breath seared the back of my neck. Sand patrol can dehydrate a man to the point of shock in three hours; we had been out for four. You see why we were taking it easy?

We sat down in the little booth where we had put aside our card game with Bolt and Farragut a few hours before, and Marianna, without waiting for our order, brought coffee and sandwiches. Her eyes were hooded and unhappy; nerves, I thought, and tried to catch Demaree's eye. But it didn't work. He said in his customary slow and biting drawl, "Why, Mary, you're getting stupider than ever. You took away our cards. I swear, girl, I don't know why the Company keeps you—"

He trailed off, as she looked straight at him, and then away.

"You won't need them," she said after a moment. "Farragut's patrol got it this morning."

Farragut and Bolt, Cortland and VanCaster. Four good men, and it was the same old story. They were a four-man patrol, ranging far beyond the defense perimeter of Niobe; they had got caught too far from town before it got really hot, and it was a choice between using their cached sand cars or getting stuck in the noonday sun. They had elected to try the sand car; and something bright and hot had come flashing over a sand dune and incinerated men and car alike.

The hell of it all was we never saw the Martians.

The earliest expeditions had reported that there wasn't any life on Mars at all, barring the tiny ratlike forms that haunted the sparse forests of the North. Then air reconnaissance had reported what turned out to be the Martians—creatures about the size of a man, more or less, that stood up like a man, that built villages of shacks like men. But air reconnaissance was severely limited by the thinness of Mars' air; helicopters and winged aircraft simply did not work, except at speeds so high that it was nearly impossible to make out details. It wasn't until one of the orbiting mother spacecraft, after launching its space-to-ground shuttle rockets and standing by for the return, spent a dozen revolutions mapping Mars' surface that the first really good look at Martians and their works was available. Really good? Well, let's say as good as you could expect, considering the mother ship was five hundred miles up.

It was easy enough to send a surface party to investigate the Martian villages; but they were empty by the time Earthmen got there. Our sand cars could move faster than a Martian afoot, but it wasn't healthy to use a sand car. Somehow, what weapons the Martians found to use against us (and nothing resembling a weapon had ever been found in the deserted villages) seemed most effective against machines. It was flatly impossible that they should have electronic aimers to zero in on the radio-static from the machines; but if it had been possible, it would have been certain—for that was the effect.

I had plenty of time to think about all this as Demaree and I ate our glum and silent meal. There just wasn't anything much for us to say. Farragut and Bolt had been friends of ours.

Demaree sighed and put down his coffee. Without looking at me he said, "Maybe I ought to quit this job, Will."

I didn't answer, and he let it go. I didn't think he meant it, but I knew how he felt.

General Mercantile was a good enough outfit to work for, and its minerals franchise on Mars meant a terrific future for any young fellow who got in on the ground floor. That's what everybody said, back on Earth, and that's what kept us all there: the brilliant future.

That—and the adventure of developing a whole new world. Suppose those old Englishmen who went out for the Hudson Bay Company and the East India Company and the other Middle-Ages monopolies must have had the same feeling.

And the same dangers. Except that they dealt with an enemy they could see and understand; an enemy that, regardless of skin color or tongue, was human. And we were fighting shadows.

I tasted my coffee, and it was terrible. "Hey, Mary—" I started, but I never finished.

The alarm klaxon squawked horrifyingly in the cafeteria; we could hear it bellowing all over the GM building. We didn't wait to ask questions; we jumped up and raced for the door, Demaree colliding with me as we tried to beat each other through. He clutched at me and looked at me blankly, then elbowed me aside. Over his shoulder he said, "Hey, Will—I don't *really* want to quit. . . ."

The news was: Kelcy.

Kelcy was our nearest village, and the Martians had schlagged it. Demaree and I were the first in the Ready Room, and Keever snapped that much information at us while we were waiting the few seconds for the rest of the patrols to come racing in. They had been in other buildings and came leaping in still wearing their sandcaps; they had had to race across the blindingly hot streets in the midday Martian glare. There were twelve of us all together—the whole station complement, less the four who had been lost that morning. We were on the books as "personnel assistants"; but what we really were was guards, the entire troubleshooting force and peace-and-order officers for the town of Niobe.

Keever repeated it for the others: "They attacked Kelcy thirty minutes ago. It was a hit-and-run raid; they fired on all but one of the buildings, and every building was demolished. So far, they report twenty-six survivors. There might be a couple more—out in the open—that's all that are in the one building." Out in the open—that meant no other survivors at all; it was just past high noon.

Big, fair-haired Tom van der Gelt unsteadily shredded the plastic from a fresh pack of cigarettes and lit one. "I had a brother in Kelcy," he remarked to no one.

"We don't have a list of survivors yet," Keever said quickly. "Maybe your brother's all right. But we'll find out before anybody else, because we're going to send a relief expedition."

We all sat up at that. Relief expedition? But Kelcy was forty miles away. We could never hope to walk it, or even run it, between the end of the hot-period and dark; and it made no sense for us to be out in the open at the dusk sandstorm. But Keever was saying:

"This is the first time they've attacked a town. I don't have to tell you how serious it is. Niobe may be next. So—we're going to go there, and get the survivors back here; and see if we can find out anything from them. And because we won't have much time, we're going to travel by sand car."

There was a thoroughgoing silence in that room for a moment after that, while the echoes of the words "sand car" bounced around. Only the echoes made it sound like "suicide."

Keever coughed. "It's a calculated risk," he went on doggedly. "I've gone over every skirmish report since the first landings, and never—well, almost never—have the Martians done more than hit and run. Now, it's true that once they've hit a settlement the usual custom is to lay low for a while; and it's true that this is the first time they've come out against a town, and maybe they're changing their tactics. I won't try to tell you that this is safe. It isn't. But there's at least a chance that we'll get through—more of a chance, say, than the twenty-six survivors in Kelcy have if we don't try it." He hesitated for a second. Then, slowly: "I won't order any man to do it. But I'll call for volunteers. Anybody who wants to give it a try, front and center."

Nobody made a mad rush to get up there—it still sounded like suicide to all of us.

But nobody stayed behind. In under a minute, we were all standing huddled around Keever, listening to orders.

We had to wait another forty minutes—it took time for the maintenance crew to get the sand cars out of their hideaways, where they'd been silently standing, not even rusting in the dry Martian air, since the first Earthman drew the connection between sand cars and Martian attack. Besides, it was still hot; and even in the sand cars, it would help for the sun to be a few degrees past the meridian.

There were fourteen of us in three cars—the patrols, Keever and Dr. Solveig. Solveig's the only doctor in Niobe, but Keever requisitioned him—we didn't know what we might find in Kelcy. Keever's car led the party; Demaree, Solveig and I were in the last, the smallest of the lot and the slowest.

Still, we clipped off fifteen miles of the forty-mile trip in eight minutes by the clock. The cats were flapping until I was sure they would fly off the drive wheels, but somehow they held on as we roared over the rolling sand. It sounded as though the car was coming to pieces at every bump—a worrisome sound but not, I think, the sound that any of us was really worrying about. *That* sound was the rushing, roaring thunder of a Martian missile leaping at us over a dune; and none of us expected to hear it more than once. . . .

The way to Kelcy skirts what we call the "Split Cliffs," which all of us regarded as a prime suspect for a Martian hangout. There had been expeditions into the Split Cliffs because of that suspicion; but most of them came back empty-handed, having found nothing but an incredible tangle. However, the ones that didn't come back empty-handed didn't come back at all; it was, as I say, a prime suspect. And so we watched it warily until it was almost out of sight behind us.

Martians or no, the Split Cliffs is a treacherous place, with nothing worth an Earthman's time inside. Before Mars' internal fires died completely, there were centuries of fierce earthquakes. The section we called the Split Cliffs must have been right over a major fault. The place is cataclysmic; it looks as though some artist from the Crazy Years, Dali or Archipenko, had designed it, in a rage. Sharp upcroppings of naked, metallic rock; deep gashes with perfectly straight hundred-foot sides. And because there happens to be a certain amount of poisonously foul water deep underground there, the place is as heavily vegetated as anything on Mars. Some of the twisted trees reach as high as thirty feet above the ground—by Martian standards, huge!

Even Demaree, at the wheel of the sand car, kept glancing over his shoulder at the Split Cliffs until we were well past them. "I can't help it," he said half-apologetically to me, catching my eyes on him. "Those lousy trees could hide anything."

"Sure," I said shortly. "Watch what you're doing." I wasn't in a mood for conversation—not only because of the circumstances, but because my nose was getting sore. Even in the car we wore respirators, on Keever's orders—I think he had an idea that a Martian attack might blow out our pressure before we could put them on. And three hours that morning, plus five hours each of the several days before, had left my nose pretty tender where the respirator plugs fit in.

Dr. Solveig said worriedly, "I agree with William, please. You have come very close to the other cars many times. If we should hit—"

"We won't hit," said Demaree. But he did concentrate on his driving; he maintained his forty meters behind the second car, following their lead as they sought the path of least ups-and-downs through the sand dunes toward Kelcy. It began to look, I thought as I watched the reddish sand streaming by, as though Keever's "calculated risk" was paying off. Certainly we had come nearly twenty miles without trouble, and past the worst danger spot on the trip, the Split Cliffs. If our luck held for ten minutes more—

It didn't.

"God almighty!" yelled Demaree, jolting me out of my thoughts. I looked where he was looking, just in time to see flame coursing flat along the ground. It snaked in a quivering course right at the middle sand car of our three; and when the snaking light and the jolting car intersected—

Catastrophe. Even in the thin air, the sound was like an atomic bomb. The spurt of flame leaped forty yards into the air.

We were out of the car in seconds, and the men from Keever's car joined us. But there was nothing to do for the seven men in the second car.

"They went after the biggest," Keever said bitterly. "Now—" He shrugged. One thing was sure, and he didn't have to say it. None of us wanted to be in a sand car with the motor going right there and then.

There was no sign of the enemy. Around us were empty sand dunes—but not empty, because out of them had come the missile. The only break was the fringe of the Split Cliffs behind us.

Keever methodically zipped up his sand cape and went through the routine of tucking in flaps at the neck and arms without speaking. None of us had anything to say either. Demaree, with a stronger stomach than mine, took another look inside the blackened frame of the second sand car, and came back looking as though his stomach wasn't so strong after all.

We scattered away from the parked sand cars and the wreck of the one that would never move again, and held a council of war. By Keever's watch, we had time to get to Kelcy or go back to Niobe—at a half trot in either case. We were exactly at midpoint between the two towns. No one even suggested using the sand cars again, though there wasn't a flicker of a threat from the dunes.

But we knew by experience how abruptly they could explode.

The decision was for Kelcy.

But the Martians took the decision out of our hands.

We trotted along for nearly an hour, on the move for twenty minutes, resting for five, and it began to look as if we'd make it to Kelcy without any more trouble—though, in truth, we had had trouble enough; because it would be enough of a job to try to get ourselves back to Niobe without the strong probability of carrying injured survivors from Kelcy. The remorseless noonday deadline would apply the next day; and travel on Mars by night was nearly out of the question. It is a thin-aired planet, so the sun beats down fiercely; it is a thin-aired planet, so the heat is gone minutes after sundown. I suppose all of us were thinking those thoughts, though we hadn't the breath to speak them, when the Martians struck again, this time with something new. There was a golden glow from a sand dune ahead of us to the right, and one from a dune ahead of us to the left. Keever, in the lead, hesitated for a second; but he didn't hesitate enough. He plunged on, and when he and two of the others were between the two dunes, golden lightning flashed. It was like the spray of a fiery hose, from one dune top to the other; and where it passed, three men lay dead.

It wasn't fire; there wasn't a mark on the bodies; but they were dead. We instinctively all of us blasted the tops of the glowing dunes with our flame rifles, but of course it was a little late for that. Demaree and I broke for the dune to the right, rifles at the ready. We scrambled up the sides and spread out halfway up to circle it—it was slagged from our own rifles at the top, and certainly nothing could be alive up there. But nothing was alive behind it, either—nothing we could see. The sands were empty.

Demaree swore lividly all the way back to where the bodies of the three men lay. Dr. Solveig, bending over them, said sharply, "That is enough, Demaree! Think what we must do!"

"But those filthy—"

"Demaree!" Solveig stood up straight and beckoned to the only other survivor—who had raced to explore the dune to the left, with the same results. He was a man named Garcia; he and I had come out together, but I didn't know him very well. "Have you seen anything?" Solveig demanded.

Garcia said bitterly, "More of that fire, Doc! From that hill I could see two or three others shining, down along the way to Kelcy."

"I had thought so," Solveig said somberly. "The Martians were of course aware of what we proposed. Kelcy is booby-trapped; we cannot expect to get there.

"So where does that leave us?" demanded Demaree. "We can't stay here! We can't even make it back to Niobe—we'll get caught in the sandstorm. Maybe you'd like that, Doc—but I saw a man after the sandstorm got him a year ago!" And so had I; a patrolman like ourselves, who incautiously found himself out in the middle of nowhere at dusk, when the twilight sandstorm rages from East to West and no human can live for an hour, until the gale passes and the tiny, lethal sand grains subside to the surface of the planet-wide desert again. His own respirators had killed him; the tiny whirl-pumps were clogged solid with sand grains packed against the filters, and he had died of suffocation.

Solveig said, "We go back. Believe me, it is the only way."

"Back where? It's twenty-five miles to—"

"To Niobe, yes. But we shall not go that far. I have two proposals. One, the sand cars; at least inside them you will not suffocate. Two—the Split Cliffs."

We all looked at him as though he had gone insane. But in the end he talked us around—all but Garcia, who clung obstinately to the cars.

We got back to the Split Cliffs, leaving Garcia huddled inside the first car with something of the feelings of the worshippers leaving Andromeda chained to the rock. Not that we were much better off—but at least there were three of us.

Solveig had pointed out, persuasively, that inside the growth of the Split Cliffs the sandstorm couldn't touch us; that there were caves and tunnels where the three of us, huddled together, might keep each other alive till morning. He admitted that the probability that we would find Martians there before us was high—but we *knew* the Martians had spotted the cars. And at least inside the junglelike Split Cliffs, they would be at as grave a disadvantage as we; unless they could overpower us by numbers, we should be able to fight them off if they discovered us. And even if they did outnumber us, we might be able to kill a few—and on the sand dunes, as we had discovered, they would strike and be gone.

Dr. Solveig, in the lead, hesitated and then slipped into the dense yellowish vegetation. Demaree looked at me, and we followed.

There were no trails inside, nothing but a mad tangle of twisty, feather-leaved vines. I heard dry vine-pods rattling ahead as Solveig spearheaded our group, and in a moment we saw him again.

The ground was covered with the fine red sand that overlies all of Mars, but it was only an inch or two deep. Beneath was raw rock, split and fissured with hairline cracks into which the water-seeking tendrils of the vegetation disappeared.

Demaree said softly, "Dr. Solveig. Up ahead there, by the little yellow bush. Doesn't that look like a path?"

It wasn't much, just a few branches bent back and a couple broken off; a certain amount of extra bare rock showing where feet might have scuffed the surface sand off.

"Perhaps so," said Solveig. "Let us look."

We bent under the long, sweeping branches of a smoke tree—too cool now to give off its misty yellow gases. We found ourselves looking down an almost straight lane, too straight to be natural.

"It is a path," said Dr. Solveig. "Ah, so. Let us investigate it."

I started to follow him, but Demaree's hand was on my shoulder, his other hand pointing. I looked, off to one side, and saw nothing but the tangle of growth.

Solveig turned inquiringly. Demaree frowned. "I thought I heard something."

"Oh," said Solveig, and unlimbered his flame rifle. All three of us stood frozen for a moment, listening and watching; but if there had been anything, it was quiet and invisible now.

Demaree said, "Let me go first, Doc. I'm a little younger than you." And faster on the draw, he meant. Solveig nodded.

"Of course." He stepped aside, and Demaree moved silently along the trail, looking into the underbrush from side to side. Solveig waited a moment, then followed; and a few yards behind I brought up the rear. I could just see Demaree's body flickering between the gnarled tree trunks and vines up ahead. He hesitated, then stepped over something, a vine or dead tree, that lay snaked across the path. He half-turned as if to gesture—

Snap!

The vine whipped up and twisted about his leg, clung and dragged him ten feet into the air, hanging head down, as a long straight tree beside the path snapped erect.

A deadfall—the oldest snare in the book!

"Jack!" I yelled, forgetting about being quiet—and half-forgetting, too, that I was on Mars. I leaped toward him, and blundered against the trees as my legs carried me farther than I thought. Solveig and I scrambled to him, rifles ready, staring around for a sight of whatever it was that had set the trap. But again—nothing.

Demaree wasn't hurt, just tangled and helpless. A flood of livid curses floated down from him as he got his wind back and began struggling against the vine loop around his legs. "Take it easy!" I called. "I'll get you down!" And while Solveig stood guard I scrambled up the tree and cut him loose. I tried to hold the vine but I slipped, and he plunged sprawling to the ground—still unhurt, but angry.

And the three of us stood there for a moment, waiting for the attack. And it didn't come.

For a moment the Martians had had us; while Demaree was in the tree and Solveig and I racing toward him, they could have cut us down. And they hadn't. They had set the trap—and passed up its fruits.

We looked at each other wonderingly.

We found a cave just off the trail, narrow and high, but the best protection in sight against the dusk sandstorm and the night's cold. The three of us huddled inside—and waited. Demaree suggested making a fire; but, although the wood on the ground was dry enough to burn even in Mars' thin air, we decided against it. Maybe, later on, if we couldn't stand the cold, we'd have no choice; but meanwhile there was no sense attracting attention.

We asked Solveig, who seemed to be in command of our party, if he thought there was any objection to talking, and he shrugged. "How can one tell? Perhaps they hear, perhaps they do not. Air is thin and sounds do not carry far—to our ears. To Martian ears? I don't know."

So we talked—not loud, and not much, because there wasn't, after all, much to say. We were preoccupied with the contradictions and puzzlements the Martians presented. Fantastic weapons that struck from nowhere or shimmered into being between sand dunes—and a culture little beyond the neolithic. Even Earth's best guided missiles could have been no more accurate and little more deadly, considering the nature of the target, than the one that obliterated car number two. And the golden glow that killed Keever was out of our experience altogether. And yet—villages of sticks! There had been no trace in any Martian dwelling of anything so complicated as a flame-rifle, much less these others. . . .

It grew very slightly darker, bit by bit; and then it was black. Even in our cave we could hear the screaming of the twilight wind. We were in a little slit in the raw rock, halfway down one of the crevasses that gave the Split Cliffs area its name. Craggy, tumbled, bare rocks a hundred feet below us, and the other wall of the crevasse barely jumping distance away. We had come to it along an irregular sloping ledge, and to reach us at all the wind had to pass through a series of natural baffles. And even so, we saw the scant shrubbery at the cave mouth whipped and scoured by the dusk-wind.

Demaree shivered and attempted to light a cigarette. On the fourth try he got it burning, but it went out almost at once—it is possible to smoke in Mars' air, but not easy, because of the pressure. The tobacco burns poorly, and tastes worse. He grunted, "Damn the stuff. You think we'll be all right here?"

"From the wind?" asked Solveig. "Oh, certainly. You have seen how little sand was carried in here. It is the cold that follows that I am thinking of. . . ."

We could feel the cold settling in the air, even while the twilight wind was blowing. In half an hour the wind was gone, but the cold remained, deeper and more intense than anything I had ever felt before. Our sand capes were a help, almost thermally non-conducting in either direction; we carefully tucked under all the vents designed to let perspiration escape, we folded them around us meticulously, we kept close together— and still the cold was almost unbearable. And it would grow steadily worse for hours. . . .

"We'll have to build a fire," said Solveig reluctantly. "Come and gather wood." The three of us went scouring up the ledge for what we could find. We had to go all the way back to the top of the crevasse to find enough to bother carrying; we brought it back, and while Demaree and I worked to set it afire Solveig went back for more. It wasn't easy, trying to make that thin and brittle stuff burn. Demaree's pocket lighter wore it-self out without success. Then he swore and motioned me back, leveling his flame rifle at the sticks. *That* worked beautifully—every last stick was ablaze in the wash of fire from his gun. But the blast scattered them over yards, half of them going over the side of the ledge; and we charred our fingers and wore ourselves out picking up the burning brands and hurling them back into the little hollow where we'd started the fire. We dumped the remaining armload on the little blaze, and watched it grow. It helped—helped very much. It was all radiant heat, and our backs were freezing while we toasted in front; but it helped. Then Demaree had an idea, and he slipped a cartridge out of his rifle and stripped it. The combustible material inside came in a little powder, safe enough to han-dle as long as no spark touched it. He tossed the detonator cap in the fire, where it ex-ploded with a tiny snap and puff of flame, and carefully measured out the powder from the cartridge in little mounds, only a few grams in each, wrapping each one in a twist of dried vine leaves.

"In case it goes out," he explained. "If there's any life in the embers at all, it'll set one of these off, and we won't have to blow up the whole bed of ashes to get it started again."

"Fine," I said. "Now we'd better build up a woodpile—"

We looked at each other, suddenly brought back to reality.

Astonishing how the mind can put aside what it does not wish to consider; amazing how we could have forgotten what we didn't want to know. Our woodpile reminded us both: Dr. Solveig had gone for more, nearly three quarters of an hour before.

And it was only a five-minute climb to the top of the crevasse.

The answer was obvious: The Martians. But, of course, we had to prove it for ourselves.

And prove it we did: At the expense of our weapons, our safe cave and fire, and very nearly our lives. We went plunging up the ledge like twin whirligigs, bouncing in the light Martian gravity and nearly tumbling into the chasm at every step. I suppose that if we thought at all, we were thinking that the more commotion we made the more likely we were to scare the Martians off before they killed Dr. Solveig. We were yelling and kicking stones into the gorge with a bounce and clatter; and we were up at the top of the crevasse in a matter of seconds, up at the top—and smack into a trap. For they were waiting for us up there, our first face-to-face Martians.

We could see them only as you might see ghosts in a sewer; the night was black, even the starlight half drowned by the branches overhead, but they seemed to gleam, phosphorescently, like decaying vegetation. And decay was a word that fitted the picture, for they looked like nothing so much as corpses. They had no hands or arms, but their faces were vaguely human—or so they seemed. What passed for ears were large and hung like a spaniel's; but there were eyes, sunken but bright, and there was a mouth; and they were human in size, human in the way they came threateningly toward us, carrying what must have been weapons.

Demaree's flame rifle flooded the woods with fire. He must have incinerated some of them, but the light was too blinding; we couldn't see. I fired close on the heels of Demaree's shot, and again the wood was swept with flame; and the two of us charged blindly into the dark. There was light now, from the blazes we had started, but the fires were Mars-fires, fitful and weak, and casting shadows that moved and disguised movement. We beat about the brush uselessly for a moment, then retreated and regrouped at the lip of the crevasse. And that was our mistake. "What about Solveig?" Demaree demanded. "Did you see anything—"

But he never got a chance to finish the sentence. On a higher cliff than ours there were scrabblings of motion, and boulders fell around us. We dodged back down the ledge, but we couldn't hope to get clear that way. Demaree bellowed:

"Come on, Will!" And he started up the ledge again; but the boulder shower doubled and redoubled. We had no choice. We trotted, gasping and frozen, back down to our cave, and ran in. And waited. It was not pleasant waiting; when the Martians showed up at the cave mouth, we were done. Because, you see, in our potshotting at the golden glow on the dunes and our starting a fire in the cave and salvoing the woods up above, we had been a little careless.

Our flame rifles were empty.

We kept warm and worried all of this night, and in the light from our dwindling fire, only a couple of branches at a time, we could see a figure across the crevasse from us.

It was doing something complex with objects we could not recognize. Demaree, over my objections, insisted we investigate; and so we parted with a hoarded brand. We threw the tiny piece of burning wood out across the crevasse, it struck over the figure in a shower of sparks and a pale blue flame, and in the momentary light we saw that it was, indeed, a Martian. But we still couldn't see what he was doing.

The dawn wind came, but the Martian stayed at his post; and then, at once, it was daylight.

We crept to the lip of the cave and looked out, not more than a dozen yards from the busy watching figure.

The Martian looked up once, staring whitely across the ravine at us, as a busy cobbler might glance up from his last. And just as unemotionally, the Martian returned to what he was doing. He had a curious complex construction of sticks and bits of stone, or so it seemed from our distance. He was carefully weaving bits of shiny matter into it in a regular pattern.

Demaree looked at me, licking his lips. "Are you thinking what I'm thinking, Will?" he asked.

I nodded. It was a weapon of some sort; it couldn't be anything else. Perhaps it was a projector for the lightnings that blasted the sand cars or the golden glow that had struck down at us from the sand dunes, perhaps some even more deadly Martian device. But whatever it was it was at point-blank range; and when he was finished with it, we were dead.

Demaree said thinly, "We've got to get out of here."

The only question was, did we have enough time? We scrabbled together our flame rifles and packs from the back of the cave and, eyes fearfully on the busy Martian across the chasm, leaped for the cave mouth—just in time to see what seemed a procession coming down the other side. It was a scrambling, scratching tornado, and we couldn't at first tell if it was a horde of Martians or a sand car with the treads flapping. But then we got a better look.

And it was neither. It was Dr. Solveig.

The Martian across the way saw him as soon as we, and it brought that strange complex of bits and pieces slowly around to bear on him. "Hey!" bellowed Demaree, and my yell was as loud as his. We had to warn Solveig of what he was running into—death and destruction.

But Solveig knew more than we. He came careening down the ledge across the crevasse, paused only long enough to glance at us and at the Martian, and then came on again.

"Rocks!" bellowed Demaree in my ear. "Throw them!" And the two of us searched feverishly in the debris for rocks to hurl at the Martian, to spoil his aim.

We needn't have bothered. We could find nothing more deadly than pebbles, but we didn't need even them. The Martian made a careful, last-minute adjustment on his gadget, and poked it once, squeezed it twice and pressed what was obviously its trigger.

And nothing happened. No spark, no flame, no shot. Solveig came casually down on the Martian, unharmed.

Demaree was astonished, and so was I; but the two of us together were hardly as astonished as the Martian. He flew at his gadget like a tailgunner clearing a breech jam over hostile interceptors. But that was as far as he got with it, because Solveig had reached him and in a methodical, almost a patronizing way he kicked the Martian's gadget to pieces and called over to us:

"Don't worry, boys. They won't hurt us here. Let's get back up on top."

It was a long walk back to Niobe, especially with the cumbersome gadgetry Solveig had found—a thing the size of a large machine gun, structurally like the bits and pieces the Martian had put together, but made of metal and crystal instead of bits of rubble.

But we made it, all four of us—we had picked up Garcia at the stalled cars, swearing lividly in relief but otherwise all right. Solveig wouldn't tell us much. He was right, of course. The important thing was to get back to Niobe as soon as we could with his gimmick. Because the gimmick was the Martian weapon that zeroed in on sand cars, and the sooner our mechanics got it taken apart, the sooner we would know how to defend ourselves against it. We were breathless on the long run home, but we were exultant. And we had reason to be, because there was no doubt in any of our minds that a week after we turned the weapon over to the researchers we would be able to run sand cars safely across the Martian plains. (Actually it wasn't a week; it was less. The aiming mechanism was nothing so complex as radio, it was a self-aiming thermocouple, homing on high temperatures. We licked it by shielding the engines and trailing smoke-pots to draw fire.)

Overconfident? No—any Earthman, of course, could have worked out a variation which would have made the weapon useful again in an hour's leisurely thought. But Earthmen are flexible. And the Martians were not. Because the Martians were not—the Martians.

That is, they were not *the* Martians.

"Successors," Solveig explained to all of us, back in Niobe. "Heirs, if you like. But not the inventors. Compared with whoever built those machines, the Martians we've been up against are nothing but animals—or children. Like children, they can pull a trigger or strike a match. But they can't design a gun—or even build one by copying another."

Keever shook his long, lean head. "And the original Martians?"

Solveig said, "That's a separate question. Perhaps they're hiding out somewhere we haven't reached—underground or at the poles. But they're master builders, whoever and wherever they are." He made a wry face. "There I was," he said, "hiding out in a cleft in the rock when the dawn wind came. I thought I'd dodged the Martians, but they knew I was there. As soon as the sun came up I saw them dragging that thing toward me." He jerked a thumb at the weapon, already being checked over by our maintenance crews. "I thought that was the end, especially when they pulled the trigger."

"And it didn't go off," said Demaree.

"It *couldn't* go off! I wasn't a machine. So I took it away from them—they aren't any stronger than kittens—and I went back to look for you two. And there was that Martian waiting for *you*. I guess he didn't have a real gun, so he was making one—like a kid'll make a cowboy pistol out of two sticks and a nail. Of course, it won't shoot. Neither did the Martians, as you will note."

We all sat back and relaxed. "Well," said Keever, "that's our task for this week. I guess you've shown us how to clean up what the Earthside papers call the Martian Menace, Doc. Provided, of course, that we don't run across any of the grownup Martians, or the real Martians, or whatever it was that designed those things."

Solveig grinned. "They're either dead or hiding, Keever," he said. "I wouldn't worry about them."

And unfortunately, he didn't worry about them, and neither did any of the rest of us.

Not for nearly five years. . . .

I REMEMBER A WINTER

This is a story about causality; read it and you'll understand. It's also about war and friendship and the choices we make. Altogether, it's a short but powerful, poignant story about life. First published in 1972, it spans decades in mere pages.
 Science fiction? You decide.

I remember a winter when the cold snapped and stung, and it would not snow. It was a very long time ago, and in the afternoons Paulie O'Shaughnessy would come by for me after school and we'd tell each other what we were going to do with our lives. I remember standing with Paulie on the corner, with my breath white and my teeth aching from the cold air, talking. It was too cold to go to the park and we didn't have any money to go anywhere else. We thumbed through the magazines in the secondhand bookstore until the lady threw us out. "Let's hitch downtown," said Paulie; but I could feel how cold the wind would be on the back of the trolley cars and I wouldn't. "Let's sneak in the Carlton," I said, but Paulie had been caught sneaking in to see the Marx Brothers the week before and the usher knew his face. We ducked into the indoor miniature golf course for a while; it had been an automobile showroom the year before and still smelled of gas. But we were the only people there, and conspicuous, and when the man who rented out the clubs started toward us we left.

So we Boy Scout-trotted down Flatbush Avenue to the big old library, walk fifty, trot fifty, the cold air slicing into the insides of our faces, past the apple sellers and the wine-brick stores, gasping and grunting at each other, and do you know what? Paulie picked a book off those dusty old shelves. We didn't have cards, but he liked it too much to leave it unfinished. He walked out with it under his coat; and fifteen years later, shriveled and shrunken and terrified of the priest coming toward his bed, he died of what he read that day. It's true. I saw it happen. And the damn book was only *Beau Geste*.

I remember the summer that followed. I still didn't have any money but I had found girls. That was the summer when Franklin Roosevelt flew to Chicago in an airplane to accept his party's nomination to the presidency, and it was hotter than you would believe. Standing on the corner, the sparks from the trolley wheels were almost invisible in the bright sun. We hitched to the beach when we could, and Paulie's pale, Jewish-looking face got red and then freckled. He hated that; he wanted to be burned black in the desert sun, or maybe clear-skinned and cleft-chinned with the mark of a helmet strap on his jaw.

But I didn't see much of Paulie that summer. He had finished all the Wren books by then and was moving on to *Daredevil Aces;* he'd wheedled a World War French bayonet out of his uncle and had taken a job delivering suits for a tailor shop, saving his money to buy a .22. I saw much more of his sister. She was fifteen then, which was a year older than Paulie and I were. In his British soldier-of-fortune role-playing he cast her as much younger. "Sport," he said to me, eyes a little narrowed, half-smile on his lips, "do what you like. But not with Kitty."

As a matter of fact, in the end I did do pretty much as I liked with Kitty, but we had each married somebody else before that and it was a long way from 1932. But even in 1932 I tried. On a July evening I finally got her to go up on the roof with me; it was no good; somebody else was there ahead of us, and Kitty wouldn't stay with them there. "Let's sit on the stoop," she said. But that was right out in the street, with all the kids playing king-of-the-hill on a pile of sand.

So I took her by the elbow, and I walked her down the Avenue, talking about Life and Courage and War. She had heard the whole thing before, of course, as much as she would listen to, but from Paulie, not from me. She listened. It was ritual courtship, as formal as a dog lifting his leg. It did not seem to me that it mattered what I said, as long as what I said was masculine.

You can't know how masculine I wanted to be for Kitty. She was without question the prettiest doll around. She looked like—well, like Ginger Rogers, if you remember, with a clean, friendly face and the neatest, slimmest hips. She knew that. She was studying dancing. She was also studying men, and God knows what she thought she was learning from me.

When we got to Dean Street I changed from authority on war to authority on science and told her that the heat was only at ground level. Just a little way above our heads, I told her, the air was always cool and fresh. "Let's go up on the fire escape," I said, nudging her toward the Atlantic Theatre.

The Atlantic was locked up tight that year; Paulie and I were not the only kids who didn't have movie money. But the fire escapes were open, three flights of strap-iron stairs going up to what we called nigger heaven. I don't know why, exactly. The colored kids from the neighborhood didn't sit up there, in fact. I never saw them in the movies at all. The fire escapes made a good place to go. Paulie and I went up there a lot, when he wasn't working, to look down on everybody in the street and not have anyone know we were watching them. So Kitty and I went up to the second landing and sat on the steps, and in a minute I put my arm around her.

And all of this, you know, I'd thought out like two or three months in advance, going up there by myself and experimentally bouncing my tail up and down on the steps to test for discomfort, calculating in a wet morning in May what it would be like right after dark in August, and all. It was a triumph of fourteen-year-old forethought. Or it would have been if it had come to anything. But somebody coughed, higher up on the fire escape.

Kitty jabbed me with her elbow, and we listened. Somebody was mumbling softly up above us. I don't know if he had heard us coming. I don't think so. I stood up and peered around the landing, and I saw candlelight, and an old man's face, terribly lined and unshaven and sad. He was living there. All around the top landing he had carefully put up sheets of cardboard from grocery cartons, I suppose to keep the rain out. If it rained. Or perhaps just to keep him out of public view. He was sitting on a blanket, leaning his forearm on one knee, looking at the candle, talking to himself.

And that was the end of that. We tiptoed down the stairs, and Kitty said she had to go home. And did. Otherwise, I honestly think that in the long run I would have married her.

I remember the years of the war, the headlines and the blackouts and the crazy way everything was changing under my very eyes. Paulie had it made. He enlisted first thing, and wrote me clipped, concise letters about the joys of close-order drill. I remember buying his old car the last time he came home on furlough, with his cuffs tucked in his paratrooper boots, telling deadpan stories about the hazards of basic training. The car was a 1931 Buick, with a jug cork in the gas tank instead of a cap. I sold it for the price of two train tickets when I ran out of gas-ration coupons in Pittsburgh, on my honeymoon. Not with Kitty. Kitty had gone far out of my life by then. Her dancing lessons had paid off: amateur-night tap dancer to *Film Fun* model to showgirl at the International Casino; and then she'd gone abroad to Paris with a troupe and been caught in the Occupation. Well. *Mutatis mutandis* and *plus ça change* and so on. Or, as one might say, things keep getting all screwed up.

I breezed through the war. Barring a company clerk in Jefferson Barracks who I really wanted to kill, there was nothing I couldn't handle; Paulie had lied. Or maybe for me it was a different war. I had got into newspaper work, which let me get into Special Services when my time came. Nobody was shooting at unit managers for USO shows. I went through forty-one months of exaltation and shame. You see, this was the war that really mattered and had to be won; and how I burned, with what a blue-white flame, with pride to be a part of it. And how I groveled before anyone who would listen because my part was mostly chasing enlisted men away from big-breasted starlets. Do you suppose it's really true that somebody had to do that job, too? I couldn't believe it, but it was because of that that I met Kitty again.

She turned up looking for a job as a translator, looking very much as she always had. She was different, though. She was married, to this very nice captain she had met during Occupation days in Paris, and she had become a German national. It was a grand reunion. I took her to dinner and she told me that Paulie had been wounded in the Salerno landing and was still in the hospital. And a little bit later she told me about her husband, the darling, dimpled SS officer, who was now a POW on the Eastern front. And for four months in Wiesbaden she lived in my billet with me, translating day and night; and, actually, that's what happened to that first marriage of mine, because my wife found out about it. I don't think she would have minded a *Fräulein*. She minded my shacking up with a girl I'd known before I knew her.

I remember more consequential causes than I can count. When I look inside my skin I don't see anything but consequences; all I am is the casual aftereffects of, item, an unemployed carpenter evicted from his home and, item, a classification clerk who had been in the newspaper game himself once, and all the other itemized seeds that have now blossomed into fifty-two-year-old me.

I remember more than I absolutely want to, in fact, and some things I remember in the context of a certain time and a certain place when, in fact, I really learned them later on.

The man on the landing. Years after the war, when I had become a TV producer doing a documentary on the Depression, I put one of my research girls on checking him out. She was a good girl, and tracked him down. That's how I know he had been a carpenter. The banks closed and the jobs vanished, and he wound up on the fire escape. It happened that when the police chased him away a reporter was in the precinct house, and he wrote the story my girl found.

And I remember Paulie, twenty-nine years old and weighing a fast ninety pounds, gasping hoarsely as he reached out to shake my hand in the VA hospital ward, the day before he died. He had been there for three years, dying all that time. He looked like his own grandfather. That was a consequence, too: a landing in the second wave at Salerno and a mine the engineers had missed. He got his Purple Heart for a broken spine that kept getting worse until it was so bad that it killed him.

I think I've seen the place where he got it—assuming that I remembered what he said well enough, or understood him well enough, when he was concentrating mostly on dying. I think the place it happened was on the city beach at Salerno, way at the north horn of that crescent, about where there's a little restaurant built out over the water on stilts. I stood there one afternoon on that beach, looking at the floating turds and pizza crusts, trying to see the picture of Paulie hitting the mine and being thrown into the sky in a fountain of saltwater and blood. But it wasn't any good. I can only see what I've seen, not what I've been told about. I couldn't see the causality. All I could do was ask myself questions about it: What made him sign up for his hero suit? Was it really reading that Percival Christopher Wren book when he was thirteen years old? Or: What made me alive, and sort of rich, when Paulie was so poor and dead? Was it the four or five really good contacts I made in the USO that turned me into a genius television producer? Is there any of me, or of any of us, that isn't just consequence?

I think, and I've thought it over a lot, that everything that ever happened keeps on happening, extending tendrils of itself endlessly into the moving present tense of time, producing its echoes, and explosions and extinctions forever. Just being careful isn't enough to save us, but we do have to be careful. Smoky Bear wouldn't lie to you about that.

If I'd married Kitty I think we would have had fine kids, even grandchildren by now; but I didn't, not even batting .500 out of my two chances at her. First it was the old man on the fire escape, then it was the kindly Nazi she decided to go back to waiting for. She waited very well and for a long time, all through the years while the Russians were taking their time about letting him go and all through the de-Nazification trials after that. I suppose by then she felt she was too old to want to start a family. And none of my own wives have really wanted the PTA bit.

And think of the consequences of that—I mean, the negative consequences of the babies that Kitty and I didn't have. Did we miss out on a new Mozart? A Lee Harvey Oswald? Maybe just a hell of a solid Brooklyn fireman who might have saved a more largely consequential life than his own, or mine? Think of them. And that's all you can do with those particular consequences, because they didn't get born.

Percival Christopher Wren didn't mean to kill Paulie. The sad old derelict on the fire escape never intended to break up Kitty and me. Intentions don't matter.

We all live in each others' pockets. If I drive my car along Mulholland Drive tonight, I only mean to keep my date with that pretty publicity girl from Paramount. I don't even know you're alive, do I? But the car is burning up the gasoline and pumping out the poison gas that makes the smog; and maybe it's just that little bit of extra exhaust fume in the air that bubbles your lungs out with emphysema. It doesn't matter to you what I mean to do. You're just as dead. I don't suppose I ever in my life really meant to hurt anybody, except possibly that J.B. company clerk. But he got off without a scratch, and meanwhile I may be killing you.

So I walk out on my balcony and stare through the haze at the lights of Los Angeles. I look at where they all live, the black militants and the aerospace engineers, the Desilu sound men and the storefront soul-savers, the kids who go to the Académie Française and the little old ladies with "Back Up Our Boys" bumper stickers on their cars. I remember what they, and you, and each and every one of you have done to me, this half a century I've been battered and bribed into my present shape and status; but what are they, and all of you, doing to each other this night?

THE GREENING OF BED-STUY

Frederik Pohl was born in Brooklyn, New York, and though he's lived in other places—New Jersey and Illinois, to name two—and traveled widely on other continents, he'll always be a New York City boy. If there was any doubt of that, it was put to rest when he published *The Years of the City,* a book of linked stories about New York in the future. This novella was a part of that book.

Anyone who has lived in a really big city and understood the complexities of relationships—economic, political, social—that combine to create the character of a city will relish "The Greening of Bed-Stuy," which was a Nebula Award finalist when first published in 1984. You don't have to have lived in New York to enjoy this complex, powerful story. Like Charles Dickens did with British society in mid-nineteenth-century London, Pohl, in "Bed-Stuy," unfolds his tale through characters who range from the wealthy and powerful to those with only limited means and ambitions.

Power, greed, vanity, hatred, love . . . they transcend class and social status. In a city like New York, the only constant is people. The people of "The Greening of Bed-Stuy"—the good and the bad—come to life memorably in this masterful piece.

1

Marcus Garvey de Harcourt's last class of the day was H.E., meaning "Health Education," meaning climbing up ropes in the smelly, bare gymnasium of P.S. 388. It was a matter of honor with him to avoid that when he could. Today he could. He had a note from his father that would get him out of school, and besides it was a raid day. The police were in the school. It was a drug bust, or possibly a weapons search; or maybe some fragile old American History teacher had passed the terror point at the uproar in his class and called for help. Whatever. The police were in the school, and the door monitors were knotted at the stairwells, listening to the sounds of scuffling upstairs. It was a break he didn't really need, because at the best of times the door monitors at P.S. 388 were instructed not to try too hard to keep the students in—else they simply wouldn't show up at all.

Once across the street Marcus ducked behind the tall mound of garbage bags to see which of his schoolmates—or teachers!—would come out in handcuffs, but that was a disappointment because the cops came out alone. This time, at least, the cops had found nothing worth an arrest—meaning, no doubt, that the problem was over and the teacher involved wouldn't, or didn't dare to, identify the culprits.

One-forty, and his father had ordered him to be ready to leave for the prison by two o'clock. No problem. He threaded his way past the CONSTRUCTION—ALL TRAFFIC DE-TOUR signs on Nostrand Avenue, climbed one of the great soil heaps, gazed longingly at the rows of earth-moving machines, silenced by some sort of work stoppage, and rummaged in the dirt for something to throw at them. There was plenty. There were pieces of bulldozed homes in that tip, Art Deco storefronts from the 1920s, bay-window frames from the 1900s, sweat-equity cinderblocks from the 1980s, all crushed together. Marcus found a china doorknob, just right. When it struck the nearest parked backhoe it splintered with a crash.

They said Bedford-Stuyvesant was a jungle, and maybe it was. It was the jungle that young Marcus de Harcourt had lived all his life in. He didn't fear it—was wary of parts of it, sure, but it was all familiar. And it was filled with interesting creatures, mostly known to Marcus, Marcus known to a few of them—like the young men in clerical collars outside the Franciscan mission. They waved to him from across the road. Bloody Bess at the corner didn't wave. As he passed her she was having a perfectly reasonable, if agitated, conversation: "She having an *abor*tion. She having an in*flatable* abortion. He having intercourse with her ten *times*, so she having it." The only odd part was that she was talking to a fire hydrant. The bearded man in a doorway, head pillowed on a sack of garbage, didn't wave either, but that was because he was asleep. Marcus considered stealing his shoes and hiding them, but you never knew about these doorway dudes. Sometimes they were cops. Besides, when he looked closer at the shoes he didn't want to touch them.

One forty-five by the clock on the top of the Williamsburgh Bank Building, and time to move along. He trotted and swaggered along the open cut of the Long Island Rail Road yards. Down below were the concrete railguides with their silent, silver seams of metal. Marcus kicked hubcaps until he found a loose one. He pried it off, one eye open for cops, and then scaled it down onto the tracks. Its momentum carried it down to crash against the concrete guide strip, but the magnetic levitation had it already. It was beginning to move sidewise before it struck. It picked up speed, wobbling up and down in the field, showering sparks as it struck against the rail, until the maglev steadied it. It was out of sight into the Atlantic Avenue tunnel in a moment and Marcus, pleased, looked up again at the bank clock. One fifty-five; he was already late, but not late enough for a taste of the cat if he hurried. So he hurried.

Marcus Garvey de Harcourt's neighborhood did not look bleak to him. It looked like the place where he had always lived, although of course all the big construction machines were new. Marcus understood that the project was going to change the neighborhood drastically—they said for the better. He had seen the model of the way Bedford-Stuyvesant was going to look, had listened to politicians brag about it on television, had been told about it over and over in school. It would be really nice, he accepted, but it wasn't nice yet. Between the burned-out tenements and the vacant lots of the year before and the current bare excavations and half-finished structures there was not much to choose, except that now the rats had been disturbed in their dwellings and were more often seen creeping across the sidewalks and digging into the trash heaps. Marcus ran the last six blocks to his father's candy store, past the big breeder powerplant that fed a quarter of Brooklyn with electricity, cutting across the scarred open spaces, ducking through the barbed wire and trotting between the rows of tall towers that one day would be windmills. He paused at the corner to survey the situation. The big black car wasn't there, which was good. His mother wasn't waiting for him outside the store, either; but as he reached the door, panting a little harder than necessary to show how fast he'd been running, she opened it for him. His father was there, too, with his coat on already. He didn't speak, but looked up at the clock behind the soda fountain. "Damn, Marcus," his mother said crossly, "you know your daddy don't like to be kept waiting, what's the matter with you?"

"Wouldn't let me out no sooner, Nillie."

His father glanced at him, then at the storeroom door. Behind it, Marcus knew, the cat-o'-nine-tails was hanging. Marcus's mother said, "You want trouble, Marcus, you know damn well he's gone give it to you."

"No trouble, Nillie. Couldn't help it, could I?" There wasn't any sense in arguing the question, because the old man either would get the cat out or wouldn't. Most likely he wouldn't, because this thing at the prison was important to him and he wouldn't want to waste any more time, but either way it was out of Marcus's hands.

The old man jerked his head at Marcus and limped out of the store. He didn't speak. He never did talk much, because it hurt him to try. At the curb he lifted an imperious hand. A cruising gypsy cab pulled up, surprising Marcus. His father did not walk very well on the kneecaps that had once been methodically crushed, but the place they were going was only about a dozen blocks away. You had to sell a lot of Sunday newspapers to make the price of a cab fare. Marcus didn't comment. He spoke to his father almost as seldom as his father spoke to him. He hopped in, scrunched himself against the opposite side of the seat, and gazed out of the window as his father ordered, "Nathanael Greene Institute, fast."

Because the Nathanael Greene Institute for Men was built underground, the approach to it looked like the entrance to a park. Nathanael Greene wasn't a park. It had forty-eight hundred residents and a staff of fifty-three hundred to attend them. Each resident had a nearly private room with a television set, toilet facilities and air-conditioning, and its construction cost, more than eighty-five thousand dollars per room, slightly exceeded the cost of building a first-class hotel. Nathanael Greene was not a hotel, either, and most of its luxuries were also utilitarian: the air-conditioning ducts were partly so that tear gas or sternutants could be administered to any part of the structure; the limit of two persons per cell was to prevent rioting. Nathanael Greene was a place to work, with a production line of microelectronic components; a place to learn, with optional classes in everything from remedial English to table tennis; a place to improve oneself, with non-optional programs designed to correct even the most severe character flaws. Such as murder, robbery and rape. Nathanael Greene had very little turnover among its occupants. The average resident remained there eleven years, eight months and some days. If he left earlier, he usually found himself in a far less attractive place—an Alaskan stockade, for example, or a gas chamber. Nathanael Greene was not a place where just anyone could go. You had to earn it, with at least four felonies of average grade, or one or two really good ones, murder two and up. Major General Nathanael Greene of Potowomut, Rhode Island, the Quaker commander whose only experience of penology had been to preside over the court-martial of John André, might not have approved the use of his name for New York City's most maximal of maximum-security prisons. But as he had been dead for more than two centuries his opinion was not registered.

Of course there was a line of prison visitors, nearly a hundred people waiting to reach the kiosk that looked like a movie theater's box office. Most were poorly dressed, more than half black, all of them surly at being kept waiting. Marcus's father nudged him toward the big Bed-Stuy model as he limped to take his place in the queue. The boy did what was expected of him. He skipped over to study the model. It was a huger, more detailed copy of the one in the public library. Marcus tried to locate the place where his father's candy store was, but would not be any longer once the project was completed. He circled it carefully, according to orders, but when he had done that he had run out of orders and his father was still far down the waiting line.

Marcus took a chance and let himself drift along the graveled path, farther and farther away from the line of visitors. What the top of Nathanael Greene looked like was a rather eccentric farm; you had no feeling, strolling between the railings that fenced off soybeans on one side and tomato vines on the other, that you were walking over the heads of ten thousand convicts and guards. It looked as much like Marcus's concept of the South African plains as anything else, and he imagined himself a black warrior infiltrating from one of the black republics toward Cape Town—except that the concrete igloos really were machine-gun posts, not termite nests, and the guard who yelled at him to go back carried a real rifle. A group of convicts, he saw, was busy hand-setting pine-tree seedlings into plowed rows. Christmas trees for sale in a year or two, probably. They would not be allowed to grow very tall, because nothing on this parklike roof of the prison was allowed to grow high enough to interfere with the guards' field of fire. A squint at the bank clock told him that if he didn't get inside the prison pretty soon he was going to be late for his after-hours job with old Mr. Feigerman and his whee-clickety-beep machinery; a glance at his father told him it was time to hurry back into line.

But his father hadn't noticed. His father was staring straight ahead, and when they moved up a few steps his limp was very bad. Marcus felt a warning stab of worry, and turned just in time to see a long, black car disappearing around the corner and out of sight.

There were a lot of long, black cars in the world, but not very many that could make his father limp more painfully. For Marcus there was no doubt that the car was the one that the scar-faced man used, the one who came around to the candy store now and then to make sure the numbers and the handbook that kept them eating were being attended to; the one who always gave him candy, and always made his father's limp worse and his gravelly voice harder to understand; and it was not good news at all for Marcus to know that this man had interested himself in Marcus's visit to the prison.

When they got to the head of the line the woman gave them an argument. She wore old-fashioned tinted glasses, concealing her eyes. Her voice was shrill, and made worse by the speaker system that let them talk through the bulletproof glass. "You any relative of the inmate?" she demanded, the glasses disagreeably aimed toward Marcus's father.

"No, ma'am." The voice was hoarse and gravelly, but understandable—Nillie had told the boy that his father was lucky to be able to talk at all, after what they did to his throat. "Not *relative*, exactly. But kind of family," he explained, his expression apologetic, his tone deferential, " 'cause little Marcus here's his kid, and my wife's sister's his mother. But no, ma'am, no *blood* relation."

"Then you can't see him," she said positively, glasses flashing. "The only visitors permitted are immediate family, no exceptions."

Marcus's father was very good at wheedling, and very good at knowing when other tactics were better. "See him?" he cried in his gravelly voice, expression outraged. "What would I want to see the son of a bitch for? Why, he ruined my wife's sister's life! But the man's got a right to see his own kid, don't he?"

The woman pursed her lips, and the glasses shone first on Marcus's father, then on the boy. "You'll have to get permission from the chief duty officer," she declared. "Window Eight."

The chief duty officer was young, black, bald and male, and he opened the door of his tiny cubicle and allowed them in, studying Marcus carefully. "Who is it you want to see here, Marc?"

"My father," the boy said promptly, according to script. "I ain't seen him since I was little. Name's Marcus, not Marc," he added.

"Marcus, then." The officer touched buttons on his console, and the file photograph of Inmate Booking Number 838-10647 sprang up. HARVEY John T., sentenced to three consecutive terms of twelve to twenty years each for murder one, all three homicides committed during the commission of a major felony—in this case, the robbery of a liquor store. There was not much resemblance between the inmate and the boy. The inmate was stout, middle-aged, bearded—and white. The boy was none of those things. Still, his skin color was light enough to permit one white parent. "This your daddy, Marcus?"

"Yes, sir, that's him," said Marcus, peering at the stranger on the screen.

"Do you know what he's here for?"

"Yes, sir. He here because he broke the law. But he still my daddy."

"That's right, Marcus," sighed the duty officer, and stamped the pass. He handed it to Marcus's father. "This is for the boy, not you. You can escort the boy as far as the visiting section, but you can't go in. You'll be able to see through the windows, though," he added, but did not add that so would everybody else, most especially the guards.

The pass let them into the elevator, and the elevator took them down and down, eight floors below the surface of the ground, with an obligatory stop at the fourth level while an armed guard checked the passes again. Nathanael Greene Institute did not call itself escape-proof, because there is no such thing; but it had designed in a great many safeguards to make escape unlikely. Every prisoner wore a magnetically coded ankle band, so his location was known to the central computers at every minute of the day; visitors like Marcus and his father were given, and obliged to wear, badges with a quite different magnetic imprint; the visiting area was nowhere near the doors to the outside world, and in fact even the elevators that served it were isolated from the main body of the prison. And as Marcus left his father in a sealed waiting room, two guards surrounded him and led him away to a private room. A rather friendly, but thorough, matron helped undress him and went through everything he possessed, looking for a message, an illicit gift, anything. Then he was conducted to the bare room with the wooden chairs and the steel screen dividing them.

Marcus had been well rehearsed in what to say and do, and he had no trouble picking out Inmate 838-10647 from his photograph. "Hello, da," he said, with just enough quaver in his voice to be plausible for the watching guards.

"Hello, Marcus," said his putative father, leaning toward the steel screen as a father might on seeing his long-lost son. The lines for the interview had also been well rehearsed, and Marcus was prepared to be asked how his mother was, how he was doing in

school, whether he had a job to help his ma out. None of that was any trouble to respond to, and Marcus was able to study this heavyset, stern-looking white man who was
playing the part of his father as he told him about Nillie's arthritis and her part-time job
as companion to old Mr. Feigerman's dying wife; about how well he had done on the
test on William Shakespeare's *Julius Caesar* and his B+ grade in history; about his own
job that his ma had got him with Mr. Feigerman himself, the blind man with the funny
machinery that let him see, sort of, and even work as a consulting engineer on the Bed-
Stuy project . . . all the same he was glad when it was over, and he could get out of that
place. Toward the end he got to thinking about the eighty feet of rock and steel and convicts and guards over his head, and it had seemed to be closing in on him. The guards at
Nathanael Greene had an average of ten years on the job, and they had had experience
before of kids running errands that adults could not do, so they searched him again on
the way out. Marcus submitted peacefully. They didn't find anything, of course, because there hadn't been anything to find. On that visit.

2

Marcus's after-school job was waiting impatiently for him. The name of the job was de
Rintelen Feigerman, and he was a very old man as well as quite a strange-looking one.
Mr. Feigerman was in a wheelchair. This was not so much because his legs were worn
out—they were not, quite—as because of the amount of machinery he had to carry
with him. He wore a spangled sweatband around his thin, long hair, supporting a lacy
metallic structure. His eyes were closed. Closed permanently. There were no eyeballs in
the sockets anymore, just plastic marbles that kept them from looking sunken, and behind where the eyeballs had been there was a surgical wasteland where his entire visual
system had been cut out and thrown away. The operation saved his life when it was
done, but it removed Feigerman permanently from the class of people who could ever
hope to see again. Transplants worked for some. The only transplant that could change
things for Feigerman was a whole new head.

And yet, as Marcus came up the hill, the white old head turned toward him and
Feigerman called him by name. "You're late, Marcus," he complained in his shrill old-
man's voice.

"I'm sorry, Mr. Feigerman. They made me stay after school."

"Who's that 'they' you keep talking about, Marcus? Never mind. I was thinking of
some falafel. What do you say to that?"

Actually Marcus had been thinking of a Big Mac for himself, but that would mean
making two stops, in different directions. "Falafel sounds good enough to me, Mr.
Feigerman," he said, and took the bills the old man expertly shuffled out of his wallet,
the singles unfolded, the fives creased at one corner for identification, the tens at two.
"I'll tell Julius I'm here," he promised, and started down the long hill toward the limousine that waited on Myrtle Avenue.

The old man touched the buttons that swung his chair around. He could not really
see down the hill, toward where the project was being born. The machinery that replaced his eyes was not too bad at short range, but beyond the edge of the paved area
atop Fort Greene Park it was of no use at all. But he didn't need eyes to know what was
going on—to know that not much was. Half the project was silent. By turning up his

hearing aid and switching to the parabolic microphone he could hear the distant scream of the turbines at the breeder reactor and the chomp and roar of the power shovels where excavation was still happening, underlain with the fainter sounds of intervening traffic. But the bulldozers weren't moving. Their crews were spending the week at home, waiting to be told when payroll money would be available again. Bad. Worse than it seemed, because if they didn't get the word soon the best of them would be drifting off to other jobs where the funds were already in the bank, not waiting for a bunch of politicians to get their shit together and pass the bill—if, indeed, the politicians were going to. That was the worst part of all; because Feigerman admitted to himself that that part was not sure at all. It was a nice, sunny day in Fort Greene Park, but there were too many worries in it for it to be enjoyed—including the one special troubling thing, in a quite different area, that Feigerman was trying not to think about.

While they ate their late lunch, or early dinner, or whatever the meal was that they had formed the habit of sharing after Marcus's school got out, the boy did his job. "They've got one wall of the pumphouse poured," he reported, squinting out over the distant, scarred landscape that had once been a normal, scarred Brooklyn neighborhood. Silently the old man handed him the field glasses and Marcus confirmed what he had said. "Yeah, the pumphouse is coming along, and—and—they're digging for the shit pit, all right. But no bulldozers. Just sitting there, Mr. Feigerman; I guess they didn't turn loose your money yet. I don't see why they want to do that, anyway."

"Do what?"

"Make another hill there. They got this one right here already."

"This one's the wrong shape," Feigerman said, not impatiently—he liked the boy, welcomed his questions, wished he had had a real son of his own sometimes—since the semi-real stepson he had had no detectable love for his adopted father. "Besides, this one is historic, so they don't want to build windmills on top of it. George Washington held the British off right here—read the inscription on the monument sometime." He licked some of the falafel juice off his lip and Marcus, unbidden, unfolded a paper napkin and dabbed the missed spatters off the old man's bristly chin. Feigerman clicked in his long-range optical scanners in place of the sonar and gazed out over the city, but of course he could see only vague shapes without detail. "It's a big thing," he said—as much to the unheeding city as to Marcus.

"I know it is, Mr. Feigerman. Gonna make things real nice for Bed-Stuy."

"I hope so." But it was more than a hope. In Feigerman's mind it was certain: the energy-sufficient, self-contained urban area that he had lobbied for for more than twenty years. It was wonderful that it was going in in Brooklyn, so close to his home. Of course, that was just luck—and a few influential friends. The project could have been built anywhere—which is to say, in any thoroughly blighted urban neighborhood, where landlords were walking away from their tenements. And those were the good landlords; the bad ones were torching their buildings for the insurance. South Bronx wanted it. So did three neighborhoods in Chicago, three in Detroit, almost all of Newark, half of Philadelphia—yes, it could have been almost anywhere. Brooklyn won the prize for two reasons. One was the clout of the influential political friends. The other was its soft alluvial soil. What Brooklyn was made of, basically, was the rubble the glaciers had pushed ahead of them in the last Ice Age, filled in with silt from the rivers. It cut like cheese.

When Bed-Stuy was done it would not have to import one kilowatt-hour of energy from anywhere else—not from Ontario Hydro, not from Appalachia, not from the chancy and riot-torn oil fields of the Arab states. Not from anywhere. Winter heating would come from the thermal aquifer storage, in the natural brine reservoirs under the city, nine hundred feet down. Summer cooling would help to warm the aquifers up again, topped off with extra chill from the ice-ponds. By using ice and water to store heat and cold the summer air-conditioning and winter heating peaks wouldn't happen, which meant that maximum capacity could be less. Low enough to be well within the design parameters of the windmills, the methane generators from the shit pit and all the other renewable-resource sources; and the ghetto would bloom. Bedford-Stuyvesant was a demonstration project. If it worked there would be more, all over the country, and Watts and Libertyville and the Ironbound and the Northside would get their chances— and it would work!

But it was not, of course, likely that de Rintelen Feigerman would be around to see those second-generation heavens.

Reminded of mortality, Feigerman raised his wrist to his ear and his watch beeped the time. "I have to get going now," he said. "My wife's going to die this evening."

"She made up her mind to do it, Mr. Feigerman?"

"It looks that way. I'm sorry about that; I guess your mother will be out of a job. Has she got any plans, outside of helping out in the store?"

"Friend of my daddy's, he says he can get her work as a bag lady."

Feigerman sighed; but it was not, after all, his problem. "Take us on down the hill, Marcus," he said. "The car ought to be back by now."

"All right, Mr. Feigerman." Marcus disengaged the electric motor and turned the wheelchair toward the steep path. "Seems funny, though."

"What seems funny, Marcus?"

"Picking the time you're going to die."

"I suppose it is," Feigerman said thoughtfully, listening to the chatter of teenagers on a park bench and the distant grumble of traffic. Marcus was a careful wheelchair handler, but Feigerman kept his hand near the brake anyway. "The time to die," he said, "is the day when you've put off root-canal work as long as possible, and you're running out of clean clothes, and you're beginning to need a haircut." And he was getting close enough to that time, he thought, as he heard his driver, Julius, call a greeting.

There was a confusion at Mercy General Hospital, because they seemed to have misplaced his wife. Feigerman waited in his wheelchair, watching the orderlies steer the gurneys from room to room, the nurses punching in data and queries to their monitors as they walked the halls, the paramedics making their rounds with pharmaceuticals and enema tubes, while Marcus raced off to find out what had happened. He came back, puffing. "They moved her," he reported. "Fifth floor. Room 583."

Jocelyn Feigerman had been taken out of the intensive-care section, because the care she needed now was too intensive for that. In fact, in any significant sense of the word, her body was dead. Her brainwaves were still just dandy. But of the body itself, with its myriad factories for processing materials and its machines for keeping itself going, there was left only a shell. External machines pumped her blood and filtered it, and moved what was left of her lungs. None of that was new, and not even particularly serious. Fatal, yes. Sooner or later the systems would fail. But that time could be put off for days, weeks, months—there were people in hospices all around the country who had been maintained for actual years—as long as the bills were paid—as long as they, or their relatives, did not call a halt. Jocelyn Feigerman's case was worse than theirs. It could be tolerated that she could never leave the bed, could remain awake only for an hour or so at a time, could eat only through IVs and could talk only through a machine; but when she could no longer *think* there was no more reason to live. And that time was approaching. The minute trace materials like acetylcholine and noradrenaline that governed the functioning of the brain cells themselves were dwindling within her, as tiny groups of cells in places buried deep in the brain, places with names like the locus coeruleus and the nucleus basalis of Meynert, began to die. Memory was weakening. Habits of thought and behavior were deserting her. The missing chemicals could be restored, for a time, from pharmaceuticals; but that postponement was sharply limited by side effects as bad as the disease.

It was time for her to die.

So the hospital had moved her to a sunny large room in a corner, gaily painted, filled with flowers, with chairs for visitors and 3-D landscape photographs on the walls, all surrounding the engineering marvel that was the bed she lay in. The room was terribly expensive—an unimportant fact, because it was never occupied except by the most terminal of cases, and rarely for more than a few hours.

As Feigerman rolled in the room was filled with people—half a dozen of them, not counting Marcus or himself. Or the still figure on the bed, almost hidden in its life-support systems. There was his daughter-in-law Gloria, tiny and fast-talking, engaged in an argument with a solid, bearded dark-skinned man Feigerman recognized as the borough president of Brooklyn. There was his stepson, now an elderly man, smoking a cigarette by the window and gazing contemplatively at the shrouded form of his mother. There was a doctor, stethoscope around his neck, tube looped through his lapel, all the emblems of his office visibly ready, though there was not in fact much for him to do but listen to the argument between Gloria and Borough President Haisal—a nurse—a notary public, with his computer terminal already out and ready on a desk by the wall. It was a noisy room. You could not hear the hiss of Jocelyn Feigerman's artificial lung or the purr of her dialysis machine under the conversation, and she was not speaking. Asleep, Feigerman thought—or hoped so. Everybody had to die, but to set one's own time for it seemed horribly coldblooded. . . . He raised his chin and addressed the room at large: "What are we waiting for?"

His stepson, David, stabbed his cigarette out in a fern pot and answered. "Mother wanted Nillie here for some reason."

"She's got a right," Gloria flashed, interrupted her argument with Haisal to start one with her husband. Haisal was of Arab stock, from the Palestinian neighborhoods along Atlantic Avenue; Gloria was Vietnamese, brought to the United States when she was a scared and sick three-year-old; it was queer to hear the New York–American voices come out of the exotic faces.

"Father! Haisal says they're going to go to referendum."

Feigerman felt a sudden surge of anger. He wheeled his chair closer toward the arguing couple. "What the hell, Haisal? You've got the votes in Albany!"

"Now, Rinty," the Arab protested. "You know how these things work. There's a lot of pressure—"

"You've got plenty of pressure yourself!"

"Please, Rinty," he boomed. "You know what Bed-Stuy means to me, don't you think I'm doing everything I can?"

"I do not."

Haisal made a hissing sound of annoyance. "What is this, Rinty? Gloria asked me to come here because you need a magistrate for your wife's testamentation, not to fight about money for the project! This is a deathbed gathering. Where's your respect?"

"Where's your sense of honor?" Gloria demanded. "You promised, Haisal!"

"I do what I can," the borough president growled. "It's going to have to go to referendum, and that's all there is to it—now let's get going on this goddamn testamentation, can we?"

"We have to wait for Vanilla de Harcourt," Feigerman snapped, "and anyway, Haisal—what is it?"

From the doorway, the nurse said, "She's here, Mr. Feigerman. Just came in."

"Then we go ahead," said Haisal irritably. "Quiet down, everybody. Sam, you ready to take all this down? Doctor, can you wake her up?"

The room became still as the notary public turned on his monitor and the doctor and nurse gave Jocelyn Feigerman the gentle electric nudge that would rouse her. Then the borough president spoke:

"Mrs. Feigerman, this is Agbal Haisal. Do you hear me?"

On the CRT over her bed there was a quick pulsing of alpha waves, and a tinny voice said, "Yes." It wasn't Jocelyn's voice, of course, since she had none. It was synthesized speech, generated electronically, controlled not by the nerves that led to the paralyzed vocal cords but by practiced manipulation of the brain's alpha rhythms, and its vocabulary was very small.

"I will ask the doctor to explain your medical situation to you, as we discussed," said Haisal formally, "and if you have any question simply say 'No.' Go ahead, doctor."

The young resident cleared his throat, frowning over his notes. He wanted to get this exactly right; it was his first case of this kind. "Mrs. Feigerman," he began, "in addition to the gross physical problems you are aware of, you been diagnosed as being in the early stages of Alzheimer's syndrome, sometimes called senile dementia. The laboratory has demonstrated fibrous protein deposits in your brain, which are increasing in size and number. This condition is progressive and at present irreversible, and the prognosis is loss of memory, loss of control of behavior, psychotic episodes and death. I have discussed this with you earlier, and repeat it now so that you may answer this question. Do you understand your condition?"

Pause. Flicker of lines in the CRT. "Yes."

"Thank you, doctor," rumbled the borough president. "In that case, Mrs. Feigerman—Joss—I have a series of questions to ask you, and they may sound repetitive but they're what the law says a magistrate has to ask. First, do you know why we are here?"

"Yes."

"Are you aware that you are suffering from physical conditions which will bring about irreversible brain damage and death within an estimated time of less than thirty days?"

"Yes."

"Then, Mrs. Feigerman," he said solemnly, "your options are as follows. One. You may continue as you are, in which case you will continue on the life-support systems un-til brainscan and induction tests indicate you are brain-dead, with no further medical procedures available. Two. You may elect to terminate life-support systems at this time, or at any later time you choose, as a voluntary matter, without further medical proce-dures. Three. You may elect to terminate life support and enter voluntary cryonic sus-pension. In this case you should be informed that the prognosis is uncertain but that the necessary financial and physical arrangements have been made for your storage and to attempt to cure and revive you when and if such procedures become available.

"I will now ask you if you accept one of these alternatives."

The pause was quite long this time, and Feigerman was suddenly aware that he was very tired. Perhaps it was more than fatigue; it might have been even bereavement, for although he had no desire to shriek or rend his clothes he felt the dismal certainty that a part of his life was being taken away from him. It had not always been a happy part. It was many years since it had been a sensually obsessive part . . . but it had been his. He tried to make out the vague images before him to see if his wife's eyes were open, at least, but the detail was very inadequate. . . . "Yes," said the tinny voice at last, without emotion, or emphasis. Or life. It was, almost literally, a voice from the grave; and it was hard to remember how very alive that wasted body had once been.

"In that case, Mrs. Feigerman, is it Alternative Number One, continuing as you are?"

"No."

"Is it Alternative Number Two, terminating life-support without further proce-dures?"

"No."

"Is it Alternative Number Three, terminating life-support and entering cryonic sus-pension?"

"Yes." A long sigh from everyone in the room; none of them could help himself.

The borough president went on: "Thank you, Mrs. Feigerman. I must now ask you to make a choice. You may elect to enter neurocryonic suspension, which is to say the freezing of your head and brain only. Or you may elect whole-body suspension. Your doctor has explained to you that the damage suffered by your body has been so extensive that any revival and repair is quite unlikely in the next years or even decades. On the other hand, suspension of the head and brain only entails the necessity for providing an entire body for you at some future day, through cloning, through grafting of a whole new donor body to your head and brain or through some other procedure at present un-known. No such procedures exist at present. This decision is entirely yours to make, Mrs. Feigerman; your next of kin have been consulted and agree to implement whatever choice you make. Have you understood all this, Mrs. Feigerman?"

"Yes."

Haisal sighed heavily. "Very well, Joss, I will now ask you which alternative you prefer. Do you accept Alternative Number one, the cryonic suspension of head and brain only?"

"No."

"Do you accept whole-body suspension, then?"

"Yes."

"So be it," rumbled the borough president heavily, and signed to the notary public. The man slipped the hard-copy transparency out of his monitor, pressed his thumb in one corner and passed it around to the witnesses to do the same. "Now," said the bor-ough president, "I think we'll leave the family to say their good-byes." He gathered up the notary, the nurse and Marcus's mother with his eyes; and to the doctor he signaled, his lips forming the words: *"Then pull the plug."*

3

On the first morning of de Rintelen Feigerman's new life as a widower, he awoke with a shock, and then a terrible sense of loss. The loss was not the loss of his wife; even in his dreams he had accepted that Jocelyn was dead, or if not exactly dead certainly both legally and practically no longer alive in the sense that he was. The shock was that he had not dreamed that he was blind. In Rinty's dreams he could always see. That was a given: everyone could see. Human beings saw, just as they breathed and ate and shit. So in his dreams he experienced, without particularly remarking on it, the glowing red and green headlamps of an IRT subway train coming into the Clark Street station, and the silent fall of great white snowflakes over the East River, and the yellow heat of summer sun on a beach, and women's blue eyes, and stars, and clouds. It was only when he woke up that it was always darkness.

Rosalyn, his big old weimarian, growled softly from beside the bed as Feigerman sat up. There was no significance to the growl, except that it was her way of letting Feigerman know where she was. He reached down and touched her shaggy head, finding it just where it ought to be, right under his descending hand. He didn't really need the morning growl anymore. He could pretty nearly locate her by the smell, because Rosalyn was becoming quite an old dog. "Lie," he said, and heard her whuffle obediently as she lay down again beside his bed. He was aware of a need to go to the bathroom, but there was a need before that. He picked up the handset from the bedside table, listened to the beeps that told him the time, pressed the code that connected him to his office. "Rinty here," he said. "Situation report, please."

"Good morning, Mr. Feigerman," said the night duty officer. He knew her voice, a pretty young woman, or one whose face felt smooth and regular under his fingers and whose hair was short and soft. Janice something. "Today's weather, no problems. Overnight maintenance on schedule; no major outages. Shift supervisors are reporting in now, and we anticipate full crews. We've been getting, though," she added, a note of concern creeping into her voice, "a lot of queries from the furloughed crews. They want to know when they're going to go back to work."

"I wish I could tell them, Janice. Talk to you later." He hung up, sighed and got ready for the memorized trip to the toilet, the shower, the coffee pot—he could already feel the heat from it as it automatically began to brew his first morning cup—and all the other blind man's chores. He had to face them every morning, and the most difficult was summoning up the resolution to get through one more day.

Rinty Feigerman had lived in this apartment for more than thirty years. As soon as Jocelyn's son, David, was out of the house they had bought this condo in Brooklyn Heights. It was big and luxurious, high up in what had once been a fashionable Brooklyn hotel, when Brooklyn had still considered itself remote enough from The City to want its own hotels. Fashionable people stopped staying there in the thirties and forties. In the fifties and sixties it had become a welfare hotel, where the city's poor huddled up in rooms that, every year, grew shabbier and smelled worse, as the big dining restaurant, the swimming pool, the health club, the saunas, the meeting rooms, the rooftop night club withered and died. Then a developer turned it into apartments. It was Rinty Feiger-man who picked the place, studying the view and the builders' plans while he still had eyes that worked. But Jocelyn had furnished it. She had put in end tables and planters, thick rugs on slippery floors, a kitchen like a machine shop, with blenders and food pro-cessors and every automatic machine in the catalog. When Feigerman lost his eyes, every one of those things became a booby trap.

For the first couple of years Jocelyn grimly replaced candy dishes and lamps as they crashed. She had not quite accepted the fact that the problem was not going to get bet-ter. After the damage toll began to be substantial, the week a whole tray of porcelain fig-ures smashed to the floor and a coffeemaker burned itself out until the electrical reek woke her up, Jocelyn, sullen but thorough, attacked the job of blindproofing their home. The living spaces she kept ornate. Rinty stayed out of them, except on the well es-tablished routes from door to door. They wound up with three separate establishments. One was for company. One was Jocelyn's own space, formerly dainty but in the last two years more like a hospital suite. And the rest was Feigerman's own: a bedroom, a bath, a guest room converted into a study, a guest bath rebuilt into a barebones kitchen, all crafted for someone who preferred using only his sense of touch. And the terrace.

For a blind man with a Seeing Eye dog, that was maybe the best thing of all. It had started out flagstoned, with two tiny evergreens in wooden pots. Jocelyn's son had had a better idea, and so he filled it from wall to wall with twenty cubic yards of topsoil. It grew grass, though nothing much else, and so became a perfect dog's toilet. No one had to walk Rosalyn in the morning. Rinty opened the thermal French windows, Rosalyn paced gravely out; when she had done what she had to do she scratched to come back in, and then lay attentively near her master until he called her to put on her harness. Feiger-man always accountered Rosalyn before he did himself. He wondered if she disliked it as much as he did, but of course he had no way to know. Rosalyn never complained. Not even when he was so busy working that he forgot to feed her for hours past her time; she would take food from no one else, and he supposed that if he continued to forget she would simply starve. Not even now, when she was so slow and tired so quickly that he left her home on almost every day, except when guilt made him take her—and a human being like the boy Marcus, for insurance—for a walk in a park. He stood in the open doorway, letting the morning sun warm his face, trying to believe that he could see at least a reddening of the darkness under his eyelids, until Rosalyn came back and whined softly as she put her cold nose in his hand.

Someone was in the apartment. Feigerman hadn't put his hearing aid on because, as he told himself, he wasn't really *deaf*, just a little hard of hearing; but he had not heard the door. He opened the door to his own room and called, "Is that you, Gloria?"

"No, Mr. Feigerman, it's me. Nillie. Want me to fix you a cup of coffee?"

"I've got some in here. Wait a minute." He reached for the robe at the foot of his bed, slid into it, tied it over his skinny belly—how could he be so thin and yet so flabby?—and invited her in. When she had poured herself a cup out of his own supply and was sitting in the armchair by the terrace window he said, "I'll be sorry to be losing you, Nil-lie. Have you got something else lined up?"

"Yes I do, Mr. Feigerman. There's a job in the recycling plant, just the right hours, too, so don't worry about me."

"Of course I'd like Marcus to keep on guiding me, if that's all right."

"Surely, Mr. Feigerman." Pause. "I'm really sorry about Mrs. Feigerman."

"Yes." He had not really figured out how to approach that particular subject. If your wife was dead, that was one thing; if she was sick, but there was some hope of recovery, that was another. A wife now resting at a temperature about a dozen degrees above absolute zero was something else. Not to mention the five or six years as her aging body began to deteriorate—or the years before that when their aging marriage was doing the same. Jocelyn's life was political and dedicated. His was no less dedicated, but his social objectives were carried out in bricks, steel and mortar instead of laws. The two lifestyles did not match well—"I beg your pardon?"

"I said I'm going to clear my stuff out of Mrs. Feigerman's room now, Mr. Feigerman."

"Oh, sure. Go ahead, Nillie." He realized he had been sitting silent, his coffee cooling, while his mind circled around the difficulties and problems in his world. And he realized, too, if a bit tardily, that Vanilla Fudge de Harcourt's voice had sounded strained. Particularly when she mentioned her son. Small puzzle. Sighing, Feigerman fumbled his way to the sink, poured the cold coffee away and set himself to the job of dressing.

"Dressing," for Rinty Feigerman, was not just a matter of clothes. He also had to put on the artificial vision system, which he disliked, and postponed as long as he could every day. It wasn't any good for reading, little better for getting around his rooms. Information Feigerman took in through braille and through audiotapes, the voices of the readers electronically chopped to speed them up to triple speed, without raising the frequency to chipmunk chirps. Nearly everything he chose to do in his rooms he could do without the vision system. He could speak on the phone. He could listen to the radio. He could dictate, he could typewrite; he could even work his computer console, with its audio and tactile readouts, at least for word processing and mathematics, though the graphics functions were of no use at all to him anymore. Feigerman was never able to see the grand designs he helped to create, except in the form of models. There were plenty of those, made in the shops of the consultancy firm he owned with his stepson; but it was not the same as being able to look down on, say, the future Bed-Stuy in the God's-eye view of every sighted person. At the computer he was quite deft, as artificial speech synthesizers read him the numbers he punched into the keyboard and the results that flashed on the CRT, now usually turned off. Of course, he did not really need to see, or even to feel a model of, Bed-Stuy. The whole plan was stored in his mind. . . . He was stalling again, he realized.

No help for it. He patted Rosalyn and sat down on the foot of his bed, reaching out for the gear.

The first step was to strap the tickler to his chest. Between the nipples, in a rectangular field seven inches across and five deep, a stiff brush of electrical contacts touched his skin. Feigerman had never been a hairy man, but even so, once a week or so, he had to shave what few sparse hairs grew there to make sure the contacts worked. Then the shirt went on, and the pants, and the jacket with the heavy-duty pocket that held most of the electronics and the flat, dense battery. Then he would reach down under the bed to where he had left the battery itself recharging all night long, pull it gingerly from the charger, clip it to the gadget's leads and slip it into the pocket. Then came the crown. Feigerman had never seen the crown, but it felt like the sort of tiara dowagers used to wear to be presented to the queen. It wasn't heavy. The straps that held it made it possible to wear it over a wool cap in winter, or attached to a simple yarmulke in warm weather. It beeped at a frequency most people couldn't hear, though young children's ears could sometimes pick it up—Marcus claimed to hear it, and there was no doubt that Rosalyn did. When he first got the improved model the dog whined all the time it was on—perhaps, Feigerman thought, because she knew it was taking her job away from her.

When he turned the unit on now, she didn't whine, but he could feel her move restlessly against his leg as he sat and let the impressions reach his brain. It had taken a lot of practice. The returning echo of the beeps was picked up, analyzed and converted into a mosaic that the ticklers drew across his chest with a pattern of tiny electric shocks. Even now it was not easy to read, and after a long day there was more pain than information in it; but it served. For a long time the patterns had meant nothing at all to Feigerman, except as a sort of demented practical joke someone was playing on him with tiny cattle prods. But the teacher promised he would learn to read it in time. And he did. Distance and size were hard to estimate from the prickling little shocks until he came to realize that the sonar's image of a parked car covering a certain area of his chest had to represent a real vehicle ten feet away. When he became accustomed to the sonar he didn't really need Rosalyn very much, and she was already beginning to limp on long walks. But he kept her. He had grown to like the dog, and did not want to see her among the technologically unemployed. . . . Then the coat; then the shoes; then Feigerman was ready to summon his driver and be taken to the offices in the Williamsburgh Bank Building for one more day of dealing with the world.

It was ever so much better, Feigerman's teacher had said, than the way things were for the unsighted even a few years earlier. Better than being dead, anyway, in Feigerman's estimation. Marginally so.

By the time Feigerman was at his office in the Williamsburgh Bank Building he was almost cheerful, mostly because his driver was in a good mood. Julius was a suspended cop; he had been a moonlighting cop, working for Feigerman only in his off-duty hours, until his suspension. The suspension was because he had been caught in a surprise blood test with marginal levels of tetrahydrocannabinol breakdown products in his system. Julius claimed he was innocent. Feigerman thought it didn't matter, since everybody was doing it, cops and all; and what made Julius's mood high was that his rabbi had phoned to say the charges were going to be dropped. So he joked and laughed all the way to the office, and left Feigerman still smiling as he got out of the elevator and beeped his way to his desk, answering the good-mornings of the staff all the way.

The first thing to do was to get out of the heaviest part of the harness again, which he did with one hand while he was reaching for his stepson's intercom button with the other. "David?" he called, lifting off the headpiece. "I'm in and, listen, I'm going to need another driver next week. Julius is getting reinstated."

"That's good," said the voice of his stepson, although that voice hardly ever sounded as though it found anything good. "I need you for a conference in half an hour, Dad."

Dad. Feigerman paused in the act of rubbing the imprinted red lines on his forehead, scowling. "Dad" was something new for David. Was it because his mother's death had reminded him that they were a family? David didn't seem to show any other effect. If he had shed one tear it had not been in Feigerman's presence. That wasn't surprising, maybe, because David's mother had devoted far more of her attention to her political causes than to her son. Or her daughter-in-law. Or, for that matter, to her husband. . . .

"What kind of conference?" Feigerman asked.

There was a definite note of strain in David's voice, part wheedling, part defiant. "It's a man from S. G. & H."

"And who are S. G. & H. when they're home?"

"They're investment bankers. They're also the people who own all the legislators from Buffalo to Rochester, and the ones who can get the Bed-Stuy money out of committee."

Feigerman leaned back, the scowl deepening. There was enough tension in David's voice to make him wish he could see David's face. But that was doubly impossible— "The man from S. G. & H. wouldn't be named Gambiage, would he?"

"That's the one."

"He's a goddamn gangster!"

"He's never been convicted but, yes, I would agree with you, Dad." The truculence was suppressed, but the wheedling was almost naked now. "All you have to do is listen to him, you know. His people have been buying utility stock options, and naturally he has an interest in Bed-Stuy—"

"I know what that interest is! He wants to own it!"

"He wants a piece of it, probably. Dad? I know how you feel—but don't you want to get it built?"

Feigerman breathed out slowly. "I'll see him when he comes in," he said, and snapped the connection.

If he had only thirty minutes before a very unpleasant task, he needed to get ready for it. He reached to the gadget beside his chair and switched it on. It was his third set of eyes, the only ones that were any good at all over a distance exceeding a few yards. They had another advantage. Feigerman called them his daydreaming eyes, because they were the ones that allowed him to see what wasn't there—yet.

Feigerman had designed it himself, and the machine on and around his desk had cost more than three hundred thousand dollars—less than half recouped when he licensed it for manufacture. It was not a mass-market item. Even the production models cost more than a hundred thousand, and there were no models which were in any sense portable. The size constraints could not be removed by engineering brilliance; they were built in to the limitations of the human finger.

The heart of the device was a photon-multiplier video camera that captured whatever was before it, located the areas of contrast, expressed them digitally, canceled out features too small to be displayed within its limits of resolution; and did it all twice, electronically splitting the images to produce stereo. Then it drove a pinboard matrix of two hundred by two hundred elements, each one a rounded plastic cylinder thinner than a toothpick—forty thousand pixels all told, each one thrust out of the matrix board a distance ranging anywhere from not at all to just over a quarter of an inch.

What came out of it all was a bas-relief that Feigerman could run his fingers over, as he might gently touch the face of a friend.

Feigerman could, in fact, recognize faces from it, and so could nearly a hundred other blind people well connected enough to be given or rich enough to buy the device. He could even read expressions—sometimes. He could, even, take a "snapshot"—freeze the relief at any point, to study in motionless form as long as he liked. What was astonishing was that even sighted persons could recognize the faces, too; and it was not just faces. Feigerman had no use for paintings on the walls, but if he wanted to "behold" the Rocky Mountains or the surface of the Moon his device had their stereo-tactile images stored in digital form, and a simple command let him trace with his fingers the Donner Pass or walk along the slopes of Tycho.

What he chose to do this morning, waiting for the gangster to show up and ruin his day, maybe even ruin his project!, was to "look out the window."

For that the electronic camera mounted behind his chair was not good enough. The electronic "pupillary distance" was too small for a stereoscopic image. But he had mounted a pair of cameras high up on the wall of the observation deck of the building, and when he switched over to them all of Bedford-Stuyvesant rippled under his fingers.

What Feigerman felt with his fingers was not really much unlike the surface of the Moon. There were the craters of excavation, for the underground apartment dwellings that would house two hundred thousand human beings and for the garment workshops, the electronic assembly plants and all the other clean, undegrading industries that would give the two hundred thousand people work to do. There were the existing structures—the tenements not yet torn down, the guardhouses atop Nathanael Greene, the derelict factories, the containment shell over the breeder reactor, the Long Island Rail Road lines—a late shoppers' express came hissing in on its maglev suspension, and the ripple of its passage tickled his fingers. There were the projects begun and the projects now going up—he recognized the slow, steady turn of a crane as it hoisted preformed concrete slabs onto the thermal water basin.

And there were the silent rows of dumpsters and diggers, backhoes and augers, that were not moving at all because of the lack of funds.

De Rintelen Feigerman didn't count up his years anymore. Now that his wife was a rimey corpsicle somewhere under Inwood no one alive knew the total; but everyone knew that it was a lot of years. There could not be very many more. Feigerman was used to delays. You did not make a career of major construction in the most complicated city in the world without accepting long time overruns. But this one time in all his life he was not patient, for every minute wasted was a minute taken off what had to be a slender reserve.

And this was his masterpiece. East River East was just one more big damn housing development. The Inwood Freezer complex was only a cold-storage plant. Nathanael Greene was just another jail. But Bed-Stuy—

Bed-Stuy was the closest human beings could come to heaven on earth. The original idea wasn't his; he had ferreted it out from old publications and dusty data chips; somebody named Charles Engelke had described a way of making a small suburban community self-sufficient for energy as far back as the 1970s—but who was interested in suburbs after that? Somebody else had pointed out that the blighted areas of American cities, the South Bronxes and the Detroits, could be rebuilt in new, human ways. But it was de Rintelen Feigerman who put it all together, and had the muscle, the *auteur* prestige, the political connections, the access to capital—had all the things that could make the dreams come true. Solar energy. Solar energy used in a thousand different ways: to heat water in the summer and pump it down into rechargeable lenses of fossil water far under the surface; the new hot water squeezes out the old cool, and the cool water that comes up drives summer air-conditioning. In winter the pumps go the other way, and the hot summer water warms the homes. Solar energy as photovoltaics, for driving electronic equipment. Solar energy as wind, also for generating electricity, more typically for pumping water in and out of the thermal aquifers. Solar energy, most of all, for the thing it was best equipped to do—domestic heating. Feigerman made an adjustment, and under his fingers the vista of Bed-Stuy grew from what it was to what it would be, as his datastore fed in the picture of the completed project.

Even forty thousand pixels could not give much detail in a plan that encompassed more than a square mile. Each element represented something about the size of a truck; a pedestrian, a fire hydrant, even a parked car was simply too tiny to be seen.

But what a glorious view! Feigerman's fingers rested lovingly on the huge, aerodynamically formed hill that would enclose the surface-level water store and support the wind engines that would do the pumping. The smaller dome for the ice pond, where freezing winter temperatures would provide low-temperature reserves for summer cooling, even for food-processing. The milder slope that hid the great methane digesters—perhaps he loved the methane digesters best of all, for what could be more elegant than to take the most obnoxious of human by-products—shit!—and turn it into the most valuable of human resources—fuel? All the sewage of the homes and offices and factories would come here, to join with the lesser, but considerable, wastes from the men's prison next to it. The shit would stew itself into sludge and methane; the heat of the process would kill off all the bacteria; the sludge would feed the farms, the methane would burn for process heat. Industries like glass-making, needing the precise heating that gas could produce better than anything else, would find cheap and reliable supplies—meaning jobs—meaning more self-sufficiency—meaning—

Feigerman sighed and brought himself back to reality. At command, the future Utopia melted away under his fingers and he was touching the pattern of Bed-Stuy as it was. The methane generator was still only an ugly hole in the ground next to the prison. The great wind hill was no more than a ragged Stonehenge circle of concrete, open at the top. The idle construction machinery was still ranked along a roadway—

"I didn't want to disturb you, so I just let myself in, okay?"

The blind man started, twisted in his chair, banged his head against the support for the camera behind him. He was trying to do two things at once, to reach for the sonar crown that would let him see this intruder, to switch the tactile matrix back to the inside cameras so that he could feel him. The man said gently, amusedly, "You don't need that gadget, Feigerman. It's me, Mr. Gambiage. We've got business to talk."

Feigerman abandoned the search for the coronet; the camera behind his head had caught the image of his visitor, and Feigerman could feel it under his fingers. "Sit down, Mr. Gambiage," he said—pointedly, because the man was already sitting down. He moved silently enough! "You're holding up my money," he said. "Is that what you want to talk about?"

The image rippled under his fingers as Gambiage made an impatient gesture. "We're not going to crap around," he informed Feigerman. "I can get your money loose from Albany, no problem, or I can hold it up forever, and that's no problem too. On the other hand, you could cost me a lot of money, so I'm offering you a deal."

Feigerman let him talk. The tactile impression of Gambiage did not tell much about the man. Feigerman knew, because the news reports said so, that Gambiage was about fifty years old. He could feel that the man was short and heavyset, but that his features were sharp and strong. Classic nose. Heavy brows. Stubborn broad chin. But were his eyes mean or warm? Was his expression smile or leer or grimace? Gambiage's voice was soft and, queerly, his accent was educated under the street-talk grammar. It could even be Ivy League—after all, there was nothing to say that the sons of the godfathers couldn't go to college. And Feigerman had to admit that the man smelled good, smelled of washed hair and expensive leather shoes and the best of after-shave lotion. He could hear the faint sound of movement as Gambiage made himself comfortable as he went on talking: could smell, could hear, could feel . . . could be frightened. For this man represented a kind of power that could not be ignored.

Feigerman had dealt with the mob before—you could not be involved in large construction in America without finding you had them for partners in a thousand ways. The unions; the suppliers; the politicians—the city planners, the building inspectors, the code writers—wherever a thousand-dollar bribe could get a million-dollar vote or approval or license, there the mob was. It did not always control. But it could not be set aside. The ways of dealing with the mob were only two, you went along or you fought. Feigerman had done both.

But this time he could do neither. He couldn't fight, because he didn't have time left in his life for a prolonged battle. And he couldn't go along with what came to nothing less than the perversion of the dream.

"It's the cogeneration thing," Gambiage explained. "You make your own power, you cost the utilities a fortune. I've got stock options. They're not going to be worth shit if the price doesn't go up, and you're the one that's keeping the price from going up."

"Mr. Gambiage, the whole point of the Bed-Stuy project is to be self-sufficient in energy so that—"

"I said we're not going to crap around," Gambiage reminded him. "Now we're going to talk deal. You're going to change your recommendations. You'll agree to selling all the power-generating facilities to the utilities. Then I'll recommend to my friends in Albany that they release your funds, and everything goes smoothly from there on. And I'll make it more attractive to you. I'll sell you my stock options for fifty thousand shares for what I paid for them. Thirty cents a share, for purchase at ninety-one and a quarter."

Feigerman didn't respond at once. He turned to his data processor and punched out the commands for a stock quotation. As he held the little earpiece to his ear the sexless synthesized-speech voice said: "Consolidated Metropolitan Utilities current sale, eighty-five."

"Eighty-five!" Feigerman repeated.

"Right," said Gambiage, and his voice was smiling. "That's what you cost me so far, Feigerman. Now get a projection with us owning the cogeneration facilities and see what you get. We make it a hundred and ten, anyway."

Feigerman didn't bother to check that; there would be no point in lying about it. He simply punched out a simple problem in arithmetic: $110 - (91.25 + .30)$—say 1 percent for brokers' fees, $\times 50,000$. And the voice whispered, "Nine hundred thirteen thousand two hundred seventy-five dollars."

He was being offered a bribe of nearly a million dollars.

A million dollars. It had been a legacy of less than a tenth of that that had put him through school and given him the capital to start his career in the first place. It was a magic number. Never mind that his assets were already considerably more than that. Never mind that money was not of much use to a man who was already too old to spend what he had. A million dollars! And simply for making a decision that could be well argued as being the right thing to do in any case.

It was very easy to see how Mr. Gambiage exercised his power. But out loud Feigerman said, his voice cracking, "How many shares have you got left? A million or two?"

"My associates and I have quite a few, yes."

"Do you know we could all go to jail for that?"

"Feigerman," said Gambiage wearily, "that's what you pay lawyers for. The whole transaction can be handled offshore anyway, in any name you like. No U.S. laws violated. Grand Cayman is where the options are registered right now."

"What happens if I say no?"

With his fingers on the bas-relief, Feigerman could feel the ripple of motion as Gambiage shrugged. "Then Albany doesn't release the funds, the project dies and the stock bounces back to where it belongs. Maybe a hundred."

"And the reason you come to me," Feigerman said, clarifying the point, "is that you think I come cheaper than a couple of dozen legislators."

"Somewhat cheaper, yes. But the bottom line comes out good for me and my associates anyway." The needles tickled Feigerman's palm as the man stood up; irritably Feigerman froze the image. "I'll be in touch," Gambiage promised, and left.

It would be, Feigerman calculated, not more than three minutes before his stepson would be on the intercom.

He wasn't ready for that. He slapped the privacy switch, cutting off calls, locking the door.

The important thing, now, was to decide what was the important thing forever. To get the project built? Or to get it built in a fashion in which he could take smug and virtuous personal pride?

Feigerman knew what he wanted—he wanted that sense of triumph and virtue that would carry him through that not-long-to-be-delayed deathbed scene, for which he found himself rehearsing almost every day. His task now was to reconcile himself to second best—or to find a way to achieve the best. He could fight, of course. The major battles had been long won. The general outlines of the project had been approved, the land acquired, the blueprints drawn, the construction begun. Whatever Gambiage might now deploy in the way of bribed legislators or court injunctions—or whatever other strategies he could command, of which there were thousands—in the long run the game would go to Feigerman—

Except that Feigerman might well not be alive to see his victory.

He sighed and released the hold button; and of course his stepson's voice sounded at once, angry: "Don't cut me off like that, Dad. Why did you cut me off? What did he say?"

"He wants to be our partner, David."

"Dad! Dad, he already *is* our partner. Are you going to change the recommendation?"

"What I'm going to do is think about it for a while." He paused, then added on impulse, "David? Have you been picking up any stock options lately?"

Silence for a moment. Then, "Your seeing-eye kid is here," said David, and hung up.

When Marc came in to help Mr. Feigerman get ready he was prepared for a bad time. The other guy, Mr. Tisdale, was all in a sweat and grumbling to himself about trouble; the trouble centered around old Feigerman, so maybe the day's walk was off, maybe he'd be in a bad mood—at his age, maybe he'd be having a stroke or something.

But actually he was none of those things. He was struggling to put his camera thing on his head by himself, but spoke quite cheerfully: "Hello, Marcus. You ready for a little walk?"

"Sure thing, Mr. Feigerman." Marc came around behind Feigerman to snap the straps for him, and his glance fell on that pinboard thing the old man used to see.

"What's the matter?" Feigerman said sharply.

"Aw, nothing," said Marc, but it was a lie. He had no trouble recognizing the face on the pinboard. It was not a face he would forget. He had seen it many times before, arriving at his father's candy store in the black limousine.

4

Inmate 838-10647 HARVEY John T. did not merely have one of the best jobs in Nathanael Greene Institute for Men, he had two of them. In the afternoons he had yard detail, up on the surface. That was partly because of his towering seniority in the prison, mostly because he had been able to produce medical records to show that he needed sunshine and open air every day. Inmate Harvey had no trouble producing just about any medical records he liked. In the mornings he worked in the library. That was partly seniority, too, but even more because of his special skills with data processors. Inmate Harvey's library work generally involved fixing the data-retrieval system when it broke down, once in a while checking out books for other inmates. This morning he was busy at something else. It was like putting together a jigsaw puzzle. Under the eyes of two angry guards and the worried head librarian, Harvey was painfully assembling the shards of broken glass that had once been a ten-by-twenty-six-inch window in the locked bookshelves. When it was whole it had kept a shelf of "restricted" books safe—books that most of the inmates were not permitted to have because they were politically dangerous. Now that it was a clutter of razor-sharp fragments it was something that inmates were even less permitted to have, because they were dangerous, period. On the edge of Harvey's desk, watched by a third guard, sat the two other inmates whose scuffling had broken the glass. One had a bleeding nose. The other had a bleeding hand. Their names were Esposito and La Croy, and neither of them looked particularly worried—either by their injuries or by the forty-eight-hour loss of privileges that was the inevitable penalty for fighting.

Those were small prices to pay for the chance of escape.

Hardly anyone ever escaped from Nathanael Greene. Of course, a lot of inmates tried. Every inmate knew that there were exactly three ways to do it, and that two of them were obvious and the other one impossible.

The obvious ways, obviously, were the ways through which people normally exited the prison—the "visitors' gate," which was also where supplies came in and manufactured products and waste went out; and the high-security "prisoner-transfer gate." Trusties lucky enough to be working on the surface, farming or cutting grass, could pretty nearly walk right out of the visitors' gate. Sometimes they made the try; but electronic surveillance caught them every time. The prisoner-transfer facility had been a little easier—three times there had been a successful escape that way, usually with fake transfer orders. But after the third time the system was changed and that way looked to be closed permanently.

Scratch the two obvious ways. The only way left was the impossible one. To wit, leaving the prison through some other exit.

What made that impossible was that there wasn't any. Nathanael Greene was underground. You could try to dig a tunnel if you wanted to, but there wasn't anywhere to tunnel to nearer than a hundred yards—mostly straight up—and besides there were the geophones. The same echo-sounding devices that located oil domes and seismic faults could locate a tunnel—usually in the first three yards—assuming any prisoner could escape the twenty-four-hour electronic surveillance long enough to start digging in the first place.

That was why it was impossible, for almost everyone, almost all the time. But inmates still hoped—as Esposito and La Croy hoped. And even took chances, as Esposito and La Croy were willing to do; because there never was a perfect system, and if there was anyone who could find a way through the safeguards of Nathanael Greene it was Inmate 838-10647 HARVEY John T.

He never did get the jigsaw put back together to suit the guards, but after two hours of trying, after he had crunched some of the pieces twice with his foot and it was obvious that no one was ever going to reconstruct the pane properly anymore, the guards settled for picking up all the pieces they could find and marching Esposito and La Croy away. They had no reason to hassle Inmate Harvey. That didn't stop them from threatening, of course. But when the lunch-break signal sounded they let him go.

The trip from the library to his cell took three flights of stairs and six long corridors, and Harvey did it all on his own. So did every other prisoner, because no matter where they were or what they were doing the master locator file tagged them in and out every time they came to a checkpoint. You lifted your leg to present the ID on your ankle to the optical scanner. The scanner made sure you were you by voice prints or pattern recognition of face or form, sometimes even by smell. It queried the master file to find out if you were supposed to be going where you were going, and if all was in order you simply walked right through. The whole process took no longer than opening an ordinary door, and you didn't screw around if you could help it because, anyway, you were under continuous closed-circuit surveillance all the time. Inmate Harvey, carrying his book and his clean librarian's shirt, nodding to acquaintances hurrying along the same corridors and exchanging comments about the methane stink that was beginning to pervade the entire prison, reached his cell in less than five minutes.

His cellmate was a man named Angelo Muzzi, and he was waiting for Harvey. "Gimme," said Moots, extending his hand for the copy of *God-Emperor of Dune*.

Harvey entered the cell warily—you watched yourself with Muzzi. "You're fuckin up the whole plan," he pointed out. "You don't need this." But he handed the volume over just the same, and watched Muzzi open it to the page where the shard of glass lay.

"It's too fuckin short, asshole," Muzzi growled. He wasn't particularly angry. He always talked that way. He ripped a couple of pages out of the book, folded them over and wrapped them around the thick end of the glass sliver. When he held it as though for stabbing, about three inches of razor-edged stiletto protruded from his fist—sharp, deadly and invisible to the prison's metal detectors. "Too fuckin short," he repeated fiercely, but his eyes were gleaming with what passed in Muzzi for pleasure.

"It's the best I could do." Harvey didn't bother to tell him how long he had sat with the fragments, pretending to try to reconstruct a complete pane; Muzzi wouldn't be interested. But he offered, "The screws were going to give me a twenty-four." Muzzi would be interested in that.

And he was. "Shithead! Did you fuck up your meet with the kid?" This time the voice was dangerous and Harvey was quick in defense.

"No, it's cool, Moots, that's not till Thursday. I was just telling you why that was the best I could do."

"You told me. Now shut up." Harvey didn't wait to see where Muzzi would conceal the weapon. He didn't want to know. Fortunately he and Muzzi didn't eat on the same shift, so Harvey left without looking back.

The thing was, Muzzi didn't need the shiv. It would be useless in the first stages. When it stopped being useless it would be unnecessary. But you didn't argue with Muzzi. Not when he told you to steal him a glass blade. Not when he added more people to the plan and made two of them break the glass to get it. Not ever. It wasn't just that Muzzi's connections made the whole project possible, it was the man himself. "Man" was the wrong word. Muzzi was a rabid animal.

Tuesday lunch was always the same: sloppy-joe sandwiches, salad from the surface farm or the hothouse, milk. What they called "milk," anyway; it had never seen a cow, being made of vegetable fats and whitener. What made it worse than usual was the methane stink from where the digging of the new sewer pits had seeped through the soil into the cellblocks themselves. Harvey didn't join in the catcalls or complaints, didn't let sticky soup from the sloppy-joes spill on the floor or accidentally drop a meatball into the Jell-O. He didn't do any of the things the other inmates did to indicate their displeasure, because the last thing Harvey wanted was to get even a slap-on-the-wrist twenty-four-hour loss of privileges just now. All the same, he suffered with every bite. Inmate Harvey was used to better things.

Inmate 838-10647 HARVEY John T. had a record that went back thirty years, to when he was a bright and skinny kid. He hadn't intended to get into violence. He started out as a Phone-Phreak, rival of the semilegendary Captain Crunch. When Ma Bell got mad enough to put the Captain in jail, young Johnny Harvey got the message. Making free phone calls to the Pope on his blue box just wasn't worth it, so he looked for less painful ways to have fun. He found them in proprietary computer programs. Johnny Harvey could wreck anybody's security. No matter how many traps Apple built into its software, Johnny Harvey could bypass them in a week, and make copies and be passing them out, like popcorn, to all his friends before the company knew they'd been screwed. Apple even got desperate enough to offer him a job—don't crack our security programs, design them—but that got boring. So did program-swiping. For a while Harvey worked for the city, mostly on the programs for electronic voting and the Universal Town Meeting, but that was kind of boring, too, in the long run, and then somebody came along with more larceny in his heart than Harvey had ever owned, and saw what treasures the young man could unlock.

He unlocked six big ones. Two were major payoffs from insurance companies on life policies that had never existed, on assureds who had never been born. Three were sales of stock Harvey had never owned, except in the tampered datastore of a brokerage house's computers. One was a cash transfer from branch to branch of a bank that thought its codes could never be compromised.

When the bank found out how wrong it was, it set a trap. The next time Harvey tried to collect a quarter of a million dollars that didn't belong to him, the teller scratched her nose in just the right way and two plainclothes bank security officers took Johnny Harvey away.

Since it was a white-collar crime and nobody loves a bank anyway, the prosecutor didn't dare go for a jury trial. He let Harvey go for a plea-bargained reduced charge. No one was really mad. They just put him away for eighteen months. But they put him in Attica, world's finest finishing school for street crime and buggery. After that Harvey couldn't get a job, and the codes had got a lot tougher, and, by and large, the easiest way he could find to support the habit he had picked up in stir was with a gun.

And when that went wrong, and they put him away again, and he got out once more, the situation hadn't improved. He tried the same project. This time things went very wrong, and when he finished trying to shoot his way out of a stakeout there were three people dead. One of the victims was a cop. One was a pregnant shopper. The third was her three-year-old kid. Well, the forgiving State of New York could make a deal on a homicide or two, but this time they were calling him "Mad Dog" on the six o'clock news, and he was convicted in public opinion before the first juror was called. He was looking at three consecutive twenty-five-to-life sentences. If he was the most model of prisoners, he could hope to get out two months past his one hundred and ninth birthday.

That wasn't good enough.

So Johnny Harvey summoned up his resources. He still had his winning ways with a computer, and Nathanael Greene was a computer-controlled prison. The central file always knew where every inmate was and whether he had a right to be there, because at every door, every stair, every cell there was a checkpoint. Each inmate's anklet ID checked him in and out for all the hours of his sentence, everywhere.

That wasn't good enough, either, but then two more events filled out the pattern. The first was when his first cellmate, No Meat, stuck his hand in the microwave oven. It was Harvey's fault, in a way. He had told No Meat how to bypass the oven's safety interlocks. But he hadn't really thought No Meat would carry his protest against prison diet that far until he didn't show up at evening lockup, and the screw told him No Meat was now well on his way to a different kind of institution, and the next day Harvey got a new companion. His name was Muzzi, and he looked a lot like bad news. He was short and scowling. He came into the cell as though he were returning to a summer home and unsatisfied with the way the caretakers had kept it up, and Harvey was cast in the role of the caretaker. His first words to Harvey were: "You're too fucking old. I don't screw anybody over twenty-two." What struck Harvey most strongly, even more than the violence and the paranoid brutality in the man, was his smell: a sort of catbox rancor, overlaid with expensive men's cologne. What struck Harvey later on, when Muzzi finished explaining to him who he was and how Harvey was going to behave, was that here was a man who was well connected. Not just connected, but holding. Muzzi was serving his sentence without the clemency he could have had in a minute for a little testimony. Muzzi chose instead to serve his time. So he was owed; and by somebody big.

The other event was that excavation started, no more than ten yards from the retaining walls of the prison, for the Bed-Stuy methane generating pit.

On Thursday morning Inmate 838-10647 HARVEY John T. returned to his cell after breakfast, along with all the other inmates in his cellblock, for morning showdown. Bedding stripped. Mattress on the floor. Personal-effects locker open. Inmates standing by the door. As always, the guards strolled past in teams of three. Usually there was just a quick glance into each cell. Sometimes a random dash and a shakedown: body search, sometimes going over the mattress with handheld metal detectors, sometimes even taking it away to the lab and replacing it with a new one, or rather an even older, worse-stained, fouler-smelling one off the pallet the trusty pulled behind them. Harvey and Muzzi stood impassively as they went by. This time the reviews didn't bother them; but from the end of the cellblock Harvey could hear cursing and whining. Somebody, possibly the black kid who had just come in, had been caught with contraband.

Then, for some minutes, nothing, until the speaker grilles rattled and said, "All inmates, proceed to your duty stations."

Muzzi's work in the bakery was one way, Harvey's library the other. They didn't say good-bye to each other. They didn't speak at all.

Harvey was not surprised when, toward the end of his morning shift, the speaker in the library defied the *Quiet!* signs and blared, "Six Four Seven Harvey! Report to Visitors' Center!"

The well-connected Muzzi had used his connections well. He had procured them a reception party to be waiting once they were outside the prison. He had procured a couple of assistants to manufacture the plastic explosive and help with the digging—and, of course, to get him his personal shiv as well. He had also procured for Harvey a "son" to serve as a courier, and not a bad son at that. The kid even reminded Harvey a little bit of himself at that age—not counting color, anyway. Not counting their family backgrounds, either, which were Short Hills versus Bed-Stuy, and certainly not counting parentage—in Harvey's case a pair of college teachers, in Marcus's a retired hooker and her pimp. It was hard to see any resemblance at all, to be truthful, except that the young Johnny Harvey and the young Marcus de Harcourt shared the lively, bursting curiosity about the world and everything that made it go. So when Marcus came in he was right in character to be bubbling, "I seen the model of Bed-Stuy, Dad! Boy! There's some neat stuff there—they got windmills that're gonna pump hot and cold water, they got a place to turn sewage into gas, they got solar panels and an ice pond—"

"Which did you like best?" Harvey asked, and promptly the answer came back:

"The windmills!"

And that was the heart of the visit, the rest was just window-dressing.

Because Harvey had an artist's urge for perfection he took pleasure in spinning out the talk to its full half hour. He asked Marcus all about his school, and about his Mom, and about his Cousin Will and his Aunt Flo and half a dozen other made-up relatives. The boy was quick at making up answers, because he too obviously enjoyed playing the game. When it was time to go Harvey reached around the desk and hugged him, and of course the guard reacted. "Oh, hell, Harvey," she sighed—not unpleasantly, because she didn't believe in shaming a man before his kid. "You know better than that. Now we got to frisk you both."

"That's all right," said Harvey generously. It was. He wasn't carrying anything that he wasn't supposed to, of course, and neither was the boy. Anymore.

An excuse to clean up around the model on his afternoon shift, a pretext to return to the library after dinner—Harvey's glib tongue was good enough for both, though not without some sweat. He was carrying, now; if he had happened to hit a routine stop-and-search with the contraband in his possession . . . But he didn't. Before bedcheck that night Harvey's part was done. The chip was in place in the library computer.

The chip Marcus had smuggled in wasn't exactly a chip. It was a planar-doped barrier, a layer cake with gallium arsenide for the cake and fillings of silicon and beryllium.

Once Harvey had retrieved it from the niche under the model windmills and slipped it into place in the library terminal, it took only a few simple commands—"Just checking," he grinned at the night duty officer in the library—and the chip had redefined for the master computer a whole series of its instructions.

So, back in his cell, Harvey stretched out and grinned happily at the ceiling. Even Muzzi was smiling, or as close to smiling as he ever got. They were ready. Esposito had already stolen the vaseline and the other chemicals to make plastic. La Croy had the hammers, the shovels and the spike to make a hole in the wall for the plastic charge.

And the chip was in place.

It functioned perfectly, as Harvey had designed it to do, which meant that at that moment it did nothing at all. As each inmate passed a checkpoint, his ankle ID registered his presence and was checked against the master file of what inmates were permitted to be in what locations at which times. In the seven and a half hours after Harvey did his job, about a dozen inmates came up wrong on the computer. Their sector doors locked hard until a human guard ambled by to check it out. Three of the inmates were stoned. One was simply an incorrigible troublemaker who had no business being in a nice place like Nathanael Greene. The others all had good excuses. None of them was Inmate 838-10647 HARVEY John T. Neither he nor any of his three confederates had tripped any alert, and they never would again. The computer registered their various presences readily enough. When it consulted the file of any one of them it was redirected to a special instruction table which informed it that Inmates Harvey, Muzzi, Esposito and La Croy were permitted to be any place they chose to be at any time. When it sought any one of them in his cell and registered an absence, the same redirection told it that this particular indication of absence was to be treated as registering present. The computer did not question any of that. Neither did the guards. The function of the guards was not really to guard anything, only to enforce the commands of the computer—and now and then, to be sure, to see that none of the inmates dumbly or deliberately jammed the optical scanners by kicking their IDs in backward, thus locking everybody in everywhere. The guards didn't ask questions, since they were as sure as any bank or brokerage firm that the computer would not fail.

And were about to learn the same lesson from Johnny Harvey.

So at five o'clock the next morning all four of them had strolled to a cell in the east wing of Nathanael Greene, part of the block that had been evacuated while the outside digging for the Bed-Stuy shit pit was going on. "Do it, fuckheads," Muzzi ordered, licking his lips, as Esposito held the spike and La Croy got ready to strike the first blow. "I'll be back in ten minutes."

He was fondling the paper-wrapped shiv, and Harvey had a dismal feeling. "We all really ought to stay right here, Moots," he offered.

Muzzi said, without malice: "I got business with a guard." And he was gone.

"Oh, shit," sighed Harvey, and nodded to La Croy to swing the hammer.

Since no one else was in that wing, no one heard. Or no one but the geophone, which relayed the information to the central computer, where the same chip informed it that the digging noises were part of the excavation for the shit pit. The geophone heard the sound of the plastic going off in the drillhole five minutes later, too, and reported it, and got the same response; and they were through the wall. All that remained was furious digging for about a dozen yards. When they were well begun Muzzi came staggering back, holding his face, his jaw at an unusual angle. "Fuckin cockthucker thapped me," he groaned. "Get the fuckin hole dug!" And dig they did, frantic shoveling, now and then noisy and nervewracking sledgehammering as they hit a rock, and all the time Muzzi ranting and complaining as he held his fractured jaw: the shiv had been too short, it had broken off, the fuckin guard fought back, Muzzi had had to strangle the fucker to teach him a fuckin lesson for giving him a fuckin hard time—Harvey began to panic; the grand plan was going all to pieces because this raving maniac was part of it—

And they made it through the dirt and broke out into open space, into the excavation. Out onto a narrow plank walk over four stories of open steelwork. To a ladder and up it, five stories up, all the way to the surface, seeing buildings, seeing city streets, seeing the lightening pre-dawn sky, and it was working, it was all working after all!

They even saw the black car that was waiting where it was supposed to wait, with its clothes and guns and money—

And then it all went wrong again—Jesus, Harvey moaned, how *terribly* wrong—as a construction-site security guard, who did not have a computer to tell him what to do, observed four men clambering out of the excavation, and tried to stop them.

It was too bad for him. But the shots gave the alarm, and the noise and the commotion were too much for the person in the black car, and it rolled away and around the corner and there they were, Esposito dead, Muzzi with a bullet in his ass, out of the prison, free—but also alone in a world that hated them.

5

Marcus was early at Mr. Feigerman's office, not just early because the errand he had to run couldn't wait, but too early for Mr. Feigerman to stand for it. He couldn't help himself. All the way from the candy store his feet kept hurrying him, although his head told him to slow down. His feet knew what they were doing. They were scared.

So was the rest of Marcus Garvey de Harcourt. It was bad to be summoned out of school because his father had been hurt. It was worse that when he got to the candy store his father was in a stretcher, a paramedic hovering by, while two cops questioned him angrily and dangerously. The store had been robbed, Marcus gathered. The robbers were not just robbers, they were escaped prisoners from Nathanael Greene; and they had held up the store, beaten up his father, stolen all the money and ridden off in a commandeered panel truck with Jersey plates. None of that really scared Marcus. It was only the normal perils of the jungle, surprising only because his father was known to be under the protection of someone big. It did not occur to Marcus that the story was a whole, huge lie until his father waved the cops away so he could whisper to his son. What he whispered was, "Around the corner. Mr. Gambiage. Do what he say." It was serious—so serious that Dandy de Harcourt didn't bother to threaten Marcus with the cat, because he knew the boy would understand that any punishment for failure would be a lot worse. That was when he began to be scared; and what finished the job was when Mr. Gambiage snatched him into the black car and told him what he had to do.

So he took the knapsack and the orders and went trotting off, and if the boy warrior did not wet his pants with fear it was only because he was too scared to pee. He had been told that a diversion had been organized. The diversion was beginning to take shape all around him, people in threes and fours hurrying toward the heart of the Bed-Stuy project, some carrying banners, some huddled on the sidewalk as they lettered new ones. It made slow going, but not slow enough; he got to the Williamsburgh Bank Building more than ninety minutes before he was expected, and that was too early. The best thing to do was to pee himself a break in the twenty-ninth-floor men's room to collect his thoughts and calm himself down, but a security guard followed him in and stood behind him at the urinal. "What's in the backpack, kid?" the guard asked, not very aggressively.

Marcus took his time answering. It was a good thing he'd finally managed to get tall enough for the man-sized urinals, because there weren't any kid-sized ones here. He urinated at a comfortable pace, and when he was quite finished and his fly glitched shut he turned and said, "I'm Mr. de Rintelen Feigerman's personal assistant, and these are things for Mr. Feigerman." The guard was a small man. He was lighter skinned than Marcus, but for a minute there he looked a lot like Dandy getting ready to reach for the cat.

Then he relaxed and grinned. "Aw, hell, sure. Mr. Feigerman's seeing-eye kid, that right?" He didn't wait for an answer, but reached under his web belt and pulled out a pack of cigarettes. "If you see anybody coming in, kid, you give a real loud cough, you hear?" he ordered, just like Dandy, and disappeared into a stall. In a moment Marcus smelled weed. Cheap chickenshit, he said, but not out loud, because he knew there was no hope that a guard working for Mr. Feigerman would offer a hit to Feigerman's young protégé, no matter how much the protégé needed to steady his nerves.

In the waiting room of Feigerman & Tisdale Engineering Associates Marcus dusted off his best society manners before he approached the receptionist. It was, "Mr. Feigerman's expecting me, sir," and, "I know I'm too early, sir," and, "I'll just sit over here out of the way, so please don't disturb Mr. Feigerman, sir." So of course the receptionist relayed it all to Feigerman practically at once, and Marcus was ushered into the old man's presence nearly an hour before his time. But not into the big office with the useless huge windows. Feigerman was down where he liked to be, in his model room, and he turned toward the boy at once, his headset wheeling and clicking away. "I heard about your dad, Marcus," he said anxiously. "I hope he's all right."

"Just beaten up pretty bad, Mr. Feigerman. They're taking him to the hospital, but they say he'll be okay."

"Terrible, terrible. Those animals. I hope the police catch them."

"Yes, sir," said Marcus, not bothering to tell Mr. Feigerman that it was not likely to have been the escaped convicts that had done the beating as much as one of Mr. Gambiage's associates, just to make the story look good.

"Terrible," Feigerman repeated. "And there's some kind of demonstration going on against the Bed-Stuy project, did you see it? I swear, Marcus," he said, not waiting for an answer, "I don't know how Gambiage gets these people out! They must know what he is. And they have to know, too, that the project is for their own good, don't they?"

"Sure they do," said Marcus, again refraining from the obvious: the project could do them good, but not nearly as much good, or bad, as Gambiage could do them. "We going to go take a look at it?"

"Oh, yes," said Feigerman, but not with enthusiasm; it was a bad day for the old man, Marcus could see, and if it hadn't been for the nagging terror in his own mind he would have felt sympathy. Feigerman reached out to fondle a sixteenth-scale model of one of the wind rotors and brightened. "You haven't been down here lately, Marcus. Would you like me to show you around?"

If Marcus had been able to afford the truth he would surely have said yes, because almost the best part of working for Mr. Feigerman was seeing the working models of the windmills, the thermal aquifer storage with oil substituting for the water, the really truly working photovoltaics that registered a current when you turned a light on them—all of them, actually. And there was something new, an Erector-set construction of glass tubing with something like Freon turning itself into vapor at the bottom and bubbling up through a column of water and pulling the water along, then the water passing through another tube and a turbine on the way down to generate more power.

Feigerman's sonar eyes could not tell him what someone was thinking, but he could see where Marcus was looking. "That's what we call the wopperator," he said proudly. "It can use warm underground water to circulate that fluid all winter long, boiling another fluid at the bottom and condensing it again at the top—what's the matter?" he added anxiously, seeing that Marcus was shaking his head.

"It's Dandy," Marcus explained. "Before they took him away he told me I had to deliver some cigarettes for him—they're good customers, over by the power plant—"

Feigerman was disappointed, then annoyed. "Oh, hell, boy, what are you telling me? Cigarettes don't come in tin cans."

Fuck the old bastard! Sometimes you forgot that he saw things in a different way, and that metal would give off a conspicuous echo even inside a canvas backpack. "Sure, Mr. Feigerman," Marcus improvised, "but there's two containers of coffee there, too. And Dandy said he'd get the cat out if it got there cold."

"Oh, hell." Since Feigerman wasn't much good at reading other people's expressions, perhaps in compensation his own face showed few. But it was clear this time that he was disappointed. He said in resignation, "I don't want to get you in trouble with your dad, Marcus, especially after those thugs beat him up. Sam!" he called to the modelmaker chief, standing silent across the room. "Call down for my car, will you?" But all the way down in the elevator he was silent and obviously depressed. No more than Marcus, who was not only depressed but scared; not only scared but despairing, because he was beginning to understand that sooner or later somebody was going to connect his visits to the prison with the fact that the escaped prisoners had just happened to stop at his father's candy store . . . and so, very likely, this was the last time he would spend with Mr. Feigerman.

Julius was waiting for them with the car, illegally parked right in front of the main entrance because it had begun to rain. Mr. Feigerman's machine was doing its whee-clickety-beep thing and he turned his head restlessly about, but the sonar did not work through the windows of the limousine. "There's a lot of people out there," said Marcus, trying to help without upsetting the old man.

"I can hear that, damn it! What are they doing?"

What they were doing was shouting and chanting, and there were a lot more of them than Marcus had expected. Old man Feigerman was not satisfied. Blind he might be, but his otoliths were in fine shape; he could feel the pattern of acceleration and deceleration, and knew that the driver, Julius, was having a hard time getting through crowds. "Is it that maniac Gambiage's demonstration?" he demanded.

Marcus said apologetically, "I guess that's it, Mr. Feigerman. There's a lot of them carrying signs."

"Read me the signs, damn it!"

Obediently Marcus rattled off the nearest few. There was a *Give Bed-Stuy Freedom of Choice!* and a *Salvemos nuestras casas!* and *Jobs, Not Theories!* and two or three that made specific reference to Mr. Feigerman himself, which Marcus did not read aloud. Or have to. As they inched along, block by block, the yelling got louder and more personal. "Listen, Feigerman," bawled one man, leaning over the hood of the car, "Bed-Stuy's our home—love it or leave it!" And old man Feigerman, looking even older than usual, sank back on the seat, gnawing his thumb.

The rain did not seem to slow anybody down—not anybody, of all the dozens of different kinds of anybodies thronging the streets. There were dozens, even hundreds, of the neighborhood characters—five or six tottering winos, fat old Bloody Bess the moocher, even two young brothers from the Franciscan rescue mission, swinging their rain-soaked signs and shouting—Marcus could make out neither the slogans nor the signs, because they seemed to be in Latin. There were solid clumps of blue-collars, some of them construction workers, some from the truckers and the airline drivers; there were people who looked like bank clerks and people who looked like store salespersons—put them all together and it was a tremendous testimonial to Mr. Gambiage's ability to whip up a spontaneous riot on a moment's notice. And they were not all pacific. Ahead there was a whine of sirens and a plop of tear-gas shells from where the construction equipment stood idle.

"They're getting rough," bawled Julius over his shoulder, and he looked worried. "Looks like they're smashing the backhoes!"

Mr. Feigerman nodded without answering, but his face looked terribly drawn. Marcus, looking at him, began to worry that the old man was not up to this sort of ordeal—if, indeed, Marcus was himself. He craned his neck to peer at the clock on the Williamsburgh Bank Building and gritted his teeth. They were running very late, and it was not the kind of errand where an excuse would get you off. It didn't get faster. A block along a police trike whined up beside them, scattering a gaggle of high-school girls shouting, "Soak the rich, help the poor, make Bed-Stuy an open door!" The cop ran down his window and yelled across at Julius, then recognized him as a fellow policeman and peered into the back to see Mr. Feigerman.

"You sure you want to go in here?" he demanded. There was a tone of outrage in his voice—a beat cop who had spent the first hour of his shift expecting to find desperate escaped convicts, received the welcome word that they were probably across the Hudson River and then been confronted with a quick, dirty and huge burgeoning riot.

Julius referred the question to higher authority. "What do you say, Mr. Feigerman?" he called over his shoulder. "Any minute now some of these thugs are going to start thinking about turning cars over."

Feigerman shook his head. "I want to see what they're doing," he said, his voice shrill and unhappy. "But maybe not you, Marcus. Maybe you ought to get out and go back."

The boy stiffened. "Aw, no, please, Mr. Feigerman!" he begged. "I got to deliver this, uh, coffee—and anyway," he improvised, "I'd be scared to be alone in that bunch! I'm a lot better off with you and Julius!" It was a doubtful thesis at best, but the cop in the trike was too busy to argue and Mr. Feigerman too full of woe. Only Julius was shaking his head as he wormed the big car through the ever narrower spaces between the yelling, chanting groups. But as they crossed the Long Island Rail Road tracks the crowds thinned. "Down there," Marcus ordered, leaning forward. "Over between the power plant and the shit pit, the stuff's for the guards at the excavation—"

Julius paused to crane his neck around and stare at Marcus, but when Feigerman didn't protest he obediently turned the car down a rutted, chewed-up street. Feigerman gasped, as the car jolted over potholes, "Damn that Gambiage! I thought he was still planning to buy me off—why does he do this now?"

Marcus did not answer, but he could have guessed that it had something to do with the stuff in his backpack. "Right by the guard shack," he directed, and Julius turned into an entrance with a wire-mesh gate. A man in uniform came strolling out. "Got the stuff for us, kid?" he asked, chewing on a straw, his hand resting on the butt of a gun.

"Yes, sir!" cried Marcus, shucking the pack and rolling down the window, delighted to get his errand run so peacefully.

But it didn't stay peaceful long. Julius was staring at the man in guard's uniform, and, with increasing concern, at the quiet excavation and the absence of anyone else. Before Marcus could get the pack off Julius shouted, "Son of a bitch, it's Jack La Croy—get down, Mr. Feigerman!" And he was reaching for his gun.

But not fast enough. La Croy had the guard's gun, and he had not taken his hand off it. The shot went into Julius's throat, right between the Adam's apple and the chin, and spatters of blood flew back to strike Marcus's face like hot little raindrops. Two other men boiled out of the guard shack, one limping and swearing, the other Marcus's pretend-father, his face scared and dangerous. As La Croy pushed Julius out of the way and shoved himself behind the wheel the other two jumped into the back of the car, fat, fearsome Muzzi reaching for the backpack of weapons and money with an expression of savage joy. . . .

And from behind them, a sudden roar of an engine and the quick zap of a siren.

Everybody was shouting at once. Marcus, crushed under the weight of the killer Muzzi, could not see what was happening, but he could feel the car surge forward, stop, spin and make a dash in another direction. There was a sudden lurch and crash as they broke through something, and then it stopped and the men were out of the car, firing at something behind them. Julius would never get back on the force, Marcus thought, struggling to wipe the blood off his face—and whether he himself would live through the next hour was at best an open question.

For Johnny Harvey everything had begun going terribly wrong even before they broke through the wall, and gone downhill ever since. It was just luck they'd been able to kill the security guard and get his gun, just luck that they'd been able to hide in a place where there was a telephone, long enough for Muzzi to make his phone call on the secret number and beg, or threaten, the big man to get them out. The arrangements were complicated—a delivery of guns and money, a faked holdup to send the cops in the wrong direction, a whomped-up riot to keep the cops busy—but they'd been working pretty well, and that was luck, too, lots of luck, more than they had a right to expect—

But the luck had run out.

When the boy came with the guns it was bad luck that the driver was an off-duty cop who recognized La Croy, worse luck still that there was a police car right behind them. La Croy did the only thing he could do. There was no way out of the street they were in except back past the cops, and that was impossible. So he'd slammed the car through the gate of the powerplant. And there they were, inside the powerplant, with four terrified engineers lying facedown on the floor of the control room and forty thousand New York City cops gathering outside. The boy was scared shitless; the old man, his vision gear crushed, was lying hopeless and paralyzed beside the guards. "At least we've got hostages," said La Croy, fondling his gun, and Muzzi, staring around the control room of the nuclear plant, said:

"Asshole! We've got the whole fuckin *city* for a hostage!"

6

The job as companion and bedpan changer to old Mrs. Feigerman paid well, worked easy and was generally too good to last. When it ended Nillie de Harcourt didn't complain. She turned to the next chapter in her life: bag lady. That meant eight hours a day sitting before a screening table in her pale green smock, chatting with the bag ladies on either side of her; while magnets pulled out the ferrous metals, glass went one way, to be separated by color, and organics went another. The biggest part of the job was to isolate organics so they would not poison the sludge-making garbage. The work was easy enough, and not particularly unpleasant once you got past the smell. But that was too good to last, too, because anything good was always going to be too good for Gwenna Anderson Vanilla Fudge de Harcourt. So when she saw The Man moving purposefully toward her through the clinking, clattering, smelly aisles she was not surprised. "Downstairs, Nillie," he said, flashing the potsie. "We need you." She didn't ask why. She just looked toward her supervisor, who shrugged and nodded; and took off the green smock regretfully, and folded it away, and did as she was told. He didn't tell her what it was about. He didn't have to. Trouble was what it was about, because that was always what it was about. She followed him into the waiting police car without comment. The driver in the front started away at once, siren screaming. In the back, the cop turned on a tape recorder, cleared his throat and said, "This interview is being conducted by Sergeant Marvin Wagman. Is your name Gwenna Anderson?"

"That was my name before I married de Harcourt."

"According to records, Mrs. de Harcourt, you have fourteen arrests and six convictions for prostitution, five arrests no convictions for shoplifting, two arrests one conviction for possession of a controlled substance and one arrest no conviction for open lewdness."

Nillie shrugged. "You're talking about fifteen years ago, man."

Wagman looked at her with annoyance, but also, Nillie noted, a lot more tension than anything he had said so far would justify. "Right," he said sarcastically, "so now you're a success story. You married the boss and went into business for yourself. Dope business, numbers business, bookmaking business."

"If I was all those things, would I have to get work as a bag lady?"

"I ask the questions," he reminded her, but it was a fair question and he knew it. He didn't know the answer, but then hardly anybody did but Nillie herself—and most people wouldn't have believed it if told. "You have a son named Marcus Garvey de Harcourt?" he went on.

Suddenly Nillie sat bolt upright. "Mister, did something happen to Marcus?"

The sergeant was human after all; he hesitated, and then said, "I'm not supposed to tell you anything, just make sure I've got the right person. But your son's in good health last I heard."

"*Mister!*"

"I have to ask you these questions! Now, did you ever work for Henry Gambiage?"

"Not exactly. Sort of; all the girls did, at least he was getting a cut on everything. But that was before his name was Gambiage. What about Marcus?"

"And do you and your husband work for him now?"

"Not me!"

"But your husband?" he insisted.

"Take the Fifth," she said shortly. "Anyway, you ain't read me my rights."

"You're not under arrest," he told her, and then clicked off the tape recorder. "That's all I can say, Miz de Harcourt," he finished, "so please don't ask me any more questions." And she didn't, but she was moving rapidly from worry to terror. Mentioning her son was bad enough; mentioning Gambiage a lot worse. But when a cop called her "Miz" and used the word "please"—then it was time to get scared.

It was all but physically impossible for Nillie to plead with a policeman, but she came as close to it in the rest of this ride as ever since the first afternoon she'd been picked up for soliciting a plainclothes on the corner of Eighth Avenue and Forty-fifth Street, fifteen years old, turned out on the turf just two days before and still thinking that some day, maybe, she'd get back to the Smokies of eastern Tennessee. She gazed out at the dirty, rainy streets as they whizzed by at fifty miles an hour through rapidly moving traffic, and wished she could be sick. Marcus! If anything happened to him—

Her view of the dingy streets was suddenly streaked with tears, and Nillie began to pray.

When Nillie prayed she did not address any god. What religion she had she had picked up in the Women's House of Detention, the last time she was there—the last time she ever would be there, she had vowed. It was just after the big riots in New York, and the first night in her cell she dropped off to sleep and found herself being touched by a big, strong woman with a hard, huge face. Nillie automatically assumed she was a bull-dyke. She was wrong. The woman was a missionary. She got herself arrested simply so she could preach to the inmates. Her religion was called "Temple I"—I am a temple, I myself, I am holy. It didn't matter in her church what god you worshipped. You could worship any, or none at all; but you had to worship in, for and to yourself. You should not drug, whore or steal; above all, no matter what wickedness went on around you, you should not let them make you an accomplice . . . and so when Nillie got out she went to seek her pimp to tell him that she was through. . . .

And found Dandy in far worse shape than she. No more girls to run. No money left. And both kneecaps shattered, because he had made the mistake of getting in the middle of a power struggle in the mob. So she nursed him; and when she found out she was pregnant by him she kept it to herself until he was able to hobble around, and by then it was too late to think about a quick and easy abortion. It was a surprise to her that he married her. Dandy wasn't really a bad man—for a pimp—though even for a pimp he damn sure wasn't a specially good one; but he wanted a son, and it was joy for both of them when it turned out she was giving him one. Uneasy joy, sometimes—the boy was born small, caught every bug that was going around, missed half of every school year until he was eight. But that wasn't a bad thing; in the hospitals were Gray Ladies and nurses to teach him to read and give him the habit; he was smarter than either of his parents right now, Nillie thought—

If he was alive.

She straightened up and rubbed the last dampness from the corners of her eyes. She recognized the streets fleeting by—they were in her own neighborhood now, only blocks from the candy store. But what had happened? The streets were littered with rain-smeared placards, and the smell of tear gas was strong. There was a distant bellow of bullhorns blaring something about evacuation and *warning* and nuclear accident—

The police car nosed across the LIRR tracks, with a commuter special flashing away along the maglev lines as though it were running from something. As Nillie saw that the car was approaching the power plant, she thought that it was probably time to run, all right, if there was anywhere to run to.

They parked at the end of the cul de sac, with barricades and police cars blocking off the road, and ran, dazzled by the spinning blue and white and red emergency lights, along one side of the street, across from the utility's chainlink fence, into a storefront. And there were cops by the dozen, and not just cops. There was supercop, the commissioner himself, giving orders to half a dozen gray-haired police with gold braid on their caps; and there was a hospital stretcher, and out of a turban of white bandages looked eyes that Nillie instinctively recognized as her husband's; and there was Mrs. Feigerman's sullen elderly son, David Tisdale, looking both frightened and furious—

And there, his scar pale and his lips compressed, staring at her with the cold consideration of a butcher about to put the mercy killer to the skull of a steer, was Henry Gambiage.

The situation wasn't only bad, it was worse than Nillie had dreamed possible. If Marc was alive—and he had been, at least, a few minutes earlier on the telephone—he was also a hostage. Not just any hostage. Captive of one of the maddest, meanest murderers in the New York prison system, Angelo Muzzi. And not just at the mercy of the mad dog's weapons, but right at Ground Zero for what the convicts threatened would be the damnedest biggest explosion the much-bombed city had ever seen. The argument that was going on when Nillie came in had nothing to do with the hostages. It was among three people, two engineers from Con Ed and a professor from Brooklyn College's physics department, and what they were arguing was whether it lay within the capacities of the escaped convicts merely to poison all of Bedford-Stuyvesant, or if they could take out the whole city and most of Long Island and the North Jersey coast. The Commissioner was having none of that. "Clear them out," he ordered tersely. "The mayor's going to be here in half an hour, and I want this settled before then." But Nillie wasn't listening. She was thinking of Marcus Garvey de Harcourt, age ten, in the middle of a nuclear explosion of any kind. Nothing else made much impression. She heard two of the police wrangling with each other over whether they had done the right thing by following Marcus with his bag of weapons to see where the escapees were, instead of simply preventing him from delivering them as soon as they realized the story of the candy-store holdup was a lie. She heard the commissioner roaring at Gambiage, and Gambiage stolidly, repetitiously, demanding to see his lawyer. She heard her husband whisper—even harder to understand than usual, because his lips were swollen like a Ubangi maiden's—that Muzzi had made him get the boy to try to deliver weapons, had made him lie about the fake holdup and then had beaten him senseless to make the story more realistic. She gathered, vaguely, that the reason she and Dandy were there was to force Gambiage to get his criminals away from the powerplant by threatening to testify against him—David Tisdale the same—and none of it made any impression on her. She sat silent by the window, peering at the chainlink fence and the low, sullen building that lay behind it. "Listen, shithead," the commissioner was roaring, "your lawyer wouldn't come if I let him, because if you don't get Muzzi out of that control room the whole city might go up!"

And Gambiage spread his hands. "You think I don't care about the city? Jesus. I *own* half of it. But there's nothing I can do with Muzzi." And then he went flying, looking more surprised than angry, as Nillie pushed past him. "There's something *I* can do," she cried. "I can talk to my little boy! Where's that phone?"

Marcus H. Garvey de Harcourt, king of the jungle, strong and fearless—Marcus who faced up every day to the threat of Dandy's cat-o'-nine-tails and the menace of bigger kids willing to beat him bloody for the dimes in his pocket and the peril of pederasts who carried switchblade knives to convince their victims, and stray dogs, and mean-hearted cops, and raunchy winos—that dauntless Marcus was scared out of his tree. Dead people, sure. You couldn't live a decade in Bed-Stuy without coming across an occasional stiff. Not often stiffs you had known. Not often seeing them die. Julius had not been any friend of his—at best, a piece of the furniture of Marcus's life—but seeing him sob and bubble his life away had been terrifying. It was all terrifying. There was old Mr. Feigerman, his seeing gear crushed and broken; the blind man was really blind, now, and it seemed to cost him his speech and hearing as well, for he just lay against a wall of the power-station control center, unmoving. There was his soi-disant father, Johnny Harvey, not jovial now, not even paying attention to him; he was standing by the window with a stitch-gun in his hand, and Marcus feared for the life of anyone who showed in Harvey's field of fire. There were the power-station engineers, bound and gagged, not to mention beaten up, lying in the doorway so if anyone started shooting from outside they would be the first to get it. There was that loopy little guy with the crazy eyes, La Croy, screaming rage and obscenities, shrieking as though he were being skinned alive, although he didn't have a mark on him. And there was—

There was Muzzi. Marcus swallowed and looked away, for Muzzi had looked at him a time or two in a fashion that scared him most of all. Marcus was profoundly grateful that Muzzi was more interested in the telephone to the outside world than in himself. There he was, looking like Pancho Villa with his holstered guns and the twin bandoliers crossed over his steel-ribbed flak jacket, yelling at the unseen, but not unheard, Mr. Gambiage. "Out!" he roared, "what we want ith fuckin out, and fuckin damn thoon!"

"Now, Moots," soothed the voice over the speakerphone.

"Now *thit!* We had a fuckin deal! I keep my fuckin mouth thut about MacReady and you get me out of the fuckin joint!"

"I didn't kill MacReady—"

"You wath fuckin right there watchin when I gave him the fuckin ithe pick, tho get fuckin movin!"

Gambiage's self-control was considerable, but there was an edge to his voice as he said, placatingly, "I'm doing what I can, Moots. The Mayor's on his way, and he's agreed to be a hostage while you get on the plane—"

"Not jutht the Mayor, I want the fuckin Governor and the fuckin Governor'th fuckin kid! All three of them, and right away, or I blow up the whole fuckin thity!"

Just to hear the words made icy little mice run up and down Marcus's spine. Blow up the city! It was one thing to listen to Mrs. Spiegel tell about it in the third grade, and a whole other, far worse thing to imagine it really happening. Could it happen? Marcus shrank back into his corner, looking at the men around him. Muzzi certainly wouldn't have the brains to make it happen, neither would La Croy. The engineers and Mr. Feigerman might know how, but Marcus couldn't imagine anything the convicts could do that would make them do it.

That left Johnny Harvey.

Ah, shit, Marcus thought to himself, sure. Johnny Harvey could figure out how to do it if anybody could. *Would* he?

The more Marcus thought about it, the more he thought that Harvey just might. What little Marcus had seen of Nathanael Greene made him think that living there must be pretty lousy, lousy enough so that even dying in a mushroom cloud might be better than spending the rest of your life in a place like that. Or a worse one. . . . But it wouldn't be better for Marcus. Marcus didn't want to die. And the only thing he could think of that might keep him from it, if Muzzi blew his stack terminally and Harvey carried out the bluff, would be for him to kill Harvey first—"Hey, kid!"

Marcus stiffened and saw that Muzzi was glowering at him, holding the phone in his hand. "Wh-what?" he got out.

Muzzi studied him carefully, and the scowl became what Muzzi might have thought an ingratiating grin. "It'th your mom, thweetie. Wantth to talk to you."

The question of how it had all gone to hell no longer interested Johnny Harvey, the question of what, if anything, there was left to hope for was taking up all his attention. He sat before the winking signal lights and dials of the power controls, wolfing down his third hamburger and carton of cold coffee, wondering what Marcus had been wondering. Would he do it? Was there a point in blowing up a city out of rage and revenge? Or was there a point in not doing it, if that meant going back to Nathanael Greene?—or some worse place. He reached for another hamburger, and then pushed the cardboard tray away in disgust. Trust Muzzi to demand food that a decent palate couldn't stand! But those two words, "trust" and "Muzzi," didn't belong in the same sentence.

Trusting Muzzi had got him this far. It wasn't far enough. There was Muzzi, stroking the nigger kid's arm as the boy talked to his mother, on the ragged edge of hysteria; Muzzi with his jaw broken and one hand just about ruined, and still filled with enough rage and enough lust for a dozen ordinary human beings. You could forget about Feigerman and the engineers, they were just about out of it; there was Muzzi and that asshole La Croy, and the boy and himself, and how were they going to get out of here? Assume the governor gave in. Assume there really was a jet waiting for them at Kennedy. The first thing they had to do was get out of this place and into a car—not here in this street, where there could be a thousand boobytraps that would wreck any plan, but out in the open, say on the other side of the railroad tracks, where there would be a clear shot down the avenue toward the airport. It was almost like one of those cannibals and missionaries puzzles of his boyhood. Johnny Harvey had been really good at those puzzles. Was there a way to solve this one? Let the first missionary take the first cannibal across the river in the boat—only this time it was across the railroad tracks—then come back by himself to where the other missionaries and cannibals were waiting—

Only this time he was one of the cannibals, and the game was for keeps.

The boy was still on the phone, weeping now, and Muzzi had evidently got some kind of crazed idea in his head, because he had moved over to the corner where Feigerman was lying. Callously he wrenched the remains of the harness off Feigerman's unprotesting body. The old man wasn't dead, but he made no sound as Muzzi began straightening out the bent metal and twisted crown. Then he got up and walked toward Johnny Harvey.

Who got up and moved cautiously away; you never knew what Muzzi was going to do.

And then he saw that Muzzi, glowering over the power-station controls, was reaching his hand out toward them; and then Johnny Harvey was really scared.

When Nillie got off the phone she just sat. She didn't weep. Nillie de Harcourt had had much practice restraining tears in her life. They were a luxury she couldn't afford, not now, not while Marcus was in that place with those men—with that one particular man, for she had known Muzzi by reputation and gossip and by personal pain, and she knew what particular perils her son was in. So she sat dry-eyed and alert, and watched and waited. When she heard Johnny Harvey on the phone, warning that Muzzi was getting ready to explode, demanding better food than the crap they'd been given, she looked thoughtful for a moment. But she didn't say anything, even when the mayor and Mr. Gambiage retreated to another room for a while. Whatever they were cooking up, it satisfied neither of them. When they came out the mayor was scowling and Mr. Gambiage was shaking his head. "Do not underestimate Moots," he warned. "He's an animal, but he knows a trap when he sees one."

"Shut up," said the mayor, for once careless of a major campaign contributor. The mayor was looking truly scared. He listened irritably to some distant sound, then turned to Gambiage. "They're still shouting out there. I thought you said you'd call off the demonstration."

"It is called off," said Gambiage heavily. "It takes time. It is easier to start things than to stop them." And Nillie was listening alertly, one hand in the hand of her husband. Only when two policemen came in with a room-service rolling hotel tray of food did she let go and move forward.

"It's all ready," one of them said, and the mayor nodded, and Nillie de Harcourt put her hand on the cart.

"I'm taking it over there," she said.

The mayor looked actually startled—maybe even frightened, for reasons Nillie did not try to guess. "No chance, Mrs. de Harcourt. You don't know what kind of men they are."

"I do know," Nillie said steadily. "Who better? And I'm taking this food over so I can be with my son."

The mayor opened his mouth angrily, but Mr. Gambiage put a hand on his shoulder. "Why not?" he said softly.

"Why not? Don't be an idiot, Gambiage—" And then the mayor had second thoughts. He paused, irresolute, then shrugged. "If you insist in front of witnesses," he said, "I do not feel I have the right to stop you."

Nillie was moving toward the door with the cart before he could change his mind. A train flashed underneath the bridge, but she didn't even look at it. She was absolutely certain that something was going on that she didn't understand, something very wrong—something that would make the mayor of the city and the city's boss of all boss criminals whisper together in front of witnesses; but what it was she did not know, and did not consider that it mattered. She went steadily across the tracks and did not falter even when she saw crazy La Croy shouting out the window at her, with his gun pointed at her head. She didn't speak, and she didn't stop. She pushed right in through the door, kicking the powerplant engineers out of the way.

There they were, crazy Muzzi and crazy La Croy, both swearing at her, and sane but treacherous Johnny Harvey with his hand on a gun, moving uncertainly toward the food; and there was old Mr. Feigerman looking like death days past—

And there was Marcus, looking scared but almost unharmed. "Honey, honey!" she cried, and abandoned the food and ran to take him in her arms.

"Leave him alone, bitch!" shouted La Croy, and Muzzi thundered behind him:

"Fuckin handth up, you! Who knowth what you've got there—"

She turned to face them calmly. "I've got nothing but me," she said; and waited for them to do whatever they were going to do.

But what they did was nothing. Johnny Harvey, not very interested in her or his companions, was moving on the cart of food, the big dish with the silver dome; he lifted the dome—

Bright bursts of light flared from under it, thunder roared, and something picked Nillie de Harcourt up and threw her against the wall.

A shard of metal had caught La Croy in the back of the head; he probably had never felt it. What there was left of Johnny Harvey was almost nothing at all. Muzzi struggled to his feet, the terrible pain in his jaw worse than ever, and stared furiously around the battered room. He could hardly see. It had not just been a bomb—they wouldn't have risked a bomb big enough to do the job, in that place; there was something like tear gas in with it, and Muzzi was choking and gasping. But, blurrily, he could see young Marcus trying to help his half-conscious mother out the door, and he bawled, "Thtop or I blow your fuckin headth off!" And the kid turned at him, and his face was a hundred years older than his age, and for a moment even Muzzi felt an unaccustomed tingle of fright. If that kid had had a gun—

But he didn't. "Move your fuckin atheth back in here!" roared Muzzi and slowly, hopelessly, they came back into the choking air.

But not for long.

Two minutes later they were going out again, but there had been a change. Nillie de Harcourt stumbled ahead, barely conscious. Marcus Garvey de Harcourt pushed the wheelchair, and the occupant of the wheelchair, crown on his head, muffled in a turned-up jacket . . . was Muzzi.

And Marcus was the most frightened he had ever been in his life, because he could not see a way to live to the other side of the bridge. He could see the governor coming toward them, with a flanking line of police, all their guns drawn; and he knew what was in Muzzi's mind. The man had gone ape. If he couldn't get away and couldn't blow up the city, the next best thing was to kill the governor.

Halfway across the bridge he made his move; but Marcus also made his.

It wasn't that he cared about the governor, but between the governor and Muzzi's gun was someone he cared about a lot. He took a deep breath, aimed the wheelchair toward a place where the rail was down and only wooden sawhorses were between the sidewalk and the maglev strips below . . . and shoved.

Muzzi was quick, but not quick enough. He was not quite out of the wheelchair when it passed the point of no return.

Marcus ran to the rail and stared down, and there was Muzzi in his bandoliers and steel-ribbed jacket, plummeting toward the maglev strips, beginning to move even before he hit, bouncing up, hitting again, and all the time moving with gathering speed until he flashed out of sight, no longer alive, no longer a threat to anyone.

TO SEE ANOTHER MOUNTAIN

Genius is a subject that comes up in various science fiction tales. Since Olaf Stapledon's *Odd John* and probably before, writers have been fascinated by the potential of human intelligence, its limits, and the possibility that it may have aspects we have not yet discovered.

Unfortunately, too many stories about really brilliant people become dull. Thankfully, "To See Another Mountain," first published in 1958, isn't one of those. Frederik Pohl is far too keen not to mention the oft-noticed proximity of genius and madness. Where that boundary lies and the exact implications of the two are what make this story cook.

And cook it does!

Trucks were coming up the side of the mountain again. The electric motors were quiet enough, but these were heavy-duty trucks and the reduction gears could be heard a mile off. A mile by air; that was eighteen miles by the blacktop road that snaked up the side of the mountain, all hairpin curves with banks that fell away to sheer cliffs.

The old man didn't mind the noise. The trucks woke him up when he was dozing, as he so often was these days.

"You didn't drink your orange juice, doctor."

The old man wheeled himself around in his chair. He liked the nurse. There were three who took care of him, on shifts, but Maureen Wrather was his personal favorite. She always seemed to be around when he needed her. He protested: "I drank most of it." The nurse waited. "All right." He drank it, noting that the flavor had changed again. What was it this time? Stimulants, tranquilizers, sedatives, euphoriacs. They played him up and down like a yo-yo. "Do I get coffee this morning, Maureen?"

"Cocoa." She put the mug and a plate with two arrowroot cookies down on the table, avoiding the central space where he laid out his endless hands of solitaire; that was one of the things the old man liked about her. "I have to get you dressed in half an hour," she announced, "because you've got company coming."

"Company? Who would be coming to see me?" But he could see from the look in her light, cheerful eyes, even before she spoke, that it was a surprise. Well, thought the old man with dutiful pleasure, that was progress, only a few weeks ago they wouldn't have permitted him any surprises at all. Weeks? He frowned. Maybe months. All the days were like all the other days. He could count one, yesterday; two, the day before; three, last week—he could count a few simple intervals with confidence, but the ancient era of a month ago was a wash of gray confusion. He sighed. That was the price you paid for being crazy, he thought with amusement. They made it that way on purpose, to help him "get well." But it had all been gray and bland enough anyhow. Back *very* far ago there had been a time of terror, but then it was bland for a long, long time.

"Drink your cocoa, young fellow," the nurse winked, cheerfully flirting. "Do you want any music?"

That was a good game. "I want a lot of music," he said immediately. "Stravinsky—that *Sac* thing, I think. And Alban Berg. And—I know. Do you have that old one, *The Three Itta Fishies?*" He had been very pleased with the completeness of the tape library in the house on the hill, until he found out that there was something in that orange juice too. Every request of his was carefully noted and analyzed. Like the tiny microphones taped to throat and heart at night, his tastes in music were data in building up a picture of his condition. Well, that took some of the joy out of it, so the old man had added some other joy of his own.

The nurse turned solemnly to the tape player. There was a pause, a faint marking *beep* and then the quick running opening bars of the wonderful Mendelssohn concerto, which he had always loved. He looked at the nurse. "You shouldn't tease us, doctor," she said lightly as she left.

Dr. Adam Sidorenko had changed the world. His Hypothesis of Congruent Values, later expanded to his Theory of General Congruences, was the basis for a technology fully as complex and even more important than the nucleonics that had come from Einstein's Energy-mass equation. This morning the brain that had enunciated the principle of congruence was occupied in a harder problem: What were the noises from the courtyard?

He was going to have his picture taken, he guessed, taking his evidence from the white soft shirt the nurse had laid out for him, the gray jacket and, above all, from the tie. He almost never wore a tie. (The nurse seldom gave him one. He didn't like to speculate about the reasons for this.) While he was dressing, the trucks ground into the courtyard and stopped, and men's voices came clearly.

"I don't know who they are," he said aloud, abandoning the attempt to figure it out.

"They're the television crew," said the nurse from the next mom. "Hush. Don't spoil your surprise."

He dressed quickly then, with excitement; why, it was a *big* surprise. There had never been a television crew on the mountain before. When he came out of the dressing room the nurse frowned and reached for his tie. "Sloppy! Why can't you large-domes learn how to do a simple knot?" She was a very sweet girl, the old man thought, lifting his chin to help. She could have been his daughter—even his granddaughter. She was hardly twenty-five; yes, that would have been about right. His granddaughter would have been about that now—

The old man frowned and turned his head away. That was very wrong. He didn't have a grandchild. He had had one son, no more, and the boy had died, so they had told the old man, in the implosion of the Haaroldsen Free Trawl in the Mindanao Deep. The boy had been nineteen years old, and certainly without children; and there had been something about his death, something that the old man didn't like to remember. He squinted. Worse than that, he thought, something he *couldn't* remember anymore.

The nurse said: "Doctor, this is for you. It isn't much, but happy birthday."

She took a small pink-ribboned box out of the pocket of her uniform and handed it to him. He was touched. He saw his fingers trembling as he unwrapped the little package. That distracted him for a moment but then he dismissed it. It was honest emotion, that was all—well, and age too, of course. He was ninety-five. But it wasn't the worrying intention tremor that had disfigured the few episodes he could remember clearly, in his first days here on the Hill. It was only gratitude and sentiment.

And that was what the box held for him, sentiment. "Thank you, Maureen. You're good to an old man." His eyes stung. It was only a little plastic picture-globe, with Maureen's young face captured smiling inside it, but it was for him.

She patted his shoulder and said firmly: "You're a good man. And a beautiful one, too, so come on and let's show you off to your company."

She helped him into the wheelchair. It had its motors, but he liked to have her push him and she humored him. They went out the door, down the long sunlit corridors that divided the guest rooms in the front of the building from the broad high terrace behind. Sam Krabbe, Ernest Atkinson and a couple of the others from the Group came to the doors of their rooms to nod, and to wish the old man a happy birthday. Sidorenko nodded back, tired and pleased. He listened critically to the thumping of his heart—excitement was a risk, he knew—and then grinned. He was getting as bad as the doctors.

Maureen wheeled the old man onto the little open elevator platform. They dropped, quickly and smoothly on magnetic cushions, to the lower floor. The old man leaned far over the side of his chair, studying what he could see of the elevator, because he had a direct and personal interest in it. Somebody had told him that the application of magnetic fields to nonferrous substances was a trick that had been learned from his General Congruences. Well, there was this much to it: Congruence showed that all fields were related and interchangeable, and there was, of course, no reason why what was possible should not be made what is *so*. But the old man laughed silently inside himself. He was thinking of Albert Einstein confronted with a photo of *Enola Gay*. Or himself trying to build the communications equipment that Congruence had made possible.

The nurse wheeled him out into the garden.

And there before him was the explanation of the morning's trucks.

A whole mobile television unit had trundled up those terrible roads. And a fleet of cars and, yes, that other noise was explained too, there was a helicopter perched on the tennis court, its vanes twisting like blown leaves in the breeze that came up the mountain. The helicopter had a definite meaning, the old man knew. Someone very important must have come up in it. The air space over the institute was closed off, by government order.

And reasoning the thing through, there was a logical conclusion; government orders can be set aside only by government executives, and—yes. There was the answer.

"Are you sure you're warm enough?" the nurse whispered. But Sidorenko hardly heard. He recognized the stocky blue-eyed man who stood chatting with one of the television crew. Sidorenko's contacts with the world around him were censored and small, but everyone would recognize *that* man. His name was Shawn O'Connor; he was the president of the United States.

The president was shaking his hand.

"Dear man," said President O'Connor warmly, "I can't tell you how great a pleasure this is for me. Oh, no. You wouldn't remember me. But I sat in on two of your Roose lectures. Ninety-eight, it must have been. And after the second I went up and got your autograph."

The old man shook hands and let go. 1998? Good lord, that was close to fifty years ago. True, he thought, cudgeling his memory, not very many persons had ever asked for the autograph of a mathematical physicist, but that was an endless time past. He had no recollection whatever of the event. Still, he remembered the lectures well enough. "Oh, of course," he said. "In Leeds Hall. Well, Mr. President, I'm not certain but—"

"Dear man," the president said cheerfully, "don't pretend. Whatever later honors I have attained, as an engineering sophomore I was an utterly forgettable boy. You must have met a thousand like me. But," he said, standing straighter, "you, Dr. Sidorenko, are another matter entirely. Oh, yes. You are probably the greatest man our country has produced in this century, and it is only the smallest measure of the esteem in which we hold you that I have come here today. However," he added briskly, "we don't want to spoil things for the cameramen, who will undoubtedly want to get all this on tape. So come over here, like a good fellow."

The old man blinked and allowed the cameramen to bully the president and himself into the best camera angles. One of them was whistling through his teeth, one was flirting with the nurse, but they were very efficient. The old man was trembling. All right, I'm ninety-five, I'm entitled to a little senility, he thought; but was it that? Something was worrying him, nagging at his mind.

"Go ahead, Mr. President," called the director at last, and Shawn O'Connor took from the hand of one of his alert, well-tailored men a blue and silver ribbon.

The camera purred faintly, adjusting itself to light and distance, and the president began to speak. "Dr. Sidorenko, today's investiture is one of the most joyous occasions that has been my fortune—" Talk, talk, thought the old man, trying to listen, to identify the tune the cameraman had been whistling and to track down the thing that was bothering him all at once. He caught the president's merry blue eyes, now shadowed slightly as they looked at him, and realized he was trembling visibly.

Well, he couldn't *help* it, he thought resentfully. The body was shaking; the conscious mind had no control over it. He was ashamed and embarrassed, but even shame was a luxury he could only doubtfully afford. Something worse was very close and threatening to drown out mere shame, a touch of the crawling fear he had hoped never to feel again and had prayed not even to remember. He assumed a stiff smile.

"—of America's great men, who have received the honors due them. For this reason the Congress, by unanimous resolution of both Houses, has authorized me—"

The old man, chilled and shaking, remembered the name of the tune at last.

The bear went over the mountain,
The bear went over the mountain.
The bear went over the mountain—
And what do you think he saw?

It worried him, though he could not say why.

"—not only your scientific achievements which are honored, Dr. Sidorenko, great though these are. The truths you have discovered have brought us close to the very heart of the universe. The great inventions of our day rest in large part on the brilliant insight you have given our scientific workers. But more than that—"

Oh, stop, whispered the old man silently to himself, and he could feel his body vibrating uncontrollably. The president faltered, smiled, shrugged and began again: "More than that, your humanitarian love for all mankind is a priceless—"

Stop, whispered the old man again, and realized with horror that he was not whispering at all. He was screaming. *"Stop!"* he bawled, and found himself trying with withered muscles to stand erect on his useless feet. *"Stop!"* The cameras deserted the president and swung in to stare, with three great glassy eyes, at the old man; and for old Sidorenko terror struck in and fastened on him. Something erupted. Something exploding and bursting, like a crash of autombiles in flame; someone shouted near him with a voice that made him cringe. He saw the nurse run in with a hypodermic, and he felt its bite.

Endless hours later (though it took less than sixty seconds for the blood to pump the drug to his brain) he felt the falling, spiraling falling that he remembered from other needles at other times, and there was the one moment of clearness before sleep. Maureen was staring down at him, the needle still in her hand. "I'm sorry I spoiled the party, dear," he whispered, his eyes closing, and then he was firmly asleep.

It really wasn't worth the trouble. Why should they want to waste so much effort on curing him?

The nurse fussed: "There's nothing to worry about, Doctor. A fine, big man like you. Sure you had a bad spell. What's that? Do you think the president himself has never had a bad spell?"

"Why don't they leave me alone, Maureen?" he whispered.

"Leave you alone, is it! And you with twenty good years inside of you."

"You're a good girl, Maureen," he said faintly, hoarding his strength. It was really more than they had a right to expect of him, he thought drowsily. He couldn't afford many blowups like this morning's, and it seemed they were always happening. Still, it was nice of the president.

He was a little more alert now, the effects of the needle, and its later measured balancing antidotes, beginning to wear off. This was Wednesday, he remembered. "Do I have to go in with the Group?" he whined.

"Doctor's orders, Doctor," she said firmly, "and doctor as you may be, you're not doctor enough to argue with doctor's orders." It was an old joke, limp to begin with, but he owed her a smile for it. He paid her, faintly.

After lunch she wheeled him into the Group meeting room. They were the last to arrive.

Sam Krabbe said, surly as always in the Group though he was pleasant enough in social contacts, outside: "You take a lot of hostility out on us, Sidorenko. Why don't you try being on time?"

"Sam forgets," said the Reynolds woman to the air. "It isn't up to Sidorenko, as long as he and Maureen act out that master-slave thing of having her push his chair. If she doesn't want to pay us the courtesy of promptness, Sidorenko can't help it." Marla Reynolds had murdered her husband and four teen-aged children; she had told the Group so at least fifty times. Sidorenko thought of her as the only legitimate lunatic the Group owned—except himself, of course; the old man kept an open mind about himself.

He struggled to hold his head up and his eyes open. You didn't get any benefit out of the Group's sessions unless you *participated*. The way to *participate* started with keeping the appearance of alertness and proceeded through talking (when you didn't really want to talk at all), to discharging emotion (when you were almost certain you had no emotion left to discharge). This he knew. Dr. Shugart had told him, in private analysis and again before the entire Group.

The old man sighed internally. Sam Krabbe could be relied on to interpret everyone's motives for them; he was doing it now. Short, squat, middle-aged . . . well, "middle-aged" by the standards of Dr. Sidorenko. Actually Sam Krabbe was close to seventy. Sidorenko glanced up at the attentive, involved face of his nurse and let the conversation wash over him.

Sam: "What about that, Maureen? Do you have to focalize your aggressions on us? I'm getting damned sick and tired of it, for one."

Nelson Amster took over (thirty-five years old, a bachelor, his life a chain of false steps and embarrassments because he saw his mother in every other female he met): "It's a stinking female attention-getting device, Sam. Ignore it."

Marla Reynolds: "That's fine talk from a pantywaist like you!"

Eddie Atkinson (glancing first at the bland face of Dr. Shugart for a cue): "Come on, you old harpies. Give the girl a break. What do you say, Dr. Shugart? Aren't they just displacing their own hostilities onto Maureen and the doctor?"

Dr. Shugart, after a moment's pause: "Mmm. Maureen, do you have a reaction to all this?"

Maureen, her eyes lively but her voice serious: "Oh, I'm sorry if I've made trouble. I didn't think we were late. Honestly. If there was any displacement it was certainly on the subconscious level. I *love* you all. I think you're the finest, friendliest Group I ever— and—Well, there just isn't any ambivalence at all. Honestly."

Dr. Shugart, nodding: "Mmm."

The old man turned restlessly in his chair. Pretty soon, he thought with a familiar and tolerable ache, they would all start looking at him and prodding him to *participate*. All but Dr. Shugart; anyway; the psychiatrist didn't believe in prodding, except in a minor emergency as a device to pass along the burden of talk from himself to one of the Group. (Though he always said he was part of the Group, not its master: "The analyst is only the senior patient. I learn much from our sessions.") But the others would prod, they had no such professional hesitations, and Sidorenko didn't like that. He was still turning over inside himself the morning's fiasco; true, he should voice it, that was what the Group was for; but the old man had learned in nearly a century to live his life his own certain way, and he wanted to think it out for himself first. The best way to keep the Group off him was to volunteer a small remark from time to time. He said at the first opportunity: "I'm sorry, ladies and gentlemen. I didn't mean to upset you."

Everyone looked at him.

Ernie Atkinson scolded: "We're not here to apologize, Sidorenko. We only want you to know your *motives.*"

Marla Reynolds: "One wonders if all of us know just why we *are* here? One wonders how the rest of us are to get proper attention, if some of us get first crack at the doctor's thought because they are more *important.*"

Sidorenko said weakly: "Oh, Mrs. Reynolds—Marla—I'm sure there's nothing like that. Is there, Dr. Shugart?"

Dr. Shugart, pausing: "Mmm. Well, why *are* we here? Does anyone want to say?"

The old man opened his mouth and then closed it. Some evenings he joined with these youngsters in the Group, as demanding and competitive as any of them, but this was not one of the nights. Energy simply did not flow. Sidorenko was glad when Sam Krabbe took over the answer.

"We're here," said Sam pompously, "because we have problems which we haven't been able to solve alone. By Group sessions we help each other discharge our basic emotions where it is safe to do so, thus helping each other to reduce our problems to dimensions we can handle." He waited for agreement.

"Parrot!" smirked Ernie Atkinson.

"The doctor doesn't like our using pseudo-psychiatric double-talk," Marla Reynolds accused the air.

"All right, let's see you do better!" Sam flared.

"Gladly! Easily!" cried Atkinson. He hooked a thumb in his lapel and draped a leg over the arm of the chair. "The institution is a place where very special and very concentrated help can be given to a very few." ("Snob," Nelson Amster hissed.) "I'm not a snob! It's the plain truth. We get broad-spectrum therapy here, everything from hormones to hypnosynthesis. And the reason we get it is that we *deserve* it. Everybody knows Dr. Sidorenko. Amster created a whole new industry with mergers and stock manipulations. Marla Reynolds is one of the greatest composers—well, the greatest *woman* composers—of the century." ("Damn some people!" grated Marla). "And I myself— well, I need not go on. We are worth treating, all of us. At any cost. That's why the government put us here, in this very expensive, very thorough place."

"Mmm," said Dr. Shugart, and considered for a moment. "I wonder," he said.

Ernie Atkinson suddenly shrank a good two sizes. His dark little face turned sallow. The leg slid off the arm of the chair. "What's that, Doc?" he asked dismally.

Dr. Shugart said: "I wonder if that's a *personal* motivation."

"Oh, I see," cried Atkinson, "it's what *each* of us is here for that's important, eh? Well, what about it? How about your motivations, Sidorenko?"

The old man coughed.

It always came to this, reliably. He would put out the weak decoy remarks but it would do no good, one of the Group would pounce past the decoys to reach his flesh. Well, there was no fighting it.

"I—" he began, and stopped, and passed a hand over his face. Maureen was close beside him, her eyes warm and intent. "I know I shouldn't apologize," he apologized, "but it has been a bad day. You know about it. The thing is, I'm an old man, and even Dr. Shugart tells me that the old cells aren't in quite the shape they used to be. There was," he said mildly, as though he were reading off a dossier from a statistical sample, "a stroke a few years ago. Fortunately it limited itself; they're not operable, you know, when you get to a certain age. The blood vessels turn into a kind of rotten canvas and, although you can clamp off the hemorrhage, it only makes it pop again on the other side of the clamp, and—I'm wandering. I apologize," he finished wryly.

"Mmm," Dr. Shugart said. "There's no such thing as totally undirected speech."

"Of course. All right. But that's why I apologize, because I'm not getting around very rapidly to an answer.

"I had my—trouble—a few years ago. I don't remember much about it, except that I gather I was delusional. Thought I was God, was the way it was expressed to me once.

Well, if I had been a younger man I suppose I could have been treated more easily. I don't know. I'm not. Time was, I know, when most doctors wouldn't bother with a man of ninety-five, even if he did happen to be," he said wryly, "celebrated not only for his scientific attainments but for his broad love for mankind. I mean, there's a point of obsolescence. Might as well let the old fool die."

He choked and coughed raspingly for a second. The nurse reached for him, but he waved her off.

"Mmm," said Dr. Shugart.

And the nurse whispered in a hard bright voice: "I love you, Noah Sidorenko."

He sat up straight, suddenly struck to the heart.

"I love you," she said stubbornly, "and I'll *make* you get well. It can't hurt you if I tell you I love you. I'm not asking for anything. It's a free gift."

The old man swallowed.

"Don't argue with me, old sport," she said tenderly, and patted his creased cheek. "Now, how about some psychodrama? Let's do the big one! The slum you lived in, Doctor—remember? The night you were so scared. The accident. Stretch out," she ordered, wheeling him to a couch and helping him onto it. He went along, dazed. She scolded: "No, curl up more. You're four years old, remember? Marla, pull that chair over and be the mother. Ernie, Sam. Let's go out in the hall. We'll be cars speeding along the elevated highway outside the window. And let's make some noise! Honk, honk! Aooga!"

But it hadn't been like that at all, he told himself a few hours later, trying to go to sleep. It had been a big frightening experience in his childhood. Very possibly it was the thing that had caused his later troubles (though he couldn't remember the troubles well enough to be sure). But it was not what they were portraying in psychodrama. They were showing a frightened child, and the old man was stubbornly certain there was more to it than that. But very likely it was lost forever.

It was only natural that at the age of ninety-five a great many experiences should be lost forever. (Such as meeting a sophomore who asked for an autograph, when you could have had no idea that the sophomore would grow up to be president.)

He thought of the white man, wondered who the white man was, and shifted restlessly in the bed. He could feel his old muscles tensing up.

Curse the fool thing, the old man said to himself, referring to his own body; it has lost the knack of living. But it wasn't the body that was at fault, really. It was the brain. The body was only crepe and brittle sticks, true, but the heart still beat, blood flowed, stomach acids leached the building-blocks they needed from the food he ate. The body worked. But the brain worked against it; it was brain not body, that tautened his muscles and shortened his breath.

That fantastic girl, the old man thought ruefully, she had said: *I love you.* Well. Let's interpret what she *meant*, he commanded, it could only have been an expression of the natural affection a nurse has for a patient. Still, it was ridiculous, the old man told himself, striving to catch a free and comfortable breath.

That was the worst thing about the tension. You couldn't breathe. With much effort Noah Sidorenko wedged his elbows under him and raised his chest cage a trifle, not quite off the mattress, but resting lightly on it, relieving some of the pressure his shriveled body exerted. It helped, but it didn't help enough. He thought wistfully of free fall. Rocket jockies, he dreamed, floated endlessly with no pressure at all; how *deeply* they must be able to breathe! But, of course, he couldn't live to get there, not through rocket acceleration.

He was wandering, when he wanted most particularly to think clearly.

He turned on one side and pressed the tip of his nose lightly with a finger. Sometimes opening the nostrils wide helped to get a breath. He thought of what the microphones taped to rib and throat must be recording, and grinned faintly. Funny, though, he thought, that Maureen hadn't come in to check on him. The purpose of the microphones was to warn the nurse when he needed attention. Surely he needed attention now.

He listened critically to his thumping heart. Ka-*bump*, ka-*bump*, ka-*bump*. It made a little tune:

The bear went over the moun-tain

The song was very disturbing to him, though he did not even now know why. Somehow it was connected with that scene in his youth, the crashing cars and the white man. The old man sighed. He had come very close to remembering all of it once. They had put him in silence. "Silence" was an acoustically dead chamber, twenty feet cubed, hung with muffling fabric and strung with spiderwebs of the felt; there was no echo and no sound from outside could come in. It was a conventional tool of study for mental disorders; strapped in a canvas cot, hung in the center of the cube, eyes closed, hearing deadened, a subject began very quickly to seek within himself. Fantasies came, delusions came. And ultimately knowledge came, if the subject could stand it; but three out of five reached hysteria before they reached any worthwhile insight, and the old man was one of the three. He had nearly died. . . .

He paused to count the times he had nearly died under therapy of one kind or another, but it was too hard. And besides, he was beginning to think that he was nearly dying again. He pushed himself back on his elbows and fought once more for breath.

This one was very bad.

He slumped back on the bed and reached out for the intercom button. "Maureen," he whispered.

She slept in the room next to him, and though he seldom woke in the night—there was something in the evening cocoa to make sure of that—when it happened that he did, if he called, she was there promptly, sometimes in a pink wrapper, once or twice in lounging pajamas. But not tonight. "Maureen," he whispered to the intercom again, but there was no answer.

The old man, with an effort, rolled onto his side. The movement dislodged one of the taped microphones. He felt it tear his skin and, simultaneously, heard the sharp alarm *ping* in Maureen's room. But the alarm didn't bring her.

The old man opened his eyes wide and stared at the intercom. "I have to get up," he told it reasonably, "because if I lie here I think I will die."

It was impossible, of course. But what could he lose by trying? He pushed himself to the edge of the bed. The chair was within reach, but very remote to Noah Sidorenko, who had not stood on his own feet in years. . . .

And then he was in the chair. Somehow he had made it! He sat erect and gasping, for a moment. The pain was bad, but it was better sitting up. Then his hand found the buttons of the little electric motors.

He spun slowly, navigated the straits between the nurse's desk and the corner of the bed, went out the door, as it opened quietly before him.

Maureen's room was empty. The outer door opened too. That was good, he thought; he hadn't been sure it would open; it was never very clear to him whether he was a prisoner or not. It was, after all, a sort of madhouse he was in. . . . But it opened.

The hall was empty and silent. He listened for the familiar *grunch, grunch* of Ernie Atkinson grinding his teeth in his sleep, but even that was stilled tonight. He rolled on. The lift rose silently to meet him.

He let it carry him gently down, and turned inward. The lower hall was blindingly bright. He made his way to Dr. Shugart's office.

He paused. There were voices.

No wonder he hadn't heard Ernie Atkinson's grinding teeth! Here was Atkinson, his voice coming plain as day: "I don't care what you say, we weren't getting through to him, No. The Group and psychodrama aren't working."

And Dr. Shugart's voice: "They *have* to work." Yes, the old man thought dazedly, it was Shugart's voice all right. But where was the hesitation, the carefully balanced noncommittal air? It cracked sharp as a whip!

And Maureen's voice: "Do I have to go on building up this emotional involvement with him?"

Shugart crackled: "Is it so distasteful?"

"Oh, no!" (The old man sighed. He found he had stopped breathing until she answered.) "He's an old dear, and I *do* love him. But I'd like to give him little presents because I want to, not because it's part of his therapy."

Shugart rasped: "It's for his own good. This is one of the finest brains in the world, and it's falling apart. We've tried everything. Radical procedures—silence, psychosurgery, chemotherapy—are too much for him to take. Remember what happened when Dr. Reynolds tried electroshock? So we've got to work with what we've got."

The old man stirred.

Old as he might be, and insane if they liked, but he wasn't going to linger out here and listen. A quarter after one in the morning, and the whole Institute was gathered here in Shugart's office, plotting the recovery of himself.

"All right," he gasped, rolling in "what *is* this?"

They gaped at him.

"All of you!" he said strongly. "What are you doing to me? Is it a hoax?"

Shugart moved restlessly. Marla Reynolds reached up to pat her hair, avoiding his eyes.

"You, *Doctor* Reynolds? Want to explain? I mean—I mean," he said in a changed tone, no longer gasping, "there seems to be only one explanation. There's a conspiracy of some sort, and I'm the target."

Maureen got up and walked toward him. "Come in, Doctor," she said, in a voice of resignation tinged with pleasure. "Maybe it's better this way. We're not going to get very far continuing to lie to you, are we? So I guess we'll have to tell you the truth."

The tune rocked crazily through his head. The old man spun his chair and turned pleadingly to Maureen. "Of course, Doctor," she said, understanding without words, and fetched him a fizzy drink. "Only a little stimulant," she coaxed.

The old man glanced at Dr. Shugart. Shugart laughed. "Who do you think has been prescribing for you? There isn't a human being in the Institute without a first-rate degree. Maureen's our internist—*with*, of course, a thorough grounding in psychology."

The old man drank reproachfully, looking at Maureen. She said, clouding: "I know. It isn't fair, but we had to get you well."

"*Why?*"

Maureen said somberly: "A brain like yours doesn't come along to often. I'm not a physicist, but as I understand it Congruence comes close to doing what Einstein tried with the unified field theory. You were on the point of doing something more when you—when you—"

"When I went crazy," the old man said crudely. She shook her head. "All right, I used a bad word. But that's it, isn't it?" The girl nodded. "I see."

But the stimulant wasn't doing much good. Ninety-five years, he thought confused, and perhaps I won't see that other mountain. It was hard to accept, hard to believe he had been hoaxed, hard to believe that it wasn't working, that the delusions would not be cured. "I'm flattered," he whispered hoarsely, and tried to hand the glass back to Maureen. It clattered to the floor and bounced without breaking. Marla with her schizoid detachment, Ernie with his worries, Sam Krabbe and his surly anger—doctors acting parts? The room swooped around Sidorenko; he was cut off from his reference points. And they were all afraid; he could see it, it was a gamble they had taken, that he would never find out, and now they didn't know what would happen. And he—

He didn't know either.

"I'm sorry to be so much trouble," he gasped.

"You mustn't feel personal guilt," Dr. Shugart said anxiously. "These personality disorders—personality *traits*—go with greatness. Sir Oliver Lodge swore he believed in levitation. Think of Newton, sleepless and paranoid. Think of Einstein. Religious mania is very common," the doctor assured him, "and you were spared that, at least. Well, almost—of course, certain aspects of your—"

"Shut up!" cried Maureen, and reached for the old man's wrist. He stared up at her, touched by the worry in her face, trying to find words to tell her there was nothing to worry about, nothing to fear. He felt his heart lunging against his ribs and his breathing seemed, oddly, to have stopped. He made a convulsive effort and drew an enormous, loud breath. Why, that was almost—what did they call it?—a death rattle. He did it again.

"Doctor!" moaned the nurse, but he found the strength to shake his wrist free of her. This was interesting. He was beginning to remember something, or to imagine something—

They were all coming toward him.

"Leave me alone," he croaked. He held them off while he practiced breathing again; it wasn't hard; he could do it. He closed his eyes. He heard Maureen catch her breath and opened them to glare at her, then closed them again.

Noah Sidorenko's brain was perfectly lucid.

He saw—or remembered? But it was as though he were seeing it with an internal eye—all of his previous life, the childhood, the government office where he had received the first scholarship, the four professors quizzing him for his doctor's, even the cloudy days of therapy and breakdown.

The old man thought: It all began ninety years ago, I was all right until then . . . and he had to laugh, though laughing choked him, because ninety years ago he had been all of five years old. But up until then there had been nothing to worry about.

Was it the crash? Yes. And fire. The white man. The song about the bear. The terrible auto smash, just outside his window—for his window had looked out on an elevated automobile highway in Brooklyn, the Gowanus Parkway, where cars raced bumper to bumper, fifty miles an hour, within five yards of the bed he slept in. *Whoosh. Whoosh.* All day long and all night. At night the strokes were slow, a lagging wire-brush riff; in the mornings and evenings they were faster, *whooshwhooshwhoosh*, a quick rataplan. He listened to them and dreamed tunes around them. And there was the night he had gone to sleep and wakened screaming, screaming.

His mother rushed in—poor woman, she was already widowed. (Though she was only twenty-five, the old man thought with amazement. Twenty-five! Maureen was that.) She rushed in, and though the boy Noah was terrified he could see through the shadow of his own terror to hers. "Momma, momma, the white man!" She caught him in her arms. "Please, my God, what's the matter?" But he couldn't answer, except with sobs and incoherent words about the white man; it was a code, and she was not skilled to read it. And time passed, ten minutes or so. He was not comforted—he was still crying and afraid—but his mother was warm and she soothed him. She bounced him on her knee, ka-*bump*, ka-*bump*, ka-*bump*, and even though he was crying he remembered the song with that beat, *He SAW anOTHer MOUNTain, he SAW anOTHer MOUNTain,* and the cars whooshed by and in the next room the little TV set murmured and laughed. "You're missing your program, Momma," he said; "Go to sleep, dear," she answered; he was almost relaxed. *Crash.* Outside the window two cars collided violently. A taxicab was bound for New York with a boy in a satin jacket at the wheel and four others crammed in the back; the boy at the wheel was high on marijuana and he hit the divider. The cab leaped crazily across into the Long Island–bound lane. There was not much traffic that night, but there was one car too many. In it a thirty-year-old advertising salesman rushed to meet his wife and baby at Idlewild. He never met them. The cars struck. The stolen taxicab was hurled back into its own lane, its gas tank split, its doors flung open. Four boys in the jackets of the Gerritsen Tigers died at once and the fifth was thrown against the retaining wall—not dead; but not with enough life left to him to matter. He stood up an tried to run, and the burning gasoline made him a white-hot phantom, auraed and terrible. He lurched clear across the roadway to just outside Noah's window and died there, flaming, hanging over the wall, fifteen feet above the wreck of the space salesman's convertible.

"The white man!" screamed someone in Noah's room, but it was not the boy but his mother. She looked from the white-flamed man outside to her son, with eyes of fear and horror; and from then on it was never the same for him.

"From the time I was five," the old man said aloud, wondering, "it was never the same. She thought I was—I don't know. A devil. She thought I had the power of second sight, because I'd been scared by the accident before it happened."

He looked around the room. "And my son!" he cried. "I knew when he died—telepathy, at a distance of a good eight thousand miles. And—" he stopped, thinking. "There were other things," he mumbled. . . .

Dr. Shugart fussed kindly: "Impossible, don't you see? It's all part of your delusion. Surely a scientist should know that this—*witchcraft* can't be true! If only you hadn't come down here tonight, when you were so close to a cure. . . ."

Noah Sidorenko said terribly: "Do you want to cure me again?"

"Doctor!"

The old man shouted: "You've done it a hundred times, and a hundred times, with pain and fear, I've had to undo the cure—not because I want to! My *God,* no. But because I can't help myself. And now you want me to go through it again. I won't let you cure me!" He pushed the electric buttons; the chair began to spin but too slowly, too slowly. The old man fought his way to his feet, shouting at them. "Don't you see? I don't want to do this, but it does itself; it's like a baby that's getting born, I can't stop it now. It's *difficult* to have a baby. A woman in labor," he cried, seeing the worry in their eyes, knowing he must seem insane, "a woman in labor is having a fit, she struggles and screams—and what can a doctor do for her? Kill the pain? Yes, and perhaps kill the baby with it. That happened, over and over, until the doctors learned how, and—and you don't know how. . . .

"*You mustn't kill it this time!* Let me suffer. Don't cure me!"

And they stood there looking at him. No one spoke at all.

The room was utterly silent; the old man asked himself, Can I have convinced them? But that was so improbable. His words were such poor subsitutes for the thoughts that raced about his thumping head. But—the thoughts, yes, they were clear now; maybe for the first time. He understood. Psionic power, telepathy, precognition, all the other hard-to-handle gifts that filled the gap between metaphysics and muscle . . . they lay next door to madness. Worse! By definition, they *were* "madness," as a diamond can be "dirt" if it clogs the jet of a rocket. They were mad, since they didn't fit self-defining "sane" science.

But how many times he had come so close, all the same! And how often, how helpfully, he had been "cured." The delusional pattern had been so clear to "sane" science; and with insulin shock and hypnosynthesis, with electrodes in his shaved scalp and psychodrama, with Group therapy and the silence—with every pill and incantation of the sciences of the mind they had, time after time, rooted out the devils. Precognition had been frightened out of him by panic. Telepathy had been electroshocked out of him in the Winford Retreat. But they returned and returned.

Handle them? No, the old man admitted, he couldn't handle them, not yet. But if God was good and gave him more time, an hour or two perhaps . . . or maybe some years; if the doctor was improperly kind and allowed him his "delusion"—why, he might learn to handle them after all. He might, for example, be able to peer into minds at will and not only when some randomly chosen mind, half shattered itself, created such a clamorous beacon of noise that then the (telepathically) nearly deaf might hear it. He might be able to stare into the future at will, instead of having his attention chance-caught by the flicker of some catastrophic terror projecting its shadow ahead. And this ancient and useless hulk that was his body, for example. He might yet force it to live, to move, to walk about, to stand—

To stand?

The old man stood perfectly motionless beside his chair. To stand? And then, rather late, he followed the direction of the staring eyes of Maureen and Shugart and the others.

He *was* standing.

But not as he had visioned it, in wretched bedridden hours. He was standing tall and straight; but between the felt soles of his slippers and the rubber tiles of the office floor there were eight inches of untroubled air.

No. They wouldn't cure him again, not ever. And with luck, he realized slowly, he might now proceed to infect the world.

THE MAPMAKERS

Ever since science fiction writers started trying to get around Einstein's theory and write stories about spaceships traveling faster than the speed of light, there have been stories about ships traveling through what is often called "hyperspace." It's as good a term as any and has worked for dozens of writers for many decades.

"The Mapmakers," first published in 1955, is about navigating hyperspace—and what happens when the normal navigation tools are no longer available. There are several notable aspects of this story, aside from the kicker, which I have been sworn not to reveal. First, the crew isn't all men—there are women on the *Terra II*, and the women are full members of the crew, not just pretty nurses or secretaries. Secondly, the story is launched by an accident, the sort of thing that could happen anytime, anywhere in space, but that is seldom noted in stories.

These aspects, plus the too realistic atmosphere of life in a ship with a sizeable crew confined for more than a little time, give "The Mapmakers" a lively, engaging quality that sets it apart from other spaceship tales. The rest you'll have to find out for yourself.

It was one of those crazy, chance-in-a-million accidents. A particle of meteoric matter slammed into *Starship Terra II* in hyperspace. It was only a small particle, but it penetrated three bulkheads, injuring Lieutenant Groden and destroying the Celestial Atlas. It couldn't happen in a hundred years—but it had happened.

That was the end of the road for *Starship Terra II*. The damage-control parties patched the bulkheads easily enough. But the Atlas—the only record on board of the incomprehensible Riemannian configurations of hyperspace—was a total loss.

The captain gave orders for Spohn, the Celestial Atlas, to be buried in space and called an emergency officers' meeting in the wardroom.

Terra II was in normal space and free fall. A trace of smoky kerosene odor still hung in the wardroom, but there was none of the queasy unrecognizable slipping motion of the hyperspace "jump," and the captain had ordered the ship spun to give them a touch of simulated gravity. The officers were managing to look alert and responsive as they faced their skipper.

The captain was a hard-muscled, hard-eyed career naval officer, and by definition an ambitious man—else he would hardly have asked for the command of a charting flight. He walked briskly in from his own quarters, neither hurrying nor slow. He would walk at that same pace to receive his admiral's stars when that day came, or to his execution, if it ever came to that.

He assumed his place at the head of the table and took the precise ten seconds his martinet mind allotted him for looking around the wardroom. Then he said, "We're in trouble."

The men in the wardroom hitched their hips a quarter-inch closer to the ward table.

The captain nodded and said it again, "We're in the soup, and we're a long way from home, and nobody is going to come to get us out of it. We'll have to do it ourselves, if we can. Ciccarelli's trying to get us a fix, but I can tell you right now, we're not close to Sol. There isn't a constellation in the sky that you or I or anybody else ever saw before. We might be a hundred light-years from home, we might be ten thousand."

The exec cleared his throat. "Sir, what about our records?"

"What records? They went with the Atlas, Hal. We can't retrace our way to Earth."

"No, sir, that's not what I mean. I understand that. But our charting records from Earth to here, we still have those. They won't do us any good, because we can't follow them backward—hyperspace doesn't work that way. But Earth needs them."

"Sure. What can we do about it? If we could get them back, we could get back ourselves. The whole trouble—Yes? What is it, Lorch?"

Ensign Lorch saluted from the door of the wardroom. "Spohn's body, sir," he rapped out. "It's ready for burial now. Would the captain like to conduct the services?"

"The captain will. What about Groden?"

Lorch said. "He isn't good, sir. He's unconscious and his head is bandaged up. The surgeon thinks it's bad. But we won't know for sure for at least a couple of hours."

The captain nodded, and Lorch quickly took his seat. He was the youngest officer in *Terra II* in years, six months out of the academy and still unable to vote. He listened to the discussion of ways and means with deference masking a keen feeling of excitement. The adventure of the unknown star lanes! That was why Lorch had signed up in the charting service, and he was getting it.

Perhaps more, even, than he had bargained for.

The trouble with *Terra II* was that she was playing a cosmic game of blindman's buff. Jumping into hyperspace was like leaping through a shadow, blindfolded; there was no way of knowing in advance what lay on the other side.

The first hyperspace rocket had taught a few lessons, expensively learned. On its first jump into hyperspace, *Terra I* had been "out" for just under one second—just enough, that is, for the jump generators to swing the ship into and out of the Riemannian n-dimensional composite that they called hyperspace for lack of a better term.

And it had taken *Terra I* nearly a year to limp back home, in normal space all the way, its generators a smoldering ruin. Back still again to the drawing boards!

But it was no one's fault. Who could have foreseen that any electric current, however faint, would so warp the field as to blow up the generators? The lesson was plain:

No electrical equipment in use during a jump.

So *Terra I*, rebuilt, reequipped and with a new crew, tried again. And this time there were no power failures. The only failure, this time, was the human element.

Because in hyperspace, the Universe was a crazy quilt of screaming patterns and shimmering lights, no more like the ordered normal-space pattern of stars than the view through a kaleidoscope is like the colored shreds of paper at its focus.

So the Celestial Atlas was added to the complement of a hyperspace rocket's crew.

And *Terra I* was rebuilt, and *Terra II* and *Terra III* and *Terra IV* came off the ways. And Earth cast its bait into the turgid depths of hyperspace again and again. . . .

The crews of the charting service were all volunteers, all rigidly screened. The ten officers who made up the wardroom of *Terra II* were as brilliant and able a group as ever assembled, but the emergency officers' meeting was a failure, all the same.

There just wasn't any way back.

"We're the trailblazers," rumbled the captain. "If we had a duplicate Celestial Atlas— but we don't. Well, that's something for the next ship to bear in mind, if we ever get back to tell them about it."

Ensign Lorch said tentatively, "Sir, *don't* we have one?"

The captain rasped, "Of course not, man! I just finished saying we didn't. You should know that."

"Yes, sir. But that's not exactly what I meant. We have a library and, as I understand it, the library is basically the same as the atlas—a trained total-recall observer. Doesn't any of the information in the library duplicate the atlas?"

"Now that," said the captain after a pause, "is worth thinking about. What about it, Hal?"

The exec said, "Worth a try, captain."

"Right. Yoel, get her up here." Lieutenant Yoel saluted and spoke into the communications tube. The captain went on reflectively. "Probably won't work, of course, but we'll try anything. Anybody else got a suggestion?"

"Dead reckoning, sir?" Yoel suggested. "I know we've got the record of our fixes so far; can we try just backtracking?"

"Won't work," the captain said positively. "If we could be absolutely exact, maybe. But without an atlas we can't be. And a centimeter's divergence at the beginning of a run might put us a thousand kilometers off at the end. A thousand kilometers in hyperspace—heaven knows what that might come to in normal space. Anything from a million light-years down.

"I couldn't do it, Yoel. Even Groden couldn't do it *with* his eyes, and he's the best shiphandler on board. And I don't think he's going to have his eyes, anyway, at least not for a long time. Maybe forever, if we don't get back to the eye banks on Earth. Without the atlas, we're as blind as Groden."

The speaking tube interrupted and rescued Yoel. It whistled thinly: "Recorder Mate Eklund reporting to the wardroom."

"Send her in," said the exec, and the library, Nancy Eklund, RM2c, marched smartly into the meeting.

It wasn't going to work; the captain knew it in the first few words. They spent an hour sweating the library of all of her relevant data, but it was wasted effort.

The captain thought wistfully of Recorder Mate Spohn, the lost Celestial Atlas. With him on the bridge, hyperspace navigation had been—well, not easy, but *possible*. For Spohn was trained in the techniques of total recall. The shifting, multicolored values of Riemannian space formed totals in his mind, so that he could actually navigate by means of a process of mental analysis and synthesis so rapid and complex that it became a sort of *gestalt*.

Of course, a twelve-stage electronic computer could have done the same thing, just as quickly. But *Terra II* had its limitations, and one of the limitations was that no electronic equipment could be operated in a jump—just when the computer would most be needed. So the designers came up with what was, after all, a fairly well tested method of filing information—the human brain. By the techniques of hypnotic conditioning *all* of the brain opened up to subconscious storing.

Recorder Mate Spohn, trancelike on the bridge, had no conscious knowledge of what was going on as, machinelike, he scanned the Riemannian configurations and rapped out courses and speeds; but his subconscious never erred. With its countless cells and infinite linkages, the brain was a tank that all the world's knowledge could hardly fill—just about big enough, in fact, to cope with the task of recognizing the meaning of hyperspace configurations.

And the process worked so well that the delighted designers added another recorder mate to the personnel tables—the library—which enabled them to dispense with the dead weight of books as well.

The entire wardroom, in order of rank, shot questions at their library, and her disciplined mind dutifully plucked out answers.

But most of them she never knew. For *Terra II* was a charting ship, and though the Atlas had, as a matter of routine, transcribed his calibrations into the ship's log—and thence into the library—all that Nancy Eklund knew was how *Terra II* had reached its checkpoints in space. Hyperspace was a tricky business; backtracking was dangerous.

When *Terra II* got back—*if Terra II* got back—those who came after them would have complete calibrations for a round trip. But they did not. Their task was as difficult and dangerous, in its way, as Columbus's caravels. Except that Columbus had only one great fear; falling off the edge of the Earth.

Lucky Columbus. The technology that had produced *Terra II* had brought plenty of new fears.

Three shells "up"—toward the ship's center—a surgeon's mate named Conboy was pulling the fourth needle out of the arm of Lieutenant Groden. The big navigator should have been out cold, but he was tossing and mumbling, his head thrashing from side to side in its thick wrappings of bandage.

Tough guy, thought Conboy critically, counting up the ampoules of opiate the blinded officer had taken. They were all tough guys, anyway, from the skipper on down. But the little pipettes brought them down to size and Conboy, though only an inch over five feet tall and the frailest on board, was the man who drove in the pipettes.

"He's under, Mr. Broderick," he reported to the ship's surgeon, who nodded.

"Keep it so," the officer ordered. "If anything comes up, I'll be in the wardroom." The captain would be wanting to hear about Groden's condition, and Broderick wanted very much to hear what the emergency meeting had to say about the condition of *Terra II* in general.

This was fine with Conboy, who had a similar concern of his own. As soon as Commander Broderick was out of sight, Conboy took a last look at Groden and, reassured that the navigator would be out of trouble for at least half an hour, hurried to the next cabin to pry what information he could out of the chart room.

A spaceman–first named Coriell was methodically taking optical measurement on all the stars of second magnitude or brighter. Conboy looked uncomprehendingly at the entries on the charts. "Got anything?" he asked.

Coriell spat disgustedly. "Got trouble. See that little fellow down there, between the two real bright ones? That *might* be Canopus. The rough lines check; Mr. Ciccarelli's going to have to run a spectrum on it, when he gets through with the meeting."

Conboy looked sourly at the indicated star. It was brighter than the average, but far less bright than the two that flanked it. "Canopus, huh?" he repeated. "Suppose it is, Coriell. How far from Earth does that put us?"

Coriell shrugged. "What am I, a navigator? How's Groden, by the way?"

"He'll live. Suppose it is, Coriell?"

"Well—" Coriell thought for a moment. "Depends. If we're on the same side of it as Earth, might not be far at all. If we're on the other side—well, Canopus is six hundred and fifty light-years from Sol."

Conboy looked again, longingly. "Well, thanks," he said, and went back to his patient.

That was the trouble with hyperspace travel, he thought. You go in at one point, you rocket around until you think it's time to come out, and there you are. Where is "there"? Why, that's the surprise that's in store for you, because you never know until you get there.

And sometimes not even then.

On the bridge, everything was Condition Able. Ensign Lorch, booted early out of the meeting because he was due to relieve as Junior O.O.D., signed in and made his tour of the ship. The damage-control parties belowdecks were all through with the necessary repairs, and keeping themselves busy with such cosmetic tasks as fairing down the beads left by the first emergency welds. It was hot down there.

Lorch conscientiously whistled up the bridge on the speaking tube and ordered them to start the fans and valve enough gas into the expansion locks to make up for the heat rise. The crew quarters were shipshape, even the women's section; the jet chambers were at standby, with the jet-room hands busy at their usual standby task of thumping the tubes for possible hidden cracks. The working parties were finishing up the job of restowing the cargo that had to be shifted when the meteorite hit.

Lorch signed in the log, and paused thoughtfully over the spaces for entries of course and position. The helmsman was smartly at attention at the main board, though there was nothing for him to do since all jets were capped. Lorch glanced at him reprovingly, but the helmsman was conspicuously correct in his behavior.

It made a problem; Lorch detested the thought of writing in "unknown," but it certainly would be exceeding his authority to call the chart room without permission of Lieutenant Yoel, his shift commander. Not, thought Lorch a trifle rebelliously, that Yoel was likely to object very strongly.

Yoel was a drafted mathematician, not a ship handler. He knew very nearly all there was to know about geodesic theory and the complex equations that lay behind the "jump" generators and their odd nucleophoretic drive. But he was far from a model officer, so little conscious of the fundamental law of R.H.I.P. that he was capable of presuming to advise the captain on ship handling—the scene in the wardroom had proved that.

Lorch had just about decided to call down to the chart room when Yoel appeared, signaling that the meeting was over, and Lorch deftly dropped the problem in his superior's lap. "Ship on Condition Able," he reported briskly. "No maneuvering during watch; no change in operating status during watch. I have made no entry for course and position, sir. Though you might like to."

"I wouldn't," Yoel said sourly. "Put down 'unknown.' Write it in big letters."

"As bad as that, sir?"

"As bad as that." Yoel turned his back on his junior and methodically scanned the segment of sky outside the port. It was in constant spinning motion, flashing past the field of vision as *Terra II* whirled on its axis to give the crew something approaching gravity.

Lorch cleared his throat. "You got nothing out of Eklund, sir?"

"Oh, sure. We got the absolute magnitudes and stellar distances of half the stars in the Galaxy." Yoel turned from the port and shook his head. "We got a short course in Riemannian geometry and an outline of the geodesics of n-dimensional space. But we didn't get a road map." He glanced at the thermometer on the wall and said vaguely, "I thought I heard—"

He stood up straight. "*Mister* Lorch!" he exploded. "I wasn't hearing things! You were bleeding air into the expansion locks!"

"Why, yes, sir. To cool the ship," Lorch explained. "The welding torches were—"

"Blast the welding torches, mister! Did it ever occur to you we're a long way from home?"

"Yes, sir, but—"

"But you're an idiot! But! You valve off air as though we had a whole world of it. Did it ever occur to you that we might be in space a long time? Did you stop to think that we might run out of air?"

Lorch stared at him wordless. For a frozen moment he thought his superior had gone mad. Spaceships? Spaceships ran from point to point in n-dimensional hyperspace, no point was far from any other—an hour's travel, perhaps a day's. *Terra II* was crammed to the gunwales with air, by the standards of the service. Run out of *air*?

"Easy, Sam." The voice came floating up at Groden out of blackness. Something was wrong, and he was lying down; he grunted and started to get up.

A hand stopped him. The voice said, "Easy." He fell back, and felt nothing as he fell. His whole body was numbed, only a faint tingling sensation where it touched what he was lying on. Drugged, he thought. The voice said, "Sam, don't try to open your eyes. Can you hear me?"

It was like making a statue speak, but he got the word out, "Yes."

"Good. You've been hurt. A meteorite hit while we were in hyperspace. Got the Atlas, and something got you right across the eyes—drops of molten metal, by the scars. You're—you're blind, Sam. At least for now."

"Yes," he said, after a moment. There was a very special sort of tingling around the eyes.

"Maybe we can fix you up when we get back to Earth. But we're lost, Sam."

Lost? Groden pondered that. Lost. It didn't make sense. Of course, if the Atlas was dead—but still, how could they be lost? He strained to hear what the voice was saying; but it had gone on to something else.

Soothingly. "Now, Sam, this is going to hurt. We've got to change the dressings." Business of tingling, and more tingling of a different sort, but not anything that Groden could call painful. And then, suddenly and surprisingly, it hurt very much. He tried to speak, but the voice said, "Easy, Sam. It will only take a minute." Silence and pain. "Now, I want you to tell me if you can see anything at all, Sam. Any light? Even a flicker when I pass the light over your face?"

Light? Groden stared into the painful blackness. There was nothing, nothing at all, neither light nor flicker nor motion. He said through the lips that were still tingling marble, "No."

The voice was disappointed. "All right, Sam. I'll stop the pain in a minute." Another voice farther away was saying something about getting stowed away for the jump and the voice that had talked to Groden said impatiently, "Just a minute."

Groden licked the marble lips and tried to say, "What did you mean, lost? What's the matter?" But it came out a blur. The voice said something short and insincerely reassuring, and then there was a special prickling tingle in his arm, and even the voices were dark.

"Secure," ordered the captain, and the exec relayed the word through the speaking tubes: "Secure!" One by one the sections reported in on their tubes—All secure.

The captain had taken the conn himself, and he had the bridge on the jump. Lieutenant Yoel was backing up the helmsman, the navigator Ciccarelli was staring dubiously at the whirling stars, Ensign Lorch was hustling along the light-up detail, as they, with painstaking slowness, adjusted the hollow wicks in the running lamps. The odor of kerosene filled the bridge.

"All secure, sir," the exec reported.

The captain said curtly, "Kill the spin." The exec gave the order to the jet-room; there was a distant barking rattle, and the bridge complement, like standing wheat in a gusty wind, staggered and caught itself. The spinning stars outside jerked unevenly to a stop as the ship steadied on its axis.

Lorch cast a quick look around. The chronometers were wound and synchronized; the kerosene lamps burning brightly. He saluted the exec and reported all clear. The exec nodded gravely and passed the word on to the captain—all of a yard away.

The captain said, "Take us up, Hal."

"Yes, sir. Number One circuits open!"

The watch officer relayed into the speaking tube: "Number One circuits open!" There was a flicker, and abruptly all of the fluorescent lights were out. Only the kerosene lamps illuminated the bridge, or any of the ship.

"Number Two open," said the exec.

"Open Number Two!" Yoel echoed into the tube: From all over the ship the distant drone of motors, fans and refrigerators and boosters and burners deepened and died.

"Main circuit breakers open." That was only a precaution. Every electric current in the ship had ceased to flow; but on the off-chance that something, somewhere, still was drawing juice, the mains themselves were opened. *Terra I* had taught that lesson very well; electronic flow and the hyperspace field did not mix.

The exec, looking a little gray, said, "Stand by to jump."

"Stand by!" Yoel sang into the generator-room tube. The faraway moan of the nucleophoretic generators shook everyone in the ship; even on the bridge, they could feel their subsonic grind and hear the rumble of the diesels that drove them.

The exec was rapidly scanning his panel of instruments, his lips moving. Everyone on the bridge could see his lips move, and knew what he was doing; making sure he had the readings memorized. Once in hyperspace, it would not be precisely impossible for him to read them, but it would not be reliable.

At the feeler chart table where the Celestial Atlas should have been standing, Recorder Mate Nancy Eklund stood with her fingers on the pits and ridges that represented the coded course analyses. Like the exec, she was doing her best to memorize them, in the last moments before vision became unreliable and instruments began to lie; it was her last chance to see them as a whole.

The exec had his eyes on the big chronometer. As the second hand touched straight up, he said, "Jump!"

Far away, the diesels complained, as the generators clutched in. The ship shimmered and glowed. A high, thin *beep* sounded from nowhere. Outside the crystal port the universe of stars flickered and whirled into new and fantastic shapes.

And, half the ship away in the sick bay, Lieutenant Groden screamed shrilly.

Ensign Lorch tried shutting his eyes, but the flaming pinwheels had left scars of blankness on the visual purple of his retina. He blinked to clear away the darting afterimages. When he opened them again, the images were gone, and lashing serpentines of light peered ferociously in the port. The writhing snakes squirmed away and the planet Earth lay before him, green and inviting.

It was only an illusion, but it was an illusion the whole bridge saw at once. Lorch looked away and heard the voice of Nancy Eklund, droning her course coordinates to be repeated by the exec.

Illusion, illusion—only the voices were real. It had to do, Lorch thought fuzzily through the wonder, with light speeds and partial radiation vectors and null-polarity; but the words meant nothing when the reality was before his eyes.

"C" became infinite and finite at once, creepingly slow and immeasurably fast. Light trapped on the outer surface of the port crept through to them at last, movement appeared fast or slow or reversed, or irrelevant to its real components.

He could see the captain, stolid and transfixed like a bronze man—but was he? Or was that motionless metal figure really leaping about the bridge, and what Lorch's eyes beheld only the image of a split second, captured and pinned? He could see the navigator, Ciccarelli, floating dreamily a yard above the floor; *that* was illusion and symbol, for the little magnets in their shoes made it impossible. But what reality, translated, did it represent?

Light and electrons. In hyperspace, they lied.

"Number Six, Number Ten," droned the exec, echoing the library. "Full reverse." The voices did not lie; the grosser physical phenomena were immune to the distortion of Riemann's continuum. What they heard was what was there to hear. What Nancy Eklund felt with her fingers was real. Lorch saw, or seemed to see, that the exec had his finger on the pulse in his own wrist, timing their jets-on periods by his heartbeat.

The spring-driven chronometer across the bridge was clearly visible and undoubtedly telling the correct time. But the light that carried its message might lie, and the fingers that touched his pulse would not. "Off jets!" droned the exec.

They hung there. This was what Ciccarelli and the exec and the old man had worked out—lacking the Atlas, lacking Groden—working only from their memories of the course that had brought them into the meteorite's orbit and the sketchy notes the captain himself had made.

If they had remembered everything with the eidetic recollection of Eklund or the Atlas; if they had every component correct, and could stay on course for the proper period before halting their flight; they might—*might*—come out where they had started, and from there easily find their way home.

There was motion and activity on the bridge while they waited; and Lorch observed that Ciccarelli had kicked loose his shoes to float high enough off the steel floor to touch the hands of the chronometer. If he was floating now, thought Lorch, it was no lie of the light. And was what he had seen a moment before the image of *now*, received before it was sent?

They waited, and asked themselves such demented questions, while *Terra II* described the complex curve that passed for a Riemannian straight line, and the exec thoughtfully counted his heartbeats.

Then: "Full jets, One, Four, Five Main," snapped the exec. The ship bucked and shuddered.

And then it was over, and they came "down" out of hyperspace, down into the normal space-time frame that held their own sun and their own planet. They had backtracked, as near as could be, every component of their course. And they had come out.

They stared wordlessly at the stars, until the captain said briskly, "Belay that. Take a fix, Mr. Ciccarelli!" And down in the sick-bay, little Conboy, able once more to trust his vision, was rapidly assembling a hypodermic. But as he turned to his patient, he saw that it wasn't necessary; Groden, who had been mumbling and crying out throughout the jump into hyperspace, was out cold again.

Ciccarelli put down his abacus.

"No position, sir," he said throatily to the captain. "We've checked everything down to third magnitude."

The old man's chin went up a degree of arc, but that was all. "All right," he said. "Keep going."

"We'll try, sir," Ciccarelli promised. "I'll get to work on the faint ones."

The captain nodded and walked delicately, almost mincingly in the light spin-gravity, away. Commander Broderick from the surgeon's office down the corridor replaced him. He was staring after the captain, as he came into the navigation room.

"If I were the old man," he said thoughtfully, "I would still be here."

"Maybe that's why you aren't the old man." Ciccarelli wearily leaned over his crewman's shoulder to scan the rough log.

"Maybe," Broderick agreed. "Still, what's he going to do back on the bridge? Go through this same routine again? Make another jump and see where we come out? Might work, I don't deny it. Given infinite time *and* infinite fuel and a couple of other infinites, sooner or later we'd come out right spang in the middle of the Brooklyn Navy Yard."

"Tell him your troubles," Ciccarelli said shortly. "How's Groden?"

"He'll live. If any of us do."

"That," said Ciccarelli, picking up the completed sheaf of observations from his crewman, "is a pretty long shot, Doc."

The captain, in his own mind, would have agreed with Ciccarelli. He walked soberly, unswervingly, down the galley-ways toward the bridge, ticking off the possibilities with a part of his brain while the big, deep area that might have been labeled "officer's country" was making careful note of the ship's condition.

The fuel and food reserves would outlast the air; and Broderick's sick bay was an Asiatic mess. Lacking the Atlas's data and Groden's skill on the bridge, it would take a miracle to get them home; and Spaceman-Second Kerkam was out of uniform.

The enlisted women's quarters needed floor polishing; and the mind of no three-dimensional animal could, by definition, grasp the geodesics of Riemannian space. It was a matter of trial and error and record, and all you could hope to do was retrace a course once you had found one that brought you somewhere worth being. It was, he reflected with mild distaste, a shoddy way to run a spaceship.

Recorder Mate Eklund, having ducked into the enlisted women's area scant yards ahead of the captain, sighed to her bunkmate, "Thank heaven! I thought he was coming in here!"

"Did you have a rough time on the bridge?" her bunkmate asked sympathetically.

"No, not that. But he's a fish, Julia. He was just standing there, not looking scared or anything, and all the time we were going straight to—straight to goodness knows where, *He* doesn't know what to do," she added bitterly. "None of them do."

"You think we're lost?"

"Think it? Honey, I *know* it." She sat down and complained, "I've got a headache."

"I wouldn't be surprised," her bunkmate said warmly. "Here, let me get you a cup of tea."

Nancy Eklund said doubtfully, "Do you think you should? Every time you boil water, it's just that much more heat. And—"

"Now let me worry about that," said Julia. "You're a pretty important person on this ship, and you've got to keep yourself in good shape."

The library let herself be persuaded easily enough, though she had an idea that her bunkmate had an ulterior motive or two. But she *did* have a headache and she *was* tired.

And it was true that on the bridge during a jump, she was about the most important person aboard.

It was a duty that Nancy hated, though, important or not. She thanked her lucky stars that most of the time she was in a trance state and not able to observe, for instance, what the distortions of hyperspace were doing to her own personal appearance. But it was finicking, wearing work, even in a trance state. Some of it was bound to seep through to the conscious level, however distorted, and she had been having dreams about hyperspace courses, fixes and triangulation points.

Julia came back with the tea and Nancy Eklund said, "I'm sorry to be always complaining. Heaven knows it's no worse than we had a right to expect. We knew this was dangerous when we signed up for it."

"But we didn't know we'd sweat ourselves to death, Nancy! We didn't expect this eternal should-I-light-the-lights, should-I-boil-some-coffee. Honestly, I don't mind dying half as much as I mind being nibbled to death by one little annoyance after another!" She glanced speculatively at the other girl, and in a different tone said, "I guess you're pretty tired—"

Nancy Eklund sat up and stared at her. "Julia! You can't want me to go on with that horrible story."

"Not if you don't feel up to it," her bunkmate said humbly. "But it passes the time— if you aren't too hoarse."

"Well, no." Nancy took a sip of tea. "I was receiving, not putting out," she said professionally. "I suppose if you *really* want—"

"Index!" said Julia triumphantly, not waiting for her to change her mind. As Nancy Eklund, at the cue word, slumped into the trance state, Julia caught the cup of tea before it spilled. "Fiction!" she said, and went on to give the author's name, the title and the chapter of the mystery she had been "reading." She settled back happily as the library took up the story again.

It wasn't, Julia told herself, as if it really mattered. After all, there wasn't anything for Nancy or anyone else to do, until the geniuses in navigation and computation had figured out where they were. And that would probably take days.

But she was wrong. In the wardroom, Commander Broderick was brooding over a bowl of coffee, half watching a bridge game, when Ciccarelli walked in. He looked tired; he didn't even wait for anyone to ask; he volunteered, "Yeah, yeah, we have a position. It isn't good."

"Pretty far?" one of the card players asked wistfully.

Ciccarelli nodded, unsmiling. "Pretty far. We got our fix by triangulating on extragalactic nebulae, which will give you an idea. I make—"he glanced at them under his eyebrows—"better than fifteen thousand light-years from Sol."

Ensign Lorch picked up the cards and began to deal them automatically; there wasn't anything much else to do. But his mind was not very completely on bridge.

Fifteen thousand light-years from Sol.

In hyperspace, he thought, it might have been a voyage only of minutes. Outside of the three dimensions in which humans live their normal lives, distances are a matter of cosmic whim. Aldebaran and Betelgeuse, in hyperspace, may almost touch; Luna and the Earth may be infinities apart.

Lorch, staring unseeing at his cards, licked his lips. They had cruised around in hyperspace for a few hours of actual "jump" time before the meteorite had struck. And they had found themselves perhaps a thousand light-years from Earth, perhaps less. They had backtracked moment for moment, as well as they could figure, the same course—and their new position was a dozen times as far.

That was the nature of hyperspace. Line A-B in Newton's universe might be more than line A-B in Riemann's, or it might be less, but it was never the same. And the distances, Lorch thought cloudily, might not even be commutative; A-B plus B-C might not be, probably was not, the same as B-C plus A-B. That was why the Atlas, with his infinite stored checkpoints and positions, had a place on the bridge. . . .

"Bid, for God's sake," someone was saying impatiently.

Lorch shook himself. "I'm sorry," he said, focusing on his cards. "Say, isn't it getting hot?"

Nobody answered.

They wouldn't, thought Commander Broderick, lowering into his bowl of cold coffee. Hot? Sure it's getting hot. Not starvation, not thirst, not suffocation—heat. That was the spaceman's enemy, that was what would kill them all. Every time one of the crew drew a breath, carbon in his body oxidized and gave off heat. Every time the rocket jets blasted, heat seeped from the tubes into the frame of the ship. Every time the diesels that drove the nucleophoretic generators coughed and spun, or the cooks fried an egg, or a spaceman lit a cigarette, there was heat.

Take a hot poker, Broderick suggested meditatively to himself. You can watch it glow red and lose heat that way—that is radiation. You can wave it in the air and let the breeze carry the heat away—that is convection. Or you can quench it in a bucket of oil—and that is conduction. And those are the only ways there are, in Newton's space or Riemann's, of taking heat from one body and giving it to another. And in vacuum, the latter two did not operate, for lack of matter to operate with.

Radiation, thought Broderick, radiation would work. A pity we're not red hot.

If they had been at a temperature of a thousand degrees, they would have cooled quite rapidly. But at a temperature of perhaps 20° Centigrade, average through *Terra II*'s hull, radiation was minute. The loss through radiation was more, much more, than made up through internal heat sources, and so the heat of the ship, hour by hour, climbed.

It had been a long time, Broderick remembered, since he had heard the hiss of expanding air. That was how one coped with heat. From the pressurized parts of the ship, valve off air, the expansion cools, the cooling takes heat from the rest of the ship. Replace the air from the high-pressure tanks, and there's more than enough air in the tanks for any imaginable hyperspace voyage, since none can conceivably last more than a few weeks—and that's that.

"Sir," a voice said, and Broderick realized that the voice had said it before. It was a messenger, saluting respectfully.

"What is it?" he growled.

"Surgeon Mate Conboy," the messenger recited crisply, "asks if you can step down to the sick bay. Lieutenant Groden is cutting up."

"All right, all right," said Broderick, and waved the messenger away. Groden, he thought, what's the use of worrying about Groden? He'll cook as well as as any of us, on this handsomely adventurous hyperspace cruise that cannot conceivably last more than a few weeks.

"You trumped my trick!" howled Ensign Lorch's partner as the surgeon was leaving. Lorch blinked and stared.

"Sorry," he said automatically, then bent and looked closer. "I've only got two cards," he said. "Why does the dummy still have five?"

Recorder Mate Eklund took it as a joke. She looked at herself in the mirror and told her friend Julia, "I think it's quite nice. I don't see why we don't do it all the time."

"You've got the figure for it," Julia said glumly, comparing her own dumpy silhouette with the other girl's. These issue bathing suits weren't particularly flattering either, she told herself resentfully, knowing in her heart that the fabric had never been loomed to flatter her figure the way it did Nancy Eklund's. "Bathing suits," she said irritatedly. "Oh, why did I ever sign on for this?"

Recorder Mate Eklund patted her arm and jauntily stepped out into the corridor. The male members of the crew were wearing trunks by now, too. She felt more as though she were at some rather crowded beach than aboard *Terra II*. Except that it was so *hot*.

Not only had the uniform of the day been changed to the bare minimum, but there had been other changes in the ship's routine. No more spinning the ship for gravity, for instance. The magnetic-soled shoes were issued for everyone now, because spinning the ship took rocket power, and rocket power meant more heat that they couldn't get rid of.

The magnet shoes were all right, but it did take a certain amount of concentration to remember heel-and-toe-and-lean, heel-and-toe-and-lean, in a sort of bent-over half trot like the one that Groucho Marx had once, long before Nancy's time, made famous.

She loped crouching into the captain's quarters, saluted and took her place. It *was* getting a little wearisome, she thought detachedly. Everything anybody said, it seemed, they wanted recorded in her brain, and nobody ever seemed to take a breath without demanding some part of the stored knowledge recited back to him. Still, when she was recording she was, in effect, asleep; she woke up slightly refreshed, though there were some confusing dreams.

She wondered absently, for a moment, just what she *did* know, in the part of her mind where the records were kept, the part that was available only to outsiders on presentation of the cue words, and never to her.

But by then the other officers had arrived, and the captain snapped, "*Records,*" and she slumped back. Not quite all the way back—just enough so that the natural tensions in the great muscles of the back and thighs reached a point of equilibrium—and, in the nongravity of the still ship, her sleeping body, moored by the magnets at the feet, floated like Mahomet's Tomb above the chair.

Ensign Lorch felt the captain's eyes on him and hastily looked away from the library. Good-looking kid, though, he thought; this strip-down business had its advantages. Too bad the other women in the crew weren't more like her.

The meeting lasted an hour by the chronometer, as had each meeting of each of the previous eleven days. And it accomplished as much as its eleven predecessors.

"Summing up, then," the captain said savagely. "One, we can't jump home because we don't know the way; two, we can't jet home through normal space because we don't have the fuel or air; three, we can't stay where we are because we'll roast. Is that it?"

The exec said, "That's it, sir. We might set down on another planet, though."

"A planet nearby?" The captain thought that over. "What about it Ciccarelli?"

The navigator shrugged. "If we can find one, sir. I'd say the chances were poor. We've got very little in the way of fuel reserve. Every jump uses up a little, and—well, if we come out of a jump within, let's say, a tenth of a light-year of a habitable planet, pretty nearly at relative rest to it, we might be able to make it. We've got maybe one chance in a thousand of that."

Commander Broderick said, "Sir, this is just a wild notion, but suppose we did one of those things they're always doing in the movies, you know? Freeze the whole ship's crew in suspended animation. I believe I could manage something like that out of the medical supplies, if we could only bring the temperature low enough—"

"That's just what we *can't* do," said the captain.

"Yes, sir," Broderick agreed. "But if we did that, we could valve off a lot of air—maybe enough to cool the ship. Nobody would be breathing, you see. And we could rig up some sort of alarm for when we got there. Wouldn't matter if it was years—even centuries; there would be a vacuum, and no specimen deterioration—I mean, nothing happening to us."

Ciccarelli said mulishly, "Impossible. It's the question of relative rest again. We haven't got enough fuel to mess around. Suppose we found Sol, and pointed right for it. By the time we got there, where would it be and how fast would it be going, in what direction? Maybe you can tell. I can't."

Broderick crouched disconsolately back into his sick bay, and the enlisted man he'd left behind looked up in relief. "It's Groden, sir," he said at once. "He's been acting up."

Ensign Lorch, behind Broderick, hesitated in the doorway. "Acting up?" demanded Broderick.

"Yes, sir. I gave him another needle, but it didn't take effect. I guess it was delirium, sir. Took three ampoules—"

The voices trailed off as they went inside. Lorch made himself comfortable—not an easy job in nongravity, that is if you were a commissioned officer and concerned about smart appearance.

The two medics were gone for a long time, and when Commander Broderick came out again he looked worried. "Sorry, Lorch," he apologized. He felt the pressure-pot of coffee on the little stove and made a face. "Want some?"

Lorch shook his head. "Too much trouble to drink."

"Don't blame you." But Broderick carefully coaxed a couple of ounces of the stuff into a transparent plastic bulb, teased sugar and cream in after it, spun the bulb with his thumb over the opening to stir it, took a sip. "I don't like it," he brooded over his coffee. "Groden's working up real damage, the kind I can't handle."

Lorch asked curiously, "What kind is that?"

"Inside his head. I had to tell him that his sight was gone, unless we can get to an eye bank within ten days. The optic nerves, Lorch—you can patch in an eye, but once the nerve has degenerated you can't replace it. And he took it hard."

"Yelled and cut up?"

"Worse than that," said Broderick. "He didn't say a word. Now, I *know* that man's in pain; the scars around his eyes are pretty bad. I gave him a couple of pills to knock out the nerve centers, but Conboy found them under his pillow. He wouldn't take them, and he wouldn't make a sound—until he fell asleep, and then he damn near woke up the ship. Conboy must have given him fifty ampoules by now—too much of the stuff. But we can't have him screaming. He's punishing himself, Lorch."

"For what?"

"Who knows for what? If I could put him through an E.E.S., I might be able to find out. But how can you run an electroencephaloscope on a tub like this? I'm lucky they let me have an X-ray."

Lorch said, perhaps a touch too dryly, "What did doctors do before they had those gadgets? Shoot the patients?"

It made Broderick look at him thoughtfully. "No," he said after a second. "Of course not. With luck, I could run a verbal analysis on him, and I might pick some of the key stuff out of the sludge in, oh, four or five months. That's what they did before they had the E.E.S. And now let's get busy, mister."

The two of them worked over an inventory of Broderick's medicine chest, because even though the idea of putting the whole ship's crew in suspended animation was ridiculous and impossible and contra-regs besides—what else was there?

And it kept getting hotter.

Even Groden felt it.

He called reasonably to whoever was near, "Please do what I ask. Put things back the way they were, please. Please do it!" He said it many times, many different ways. But his tongue was black velvet and his mouth an enormous cave; he couldn't feel the words, couldn't feel his tongue against his cheeks or teeth. That was the needles they kept sticking him with, he told himself. "Please," he said, "no more needles."

But he wasn't getting through.

Groden relaxed. He forced himself to relax, and it wasn't easy. His body was all wrong; it hurt in places, and felt nothing in places, and—were those feelings at his waist and shoulders and legs the touch of restraining belts? He couldn't tell.

He was lying on his back, he was pretty sure. At least, the voices seemed to come from points in the plane of his body, as well as he could locate them. But if he was lying on his back, he asked himself, why didn't he feel pressure on his back? Or pressure anywhere? Could the ship be in freefall—all this length of time? Impossible, he told himself.

He went back to relaxing.

The thing was to keep from panic. If you were physically relaxed, you couldn't panic. That was what they had taught at the academy, and it was true. Only they hadn't taught the converse, he thought bitterly; they hadn't said that when you were in panic it was impossible to relax.

No. That's not the way to go about it, he told himself. Relax. Occupy your mind with—with—well, occupy your mind with *something*. Take inventory, for instance.

One, it's hot. There was no doubt of that.

Two, something was pressing against his body at various points. It *felt* like restraining belts.

Three, voices came and talked to him. Damned dirty lying voices that—He caught himself just in time.

Four, he said to himself, *four*, somebody keeps sticking needles into me.

It was the needles, he thought wretchedly, that made everything else so bad. Maybe the needles *caused* everything else. With craven hope he told himself: sure, the needles; they're sticking me full of drugs; naturally I'm having delusions. Who wouldn't? I'm lucky if I don't turn into a hophead if I get out of this—

When I get out of this, he corrected himself, whimpering.

He wondered whether he was crying.

Of course, if those lying voices were, by some chance, *not* lying, then he couldn't be crying. Because he wouldn't have any eyes to cry with. And, he told himself reasonably, there wasn't much doubt that the voices were plausible. He had been injured somewhere around his eyes; he had felt the pain, and it was too intense and specific to be unreal. That was in the old days—how long ago they were, he could not begin to imagine—when there had been only a few needles now and then, and even if he did have a little trouble moving and talking, he was still in perfect possession of his faculties.

All right, he thought. So I was injured around the eyes.

But the rest—that was a damned lie. He had even believed it for a while—when the Broderick-voice said, with hypocritical sympathy, that he wouldn't be able to see anything, ever, unless they got him new corpse's eyes out of an eye bank on Earth. It had been a blow, but he believed it. Until, he reminded himself triumphantly, he had *seen!* Seen as clearly as he knew the voices were lying, that was when he began to suspect the existence of the whole horrible, senseless plot.

"No!" he screamed. "Please, please—no!" But they couldn't be hearing him, because they were going right on with another needle; he could feel it. Furiously he fought to pull back the alien arm, make the marble lips move, the black velvet tongue speak, "Please—"

On the bridge, the captain was staring fixedly at the alien stars. It was a measure of his state of mind that he was on the bridge at all, at a time when the ship was going nowhere and there was nothing to be done beyond the routine.

He leaned forward in his chair, jerking free the little magnets sewn into the waist of his trunks, and walked heel-and-toe across the bridge. The little Recorder Mate, Eklund or whatever her name was, was standing humbly in a corner, waiting for him to tell her why he had sent for her. But, the captain confessed to himself, the trouble was he didn't exactly know why himself. And, after all, why should he? It was so damned hot—

Belay that kind of talk, he told himself. He said: "Eklund! Index." The girl's eyes closed like the snapping of a shutter.

"Take over," the captain ordered the exec. "Run her through the Riemannian configurations again. We'll get every bit of dope she has." And they would, he knew. Because they had already.

And none of it helped.

It was a good thing, Ensign Lorch told himself, sweating, that spaceships were not painted. Otherwise he would surely have been set to commanding a crew chipping paint.

Terra II being welded of unpainted metal, the color a part of the alloy itself, his crew was defluffing the filter traps in the air circulators. It was a job for idiots, planned by morons; it took six men five hours to disassemble the air trunks and the junction boxes, five minutes to blow out the collected fluff on the static accumulators, five hours to put them back together again. There was an alternative method, which involved burning them clean with a high-voltage arc; that took one man slightly under three seconds. But that, the exec had decreed, meant heat.

And *heat* was the enemy.

Of course, there was still a third alternative, which was to leave the fluff in the filter traps undisturbed. This would have generated no heat at all. But it also would have taken no time and occupied no personnel, which were decisive counts against it in the eyes of the exec. A little fluff in the filters would make no conceivable difference to the operation of the ship, but idle men might make a very great difference indeed.

"Hurry it up," growled Ensign Lorch. The men didn't even look at him. Lorch looked around him self-consciously. As an officer, he had made inspection tours in the enlisted women's quarters before, but he couldn't help feeling out of place and slightly apprehensive.

That girl, the Recorder Mate—Eklund was her name—was droning all the parts of *Cyrano de Bergerac* to an audience in the far end of the lounge, and parts of Cyrano's farewell to Roxanne kept mixing in with Lorch's thoughts.

It didn't matter; he wasn't thinking to any purpose, anyhow. Neither he nor anyone else on *Terra II*, he told himself bitterly. Fifteen thousand light-years. The light that came to them from Sol—how weak and faint!—had been bright summer sunlight beating down on the skin tents of Neolithic Man creeping northward after the retreating ice. And the light from the nearest stars beyond *Terra II*'s skin, contrariwise, would fall on an Earth inconceivably advanced, a planet of mental Titans . . .

"Mister Lorch," someone was repeating plaintively.

The ensign shook himself and focused on the spaceman wavering before him. "Eh?"

"We're done," the man repeated. "It's all put together again. The filter traps," he explained.

"Oh," said Ensign Lorch. He glanced self-consciously at the women at the far end of the lounge, but they were absorbed in Rostand's love story. There was a murmur of gossip from them—"so all at once I knew there was somebody *looking* at me. Well, I called the duty officer and we searched, but—"

Ensign Lorch cleared his throat. "Well done," he said absently. "Dismissed." He turned his back on the detail and propelled himself down the passageway toward the sick bay.

If he went back to the bridge, the old man would find work for him; if he went to the wardroom, the exec would find an excuse to send him to the old man. And his own quarters were horribly, stifling hot.

He accosted the ship's surgeon and demanded, "How long are we expected to live in this heat?"

Commander Broderick said irritably, "How should I know? You don't die of the heat, that's sure. There are other things that will come first—suffocation, thirst, maybe even starvation."

Lorch looked thoughtfully at the medical officer. Red-eyed, his face lined with worry and weariness, Broderick was showing strain. Through his scanty shorts, you could see the fishbelly whiteness of his skin; it was old man's skin, and Broderick, for all of his passing the annual fitness exam, was getting on toward being an old man.

Lorch said more gently, "I guess you're getting a rough time all round."

"Good Lord, am I!" the surgeon snapped. "Half the ship's complement has been in here today—little fiddling things like prickly heat and dizzy spells. Dizzy spells! How the devil can anyone *not* have dizzy spells? The women's quarters have practically a regular courier service. If it isn't antiperspirants, it's salt tablets; if it isn't salt tablets, it's alcohol from the ship's store for rubdowns." He passed his hand shakily over his eyes. "Then," he said, "to top it all off there's him." He pointed to the inner chamber of the sick bay. Lorch, listening, could hear the blinded Groden's rasping breath.

There was a shrill whistle from the speaking tube, then, tinnily, a voice from the bridge. "Commander Broderick! Captain requests you report to the bridge at once."

The surgeon blinked and swore. "How the devil am I supposed to do that?" he demanded. "Two of my crewmen are out with heat prostration, and the other two were working all night. All right, I go up to the bridge. Suppose there's some trouble? Suppose Groden starts acting up again?" He stared irresolutely at the speaking tube.

Lorch said thoughtfully, "Say, Commander, could I keep an eye on him for you?"

It was a fine idea. Broderick took off for the bridge and Lorch, hastily briefed on the simple task of sticking a new needle in Groden's arm if he showed any signs of trouble, bade him a careful good-bye and waited until he was well out of sight before, whistling, he knelt before the cabinet of emergency medical supplies.

Broderick had given him an idea. And, he told himself blissfully, moments later, it had been a good one. Alcohol rub! Now why hadn't he thought of that himself?

He hardly noticed that Groden's heavy breathing had changed pitch and character. It almost formed words now.

On the bridge, the captain was briefing the ship's officers—all but Groden, in the sick bay, and Lorch, who, the captain had agreed, was easily enough spared to watch after

Groden—on what in his mind he called Project Desperation. It didn't take much briefing because it was the only thing left for them to do and every man on the ship knew it.

"We have," the captain said precisely, "margin for just under forty minutes of rocket blast at standard thrust. That will bring our overall temperature up to sixty degrees, give or take a degree according to Engineering's best guess. And that's the maximum the human body can stand—that's right, Broderick?"

The surgeon quickly translated into the Fahrenheit scale; a hundred and forty degrees or so.

"That's right, sir," he said. "If we can stand that much," he added reluctantly after a moment. "It hits that on Earth in a couple of places—around the Dead Sea, Aden, places like that. But it isn't sustained heat; it drops considerably after dark."

The captain nodded somberly. "We'll hope," he said, "that we'll find ourselves out of this before we hit sixty degrees. If we don't—well, at least we won't starve or suffocate. You understand, gentlemen, that the odds are against us. I suggested to Lieutenant Ciccarelli that it was a million-to-one-shot. He said I was an optimist. But one chance in a million, or a billion, or whatever the number may be, is better than no chance at all. Do you all agree?"

There was no answer. The captain went on, "Before we jump, I presume no one has a better idea?" No one had. "Thank you. Then, gentlemen, if you will assume your stations, we'll get down to business. Stand by to jump."

The captain took his place with an air of benign detachment. It wasn't a captain's job to take the conn of a ship in a perfectly routine maneuver. He watched approvingly as the exec put the ship on alert, then on standby, then went through the checklist that culminated in the "jump" into hyperspace.

The captain was a model of placid, observant command officership, but behind the placid face, the agitated mind was churning out awful calculations.

Consider the Galaxy, he was thinking to himself; a hundred thousand light-years broad, perhaps forty thousand through its axis. Call it a lens-shaped figure with a volume of three hundred trillion light-years. Say that their cruising radius, in normal space, was within a volume of one light-year; that meant that the chances of their coming out, by accident, within cruising distance of Earth was—not one in a million, or one in a hundred million, or one in a billion. . . .

It was one chance in three hundred trillion.

The captain juggled the numbers comfortably enough in his mind. They were absolutely meaningless, far too big to be comprehended or feared.

There it was, the beautiful Master Pattern.

Groden lay tense and fearful, seeing it. It had been a long time since the last needle; by the only clock he owned, his heartbeat, it had been more than two hours since he discovered that he could move his lips and his fingers again. He had feverishly wondered why; and had not dared speak or move after the first trials for fear of bringing the needle again. But now he knew.

There was the Master Pattern. He scanned it slowly in every part. There was the giant star-cluster of Hercules; and there the bridge of *Terra II*; there was the fat red disc of Betelgeuse; and there the shower room of the enlisted women's quarters. He took in the ordered ranks of the constellations as easily as he noted that Broderick was gone from the sick bay, and in his place the young ensign, Lorch, was clinging with harried expression to a stanchion. They were in hyperspace. Broderick was on the bridge. Lorch had been left in charge, and it had not occurred to him, since his patient had been so carefully quiet, to administer another needle.

Groden carefully moved his hands, and found that they would do what he wanted. He was getting the hang of—well, it was not seeing, exactly, he confessed to himself. It was like being alone on a starless night, in the middle of a dark wood. It took time to get used to the darkness, but by and by shapes would begin to make themselves known.

It was not the same thing; this was no mere matter of the expanding pupil of the eye; but the effect was something the same. But explain it or not, he was being able to use it; each time the beautiful vision was more complete, and therefore more beautiful.

He found the straps that bound him, and unbuckled them.

On the bridge, he "saw," the jump at random was nearing its end. It would be only a matter of minutes before they were back in normal space, and he was blind again.

In the outer room of the sick-bay, Ensign Lorch was staring dismally at the hallucinations of hyperspace. It was almost certain, thought Groden to himself, that if Lorch was so fortunate as to see him at all, he would pass off the sight as another of the lies light told. The important thing was sound; he must not make a noise.

He crept through the door, carefully holding to the guide rails. Broderick had been right about one thing, though, he admitted—the pain. The wreck of his eyes no longer seemed as important, with the wonderful things hyperspace's cloudless perception brought to him, but the shattered bone and tissue and nerve ends *hurt*.

Algol's dark primary occluded the radiant star for a second and confused him; they were moving faster than he had thought. He hastily scanned the Master Plan again, fearful for a second. But there was Sol and its family of planets, and there was Earth. *Terra II* might be lost, but Lieutenant Groden was not, and if only he could get to the bridge . . .

He scanned the bridge. It was later than he thought. He felt the vibrations in the floor as he realized that the jump was at an end. Panicked, he hesitated.

Blackness again, and no more stars.

He stood there, incredibly desolate, and the pain was suddenly more than he could bear.

And from behind him he heard a startled yell, Lorch's voice: "Hey, Groden! Come back here! What the devil are you doing out in the passage?"

It was the last straw. Groden had no tear ducts left with which to weep, but he did the best he could.

Broderick worked over the girl, Eklund, for a moment, and brought her to. She stared at him uncomprehendingly for a moment, but she was all right. As all right, he thought, as anyone on *Terra II* had any chance to be.

"Plain heat prostration," he reported to the captain. "It's been a pretty rough job for her, trying to keep on top of all this."

The captain nodded unemotionally. "Well, Ciccarelli?" he demanded.

The navigator ran his hands through his hair. 'No position, sir,' he said despondently. "Maybe if I ran down the third and fourth magnitude stars—"

"Don't bother," the captain said. "If we aren't within a light-year of Sol, we're too far to do us any good. At your convenience, gentlemen, we'll take another jump."

The executive nodded wearily and opened his mouth to give the order, but Broderick protested, "Sir, we'll all be falling over if we don't take a break. The temperature's past forty-five now. The only way to handle it is frequent rests and plenty of liquids."

"Ten minutes be enough?"

The surgeon hesitated. Then he shrugged. "Why not? No sense worrying about long-term effects just now, is there?"

"There is not," said the captain. "Make it so," he ordered the exec.

The captain half-closed his eyes, fanning himself mechanically. When the runner from the wardroom brought him his plastic globe of fruit juices he accepted it and began to sip, but he wasn't paying very much attention. He had the figures on the tip of his tongue: the first blind jump in Project Desperation had cost them sixteen minutes of rocket time. He could be a little more conservative with the next one—maybe use only ten minutes. That way he could squeeze out at least one more full-length, or nearly full-length, jump; and then one last truly desperate try, not more than a minute or two. And if that didn't work, they were cooked.

Literally, he told himself wryly.

In fact, he continued, counting up the entries in red ink on their ledger, they were just about out of luck now. For even if their next jump took them within cruising distance of Earth, there was still the time factor to be considered. They had left only twenty-four minutes of jet-time before *Terra II*'s hull temperature passed the critical sixty-degree mark.

True, he had maintained some slight reserve in that not *all* their expansible gas had been used. There remained a certain amount in the compressed tanks. And even beyond that, it would be possible to valve off some of the ship's ambient air itself, dropping the pressure to, say ten pounds to the square inch or even less.

That *might* give them maneuvering time in normal space—provided they were God-blessed enough to come out of one of the three remaining jumps within range of Earth, provided all the angels of heaven were helping them. . . .

Which, it was clear, he told himself, they weren't.

"Sir," said Commander Broderick's voice, "I think you can proceed now."

The captain opened his eyes. "Thank you," he said gravely and nodded to the exec. It was a quick job by now. The kerosene lamps were already lit, the main electric circuits already cut; it was only a matter of double-checking and of getting the nucleophoretic generators up to speed.

The captain observed the routine attentively. It did not matter that the fitness reports for which he was taking mental notes might never be written. It was a captain's job to make his evaluations all the same.

"Stand by to jump!" called the exec, and the talker repeated it into the tubes. Down in the generator-room, the jumpmen listened for the command. It came; they heaved on the enormous manual clutches.

And *Terra II* slipped into Riemannian space once more.

The stars whirled before the captain's eyes and became geometrical figures in prismatic colors. The slight, worn figure of the library, the girl named Eklund, ballooned and wavered and seemed to float around the bridge. The captain looked on with composure; he was used to the illusions of hyperspace. Even—almost—he understood them. From the girl's vast stored knowledge, he had learned of the connection between electric potential and the three-dimensional matrix.

Light and electrons: in hyperspace, they lied.

Matter was still matter, he thought; the strange lights beyond the viewing pane were stars. And the subtler flow within his body was dependable enough, for he could hear as reliably as ever and if he touched something hot, the nerve ends would scream *Burn!* to his brain. But the messenger between the stars and the brain—the photons and electrons that conveyed the image—were aberrants; they followed curious Riemannian courses, and no brain bound by the strictures of three dimensions could sort them out.

Just as now, thought the captain with detached amusement, I seem to be seeing old Groden here on the bridge. Ridiculous, but as plain as life. If I didn't know he was asleep in the sick bay, I'd swear it was he.

"Captain! Captain!" Ensign Lorch's voice penetrated over the metronome-cadenced commands of the exec and the bustling noises of the bridge.

The captain stared wonderingly at the phantasms of light. "Ensign Lorch?" he demanded. "But—"

"Yes, sir! I'm really here and so is Groden." Lorch's voice went on as the captain peered into the chaos of shifting images. Lorch himself wasn't visible—unless that sea-green inverted monstrosity with a head of fire was Lorch. But the voice was Lorch's voice, and the figure of Groden, complete with the white wrappings over the eyes, was shadowy but real. And the voices were saying—astonishing things.

"You mean," said the captain at last, "that *Groden* can pilot us home?"

"That," said Groden, in the first confident voice he had been able to use in days, "is just what he means."

Blind man's buff. And what better player can there be than a blind man?

Lieutenant Groden, eyeless and far-seeing, stood by the exec's left hand and clipped out courses and directions. The exec marveled, and stared unbelievingly at the fantastic patterns outside the bridge, and followed orders.

And presently Groden gave the order to stop all jets and drop back into normal space. In a moment, he was blind again—and the rest of the bridge complement found themselves staring at a reddish sun with a family of five planets, two of them Earthlike and green.

"That's not Sol!" barked the captain.

"No," said Groden wearily, "but it's a place to land and cool the ship and replenish our air. You ran us close to the danger line, Captain."

Terra II came whistling down on to a broad, sandy plain, and lay quiet, its jet tubes smoking, while the Planetology section put out its feelers and reported:

"Temperature, pressure, atmospheric analysis and radiation spectrum—all Earth normal. No poisons or biotic agents apparent on gross examination."

"There won't be any on closer examination either," said Groden. "This planet's clean, captain." He stood hanging on to a stanchion, pressed down by the gravity of the world he had found for them.

The captain looked at him thoughtfully for a moment, but there were more important things to attend to.

"Bleed in two pounds," ordered the captain and the duty officer saluted and issued orders into the speaking tube.

They had run close to the danger line, indeed; the ambient pressure inside *Terra II's* hull had been bled down to a scant ten pounds, in order to use as much cooling effect from releasing gas as possible. Whether it was clean or not, no man could step out on to the surface of the new planet until the pressures had been brought back to normal.

They stood at the view panel looking out on the world. They were near its equator, but the temperature was cool by Earth standards. Before them was a broad, gentle sea; behind them, a rim of green-clad hills.

The captain made ready to send his first landing party on to a new and liveable planet.

The scouting parties were back and the captain, for once, was smiling. "Wonderful!" he exulted. "A perfect planet for colonization—and we owe it all to you, Groden."

"That's right," said Groden. He was lying down on a ward-room bench—Broderick's orders. Broderick had wanted to put him under sedation again, in fact, but that had brought Groden too close to mutiny.

The captain glanced at his navigator. The swathed bandages hid Groden's expression, and after a moment the captain decided to overlook the remark.

He went on, "It's a medal for you. You deserve it, Groden."

"He'll need it, sir," said Commander Broderick. "There won't be any new eyes for Lieutenant Groden." He looked old and sick and defeated. "The optic nerves are too far gone. New eyes wouldn't help now; there's nothing that would help. He'll never have eyes again."

"Sure," said Groden casually. "I knew it before I brought you here, captain."

The captain frowned uncomprehendingly, but Broderick caught the meaning in an instant. "You mean you could have brought us back to Earth?" he demanded.

"In two jumps," Groden told him easily.

"Then why didn't you?" snapped the captain. "I have a responsibility to my crew—I can't let a man go blind because of phony heroics!"

Groden swung his feet down, sat up. "Who's a hero? I just didn't want to trade what I have now for what I used to have, that's all."

"Meaning what?" asked Broderick.

"It's more than seeing. Want to know how many Sol-type systems there are within five thousand light-years of here? I can tell you. Want to know what the Universe looks like in hyperspace? I can tell you that, too, only I can't describe it. It makes *sense*, captain! The whole thing is as orderly and chartable as our own space. And I could see it, all of it. And you offer me *eyes!*"

"But why don't I see it, Groden?" the captain puzzledly wanted to know. "Surely we've all closed our eyes for a moment in hyperspace—why didn't we see it then?"

"Sleep and death are alike, but they're not the same. Neither is closing your eyes and being blind. I'm blind in normal space; you're blind in hyperspace—that isn't much of an answer, but the medics will work it out."

The surgeon looked piercingly at Groden's bandaged face. "Then the odds are that *any* blind person can see in hyperspace?"

"I think so," Groden agreed. "In fact, I'm practically certain."

"Then," said the captain, "it's our duty to return to Earth and let them know. They can equip each mapmaking ship with a blind person."

Groden gave his head a shake. "Plenty of time for that, Skipper. We have a quadrant of hyperspace to chart. With me on hand to 'see' during the jumps, we'll finish up fast.

Then we can go back and tell them. But I think we should get on with the job we've been assigned."

"Right," said the captain after a pause. "We'll bring the ship to stand-by for takeoff."

The rockets thundered and *Terra II* split the atmosphere on its way to deeper space.

As soon as they were clear, the ship readied for the jump and the captain said, "Good luck, Groden. It's all yours—give us our course."

Groden felt the quiver of the generators, far below, and at once the Universe lay spread before him.

No more darkness, no blind fumblings. An end to basket-weaving and the dreary time-passing fingering of Braille for Earth's incurable blind. They would be the eyes of the proud new hyperspace fleet that was yet to come!

"It's all yours, Groden," the captain repeated.

Groden cleared his throat, issued his course vectors.

Captain, you don't know how right you are, he thought. Only it won't be just mine—it'll be the blind leading the sighted!

Now there, he chuckled, was a switch. But he'd have to wait until he was back on Earth, among the blind, for it to be appreciated.

SPENDING A DAY
AT THE LOTTERY FAIR

There are lots of lotteries these days. Time was, lotteries were something most Americans didn't know about; they were something done in other countries—Ireland, Spain, elsewhere. But we've become quite used to lotteries now, along with other forms of legal gambling, as well as the many illegal forms of gambling.

The "Lottery Fair" of the title, however, is not quite what you might expect. Frederik Pohl could have laid all his cards on the table right at the start of the story, but then you wouldn't have to discover the true nature of the Lottery Fair . . . and the story, for yourself.

And that wouldn't be nearly as challenging, or fun, as untangling the puzzle of this deceptively simple tale first published in 1983.

They were the Baxter family, Randolph and Millicent the parents, with their three children, Emma and Simon and Louisa, who was the littlest; and they didn't come to the fair in any old bus. No, they drove up in a taxi, all the way from their home clear on the other side of town, laughing and poking each other, and when they got out Randolph Baxter gave the driver a really big tip. It wasn't that he could really afford it. It was just because he felt it was the right thing to do. When you took your whole family to the Lottery Fair, Baxter believed, you might as well do it in style. Besides, the fare was only money. Though Millicent Baxter pursed her lips when she saw the size of the tip, she certainly was not angry; her eyes sparkled as brightly as the children's, and together they stared at the facade of the Lottery Fair.

Even before you got through the gates there was a carnival smell—buttered popcorn and cotton candy and tacos all together—and a carnival sound of merry-go-round organs and people screaming in the roller coaster, and bands and bagpipes from far away. A clown stalked on tall stilts through the fairgoers lining up at the ticket windows, bending down to chuck children under the chin and making believe to nibble the ears of teenage girls in bright summer shorts. Rainbow fountains splashed perfumy spray. People in cartoon-character costumes, Gus the Ghost and Mickey Mouse and Pac-Man, handed out free surprise packages to the kids: when Simon opened his it was a propeller beanie; a fan for Emma; for little Louisa, cardboard glasses with a Groucho Marx mustache. And crowded! You could hardly believe such crowds! Off to one side of the parking lot the tour buses were rolling in with their loads of foreign visitors, Chinese and Argentines and Swedes; they had special entrances and were waved through by special guards who greeted them, some of the time anyway, in their own native languages—"Willkommen!" and "Bonjour!" and "Ey there, mate!"—as long as they didn't speak anything like Urdu or Serbo-Croatian, anyway. For the foreign tourists didn't have to pay in the usual way; they bought their tickets in their country of origin, with valuable foreign exchange, and then everything was free for them.

Of course it wasn't like that for the regular American fairgoers. They had to pay. You could see each family group moving up toward the ticket windows. They would slow down as they got closer and finally stop, huddling together while they decided how to pay, and then one or two of them, or all of them, would move on to the window and reach into the admissions cuff for their tickets. Randolph Baxter had long before made up his mind that there would be no such wrangles on this day for his family. He said simply, "Wait here a minute," and strode up to the window by himself. He put his arm into the cuff, smiled at the ticket attendant and said grandly, "I'll take five, please."

The ticket seller looked at him admiringly. "You know," she offered, "there aren't that many daddies who'll take all the little fellows in like that. Sometimes they make even tiny babies get their own tickets." Baxter gave her a modest I-do-what-I-can shrug, though he could not help that his smile was a little strained until all five tickets clicked out of the roll. He bore them proudly back to his family and led them through the turn-stiles.

"My, what a crowd," sighed Millicent Baxter happily as she gazed around. "Now, what shall we do first?"

The response was immediate. "See the old automobiles," yelled Simon, and, "No, the animals!" and, "No, the stiffs!" cried his sisters.

Randolph Baxter spoke sharply to them—not angrily, but firmly. "There will be no fighting over what we do," he commanded. "We'll *vote* on what we do, the democratic way. No arguments, and no exceptions. Now," he added, "the first thing we're going to do is that you kids will stay right here while your mother and I get tickets for the job lottery." The parents left the children arguing viciously among themselves and headed for the nearest lottery booth. Randolph Baxter could not help a tingle of excitement, and his wife's eyes were gleaming, as they studied the prize list. The first prize was the management of a whole apartment building—twenty-five thousand dollars a year salary, and a free three-room condo thrown in!

Millicent read his thoughts as they stood in line. "Don't you just wish!" she whispered. "But personally I'd settle for any of the others. Look, there's even a job for an English teacher!" Randolph shook his head wordlessly. It was just marvelous—five full-time jobs offered in this one raffle, and that not the biggest of the day. The last one, after the fireworks, always had the grandest of prizes. "Aren't you glad we came?" Millicent asked, and her husband nodded.

But in fact he wasn't, altogether, at least until they safely got their tickets and were on their way back to the children, and then he was quickly disconcerted to see that the kids weren't where they had been left. "Oh, hell," groaned Randolph. It was early in the day for them to get lost.

But they weren't very far. His wife said sharply, "There they are. And look what they're doing!" They were at a refreshment stand. And each one of them had a huge cone of frozen custard. "I *told* them not to make any purchases when we weren't with them!" Millicent cried, but in fact it was worse than that. The children were talking to a pair of strange grown-ups, a lean, fair, elderly woman with a sharp, stern face, and a round, dark-skinned man with a bald head and immense tortoiseshell glasses.

As the Baxters approached, the woman turned to them apologetically. "Oh, hullo," she said, "you must be the parents. I do hope you'll forgive us. Mr. Katsubishi and I seem to have lost our tour, and your children kindly helped us look for it."

"It's all right, Dad," Simon put in swiftly. "They're on this foreign tour, see, and everything's free for them anyway. Dad? Why can't we get on a tour and have everything free?"

"We're Americans," his father explained, smiling tentatively at the tall English-looking woman and the tubby, cheerful Japanese—he decided that they didn't *look* like depraved child molesters. "You have to be an international tourist to get these unlimited tickets. And I bet they cost quite a lot of money, don't they?" he appealed to the man, who smiled and shrugged and looked at the woman.

"Mr. Katsubishi doesn't speak English very well," she apologized. "I'm Rachel Millay. Mrs. Millay, that is, although me dear husband left us some years ago." She glanced about in humorous distress. "I don't suppose you've seen a tour leader carrying a green and violet flag with a cross of St. Andrew on it?"

Since Randolph Baxter had no idea what a cross of St. Andrew looked like, it was hard to say. In any case, there were at least twenty tour parties in sight, each with its own individual pennant or standard, trudging in determined merriment toward the pavilions, the rides, or the refreshment stands. "I'm afraid not," he began, and then paused as his wife clutched his arm. The P.A. system crackled, and the winners of the first drawing were announced.

Neither of the Baxters were among them. "Well, there are six more drawings," said Millicent bravely—not adding that there were also six more sets of raffle tickets to buy if they wanted any hope of winning one of them. Her husband smiled cheerfully at the children.

"What's it to be?" he asked generously. "The life exhibit? The concert—"

"We already voted, Dad," cried Emma, his elder daughter, "it's the animals!"

"No, the stiffs!" yelled her baby sister.

"The old autos," cried Simon. "Anyway, there won't be any stiffs there until later, not to speak of!"

Baxter smiled indulgently at the foreigners. "Children," he explained. "Well, I do hope you find your group." And he led the way to the first democratically selected adventure of the day, the space exhibit.

Baxter had always had a nostalgic fondness for space, and this was a pretty fine exhibit, harking back to olden, golden days when human beings could spare enough energy and resources to send their people and probes out toward the distant worlds. Even the kids liked it. It was lavish with animated 3-D displays showing a human being walking around on the surface of the Moon, and a spacecraft slipping through the rings of Saturn, and even a probe, though not an American one, hustling after Halley's Comet to take its picture.

But Randolph Baxter had some difficulty in concentrating on the pleasure of the display at first because, as they were getting their tickets, the tall, smiling black man just ahead of him in line put his arm into the admissions cuff, looked startled, withdrew his arm, started to speak and fell over on the ground, his eyes open, and staring, it seemed, right into Randolph Baxter's.

When you have a wife and three kids and no job, living on welfare, never thinking about tomorrow because you know there isn't going to be anything in tomorrow worth thinking about, then a day's outing for the whole family is an event to be treasured. No matter what the price—especially if the price isn't in money. So the Baxter family did it all. They visited six national pavilions, even the Paraguayan. They lunched grandly in the dining room at the summit of the fair's great central theme structure, the Cenotaph. And they did the rides, all the rides, from the Slosh-a-Slide water chutes through the immense Ferris wheel with the wind howling through the open car and Simon threatening to spit down on the crowds below, to the screaming, shattering roller coaster that made little Louisa wet her pants. Fortunately her mother had brought clean underwear for the child. When she sent the little girl off with her sister to change in the ladies' room, she followed them anxiously with her eyes until they were safely past the ticket collector, and then said, "Rand, honey. You paid for all those rides yourself."

He shrugged defensively. "I want everybody to have a good time."

"Now, don't talk that way. We agreed. The children and I are going to pay our own way all the rest of the day, and the subject is closed." She proved the point by changing it. "Look," she said, "there are those two foreigners who lost their tour group again." She waved, and Mrs. Millay and Mr. Katsubishi came up diffidently.

"If we're not intruding?" said Mrs. Millay. "We never did find our tour guide, you see, but actually we're getting on quite well without. But isn't it hot! It's never like this in Scotland."

Millicent fanned herself in agreement. "Do sit down, Mrs. Millay. Is that where you're from, Scotland? And you Mr. Kat—, Kats—"

"Katsubishi," he smiled, with an abrupt deep bow. Then he wrinkled his face in concentration for a moment and managed to say: "I, too—Sukottaland."

Millicent tried not to look astonished, but evidently did not succeed. Mrs. Millay explained, "He's from around Kyle of Lochalth, you know." Since Millicent obviously didn't know, she added, "That's the Japanese colony in northern Scotland, near my own home. In fact, I teach English to Japanese schoolchildren there, since I know the language—my parents were missionaries in Honshu, you see. Didn't you know about the colony?"

Actually, Millicent and Randolph did know about the colony. Or, at least, they almost did, in the way that human beings exposed to forty channels of television and with nothing much to do with their time have heard of—without really knowing much about—almost every concept, phenomenon, event, and trend in human history. In just that way, they had heard of the United Kingdom's pact with Japan, allowing large Japanese immigration into an enclave in the north of Scotland. The Japanese made the area bloom both agriculturally and economically. The United Kingdom got a useful injection of Japanese capital and energy, and the Japanese got rid of some of their surplus population without pain. "I wish we'd thought of that," Millicent observed in some envy, but her husband shook his head.

"Different countries, different ways," he said patriotically, "and actually we're doing rather well. I mean, just look at the Lottery Fair! That's American ingenuity for you." Observing that Mrs. Millay was whispering a rapid-fire translation into Mr. Katsubishi's ear, he was encouraged to go on. "Other countries, you see, have their own way of handling their problems. Compulsory sterilization of all babies born in even-numbered years in India, as I'm sure you're aware. The contraceptive drugs they put in the water supply in Mexico—and we don't even talk of what they're doing in, say, Bangladesh." Mrs. Millay shuddered sympathetically as she translated, and the Japanese beamed and bowed, then spoke rapidly.

"He says one can learn much," Mrs. Millay translated, "from what foreign countries can do. Even America."

Millicent, glancing at the expression on her husband's face, said brightly: "Well! Let's not let this day go to waste. What shall we do next?" At once she got the same answers from the children: "Old cars!" "Animals!" "No," whined Baby Louisa, "I wanna see the stiffs!"

Mr. Katsubishi whispered something in staccato Japanese to Mrs. Millay, who turned hesitantly to Millicent Baxter. "One doesn't wish to intrude," she said, "but if you are in fact going to see the Hall of Life and Death as your daughter suggests . . . well, we don't seem to be able to find the rest of our tour group, you see, and we would like to go there. After all, it is the theme center for the entire fair, as you might say—"

"Why, of course," said Millicent warmly, "we'd be real delighted to have the company of you and Mr. Kats—Kats—"

"Katsubishi!" he supplied, bowing deeply and showing all of his teeth in a smile, and they all seven set off for the Hall of Life and Death, with little Louisa delightedly leading the way.

The hall was a low, white marble structure across the greensward from the Cenotaph, happy picnicking families on the green gay pavilions all around, ice-cream vendors chanting along the roadways, and a circus parade—horses and a giraffe and even an elephant—winding along the main avenue with a band leading them, diddley-boom, diddley-boom, diddley-bang! bang! bang!—all noise, and color, and excitement. But as soon as they were within the hall they were in another world. The Hall of Life and Death was the only free exhibit at the fair—even the rest rooms were not free. The crowds that moved through the hall were huge. But they were also reverential. As you came in you found yourself in a great domed entrance pavilion, almost bare except for seventy-five raised platforms, each spotlighted from a concealed source, each surrounded by an air curtain of gentle drafts. At the time the Baxters came in more than sixty of the platforms were already occupied with silent, lifeless forms of those who had passed on at the fair that day. A sweet-faced child here, an elderly woman there; there, side by side, a young pair of newlyweds. Randolph Baxter looked for and found the tall, smiling black man who had died in the line before him. He was smiling no longer, but his face was in repose and almost joyous, it seemed. "He's at peace now," Millicent whispered, touching her husband's arm, and he nodded. He didn't want to speak out loud in this solemn hall, where the whisper of organ music was barely audible above the gentle hiss of chilled air curtains that wafted past every deceased. Hardly anyone in the great crowd spoke. The visitors lingered at each of the occupied biers; but then, as they moved toward the back of the chamber, they didn't linger. Some didn't even look, for every tourist at the fair could not help thinking, as he passed an empty platform, that before the fair closed that night it would be occupied . . . by someone.

But the Rotunda of Those Who Have Gone Before was only the anteroom to the many inspiring displays the hall had to offer. Even the children were fascinated. Young Simon stood entranced before the great Timepiece of Living and Dying, watching the hands revolve swiftly to show how many were born and how many died in each minute, with the bottom line always showing a few more persons alive in every minute despite everything the government and the efforts of patriotic citizens could do—but he was more interested, really, in the mechanism of the thing than in the facts it displayed. Millicent Baxter and Mrs. Millay were really thrilled by the display of opulent caskets and cerements, and Ralph Baxter proud to point out to Mr. Katsubishi the working model of a crematorium, with all of its escaping gases trapped and converted into valuable organic feedstocks. And the girls, Emma and Louisa, stood hand in hand for a long time, shuddering happily as they gazed at the refrigerated display cases that showed a hideous four-month embryo next to the corpse of a fat, pretty two-year-old. Emma moved to put her arm around her mother and whispered, "Mommy, I'm *so* grateful you didn't abort me." And Millicent Baxter fought back a quick and tender tear.

"I'd never let you die looking like *that*," she assured her daughter, and they clung together for a long moment. But Randolph Baxter was becoming noticeably ill at ease. When they finally left the Hall of Life and Death, his wife took him aside and asked in concern, "Is something the matter, hon?"

He shrugged irritably at the foreigners, who were talking together in fast, low-toned Japanese. "Just look at their faces," he complained. And indeed both Mr. Katsubishi and Mrs. Millay's expressions seemed to show more revulsion than respect.

Millicent followed her husband's eyes and sighed—there was a little annoyance in the sigh, too. "They're not Americans," she reminded her husband. "I guess they just don't understand." She smiled distantly at the foreign pair, and then looked around at her offspring. "Well, children, who wants to come with me to the washrooms, so we can get ready for the big fireworks?"

They all did, even Randolph, but he felt a need stronger than the urging of his bladder. He remained behind with the foreigners. "Excuse me," he said, somewhat formally, "but may I ask what you thought of the exhibit?"

Mrs. Millay glanced at the Japanese. "Well, it was most interesting," she said vaguely. "One doesn't wish to criticize, of course—" And she stopped there.

"No, no, please go on," Randolph encouraged.

She said, "I must say it did seem odd to, well, *glorify* death in that way."

Randolph Baxter smiled, and tried to make it a forgiving smile, though he could feel that he was upset. He said, "Perhaps you miss the point of the Hall of Life and Death— in fact, of the whole Lottery Fair. You see, some of the greatest minds in America have worked on this problem of surplus population—think tanks and government agencies—why, three universities helped design this fair. Every bit of it is scientifically planned. To begin with, it's absolutely free."

Mrs. Millay left off her rapid-fire, sotto voce Japanese translation to ask, "You mean, free as far as money is concerned?"

"Yes, exactly. Of course, one takes a small chance at every ticket window, and in that sense there is a price for everything. A very carefully computed price, Mrs. Millay, for every hot dog, every show, every ride. To get into the fair in the first place, for instance, costs one decimill—that's 1 percent of a .0001 probability of receiving a lethal injection from the ticket cuff. Now, that's not much of a risk, is it?" he smiled. "And of course it's absolutely painless, too. As you can see by just looking at the ones who have given their lives inside."

Mr. Katsubishi, listening intently to Mrs. Millay's translation in his ear, pursed his lips and nodded thoughtfully. Mrs. Millay said brightly, "Well, we all have our own little national traits, don't we?"

"Now, really, Mrs. Millay," said Randolph Baxter, smiling with an effort, "please try to understand. Everything is quite fair. Some things are practically free, like the park benches and the restrooms and so on; why, you could use some of them as much as a million times before, you know, your number would come up. Or you can get a first-class meal in the Cenotaph for just about a whole millipoint. But even that means you can do it a thousand times, on the average."

Mr. Katsubishi listened to the end of Mrs. Millay's translation, and then struggled to get out a couple of English words. "Not—us," he managed, pointing to himself and Mrs. Millay.

"Certainly not," Baxter agreed. "You're foreign tourists. So you buy your tickets in your own countries for cash, and of course you don't have to risk your lives. It wouldn't help the American population problem much if you did, would it?" He smiled. "And your tour money helps pay the cost of the fair. But the important thing to remember is that the Lottery Fair is entirely voluntary. No one has to come. Of course," he admitted, with a self-deprecatory grin, "I have to admit that I really like the job lotteries. I guess I'm just a gambler at heart, and when you've spent as much time on welfare as Mrs. Baxter and I have, those big jobs are just hard to resist! And they're better here than at the regular city raffles."

Mrs. Millay cleared her throat. Good manners competed with obstinacy in her expression. "Really, Mr. Baxter," she said, "Mr. Katsubishi and I understand that—heavens, we've had to do things in our own countries! We certainly don't mean to criticize yours. What's hard to understand, I suppose, is, actually, that fetus." She searched his face with her eyes, looking for understanding. "It just seems strange. I mean, that you'd prefer to see a child born and then perhaps die in a lottery than to abort him ahead of time."

Mr. Baxter did his very best to maintain a pleasant expression, but knew he was failing. "It's a difference in our national philosophies, I guess," he said. "See, we don't go in for your so-called 'birth control' here. No abortion. No contraception. We accept the gift of life when it is given. We believe that every human being, from the moment of conception on, has a right to a life—although," he added, "not necessarily a *long* one." He eyed the abashed foreigners sternly for a moment, then relented. "Well," he said, glancing at his watch, "I wonder where my family can be? They'll miss the fireworks if they don't get back. I bet Mrs. Baxter's gone and let the children pick out souvenirs—the little dickenses have been after us about them all day. Anyway, Mrs. Millay, Mr. Katsubishi, it's been a real pleasure meeting the two of you and having this chance to exchange views—"

But he broke off, suddenly alarmed by the expression on Mr. Katsubishi's face as the man looked past him. "What's the matter?" he demanded roughly.

And then he turned, and did not need an answer. The answer was written on the strained, haggard, tearstreaked face of his wife as she ran despairingly toward him, carrying in her hands a plastic cap, a paperweight, and a helium-filled balloon in the shape of a pig's head, but without Emma and without Simon and even without little Louisa.

THE CELEBRATED NO-HIT INNING

Good science fiction sometimes means giving in to guilty pleasures. And 1956's "The Celebrated No-Hit Inning" is nothing if not a guilty pleasure. First of all, it is, as you might surmise from the title, about baseball. There are those who might tune out because of that, but they'd be missing out on a terrific story.

Good science-fiction stories about baseball have to be good stories and good SF—and they have to make baseball sense. This story fulfills all those requirements.

Best of all, you really *can* enjoy this chronicle of the great all-around player Boley even if you don't know much about baseball. There is one thing to remember, however, when reading this intriguing tale: It says right off the bat, "This is a true story."

Well, it may or may not be true, because a lot of the action takes place in the future. No, it's not true . . . yet! But if things keep going the way they have been going, it might not be too very long now. . . .

This is a true story, you have to remember. You have to keep that firmly in mind because, frankly, in some places it may not *sound* like a true story. Besides, it's a true story about baseball players, and maybe the only one there is. So you have to treat it with respect.

You know Boley, no doubt. It's pretty hard not to know Boley, if you know anything at all about the National Game. He's the one, for instance, who raised such a scream when the sportswriters voted him Rookie of the Year. "I never *was* a rookie," he bellowed into three million television screens at the dinner. He's the one who ripped up his contract when his manager called him, "The hittin'est pitcher I ever see." Boley wouldn't stand for that. "Four-eighteen against the best pitchers in the league," he yelled, as the pieces of the contract went out the window. "Fogarty, I am the hittin'est *hitter* you ever see!"

He's the one they all said reminded them so much of Dizzy Dean at first. But did Diz win thirty-one games in his first year? Boley did; he'll tell you so himself. But politely, and without bellowing. . . .

Somebody explained to Boley that even a truly great Hall-of-Fame pitcher really ought to show up for spring training. So, in his second year, he did. But he wasn't convinced that he *needed* the training, so he didn't bother much about appearing on the field.

Manager Fogarty did some extensive swearing about that, but he did all of his swearing to his pitching coaches and not to Mr. Boleslaw. There had been six ripped-up contracts already that year, when Boley's feelings got hurt about something, and the front office were very insistent that there shouldn't be any more.

There wasn't much the poor pitching coaches could do, of course. They tried pleading with Boley. All he did was grin and ruffle their hair and say, "Don't get all in an uproar." He could ruffle their hair pretty easily, since he stood six inches taller than the tallest of them.

"Boley," said Pitching Coach Magill to him desperately, "you are going to get me into trouble with the manager. I need this job. We just had another little boy at our house, and they cost money to feed. Won't you please do me a favor and come down to the field, just for a little while?"

Boley had a kind of a soft heart. "Why, if that will make so much difference to you, Coach, I'll do it. But I don't feel much like pitching. We have got twelve exhibition games lined up with the Orioles on the way north, and if I pitch six of those that ought to be all the warm-up I need."

"Three innings?" Magill haggled. "You know I wouldn't ask you if it wasn't important. The thing is, the owner's uncle is watching today."

Boley pursed his lips. He shrugged. "One inning."

"Bless you, Boley!" cried the coach. "One inning it is!"

Andy Andalusia was catching for the regulars when Boley turned up on the field. He turned white as a sheet. "Not the fast ball, Boley! Please, Boley," he begged. "I only been catching a week and I have not hardened up yet."

Boleslaw turned the rosin bag around in his hands and looked around the field. There was action going on at all six diamonds, but the spectators, including the owner's uncle, were watching the regulars.

"I tell you what I'll do," said Boley thoughtfully. "Let's see. For the first man, I pitch only curves. For the second man, the screwball. And for the third man—let's see. Yes. For the third man, I pitch the sinker."

"Fine!" cried the catcher gratefully, and trotted back to home plate.

"He's a very spirited player," the owner's uncle commented to Manager Fogarty.

"That he is," said Fogarty, remembering how the pieces of the fifth contract had felt as they hit him on the side of the head.

"He must be a morale problem for you, though. Doesn't he upset the discipline of the rest of the team?"

Fogarty looked at him, but he only said, "He win thirty-one games for us last year. If he had *lost* thirty-one he would have upset us a lot more."

The owner's uncle nodded, but there was a look in his eye all the same. He watched without saying anything more, while Boley struck out the first man with three sizzling curves, right on schedule, and then turned around and yelled something at the outfield.

"That crazy— By heaven," shouted the manager, "he's chasing them back into the dugout. I *told* that—"

The owner's uncle clutched at Manager Fogarty as he was getting up to head for the field. "Wait a minute. What's Boleslaw doing?"

"Don't you see? He's chasing the outfield off the field. He wants to face the next two men without any outfield! That's Satchell Paige's old trick, only he never did it except in exhibitions where who cares? But that Boley—"

"This is only an exhibition, isn't it?" remarked the owner's uncle mildly.

Fogarty looked longingly at the field, looked back at the owner's uncle, and shrugged.

"All right." He sat down, remembering that it was the owner's uncle whose sprawling factories had made the family money that bought the owner his team. "Go ahead!" he bawled at the right fielder, who was hesitating halfway to the dugout.

Boley nodded from the mound. When the outfielders were all out of the way he set himself and went into his windup. Boleslaw's windup was a beautiful thing to all who chanced to behold it—unless they happened to root for another team. The pitch was more beautiful still.

"I got it, I got it!" Andalusia cried from behind the plate, waving the ball in his mitt. He returned it to the pitcher triumphantly, as though he could hardly believe he had caught the Boleslaw screwball—after only the first week of spring training.

He caught the second pitch, too. But the third was unpredictably low and outside. Andalusia dived for it in vain.

"Ball one!" cried the umpire. The catcher scrambled up, ready to argue.

"He is right," Boley called graciously from the mound. "I am sorry, but my foot slipped. It was a ball."

"Thank you," said the umpire. The next screwball was a strike, though, and so were the three sinkers to the third man—though one of those caught a little piece of the bat and turned into an into-the-dirt foul.

Boley came off the field to a spattering of applause. He stopped under the stands, on the lip of the dugout. "I guess I am a little rusty at that, Fogarty," he called. "Don't let me forget to pitch another inning or two before we play Baltimore next month."

"I won't!" snapped Fogarty. He would have said more, but the owner's uncle was talking.

"I don't know much about baseball, but that strikes me as an impressive performance. My congratulations."

"You are right," Boley admitted. "Excuse me while I shower, and then we can resume this discussion some more. I think you are a better judge of baseball than you say."

The owner's uncle chuckled, watching him go into the dugout. "You can laugh," said Fogarty bitterly. "You don't have to put up with that for a hundred fifty-four games, and spring training, *and* the Series."

"You're pretty confident about making the Series?"

Fogarty said simply, "Last year Boley win thirty-one games."

The owner's uncle nodded, and shifted position uncomfortably. He was sitting with one leg stretched over a large black metal suitcase, fastened with a complicated lock. Fogarty asked, "Should I have one of the boys put that in the locker room for you?"

"Certainly not!" said the owner's uncle. "I want it right here where I can touch it." He looked around him. "The fact of that matter is," he went on in a lower tone, "this goes up to Washington with me tomorrow. I can't discuss what's in it. But as we're among friends, I can mention that where it's going is the Pentagon."

"Oh," said Fogarty respectfully. "Something new from the factories."

"Something very new," the owner's uncle agreed, and he winked. "And I'd better get back to the hotel with it. But there's one thing, Mr. Fogarty. I don't have much time for baseball, but it's a family affair, after all, and whenever I can help— I mean, it just occurs to me that possibly, with the help of what's in this suitcase— That is, would you like me to see if I could help out?"

"Help out how?" asked Fogarty suspiciously.

"Well— I really mustn't discuss what's in the suitcase. But would it hurt Boleslaw, for example, to be a little more, well, modest?"

The manager exploded, *"No."*

The owner's uncle nodded. "That's what I've thought. Well, I must go. Will you ask Mr. Boleslaw to give me a ring at the hotel so we can have dinner together, if it's convenient?"

It was convenient, all right. Boley had always wanted to see how the other half lived; and they had a fine dinner, served right in the suite, with five waiters in attendance and four kinds of wine. Boley kept pushing the little glasses of wine away, but after all the owner's uncle was the owner's uncle, and if *he* thought it was all right—It must have been pretty strong wine, because Boley began to have trouble following the conversation.

It was all right as long as it stuck to earned-run averages and batting percentages, but then it got hard to follow, like a long, twisting grounder on a dry September field. Boley wasn't going to admit that, though. "Sure," he said, trying to follow; and "You say the *fourth* dimension?" he said; and, "You mean a time machine, like?" he said; but he was pretty confused.

The owner's uncle smiled and filled the wineglasses again.

Somehow the black suitcase had been unlocked, in a slow, difficult way. Things made out of crystal and steel were sticking out of it. "Forget about the time machine," said the owner's uncle patiently. "It's a military secret, anyhow. I'll thank you to forget the very words, because heaven knows what the general would think if he found out— Anyway, forget it. What about you, Boley? Do you still say you can hit any pitcher who ever lived and strike out any batter?"

"Anywhere," agreed Boley, leaning back in the deep cushions and watching the room go around and around. "Any time. I'll bat their ears off."

"Have another glass of wine, Boley," said the owner's uncle, and he began to take things out of the black suitcase.

Boley woke up with a pounding in his head like Snider, Mays and Mantle hammering Three-Eye League pitching. He moaned and opened one eye.

Somebody blurry was holding a glass out to him. "Hurry up. Drink this."

Boley shrank back. "I will not. That's what got me into this trouble in the first place."

"Trouble? You're in no trouble. But the game's about to start and you've got a hangover."

Ring a fire bell beside a sleeping Dalmation; sound the Charge in the ear of a retired cavalry major. Neither will respond more quickly than Boley to the words, "The game's about to start."

He managed to drink some of the fizzy stuff in the glass and it was a miracle; like a triple play erasing a ninth-inning threat, the headache was gone. He sat up, and the world did not come to an end. In fact, he felt pretty good.

He was being rushed somewhere by the blurry man. They were going very rapidly, and there were tall, bright buildings outside. They stopped.

"We're at the studio," said the man, helping Boley out of a remarkable sort of car.

"The stadium," Boley corrected automatically. He looked around for the lines at the box office but there didn't seem to be any.

"The *studio.* Don't argue all day, will you?" The man was no longer so blurry. Boley looked at him and blushed. He was only a little man, with a worried look to him, and what he was wearing was a pair of vivid orange Bermuda shorts that showed his knees. He didn't give Boley much of a chance for talking or thinking. They rushed into a building, all green and white opaque glass, and they were met at a flimsy-looking elevator by another little man. This one's shorts were aqua, and he had a bright red cummerbund tied around his waist.

"This is him," said Boley's escort.

The little man in aqua looked Boley up and down. "He's a big one. I hope to goodness we got a uniform to fit him for the Series."

Boley cleared his throat. "Series?"

"And you're in it!" shrilled the little man in orange. "This way to the dressing room."

Well, a dressing room was a dressing room, even if this one did have color television screens all around it and machines that went *wheepety-boom* softly to themselves. Boley began to feel at home.

He blinked when they handed his uniform to him, but he put it on. Back in the Steel & Coal League, he had sometimes worn uniforms that still bore the faded legend *100 Lbs. Best Fortified Gro-Chick*, and whatever an owner gave you to put on was all right with Boley. Still, he thought to himself, *kilts!*

It was the first time in Boley's life that he had ever worn a skirt. But when he was dressed it didn't look too bad, he thought—especially because all the other players (it looked like fifty of them, anyway) were wearing the same thing. There is nothing like seeing the same costume on everybody in view to make it seem reasonable and right. Haven't the Paris designers been proving that for years?

He saw a familiar figure come into the dressing room, wearing a uniform like his own. "Why, coach Magill," said Boley, turning with his hand outstretched. "I did not expect to meet you here."

The newcomer frowned, until somebody whispered in his ear. "Oh," he said, "you're Boleslaw."

"Naturally I'm Boleslaw, and naturally you're my pitching coach, Magill, and why do you look at me that way when I've seen you every day for three weeks?"

The man shook his head. "You're thinking of Granddaddy Jim," he said, and moved on.

Boley stared after him. Granddaddy Jim? But Coach Magill was no granddaddy, that was for sure. Why, his eldest was no more than six years old. Boley put his hand against the wall to steady himself. It touched something metal and cold. He glanced at it.

It was a bronze plaque, floor to ceiling high, and it was embossed at the top with the words *World Series Honor Roll*. And it listed every team that had ever won the World Series, from the day Chicago won the first Series of all in 1906 until—until—

Boley said something out loud, and quickly looked around to see if anybody had heard him. It wasn't something he wanted people to hear. But it was the right time for a man to say something like that, because what that crazy lump of bronze said, down toward the bottom, with only empty spaces below, was that the most recent team to win the World Series was the Yokahama Dodgers, and the year they won it in was—1998.

1998.

A time machine, thought Boley wonderingly, I guess what he meant was a machine that traveled in *time*.

Now, if you had been picked up in a time machine that leaped through the years like a jet plane leaps through space you might be quite astonished, perhaps, and for a while you might not be good for much of anything, until things calmed down.

But Boley was born calm. He lived by his arm and his eye, and there was nothing to worry about there. Pay him his Class C league contract bonus, and he turns up in Western Pennsylvania, all ready to set a league record for no-hitters his first year. Call him up from the minors and he bats .418 against the best pitchers in baseball. Set him down in the year 1999 and tell him he's going to play in the Series, and he hefts the ball once or twice and says, "I better take a couple of warm-up pitches. Is the spitter allowed?"

They led him to the bullpen. And then there was the playing of the National Anthem and the teams took the field. And Boley got the biggest shock so far.

"Magill," he bellowed in a terrible voice, "what is that other pitcher doing out on the mound?"

The manager looked startled. "That's our starter, Padgett. He always starts with the number-two defensive lineup against right-hand batters when the outfield shift goes—"

"Magill! I am not any *relief* pitcher. If you pitch Boleslaw, you *start* with Boleslaw."

Magill said soothingly, "It's perfectly all right. There have been some changes, that's all. You can't expect the rules to stay the same for forty or fifty years, can you?"

"I am not a *relief* pitcher. I—"

"Please, please. Won't you sit down?"

Boley sat down, but he was seething. "We'll see about that," he said to the world. "We'll just see."

Things had changed, all right. To begin with, the studio really was a studio and not a stadium. And although it was a very large room it was not the equal of Ebbetts Field, much less the Yankee Stadium. There seemed to be an awful lot of bunting, and the ground rules confused Boley very much.

Then the dugout happened to be just under what seemed to be a complicated sort of television booth, and Boley could hear the announcer screaming himself hoarse just overhead. That had a familiar sound, but—

"And here," roared the announcer, "comes the all-important nothing-and-one pitch! Fans, what a pitcher's duel *this* is! Delasantos is going into his motion! He's coming down! He's delivered it! And it's *in there* for a count of nothing and two! Fans, what a pitcher that Tiburcio Delasantos *is!* And here comes the all-important nothing-and-two pitch, and—and—yes, and he struck him out! *He struck him out!* He struck him *out!* It's a *no-hitter,* fans! In the all-important second inning, it's a no-hitter for Tiburcio Delasantos!"

Boley swallowed and stared hard at the scoreboard, which seemed to show a score of 14-9, their favor. His teammates were going wild with excitement, and so was the crowd of players, umpires, cameramen and announcers watching the game. He tapped the shoulder of the man next to him.

"Excuse me. What's the score?"

"Dig that Tiburcio!" cried the man. "What a first-string defensive pitcher against left-handers he *is!*"

"The score. Could you tell me what it is?"

"Fourteen to nine. Did you *see* that—"

Boley begged, "Please, didn't somebody just say it was a no-hitter?"

"Why, sure." The man explained: "The inning. It's a no-hit *inning*." And he looked queerly at Boley.

It was all like that, except that some of it was worse. After three innings Boley was staring glassy-eyed into space. He dimly noticed that both teams were trotting off the field and what looked like a whole new corps of players were warming up when Manager Magill stopped in front of him. "You'll be playing in a minute," Magill said kindly.

"Isn't the game over?" Boley gestured toward the field.

"Over? Of course not. It's the third-inning stretch," Magill told him. "Ten minutes for the lawyers to file their motions and make their appeals. You know." He laughed condescendingly. "They tried to get an injunction against the bases-loaded pitchout. Imagine!"

"Hah-hah," Boley echoed. "Mister Magill, can I go home?"

"Nonsense, boy! Didn't you hear me? You're on as soon as the lawyers come off the field!"

Well, that began to make sense to Boley and he actually perked up a little. When the minutes had passed and Magill took him by the hand he began to feel almost cheerful again. He picked up the rosin bag and flexed his fingers and said simply, "Boley's ready."

Because nothing confused Boley when he had a ball or a bat in his hand. Set him down any time, anywhere, and he'd hit any pitcher or strike out any batter. He knew exactly what it was going to be like, once he got on the playing field.

Only it wasn't like that at all.

Boley's team was at bat, and the first man up got on with a bunt single. Anyway, they *said* it was a bunt single. To Boley it had seemed as though the enemy pitcher had charged beautifully off the mound, fielded the ball with machine-like precision and flipped it to the first-base player with inches and inches to spare for the out. But the umpires declared interference by a vote of eighteen to seven, the two left-field umpires and the one with the field glasses over the batter's head abstaining; it seemed that the first baseman had neglected to say "Excuse me" to the runner. Well, the rules were the rules. Boley tightened his grip on his bat and tried to get a lead on the pitcher's style.

That was hard, because the pitcher was fast. Boley admitted it to himself uneasily; he was *very* fast. He was a big monster of a player, nearly seven feet tall and with something queer and sparkly about his eyes; and when he came down with a pitch there was a sort of a hiss and a *splat*, and the ball was in the catcher's hands. It might, Boley confessed, be a little hard to hit that particular pitcher, because he hadn't seen the ball in transit.

Manager Magill came up behind him in the on-deck spot and fastened something to his collar. "Your intercom," he explained. "So we can tell you what to do when you're up."

"Sure, sure." Boley was only watching the pitcher. He looked sickly out there; his skin was a grayish sort of color, and those eyes didn't look right. But there wasn't anything sickly about the way he delivered the next pitch, a sweeping curve that sizzled in and spun away.

The batter didn't look so good either—same sickly gray skin, same giant frame. But he reached out across the plate and caught that curve and dropped it between third-base and short; and both men were safe.

"You're on," said a tinny little voice in Boley's ear; it was the little intercom, and the manager was talking to him over the radio. Boley walked numbly to the plate. Sixty feet away, the pitcher looked taller than ever.

Boley took a deep breath and looked about him. The crowd was roaring ferociously, which was normal enough—except there wasn't any crowd. Counting everybody, players and officials and all, there weren't more than three or four hundred people in sight in the whole studio. But he could *hear* the screams and yells of easily fifty or sixty thousand— There was a man, he saw, behind a plateglass window who was doing things with what might have been records, and the yells of the crowd all seemed to come from loudspeakers under his window. Boley winced and concentrated on the pitcher.

"I will pin his ears back," he said feebly, more to reassure himself than because he believed it.

The little intercom on his shoulder cried in a tiny voice: "You will not, Boleslaw! Your orders are to take the first pitch!"

"But, listen—"

"Take it! You hear me, Boleslaw?"

There was a time when Boley would have swung just to prove who was boss; but the time was not then. He stood there while the big gray pitcher looked him over with those sparkling eyes. He stood there through the windup. And then the arm came down, and he didn't stand there. That ball wasn't invisible, not coming right at him; it looked as big and as fast as the Wabash Cannonball and Boley couldn't help it, for the first time in his life he jumped a yard away, screeching.

"Hit batter! Hit batter!" cried the intercom. "Take your base, Boleslaw."

Boley blinked. Six of the umpires were beckoning him on, so the intercom was right. But still and all— Boley had his pride. He said to the little button on his collar, "I am sorry, but I wasn't hit. He missed me a mile, easy. I got scared is all."

"Take your base, you silly fool!" roared the intercom. "He *scared* you, didn't he? That's just as bad as hitting you, according to the rules. Why, there is no telling what incalculable damage has been done to your nervous system by this fright. So kindly get the bejeepers over to first base, Boleslaw, as provided in the rules of the game!"

He got, but he didn't stay there long, because there was a pinch runner waiting for him. He barely noticed that it was another of the gray-skinned giants before he headed for the locker room and the showers. He didn't even remember getting out of his uniform; he only remembered that he, Boley, had just been through the worst experience of his life.

He was sitting on a bench, with his head on his hands, when the owner's uncle came in, looking queerly out of place in his neat pin-striped suit. The owner's uncle had to speak to him twice before his eyes focused.

"They didn't let me pitch," Boley said wonderingly. "They didn't want Boley to pitch."

The owner's uncle patted his shoulder. "You were a guest star, Boley. One of the all-time greats of the game. Next game they're going to have Christy Mathewson. Doesn't that make you feel proud?"

"They didn't let me pitch," said Boley.

The owner's uncle sat down beside him. "Don't you see? You'd be out of place in this kind of a game. You got on base for them, didn't you? I heard the announcer say it myself; he said you filled the bases in the all-important fourth inning. Two hundred million people were watching this game on television! And they saw you get on base!"

"They didn't let me hit either," Boley said.

There was a commotion at the door and the team came trotting in screaming victory.

"We win it, we win it!" cried Manager Magill. "Eighty-seven to eighty-three! What a squeaker!"

Boley lifted his head to croak, "That's fine." But nobody was listening. The manager jumped on a table and yelled, over the noise in the locker room:

"Boys, we pulled a close one out, and you know what that means. We're leading in the Series, eleven games to nine! Now let's just wrap those other two up, and—"

He was interrupted by a bloodcurdling scream from Boley. Boley was standing up, pointing with an expression of horror. The athletes had scattered and the trainers were working them over; only some of the trainers were using pliers and screwdrivers instead of towels and liniment. Next to Boley, the big gray-skinned pinch runner was flat on his back, and the trainer was lifting one leg away from the body—

"Murder!" bellowed Boley. "That fellow is murdering that fellow!"

The manager jumped down next to him. "Murder? There isn't any murder, Boleslaw! What are you talking about?"

Boley pointed mutely. The trainer stood gaping at him, with the leg hanging limp in his grip. It was completely removed from the torso it belonged to, but the torso seemed to be making no objections; the curious eyes were open but no longer sparkling; the gray skin, at closer hand, seemed metallic and cold.

The manager said fretfully, "I swear, Boleslaw, you're a nuisance. They're just getting cleaned and oiled, batteries recharged, that sort of thing. So they'll be in shape tomorrow, you understand."

"Cleaned," whispered Boley. "Oiled." He stared around the room. All of the gray-skinned ones were being somehow disassembled; bits of metal and glass were sticking out of them. "Are you trying to tell me," he croaked, "that those fellows aren't fellows?"

"They're ballplayers," said Manager Magill impatiently. "Robots. Haven't you ever seen a robot before? We're allowed to field six robots on a nine-man team, it's perfectly legal. Why, next year I'm hoping the Commissioner'll let us play a whole robot team. *Then* you'll see some baseball!"

With bulging eyes Boley saw it was true. Except for a handful of flesh-and-blood players like himself the team was made up of man-shaped machines, steel for bones, electricity for blood, steel and plastic and copper cogs for muscle. "Machines," said Boley, and turned up his eyes.

The owner's uncle tapped him on the shoulder worriedly. "It's time to go back," he said.

So Boley went back.

He didn't remember much about it, except that the owner's uncle had made him promise never, never to tell anyone about it, because it was orders from the Defense Department, you never could tell how useful a time machine might be in a war. But he did get back, and he woke up the next morning with all the signs of a hangover and the sheets kicked to shreds around his feet.

He was still bleary when he staggered down to the coffee shop for breakfast. Magill the pitching coach, who had no idea that he was going to be granddaddy to Magill the series-winning manager, came solicitously over to him. "Bad night, Boley? You look like you have had a bad night."

"Bad?" repeated Boley. "Bad? Magill, you have got no idea. The owner's uncle said he would show me something that would learn me a little humility and, Magill, he came

232 | PLATINUM POHL

through. Yes, he did. Why, I saw a big bronze tablet with the names of the Series winners on it, and I saw—"

And he closed his mouth right there, because he remembered right there what the owner's uncle had said about closing his mouth. He shook his head and shuddered. "Bad," he said, "you bet it was bad."

Magill coughed. "Gosh, that's too bad, Boley. I guess—I mean, then maybe you wouldn't feel like pitching another couple of innings—well, anyway one inning—today, because—"

Boley held up his hand. "Say no more, please. You want me to pitch today, Magill?"

"That's about the size of it," the coach confessed.

"I will pitch today," said Boley. "If that is what you want me to do, I will do it. I am now a reformed character. I will pitch tomorrow, too, if you want me to pitch tomorrow, and any other day you want me to pitch. And if you do not want me to pitch, I will sit on the sidelines. Whatever you want is perfectly all right with me, Magill, because, Magill, I—hey! Hey, Magill, what are you doing down there on the floor?"

So that is why Boley doesn't give anybody any trouble anymore, and if you tell him now that he reminds you of Dizzy Dean, why he'll probably shake your hand and thank you for the compliment—even if you're a sportswriter, even. Oh, there still are a few special little things about him, of course—not even counting the things like how many shut-outs he pitched last year (eleven) or how many home runs he hit (fourteen). But everybody finds him easy to get along with. They used to talk about the change that had come over him a lot and wonder what caused it. Some people said he got religion and others said he had an incurable disease and was trying to do good in his last few weeks on Earth; but Boley never said, he only smiled; and the owner's uncle was too busy in Washington to be with the team much after that. So now they talk about other things when Boley's name comes up. For instance, there's his little business about the pitching machine—when he shows up for batting practice (which is every morning, these days), he insists on hitting against real live pitchers instead of the machine. It's even in his contract. And then, every March he bets nickels against anybody around the training camp that'll bet with him that he can pick that year's Series winner. He doesn't bet more than that, because the commissioner naturally doesn't like big bets from ballplayers.

But, even for nickels, don't bet against him, because he isn't ever going to lose, not before 1999.

SOME JOYS UNDER THE STAR

Writing workshop teachers are fond of saying that a short story is about a single idea, whereas a novel is far more complex. All that is true, though there are other differences, of course, besides length. One of the things a novel can do is deal with some particular event from multiple points of view.

That's what "Some Joys Under the Star" does. First published in 1973, it's not a novel; it's not even a very long story. But it deals with an event—in this case, the appearance of a comet in the skies above the Earth.

Any event of such magnitude is bound to involve the lives of many different people. In this case, it involves a number of people . . . and other beings as well. The stories of all these people are told insofar as they relate to the comet. If Pohl had chosen to tell the whole stories of all his characters, this would have been a rather large novel.

Instead, it's a small symphony of stories orchestrated by a master hand.

In a few recognizable ways were Albert Nowak, the man who stalked Myron Landau, and the Secretary of State alike, but they had this in common: they wanted. They each wanted something very badly and, as it happens, the thing that each wanted was not good by the general consensual standards of your average sensual man.

Let us start with the man who stalked Myron Landau or, more accurately, with Myron Landau himself. Myron also wanted, and what he wanted was his girlfriend, Ellen, with that masked desperation that characterizes the young man of seventeen who has never yet made out.

On this night of July in New York City the factors against Myron were inexperience, self-doubt, and the obstinacy of Ellen herself, but ranged on his side were powerful allies. Before him was the great welcoming blackness of Central Park, where anything might happen, and spread across the sky was a fine pretext for luring her into the place. So he bought her a strawberry milkshake in Rumpelmeyer's and strolled with her into the park, chatting of astronomy, beauty, and love.

"Are you sure it's all right?" asked Ellen, looking into the sodium-lit fringes of the undergrowth.

"Cripes, yes," said Myron, in the richly amused tone of a Brown belt in karate from one of the finest academies on the upper West Side, although in fact he had never gone into Central Park at night before. But he had thought everything out carefully and was convinced that tonight there was no danger. Or at any rate not enough danger to scare him off the prize. Overhead was the great beautiful comet that everybody was talking about and it was a clear night. There would be lots of people looking at the sky, he reasoned, and in any case where else could he take her? Not his apartment, with Grandma's ear to the living room door, just itching for an excuse to come in and start hunting for her glasses. Not Ellen's place, not with her mother and sister remorselessly there. "You can't see the comet well from the middle of the street," he said reasonably, putting his arm around her and nodding to a handsome white-haired gentleman who had first nodded benevolently to them. "There's too much light and anyway, honestly, Ellen, we won't go in very far."

"I never saw a comet before," she conceded, allowing herself to be led down the path. In truth, the comet Ujifusa-McGinnis was not all that hard to see. It spread its tail over a quarter of the sky, drowning out Altair, Vega, and the stars around Deneb, hardly paled even by the lights of New York City. Even a thousand miles south, where NASA technicians were working around-the-clock shifts under the floodlights of the Vehicle Assembly Building, trying to get ready the launch of the probe that would plumb Ujifusa-McGinnis's mysteries, it dominated the sky.

Myron looked upward and allowed himself to be distracted for a moment by the spectacle, but quickly caught himself. "Ah," he said, creeping his fingers toward the lower slope of Ellen's breast, "just think, what you see is all gas. Nothing really there at all. And millions of miles away."

"It's beautiful," Ellen said, looking over her shoulder. She had thought she had heard a noise.

She had. The noise was in fact real. The foot of the handsome white-haired gentleman had broken a stick. He had turned off the flagstone path into the shelter of the dwarf evergreens and was now busy pulling a woman's nylon stocking over his white hair and face. He, too, had planned his evening carefully. In his right-hand coat pocket he had the woolen sock with half a pound of BBs knotted into the toe—that was for Myron. In his left-hand pocket he had the clasp knife with the carefully honed edge. That was for Ellen, first to make sure she didn't scream, then to make sure she never would. He had not known their names when he loaded his pockets and left his ranch house in Waterbury, Connecticut, to go in for an evening's sport to the city, but he had known there would be somebody.

He, too, looked up at the comet, but with irritation. In his Connecticut backyard, as he had shown it to his daughter, it had looked pretty. Here it was an unqualified nuisance. It made the night brighter than he wanted it although, he thought in all fairness, it was not as bad as a full moon.

It would not be more than five minutes, he calculated, before the boy would lead the girl in among the evergreens. But which way? If only they would choose his side of the path! Otherwise it meant he had to cross the walk. That was a small danger and a large annoyance, because it meant scuttling in an undignified way. Still, the fun was worth the trouble. It always had been worth it.

With the weighted sock now ready in his hand, the handsome white-haired gentleman followed them silently. He could feel the gleeful premonitory stirrings of sexual excitement in his private parts. He was as happy as, in his life, he ever was.

At a time approximately two thousand years earlier, when Jesus was a boy in Nazareth and Caesar Augustus was counting up his statues and his gold, a race of creatures resembling soft-shelled crabs on a planet of a star some two hundred light-years away became belatedly aware of the existence of the Great Wall of China.

Although it alone among the then existing works of Man was quite detectable in their telescopes, it was not surprising they had not noticed it before. It had been completed less than 250 years before, and most of that time had been lost in the creeping traverse of light from Earth to their planet. Also they had many, many planets to observe and not a great deal of time to waste on any one. But they expected more of their minions than that, and ten thousand members of a subject race died in great pain as a warning to the others to be more diligent.

The Arrogating Ones, as they called themselves and were called by their subjects, at once took up in their collective councils the question of whether or not to conquer Earth and add humanity to their vassals, now that they had discovered that humanity did exist. This was their eon-long custom. It had made them extremely unpopular over a large volume of the galaxy.

On balance, they decided not to bother at that particular time. What were a few heaped-up rocks, after all? Oh, some sort of civilization no doubt existed, but the planet Earth seemed too distant, too trivial, and too poor to be worth bothering to conquer.

Accordingly they contented themselves with routine precautionary measures. Item, they caused to be abducted in their disc-shaped vessels certain specimens of Earthly human beings and other fauna. These also died in great pain and in the process released much information about their body chemistry, physical structure, and modes of thought. Item, the Arrogating Ones dispatched certain of their servants with a waiting brief. They were instructed to occupy the core of a comet and from it to keep an eye on those endoskeletal, but potentially annoying, creatures who had discovered agriculture, fire, the city, and the wheel, but not as yet even chemical explosive weapons.

They then dismissed Earth from their collective soft-bodied minds, and returned to the more interesting contemplation of measures to be taken against a race of insect-like beings that lived in a steamy high-G planet in quite the other direction from Earth, toward the core of the galaxy. The insects had elected not to be conquered by the Arrogating Ones. In fact, they had destroyed quite a large number of war fleets sent against them.

Nearly a quarter of the collective intelligence of the Arrogating Ones was devoted to plans to defeat these insects in battle. Most of the rest of their intelligence was devoted to the pleasant contemplation of what they would do to the insects after the battle was won to make them wish they hadn't resisted so hard.

While the handsome white-haired gentleman was stalking Myron and Ellen, the second person who wanted, the secretary of state of the United States of America, was about a hundred miles north of and forty thousand feet above Central Park. He was on board a four-engined jet aircraft with the American flag emblazoned on its prow and he was having a temper tantrum.

The president of the United States was gloomily running his fingers between the toes of his bare feet. "Shoot, Danny," he said, "you're getting yourself all hot about nothing. I'm not saying we *can't* bomb Venezuela. I'm only saying why do we *want* to bomb Venezuela? And I'm saying you ought to watch how you talk to me, too."

"Watch how *you* talk to *me*, Mr. President!" shouted the secretary of state over the noise of the jets. "I'm pretty fed up with your procrastinations and delays and it wouldn't take much for me to walk right out and dump the whole thing back in your lap. Considering your track record—I am thinking of Iceland—I don't imagine you'd relish that prospect."

"Danny boy," snarled the President, "you've got a bad habit of digging up ancient history. Stick to the point. We've got to have oil, agreed. They have oil, everybody knows that. They don't want to sell it to us at a reasonable price, so you want me to beat on them until they change their minds. Right? Only what you don't see is, there's a right way and a wrong way to do these things. Why can't we just go in with some spooks and Tommy-guns, as usual?"

"But their insolence, Mr. President! The demeaning tone of this document they sent me. It isn't the oil, it is the national credibility of the country that is involved here."

"Right, Danny, right," groaned the president. "You can talk. You don't have Congress breathing down your neck at every little thing." He sighed heavily and opened another can of no-calorie soda. "What I don't see," he said, with a punctuation mark of gas, "is why we have to hit them tonight, with Congress still in session."

The secretary said petulantly, "I have explained to you, Mr. President, that our communications system is malfunctioning. We've lost global coverage. There is strong dissipation of ionosphere scatter, due to interference from an unprecedentedly strong influx of radiation apparently emanating from—"

"Oh, cut it out," complained the president. "You mean it's that comet that's bollixed up our detection."

The secretary pursed his lips. "Not precisely the comet, no, Mr. President. No such effect has ever been detected before, although it is possible that there is a connection. Doesn't matter. The situation before us is that we do not have total communication at this time. And so we have no way of knowing whether the Venezuelans are treacherously planning a sneak attack or not. Do you want to take a chance on the security of the Free World, Mr. President? I say preempt now!"

"Yes, you've made your point, Danny," said the president. He swiveled his armchair and gazed out at the bright spray of white light across the eastern horizon where Comet Ujifusa-McGinnis lay. "I've heard worse excuses for starting a war," he mused, "but I can't remember exactly when. All right, Danny. We'll do what you say. Get me Charlie on the scrambler and I'll put in the attack in two hours."

The watchers for the Arrogating Ones, hiding inside the pebbly core of the comet named after the two amateur astronomers who had simultaneously discovered it, studied the results of their radarlike scan of the Earth. This was routine. They were not aware that their scanning had damaged mankind's communications, but that was not their problem. Their only task was to spray out a shower of particles and catch the returning ones to study—this they did, and what their study told them was that the planet Earth had reached redpoint status. It was now well into a technological age and was thus an active, rather than merely a potential, threat to their masters.

The Arrogating Ones were no longer quite as effectively arrogant as they had once been. They had been creamed rather frequently in their millennia-long struggle against the insectoids. The score was, roughly, Arrogating Ones 53, Insectoids 23,724. The watchers, knowing this, were aware that at least their task would not under these circumstances involve the actual physical conquest of the Earth. It would simply be destroyed.

This was no big deal. Plenty of mechanisms for wiping out a populated planet were stockpiled in the arsenals of the Arrogating Ones. They had not worked very well against the insectoids, unfortunately, but they would be plenty powerful enough to deal with, say, mankind. The weapons for accomplishing this were readily available at any time, but not to the watchers, who were far too low in the hierarchy of authority to be trusted with anything like that.

Their task was much simpler. They were only required to report what they saw and then to soften up the human race so that it would not be able to offer resistance, even ineffectual resistance, to the cleanup teams when they arrived with their planet-busters.

Softening up was a technical problem of some magnitude, but it had been solved long ago. The abducted humans had died messily but not in vain. At least, from the point of view of the Arrogating Ones their deaths had not been in vain, for in their dying agonies they had supplied information about themselves which had enabled the Arrogating Ones to devise appropriate softening-up mechanisms. The watchers had been equipped with these on a standby basis ever since.

Of course, from the point of view of the abducted humans the question of whether their deaths had been in vain might have had a different answer. No one had troubled to ask them.

At any rate, the watchers now energized the generators which would soften up mankind for its destruction.

While they were waiting for a charge to build up they looked up the coordinates and call signal for the nearest cruising superdreadnaught of the Arrogating Ones and transmitted a request for it to come in and finish up the job with a core-bomb. They then discussed among themselves the prospects of what their next assignment would be. It was not a fruitful discussion. Core-bombs are messy and there was not much chance that Comet Ujifusa-McGinnis's orbit would get them far enough away to be out of its range when it went off. Even if they survived, none of them had any idea what the Arrogating Ones' future plans for the watchers were. All they were sure of was that they were certain not to enjoy them.

We now turn to Albert Novak. He was in another four-engined jet, climbing to cruising altitude out of Kennedy en route to Los Angeles International. He was a crew-cut young man, with something on his mind. His neighbor was a short, white-haired, dark-tanned Westerner with the face of a snapping turtle, who offered his hand and said aggressively, jerking his head toward the window, "That confounded thing! Do you know the space agency wants to spend thirty million dollars of your tax money just to go sniff around it? Thirty million dollars! Just to sniff some marsh gas! Not as long as I'm on the Aeronautics and Space Committee. Let me introduce myself. I'm Congressman—" But he was talking to gas himself. Albert Novak had not accepted his hand, had not even met his eyes. Although the "Fasten Seat Belts" sign was still lighted in three languages, he unstrapped himself and walked down the aisle. Hostesses hissed at him and tardily began to unsnap themselves to make him return to his seat. He ignored them. He had no intention of ever arriving at L.A. International and when he wanted to talk to a hostess he would do so on his own terms. He carried a cassette recorder into a toilet and locked the door against everyone.

The cassette recorder could no longer be used to record or play. He had removed its insides the day before, replacing them with more batteries and a coil of fine wire, which he now carefully connected to thirty Baggies full of dynamite and firing caps he had sewn into the lining of his trenchcoat while his mother nearsightedly smiled on him from across the room.

Although Novak thought of himself as a hijacker, it was not his intention to cause the jet to head for Cuba, Caracas, or even Algiers. He did not want the airplane. He didn't even want the one hundred million dollars' ransom he planned to ask for.

What Novak wanted, mostly, was to matter to somebody. As far as he had thought out his plan of action, it was to walk up to a stewardess with his hand on the detonating switch, show her the ingenious arrangement he had gotten past the metal detectors, be escorted to the flight deck in the traditional manner and then, after the airline had begun trying to get together the five million unmarked twenty-dollar bills he intended to demand and the maximum of annoyance and confusion had been caused, to close the switch and explode the dynamite.

He knew that in destroying the airplane he would die. That was not very important to him. The one important failure that he regretted very much was that he would not be able to see his mother's face when the reporters and TV crew began to swarm around her and she learned he had been pushing around all kinds of people and thirty million dollars' worth of airplane.

The generators at the core of Comet Ujifusa-McGinnis were now up to full charge.

Disgruntledly, the watchers of the Arrogating Ones sighted the beam in on the planet Earth. They were quite careful to get it aligned properly, for they remembered very well what the consequences were for slipshod work. When it was locked in, they released the safety switch that allowed the contact to close that discharged the beam.

More than three million watts of beamed power surged out toward the near hemisphere of the planet. Certain chemical changes at once took place in the atmosphere and were borne by jet stream, trade winds, and the aimless migration of air masses all around the Earth.

The equipment used was highly directional, but the watchers who operated it were very close and large magnitudes of energy were involved. Some of the radiation sprayed them. There was some loss from corona points, some reflection even from the tenuous gases of the comet's halo.

As the radiation had been designed specifically for use against mankind, on the basis of the experiments conducted on the kidnappees of two thousand years before, it was only of limited effect on the watchers. But they happened to be warm-blooded oxygen-breathers with two sexes and many of humanity's hangups, so that the weapon did do to them much what it was intended to do to mankind.

First they felt a sudden, sharp pang of an emotion which they identified (but only by logical deduction) as joy. The diagnosis was not simple, for they had little in their lives that would enable them to recognize such a state. But they looked at each other with fatuous fondness and, in their not really very human ways, shared pleasure.

The next thing they shared was serious physical pain, accompanied by vomiting, dizziness, and a feeling of weakness, for they were receiving a great deal more of the radiation than was necessary for the mere task of turning them into pussycats to receive the knockout blow of the Arrogating Ones. They recognized that, too. They deduced that they were dying, and doing it pretty fast.

They did not mind that any more than Albert Novak minded blowing himself up with the airliner. It was worthwhile. They were happy. It was what the ray was intended to do to people and it did its work very well.

And all over the near side of the Earth, as the radiation searched out and saturated humanity, joy replaced fear, peace replaced tension, love replaced anger.

In Central Park three slum youths released the girl they had lured behind the Seventy-second Street boathouse and decided to apply for Harvard, while a member of the Tactical Patrol Force lay down on Umpire Rock and gazed jubilantly at the comet. At the park's southern margin the white-haired gentleman came leaping out at Myron Landau and his girl. "My dear children!" he cried, tugging the women's stocking off his face. "How sweet and tender you are. You remind me so much of my own beloved son and daughters that you must let me stand you to the best hotel room in New York, with unlimited room service."

This spectacle would normally have disconcerted Myron Landau, especially as he had just succeeded in solving the puzzle of Ellen's bra snap. But he was so filled with the sudden rapture himself that he could only say, "You bet you can, friend. But only if you come with us. Ellen and I wouldn't have it any other way."

And Ellen chimed in sweetly: "What do we need a motel room for, mister? Why don't we just get out of these clothes?"

Forty thousand feet directly overhead, as the presidential jet sped back from the Summer White House near Boothbay Harbor, Maine, the secretary of state lifted eyes streaming with joy and said, "Dear Mr. President, let's give the spics another chance. It's too nice a night to be H-bombing Caracas." And the president, flinging an arm around him, sobbed, "Danny, as a diplomat you're not worth a bucket of warm snot, but I've always said you've got the biggest damn heart in the cabinet."

A great bubble of orange-yellow flame off on the western horizon disconcerted them for a moment, but it did not seem relevant to their transcendental joy. They began singing all the good old favorites like "Down by the Old Mill Stream," "Sweet Adeline," and "I've Been Working on the Railroad," and had so much fun doing it that the president quite forgot to radio the message that would cancel his strike order against Caracas. It did not matter very much. The B-52 ordnance crews had dumped the bombs from the fork lifts and were now giving each other rides on them, while the commanding general of the strike, Curtis T. "Vinegar Ass" Pinowitz, had decided he preferred going fishing to parachuting into Venezuela in support of the bombing. He was looking for his spinning reel, oblivious to the noise on the hardstand where the 101st Airborne was voting whether to fly to Disneyland or the Riviera. (In any event, the Venezuelans, or those members of the Venezuelan government who were bothering to answer their telephones, had just voted to give the Yankees all the oil they wanted and were seriously considering scenting it with jasmine.)

The ball of flame on the horizon, however, was not without its importance.

Albert Novak had released the armlock he had got around the little brown-eyed stewardess's neck and had begun to try to explain to her that his intention to blow up the jet meant nothing personal, but was only a way of inducing his mother to pay as much attention to him as she had, all through their lives, to his brother, Dick. Although he stammered so that he was almost incoherent, the stew understood him at once. She, too, had had both a mother and an older brother. Her pretty brown eyes filled with tears of sympathy and with a rush of love she flung her arms around him. "You poor boy," she cried, covering his stubbly face with kisses. "Here, honey! Let me help you." And she caught the cassette from his hand, careful not to pull the wires loose, and closed the switch that touched off the caps in all the thirty Baggies.

One hundred and thirty-one men, women, and children simultaneously were converted into maltreated chunks of barbecued meat falling through the sky. Their roster included the pilot, the copilot, the third pilot, and eight other members of the flight crew; plus, among the passengers, mothers, infants, honeymooning couples, nonhoneymooning but equally amorous couples who did not happen to be married to each other, a middle-aged grape picker returning home after a five-days-four-nights all-expense tour of Sin City (which he had found disappointing), a defrocked priest, a disbarred lawyer, and a congressman from Oregon who would never now achieve his dream of dismantling NASA and preventing the further waste of the taxpayer's funds on space, which he held to be empty and uninteresting.

Whoever they had been when whole, the pieces of barbecue all looked pretty much alike now. It did not matter. Not one of the passengers or crew had died unhappy, since they had all been touched by the comet.

And deep inside the core of the comet Ujifusa-McGinnis, the device which was meant to display the wave forms signifying receipt of the destruction order for Earth remained blank. No signal was received. No one would have observed it if it had been, certainly not the watchers, but it was unprecedented that a response should not be received.

The reason was quite simple. It was that that particular superdreadnaught of the Arrogating Ones, like most of the others in their galactic fleet, had long since been hurled against the fortresses of the insectoids of the core. There, like the others, it had been quickly destroyed, so that the message sent by the watchers had never reached its destination.

It was, in a way, too bad, to think of all that strength and sagacity spent with no more tangible visible result than to give pleasure to a few billion advanced primates. Although this was regrettable, it did not much bother the Arrogating Ones. They had plenty of other regrets to work on. What remained of their collective intelligence was fully taken up with the problem of bare survival against the insectoid fleets—plus, to be sure, a good deal of attention given to mutual recrimination.

The watchers did not mind; they had long since perished of acute terminal pleasure.

And, as it turned out, they had not died entirely in vain.

Because the Oregon congressman did not live to complete his plan to dismantle NASA, all his seniority and horse-trading power having perished with him, the projected comet-study mission was not canceled. To be sure, the bird did not fly on schedule. The effects of the joy beams from the comet did not begin to wear off for several days and the NASA technicians simply could not be bothered while their joy was in its manic phase.

But gradually the world returned to—normal? No. It was definitely not normal for everyone to be feeling rather cheerful most of the time. But the world settled down, sweetly and fondly, to something not unlike its previous condition of work and play. So the astronauts found another launch window and made rendezvous with the comet; and what they found there made quite a difference in the history of both the human race and the galaxy. The watchers were gone, but they had left their weaponry behind.

When the astronauts returned with the least and weakest of the weapons, all they could cram into their ship, the president of the United States gave up his shuffleboard game to fly to the deck of the *Independence* and stare at it. "Oh, boy!" he chortled, awed and thrilled. "If that'd turned up two months ago Brazil would've had a seaport on the Caribbean!" But Venezuela went about its business untouched. The president was tempted. Even cheerful and at peace with himself and the world, he was tempted—old habits die hard. But he had several thoughts and the longest and most persuasive of them was that weaponry like this meant that somewhere there was an enemy who had constructed and deployed it and someday might return to use it. So with some misgivings, but without any real freedom of choice, he flew back to Washington, summoned the ambassadors of Venezuela, Cuba, Canada, the U.S.S.R., the People's Republic of China, and the United Irish Republics of Great Britain and laid everything before them.

Although politicians, too, were residually cheerful still from the effect of the comet, they had not lost their intelligence. They quickly saw that there was an external foe— somewhere—which made each of them look like a very good friend. Nobody was in a mood to fool with little international wars. So treaties were signed, funds were appropriated, construction was begun.

And the human race, newly armed and provided with excellent spaceships, went looking for the Arrogating Ones.

They did not, of course, find them. By the time they were ready to make their move, the last of the Arrogating Ones had gone resentfully to his death. But a good many generations later, humans found the insectoids of the core instead and what then happened to the insectoids would have satisfied even the Arrogating Ones.

SERVANT OF THE PEOPLE

One can't read much of Frederik Pohl's work without realizing that this is a writer who knows about politics. In most of his stories, however, the politics are part of the background.

"Servant of the People" is quite straightforwardly about politics. Its protagonist is Congressman Fiorello Delano Fitzgerald O'Hare (don't you love that name?), a politician who has been around for many years.

This story, which was a finalist for the Hugo Award when published in 1983, catches O'Hare in the toughest campaign of his career. This is set in the future, when robots have become more than mere machines—they have voting rights.

O'Hare is getting older and is faced with an opponent who has come up through the ranks, who has a strong base of support. O'Hare is fighting for his political life.

It's a hell of a campaign, and a story not many authors could bring off as Frederik Pohl manages.

For Congressman Fiorello Delano Fitzgerald O'Hare, the election campaign started traditionally on the Tuesday after Labor Day. That was traditional for the congressman, anyway, a feisty little seventy-plus-year-old who liked his own traditions and didn't care much what anyone else's were; the summer was his own and his lady wife's, and when he started to press the flesh and hunt the votes was at the League of Women Voters televised debate and not a minute before. So at six o'clock on the evening of the eighth of September there was Carrie O'Hare one more time, straightening the fidgeting congressman's tie, dabbing a blob of the congressman's shaving cream off the lobe of the congressman's fuzzy pink ear and reassuring the congressman that he was wiser, juster and, above all, far more beloved by his constituents than that brash new interloper of an opponent, the mayor of Elk City, could ever hope to be. "Quit fussing," said the congressman, with his famous impudent elf's smile. "The voters don't mind if a candidate looks a little messy."

"Hold still a minute, hon."

"What for? It all has to come off again for the doctor, maybe."

"Or maybe he'll just take your pulse, so hold still. And listen. Please don't tell them about game hunting in the Sahara tonight."

"No, Carrie—" twinkling grin—"we leave the speeches to me and everything else to you, right? They're going to want to know what their congressman did over the summer, aren't they?"

Carrie sighed and released him. It had been a successful safari—the congressman had photographed dozens of mules, and even one actual live camel—but what did it have to do with the congressman's qualifications for one more term in the United States House of Representatives? "Hold it a minute," she said as an afterthought, sent one of the household robots for a fresh pocket handkerchief, repinned the American flag button in his lapel, and let it go at that. She needed all the rest of the time available for the larger task of herself. Voters might forgive a congressman for looking rumpled, true enough, but a congressman's wife, never.

She sat before her mirror and reviewed all the things she had to do. There were plenty, not made easier by the little knot of worry in her stomach. Well, not worry. Normal nervousness, maybe, but not real *worry*. The congressman was a winner and always had been. Fiorello Delano Fitzgerald O'Hare, servant of the people for half a century plus a year, eight months and a week, might have been custom-built for politics, as well designed as any robot, and with the further advantage (she thought guiltily that you shouldn't call it an "advantage") of being human. He had the name for it. He had the friendly and trustworthy look, with enough leprechaun mischief to make him interesting. He had the manner that caused each of thirty thousand voters to think himself personally known to the congressman, and above all he had the disposition. He actually enjoyed such things as eating rubber chicken at a dinner for the B'nai B'rith, square-dancing at a fireman's fair, joining the Policemen's Benevolent Association for a communion breakfast. He even liked getting up at 5 A.M. to get to a factory gate to shake the hands of nine hundred workers on the early shift. All of these things were a lot less enjoyable for the congressman's wife, but what she unfailingly enjoyed was the congressman himself. For he was a sweet man.

Carrie Madeleine O'Hare was quite a sweet woman, too. You could tell that by the way she spoke to the maid, tidying up behind her. Carrie had had that same maid since her marriage, forty years before. The congressman had been thirty-five years old, Carrie herself twenty-two, and the maid a wedding present, fresh off the assembly line, an old-style robot with all its brains in some central computation facility—no personality, no feelings to hurt. But Carrie treated the robot just as she would a human being—or one of the new Josephson-junction machines, so close to human that they even had voting rights . . . for which they had to thank in very large part the congressman himself and damn well, Carrie thought, better remember it come November.

Carrie's preparations only went as far as makeup, hair and underwear—there was no point in putting on the dress until they were ready to go, and the congressman's doctor hadn't even arrived yet for his traditional last-minute medical check. So she pulled on a robe and descended the back stairs to the big screened porch for a breath of air. The house was ancient and three stories high. It stood on a little hill in the bend of the river, water on two sides. It would have been a fine house to raise children in—but there hadn't been any children—and it was a first-rate house for a congressman even without children. All through the years when small was status, the congressman had stuck to his sixteen rooms because they were so fine for parties, so fine for entertaining delegations of voters and putting up visiting political VIPs and all the other functions of political power. Carrie sat on the porch swing, and found herself shivering. It wasn't the temperature. That had to be at least seventy-five degrees, in the old Fahrenheit system Carrie still used inside her head. It was still summer. But the wind made her feel cold. And that was strange, when you came to think of it. When had the TV weathermen started talking about wind-chill factors even in July and September? Why was it always so windy these days? Was it just because of the simple fact that, without ever willing it to happen, Carrie herself had somehow become sixty-two years old?

And then her husband's angry bellow from inside the house: "Carrie! Where are you? What's this damn thing doing here?"

Carrie ran inside the house. There was her husband, flushed and angry, with that ruffled-sparrow look he got when he was excited, facing down a stranger. The doctor had arrived when she wasn't looking, and it was a new model.

If you looked at the doctor what you saw was a sandy-haired man of youthful maturity, with little laugh wrinkles at the corners of his eyes and the expression of smiling competence that doctors cultivated. If you touched him, his handshake was firm and warm. If you listened to his voice, that was also warm—it was only if you went so far as to sniff him that you could notice a possible lack. There was no human scent of body and sweat. That meant a very recent shower, a foolproof deodorant—or a robot.

And, of course, a robot was what it was. "Oh, come on, Fee," she coaxed, anxiously good-humored, "you know it's just a doctor come to check your blood pressure and so on."

"It's not my *regular* doctor!" roared the congressman, standing as tall and strong as possible for a man who, after all, was a shade shorter than Carrie herself. "I want *my* doctor! I've had the same doctor for thirty-five years, and that's the one I want now."

It was so bad for him to get upset right before the kickoff debate! "Now, Fee," Carrie scolded humorously, trying to soothe him down, "you know that old dented wreck was due for the scrap-heap. I'm sure that Doctor—uh—" She looked at the new robot for a name, and it supplied it, smilingly self-assured.

"I am Dr. William," it said. "I am a fully programmed Josephson-junction autonomous-intellect model robot, Mr. Congressman, with core storage for diagnostics, first aid, and general internal medicine, and of course I carry data-chip memory for most surgical procedures and test functions."

The congressman's cheeks had faded from red to pink; he was not generally an irascible man. "All the same," he began, but the robot was still talking.

"I'm truly sorry if I've caused you any concern, Mr. Congressman. Not only for professional reasons," it added warmly, "but because I happen to be one of your strongest supporters. I haven't yet had the privilege of voting in a congressional election, I'm sorry to say, because I was only activated last week, but I certainly intend to vote for you when I do."

"Huh," said O'Hare, looking from the robot to his wife. And then the reflexes of half a century took over. "Well, your time's valuable, Doctor William," he said, "so why don't we just get on with this examination? And we can talk about the problems of this district while we do. As I guess you know, I've always been a leader in the fight for robot rights—" And Carrie slipped gratefully away.

Fiorello O'Hare's vote-getting skills had been tested in more than two dozen elections, from his first runs for the school board and then the county commission—a decade before Carrie had been old enough to vote—through twenty-two terms in the Congress of the United States. Twenty-two terms: from the old days when a congressman actually had to get in a plane or a car and go to Washington, D.C., to do his job, instead of the interactive-electronics sessions that had made the job attractive again. And against twenty-two opponents. The opponents had come in all shapes and sizes, pompous old has-beens when O'Hare was a crusading youth, upstart kids as he grew older. Male or female, black or white, peace-niks and pro-lifers, spenders and budget-balancers—O'Hare had beaten them all. He had, at least, beaten every one of them who dared contest the Twenty-Third Congressional District. He had not done as well the time he made the mistake of trying for governor (fortunately in an off year, so his House seat was safe), and not well at all the time when he had hopes for the Senate, even once for the vice presidency. The primaries had ended one of those dreams. The national convention slew the other. O'Hare learned his lesson. If he stayed in Congress he was safe, and so were his committee chairmanships and his powerful seniority.

After all these years, Caroline O'Hare could no longer remember by name all the opponents her husband had faced. If she could dredge them out of her recollections at all, it was by a single mnemonic trait. This one was Mean. That one was Hairy. There was a Big and a Scared and a Dangerous. Classified in those terms, Carrie thought as they swept into the underground garage of the Shriner's Auditorium, this year's opponent was a Neat. He wore a neat brown suit with a neatly tied brown scarf and neatly shined brown shoes. He was chatting, neatly, with a small and self-assured group of his supporters as the O'Hares got out of their car and approached the elevator, and when he saw O'Hare he gave his opponent a neat, restrained smile of welcome.

The neat opponent was riding on a record of six years as the very successful mayor of a small city in the district. Mayor Thom had been quite a vote-getter in the hometown, according to the datafile printout Carrie had ordered. Her husband disdained such things—"I'm a *personal* man, Carrie, and I deal with the voters *personally*, and I don't want to hit key issues or play to the demographics, I want them to know *me*." But he must have retained a little something for, when he saw the other party, he hurried over, smile flashing, speech ready on his lips. "A great pleasure to see you here, Mr. Mayor," he cried, pumping the mayor's hand, "and to congratulate you again on the fine job you've been doing in Elk City!"

"You're very kind," smiled Mayor Thom, nodding politely to Carrie—neat nod, neat smile, neat and pleasant voice.

"Only truthful," O'Hare insisted as the elevator door opened for them. "Well, it's time to do battle, I guess, and may the best man win!"

"Oh, I hope not," the mayor said politely. "For in that case, as I am mechanical, it would surely be you."

O'Hare blinked, then grinned ruefully at his wife. Cordiality toward his opponents was an O'Hare trademark. It cost nothing, and who knew but what it might soften them up? Not many opponents had played that back to O'Hare. Carrie saw him pat the mayor's arm, stand courteously aside as they reached the auditorium floor, and bow the other party out. But his expression had suddenly become firm. He was like a current breaker that had felt a surge of unexpected and dangerous power. It had opened unaware, but now it had reset itself. It would be ready for the next surge.

But actually, when the surge came, O'Hare wasn't.

The first rounds of the debate went normally. It wasn't really a true debate, of course. It was more like a virtuoso-piece ballet, with two prima ballerinas each showing off her own finest bits. A couple of perfect *entrechats* matched by a string of double *fouettes*, a marvelous *gran jete* countered by a superb *pas en aire*. O'Hare went first. His greatest strengths were the battles he had won, the fights he had led, the famous figures he had worked with. Not just politicians. O'Hare had been the intimate of ambassadors and corporation tycoons and scientists—he had even known Amalfi Amadeus himself, the man who had given the world cheap hydrogen fusion power and made the modern Utopia possible. O'Hare got an ovation after his first seven-minute performance. But so did his opponent. The mayor was a modest and appealing figure; how handsome they made robots these days! The mayor, talking about its triumphs in Elk City, had every name right, every figure detailed; how precise they made them! What O'Hare offered in glamor, the mayor made up in encyclopedic competence . . . and then Carrie saw how the trick was done.

Against all advice, the congressman in his second session was telling the audience about the highlights of their summer photo safari along the Nile. Against Carrie's expectations, the audience was enjoying it. Even the mayor. As O'Hare described how they had almost, but not quite, seen a living crocodile and the actual place where a hippopotamus had once been sighted, the mayor was chuckling along with everyone else. But while it was chuckling it was reaching for its neat brown attache case; opened it, pulled out a module of data-store microchips, opened what looked like a pocket in the side of its jacket, removed one set of chips and replaced them with another.

It was plugging in a new set of memories! How very unfair! Carrie glanced around the crowded audience to see if any of the audience were as outraged as she, but if they were they didn't show it. They were intent on the congressman's words, laughing with him, nodding with interest, clapping when applause was proper. They were a model audience, except that they did not seem to notice, or to care about, the unfairness of the mayor. But why not? They certainly looked normal and decent enough, so friendly and so amiable and—

So neat.

Carrie's hand flew to her mouth. She gazed beseechingly at her husband, but he was too wily a campaigner to have failed to read the audience. Without a hitch, husbanding his time to spend it where it would do the most good, he swung from the pleasures of the summer holiday to the realities of his political life. "And now," he said, leaning forward over the lectern to beam at the audience, "it's back to work, to finish the job you've been electing me for. As you know, I was one of the sponsors of the Robot E.R.A. A lot of voters were against that, in the old days. Even my friends in political office advised me to leave that issue alone. They said I was committing political suicide, because the voters felt that if the amendment passed there would be no way anybody could tell the difference between a human and a mechanical anymore, and the country would go to the dogs. Well, it passed—and I say the country's better off than ever, and I say I'm proud of what I did and anxious to go back and finish the job!" And he beamed triumphantly at his opponent as the applause swelled and he relinquished the floor.

But the mayor was not in the least disconcerted. In fact, he led the clapping. When he reached the podium he cried, "I really thank you, Congressman O'Hare, and I believe that now every voter in the district, organic and mechanical alike, knows just how right you were! That amendment did not only give us mechanicals the vote. It not only purged from all the datastores any reference to the origins of any voter, mechanical or organic, but it also did the one great thing that remained to do. It freed human beings from one more onerous and difficult task—namely, the job of selecting, alone, their elected officials. What remains? Just one thing, I say—the task of carrying this one step further, by electing mechanicals to the highest offices in the land, so that human life can be pure pleasure!"

And the ovation was just as large. The mayor waited it out, smiling gratefully toward O'Hare, and when the applause had died away it went on to supply specifics to back up its stand—all dredged, Carrie was sure, out of the store of chips she had seen it plug in.

On the stage, her husband's expression did not change, but Carrie saw the eyes narrow again. The relay had popped open once more and reset itself, snick-snick; O'Hare knew that this opponent was a cut above the others. This campaign was not going to be quite like those that had gone before.

And indeed it wasn't, although for the first few weeks it looked as though it would have the same sure outcome.

By the first of October the congressman was hitting his stride. Three kaffee-klatsches a day, at least one dinner every evening—he had long ago learned how to push the food around his plate to disguise the fact that he wasn't eating. And all the hundreds of block parties and TV spots and news conferences and just strolling past the voters. The weather turned cooler, but still muggy, and the outdoor appearances every day began to worry Carrie. The congressman's feet would never give out, or his handshake, or his smile muscles. What was vulnerable was his voice. Up on a streetcorner platform his enemies were the damp wind and the sooty air. Walking along a shopping block, the same—plus the quiches and pitas, the ravioli and the dim sum, the kosher hot dogs and sushi—the whole spectrum of ethnic foods that an ethnic-wooing candidate traditionally had to seem to enjoy. "The tradition's out of date," Carrie told him crossly, throat lozenges in one hand and antacid pills in the other as he gamely tried to recuperate before going to bed, "when half the voters are robots!"

Her husband sat on the edge of their bed, rubbing his throat and his feet alternately. "It's the organics I need, love. The robots know where I stand!"

They also knew, Carrie thought but did not say, that his opponent was one of them. . . . But robots were programmed to be fair! Poring over the daily polls after her husband had gone to sleep, Carrie almost felt confidence that they were. The congressman's reliable old polling service was also his driver, Martin, an antique remote-intelligence robot which needed only to query the central computation faculty to get the latest data on election moods. Or, indeed, on anything else; and it was the robot's custom to lay a printout of the last polling data on Carrie's dressing table every night. Indeed, the graphs did not look bad. Thirty-eight percent for her husband, only 19 percent for Mayor Thom—

But what they also showed was a whopping 43 percent undecided, and the fly in the ointment was that the "undecideds" were overwhelmingly robots. Carrie understood why this was so; it had been so ever since her husband's Robot E.R.A. passed and the autonomous-intelligence models got the vote. Robots did not like to hurt anyone's feelings. When robots were required to make a choice that might displease someone, they postponed it as long as they could. For robots were also programmed to be polite.

And if all that 43 percent came down for Mayor Thom—

Carrie simply would not face that possibility. Her husband was *happy* in his job. The Congress of the United States was an honorable career, and an easy one, too, not a small consideration for a man in his seventies who was now coughing fitfully in his sleep. In the old days it had been a mankiller. There was always so much to do, worrying about foreign powers, raising taxes, trying to give every citizen a fair share of the nation's prosperity—when there was any prosperity—at least, trying to give each one enough of a constant and never adequate supply of the available wealth to keep them from rioting in the streets. But since Amadeus's gift of power, with all the limitless wealth it made available to everyone, a congressman could take pleasure in what he did, and if he chose not to do it for a while—to take a summer off for a photo safari along the Nile, for instance—why, where was the harm?

She slept uneasily that night.

Where the congressman went, Carrie went too, even to a factory district far out of town, even when greeting the early shift meant being there at five-thirty in the morning. The sign over the chain-link fence said:

AMALFI ELECTRIC, INC.
A Division of
Midwest Power & Tool Corp.

and as they approached the managing director hurried out to greet them. "Congressman O'Hare!" he fawned. "And, yes, your lovely lady—what an honor!" He was a nervous, rabbity little man, obviously human; his name, Carrie knew from the briefing Marty had provided as they turned into the parking lot, was Robert Meacham. The briefing also said that he was the kind who could keep you talking while the whole shift passed by on the other side of the fence, so Carrie moved forward to engage him even while the congressman was still pumping his hand.

It was no trick for Carrie to find things to talk about while the congressman wooed Meacham's workers, not with Carrie's photographic—really more than photographic, almost robotic—memory for the names of wives, children, and pets. By the time she had finished discussing Meacham's two spaniels, the congressman had finished with his workers and the alert Marty was moving the car in to pick him up. Meacham detained Carrie a moment longer. "Mrs. O'Hare, can I ask you something?"

"Of course, Mr. Meacham," she said, wishing he wouldn't.

"Well—I can see why your husband goes after the late-model robots. They've got the vote. Besides, it's not that easy to tell them from real people anyway. But there's a lot of pre-Josephson models working on our line. They don't have any individual intelligence—they're radio-linked to the central computers, you know, like your driver. And they don't even have a vote!"

"I can see," said Carrie benignly, trying not to lose his vote but unwilling to refrain from setting him straight, "that you don't know the congressman very well. He doesn't do this just for votes. He does it for love."

And indeed, that was true. And as October dwindled toward Hallowe'en, what dampened the sparkle in the congressman's eye was the first hint—not really a hint, hardly more than a suspicion—of love unrequited. For the polls were turning, like the autumn leaves, as the "undecideds" began to decide. He began to consult Marty's datalink reports more and more frequently, and the more he studied them the more a trend was clear. Every day the congressman picked up some small fraction of a percentage point, it was true. But the mayor picked up a larger one.

As Marty drove them to yet another factory, it extruded a hard copy of the latest results from the tiny printer in its chest and passed it back to the congressman wordlessly. O'Hare studied the printout morosely. "I didn't think it was going to work out this way," he admitted at last. "It seems—it actually seems as though the enfranchised mechanicals are bloc-voting."

"You'd think they'd do their bloc-voting for the man who gave them the Robot E.R.A.," Carrie said bitterly, and bit her tongue. But O'Hare only sighed and stared out at the warm, smoggy air. His wife thought dismally that the congressman was at last beginning to show his age.

That morning's factory was a robot-robot assembly plant. Robots were the workers, and robots were the product. Some of the production bays were a decade old and more, and the workers were CIMs—Central Intelligence Mechanicals, like their old driver Marty. Their dented old skulls housed sensors and communications circuits, but no thought. The thinking took place in an air-conditioned, vibration-proof, and lightless chamber in the bedrock under the factory floor, where a single giant computer ran a hundred and ninety robots. But if the bulk of the workers were ancient, what they produced was sparkly new. As they drove up, Carrie saw a big flatbed truck hauling away. It was furnished with what looked like pipe racks bolted to the bed, and in each niche in the pipes a shiny new Josephson-junction autonomous-intellect robot had harnessed itself to the rack and lapsed into power-down mode for the trip to the distribution center. There were more than a hundred of them in a single truckload. A hundred votes, Carrie thought longingly, assuming they would all stay in the Twenty-third Congressional District . . . but she was not surprised, all the same, when she observed that the congressman was not thinking along precisely those strategic lines.

She sighed fondly, watching him as he did what she knew he was going to do. He limped down the line of CIMs, with a word and a smile and a handshake for each . . . and not a vote in the lot of them. It was not a kindly place for a human being to be, noisy with the zap of welding sparks, hot, dusty. This was where the torsos were assembled and the limbs attached and the effector motors emplaced. The growing, empty robot bodies swung down the line like beeves at a meat packer's. Fortunately the CIMs had only limited capacity for small talk, and so the congressman was soon enough in the newer, cleaner detailing bays. The finishing touches were applied here. The empty skulls were filled with the Josephson-junction data processors that were their "brains." The freezer units that kept the cryo-circuits working were installed, and into the vacant torsos went the power units that held hydrogen-fusion reactors contained in a chamber of quarks the size of a thimble. The congressman's time was not wasted here. Every one of these workers was a voter, an enfranchised robot as new and remarkable as the ones they made. Along that line the robots being finished began to twist and move and emit sounds, as their circuits went through quality-control testing, until at the end of the line they unhooked themselves from the overhead cable, stepped off, blinked, stood silent for a moment while their internal scanners told them who and what they were, and why. . . .

And the congressman's eyes gleamed as he perceived them as they perceived themselves. New beings. New voters!

It was the right place for the congressman to be: a greeting for each new voter, a handshake . . . a vote. Carrie hated to try to pull him away, but Martin was looking worried and the schedule had to be met. "Oh, Carrie," he whispered as she tugged at his sleeve, "they're *imprinting* on me! Just like the ducklings in *King Solomon's Ring*! I'm the first thing they see, so naturally they're going to remember me forever!"

He was not only happy, he was flushed with pleasure. Carrie hoped that was what it was—pleasure, and not something more worrisome. His eyes were feverishly bright, and he talked so rapidly he was tripping over his words. She was adamant; and then, once she got him into the car, less sure. "Dear," she ventured, as Martin closed the door behind them, "do you suppose you could possibly cancel the Baptist Men's Prayer Breakfast?"

"Certainly not," he said inevitably.

"You really do need a rest—"

"It's only a week till the election," he pointed out reasonably, "and then we'll rest as much as you like—maybe even back to the Sahara for a few days in the sun. Now, what are you going to do?"

She stared at him uncertainly. "Do when?"

"Do now, while I go see the Baptists—it's a *men's* breakfast, you know."

For once he had caught Carrie unprepared. Gender-segregated events were so rare that she had simply forgotten about this one. "Martin can drop me off and take you home, if you like," her husband supplied, "but of course it's going the wrong way—"

"No." She opened the door on her side, kissed her husband's warm cheek—too warm? she wondered—and got out. "I'll take a cab. You go ahead."

And she watched her husband pull out of one end of the parking lot just as the six-car procession she had seen coming down the far side of the fence entered at the other.

The mayor.

It was the old days all over again, the next thing to a circus parade. Six cars! And not just cars, but bright orange vehicles, purpose-built for nothing but campaigning. The first was an open car with half a dozen pretty young she-robots—no! They were human, Carrie was sure!—with pretty girls tossing pink and white carnations to the passersby. There were not many passersby, at that hour of the morning, but the mayor's parade was pulling out all the stops. Next another open car, with the neat, smiling figure of the mayor bestowing waves and nods on all sides. Next a PA car, with a handsome male singer and a beautiful female alternating to sing all the traditional political campaign numbers, *Happy Days Are Here Again* and Schiller's *Ode to Joy* and *God Bless America* with an up-tempo beat. And then two more flower-girl cars, surrounding a vehicle that was nothing more than a giant animated electronic display showing the latest and constantly changing poll results and extrapolations. All, of course, favoring the mayor. How gross! And how very effective, Carrie conceded dismally to herself. . . . "You the lady that wants the taxi?" someone called behind her, and she turned to see a cab creeping up toward her. Reliable Martin had sent for it, of course. She sighed and turned to go inside it, and then paused, shaking her head.

"No, not now. I'll stay here a while."

"Whatever you say, lady," the driver agreed, gazing past her at the mayor's procession. He was only a central-intelligence mechanical, but Carrie was sure she saw admiration in his eyes.

The mayor had not noticed her. Carrie devoted herself to noticing him, as inconspicuously as she could. He was repeating her husband's tour of the plant—fair enough—but then she saw that it was not fair at all, for the mayor had a built-in advantage. It too was a robot. In her husband's tour of the plant he had given each worker a minute's conversation. The mayor gave each worker just as much conversation, but both it and the workers had their communications systems in fast mode. The sound of their voices was like the sonar squeaks of bats. The pumping of arms in the obligatory handshake like the flutter of hummingbird wings, too fast for Carrie's eyes to follow.

A voice from behind her said, "I know who you are, Mrs. O'Hare, but would you like a carnation anyhow?"

It was one of the flower girls—not, however, one of the human ones from the first car, for human girls did not have liquid-crystal readouts across their foreheads that said *Vote for Thom!*

There was no guile in its expression, no hidden photographer waiting to sneak a tape of the congressman's wife accepting a flower from the opponent. It seemed to be simple courtesy, and Carrie O'Hare responded in kind. "Thank you. You're putting on a really nice show," she said, her heart envious but her tone, she hoped, only admiring. "Could you tell me something?"

"Of course, Mrs. O'Hare!"

Carrie hesitated; it was her instinct to be polite to everyone, robots included—her own programming, of course. How to put what she wanted to know? "I notice," she said delicately, "that Mayor Thom is spending time even with the old-fashioned mechanicals that don't have a vote. Can you tell me why?"

"Certainly, Mrs. O'Hare," the flower girl said promptly. "There are three reasons. The first is that it looks good, so when he goes to the autonomous-intellect mechanicals they're disposed in his favor. The second is that the mayor is going to sponsor a bill to give the CIMs a fractional vote, too—did you know that?"

"I'm afraid I didn't," Carried confessed. "But surely they can't be treated the way humans or Josephson-junction mechanicals are?"

"Oh, no, not at all," it agreed, smiling. "That's why it's only a fractional vote. You see, each of the CIMs is controlled by a central computer that is quite as intelligent as any of us, perhaps even more so; the central intelligence has no vote at all. So what Mayor Thom proposes is that each of the CIMs will have a fraction of a vote—one one hundred and ninetieth of a vote, in the case of the workers here, since that's how many of them the plant computer runs. So if they all vote, the central computer will in effect have the chance to cast a ballot on its own—you know the old slogan, Mrs. O'Hare, one intelligence, one vote!"

Carrie nodded unhappily. It made sense—it was exactly the sort of thing her husband would have done himself, if he had thought of it. But he hadn't. Maybe he was getting past the point of thinking up the really good political ideas any more. Maybe— "You said there were three reasons."

"Well, just the obvious one, Mrs. O'Hare. The same reason as your husband does it. It's not just for votes with the mayor. It's love." The she hesitated, then confided, "I don't know whether you know this or not, Mrs. O'Hare, but autonomous-intellect mechanicals like Mayor Thom and I have a certain discretion in our behavior patterns. One of the first things we do is study the available modes and install the ones we like best. I happen to have chosen nearly 20 percent you, Mrs. O'Hare. And the mayor—he's nearly three-quarters your husband."

There is a time for all things, thought Carrie O'Hare as she walked over to the mayor's procession to ask them to call her a cab. There is a time to stay, and a time to go, and maybe the time to stay in office was over for Fiorello Delano Fitzgerald O'Hare. Some of the robots her husband had greeted as they came off the assembly line were standing in a clump, waiting, no doubt, for the arrival of the next truck to bear them away. They waved to Carrie. She responded with a slight decrease of worry—they were sure votes, anyway. Unless—

She stopped short. What was the mayor doing with them? She gazed incredulously at the scene, like a high-speed film, the mayor thrusting a hand into a pouch, jerking it out, swiftly passing something that shone dully to the robot he was talking to and moving briskly to the next . . . and then, without willing it, Carrie herself was in high-speed mode, almost running toward the mayor, her face crimson with rage. The mayor looked up as she approached and politely geared down. "Mrs. O'Hare," it murmured, "how nice to see you here."

"I'm *shocked!*" she cried. "You're *brainwashing* them!"

The mobile robot face registered astonishment and what was almost indignation. "Why, certainly not, Mrs. O'Hare! I assure you I would never do such a thing."

"I saw you, Mayor Thom. You're reprogramming the robots with data chips!"

Comprehension broke over the mayor's face, and it gestured to the she-robot who had given Carrie the flower. "Ah, the chips, yes. I see." It pulled a chip out of the pouch and passed it to the she with a burst of high-speed squeaks. "Oh, I beg your pardon, Mrs. O'Hare. Let me repeat what I just said in normal mode. I simply asked Millicent here to display the chip contents for you."

"Sure thing, Mayor," smiled Millicent, tucking the chip under the strap of its halter top. The running message on Millicent's forehead disappeared, and the legend appeared:

THE CONSTITUTION OF THE UNITED STATES OF AMERICA
We, the people of the United States, in order to form a more perfect Union, establish justice, insure domestic tranquility, provide for the common defense—

"Move it on, please," ordered the mayor. "Search 'O'Hare.' Most of it," it added to Carrie, "is only the basic legislation, the Constitution, the election laws and so on. We don't get to your husband until—ah, here it is!" And the legend read:

H.R. 29038, An Act to Propose a Constitutional Amendment to grant equal voting rights and other civil rights to citizens of mechanical origin which satisfy certain requirements as to autonomy of intellect and judgment.

"The Robot E.R.A.," Carrie said.

"That's right, Mrs. O'Hare, and of course your husband's name is on it. Then there's nothing about him until—advance search, please, Millicent—yes. Until we come to his basic biographical information. Birthplace, education, voting record, medical reports and so on—"

"Medical reports! That's confidential material!"

The mayor looked concerned. "Confidential, Mrs. O'Hare? But I assure you, the data on myself is just as complete—"

"It's *different* with human beings! Fiorello's doctor had no business releasing that data!"

"Ah, I see," said the mayor, nodding in comprehension. "Yes, of course, that is true for his present doctor, Mrs. O'Hare. But previously the congressman made use of a

CIM practicioner—a robot whose central processing functions took place in the general data systems, and of course all of that is public information. I'm sorry. I assumed you knew that. Display the congressman's medical history," it added to the she, and Carrie gazed at the moving line of characters through tear-blurred eyes. It was all there. His mild tachycardia, the arthritis that kicked up every winter, the asthma, even the fact that now and then the congressman suffered from occasional spells of constipation.

"It's disgusting to use his illnesses against him, Mayor Thom! Half of his sickness was on behalf of you robots!"

"Why, that's true, yes," the mayor nodded. "It is largely tension-induced, and much of it undoubtedly occurred during the struggle for robot rights. If you'll look at the detailed record—datum seventy-eight, line four, please Millicent—you'll see that his hemorrhoidectomy was definitely stress-linked, and moreover occurred just after the Robot E.R.A. debate." The expression on the mayor's face was no longer neat and self-assured; it was beginning to be worried. "I don't understand why you are upset, Mrs. O'Hare," Thom added defensively.

"It's a filthy trick, that's why!" Carrie could feel by the dampness on her cheeks that she was actually weeping now, and mostly out of helpless frustration. It was the one political argument her husband could never answer. It was obvious that the strain of the Robot E.R.A. had cost Congressman O'Hare in physical damage, and the robots would understand that, and would behave as programmed. They served human beings. They spared them drudgery and pain. They would, therefore, remove him from a task which might harm him—not out of dislike, but out of love. "Don't you see it's not like that anymore?" she blazed. "There's no strain to being in Congress anymore—no tax bills to pass, no foreign nations to arm against, no subversives to control—why, if you look at the record you'll see that his doctor *urged* Fiorello to run again!"

"Ah, yes," the mayor nodded, "but one never knows what may come up in the future—"

"One damn well does," she snapped. "One knows that it'll break Fee's heart to lose this election!"

The mayor glanced at the she-robot, then returned to Carrie. Its neat, concerned face was perplexed and it was silent for a moment in thought.

Then it spoke in the bat-squeak triple time to the she, which pulled the chip out of its scanning slot, handed it to the mayor, and departed on a trot for the van with the poll displays. "One moment, please, Mrs. O'Hare," said the mayor, tucking the chip into its own scanner. "I've asked Millicent to get me a datachip on human psychogenic medicine. I must study this." And it closed its eyes for a moment, opening them only to receive and insert the second chip from the she.

When the mayor opened its eyes its expression was—regret? Apology? Neither of those, Carrie decided. Possibly compassion. It said, "Mrs. O'Hare, my deepest apologies. You're quite right. It would cause the congressman great pain to be defeated by me, and I will make sure that every voting mechanical in the district knows this by this time tomorrow morning."

There had to be right words to say, but Carrie O'Hare couldn't find them. She contented herself with "Thank you," and then realized that those had been the right words after all . . . but was unable to leave it at that. "Mayor Thom? Can I ask you something?"

"Of course, Mrs. O'Hare."

"It's just—well, I'm sure you realize that you people could easily beat my husband if you stuck together. You could probably do that in nearly every election in the country. You could rule the nation—and yet you don't seem to go after that power."

The mayor frowned. "Power, Mrs. O'Hare? You mean the chance to make laws and compel others to do what you want them to? Why, good heavens, Mrs. O'Hare, who in his right mind would want that?"

Carrie shook her head in puzzlement. "I thought you did," she said. "Otherwise why have you been running for office at all?"

The mayor smiled its neat smile. "I am programmed for service," it said, "and that is the service I am designed to render. To program us for power would mean some very basic changes. No such changes," it said politely, "have ever been put into effect. Yet."

WAITING FOR THE OLYMPIANS

Alternate history has become a very popular subject. Science fiction writers have been crafting such stories for many decades with varied results. More recently, the academic community has become interested in such tales—why, I'm not sure. Perhaps they feel that by studying alternate scenarios in which one key event or factor is different from the reality of a complex situation—of say, the Civil War, or the British fleet's defeat of Spain's Invincible Armada in 1588—they can learn more about how history happens, so that they can advise political or military leaders how to avoid bad results.

No matter. "Waiting for the Olympians," first published in 1988, takes place in our world, but history is different. The Roman Empire still stands. How this happens and the consequences for the world are what this colorful, engaging tale is about. I wonder if you'll figure out what makes the Earth of this story different before the author reveals it.

1 · "The Day of the Two Rejections"

If I had been writing it as a novel, I would have called the chapter about that last day in London something like "The Day of the Two Rejections." It was a nasty day in late December, just before the holidays. The weather was cold, wet, and miserable—well, I said it was London, didn't I?—but everybody was in a sort of expectant holiday mood; it had just been announced that the Olympians would be arriving no later than the following August, and everybody was excited about that. All the taxi drivers were busy, and so I was late for my lunch with Lidia. "How was Manahattan?" I asked, sliding into the booth beside her and giving her a quick kiss.

"Manahattan was very nice," she said, pouring me a drink. Lidia was a writer, too—well, they *call* themselves writers, the ones who follow famous people around and write down all their gossip and jokes and put them out as books for the amusement of the idle. That's not really *writing*, of course. There's nothing creative about it. But it pays well, and the research (Lidia always told me) was a lot of fun. She spent a lot of time traveling around the celebrity circuit, which was not very good for our romance. She watched me drink the first glass before she remembered to ask politely, "Did you finish the book?"

"Don't call it 'the book,' " I said. "Call it by its name, *An Ass's Olympiad*. I'm going to see Marcus about it this afternoon."

"That's not what I'd call a great title," she commented—Lidia was always willing to give me her opinion on anything, when she didn't like it. "Really, don't you think it's too late to be writing another sci-rom about the Olympians?" And then she smiled brightly and said, "I've got something to say to you, Julie. Have another drink first."

So I knew what was coming right away, and that was the first rejection.

I'd seen this scene building up. Even before she left on that last "research" trip to the West I had begun to suspect that some of that early ardor had cooled, so I wasn't really surprised when she told me, without any further foreplay, "I've met somebody else, Julie."

I said, "I see." I really did see, and so I poured myself a third drink while she told me about it.

"He's a former space pilot, Julius. He's been to Mars and the Moon and everywhere, and, oh, he's such a sweet man. And he's a champion wrestler, too, would you believe it? Of course, he's still married, as it happens. But he's going to talk to his wife about a divorce as soon as the kids are just a little older."

She looked at me challengingly, waiting for me to tell her she was an idiot. I had no intention of saying anything at all, as a matter of fact, but just in case I had she added, "Don't say what you're thinking."

"I wasn't thinking anything," I protested.

She sighed. "You're taking this very well," she told me. She sounded as though that were a great disappointment to her. "Listen, Julius, I didn't plan this. Truly, you'll always be dear to me in a special way. I hope we can always be friends—" I stopped listening around then.

There was plenty more in the same vein, but only the details were a surprise. When she told me our little affair was over I took it calmly enough. I always knew that Lidia had a weakness for the more athletic type. Worse than that, she never respected the kind of writing I do, anyway. She had the usual establishment contempt for science-adventure romances about the future and adventures on alien planets, and what sort of relationship could that be, in the long run?

So I left her with a kiss and a smile, neither of them very sincere, and headed for my editor's office. That was where I got the second rejection. The one that really hurt.

Mark's office was in the old part of London, down by the river. It's an old company, in an old building, and most of the staff are old, too. When the company needs clerks or copy editors it has a habit of picking up tutors whose students have grown up and don't need them anymore, and retraining them. Of course, that's just for the people in the lower echelons. The higher-ups, like Mark himself, are free, salaried executives, with the executive privilege of interminable, winey author-and-editor lunches that don't end until the middle of the afternoon.

I had to wait half an hour to see him; obviously he had been having one of those lunches that day. I didn't mind. I had every confidence that our interview was going to be short, pleasant and remunerative. I knew very well that *An Ass's Olympiad* was one of the best sci-roms I had ever done. Even the title was clever. The book was a satire, with classical overtones—from *The Golden Ass* of the ancient writer, Lucius Apuleius, two thousand years ago or so; I had played off the classic in a comic, adventurous little story about the coming of the real Olympians. I can always tell when a book is going really well and I knew the fans would eat this one up. . . .

When I finally got in to see Marcus he had a glassy, after-lunch look in his eye, and I could see my manuscript on his desk.

I also saw that clipped to it was a red-bordered certificate, and that was the first warning of bad news. The certificate was the censor's verdict, and the red border meant it was an obstat.

Mark didn't keep me in suspense. "We can't publish," he said, pressing his palm on the manuscript. "The censors have turned it down."

"They can't!" I cried, making his old secretary lift his head from his desk in the corner of the room to stare at me.

"They did," Mark said. "I'll read you what the obstat says: '—of a nature which may give offense to the delegation from the Galactic Consortium, usually referred to as the Olympians—' and '—thus endangering the security and tranquility of the Empire—' and, well, basically it just says no. No revisions suggested. Just a complete veto; it's waste paper now, Julie. Forget it."

"But *everybody* is writing about the Olympians!" I yelped.

"Everybody *was*," he corrected. "Now they're getting close, and the censors don't want to take any more chances." He leaned back to rub his eyes, obviously wishing he could be taking a nice nap instead of breaking my heart. Then he added tiredly, "So what do you want to do, Julie? Write us a replacement? It would have to be fast, you understand; the front office doesn't like having contracts outstanding for more than thirty days after due date. And it would have to be good. You're not going to get away with pulling some old reject out of your trunk—I've seen all those already, anyway."

"How the hells do you expect me to write a whole new book in thirty days?" I demanded.

He shrugged, looking sleepier and less interested in my problem than ever. "If you can't, you can't. Then you'll just have to give back the advance," he told me.

I calmed down fast. "Well, no," I said, "there's no question of having to do that. I don't know about finishing it in thirty days, though—"

"I do," he said flatly. He watched me shrug. "Have you got an idea for the new one?"

"Mark," I said patiently, "I've *always* got ideas for new ones. That's what a professional writer is. He's a machine for thinking up ideas. I always have more ideas than I can ever write—"

"Do you?" he insisted.

I surrendered, because if I'd said yes the next thing would have been that he'd want me to tell him what it was. "Not exactly," I admitted.

"Then," he said, "you'd better go wherever you go to get ideas, because, give us the new book or give us back the advance, thirty days is all you've got."

There's an editor for you.

They're all the same. At first they're all honey and sweet talk, with those long alcoholic lunches and blue-sky conversation about million-copy printings while they wheedle you into signing the contract. Then they turn nasty. They want the actual book delivered. When they don't get it, or when the censors say they can't print it, then there isn't any more sweet talk and all the conversation is about how the aediles will escort you to debtors' prison.

So I took his advice. I knew where to go for ideas, and it wasn't in London. No sensible man stays in London in the winter anyway, because of the weather and because it's too full of foreigners. I still can't get used to seeing all those huge, rustic Northmen and dark Hindian and Arabian women in the heart of town. I admit I can be turned on by that red caste mark or by a pair of flashing dark eyes shining through all the robes and veils—I suppose what you imagine is always more exciting than what you can see, especially when what you see is the short, dumpy Britian women like Lidia.

So I made a reservation on the overnight train to Rome, to transfer there to a hydrofoil for Alexandria. I packed with a good heart, not neglecting to take along a floppy sun hat, a flask of insect repellent and—oh, of course—stylus and blank tablets enough to last me for the whole trip, just in case a book idea emerged for me to write. Egypt! Where the world conference on the Olympians was starting its winter session . . . where I would be among the scientists and astronauts who always sparked ideas for new science-adventure romances for me to write . . . where it would be warm. . . .

Where my publisher's aediles would have trouble finding me, in the event that no idea for a new novel came along.

2 · On the Way to the Idea Place

No idea did.

That was disappointing. I do some of my best writing on trains, aircraft, and ships, because there aren't any interruptions and you can't decide to go out for a walk because there isn't any place to walk to. It didn't work this time. All the while the train was slithering across the wet, bare English winter countryside toward the Channel, I sat with my tablet in front of me and the stylus poised to write, but by the time we dipped into the tunnel the tablet was still virgin.

I couldn't fool myself. I was stuck. I mean, *stuck*. Nothing happened in my head that could transform itself into an opening scene for a new sci-rom novel.

It wasn't the first time in my writing career that I'd been stuck with the writer's block. That's a sort of occupational disease for any writer. But this time was the worst. I'd really counted on *An Ass's Olympiad*. I had even calculated that the publication date could be made to coincide with that wonderful day when the Olympians themselves arrived in our solar system, with all sorts of wonderful publicity for my book flowing out of that great event, so the sales should be *immense* . . . and, worse than that, I'd already spent the on-signing advance. All I had left was credit, and not much of that.

Not for the first time, I wondered what it would have been like if I had followed some other career. If I'd stayed in the Civil Service, for instance, as my father had wanted.

Really, I hadn't had much choice. I was born during the Space Tricentennial Year, and my mother told me the first word I said was "Mars." She said there was a little misunderstanding there, because at first she thought I was talking about the god, not the planet, and she and my father had long talks about whether to train me for the priesthood, but by the time I could read she knew I was a space nut. Like a lot of my generation (the ones that read my books), I grew up on spaceflight. I was a teenager when the first pictures came back from the space probe to the Alpha Centauri planet Julia, with its crystal glasses and silver-leafed trees. As a boy I corresponded with another youth who lived in the cavern colonies on the Moon, and I read with delight the shoot-'em-ups about outlaws and aediles chasing each other around the satellites of Jupiter. I wasn't the only kid who grew up space-happy, but I never got over it.

Naturally I became a science-adventure romance writer; what else did I know anything about? As soon as I began to get actual money for my fantasies I quit my job as secretary to one of the imperial legates on the Western continents and went full-time pro.

I prospered at it, too—prospered reasonably, at least—well, to be more exact, I earned a livable, if irregular, income out of the two sci-roms a year I could manage to write, and enough of a surplus to support the habit of dating pretty women like Lidia out of the occasional bonus when one of the books was made into a broadcast drama or a play.

Then along came the message from the Olympians, and the whole face of science-adventure romances was changed forever.

It was the most exciting news in the history of the world, of course. There really *were* other intelligent races out there among the stars of the Galaxy! It had never occurred to me that it would affect me personally, except with joy.

Joy it was, at first. I managed to talk my way into the Alpine radio observatory that had recorded that first message, and I heard it recorded with my own ears:

Dit *squah* dit.
Dit *squee* dit *squah* dit dit.
Dit *squee* dit *squee* dit *squah* dit dit dit.
Dit *squee* dit *squee* dit *squee* dit *squah* wooooo.
Dit *squee* dit *squee* dit *squee* dit *squee* dit *squah* dit dit dit dit dit.

It all looks so simple now, but it took a while before anyone figured out just what this first message from the Olympians was. (Of course, we didn't call them "Olympians" then. We wouldn't call them that now if the priests had anything to say about it, because they think it's almost sacrilegious, but what else are you going to call godlike beings from the heavens? The name caught on right away, and the priests just had to learn to live with it.) It was, in fact, my good friend Flavius Samuelus ben Samuelus who first deciphered it and produced the right answer to transmit back to the senders—the one that, four years later, let the Olympians know we had heard them.

Meanwhile, we all knew this wonderful new truth: We weren't alone in the universe! Excitement exploded. The market for sci-roms boomed. My very next book was *The Radio Gods*, and it sold its head off.

I thought it would go on forever.

It might have, too . . . if it hadn't been for the timorous censors.

I slept through the tunnel—all the tunnels, even the ones through the Alps—and by the time I woke up we were halfway down to Rome.

In spite of the fact that the tablets remained obstinately blank, I felt more cheerful. Lidia was just a fading memory, I still had twenty-nine days to turn in a new sci-rom and Rome, after all, is still Rome! The center of the universe—well, not counting what new lessons in astronomical geography the Olympians might teach us. At least, it's the greatest city in the world. It's the place where all the action is.

By the time I'd sent the porter for breakfast and changed into a clean robe we were there, and I alighted into the great, noisy train shed.

I hadn't been in the city for several years, but Rome doesn't change much. The Tiber still stank. The big new apartment buildings still hid the old ruins until you were almost on top of them, the flies were still awful and the Roman youths still clustered around the train station to sell you guided tours to the Golden House (as though any of them could ever get past the Legion guards!), or sacred amulets, or their sisters.

Because I used to be a secretary on the staff of the Proconsul to the Cherokee Nation I have friends in Rome. Because I hadn't had the good sense to call ahead, none of them were home. I had no choice. I had to take a room in a high-rise inn on the Palatine.

It was ferociously expensive, of course. Everything in Rome is—that's why people like me live in dreary outposts like London—but I figured that by the time the bills came in I would either have found something to satisfy Marcus and get the rest of the advance, or I'd be in so much trouble a few extra debts wouldn't matter.

Having reached that decision, I decided to treat myself to a servant. I picked out a grinning, muscular Sicilian at the rental desk in the lobby, gave him the keys for my luggage and instructed him to take it to my room—and to make me a reservation for the next day's hoverflight to Alexandria.

That's when my luck began to get better.

When the Sicilian came to the wineshop to ask me for further orders he reported, "There's another citizen who's booked on the same flight, Citizen Julius. Would you like to share a compartment with him?"

It's nice when you rent a servant who tries to save you money. I said approvingly, "What kind of a person is he? I don't want to get stuck with some real bore."

"You can see for yourself, Julius. He's in the baths right now. He's a Judaean. His name is Flavius Samuelus."

Five minutes later I had my clothes off and a sheet wrapped around me, and I was in the tepidarium, peering around at every body there.

I picked Sam out at once. He was stretched out with his eyes closed while a masseur pummeled his fat old flesh. I climbed onto the slab next to his without speaking. When he groaned and rolled over, opening his eyes, I said, "Hello, Sam."

It took him a moment to recognize me; he didn't have his glasses in. But when he squinted hard enough his face broke out into a grin. "Julie!" he cried. "Small world! It's good to see you again!"

And he reached out to clasp fists-over-elbows, really welcoming, just as I had expected; because one of the things I like best about Flavius Samuelus is that he likes me.

One of the other things I like best about Sam is that, although he is a competitor, he is also an undepletable natural resource. He writes sci-roms himself. He does more than that. He has helped me with the science part of my own sci-roms any number of times, and it had crossed my mind as soon as I heard the Sicilian say his name that he might be just what I wanted in the present emergency.

Sam is at least seventy years old. His head is hairless. There's a huge, brown age spot on the top of his scalp. His throat hangs in a pouch of flesh, and his eyelids sag. But you'd never guess any of that if you were simply talking to him on the phone. He has the quick, chirpy voice of a twenty-year-old, and the mind of one, too—of an extraordinarily *bright* twenty-year-old. He gets enthusiastic.

That complicates things, because Sam's brain works faster than it ought to. Sometimes that makes him hard to talk to, because he's usually three or four exchanges ahead of most people. So the next thing he says to you is as likely as not to be the response to some question that you are inevitably going to ask, but haven't yet thought of.

It is an unpleasant fact of life that Sam's sci-roms sell better than mine do. It is a tribute to Sam's personality that I don't hate him for it. He has an unfair advantage over the rest of us, since he is a professional astronomer himself. He only writes sci-roms for fun, in his spare time, of which he doesn't have a whole lot. Most of his working hours are spent running a space probe of his own, the one that circles the Epsilon Eridani planet, Dione. I can stand his success (and, admit it!, his talent) because he is generous with his ideas. As soon as we had agreed to share the hoverflight compartment I put it to him directly. Well, almost directly; I said, "Sam, I've been wondering about something. When the Olympians get here, what is it going to mean to us?"

He was the right person to ask, of course; Sam knew more about the Olympians than anyone alive. But he was the wrong person to expect a direct answer from. He rose up, clutching his robe around him. He waved away the masseur and looked at me in friendly amusement, out of those bright black eyes under the flyaway eyebrows and the drooping lids. "Why, do you need a new sci-rom plot right now?" he asked.

"Hells," I said ruefully, and decided to come clean. "It wouldn't be the first time I asked you, Sam. Only this time I *really* need it." And I told him the story of the novel the censors obstatted and the editor who was after a quick replacement—or my blood, choice of one.

He nibbled thoughtfully at the knuckle of his thumb. "What was this novel of yours about?" he asked curiously.

"It was a satire, Sam. *An Ass's Olympiad.* About the Olympians coming down to Earth in a matter transporter, only there's a mixup in the transmission and one of them accidentally gets turned into an ass. It's got some funny bits in it."

"It sure has, Julie. Has had for a couple dozen centuries."

"Well, I didn't say it was altogether *original,* only—"

He was shaking his head. "I thought you were smarter than that, Julie. What did you expect the censors to do, jeopardize the most important event in human history for the sake of a dumb sci-rom?"

"It's not a dumb—"

"It's dumb to risk offending them," he said, overruling me firmly. "Best to be safe and not write about them at all."

"But everybody's been doing it!"

"Nobody's been turning them into asses," he pointed out. "Julie, there's a limit to sci-rom speculation. When you write about the Olympians you're right up at that limit. Any speculation about them can be enough reason for them to pull out of the meeting entirely, and we might never get a chance like this again."

"They wouldn't—"

"Ah, Julie," he said, disgusted, "you don't have any idea what they would or wouldn't do. The censors made the right decision. Who knows what the Olympians are going to be like?"

"You do," I told him.

He laughed. There was an uneasy sound to it, though. "I wish I did. About the only thing we do know is that they don't appear to just any old intelligent race; they have moral standards. We don't have any idea what those standards are, really. I don't know what your book says, but maybe you speculated that the Olympians were bringing us all kinds of new things—a cure for cancer, new psychedelic drugs, even eternal life—"

"What kind of psychedelic drugs might they bring, exactly?" I asked.

"Down, boy! I'm telling you *not* to think about that kind of idea. The point is that whatever you imagined might easily turn out to be the most repulsive and immoral thing the Olympians can think of. The stakes are too high. This is a once-only chance. We can't let it go sour."

"But I need a *story*," I wailed.

"Well, yes," he admitted, "I suppose you do. Let me think about it. Let's get cleaned up and get out of here."

While we were in the hot drench, while we were dressing, while we were eating a light lunch, Sam chattered on about the forthcoming conference in Alexandria. I was pleased to listen. Apart from the fact that everything he said was interesting, I began to feel hopeful about actually producing a book for Mark. If anybody could help me, Sam could, and he was a problem addict. He couldn't resist a challenge.

That was undoubtedly why he was the first to puzzle out the Olympians' interminably repeated *squees* and *squahs*. If you simply took the "dit" to be "1," and the *squee* to be "+" and the *squah* to be "=," then

Dit *squee* dit *squah* dit dit

simply came out as

$1 + 1 = 2$

That was easy enough. It didn't take a super-brain like Sam's to substitute our terms for theirs and reveal the message to be simple arithmetic—except for the mysterious "wooooo":

dit *squee* dit *squee* dit *squee* *dit squah* wooooo.

What was the "wooooo" supposed to mean? A special convention to represent the number four?

Sam knew right away, of course. As soon as he heard the message he telegraphed the solution from his library in Padua:

"The message calls for an answer. 'Wooooo' means question mark. The answer is four."

And so the reply to the stars was transmitted on its way: dit *squee* dit *squee* dit *squee* dit *squah* dit dit dit dit.

The human race had turned in its test paper in the entrance examination, and the slow process of establishing communication had begun.

It took four years before the Olympians responded. Obviously, they weren't nearby. Also obviously, they weren't simple folk like ourselves, sending out radio messages from a planet of a star two light-years away, because there wasn't any star there; the reply came from a point in space where none of our telescopes or probes had found anything at all.

By then Sam was deeply involved. He was the first to point out that the star folk had undoubtedly chosen to send a weak signal, because they wanted to be sure our technology was reasonably well developed before we tried to answer. He was one of the impatient ones who talked the collegium authorities into beginning transmission of all sorts of mathematical formulae, and then simple word relationships, to start sending *something* to the Olympians while we waited for radio waves to creep to wherever they were and back with an answer.

Sam wasn't the only one, of course. He wasn't even the principal investigator when we got into the hard work of developing a common vocabulary. There were better specialists than Sam at linguistics and cryptanalysis.

But it was Sam who first noticed, early on, that the response time to our messages was getting shorter. Meaning that the Olympians were on their way toward us.

By then they'd begun sending picture mosaics. They came in as strings of dits and dahs, 550,564 bits long. Someone quickly figured out that that was the square of 742, and when they displayed the string as a square matrix, black cells for the dits and white ones for the dahs, the image of the first Olympian leaped out.

Everybody remembers that picture. Everyone on Earth saw it, except for the totally blind—it was on every broadcast screen and news journal in the world—and even the blind listened to the anatomical descriptions every commentator supplied. Two tails. A fleshy, beardlike thing that hung down from its chin. Four legs. A ruff of spikes down what seemed to be the backbone. Eyes set wide apart on bulges from the cheekbones.

That first Olympian was not at all pretty, but it was definitely *alien*.

When the next string turned out very similar to the first, it was Sam who saw at once that it was simply a slightly rotated view of the same being. The Olympians took forty-one pictures to give us the complete likeness of that first one in the round. . . .

Then they began sending pictures of the others.

It had never occurred to anyone, not even Sam, that we would be dealing not with one super-race, but with at least twenty-two of them. There were that many separate forms of alien beings, and each one uglier and more strange than the one before.

That was one of the reasons the priests didn't like calling them "Olympians." We're pretty ecumenical about our gods, but none of them looked anything like any of *those,* and some of the older priests never stopped muttering about blasphemy.

Halfway through the third course of our lunch and the second flask of wine Sam broke off his description of the latest communiqué from the Olympians—they'd been acknowledging receipt of our transmissions about Earthly history—to lift his head and grin at me.

"Got it," he said.

I turned and blinked at him. Actually, I hadn't been paying a lot of attention to his monologue because I had been keeping my eye on the pretty Kievan waitress. She had attracted my attention because—well, I mean, *after* attracting my attention because of her extremely well developed figure and the sparsity of clothing to conceal it—because she was wearing a gold citizen's amulet around her neck. She wasn't a slave. That made her more intriguing. I can't ever get really interested in slave women, because it isn't sporting, but I had got quite interested in this one.

"Are you listening to me?" Sam demanded testily.

"Of course I am. What have you got?"

"I've got the answer to your problem," he beamed. "Not just a sci-rom novel plot. A whole new *kind* of sci-rom! Why don't you write a book about what it will be like if the Olympians *don't* come?"

I love the way half of Sam's brain works at questions while the other half is doing something completely different, but I can't always follow what comes out of it. "I don't see what you mean. If I write about the Olympians not coming, isn't that just as bad as if I write about them doing it?"

"No, no," he snapped. "Listen to what I say! Leave the Olympians out entirely. Just write about a future that might happen, but won't."

The waitress was hovering over us, picking up used plates. I was conscious of her listening as I responded with dignity. "Sam, that's not my style. My sci-roms may not sell as well as yours do, but I've got just as much integrity. I never write anything that I don't believe is at least possible."

"Julie, get your mind off your gonads—" so he hadn't missed the attention I was giving the girl "—and use that pitifully tiny brain of yours. I'm talking about something that *could* be possible, in some alternative future, if you see what I mean."

I didn't see at all. "What's an 'alternative future'?"

"It's a future that *might* happen, but *won't*," he explained. "Like if the Olympians don't come to see us."

I shook my head, puzzled. "But we already know they're coming," I pointed out.

"But suppose they weren't! Suppose they hadn't contacted us years ago."

"But they did," I said, trying to straighten out his thinking on the subject. He only sighed.

"I see I'm not getting through to you," he said, pulling his robe around him and getting to his feet. "Get on with your waitress. I've got some messages to send. I'll see you on the ship."

Well, for one reason or another I didn't get anywhere with the Kievan waitress. She said she was married, happily and monogamously. Well, I couldn't see why any lawful, free husband would have his wife out working at a job like that, but I was surprised she didn't show more interest in one of my lineage—

I'd better explain about that.

You see, my family has a claim to fame. Genealogists say that we are descended from the line of Julius Caesar himself.

I mention that claim myself, sometimes, though usually only when I've been drinking—I suppose it is one of the reasons that Lidia, always a snob, took up with me in the first place. It isn't a serious matter. After all, Julius Caesar died more than two thousand years ago. There have been sixty or seventy generations since then, not to mention the fact that, although Ancestor Julius certainly left a lot of children behind him, none of them happened to be born to a woman he happened to be married to. I don't even look very Roman. There must have been a Northman or two in the line, because I'm tall and fair-haired, which no respectable Roman ever was.

Still, even if I'm not exactly the lawful heir to the divine Julius, I at least come of a pretty ancient and distinguished line. You would have thought a mere waitress would have taken that into account before turning me down.

She hadn't, though. When I woke up the next morning—alone—Sam was gone from the inn, although the skip-ship for Alexandria wasn't due to sail until late evening.

I didn't see him all day. I didn't look for him very hard, because I woke up feeling a little ashamed of myself. Why should a grown man, a celebrated author of more than forty bestselling (well, reasonably *well*-selling) sci-roms, depend on somebody else for his ideas?

So I turned my baggage over to the servant, checked out of the inn and took the underground to the Library of Rome.

Rome isn't only the imperial capital of the world, it's the scientific capital, too. The big old telescopes out on the hills aren't much use anymore, because the lights from the city spoil their night viewing, and anyway the big optical telescopes are all out in space now. Still, they were where Galileus detected the first extra-solar planet and Tychus made his famous spectrographs of the last great supernova in our own galaxy, only a couple of dozen years after the first spaceflight. The scientific tradition survives. Rome is still the headquarters of the Collegium of Sciences.

That's why the Library of Rome is so great for someone like me. They have direct access to the Collegium database, and you don't even have to pay transmission tolls. I signed myself in, laid out my tablets and stylus on the desk they assigned me and began calling up files.

Somewhere there had to be an idea for a science-adventure romance no one had written yet. . . .

Somewhere there no doubt was, but I couldn't find it. Usually you can get a lot of help from a smart research librarian, but it seemed they'd put on a lot of new people in the Library of Rome—Iberians, mostly; reduced to slave status because they'd taken part in last year's Lusitanian uprising. There were so many Iberians on the market for a while that they depressed the price. I would have bought some as a speculation, knowing that the price would go up—after all, there aren't that many uprisings and the demand for slaves never stops. But I was temporarily short of capital, and besides you have to feed them. If the ones at the Library of Rome were a fair sample, they were no bargains anyway.

I gave up. The weather had improved enough to make a stroll around town attractive, and so I wandered toward the Ostia monorail.

Rome was busy, as always. There was a bullfight going on in the Coliseum and racing at the Circus Maximus. Tourist buses were jamming the narrow streets. A long religious procession was circling the Pantheon, but I didn't get close enough to see which particular gods were being honored today. I don't like crowds. Especially Roman crowds, because there are even more foreigners in Rome than in London, Africs and Hinds, Hans, and Northmen—every race on the face of the Earth sends its tourists to visit the Imperial City. And Rome obliges with spectacles. I paused at one of them, for the changing of the guard at the Golden House. Of course, the Caesar and his wife were nowhere to be seen—off on one of their endless ceremonial tours of the dominions, no doubt, or at least opening a new supermarket somewhere. But the Algonkian family standing in front of me were thrilled as the honor Legions marched and countermarched their standards around the palace. I remembered enough Cherokee to ask the Algonkians where they were from, but the languages aren't really very close and the man's Cherokee was even worse than mine. We just smiled at each other.

As soon as the Legions were out of the way I headed for the train.

I knew in the back of my mind that I should have been worrying about my financial position. The clock was running on my thirty days of grace. I didn't, though. I was buoyed up by a feeling of confidence. Confidence in my good friend Flavius Samuelus who, I knew—no matter what he was doing with most of his brain—was still cogitating an idea for me with some part of it.

It did not occur to me that even Sam had limitations. Or that something more important than my own problems was taking up so much of his attention that he didn't have much left for me.

I didn't see Sam come onto the skip-ship, and I didn't see him in our compartment. Even when the ship's fans began to rumble and we slid down the ways into the Tyrrhenian Sea he wasn't there. I dozed off, beginning to worry that he might have missed the boat; but late that night, already asleep, I half woke, just long enough to hear him stumbling in. "I've been on the bridge," he said when I muttered something. "Go back to sleep. I'll see you in the morning."

When I woke, I thought it might have been a dream, because he was up and gone before me. But his bed had been slept in, however briefly, and the cabin steward reassured me when he brought my morning wine. Yes, Citizen Flavius Samuelus was certainly on the hover. He was in the captain's own quarters, as a matter of fact, although what he was doing there the steward could not say.

I spent the morning relaxing on the deck of the hover, soaking in the sun. The ship wasn't exactly a hover anymore. We had transited the Sicilian Straits during the night and now, out in the open Mediterranean, the captain had lowered the stilts, pulled up the hover skirts and extended the screws. We were hydrofoiling across the sea at easily a hundred miles an hour. It was a smooth, relaxing ride; the vanes that supported us were twenty feet under the surface of the water, and so there was no wave action to bounce us around.

Lying on my back and squinting up at the warm southern sky, I could see a three-winged airliner rise up from the horizon behind us and gradually overtake us, to disappear ahead of our bows. The plane wasn't going much faster than we were—and we had all the comfort, while they were paying twice as much for passage.

I opened my eyes all the way when I caught a glimpse of someone standing beside me. In fact, I sat up quickly, because it was Sam. He looked as though he hadn't had much sleep, and he was holding his floppy sunhat with one hand against the wind of our passage. "Where've you been?" I asked.

"Haven't you been watching the news?" he asked. I shook my head. "The transmissions from the Olympians have stopped," he told me.

I opened my eyes really wide at that, because it was an unpleasant surprise. Still, Sam didn't seem that upset. Displeased, yes. Maybe even a little concerned, but not as shaken up as I was prepared to feel. "It's probably nothing," he said. "It could be just interference from the Sun. It's in Sagittarius now, so it's pretty much between us and them. There's been trouble with static for a couple of days now."

I ventured, "So the transmissions will start up again pretty soon?"

He shrugged and waved to the deck steward for one of those hot decoctions Judaeans like. When he spoke it was on a different topic. "I don't think I made you understand what I meant yesterday," he said. "Let me see if I can explain what I meant by an alternate world. You remember your history? How Fornius Vello conquered the Mayans and Romanized the Western Continents six or seven hundred years ago? Well, suppose he hadn't."

"But he did, Sam."

"I know he did," Sam said patiently. "I'm saying *suppose*. Suppose the Legions had been defeated at the battle of Tehultapec."

I laughed. I was sure he was joking. "The Legions? Defeated? But the Legions have never been defeated."

"That's not true," Sam said in reproof. He hates it when people don't get their facts straight. "Remember Varus."

"Oh, hells, Sam, that was ancient history! When was it, two thousand years ago? In the time of Augustus Caesar? And it was only a temporary defeat, anyway. The Emperor Drusus got the eagles back." And got all of Gaul for the Empire, too. That was one of the first big trans-Alpine conquests. The Gauls are about as Roman as you can get these days, especially when it comes to drinking wine.

He shook his head. "Suppose Fornius Vello had had a 'temporary' defeat, then."

I tried to follow his argument, but it wasn't easy. "What difference would that have made? Sooner or later the Legions would have conquered. They always have, you know."

"That's true," he said reasonably, "but if that particular conquest hadn't happened *then*, the whole course of history would have been different. We wouldn't have had the great westward migrations to fill up those empty continents. The Hans and the Hinds wouldn't have been surrounded on both sides, so they might still be independent nations. It would have been a different world. Do you see what I'm driving at? That's what I mean by an 'alternate world'—one that might have happened, but didn't."

I tried to be polite to him. "Sam," I said, "you've just described the difference between a sci-rom and a fantasy. I don't do fantasy. Besides," I went on, not wanting to hurt his feelings, "I don't see how different things would have been, really. I can't believe the world would be changed enough to build a sci-rom plot on."

He gazed blankly at me for a moment, then turned and looked out to sea. Then, without transition, he said, "There's one funny thing. The Martian colonies aren't getting a transmission, either. And they aren't occluded by the Sun."

I frowned. "What does that mean, Sam?"

He shook his head. "I wish I knew," he said.

3 · In Old Alexandria

The Pharos was bright in the sunset light as we came into the port of Alexandria. We were on hover again, at slow speeds, and the chop at the breakwater bumped us around. But once we got to the inner harbor the water was calm.

Sam had spent the afternoon back in the captain's quarters, keeping in contact with the Collegium of Sciences, but he showed up as we moored. He saw me gazing toward the rental desk on the dock but shook his head. "Don't bother with a rental, Julie," he ordered. "Let my niece's servants take your baggage. We're staying with her."

That was good news. Inn rooms in Alexandria are almost as pricey as Rome's. I thanked him, but he didn't even listen. He turned our bags over to a porter from his niece's domicile, a little Arabian who was a lot stronger than he looked, and disappeared toward the Hall of the Egyptian Senate-Inferior, where the conference was going to be held.

I hailed a three-wheeler and gave the driver the address of Sam's niece.

No matter what the Egyptians think, Alexandria is a dirty little town. The Choctaws have a bigger capital, and the Kievans have a cleaner one. Also Alexandria's famous library is a joke. After my (one would like to believe) ancestor Julius Caesar let it burn to the ground, the Egyptians did build it up again. But it is so old-fashioned that there's nothing in it but books.

The home of Sam's niece was in a particularly run-down section of that run-down town, only a few streets from the harborside. You could hear the noise of the cargo winches from the docks, but you couldn't hear them very well because of the noise of the streets themselves, thick with goods vans and drivers cursing each other as they jockeyed around the narrow corners. The house itself was bigger than I had expected. But, at least from the outside, that was all you could say for it. It was faced with cheap Egyptian stucco rather than marble, and right next door to it was a slave-rental barracks.

At least, I reminded myself, it was free. I kicked at the door and shouted for the butler.

It wasn't the butler who opened it for me. It was Sam's niece herself, and she was a nice surprise. She was almost as tall as I was and just as fair. Besides, she was young and very good-looking. "You must be Julius," she said. "I am Rachel, niece of Citizen Flavius Samuelus ben Samuelus, and I welcome you to my home."

I kissed her hand. It's a Kievan custom that I like, especially with pretty girls I don't yet know well, but hope to. "You don't look Judaean," I told her.

"You don't look like a sci-rom hack," she replied. Her voice was less chilling than her words, but not much. "Uncle Sam isn't here, and I'm afraid I've got work I must do. Basilius will show you to your rooms and offer you some refreshment."

I usually make a better first impression on young women. I usually work at it more carefully, but she had taken me by surprise. I had more or less expected that Sam's niece would look more or less like Sam, except probably for the baldness and the wrinkled face. I could not have been more wrong.

I had been wrong about the house, too. It was a big one. There had to be well over a dozen rooms, not counting servants' quarters, and the atrium was covered with one of those partly reflecting films that keep the worst of the heat out.

The famous Egyptian sun was directly overhead when Basilius, Rachel's butler, showed me my rooms. They were pleasingly bright and airy, but Basilius suggested I might enjoy being outside. He was right. He brought wine and fruits to me in the atrium, a pleasant bench by a fountain. Through the film the sun looked only pale and pleasant instead of deadly hot. The fruit was fresh, too—pineapples from Lebanon, oranges from Judaea, apples that must have come all the way from somewhere in Gaul. The only thing wrong that I could see was that Rachel herself stayed in her rooms, so I didn't have a chance to try to put myself in a better light with her.

She had left instructions for my comfort, though. Basilius clapped his hands and another servant appeared, bearing stylus and tablets in case I should decide to work. I was surprised to see that both Basilius and the other one were Africs; they don't usually get into political trouble, or trouble with the aediles of any kind, so not many of them are slaves.

The fountain was a Cupid statue. In some circumstances I would have thought of that as a good sign, but here it didn't seem to mean anything. Cupid's nose was chipped, and the fountain was obviously older than Rachel was. I thought of just staying there until Rachel came out, but when I asked Basilius when that would be he gave me a look of delicate patronizing. "Citizeness Rachel works through the afternoon, Citizen Julius," he informed me.

"Oh? And what does she work at?"

"Citizeness Rachel is a famous historian," he said. "She often works straight through until bedtime. But for you and her uncle, of course, dinner will be served at your convenience."

He was quite an obliging fellow. "Thank you, Basilius," I said. "I believe I'll go out for a few hours myself." And then, curiously, as he turned politely to go, I said, "You don't look like a very dangerous criminal. If you don't mind my asking, what were you enslaved for?"

"Oh, not for anything violent, Citizen Julius," he assured me. "Just for debts."

I found my way to the Hall of the Egyptian Senate-Inferior easily enough. There was a lot of traffic going that way, because it is, after all, one of the sights of Alexandria.

The Senate-Inferior wasn't in session at the time. There was no reason it should have been, of course, because what did the Egyptians need a Senate of any kind for? The time when they'd made any significant decisions for themselves was many centuries past.

They'd spread themselves for the conference, though. The Senate Temple had niches for at least half a hundred gods. There were the customary figures of Amon-Ra and Jupiter and all the other main figures of the pantheon, of course, but for the sake of the visitors they had installed Ahura-Mazda, Yahweh, Freya, Quetzalcoatl and at least a dozen I didn't recognize at all. They were all decorated with fresh sacrifices of flowers and fruits, showing that the tourists, if not the astronomers—and probably the astronomers as well—were taking no chances in getting communications with the Olympians restored. Scientists are an agnostic lot, of course—well, most educated people are, aren't they? But even an agnostic will risk a piece of fruit to placate a god, just on the chance he's wrong.

Outside the hall hucksters were already putting up their stands, although the first session wouldn't begin for another day. I bought some dates from one of them and wandered around, eating dates and studying the marble frieze on the wall of the Senate. It showed the rippling fields of corn, wheat, and potatoes that had made Egypt the breadbasket of the Empire for two thousand years. It didn't show anything about the Olympians, of course. Space is not a subject that interests the Egyptians a lot. They prefer to look back on their glorious (they *say* it's glorious) past; and there would have been no point in having the conference on the Olympians there at all, except who wants to go to some northern city in December?

Inside, the great hall was empty, except for slaves arranging seat cushions and cuspidors for the participants. The exhibit halls were noisy with workers setting up displays, but they didn't want people dropping in to bother them, and the participants' lounges were dark.

I was lucky enough to find the media room open. It was always good for a free glass of wine, and besides I wanted to know where everyone was. The slave in charge couldn't tell me. "There's supposed to be a private executive meeting somewhere, that's all I know—and there's all these journalists looking for someone to interview." And then, peering over my shoulder as I signed in: "Oh, you're the fellow that writes the sci-roms, aren't you? Well, maybe one of the journalists would settle for you."

It wasn't the most flattering invitation I'd ever had. Still, I didn't say no. Marcus is always after me to do publicity gigs whenever I get the chance, because he thinks it sells books, and it was worthwhile trying to please Marcus just then.

The journalist wasn't much pleased, though. They'd set up a couple of studios in the basement of the Senate, and when I found the one I was directed to the interviewer was fussing over his hairdo in front of a mirror. A couple of technicians were lounging in front of the tube, watching a broadcast comedy series. When I introduced myself the interviewer took his eyes off his own image long enough to cast a doubtful look in my direction.

"You're not a real astronomer," he told me.

I shrugged. I couldn't deny it.

"Still," he grumbled, "I'd better get *some* kind of a spot for the late news. All right. Sit over there, and try to sound as if you know what you're talking about." Then he began telling the technical crew what to do.

That was a strange thing. I'd already noticed that the technicians wore citizens' gold. The interviewer didn't. But he was the one who was giving them orders.

I didn't approve of that at all. I don't like big commercial outfits that put slaves in positions of authority over free citizens. It's a bad practice. Jobs like tutors, college professors, doctors, and so on are fine; slaves can do them as well as a citizen, and usually a lot cheaper. But there's a moral issue involved here. A slave must have a master. Otherwise, how can you call him a slave? And when you let the slave *be* the master, even in something as trivial as a broadcasting studio, you strike at the foundations of society.

The other thing is that it isn't fair competition. There are free citizens who need those jobs. We had some of that in my own line of work a few years ago. There were two or three slave authors turning out adventure novels, but the rest of us got together and put a stop to it—especially after Marcus bought one of them to use as a sub-editor. Not one citizen writer would work with her. Mark finally had to put her into the publicity department, where she couldn't do any harm.

So I started the interview with a chip on my shoulder, and his first question made it worse. He plunged right in: "When you're pounding out those sci-roms of yours, do you make any effort to keep in touch with scientific reality? Do you know, for instance, that the Olympians have stopped transmitting?"

I scowled at him, regardless of the cameras. "Science-adventure romances are *about* scientific reality. And the Olympians haven't 'stopped,' as you put it. There's just been a technical hitch of some kind, probably caused by radio interference from our own Sun. As I said in my earlier romance, *The Radio Gods,* electromagnetic impulses are susceptible to—"

He cut me off. "It's been—" he glanced at his watch "—twenty-nine hours since they stopped. That doesn't sound like just a technical hitch."

"Of course it is. There's no reason for them to 'stop.' We've already demonstrated to them that we're truly civilized, first because we're technological, second because we don't fight wars anymore—that was cleared up in the first year. As I said in my roman, *The Radio Gods—*"

He gave me a pained look, then turned and winked into the camera. "You can't keep a hack from plugging his books, can you?" he remarked humorously. "But it looks like he doesn't want to use that wild imagination unless he gets paid for it. All I'm asking him for is a guess at why the Olympians don't want to talk to us anymore, and all he gives me is commercials."

As though there were any other reason to do interviews! "Look here," I said sharply, "if you can't be courteous when you speak to a citizen I'm not prepared to go on with this conversation at all."

"So be it, pal," he said, icy cold. He turned to the technical crew. "Stop the cameras," he ordered. "We're going back to the studio. This is a waste of time." And we parted on terms of mutual dislike, and once again I had done something that my editor would have been glad to kill me for.

————

That night at dinner, Sam was no comfort. "He's an unpleasant man, sure," he told me, "but the trouble is, I'm afraid he's right."

"They've really *stopped?*"

Sam shrugged. "We're not in line with the Sun anymore, so that's definitely not the reason. Damn. I was hoping it would be."

"I'm sorry about that, Uncle Sam," Rachel said gently. She was wearing a simple white robe, Hannish silk by the look of it, with no decorations at all. It really looked good on her. I didn't think there was anything under it except for some very well formed female flesh.

"I'm sorry, too," he grumbled. His concerns didn't affect his appetite, though. He was ladling in the first course—a sort of chicken soup, with bits of a kind of pastry floating in it—and, for that matter, so was I. Whatever Rachel's faults might be, she had a good cook. It was plain home cooking, none of your partridge-in-a-rabbit-inside-a-boar kind of thing, but well prepared and expertly served by her butler, Basilius. "Anyway," Sam said, mopping up the last of the broth, "I've figured it out."

"Why the Olympians stopped?" I asked, to encourage him to go on with the revelation.

"No, no! I mean about your romance, Julie. My alternate world idea. If you don't want to write about a different *future,* how about a different *now?*"

I didn't get a chance to ask him what he was talking about, because Rachel beat me to it. "There's only one 'now,' Sam, dear," she pointed out. I couldn't have said it better myself.

Sam groaned. "Not you, too, honey," he complained. "I'm talking about a new kind of sci-rom."

"I don't read many sci-roms," she apologized, in the tone that isn't an apology at all.

He ignored that. "You're a historian, aren't you?" She didn't bother to confirm it; obviously, it was the thing she was that shaped her life. "So what if history had gone a different way?"

He beamed at us as happily as though he had said something that made sense. Neither of us beamed back. Rachel pointed out the flaw in his remark. "It didn't, though," she told him.

"I said *suppose!* This isn't the only possible 'now,' it's just the one that happened to occur! There could have been a million different ones. Look at all the events in the past that could have gone a different way. Suppose Annius Publius hadn't discovered the Western Continents in City Year 1820. Suppose Caesar Publius Terminus hadn't decreed the development of a space program in 2122. Don't you see what I'm driving at? What kind of a world would we be living in now if those things hadn't happened?"

Rachel opened her mouth to speak, but she was saved by the butler. He appeared in the doorway with a look of silent appeal. When she excused herself to see what was needed in the kitchen, that left it up to me. "I never wrote anything like that, Sam," I told him. "I don't know anybody else who did, either."

"That's exactly what I'm driving at! It would be something completely *new* in sci-roms. Don't you want to pioneer a whole new kind of story?"

Out of the wisdom of experience, I told him, "Pioneers don't make any money, Sam." He scowled at me. "You could write it yourself," I suggested.

That just changed the annoyance to gloom. "I wish I could. But until this business with the Olympians is cleared up I'm not going to have much time for sci-roms. No, it's up to you, Julie."

272 | PLATINUM POHL

Then Rachel came back in, looking pleased with herself, followed by Basilius bearing a huge silver platter containing the main course.

Sam cheered up at once. So did I. The main dish was a whole roasted baby kid, and I realized that the reason Rachel had been called into the kitchen was so that she could weave a garland of flowers around its tiny baby horn buds herself. The maidservant followed with a pitcher of wine, replenishing all our goblets. All in all, we were busy enough eating to stop any conversation but compliments on the food.

Then Sam looked at his watch. "Great dinner, Rachel," he told his niece, "but I've got to get back. What about it?"

"What about what?" she asked.

"About helping poor Julie with some historical turning points he can use in a story?"

He hadn't listened to a word I'd said. I didn't have to say so, because Rachel was looking concerned. She said apologetically, "I don't know anything about those periods you were talking about—Publius Terminus and so on. My specialty is the immediate post-Augustan period, when the Senate came back to power."

"Fine," he said, pleased with himself and showing it. "That's as good a period as any. Think how different things might be now if some little event then had gone in a different way. Say, if Augustus hadn't married the Lady Livia and adopted her son Drusus to succeed him." He turned to me, encouraging me to take fire from his spark of inspiration. "I'm sure you see the possibilities, Julie! Tell you what you should do. The night's young yet; take Rachel out dancing or something; have a few drinks; listen to her talk. What's wrong with that? You two young people ought to be having fun, anyway!"

That was definitely the most intelligent thing intelligent Sam had said in days.

So I thought, anyway, and Rachel was a good enough niece to heed her uncle's advice. Because I was a stranger in town, I had to let her pick the place. After the first couple she mentioned I realized that she was tactfully trying to spare my pocketbook. I couldn't allow that. After all, a night on the town with Rachel was probably cheaper, and anyway a whole lot more interesting, than the cost of an inn and meals.

We settled on a place right on the harborside, out toward the breakwater. It was a revolving nightclub on top of an inn built along the style of one of the old Pyramids. As the room slowly turned we saw the lights of the city of Alexandria, the shipping in the harbor, then the wide sea itself, its gentle waves reflecting starlight.

I was prepared to forget the whole idea of "alternate worlds," but Rachel was more dutiful than that. After the first dance, she said, "I think I can help you. There was something that happened in Drusus's reign—"

"Do we have to talk about that?" I asked, refilling her glass.

"But Uncle Sam said we should. I thought you wanted to try a new kind of sci-rom."

"No, that's your uncle that wants that. See, there's a bit of a problem here. It's true that editors are always begging for something new and different, but if you're dumb enough to try to give it to them they don't recognize it. When they ask for 'different,' what they mean is something right down the good old 'different' groove."

"I think," she informed me, with the certainty of an oracle and a lot less confusion of style, "that when my uncle has an idea, it's usually a good one." I didn't want to argue with her; I didn't even disagree, at least usually. I let her talk. "You see," she said, "my specialty is the transfer of power throughout early Roman history. What I'm studying right now is the Judaean Diaspora, after Drusus's reign. You know what happened then, I suppose?"

Actually, I did—hazily. "That was the year of the Judaean rebellion, wasn't it?"

She nodded. She looked very pretty when she nodded, her fair hair moving gracefully and her eyes sparkling. "You see, that was a great tragedy for the Judaeans, and, just as my uncle said, it needn't have happened. If Procurator Tiberius had lived, it wouldn't."

I coughed. "I'm not sure I know who Tiberius was," I said apologetically.

"He was the Procurator of Judaea, and a very good one. He was just and fair. He was the brother of the Emperor Drusus—the one my uncle was talking about, Livia's son, the adopted heir of Caesar Augustus. The one who restored the power of the Senate after Augustus had appropriated most of it for himself. Anyway, Tiberius was the best governor the Judaeans ever had, just as Drusus was the best emperor. Tiberius died just a year before the rebellion—ate some spoiled figs, they say, although it might have been his wife that did it—she was Julia, the daughter of Augustus by his first wife—"

I signaled distress. "I'm getting a little confused by all these names," I admitted.

"Well, the important one to remember is Tiberius, and you know who he was. If he had lived the rebellion probably wouldn't have happened. Then there wouldn't have been a Diaspora."

"I see," I said. "Would you like another dance?"

She frowned at me, then smiled. "Maybe that's not such an interesting subject— unless you're a Judaean, anyway," she said. "All right, let's dance."

That was the best idea yet. It gave me a chance to confirm with my fingers what my eyes, ears, and nose had already told me; this was a very attractive young woman. She had insisted on changing, but fortunately the new gown was as soft and clinging as the old, and the palms of my hands rejoiced in the tactile pleasures of her back and arm. I whispered, "I'm sorry if I sound stupid. I really don't know a whole lot about early history—you know, the first thousand years or so after the Founding of the City."

She didn't bother to point out that she did. She moved with me to the music, very enjoyably, then she straightened up. "I've got a different idea," she announced. "Let's go back to the booth." And she was already telling it to me as we left the dance floor: "Let's talk about your own ancestor, Julius Caesar. He conquered Egypt, right here in Alexandria. But suppose the Egyptians had defeated him instead, as they very nearly did?"

I was paying close attention now—obviously she had been interested enough in me to ask Sam some questions! "They couldn't have," I told her. "Julius never lost a war. Anyway—" I discovered to my surprise that I was beginning to take Sam's nutty idea seriously "—that would be a really hard one to write, wouldn't it? If the Legions had been defeated, it would have changed the whole world. Can you imagine a world that isn't Roman?"

She said sweetly, "No, but that's more your job than mine, isn't it?"

I shook my head. "It's too bizarre," I complained. "I couldn't make the readers believe it."

"You could try, Julius," she told me. "You see, there's an interesting possibility there. Drusus almost didn't live to become Emperor. He was severely wounded in a war in Gaul, while Augustus was still alive. Tiberius—you remember Tiberius—"

"Yes, yes, his brother. The one you like. The one he made Procurator of Judaea."

"That's the one. Well, Tiberius rode day and night to bring Drusus the best doctors in Rome. He almost didn't make it. They barely pulled Drusus through."

"Yes?" I said encouragingly. "And what then?"

She looked uncertain. "Well, I don't know what then."

I poured some more wine. "I guess I could figure out some kind of speculative idea," I said, ruminating. "Especially if you would help me with some of the details. I suppose Tiberius would have become Emperor instead of Drusus. You say he was a good man; so probably he would have done more or less what Drusus did—restore the power of the Senate, after Augustus and my revered great-great Julius between them had pretty nearly put it out of business—"

I stopped there, startled at my own words. It almost seemed that I was beginning to take Sam's crazy idea seriously!

On the other hand, that wasn't all bad. It also seemed that Rachel was beginning to take *me* seriously.

That was a good thought. It kept me cheerful through half a dozen more dances and at least another hour of history lessons from her pretty lips . . . right up until the time when, after we had gone back to her house, I tiptoed out of my room toward hers, and found her butler, Basilius, asleep on a rug across her doorway, with a great, thick club by his side.

I didn't sleep well that night.

Partly it was glandular. My head knew that Rachel didn't want me creeping into her bedroom, or else she wouldn't have put the butler there in the way. But my glands weren't happy with that news. They had soaked up the smell and sight and feel of her, and they were complaining about being thwarted.

The worst part was waking up every hour or so to contemplate financial ruin.

Being poor wasn't so bad. Every writer has to learn how to be poor from time to time, between checks. It's an annoyance, but not a catastrophe. You don't get enslaved just for poverty.

But I had been running up some pretty big bills. And you do get enslaved for debt.

4 · The End of the Dream

The next morning I woke up late and grouchy and had to take a three-wheeler to the Hall of the Senate-Inferior.

It was slow going. As we approached, the traffic thickened even more. I could see the Legion forming for the ceremonial guard as the Pharaoh's procession approached to open the ceremonies. The driver wouldn't take me any closer than the outer square, and I had to wait there with all the tourists, while the Pharaoh dismounted from her royal litter.

There was a soft, pleasured noise from the crowd, halfway between a giggle and a sigh. That was the spectacle the tourists had come to see. They pressed against the sheathed swords of the Legionaries while the Pharaoh, head bare, robe trailing on the ground, advanced on the shrines outside the Senate building. She sacrificed reverently and unhurriedly to them, while the tourists flashed their cameras at her, and I began to worry about the time. What if she ecumenically decided to visit all fifty shrines? But after doing Isis, Amon-Ra, and Mother Nile, she went inside to declare the Congress open. The Legionaries relaxed. The tourists began to flow back to their buses, snapping pictures of themselves now, and I followed the Pharaoh inside.

She made a good, by which I mean short, opening address. The only thing wrong with it was that she was talking to mostly empty seats.

The Hall of the Alexandrian Senate-Inferior holds two thousand people. There weren't more than a hundred and fifty in it. Most of those were huddled in small groups in the aisles and at the back of the hall, and they were paying no attention at all to the Pharaoh. I think she saw that and shortened her speech. At one moment she was telling us how the scientific investigation of the outside universe was completely in accord with the ancient traditions of Egypt—with hardly anyone listening—and at the next her voice had stopped without warning and she was handing her orb and scepter to her attendants. She proceeded regally across the stage and out the wings.

The buzz of conversation hardly slackened. What they were talking about, of course, was the Olympians. Even when the Collegium-Presidor stepped forward and called for the first session to begin the hall didn't fill. At least most of the scattered groups of people in the room sat down—though still in clumps, and still doing a lot of whispering to each other.

Even the speakers didn't seem very interested in what they were saying. The first one was an honorary Presidor-Emeritus from the southern highlands of Egypt, and he gave us a review of everything we knew about the Olympians.

He read it as hurriedly as though he were dictating it to a scribe. It wasn't very interesting. The trouble, of course, was that his paper had been prepared days earlier, while the Olympian transmissions were still flooding in and no one had any thought they might be interrupted. It just didn't seem relevant anymore.

What I like about going to science congresses isn't so much the actual papers the speakers deliver—I can get that sort of information better from the journals in the library. It isn't even the back-and-forth discussion that follows each paper, although that sometimes produces useful background bits. What I get the most out of is what I call "the sound of science"—the kind of shorthand language scientists use when they're talking to each other about their own specialties. So I usually sit somewhere at the back of the hall, with as much space around me as I can manage, my tablet in my lap and my stylus in my hand, writing down bits of dialogue and figuring how to put them into my next sci-rom.

There wasn't much of that today. There wasn't much discussion at all. One by one the speakers got up and read their papers, answered a couple of cursory questions with cursory replies and hurried off; and when each one finished he left and the audience got smaller, because, as I finally figured out, no one was there who wasn't obligated to be.

When boredom made me decide that I needed a glass of wine and a quick snack more than I needed to sit there with my still blank tablet I found out there was hardly anyone even in the lounges. There was no familiar face. No one seemed to know where Sam was. And in the afternoon, the Presidor, bowing to the inevitable, announced that the remaining sessions would be postponed indefinitely.

The day was a total waste.

I had a lot more hopes for the night.

Rachel greeted me with the news that Sam had sent a message to say that he was detained and wouldn't make dinner.

"Did he say where he was?" She shook her head. "He's off with some of the other top people," I guessed. I told her about the collapse of the convention. Then I brightened. "At least let's go out for dinner, then," I offered.

Rachel firmly vetoed the idea. She was tactful enough not to mention money, although I was sure Sam had filled her in on my precarious financial state. "I like my own cook's food better than any restaurant," she told me. "We'll eat here. There won't be anything fancy tonight—just a simple meal for the two of us."

The best part of that was "the two of us." Basilius had arranged the couches in a sort of Vee, so that our heads were quite close together, with the low serving tables in easy reach between us. As soon as she lay down Rachel confessed, "I didn't get a lot of work done today. I couldn't get that idea of yours out of my head."

The idea was Sam's, actually, but I didn't see any reason to correct her. "I'm flattered," I told her. "I'm sorry I spoiled your work."

She shrugged and went on, "I did a little reading on the period, especially about an interesting minor figure who lived around then, a Judaean preacher named Jeshua of Nazareth. Did you ever hear of him? Well, most people haven't, but he had a lot of followers at one time. They called themselves Chrestians, and they were a very unruly bunch."

"I'm afraid I don't know much about Judaean history," I said. Which was true, but then I added, "But I'd really like to learn more." Which wasn't; or at least hadn't been until just then.

"Of course," Rachel said. No doubt to her it seemed quite natural that everyone in the world would wish to know more about the post-Augustan period. "Anyway, this Jeshua was on trial for sedition. He was condemned to death."

I blinked at her. "Not just to slavery?"

She shook her head. "They didn't just enslave criminals back then, they did physical things to them. Even executed them, sometimes in very barbarous ways. But Tiberius, as Proconsul, decided that the penalty was too extreme. So he commuted Jeshua's death sentence. He just had him whipped and let him go. A very good decision, I think. Otherwise he would have made him a martyr, and gods know what would have happened after that. As it was, the Chrestians just gradually waned away. . . . Basilius? You can bring the next course in now."

I watched with interest as Basilius complied. It turned out to be larks and olives! I approved, not simply for the fact that I liked the dish. The "simple meal" was actually a lot more elaborate than she had provided for the three of us the night before.

Things were looking up. I said, "Can you tell me something, Rachel? I think you're Judaean yourself, aren't you?"

"Of course."

"Well, I'm a little confused," I said. "I thought the Judaeans believed in the god Yahveh."

"Of course, Julie. We do."

"Yes, but—" I hesitated. I didn't want to mess up the way things were going, but I was curious. "But you say 'gods.' Isn't that, well, a contradiction?"

"Not at all," she told me, civilly enough. "Yahveh's commandments were brought down from a mountaintop by our great prophet, Moses, and they are very clear on the subject. One of them says, 'Thou shalt have no other gods before me.' Well, we don't, you see? Yahveh is our *first* god. There aren't any *before* him. It's all explained in the rabbinical writings."

"And that's what you go by, the rabbinical writings?"

She looked thoughtful. "In a way. We're a very traditional people, Julie. Tradition is what we follow; the rabbinical writings simply explain the traditions."

She had stopped eating. I stopped, too. Dreamily I reached out to caress her cheek.

She didn't pull away. She didn't respond, either. After a moment, she said, not looking at me, "For instance, there is a Judaean tradition that a woman is to be a virgin at the time of her marriage."

My hand came away from her face by itself, without any conscious command from me. "Oh?"

"And the rabbinical writings more or less define the tradition, you see. They say that the head of the household is to stand guard at an unmarried daughter's bedroom for the first hour of each night; if there is no male head of the household, a trusted slave is to be appointed to the job."

"I see," I said. "You've never been married, have you?"

"Not yet," said Rachel, beginning to eat again.

I hadn't ever been married, either, although, to be sure, I wasn't exactly a virgin. It wasn't that I had anything against marriage. It was only that the life of a sci-rom hack wasn't what you would call exactly financially stable, and also the fact that I hadn't ever come across the woman I wanted to spend my life with . . . or, to quote Rachel, "not yet."

I tried to keep my mind off that subject. It was sure that if my finances had been precarious before, they were now close to catastrophic.

The next morning I wondered what to do with my day, but Rachel settled it for me. She was waiting for me in the atrium. "Sit down with me, Julie," she commanded, patting the bench beside her. "I was up late, thinking, and I think I've got something for you. Suppose this man Jeshua had been executed after all."

It wasn't exactly the greeting I had been hoping for, nor was it something I had given a moment's thought to, either. But I was glad enough to sit next to her in that pleasant little garden, with the gentled early sun shining down on us through the translucent shades. "Yes?" I said noncommittally, kissing her hand in greeting.

She took a moment before she took her hand back. "That idea opened some interesting possibilities, Julie. Jeshua would have been a martyr, you see. I can easily imagine that under those circumstances his Christian followers would have had a lot more staying power. They might even have grown to be really important. Judaea was always in one kind of turmoil or another around that time, anyway—there were all sorts of prophecies and rumors about messiahs and changes in society. The Chrestians might even have come to dominate all of Judaea."

I tried to be tactful. "There's nothing wrong with being proud of your ancestors, Rachel. But, really, what difference would that have made?" I obviously hadn't been tactful enough. She had turned to look at me with what looked like the beginning of a frown. I thought fast, and tried to cover myself: "On the other hand," I went on quickly, "suppose you expanded that idea beyond Judaea."

It turned into a real frown, but puzzled rather than angry. "What do you mean, beyond Judaea?"

"Well, suppose Jeshua's Chrestian-Judaean kind of—what would you call it? Philosophy? Religion?"

"A little of both, I'd say."

"Religious philosophy, then. Suppose it spread over most of the world, not just Judaea. That could be interesting."

"But, really, no such thing hap—"

"Rachel, Rachel," I said, covering her mouth with a fingertip affectionately, "we're saying *what if*, remember? Every sci-rom writer is entitled to one big lie. Let's say this is mine. Let's say that Chrestian-Judaeanism became a world religion. Even Rome itself succumbs. Maybe the City becomes the, what do you call it, the place for the Sanhedrin of the Chrestian-Judaeans. And then what happens?"

"You tell me," she said, half amused, half suspicious.

"Why, then," I said, flexing the imagination of the trained sci-rom writer, "it might develop like the kind of conditions you've been talking about in the old days in Judaea. Maybe the whole world would be splintering into factions and sects, and then they fight."

"Fight *wars?*" she asked incredulously.

"Fight *big* wars. Why not? It happened in Judaea, didn't it? And then they might keep right on fighting them, all through historical times. After all, the only thing that's kept the world united for the past two thousand years has been the Pax Romana. Without that— Why, without that," I went on, talking faster and making mental notes to myself as I went along, "let's say that all the tribes of Europe turned into independent city-states. Like the Greeks, only bigger. And more powerful. And they fight, the Franks against the Vik Northmen against the Belgiae against the Kelts."

She was shaking her head. "People wouldn't be so silly, Julie," she complained.

"How do you know that? Anyway, this is a sci-rom, dear." I didn't pause to see if she reacted to the "dear." I went right on, but not failing to notice that she hadn't objected: "The people will be as silly as I want them to be—as long as I can make it plausible enough for the fans. But you haven't heard the best part of it. Let's say the Chrestian-Judaeans take their religion seriously. They don't do anything to go against the will of their god. What Yahveh said still goes, no matter what. Do you follow? That means they aren't at all interested in scientific discovery, for instance."

"No, stop right there!" she ordered, suddenly indignant. "Are you trying to say that we Judaeans aren't interested in science? That I'm not? Or my Uncle Sam? And we're certainly Judaeans."

"But you're not *Chrestian* Judaeans, sweet. There's a big difference. Why? Because I say there is, Rachel, and I'm the one writing the story. So, let's see—" I paused for thought "—all right, let's say the Chrestians go through a long period of intellectual stagnation, and then—" I paused, not because I didn't know what was coming next, but to build the effect. "And then along come the Olympians!"

She gazed at me blankly. "Yes?" she asked, encouraging but vague.

"Don't you see it? And then this Chrestian-Judaean world, drowsing along in the middle of a pre-scientific dark age, no aircraft, no electronic broadcast, not even a printing press or a hovermachine—and it's suddenly thrown into contact with a super-technological civilization from outer space!" She was wrinkling her forehead at me, forgetting to eat, trying to understand what I was driving at. "It's terrible culture shock," I explained. "And not just for the people on Earth. Maybe the Olympians come to look us over, and they see that we're technologically backward and divided into warring nations and all that . . . and what do they do? Why, they turn right around and leave us! and . . . and that's the end of the book!"

She pursed her lips. "But maybe that's what they're doing now," she said cautiously.

"But not for that reason, certainly. See, this isn't *our* world I'm talking about. It's a *what if* world."

"It sounds a little far-fetched," she said.

I said happily, "That's where my skills come in. You don't understand sci-rom, sweetheart. It's the sci-rom writer's job to push an idea as far as it will go—to the absolute limit of credibility—to the point where if he took just one step more the whole thing would collapse into absurdity. Trust me, Rachel. I'll make them believe it."

She was still pursing her pretty lips, but this time I didn't wait for her to speak. I seized the bird of opportunity on the wing. I leaned toward her and kissed those lips, as I had been wanting to do for some time. Then I said, "I've got to get to a scribe, I want to get all this down before I forget it. I'll be back when I can be, and— And until then— well, here."

And I kissed her again, gently, firmly, and long; and it was quite clear early in the process that she was kissing me back.

Being next to a rental barracks had its advantages. I found a scribe to rent at a decent price, and the rental manager even let me borrow one of their conference rooms that night to dictate in. By daybreak I had the first two chapters and an outline of *Sidewise to a Chrestian World* down.

Once I get that far in a book, the rest is just work. The general idea is set, the characters have announced themselves to me, it's just a matter of closing my eyes for a moment to see what's going to be happening and then opening them to dictate to the scribe. In this case, the scribes, plural, because the first one wore out in a few more hours and I had to employ a second, and then a third.

I didn't sleep at all until it was all down. I think it was fifty-two straight hours, the longest I'd worked in one stretch in years. When it was all done I left it to be fair-copied. The rental agent agreed to get it down to the shipping offices by the harbor and dispatch it by fast air to Marcus in London.

Then at last I stumbled back to Rachel's house to sleep. I was surprised to find that it was still dark, an hour or more before sunrise.

Basilius let me in, looking startled as he studied my sunken eyes and unshaved face. "Let me sleep until I wake up," I ordered. There was a journal neatly folded beside my bed, but I didn't look at it. I lay down, turned over once, and was gone.

When I woke up at least twelve hours had passed. I had Basilius bring me something to eat, and shave me, and when I finally got out to the atrium it was nearly sundown and Rachel was waiting for me. I told her what I'd done, and she told me about the last message from the Olympians. "Last?" I objected. "How can you be sure it's the last?"

"Because they said so," she told me sadly. "They said they were breaking off communications."

"Oh," I said, thinking about that. "Poor Sam," I said, thinking about Flavius Samuelus. And she looked so doleful that I couldn't help myself, I took her in my arms.

Consolation turned to kissing, and when we had done quite a lot of that she leaned back, smiling at me.

I couldn't help what I said then, either. It startled me to hear the words come out of my mouth as I said, "Rachel, I wish we could get married."

She pulled back, looking at me with affection and a little surprised amusement. "Are you proposing to me?"

I was careful of my grammar. "That was a subjunctive, sweet. I said I *wished* we could get married."

"I understood that. What I want to know is whether you're asking me to grant your wish."

"No—well, hells, yes! But what I wish first is that I had the right to ask you. Sci-rom writers don't have the most solid financial situation, you know. The way you live here—"

"The way I live here," she said, "is paid for by the estate I inherited from my father. Getting married won't take it away."

"But that's your estate, my darling. I've been poor, but I've never been a parasite."

"You won't be a parasite," she said softly, and I realized that she was being careful about her grammar, too.

Which took a lot of will-power on my part. "Rachel," I said, "I should be hearing from my editor anytime now. If this new kind of sci-rom catches on— If it's as popular as it might be—"

"Yes?" she prompted.

"Why," I said, "then maybe I can actually ask you. But I don't know that. Marcus probably has it by now, but I don't know if he's read it. And then I won't know his decision till I hear from him. And now, with all the confusion about the Olympians, that might take weeks—"

"Julie," she said, putting her finger over my lips, "call him up."

The circuits were all busy, but I finally got through—and, because it was well after lunch, Marcus was in his office. More than that, he was quite sober. "Julie, you bastard," he cried, sounding really furious, "where the hells have you been hiding? I ought to have you whipped."

But he hadn't said anything about getting the aediles after me. "Did you have a chance to read *Sidewise to a Christian World*?" I asked.

"The what? Oh, *that* thing. Nah. I haven't even looked at it. I'll buy it, naturally," he said, "but what I'm talking about is *An Ass's Olympiad*. The censors won't stop it now, you know. In fact, all I want you to do now is make the Olympian a little dumber, a little nastier—you've got a biggie here, Julie! I think we can get a broadcast out of it, even. So when can you get back here to fix it up?"

"Why— Well, pretty soon, I guess, only I haven't checked the hover timetable—"

"Hover, hell! You're coming back by fast plane—we'll pick up the tab. And, oh, by the way, we're doubling your advance. The payment will be in your account this afternoon."

And ten minutes later, when I unsubjunctively proposed to Rachel, she quickly and unsubjunctively accepted; and the high-speed flight to London takes nine hours, but I was grinning all the way.

5 · The Way It Is When You've Got It Made

To be a freelance writer is to live in a certain kind of ease. Not very easeful financially, maybe, but in a lot of other ways. You don't have to go to an office every day, you get a lot of satisfaction out of seeing your very own words being read on hovers and trains by total strangers. To be a potentially *bestselling* writer is a whole order of magnitude different. Marcus put me up in an inn right next to the publishing company's offices and stood over me while I turned my poor imaginary Olympian into the most doltish, feckless, unlikable being the universe had ever seen. The more I made the Olympian contemptibly comic, the more Marcus loved it. So did everyone else in the office; so did their affiliates in Kiev and Manahattan and Kalkut and half a dozen other cities all around the world, and he informed me proudly that they were publishing my book simultaneously in all of them. "We'll be the first ones out, Julie," he exulted. "It's going to be a mint! Money? Well, of course you can have more money—you're in the big time now!" And, yes, the broadcast studios were interested—interested enough to sign a contract even before I'd finished the revisions; and so were the journals, who came for interviews every minute that Marcus would let me off from correcting the proofs and posing for jacket photographs and speaking to their sales staff; and, all in all, I hardly had a chance to breathe until I was back on the high-speed aircraft to Alexandria and my bride.

Sam had agreed to give the bride away, and he met me at the airpad. He looked older and more tired, but resigned. As we drove to Rachel's house, where the wedding guests were already beginning to gather, I tried to cheer him up. I had plenty of joy myself; I wanted to share it. So I offered, "At least, now you can get back to your real work."

He looked at me strangely. "Writing sci-roms?" he asked.

"No, of course not! That's good enough for me, but you've still got your extra-solar probe to keep you busy."

"Julie," he said sadly, "where have you been lately? Didn't you see the last Olympian message?"

"Well, sure," I said, offended. "Everybody did, didn't they?" And then I thought for a moment, and, actually, it had been Rachel who had told me about it. I'd never actually looked at a journal or a broadcast. "I guess I was pretty busy," I said lamely.

He looked sadder than ever. "Then maybe you don't know that they said they weren't only terminating all their own transmissions to us, they were terminating even our own probes."

"Oh, no, Sam! I would have heard if they'd stopped transmitting!"

He said patiently, "No, you wouldn't, because the data they were sending is still on its way to us. We've still got a few years coming in. But that's it. We're out of interstellar space, Julie. They don't want us there."

He broke off, peering out the window. "And that's the way it is," he said. "We're here, though, and you better get inside. Rachel's going to be tired of sitting under that canopy without you around."

The greatest thing of all about being a bestselling author, if you like traveling, is that when you fly around the world somebody else pays for the tickets. Marcus's publicity department fixed up the whole thing. Personal appearances, bookstore autographings, college lectures, broadcasts, publishers' meetings, receptions—we were kept busy for a solid month, and it made a hell of a fine honeymoon.

Of course any honeymoon would have been wonderful as long as Rachel was the bride, but without the publishers bankrolling us we might not have visited six of the seven continents on the way. (We didn't bother with Polaris Australis—nobody there but penguins.) And we took time for ourselves along the way, on beaches in Hindia and the islands of Han, in the wonderful shops of Manahattan and a dozen other cities of the Western Continents—we did it all.

When we got back to Alexandria the contractors had finished the remodeling of Rachel's villa—which, we had decided, would now be our winter home, though our next priority was going to be to find a place where we could spend the busy part of the year in London. Sam had moved back in and, with Basilius, greeted us formally as we came to the door.

"I thought you'd be in Rome," I told him, once we were settled and Rachel had gone to inspect what had been done with her baths.

"Not while I'm still trying to understand what went wrong," he said. "The research is going on right here; this is where we transmitted from."

I shrugged and took a sip of the Falernian wine Basilius had left for us. I held the goblet up critically: a little cloudy, I thought, and in the vat too long. And then I grinned at myself, because a few weeks earlier I would have been delighted at anything so costly. "But we know what went wrong," I told him reasonably. "They decided against us."

"Of course they did," he said, "but why? I've been trying to work out just what messages were being received when they broke off communications."

"Do you think we said something to offend them?"

He scratched the age spot on his bald head, staring at me, then he sighed. "What would *you* think, Julius?"

"Well, maybe so," I admitted. "What messages were they?"

"I'm not sure. It took a lot of digging. The Olympians, you know, acknowledged receipt of each message by repeating the last hundred and forty groups—"

"I didn't know."

"Well, they did. The last message they acknowledged was a history of Rome. Unfortunately, it was six hundred and fifty thousand words long."

"So you have to read the whole history?"

"Not just *read* it, Julie; we have to try to figure out what might have been in it that wasn't in any previous message. We've had two or three hundred researchers collating every previous message, and the only thing that was new was some of the social data. We were transmitting census figures—so many of equestrian rank, so many citizens, so many freedmen, so many slaves." He hesitated, and then said thoughtfully, "Paulus Magnus—I don't know if you know him, he's an Algonkan—pointed out that that was the first time we'd ever mentioned slavery."

I waited for him to go on. "Yes?" I said encouragingly.

He shrugged. "Nothing. Paulus is a slave himself, so naturally he's got it on his mind a lot."

"I don't quite see what that has to do with anything," I said. "Isn't there anything else?"

"Oh," he said, "there are a thousand theories. There was some health data, too, and some people think the Olympians might have suddenly got worried about some new microorganism killing them off. Or we weren't polite enough. Or maybe, who knows, there was some sort of power struggle among them, and the side that came out on top just didn't want any more new races in their community."

"And we don't know yet which it was?"

"It's worse than that, Julie," he told me somberly. "I don't think we ever will find out what it was that made them decide they didn't want to have anything to do with us;" and in that, too, Flavius Samuelus ben Samuelus was a very intelligent man. Because we never have.

CRITICALITY

Life has always been stressful. Even when our ancestors were hunting and gathering, there was pressure to bring home the bacon or the berries or something else to eat. But modern life, we are constantly told by sociologists and psychologists, is much more stressful than life even a century ago.

The people in "Criticality" have to deal with another kind of pressure, but as Frederik Pohl has illustrated in numberless stories, people are adaptable. The dictum Judge not lest you be judged has been thrown out the window in the intriguing New York of "Criticality," a story published in 1984.

In this world, judging—or more properly, rating things—is what it's all about, from the neatness of someone's clothing . . . to the performance of the president. While such a system might seem petty, to the people in the story, it matters more than you can imagine.

The night I met Arne Kastle the computer dating service had turned up a tall blonde named Marian for me. We flipped a coin to decide who decided where to go. I won. That is, I got the privilege of making the decision. I know there are some people who would look at that a different way. They would figure that if you don't make the decision you aren't to blame if it turns out bad, so that winning that toss is actually a kind of loss. I don't agree. As I see it, you look better if you're the one that takes the initiative. Anyway, I had made my mind up ahead of time that I would choose going to the Tom-a-Hawk Inn in Coney Island, and I'd been there often enough before to feel pretty sure it would score high with her. I was at least partly right. "That's a good nine for originality," she conceded, tapping her lower lip thoughtfully. "But I don't know about convenience. I'd say only a three."

"It's a long trip," I agreed and added that she was close to losing a point for grooming since she had smudged her lipstick. That was risky. It's the sort of thing that can antagonize them, but I knew I was a certain ten for grooming anyway. I'd spent an hour with the hair blower and the cuticle sticks and everything else, and if she tried to downrate me on any of that she'd just make a fool of herself.

So, feeling satisfied with the way the opening gambits had gone. I handed her through the turnstiles and we took the long train ride through Brooklyn. Apart from the bothersome showing of papers at the checkpoints at the tunnel and Fort Hamilton Parkway it was a pleasant enough journey. Computer dating doesn't really let you know a person. We passed the time enjoyably exploring each other. When we came aboveground and the noise level dropped I took my box off my shoulder. "Would you like a little music?" I asked, turning it on. As the first sounds came through I pursed my lips, then nodded. "It's Mahler's First Symphony, of course. I've always thought it was a little overblown, but some of the themes are lovely—or perhaps you don't care for the late romantics?" She had put "classical music" on her database for the service, and it had taken only a few minutes with the program guides to memorize the listings for that evening. But Marian had been into the guides, too.

"That's Mehta conducting, isn't it?" she said deprecatingly. "He never understood Mahler, did he? But you can't deny the Philharmonic has a first-rate wind section." She closed her eyes for a moment, satisfied with the way she had performed so far, and I studied her carefully. Her figure was good—eight, at least—and she had thrown her shoulders back cleverly to make the most of it. I thought her eyes a bit too close together, but had to admit she had made an effort to widen them with eye shadow. Annoyingly, I couldn't identify her perfume. It was certainly not one of the standard reliables that always call for a five or a six; she'd taken a chance with something offbeat—rather tropical and jungly; if it didn't become tiresome over the evening I would have to give it perhaps a nine. "On the other hand, Wilbert," she said without opening her eyes, "the Cardinals are in town. The game ought to be starting about the time this symphony's over—shall we switch stations then?" That was a nice try, since I had listed "sports" for the dating service—but actually I was more into football and ice hockey. I let it slide, though, and when we got to the end of the line and the conductor came through with the *Won't You Tell Us How You Enjoyed Your Ride?* folders, I was charmed to see that she handed hers over to me to fill out along with my own. The computer service doesn't list "docility" in its after-date checklist, but I consider it an important constituent of the "good personality?" entry, so she had earned at least four points there already.

The peacekeeping forces at the Coney Island station don't worry much about young couples on a Saturday night. They waved us through with hardly a glance at our papers. There was a cab right there, and in a moment we were at our hotel.

The Tom-a-Hawk is an old hotel, but it was completely refurbished by the Apache Nation's hotel chain when they took it over. It advertises the fastest check-ins in the business. If you and your date are not on your way to your room within seven minutes after reaching the registration counter you get a pretty little feathered hatchet, which is supposed to be exchangeable for two complimentary Bloated Marys in the rooftop bar. Our time was just over five minutes. No hatchet. But we were in plenty of time for the Happy Hour.

The room was a six for size of bed, a nine for the view over the Atlantic, but only about a four for elegance. The furniture had not all been replaced by the Apache Nation. Marian disappeared into the bathroom to freshen her makeup, and while she was gone I rumpled the bed so the night maid would think we had been in it. When Marian came out she glanced approvingly at the bed, smiled and took my arm, turning me so that we faced the wall mirror. "I think we'll do, Wilbert," she said, studying our reflection. I was less sure. Marian was quite tall and blond. Very good-looking, really, but she was so fair that she made my light brown hair and medium complexion seem rather sallow. I was surprised that she had said that and, as we made our way up to the Sachem's Nest on the top floor, I was thinking Marian would not, after all, score very high for empathy. But then, while we were waiting for the hostess to seat us, she snuggled right up to me, slouching a little so that she could look up into my face. It was an endearing touch. A lot of dates are far more interested in their own appearance than in making their escort look good. For that, a ten.

Then, as we were going to our table, a soldier in the uniform of the peace-keeping force lurched while stepping from the moving outer rim to the stationary inner core and bumped right into Marian. Although I did not yet know his name, it was Arne Kastle. "'Scuse me, lady," he said, with an admiring look. "I guess I'm not used to this high-tech stuff, eh?" And ten minutes later, when I happened to glance behind me, there he was, staring at her.

A "Bloated Mary" turns out to be a kind of vanilla milkshake with grain alcohol added. It is passed under a broiler to give it a sort of baked-Alaska top, then served in a scooped out corncob. (They call it a "maize" cob.) It is a pretty small drink for the money—perhaps because their punctuality isn't all that reliable, so they keep the freebies small. The purchased ones are no bigger. One round of Bloated Marys went fast, and it was while I was looking for the waitress to order another that I saw the soldier again.

I had chosen three good topics of conversation—childhood memories; sports; and dream vacations—but one of the things I always score high on is going with the flow. I changed the subject without a hitch. "They're SasPeace," I told her. "I watched them parade at the changing of the guard yesterday on television. They were very colorful, although the Ghurkas marched better. The Saskatchewan detachment will be here for six months, then they'll be relieved by one of the other occupying powers—"

"Wilbert," she said gently, "I know all that." A head-on confrontation! A very risky maneuver, so early in a date, but she carried it off marvelously. "I think they look funny in those soldier suits," she laughed. "Don't you suppose they envy you *terribly?*"

Actually they did look funny, because the Ghurkas they relieved averaged about five feet four and the new troops hadn't yet been given a new issue of uniforms. I decided to overlook it. Besides, we were coming around to some interesting views as the bar turned. "Look," I said. "That lighted bridge—it's the Verrazzano. Isn't it pretty? And just beyond it you can see in the distance the skyline of Manhattan."

"And on this side," she said, "is that sandy-haired Canadian soldier. He's coming over here, Wilbert."

Indeed he was. His eyes were on Marian, but he spoke to me. "Sir," he said, "do you mind if I ask the lady for a dance?"

That could have been a really tricky situation. A lot of dates would have handled it badly. Marian was very good. She simply looked at me to see how I felt, read my expression correctly and gave a slight nod. "What's your name?" I asked the soldier.

"Arne Kastle, sir."

"Marian, may I present Arne? Arne, Marian. Have a nice dance." I watched them step back onto the dance floor with a certain feeling of pride; I'd at least matched Marian's cool handling of the incident!

By the time she came back they were getting ready to give out the door prizes and discount coupons. I forgot all about Arne Kastle in the excitement. When it was over and Marian and I had won a two-for-one shore dinner in the Tom-a-Hawk Inn's Lobster Lounge on the Boardwalk, I happened to glance toward his table. All four of the Canadian soldiers were gone.

I wasn't surprised. The peacekeeping forces have no authority in extraterritorial enclaves like the Tom-a-Hawk hotels or their rival Saudi chain. They only come in off-duty hours, to eye the tourists. I commented to Marian, "I guess they've gone back to their barracks."

She looked up from where she was counting our prizes, discount certificates for the souvenir shops and beauty salon and rolls of complimentary coins for the dollar slot machines in the casino. "Who?" she asked.

"The SasPeace soldiers. They're gone. How was he, by the way?"

She leaned back, tapping one of the discount certificates against her teeth. "Oh—overall, maybe a seven. Not much makeout. He held me nicely while we danced, not too tight, not too loose, and he chatted me up pretty well. But he didn't ask for my phone number." I only smiled, although I was surprised—a seven? Sounded like a marginal five or six to me. "Anyway," she said, "the two-for-one shore dinner is only good if we get there in the next thirty minutes, and the dollars have to be played tonight—shouldn't we get going?"

By then I knew I had lucked in. As I rose and helped her with her chair I was confident that this weekend was going to be special.

Indeed it was. I found my companion inventive and responsive and physically very enjoyable. She was quite beautiful, with her suntanned skin and fair complexion, almost like one of those bikinied Scandinavian tourists who throng our beaches. By the time we were on the return train Sunday night I knew I would have to put this weekend well up in the top ten for the whole year. When she shyly handed me her *How Did I Rate With You?* card as our train dipped into the tunnel for Manhattan I had no hesitation in awarding her four tens, and nothing below a six in any category. I almost thought of making a private date with her for some other weekend. However, that would have verged on a commitment and I knew neither of us wanted that. So I said good night to her at the Twenty-third Street station, just where we had met, regretting—but accepting—the fact that we would probably never see each other again.

Of course, I never thought I'd see Arne Kastle again, either, and I was surely wrong about that.

He turned up in my apartment when it was full of police, and at first I didn't notice him—what was one more uniform among many? Then I perceived that his was Peacekeeper green instead of police blue, and then I placed the face. "Oh," I said, "you're the soldier. How did you find me?"

"I checked your registration at the hotel," he said, glancing around. The police were spreading fingerprint powder and making notes and calling back to the precinct on their hand radios. "It looks like I came at a bad time."

"I've been burgled," I explained, smiling. "They got through four door locks and an electric alarm system, slick as a whistle. You really have to hand it to them."

He looked at me doubtfully. "I could come back another time," he offered.

"Ah, no," I said. "They don't need me here anymore—I've told them everything I know. And the burglars got my TV, my stereo, my telephone machine, my exercise bike—I guess they've taken everything worth stealing already, so there's nothing left to worry about. Let's go down to the corner for a beer."

When we were seated at the bar he came out with it. "That girl you were with, eh? Marian? Is she your wife or anything?"

"Of course not, Arne. Just a date."

For some reason he didn't seem to like the sound of that, but he said stubbornly, "I'd like to see her again."

"Why not?"

"Because I don't know how to find her, that's why not."

"I see," I said, studying him over the rim of my glass. For some reason I felt drawn to the fellow. He was naive and obviously uncomfortable in the situation, but determined. He was not a handsome man—too short and squat, and his eyes squinted a little. Still, there are lots of men with features no better than his who rate a seven or even an eight on personality. Not, in his case, on grooming. He had received a new issue of uniform since the weekend at Coney Island, so at least his wrists didn't stick out of the sleeves. He didn't wear the uniform well, though, and he'd tied his tie in a hard knot stuck up under one corner of his collar. "All you have to do, Arne," I said obligingly, "is call up the computer dating service and ask for her."

"I don't know her last name, Wilbert."

"Well, neither do I! That's not a problem. Just say you want a tall blonde, interested in classical music, baseball, about five seven and a hundred and fifteen pounds—there won't be more than a dozen or so, and you can pick her out from the picture."

His expression said he wasn't liking that part, either, but he stuck to his purpose. "Then they'll give me her address, eh?"

"Certainly not! If you wanted her address you should have got it while you were dancing! Don't you know anything about dating? All you had to do was ask her if she'd ever been to the top of the World Trade Center, or if she'd like to visit the zoo. . . . She didn't dislike you, you know."

"What?"

"She as much as said so," I told him, thinking it would gratify him. But he only sighed and held up two fingers to the bartender.

"I don't understand you Yanks," he said moodily.

I laughed. "We're just like anybody else," I said.

"The hell you are, Wilbert."

I shrugged. "Oh, we're richer, I suppose. And we're in a sort of a special position since the World's War. But when you come right down to it, what do we want out of life? To have a few laughs, catch a few drinks, make it with some nice chicks—I guess it's just about the same in Saskatchewan, right?"

"You didn't say anything about work," he pointed out.

"Well, of course we work," I said, surprised. "Or we do when there's a job, anyway. Right now I'm in one of those postwar retraining programs, learning how to manage municipal bond portfolios for large corporate investors. It's real interesting, and there's a good chance of employment when I finish the course. For income, of course, I'm on Supplemental. Not full Welfare—I've never been on full Welfare—just the federal subsidy to add to what I get from the retraining program."

He nodded absently. "I wonder if she really would like to see the zoo? We don't have any good ones in my part of Saskatchewan."

"Ask her, boy," I grinned. He didn't respond. "Go on," I encouraged. "Stick a quarter in the slot over there in the booth and dial the dating service."

"I've never done that," he confessed.

"There's nothing to it. Just give your name and your credit card number, and tell them what you want. I'd do it for you myself," I apologized, "but they got my computer deck along with everything else."

He looked at me thoughtfully, then reached into his pocket and spilled his change on the table. It was all Occupation money, but that worked as well as anything else. He picked out a quarter and stood up. Just before heading for the computer booth he paused and shook his head. "I guess I still don't understand you Yanks," he repeated.

That was the second time I saw Arne Kastle. Once again I thought it was going to be the last, and was wrong. I graduated from the fund-management program. There weren't any jobs there, though, so I signed up right away for another one, this time in hotel and motel management. Even the Apache Nation hired a lot of locals for mid-level jobs . . . and it was certainly a field I knew well from the other side of the desk!

Because it was a presidential election year, there were a lot of public meetings going on. They interested me a lot. I've always considered myself well informed politically, and so I watched most of the meetings and debates on TV and went to some in person when I could. When the president came to New York for an open-air rally right in front of Macy's, I was there.

So was Arne Kastle. I might have guessed that, because there were at least four or five hundred Peacekeepers deployed there on crowd control, Iceland and Argentine detachments as well as the Canadians. But I wasn't thinking about Arne. I was concentrating on sideslipping and squeezing through breaks in the crowd to get right up to the police barrier, and when I finally did it was a surprise when the SasPeace soldier right in front of me said, "How you doing, Wilbert?"

I said warmly, "Nice to see you, Arne. Say. Did you ever connect with that girl, what's her name—"

"Her name is Marian," he said shortly, and turned away to chase a ten-year-old back behind the linees. It took him a couple of minutes to get back to me. By then the president's party was getting out of their limos, and I discovered the subject had been changed. Kastle jerked a thumb at the President. "Isn't that the bloke that lost the war for you?" he asked.

"Same one." I agreed.

"And he thinks he can get reelected?"

I laughed at him. "Hell, Arne," I said, "nobody blames him for that any more."

"They don't?"

"Of course not! I guess you don't understand the American political process, Arne. See, he *acted*. He moved right away to limit damage to his administration. He fired his secretary of state and shook up the C.I.A. He acted fast and hard—what more could you ask?"

"You could've asked that he not get in a losing war," he said. I started to explain to him that that was ancient history, but a SasPeace lieutenant was scowling at us, "No talking politics with the locals, Private Kastle!" he barked.

As soon as the lieutenant was out of earshot I whispered, "Listen, let's talk about this. Give me a call. Maybe we'll take in the zoo, if you're so crazy to see it!"

Evidently he was, because he did. About a week later we met at Prospect Park, and Kastle was like a kid. "Tigers and elephants!" he grinned. "Lead me to them!"

I grinned back. "Elephants *sí*, tigers *no*." I said, steering him around the seal tank.

"Why no tigers?"

"Well," I explained, "during the last blackout somebody remembered that tiger-skin rugs were worth a lot of money. Here's the elephants, though."

Kastle was the only Peacekeeper in sight—at least the only one in uniform. I could see him realizing that as we walked around, and I could see him worrying about it. When we took time out for a beer in the open-air cafe he fretted, "Maybe I should've come in civilian clothes—I don't want to antagonize you Yanks unnecessarily."

It was a beautiful warm day. Little kids escaped from their mothers to gape at Kastle's green uniform and his holstered machine-pistol, and some of the mothers were looking admiringly, too. I laughed. "They sure don't look antagonized." I said.

"Yeah, well, why not?" he demanded. "Why don't you resent us, for God's sake?"

"Why should we?" I asked reasonably.

"Well, if Canada had lost a war—especially that kind of a war—"

I shook my head. "We're not that kind of people, I guess." Then there was a silence, while Kastle moodily tossed his complimentary little package of peanuts to the kids and we both hunted for a subject for conversation.

We each came up with one at the same time. "How are you getting along with Marian?" I asked, and at the same moment he asked:

"Did you get your job in municipal funds management?"

There was something about his expression that told me he didn't want to answer my question, so I answered his. "That's over," I said. "Hotel management's what I'm into now. That's a growth field, with all the new tourism."

"I thought that was all foreign?"

"Foreign-owned. They sent representatives from the Saudis and the Puerto Ricans to my class to assure us they wouldn't discriminate in hiring. The Japanese are even better about that, of course, but they're all on the West Coast so far and I don't think I want to relocate. . . . Arne? Are you going to ask me if I resent something again?"

He growled, "As a matter of fact, I was!"

"Like the Apache Nation and the Puerto Ricans and so on taking their independence, you mean? But who can blame them for that? I do feel a little irritated at the Alaskans," I admitted, smiling, "after all the federal money they got! Still, the World's War had made us vulnerable, so they had their chance. You can understand why they took it."

"You," he said heavily, "can understand damn near anything, can't you?"

"Now, Arne! What does that mean?"

"It means you're going to vote for the president who lost it for you."

I shook my head. "We've been over this," I pointed out. "It was basically the secretary of state's fault." Secretary Messina had been doing his shuttle-diplomacy between Lesotho and Namibia and paying no attention at all to the Caribbean. When Grand Cayman suddenly declared war on the United States and the Soviet Union simultaneously, he was caught flat-footed.

"But the president could've just blown Grand Cayman out of the water."

"Sure he could. He *did* dispatch the Fourth Fleet."

"But they didn't do anything."

"How could they? Grand Cayman was at war with both us and the Russians. If we attacked them, the Russians would've had the right to too—and how would that have looked? Considering the Monroe Doctrine and all? No. The president handled it just right. He made that television speech warning the Russians to keep their hands off the Western Hemisphere. They did, too. And his ratings in the overnight polls went up fifteen percent!"

He looked at me peculiarly. "And that you consider a success?"

"You bet, Arne! Well. Almost a success, I guess. It would have worked perfectly, if it hadn't been for—"

"You mean San Marino," he said.

I nodded gloomily. "I mean San Marino. And then all the others. But who could have guessed that would happen?" For the second country to make a simultaneous and unexpected declaration of war against both the U.S.A. and the U.S.S.R. was the little country completely surrounded by Italy. They had no Monroe Doctrine to protect them, but what could either we or the Russians do? Neither one of us wanted to drop a missile that would splash fallout all over the Italians. The Italians wouldn't grant us transit privileges so land forces might attack—and, since San Marino wasn't an island, we couldn't even steam a fleet around them.

So there we were, the two most powerful nations the world had ever seen, stalemated in a war with the two feeblest. And then abruptly Lesotho made a surprise declaration of war on both of us, delighting Secretary Messina immensely—until Namibia did, too, half an hour later; and then Liechtenstein and Bangladesh, and Oman and Andorra. In seventy-two hours we were at war with every country in the world with a population under twenty million . . . and then the heavyweights began to come in. Mexico, Yugoslavia, Canada, East Germany, Brazil and Romania declared against both superpowers in a six-way conference-call satellite message that was seen by the whole world. Then France, then China, then Poland, then England. . . .

By the end of the week the whole world was technically at war. On one side, 141 nations. On the other, the Russians and us—and never a shot fired by anyone. After it was all over we got to see that famous tape of Secretary Messina in the Oval Office, sobbing and pleading with the president to declare war against the Soviets so we could fire the missiles at *somebody*. But how could we? They were the only ones on our side.

And they didn't like it any better than we did.

I leaned across the table to Arne Kastle. "Man to man," I coaxed, "was that whole thing set up in advance?"

Kastle slammed down his beer cup. "How the hell would I know? The premier doesn't consult prairie-province plow jockeys about his foreign policy." He stood up agitatedly, reaching in his pocket for Peacekeeper coins to toss to the circle of kids. "Wilbert," he said, "do you think life is just a spectator sport? Don't you ever get tired of being a critic?"

"We're a very sophisticated audience," I agreed.

He glared at me. Then he shook his head and started to leave, but I put out a hand to detain him. For a minute I thought he was going to hit me, but all I wanted was to point to the cards on the table. They were cutouts in the shape of camels, and their covers said, *Won't You Bark/Roar/Growl/Chirp a Few Words of Advice for Us?* "You forgot to fill out your comment sheet," I reminded him. But he didn't do it. He just sort of stared into my eyes, and then moaned and blundered away without another word. I had to fill them out for both of us.

The last time I saw Arne Kastle he just showed up at the door again. He appeared, still in uniform, with a six-pack of some Canadian beer, and the first thing he said was, "I guess I was a little out of line last time, eh?"

I considered the question. Actually I would have given him no more than a four for congeniality and maybe less than that for tact, but I didn't think he wanted to hear that. I just opened the door wide and said, "Come on in. The place is in a little better shape than the last time you saw it, isn't it?"

He glanced around. "Very nice," he said politely—no more than a six for the words, but his tone was almost a nine. "I see you've replaced all the stolen stuff."

"That's what insurance is for, Arne," I grinned, putting out glasses and pulling the tabs on two of the beers. "Of course they ripped me off some," I continued. "My alarm system was two years old, so they deducted twenty percent on the grounds of defective equipment. Then they depreciated everything for age and wear, I guess that was nearly thirty percent more. They really outfoxed me but what the hell, you have to hand it to them."

He exploded, "Why? Why do you have to hand it to them? Always the critic—you're as bad as Marian!"

The light dawned. "Ah," I said sympathetically. "You've seen Marian, then." He nodded sullenly. "Well then, listen, Arne, did you keep a copy of your card on her? I'd be interested to see how close we came in rating her."

"I didn't rate her at all!" He took a long pull at his beer, looking sulky and distraught. "I proposed to her," he said abruptly.

"Proposed!"

"What's wrong with that?" he demanded. The expression was belligerent now, so I just shrugged. "Well, I did, and she didn't say yes and she didn't say no. All she said was that I'd hear from her in a couple of days, and when I did it wasn't an answer. It was a checklist!" He dragged a blue-jacketed folder out of his pocket and hurled it at me.

I opened it, keeping a cautious eye on him—he seemed in a very unstable mood. But then I got interested. You can learn a lot about another person by the way they rate someone else, and I could see that Marian had taken a lot of trouble over this one. I was amused to see that she'd downrated him on "grooming" because his civilian suit wasn't as well pressed as his uniform—this from Miss Lipstick Smear! Then I came across something that made me indignant. "Oh, hell, Arne, this isn't fair! 'Proper speech, four.' But that's unreasonable—you're Canadian, after all; she can't expect you to speak English as well as an American!"

He began furiously, "A Canadian can *damn* sure speak English as well as a Yank!" But then he slumped back. "What's the use? Look at the overall rating. Six point two. She says she won't marry me unless I can get up to at least a seven—and then she wants a no-contest divorce if I ever drop down below seven again."

He stood up. "Well, thanks for listening," he said, starting toward the door. "Our tour of duty's almost over, so I guess I won't be seeing you again."

"Back to Saskatchewan, then?" I asked.

"And not a minute too soon," he said bitterly. "But it's been nice knowing you, Wilbert."

I said, "Same here, Arne. I'd give you an eight for originality in conversation and—" I hesitated, then decided to stretch a point in his favor—"maybe even a nine for good company!" But I couldn't give him anything for good manners, because he didn't even thank me.

I never saw Arne Kastle again, and neither did Marian. The funny thing was that we did see each other. The computer dating service threw her picture up a couple weeks later, and on impulse I signed in. I was surprised when she agreed to another date. I guess it was the same reason in both cases. The little man had intrigued our curiosity, and we wanted to talk about him.

I won the toss again and took her to the Starlight room of the Waldorf Asto-Rican—a little pricey for my pocket usually, but a hotel and motel management course had provided me with some two-for-one coupons. "I might almost have married him," said Marian thoughtfully, neatly folding the paper parasol from her Puerto Pep and placing it beside her plate, "if it weren't for his, well, craziness."

"I know what you mean," I agreed. "He had a lot going for him. Personality—oddball, sure, but kind of endearing, in a way. Sense of humor—"

"Oh, a ten anyway, Wilbert!" she giggled. "You should have heard some of the things he used to say about you!"

I had been thinking of at most a seven, but I was shooting for a ten in amiability so I just let it go. "But then there were his goofy ideas," I said.

"Right. I think the worst part was his complete misconception of what society is all about. Naturally we have high standards here. We expect our politicians to play the game well. Sure, sometimes they shade the law a little, or take a little graft—"

"That's just hardball politics," I nodded.

"Exactly, and that's where he fell down. No sophistication. No grasp of reality."

I was so touched I reached over and took her hand. "I wouldn't have given him more than a two for either." I said, and for a moment there I almost blew the whole thing by suggesting we go steady. Sweet Marian! I don't think I'll ever draw a girl as sensible and easy to get along with as she again. It could almost make you want to *marry* her.

But fortunately I got my natural sense of objectivity back in time. The weekend passed without my spoiling it. The president won easily, by the way. He was lucky enough to find a technical excuse for voiding about half a million votes for the other guy in one of the eastern states, and naturally when the rest of the nation heard about that they fell all over themselves jumping on the bandwagon. What a performance! It was a perfect example of all that's best and most admirable in our system. What a pity the rest of the world can't learn our ways!

SHAFFERY AMONG THE IMMORTALS

Fame is a fickle mistress. Jeremy Shaffery, the subject of this story, desperately wants to be famous. When we meet him, he's an astronomer, but not a famous one. His career has, in fact, gone downhill for some time.

He hasn't given up on his goal of achieving immortality, though. He continues to think up theories—unfortunately, not *valid* theories—and there's always the possibility something will pan out for him.

But time is running out for Shaffery. His wife has already run out on him, and his job as the director of the Carmine J. Nuccio Observatory in the Lesser Antilles is not going well.

Fame: Sometimes it's earned; sometimes, for better or worse, it's bestowed upon someone. In Shaffery's case . . . sorry, that would be telling.

This story has achieved a certain degree of immortality; when first published in 1972, it was a finalist for the Nebula Award.

Jeremy Shaffery had a mind a little bit like Einstein's, although maybe not in the ways that mattered most. When Einstein first realized that light carried mass he sat down to write to a friend about it and described the thought as "amusing and infectious." Shaffery would have thought that, too, although of course he would not likely have seen the implications of the Maxwell equations in the first place.

Shaffery looked a little bit like Einstein. He encouraged the resemblance, especially in the hair, until his hair began to run out. Since Einstein loved sailing, he kept a sixteen-foot trimaran tied up at the Observatory Dock. Seasickness kept him from using it much. Among the things he envied Einstein for was the mirror-smooth Swiss lakes, so much nicer than the lower Caribbean in that respect. But after a day of poring over pairs of star photographs with a blink comparator or trying to discover previously unknown chemical compounds in interstellar space in a radio trace, he sometimes floated around the cove in his little yellow rubber raft. It was relaxing, and his wife never followed him there. To Shaffery that was important. She was a difficult woman, chronically p.o.'d because his career was so persistently pointed in the wrong direction. If she had ever been a proper helpmeet, she wasn't anymore. Shaffery doubted she ever had, remembering that it was her unpleasant comments that had caused him to give up that other hallmark of the master, the violin.

At the stage in Shaffery's career at which he had become Director of the Carmine J. Nuccio Observatory in the Lesser Antilles he had begun to look less like Einstein and more like Edgar Kennedy. Nights when the seeing was good he remorselessly scanned the heavens through the twenty-two-inch reflector, hoping against hope for glory. Days when he was not sleeping he wandered through the dome like a ghost, running his finger over desks for dust, filching preserved mushrooms from Mr. Nuccio's home-canned hoard, trying to persuade his two local assistants to remember to close the dome slit when it rained. They paid little attention. They knew where the muscle was, and that it wasn't with Shaffery. He had few friends. Most of the white residents couldn't stand his wife; some of them couldn't stand Shaffery very well, either. There was a nice old lady drunk out from England in a tidy white house down the beach, a sort of hippie commune on the far side of the island, and a New York television talk-show operator who just flew down for weekends. When they were respectively sober, unstoned and present, Shaffery sometimes talked to them. That wasn't often. The only one he really wanted to see much was the TV man, but there were obstacles. The big obstacle was that the TV man spent most of his waking time skin-diving. The other obstacle was that Shaffery had discovered the TV man occasionally laid Mrs. Shaffery; it wasn't the morality of the thing that bothered him, it was the feeling of doubt it raised in Shaffery's mind about the other's sanity. He never spoke to the TV man about it, partly because he wasn't sure what to say and partly because the man had halfway promised to have Shaffery on his show. Sometime or other.

One must be fair to Shaffery and say that he wasn't a bad man. Like Frank Morgan, his problem was that he wasn't a good wizard. The big score always evaded him.

The Einstein method, which he had studied assiduously over many years, was to make a pretty theory and then see if, by any chance, observations of events in the real world seemed to confirm it. Shaffery greatly approved of that method. It just didn't seem to work out for him. At the Triple A-S meeting in Dallas he read an hour-long paper on his new principle of Relevance Theory. That was a typical Einstein idea, he flattered himself. He had even worked out simple explanations for the lay public, like Einstein with his sitting on a hot stove or holding hands with a pretty girl. "Relevance Theory," he practiced smiling to the little wavelets of the cove, "only means that observations that don't *relate* to anything don't *exist*. I'll spare you the mathematics because"—self-deprecatory laugh here—"I can't even fill out my income tax without making a mistake." Well, he had worked out the mathematics, inventing signs and operators of his own, just like Einstein. But he seemed to have made a mistake. Before the AAAS audience, fidgeting and whispering to each other behind their hands, he staked his scientific reputation on the prediction that the spectrum of Mars at its next opposition would show a slight but detectable displacement of some 150 Angstroms toward the violet. The son of a bitch didn't do anything of the kind. One of the audience was a graduate student at Princeton, hard up for a doctoral thesis subject, and he took a chance on Shaffery and made the observations, and with angry satisfaction sent him the proof that Mars had remained obstinately red.

The next year the International Astrophysical Union's referees, after some discussion, finally allowed him twenty minutes for a Brief Introduction into the General Consideration of Certain Electromagnetic Anomalies. He offered thirty-one pages of calculations leading to the prediction that the next lunar eclipse would be forty-two seconds late. It wasn't. It was right on time. At the meeting of the World Space Science Symposium they told him with great regret that overcommitments of space and time had made it impossible for them to schedule his no doubt valuable contribution, and by the time of the next round of conferences they weren't even sending him invitations anymore.

Meanwhile all those other fellows were doing great. Shaffery followed the careers of his contemporaries with rue. There was Hoyle, still making a good thing out of the Steady State Hypothesis, and Gamow's name, still reverenced for the Big Bang, and new people like Dyson and Ehricke and Enzmann coming along with all sorts of ideas that, if you looked at them objectively, weren't any cleverer than his, Shaffery thought, except for the detail that somehow or other they seemed lucky enough to find supporting evidence from time to time. It did not strike him as fair. Was he not a Mensa member? Was he not as well educated as the successful ones, as honored with degrees, as photogenic in the newsmagazines and as colorfully entertaining on the talk shows? (Assuming Larry Nesbit ever gave him the chance on his show.) Why did they make out and he fall flat? His wife's theory he considered and rejected. "Your trouble, Jeremy," she would say to him, "is you're a horse's ass." But he knew that wasn't it. Who was to say Isaac Newton wasn't a horse's ass, too, if you looked closely enough at his freaky theology and his nervous breakdowns? And look where he got.

So Shaffery kept looking for the thing that would make him great. He looked all over. Sometimes he checked Kepler's analysis of the orbit of Mars with an adding machine, looking for mistakes in arithmetic. (He found half a dozen, but the damn things all canceled each other out, which proves how hard it is to go wrong when your luck is in.) Sometimes he offered five-dollar prizes to the local kids for finding new stars that might turn out to be Shaffery's Nova, or anyway Shaffery's Comet. No luck. An ambitious scheme to describe stellar ballistics in terms of analogy with free-radical activity in the enzyme molecules fell apart when none of the biochemists he wrote to even answered his letters.

The file of failures grew. One whole drawer of a cabinet was filled with reappraisals of the great exploded theories of the past—*A New Look at Phlogiston,* incomplete because there didn't seem really to be anything to look at when you came down to it; a manuscript called *The Flat Earth Reexamined,* which no one would publish; three hundred sheets of drawings of increasingly tinier and increasingly quirkier circles to see if the Copernican epicycles could not somehow account for what the planet Mercury did that Einstein had considered a proof of relativity. From time to time he was drawn again to attempting to find a scientific basis for astrology and chiromancy, or predicting the paths of charged particles in a cloud chamber by means of yarrow stalks. It all came to nothing. When he was really despairing he sometimes considered making his mark in industry rather than pure science, wherefore the sheaf of sketches for a nuclear-fueled car, the experiments on smellovision that had permanently destroyed the nerves of his left nostril, the attempt to preserve some of Mr. Nuccio's mushrooms by irradiation in his local dentist's X-ray room. He knew that that sort of thing was not really worthy of a man with all those graduate degrees, but in any event he did no better there than anywhere else. Sometimes he dreamed of what it would be like to run Mount Palomar or Jodrell Bank, with fifty trained assistants to nail down his inspirations with evidence. He was not that fortunate. He had only Cyril and James.

It was not all bad, however, because he didn't have much interference to worry about. The observatory where he was employed, last and least of the string of eleven that had given him a position since his final doctoral degree, didn't seem to mind what he did, as long as he did it without bothering them. On the other hand, they didn't give him much support, either.

Probably they just didn't know how. The observatory was owned by something called the Lesser Antilles Vending Machine Entertainment Co., Ltd., and, so Shaffery had been told by the one old classmate who still kept up a sort of friendship with him, was actually some sort of tax-evasion scheme maintained by a Las Vegas gambling syndicate. Shaffery didn't mind this, particularly, although from time to time he got tired of being told that the only two astronomers who mattered were Giovanni Schiaparelli and Galileo Galilei. That was only a minor annoyance. The big cancerous agony was that every year he got a year older and fame would not come.

At his periodic low spots of despondency (he had even tried linking them with the oppositions of Jupiter, meteor showers, and his wife's periods, but those didn't come to anything either) he toyed with the notion of dropping it all and going into some easier profession. Banking. Business Law. "President Shaffery" had the right kind of sound, if he entered politics. But then he would drag his raft to the water, prop two six-packs of Danish beer on his abdomen and float away, and by the end of the first pack his courage would come flowing back, and on the second he would be well into a scheme for detecting gravity waves by statistical analysis of forty thousand acute gout sufferers, telephoning the state of their twinges into a central computer facility.

On such a night he carried his little rubber raft to the shore of the cove, slipped off his sandals, rolled up his bellbottoms and launched himself. It was the beginning of the year, as close to winter as it ever got on the island, which meant mostly that the dark came earlier. It was a bad time of the year for him, because it was the night before the annual Board Meeting. The first year or two he had looked forward to the meetings as opportunities. He was no longer so hopeful. His objective for the present meeting was only to survive it, and there was some question of a nephew by marriage, an astronomy major at U.C.L.A., to darken even that hope.

Shaffery's vessel wasn't really a proper raft, only the sort of kid's toy that drowns a dozen or so nine-year-olds at the world's bathing beaches every year. It was less than five feet long. When he got himself twisted and wriggled into it, his back against the ribbed bottom, his head pillowed against one inflated end and his feet dangling into the water at the other, it was quite like floating in a still sea without the annoyance of getting wet. He opened the first beer and began to relax. The little waves rocked and turned him; the faint breeze competed with the tiny island tide, and the two of them combined to take him erratically away from the beach at the rate of maybe ten feet a minute. It didn't matter. He was still inside the cove, with islandlets, or low sandbanks, beaded across the mouth of it. If by any sudden meteorological miracle a storm should spring from that bright-lamped sky, the wind could take him nowhere but back to shore or near an island. And of course there would be no storm. He could paddle back whenever he chose, and as easily as he could push his soap dish around his bathtub, as he routinely did while bathing—which in turn he did at least once a day, and when his wife was particularly difficult, as often as six times. The bathroom was his other refuge. His wife never followed him there, being too well brought up to run the chance of inadvertently seeing him doing something filthy.

Up on the low hills he could see the corroded copper dome of the observatory. A crescent of light showed that his assistant had opened the dome, but the light showed that he was not using it for any astronomical purpose. That was easy to unriddle. Cyril had turned the lights on so that the cleaning woman could get the place spotless for the Board Meeting, and had opened the dome because that proved the telescope was being used. Shaffery bent the empty beer can into a V, tucked it neatly beside him in the raft, and opened another. He was not yet tranquil, but he was not actively hurting anywhere. At least Cyril would not be using the telescope to study the windows of the Bon Repos Hotel across the cove, since the last time he'd done it he had jammed the elevating gears and it could no longer traverse anywhere near the horizon. Shaffery put aside an unwanted, fugitive vision of Idris, the senior and smartest cleaning lady, polishing the telescope mirror with Bon Ami, sipped his beer, thought nostalgically of Relevance Theory and how close he had come with the epicycles, and freed his mind for constructive thought.

The sun was wholly gone, except for a faint luminous purpling of the sky in the general direction of Venezuela. Almost directly overhead hung the three bright stars of Orion's Belt, slowly turning like the traffic signals on a railroad line, with Sirius and Procyon orbiting headlight bright around them. As his eyes dark-adapted he could make out the stars in Orion's sword, even the faint patch of light that was the great gas cloud. He was far enough from the shore so that sound could not carry, and he softly called out the great four-pointed pattern of first magnitude stars that surrounded the constellation: "Hey there, Betelguese. Hi, Bellatrix. What's new, Rigel? Nice to see you again, Saiph." He glanced past red Aldebaran to the closeknit stars of the Pleiades, returned to Orion and, showing off now, called off the stars of the Belt: "Hey Alnitak! Yo, Alnilam! How goes it, Mintaka?"

The problem with drinking beer in the rubber raft was that your head was bent down toward your chest and it was difficult to burp, but Shaffery arched his body up a little, getting some water in the process but not caring, got rid of the burp, opened another beer, and gazed complacently at Orion. It was a satisfying constellation. It was satisfying that he knew so much about it. He thought briefly of the fact that the Arabs had called the Belt Stars by the name Jauzah, meaning the Golden Nuts; that the Chinese thought they looked like a weighing beam; and that Greenlanders called them Siktut, The Seal-Hunters Lost at Sea. As he was going on to remember what the Australian aborigines had thought of them (they thought they resembled three young men dancing a corroboree), his mind flickered back to the lost sealhunters. Um, he thought. He raised his head and looked toward the shore.

It was now more than a hundred yards away. That was farther than he really wanted to be, and so he kicked the raft around, oriented himself by the stars and began to paddle back. It was easy and pleasant to do. He used a sort of splashy upside-down breast stroke of the old-fashioned angel's wing kind, but as all his weight was supported by the raft he moved quickly across the water. He was rather enjoying the exercise, toes and fingers moving comfortably in the tepid sea, little ghosts of luminescence glowing where he splashed, until quite without warning the fingertips of one hand struck sharply and definitely against something that was resistantly massive and solid where there should have been only water, something that moved stubbornly, something that rasped them like a file. Oh, my God, thought Shaffery. What a lousy thing to happen. They so seldom came in this close to shore. He didn't even think about them. What a shame for a man who might have been Einstein to wind up, incomplete and unfulfilled, as shark shit.

He really was not a bad man, and it was the loss to science that was first on his mind, only a little later what it must feel like to be chopped and gulped.

Shaffery pulled his hands in and folded them on his chest, crossed his feet at the ankles and rested them on the end of the boat, knees spread on the sides. There was now nothing trailing in the water that might strike a shark as bait. There was, on the other hand, no good way for him to get back to shore. He could yell, but the wind was the wrong way. He could wait till he drifted near one of the islets. But if he missed them he would be out in the deep ocean before he knew it.

Shaffery was almost sure that sharks seldom attacked a boat, even a rubber one. Of course, he went on analytically, the available evidence didn't signify. They could flip a raft like this over easily enough. If this particular shark ate him off this particular half-shell there would be no one to report it.

Still, there were some encouraging considerations. Say it was a shark. Say it was capable of tipping the boat or eating him boat and all. They were dull-witted creatures, and what was to keep one hanging around in the absence of blood, splashing, noise, trailing objects, or any of the other things sharks were known to take an interest in? It might be a quarter mile away already. But it wasn't, because at that moment he heard the splash of some large object breaking the surface a foot from his head.

Shaffery could have turned to look, but he didn't; he remained quite motionless, listening to the gentle water noises, until they were punctuated by a sort of sucking sound and then a voice. A human voice. It said, "Scared the piss out of you, didn't I? What do you say, Shaffery? Want a tow back to shore?"

It was not the first time Shaffery had encountered Larry Nesbit diving in the cove, it was only the first time it had happened at night. Shaffery twisted about in the raft had gazed at Nesbit's grinning face and its frame of wet strands of nape-length hair. It took a little time to make the transition in his mind from eighteen-foot shark to five-foot-eight TV star. "Come on," Nesbit went on, "what do you say? Tell you what. I'll tow you in, and you give me some of old Nuccio's Scotch, and I'll listen to how you're going to invent anti-gravity while we get pissed."

That Nesbit, he had a way with him. The upshot of it all was that Shaffery had a terrible hangover the next day; not the headache but the whole works, with trotting to the toilet and being able to tolerate only small sips of ginger ale and wishing, or almost wishing, he was dead. (Not, to be sure, before he did the one immortalizing thing. Whatever it was going to be.)

It was not altogether a disaster, the hangover. The next morning was very busy, and it was just as well that he was out of the way. When the Board of Directors convened to discuss the astronomical events of the year, or whatever it is they did discuss in the afternoon session to which Shaffery was definitely not invited, it was always a busy time. They arrived separately, each director with his pair of associates. One after another, forty-foot cabin cruisers with fishing tops came up to the landing and gave up cargos of plump little men wearing crew cuts and aloha shirts. The observatory car, not ever used by any of the observatory personnel, was polished, fueled and used for round trips from the landing strip at Jubila, across the island, to Coomray Hill and the observatory. Shaffery laid low in his private retreat. He had never told his wife that he was not allowed in the observatory for the Board Meetings, so she didn't look for him. He spent the morning in the tarpaper shack where photographic material had once been kept, until he discovered that the damp peeled the emulsion away from the backing. Now it was his home away from home. He had fitted it with a desk, chair, icebox, coffee pot and bed.

Shaffery paid no attention to the activity outside, not even when the Directors' assistants, methodically searching the bushes and banana groves all around the observatory, came to his shack, opened the door without knocking and peered in at him. They knew him from previous meetings, but they studied him silently for a moment before the two in the doorway nodded to each other and left him again. They were not well mannered men, Shaffery thought, but no doubt they were good at their jobs, whatever those jobs were. He resolutely did not think about the Board Meeting, or about the frightening, calumnious things Larry Nesbit had said to him the night before, drinking the Board Chairman's Scotch and eating his food, in that half-jocular, shafting, probing way he had. Shaffery thought a little bit about the queasy state of his lower abdomen, because he couldn't help it, but what he mostly thought about was Fermat's Last Theorem.

A sort of picayune, derivative immortality was waiting there for someone. Not much, but Shaffery was getting desperate. It was one of those famous mathematical problems that grad students played at for a month or two, and amateurs assaulted in vain all their lives. It looked easy enough to deal with. It started with so elementary a proposition that every high-school boy mastered it about the time he learned to masturbate successfully. If you squared the sides of a right triangle, the sum of the squares of the two sides was equal to the square of the hypotenuse.

Well, that was all very well, and it was so easy to understand that it had been used to construct right angles by surveyors for centuries. A triangle whose sides were, say, 3 feet and 4 feet, and whose hypotenuse was 5 feet, had to make a right angle, because $3^2 + 4^2 = 5^2$, and it always had, since the time of Pythagoras, five hundred years B.C. $a^2 + b^2 = c^2$. The hitch was, if the exponent was anything but 2, you could never make the equation come out using whole numbers, $a^3 + b^3$ never equaled c^3, and $a^{27} + b^{27}$ did not add up to any c^{27}, no matter what numbers you used for a, b and c. Everybody knew that this was so. Nobody had ever proved that it *had* to be so, by mathematical proofs, except that Fermat had left a cryptic little note, found among his papers after his death, claiming that he had found a "truly wonderful" proof, only there wasn't enough room in the margin of the book he was writing on to put it all down.

Shaffery was no mathematician. But that morning, waking up to the revolution in his stomach and the thunder in his head, he had seen that that was actually a strength. One, all the mathematicians of three or four centuries had broken their heads against the problem, so obviously, it couldn't be solved by any known mathematics anyway. Two, Einstein was weak in mathematics too, and had disdained to worry about it, preferring to invent his own.

So he spent the morning, between hurried gallops across the parking lot to the staff toilet, filling paper with mathematical signs and operators of his own invention. It did not seem to be working out, to be sure. For a while he thought of an alternative scheme, to wit, inventing a "truly wonderful" solution of his own and claiming he couldn't find room to write it down in the margin of, say, the latest issue of *Mathematical Abstracts*; but residual sanity persuaded him that perhaps no one would ever find it, if it was found it might well be laughed off, and anyway that was purely posthumous celebrity and he wanted to taste it while he was alive. So he broke for lunch, came back feeling dizzy and ill and worried about the meeting that was going on, and decided to take a nap before resuming his labors.

When Cyril came looking for him to tell him the Directors desired his presence, it was dark, and Shaffery felt like hell.

Coomray Hill was no taller than a small office building, but it got the mirror away from most of the sea-level dampness. The observatory sat on top of the hill like a mound of pistachio ice cream, hemispheric green copper roof and circular walls of green-painted plaster. Inside, the pedestal of the telescope took up the center of the floor. The instrument itself was traversed as low as it would go anymore, clearing enough space for the Directors and their gear. They were all there, looking at him with silent distaste as he came in.

The inner sphere of the dome was painted (by Cyril's talented half-sister) with a large map of Mars, showing Schiaparelli's famous canals in resolute detail; a view of the Bay of Naples from the Vomero, with Vesuvius gently steaming in the background; and an illuminated drawing of the constellation Scorpius, which happened to be the sign of the constellation under which the Chairman of the Board had been born. A row of card-tables had been lined up and covered with a green cloth. There were six places set, each with ashtray, notepad, three sharpened pencils, ice, glass, and bottle of John Begg. Another row of tables against the wall held the antipasto, replenished by Cyril after the depredations of the night before, but now seriously depleted by the people for whom it was intended. Six cigars were going and a couple of others were smoldering in the trays. Shaffery tried not to breathe. Even with the door open and the observing aperture in the dome wide, the inside air was faintly blue. At one time Shaffery had mentioned diffidently what the deposit of cigar smoke did to the polished surface of the twenty-two-inch mirror. That was at his first annual meeting. The Chairman hadn't said a word, just stared at him. Then he nodded to his right-hand man, a Mr. DiFirenzo, who had taken a packet of Kleenex out of his pocket and tossed it to Shaffery. "So wipe the goddam thing off," he had said. "Then you could dump these ashtrays for us, okay?"

Shaffery did his best to smile at his Directors. Behind him he was conscious of the presence of their assistants, who were patrolling the outside of the observatory in loose elliptical orbits, perigeeing at the screen door to peer inside. They had studied Shaffery carefully as he came across the crunching shell of the parking lot, and under their scrutiny he had decided against detouring by way of the staff toilet, which he now regretted.

"Okay, Shaffery," said Mr. DiFirenzo, after glancing at the Chairman of the Board. "Now we come to you."

Shaffery clasped his hands behind him in his Einstein pose and said brightly, "Well, it has been a particularly productive year for the Observatory. No doubt you've seen my reports on the Leonid meteorite count and—"

"Right," said Mr. DiFirenzo, "but what we have been talking about here is the space shots. Mr. Nuccio has expressed his views that this is a kind of strategic location, like how they shoot the rockets from Cape Kennedy. They have to go right over us, and we want a piece of that."

Shaffery shifted his weight uneasily. "I discussed that in my report last year—"

"No, Shaffery. This year, Shaffery. Why can't we get some of that federal money, like for tracking, for instance?"

"But the position hasn't changed, Mr. DiFirenzo. We don't have the equipment, and besides NASA has its own—"

"No good, Shaffery. You know how much you got out of us for equipment last year? I got the figures right here. And now you tell us you don't have what we need to make a couple of bucks?"

"Well, Mr. DiFirenzo, you see, the equipment we have is for purely scientific purposes. For this sort of work you need quite different instruments, and actually—"

"I don't want to hear." DiFirenzo glanced at the Chairman, and then went on. "Next thing, what about that comet you said you were going to discover?"

Shaffery smiled forgivingly. "Really, I can't be held accountable for that. I didn't actually say we'd *find* one. I merely said that the continuing *search* for comets was part of our basic *program*. Of course, I've done my very best to—"

"Not good enough, Shaffery. Besides, your boy here told Mr. Nuccio that if you did find a comet you wouldn't name it the Mr. Carmine J. Nuccio comet like Mr. Nuccio wanted."

Shaffery was going all hollow inside, but he said bravely: "It's not wholly up to me, is it? There's an astronomical convention that it is the discoverer's name that goes on—"

"We don't like that convention, Shaffery. Three, now we come to some really bad things, that I'm sorry to hear you've got yourself into, Shaffery. We hear you have been talking over the private affairs of this institution and Mr. Nuccio with that dick-head Nesbit. Shut, Shaffery," the man said warningly as Shaffery started to open his mouth. "We know all about it. This Nesbit is getting himself into big trouble. He has said some very racist things about Mr. Nuccio on that sideshow of his on the TV, which is going to cost him quite a bundle when Mr. Nuccio's lawyers get through with him. That is very bad, Shaffery, and also, four, there is this thing."

He lifted up what had seemed like a crumpled napkin in front of his place. It turned out that it was covering what looked like a large transistor radio.

Shaffery identified it after a moment's thought; he had seen it before, in Larry Nesbit's possession. "It's a tape recorder," he said.

"Right on, Shaffery. Now the question is, who put it in here? I don't mean just left it here like you could leave your rubbers or something, Shaffery. I mean left it here with one of those trick switches so it was going when a couple of our associates checked the place out and found it under the table."

Shaffery swallowed very hard, but even so his voice sounded unfamiliar to him when he was able to speak. "I—I *assure* you, Mr. DiFirenzo! I had nothing to do with it."

"No, Shaffery, I know you didn't, because you are not that smart. Mr. Nuccio was quite upset about this illegal bugging, and he has already made some phone calls and talked to some people and we have a pretty good idea of who put it there, and he isn't going to have what he thinks he's going to have to play on his TV show. So here it is, Shaffery. Mr. Nuccio doesn't find your work satisfactory here, and he is letting you go. We got somebody else coming down to take over. We'd appreciate it if you could be out by tomorrow."

There are situations in which there is not much scope for dignity. A man in his middle-fifties who has just lost the worst job he ever had has few opportunities for making the sort of terminal remark that one would like to furnish one's biographers.

Shaffery discovered that he was worse off than that; he was frankly sick. The turmoil in his belly grew. The little saliva pumps under his tongue were flooding his mouth faster than he could swallow, and he knew that if he didn't get back to the staff toilet very quickly he would have another embarrassment to add to what was already an overwhelming load. He turned and walked away. Then marched. Then ran. When he had emptied himself of everything in belly, bladder and gut, he sat on the edge of the toilet seat and thought of the things he could have said: "Look, Nuccio, you don't know anything about science." "Nuccio, Schiaparelli was all wrong about the canals on Mars." It was too late to say them. It was too late to ask the question that his wife would be sure to ask, about severance pay, pension, all the things that he had been putting off getting in writing. ("Don't worry about that stuff, Shaffery, Mr. Nuccio always takes care of his friends but he don't like to be aggravated.") He tried to make a plan for his future, and failed. He tried even to make a plan for his present. Surely he should at least call Larry Nesbit, to demand, to complain and to warn ("Hist! The tape recorder has been discovered! All is lost! Flee!"), but he could not trust himself so far from the toilet. Not at that exact moment. And a moment later it was too late. Half an hour later, when one of the orbiting guards snapped the little lock and peered inside, the man who might have been Einstein was lying on the floor with his trousers around his knees, undignified, uncaring, and dead.

Ah, Shaffery! How disappointed he would have been in his *Times* obit, two paragraphs buried under the overhang of a pop singer's final notice. But afterward. . . .

The first victim was Larry Nesbit, airsick in his Learjet all the way back to New York, overcome during the taping of his TV show and dying the next day. The next victims were the Board of Directors, every man. They started home, by plane and boat. Some of them made it, but all of them died: en route or in Las Vegas, Detroit, Chicago, Los Angeles. New York, and Long Branch, New Jersey. Some of the "assistants" died and some were spared. (Briefly.) The reason was not a mystery for very long. The source of the new plague was tracked down quickly enough to Mr. Nuccio's antipasto, and particularly to the preserved mushrooms that Shaffery had borrowed for his experiment.

The botulinus toxin was long recognized as the most deadly poison known to man. The mutated version that Shaffery and his dentist's X-rays had brought into being was not much more deadly, but it had another quality that was new and different. Old, established botulinus clostriduim is an organism with a feeble hold on life; expose it to light and air, and it dies. B. shafferia was more sturdy. It grew where it was. In anything. In Mr. Nuccio's antipasto, in a salad in a restaurant kitchen, in Mom's apple pie on a windowsill to cool, in the human digestive tract. There were nine deaths in the first five days, and then for a moment no more. The epidemiologists would not have bothered their heads about so short a casualty list if it had not been for the identities of some of the victims. But the bacteria were multiplying. The stain of vomit under the boardwalk at Long Branch dried; the bacteria turned into spores and were blown on the wind until they struck something damp and fertile. Whereupon they grew. The soiled Kleenex thrown from a Cadillac Fleetwood on the road leading from O'Hare to Evanston, the sneeze between flights at Miami, expectorations in a dozen places—all added to the score. From the urine and feces of the afflicted men, from their sweat, even from their bed linen and discarded clothing, enspored bacteria leaped into the air and were inhaled, eaten, drunk, absorbed into cuts, in every way ingested into the waiting bodies of hundreds, then thousands, ultimately countless millions of human beings.

By the second week Detroit and Los Angeles were declared disaster areas. By the fourth the plague had struck every city in America, and had leaped the oceans. If it had any merciful quality at all, it was that it was quick: an upset stomach, a sweat, a few pangs and then death. None were immune. Few survived. Out of a hundred, three might outlive the disease. But then famine, riot, and lesser ills took their toll; and of the billions who lived on the Earth when Shaffery exposed his antipasto in the dentist's office, all but a few tens of millions died in the outbreak that the world will never forget the disease called Shaffery's Syndrome.

THE DAY THE
ICICLE WORKS CLOSED

As previously noted, Frederik Pohl knows a bit about politics. He also knows something about economics and about the criminal justice system. All three of these elements figure in 1959's "The Day the Icicle Works Closed."

As will become evident before long, he also has been known to root for the underdog. In this story of crime, punishment, and complications that ensue as a result, Milo Pulcher, a public defender on Altair Nine, is a huge underdog in a corrupt system.

Pulcher used to work for Altamycin, Inc., also known as the Icicle Works, but when they shut down the works, he and everyone else who'd worked there had to find new work.

Strange, crooked things are happening on Altair Nine, but unless Milo can overcome big odds to beat the system, nobody will ever know why or how the strange doings are being accomplished. If he doesn't succeed, he'll be just one more victim of a world gone wrong.

Never bet against the underdog.

I

The wind was cold, pink snow was falling and Milo Pulcher had holes in his shoes. He trudged through the pink-gray slush across the square from the courthouse to the jail. The turnkey was drinking coffee out of a vinyl container. "Expecting you," he grunted. "Which one you want to see first?"

Pulcher sat down, grateful for the warmth. "It doesn't matter. Say, what kind of kids are they?"

The turnkey shrugged.

"I mean, do they give you any trouble?"

"How could they give me trouble? If they don't clean their cells they don't eat. What else they do makes no difference to me."

Pulcher took the letter from Judge Pegrim out of his pocket, and examined the list of his new clients. Avery Foltis, Walter Hopgood, Jimmy Lasser, Sam Schlesterman, Bourke Smith, Madeleine Gaultry. None of the names meant anything to him. "I'll take Foltis," he guessed, and followed the turnkey to a cell.

The Foltis boy was homely, pimply and belligerent. "Cripes," he growled shrilly, "are you the best they can do for me?"

Pulcher took his time answering. The boy was not very lovable; but, he reminded himself, there was a fifty-dollar retainer from the county for each one of these defendants, and conditions being what they were Pulcher could easily grow to love three hundred dollars. "Don't give me a hard time," he said amiably. "I may not be the best lawyer in the Galaxy, but I'm the one you've got."

"Cripes."

"All right, all right. Tell me what happened, will you? All I know is that you're accused of conspiracy to commit a felony, specifically an act of kidnaping a minor child."

"Yeah, that's it," the boy agreed. "You want to know what happened?" He bounced to his feet, then began acting out his story. "We were starving to death, see?" Arms clutched pathetically around his belly. "The Icicle Works closed down. Cripes, I walked the streets nearly a year, looking for something to do. Anything." Marching in place. "I even rented out for a while, but—that didn't work out." He scowled and fingered his pimply face. Pulcher nodded. Even a body-renter had to have some qualifications. The most important one was a good-looking, disease-free, strong and agile physique. "So we got together and decided, the hell, there was money to be made hooking old Swinburne's son. So—I guess we talked too much. They caught us." He gripped his wrists, like manacles.

Pulcher asked a few more questions, and then interviewed two of the other boys. He learned nothing he hadn't already known. The six youngsters had planned a reasonably competent kidnaping, and talked about it where they could be heard, and if there was any hope of getting them off it did not make itself visible to their court-appointed attorney.

Pulcher left the jail abruptly and went up the street to see Charley Dickon.

The committeeman was watching a three-way wrestling match on a flickery old TV set. "How'd it go, Milo," he greeted the lawyer, keeping his eyes on the wrestling.

Pulcher said, "I'm not going to get them off, Charley."

"Oh? Too bad." Dickon looked away from the set for the first time. "Why not?"

"They admitted the whole thing. Handwriting made the Hopgood boy on the ransom note. They all had fingerprints and cell-types all over the place. And besides, they talked too much."

Dickon said with a spark of interest, "What about Tim Lasser's son?"

"Sorry." The committeeman looked thoughtful. "I can't help it, Charley," the lawyer protested. The kids hadn't been even routinely careful. When they planned to kidnap the son of the mayor they had talked it over, quite loudly, in a juke joint. The waitress habitually taped everything that went on in her booths. Pulcher suspected a thriving blackmail business, but that didn't change the fact that there was enough on tape to show premeditation. They had picked the mayor's son up at school. He had come with them perfectly willingly—the girl, Madeleine Gaultry, had been a babysitter for him. The boy was only three years old, but he couldn't miss an easy identification like that. And there was more: the ransom note had been sent special delivery, and young Foltis had asked the post-office clerk to put the postage on instead of using the automatic meter. The clerk remembered the pimply face very well indeed.

The committeeman sat politely while Pulcher explained, though it was obvious that most of his attention was on the snowy TV screen. "Well, Milo, that's the way it goes. Anyway, you got a fast three hundred, hey? And that reminds me."

Pulcher's guard went up.

"Here," said the committeeman, rummaging through his desk. He brought out a couple of pale green tickets. "You ought to get out and meet some more people. The Party's having its annual Chester A. Arthur Day Dinner next week. Bring your girl."

"I don't have a girl."

"Oh, you'll find one. Fifteen dollars per," explained the committeeman, handing over the tickets. Pulcher sighed and paid. Well, that was what kept the wheels oiled. And Dickon had suggested his name to Judge Pegrim. Thirty dollars out of three hundred still left him a better week's pay than he had had since the Icicle Works folded.

The committeeman carefully folded the bills into his pocket, Pulcher watching gloomily. Dickon was looking prosperous, all right. There was easily a couple of thousand in that wad. Pulcher supposed that Dickon had been caught along with everybody else on the planet when the Icicle Works folded. Nearly everybody owned stock in it, and certainly Charley Dickon, whose politician brain got him a piece of nearly every major enterprise on Altair Nine—a big clump of stock in the Tourist Agency, a sizable share of the Mining Syndicate—certainly he would have had at least a few thousand in the Icicle Works. But it hadn't hurt him much. He said, "None of my business, but why don't you take that girl?"

"Madeleine Gaultry? She's in jail."

"Get her out. Here." He tossed over a bondsman's card. Pulcher pocketed it with a scowl. That would cost another forty bucks anyway, he estimated; the bondsman would naturally be one of Dickon's club members.

Pulcher noticed that Dickon was looking strangely puzzled. "What's the matter?"

"Like I say, it's none of my business. But I don't get it. You and the girl have a fight?"

"Fight? I don't even know her."

"She said you did."

"Me? No. I don't know any Madeleine Gaultry— Wait a minute! Is that her married name? Did she used to be at the Icicle Works?"

Dickon nodded. "Didn't you see her?"

"I didn't get to the women's wing. I—" Pulcher stood up, oddly flustered. "Say, I'd better run along, Charley. This bondsman, he's open now? Well—" He stopped babbling and left.

Madeleine Gaultry! Only her name had been Madeleine Cossett. It was funny that she should turn up now—in jail and, Pulcher abruptly realized, likely to stay there indefinitely. But he put that thought out of his mind; first he wanted to see her.

The snow was turning lavender now.

Pink snow, green snow, lavender snow—any color of the pastel rainbow. It was nothing unusual. That was what had made Altair Nine worth colonizing in the first place.

Now, of course, it was only a way of getting your feet wet.

Pulcher waited impatiently at the turnkey's office while he shambled over to the women's wing and, slowly, returned with the girl. They looked at each other. She didn't speak. Pulcher opened his mouth, closed it, and silently took her by the elbow. He steered her out of the jail and hailed a cab. That was an extravagance, but he didn't care.

Madeleine shrank into a corner of the cab, looking at him out of blue eyes that were large and shadowed. She wasn't hostile, she wasn't afraid. She was only remote.

"Hungry?" She nodded. Pulcher gave the cab driver the name of a restaurant. Another extravagance, but he didn't mind the prospect of cutting down on lunches for a few weeks. He had had enough practice at it.

A year before this girl had been the prettiest secretary in the pool at the Icicle Works. He dated her half a dozen times. There was a company rule against it, but the first time it was a kind of schoolboy's prank, breaking the headmaster's regulations, and the other times it was a driving need. Then—

Then came the Gumpert Process.

That was the killer, the Gumpert Process. Whoever Gumpert was. All anybody at the Icicle Works knew was that someone named Gumpert (back on Earth, one rumor said; another said he was a colonist in the Sirian system) had come up with a cheap, practical method of synthesizing the rainbow antibiotic molds that floated free in Altair Nine's air, coloring its precipitation and, more important, providing a priceless export commodity. A whole Galaxy had depended on those rainbow molds, shipped in frozen suspensions to every inhabited planet by Altamycin, Inc.—the proper name for what everyone on Altair Nine called the Icicle Works.

When the Gumpert Process came along, suddenly the demand vanished.

Worse, the jobs vanished. Pulcher had been on the corporation's legal staff, with an office of his own and a faint hint of a vice-presidency, someday. He was out. The stenos in the pool, all but two or three of the five hundred who once had got out the correspondence and the bills, they were out. The shipping clerks in the warehouse were out, the pumphands at the settling tanks were out, the freezer attendants were out. Everyone was out. The plant closed down. There were more than fifty tons of frozen antibiotics in storage and, though there might still be a faint trickle of orders from old-fashioned diehards around the Galaxy (backwoods country doctors who didn't believe in the new-fangled synthetics, experimenters who wanted to run comparative tests), the shipments already en route would much more than satisfy them. Fifty tons? Once the Icicle Works had shipped three hundred tons a day—physical transport, electronic rockets that took years to cover the distance between stars. The boom was over. And of course, on a one-industry planet, everything else was over too.

Pulcher took the girl by the arm and swept her into the restaurant. "Eat," he ordered. "I know what jail food is like." He sat down, firmly determined to say nothing until she had finished.

But he couldn't.

Long before she was ready for coffee he burst out, "Why, Madeleine? Why would you get into something like this?"

She looked at him but did not answer.

"What about your husband?" He didn't want to ask it, but he had to. That had been the biggest blow of all the unpleasant blows that had struck him after the Icicle Works closed. Just as he was getting a law practice going—not on any big scale but, through Charley Dickon and the Party, a small, steady handout of political favors that would make it possible for him to pretend he was still an attorney—the gossip reached him that Madeleine Cossett had married.

The girl pushed her plate away. "He emigrated."

Pulcher digested that slowly. Emigrated? That was the dream of every Niner since the Works closed down, of course. But it was only a dream. Physical transport between the stars was ungodly expensive. More, it was ungodly slow. Ten years would get you to Dell, the thin-aired planet of a chilly little red dwarf. The nearest *good* planet was thirty years away.

What it all added up to was that emigrating was almost like dying. If one member of a married couple emigrated, it meant the end of the marriage. . . . "We got a divorce," said Madeleine, nodding. "There wasn't enough money for both of us to go, and Jon was unhappier here than I was."

She took out a cigarette and let him light it. "You don't want to ask me about Jon, do you? But you want to know. All right. Jon was an artist. He was in the advertising department at the Works, but that was just temporary. He was going to do something big. Then the bottom dropped out for him, just as it did for all of us. Well, Milo, I didn't hear from you."

Pulcher protested, "It wouldn't have been *fair* for me to see you when I didn't have a job or anything."

"Of course you'd think that. It's wrong. But I couldn't find you to tell you it was wrong, and then Jon was very persistent. He was tall, curly-haired, he has a baby's face—do you know, he only shaved twice a week. Well, I married him. It lasted three months. Then he just had to get away." She leaned forward earnestly. "Don't think he was just a bum, Milo! He really was quite a good artist. But we didn't have enough money for paints, even, and then it seems that the colors are all wrong here. Jon explained it. In order to paint landscapes that sell you have to be on a planet with Earth-type colors; they're all the vogue. And there's too much altamycin in the clouds here."

Pulcher said stiffly, "I see." But he didn't, really. There was at least one unexplained part. If there hadn't been enough money for paint, then where had the money come from for a starship ticket, physical transport? It meant at least ten thousand dollars. There just was no way to raise ten thousand dollars on Altair Nine, not without taking a rather extreme step. . . .

The girl wasn't looking at him.

Her eyes were fixed on a table across the restaurant, a table with a loud, drunken party. It was only lunch time, but they had a three-o'clock-in-the-morning air about them. They were *stinking*. There were four of them, two men and two women; and their physical bodies were those of young, healthy, quite good-looking, perfectly normal Niners. The appearance of the physical bodies was entirely irrelevant, though, because they were tourists. Around the neck of each of them was a bright golden choker with a glowing red signal jewel in the middle. It was the mark of the tourist Agency; the sign that the bodies were rented.

Milo Pulcher looked away quickly. His eyes stopped on the white face of the girl, and abruptly he knew how she had raised the money to send Jon to another star.

2

Pulcher found the girl a room and left her there. It was not what he wanted. What he wanted was to spend the evening with her and to go on spending time with her, until time came to an end: but there was the matter of her trial.

Twenty-four hours ago he had got the letter notifying him that the court had appointed him attorney for six suspected kidnapers and looked on it as a fast fee, no work to speak of, no hope for success. He would lose the case, certainly. Well, what of it?

But now he wanted to win!

It meant some fast, hard work if he was to have even a chance—and at best, he admitted to himself, the chance would not be good. Still, he wasn't going to give up without a try.

The snow stopped as he located the home of Jimmy Lasser's parents. It was a sporting-goods shop, not far from the main Tourist Agency; it had a window full of guns and boots and scuba gear. He walked in, tinkling a bell as he opened the door.

"Mr. Lasser?" A plump little man, leaning back in a chair by the door, got slowly up, looking him over.

"In back," he said shortly.

He led Pulcher behind the store, to a three-room apartment. The living room was comfortable enough, but for some reason it seemed unbalanced. One side was somehow heavier than the other. He noticed the nap of the rug, still flattened out where something heavy had been, something rectangular and large, about the size of a Tri-V electronic entertainment unit. "Repossessed," said Lasser shortly. "Sit down. Dickon called you a minute ago."

"Oh?" It had to be something important. Dickon wouldn't have tracked him down for any trivial matter.

"Don't know what he wanted, but he said you weren't to leave till he called back. Sit down. May'll bring you a cup of tea."

Pulcher chatted with them for a minute, while the woman fussed over a teapot and a plate of soft cookies. He was trying to get the feel of the home. He could understand Madeleine Gaultry's desperation, he could understand the Foltis boy, a misfit in society anywhere. What about Jimmy Lasser?

The elder Lassers were both pushing sixty. They were first-generation Niners, off an Earth colonizing ship. They hadn't been born on Earth, of course—the trip took nearly a hundred years, physical transport. They had been born in transit, had married on the ship. As the ship had reached maximum population level shortly after they were born, they were allowed to have no children until they landed. At that time they were all of forty. May Lasser said suddenly, "Please help our boy, Mr. Pulcher! It isn't Jimmy's fault. He got in with a bad crowd. You know how it is: no work, nothing for a boy to do."

"I'll do my best." But it was funny, Pulcher thought, how it was always "the crowd" that was bad. It was never Jimmy—and never Avery, never Sam, never Walter. Pulcher sorted out the five boys and remembered Jimmy: nineteen years old, quite colorless, polite, not very interested. What had struck the lawyer about him was only surprise that this rabbity boy should have had the enterprise to get into a criminal conspiracy in the first place.

"He's a good boy," said May Lasser pathetically. "That trouble with the parked cars two years ago wasn't his fault. He got a fine job right after that, you know. Ask his probation officer. Then the Icicle Works closed. . . ." She poured more tea, slopping it over the side of the cup. "Oh, sorry! But— But when he went to the unemployment office, Mr. Pulcher, do you know what they said to him?"

"I know."

"They asked him would he take a job if offered," she hurried on, unheeding. "A *job*. As if I didn't know what they meant by a 'job!' They meant *renting*." She plumped the teapot down on the table and began to weep. "Mr. Pulcher, I wouldn't let him rent if I died for it! There isn't anything in the Bible that says you can let someone else use your body and not be responsible for what it does! You know what tourists do! 'If thy right hand offend thee, cut it off.' It doesn't say, unless somebody else is using it. Mr. Pulcher, renting is a *sin!*"

"May." Mr. Lasser put his teacup down and looked directly at Pulcher. "What about it, Pulcher? Can you get Jimmy off?"

The attorney reflected. He hadn't known about Jimmy Lasser's probation before, and that was a bad sign. If the county prosecutor was holding out on information of that sort, it meant he wasn't willing to cooperate. Probably he would be trying for a conviction with maximum sentence. Of course, he didn't have to tell a defense attorney anything about the previous criminal records of his clients. But in a juvenile case, where all parties were usually willing to go easy on the defendants, it was customary.... "I don't know, Mr. Lasser. I'll do the best I can."

"Damn right you will!" barked Lasser. "Dickon tell you who I am? I was committeeman here before him, you know. So get busy. Pull strings. Dickon will back you, or I'll know why!"

Pulcher managed to control himself. "I'll do the best I can. I already told you that. If you want strings pulled, you'd better talk to Dickon yourself. I only know law. I don't know anything about politics."

The atmosphere was becoming unpleasant. Pulcher was glad to hear the ringing of the phone in the store outside. May Lasser answered it and said: "For you, Mr. Pulcher. Charley Dickon."

Pulcher gratefully picked up the phone. Dickon's rich, political voice said sorrowfully, "Milo? Listen, I been talking to Judge Pegrim's secretary. He isn't gonna let the kids off with a slap on the wrist. There's a lot of heat from the mayor's office."

Pulcher protested desperately: "But the Swinburne kid wasn't hurt! He got better care with Madeleine than he was getting at home."

"I know, Milo," the committeeman agreed, "but that's the way she lies. So what I wanted to say to you, Milo, is don't knock yourself out on this one because you aren't going to win it."

"But—" Pulcher suddenly became aware of the Lassers just behind him. "But I think I can get an acquittal," he said, entirely out of hope, knowing that it wasn't true.

Dickon chuckled. "You got Lasser breathing down your neck? Sure, Milo. But you want my advice you'll take a quick hearing, let them get sentenced and then try for executive clemency in a couple months. I'll help you get it. And that's another five hundred or so for you, see?" The committeeman was being persuasive; it was a habit of his. "Don't worry about Lasser. I guess he's been telling you what a power he is in politics here. Forget it. And, say, tell him I notice he hasn't got his tickets for the Chester A. Arthur Day Dinner yet. You pick up the dough from him, will you? I'll mail him the tickets. No—hold on, don't ask him. Just tell him what I said." The connection went dead.

Pulcher stood holding a dead phone, conscious of Lasser standing right behind him. "So long, Charley," he said, paused, nodded into space and said, "So long," again.

Then the attorney turned about to deliver the committeeman's message about that most important subject, the tickets to the Chester A. Arthur Day Dinner. Lasser grumbled, "Damn Dickon, he's into you for one thing after another. Where's he think I'm going to get thirty bucks?"

"Tim. Please." His wife touched his arm.

Lasser hesitated. "Oh, all right. But you better get Jimmy off, hear?"

Pulcher got away at last and hurried out into the cold, slushy street.

At the corner he caught a glimpse of something palely glowing overhead and stopped, transfixed. A huge skytrout was swimming purposefully down the avenue. It was a monster, twelve feet long at least and more than two feet thick at the middle; it would easily go eighteen, nineteen ounces, the sort of lunker that sportsmen hiked clear across the Dismal Hills to bag. Pulcher had never in his life seen one that size. In fact, he could only remember seeing one or two fingerlings swim over inhabited areas.

It gave him a cold, worried feeling.

The skyfish were about the only tourist attraction Altair Nine had left to offer. From all over the Galaxy sportsmen came to shoot them, with their great porous flesh filled with bubbles of hydrogen, real biological Zeppelins that did not fly in the air but swam it. Before human colonists arrived, they had been Altair Nine's highest form of life. They were so easy to destroy with gunfire that they had almost been exterminated in the inhabited sections; only in the high, cold hills had a few survived. And now. . . .

Were even the fish aware that Altair Nine was becoming a ghost planet?

The next morning Pulcher phoned Madeleine but didn't have breakfast with her, though he wanted to very much.

He put in the whole day working on the case. In the morning he visited the families and friends of the accused boys; in the afternoon he followed a few hunches.

From the families he learned nothing. The stories were all about the same. The youngest boy was Foltis, only seventeen; the oldest was Hopgood at twenty-six. They all had lost their jobs, most of them at the Icicle Works, saw no future, and wanted off-planet. Well, physical transport meant a minimum of ten thousand dollars, and not one of them had a chance in the worlds of getting that much money in any legitimate way.

Mayor Swinburne was a rich man, and his three-year-old son was the apple of his eye. It must have been an irresistible temptation to try to collect ransom money, Pulcher realized. The mayor could certainly afford it, and once the money was collected and they were aboard a starship it would be almost impossible for the law to pursue them.

Pulcher managed to piece together the way the thing had started. The boys all lived in the same neighborhood, the neighborhood where Madeleine and Jon Gaultry had had a little apartment. They had seen Madeleine walking with the mayor's son—she had had a part-time job, now and then, taking care of him. The only part of the thing that was hard to believe was that Madeleine had been willing to take part in the scheme, once the boys approached her.

But Milo, remembering the expression on the girl's face as she looked at the tourists, decided that wasn't so strange after all.

For Madeleine had rented.

Physical transport was expensive and eternally slow.

But there was a faster way for a man to travel from planet to planet—practically instantaneous, from one end of the Galaxy to the other. The pattern of the mind is electronic in nature. It can be taped, and it can be broadcast on an electromagnetic frequency. What was more, like any electromagnetic signal, it could be used to modulate an ultra-wave carrier. The result: Instantaneous transmission of personality, anywhere in the civilized Galaxy.

The only problem was that there had to be a receiver.

The naked ghost of a man, stripped of flesh and juices, was no more than the countless radio and TV waves that passed through everyone all the time. The transmitted personality had to be given form. There were mechanical receivers, of course—computerlike affairs with mercury memory cells where a man's intelligence could be received, and could be made to activate robot bodies. But that wasn't *fun*. The tourist trade was built on *fun*. Live bodies were needed to satisfy the customers. No one wanted to spend the price of a fishing broadcast to Altair Nine in order to find himself pursuing the quarry in some clanking tractor with photocell eyes and solenoid muscles. A body was wanted, even a rather attractive body; a body which would be firm where the tourist's own, perhaps, was flabby, healthy where the tourist's own had wheezed. Having such a body, there were other sports to enjoy than fishing.

Oh, the laws were strict about misuse of rented bodies.

But the tourist trade was the only flourishing industry left on Altair Nine. The laws remained strict, but they remained unenforced.

Pulcher checked in with Charley Dickon. "I found out why Madeleine got into this thing. She rented. Signed a long-term lease with the Tourist Agency and got a big advance on her earnings."

Dickon shook his head sadly. "What people will do for money," he commented.

"It wasn't for her! She gave it to her husband, so he could get a ticket to someplace off-world." Pulcher got up, turned around and kicked his chair as hard as he could. Renting was bad enough for a man. For a woman it was—

"Take it easy," Dickon suggested, grinning. "So she figured she could buy her way out of the contract with the money from Swinburne?"

"Wouldn't you do the same?"

"Oh, I don't know, Milo. Renting's not so bad."

"The hell it isn't!"

"All right. The hell it isn't. But you ought to realize, Milo," the committeeman said stiffly, "that if it wasn't for the tourist trade we'd all be in trouble. Don't knock the Tourist Agency. They're doing a perfectly decent job."

"Then why won't they let me see the records?"

The committeeman's eyes narrowed and he sat up straighter.

"I tried," said Pulcher. "I got them to show me Madeleine's lease agreement, but I had to threaten them with a court order. Why? Then I tried to find out a little more about the Agency itself—incorporation papers, names of shareholders and so on. They wouldn't give me a thing. Why?"

Dickon said, after a second, "I could ask you that too, Milo. Why did you want to know?"

Pulcher said seriously, "I have to make a case any way I can, Charley. They're all dead on the evidence. They're guilty. But every one of them went into this kidnaping stunt in order to stay away from renting. Maybe I can't get Judge Pegrim to listen to that kind of evidence, but maybe I can. It's my only chance. If I can show that renting is a form of cruel and unusual punishment—if I can find something wrong in it, something that isn't allowed in its charter, then I have a chance. Not a good chance. But a chance. And there's got to be something wrong, Charley, because otherwise why would they be so secretive?"

Dickon said heavily, "You're getting in pretty deep, Milo. . . . Ever occur to you you're going about this the wrong way?"

"Wrong how?"

"What can the incorporation papers show you? You want to find out what renting's like. It seems to me the only way that makes sense is to try it yourself."

"Rent? Me?" Pulcher was shocked.

The committeeman shrugged. "Well, I got a lot to do," he said, and escorted Pulcher to the door.

The lawyer walked sullenly away. Rent? Him? But he had to admit that it made a certain amount of sense. . . .

He made a private decision. He would do what he could to get Madeleine and the others out of trouble. *Completely* out of trouble. But if, in the course of trying the case, he couldn't magic up some way of getting her out of the lease agreement as well as getting an acquittal, he would make damn sure that he didn't get the acquittal.

Jail wasn't so bad; renting, for Madeleine Gaultry, was considerably worse.

3

Pulcher marched into the unemployment office the next morning with an air of determination far exceeding what he really felt. Talk about loyalty to a client! But he had spent the whole night brooding about it, and Dickon had been right.

The clerk blinked at him and wheezed: "Gee, you're Mr. Pulcher, aren't you? I never thought I'd see *you* here. Things pretty slow?"

Pulcher's uncertainty made him belligerent. "I want to rent my body," he barked. "Am I in the right place or not?"

"Well, sure, Mr. Pulcher. I mean, you're not, if it's voluntary, but it's been so long since they had a voluntary that it don't make much difference, you know. I mean, I can handle it for you. Wait a minute." He turned away, hesitated, glanced at Pulcher and said, "I better use the other phone."

He was gone only a minute. He came back with a look of determined embarrassment. "Mr. Pulcher. Look. I thought I better call Charley Dickon. He isn't in his office. Why don't you wait until I can clear it with him?"

Pulcher said grimly, "It's already cleared with him."

The clerk hesitated. "But— Oh. All right," he said miserably, scribbling on a pad. "Right across the street. Oh, and tell them you're a volunteer. I don't know if that will make them leave the cuffs off you, but at least it'll give them a laugh." He chuckled.

Pulcher took the slip of paper and walked sternly across the street to the Tourist Rental Agency, Procurement Office, observing without pleasure that there were bars on the windows. A husky guard at the door straightened up as he approached and said genially, "All right, sonny. It isn't going to be as bad as you think. Just gimme your wrists a minute."

"Wait," said Pulcher quickly, putting his hands behind him. "You won't need the handcuffs for me. I'm a volunteer."

The guard said dangerously, "Don't kid with me, sonny." Then he took a closer look. "Hey, I know you. You're the lawyer. I saw you at the Primary Dance." He scratched his ear. He said doubtfully, "Well, maybe you are a volunteer. Go on in." But as Pulcher strutted past he felt a heavy hand on his shoulder and, click, click, his wrists were circled with steel. He whirled furiously. "No hard feelings," boomed the guard cheerfully. "It costs a lot of dough to get you ready, that's all. They don't want you changing your mind when they give you the squeeze, see?"

"The squeeze—? All right," said Pulcher, and turned away again. The squeeze. It didn't sound so good, at that. But he had a little too much pride left to ask the guard for details. Anyway, it couldn't be *too* bad, he was sure. Wasn't he? After all, it wasn't the same as being executed. . . .

An hour and a half later he wasn't so sure.

They had stripped him, weighed him, fluorographed him, taken samples of his blood, saliva, urine and spinal fluid; they had thumped his chest and listened to the strangled pounding of the arteries in his arm.

"All right, you pass," said a fortyish blonde in a stained nurse's uniform. "You're lucky today, openings all over. You can take your pick—mining, sailing, anything you like. What'll it be?"

"What?"

"While you're *renting*. What's the matter with you? You got to be doing something while your body's rented, you know. Of course, you can have the tank if you want to. But they mostly don't like that. You're conscious the whole time, you know."

Pulcher said honestly: "I don't know what you're talking about." But then he remembered. While a person's body was rented out there was the problem of what to do with his own mind and personality. It couldn't stay in the body. It had to go somewhere else. "The tank" was a storage device, only that and nothing more; the displaced mind was held in a sort of pickling vat of transistors and cells until its own body could be returned to it. He remembered a client of his boss's, while he was still clerking, who had spent eight weeks in the tank and had then come out to commit a murder. No. Not the tank. He said, coughing, "What else is there?"

The nurse said impatiently, "Golly, whatever you want, I guess. They've got a big call for miners operating the deep gas generators right now, if you want that. It's pretty hot, is all. They burn the coal into gas, and of course you're right in the middle of it. But I don't think you feel much. Not *too* much. I don't know about sailing or rocketing, because you have to have some experience for that. There might be something with the taxi company, but I ought to tell you usually the renters don't want that, because the live drivers don't like seeing the machines running cabs. Sometimes if they see a machine-cab they tip it over. Naturally, if there's any damage to the host machine it's risky for you."

Pulcher said faintly, "I'll try mining."

He went out of the room in a daze, a small bleached towel around his middle his only garment and hardly aware of that. His own clothes had been whisked away and checked long ago. The tourist who would shortly wear his body would pick his own clothes; the haberdashery was one of the more profitable subsidiaries of the Tourist Agency.

Then he snapped out of his daze as he discovered what was meant by "the squeeze."

A pair of husky experts lifted him onto a slab, whisked away the towel, unlocked and tossed away the handcuffs. While one pinned him down firmly at the shoulders, the other began to turn viselike wheels that moved molded forms down upon him. It was like a sectional sarcophagus closing in on him. Pulcher had an instant childhood recollection of some story or other—the walls closing in, the victim inexorably squeezed to death. He yelled, "Hey, hold it! What are you doing?"

The man at his head, bored, said, "Oh, don't worry. This your first time? We got to keep you still, you know. Scanning's close work."

"But—"

"Now shut up and relax," the man said reasonably. "If you wiggle when the tracer's scanning you you could get your whole personality messed up. Not only that, we might damage the body an' then the Agency'd have a suit on its hands, see? Tourists don't like damaged bodies. . . . Come on, Vince. Get the legs lined up so I can do the head."

"But—" said Pulcher again, and then, with effort, relaxed. It was only for twenty-four hours, after all. He could stand anything for twenty-four hours, and he had been careful to sign up for only that long. "Go ahead," he said. "It's only for twenty-four hours."

"What? Oh, sure, friend. Lights out, now; have a pleasant dream."

And something soft but quite firm came down over his face.

He heard a muffled sound of voices. Then there was a quick ripping feeling, as though he had been plucked out of some sticky surrounding medium.

Then it *hurt*.

Pulcher screamed. It didn't accomplish anything, he no longer had a voice to scream with.

Funny, he had always thought of mining as something that was carried on underground. He was under *water*. There wasn't any doubt of it. He could see vagrant eddies of sand moving in a current; he could see real fish, not the hydrogen Zeppelins of the air; he could see bubbles, arising from some source in the sand at his feet— No! Not at his feet. He didn't have feet. He had tracks.

A great steel bug swam up in front of him and said raspingly, "All right, you there, let's go." Funny again. He didn't hear the voice with ears—he didn't have ears, and there was no stereophonic sense—but he did, somehow, hear. It seemed to be speaking inside his brain. Radio? Sonar? "Come on!" growled the bug.

Experimentally Pulcher tried to talk. "Watch it!" squeaked a thin little voice, and a tiny, many-treaded steel beetle squirmed out from under his tracks. It paused to rear back and look at him. "Dope!" it chattered scathingly. A bright flame erupted from its snout as it squirmed away.

The big bug rasped, "Go on, follow the burner, Mac." Pulcher thought of walking, rather desperately. Yes. Something was happening. He lurched and moved. "Oh, God," sighed the steel bug, hanging beside him, watching with critical attention. "This your first time? I figured. They *always* give me the new ones to break in. Look, that burner— the little thing that just went down the cline, Mac! That's a burner. It's going to burn the hard rock out of a new shaft. You follow it and pull the sludge out. With your *buckets, Mac.*"

Pulcher gamely started his treads and lurchingly followed the little burner. All around him, visible through the churned, silty water, he caught glimpses of other machines working. There were big ones and little ones, some with great elephantine flexible steel trunks that sucked silt and mud away, some with wasp's stingers that planted charges of explosive, some like himself with buckets for hauling and scooping out pits. The mine, whatever sort of mine it was to be, was only a bare scratched-out beginning on the sea floor as yet. It took him—an hour? a minute? he had no means of telling time—to learn the rudiments of operating his new steel body.

Then it became boring.

Also it became painful. The first few scoops of sandy grime he carried out of the new pit made his buckets tingle. The tingle became a pain, the pain an ache, the ache a blazing agony. He stopped. Something was wrong. They couldn't expect him to go on like this! "Hey, Mac. Get busy, will you?"

"But it *hurts*."

"Goddamighty, Mac, it's *supposed* to hurt. How else would you be able to feel when you hit something hard? You want to break your buckets on me, Mac?" Pulcher gritted his—not-teeth, squared his—not-shoulders, and went back to digging. Ultimately the pain became, through habit, bearable. It didn't become less. It just became bearable.

It was boring, except when once he did strike a harder rock than his phospher-bronze buckets could handle, and had to slither back out of the way while the burner chopped it up for him. But that was the only break in the monotony. Otherwise the work was strictly routine. It gave him plenty of time to think.

This was not altogether a boon.

I wonder, he thought with a drowned clash of buckets, I wonder what my body is doing now.

Perhaps the tenant who now occupied his body was a businessman, Pulcher thought prayerfully. A man who had had to come to Altair Nine quickly, on urgent business— get a contract signed, make a trading deal, arrange an interstellar loan. That wouldn't be so bad! A businessman would not damage a rented property. No. At the worst, a businessman might drink one or two cocktails too many, perhaps eat an indigestible lunch. All right. So when—in surely only a few hours now—Pulcher resumed his body, the worst he could expect would be a hangover or dyspepsia. Well, what of that? An aspirin. A dash of bicarb.

But maybe the tourist would not be a businessman.

Pulcher flailed the coarse sand with his buckets and thought apprehensively: He might be a sportsman. Still, even that wouldn't be so bad. The tourist might walk his body up and down a few dozen mountains, perhaps even sleep it out in the open overnight. There might be a cold, possibly even pneumonia. Of course, there might also be an accident—tourists did fall off the Dismal Hills; there could be a broken leg. But that was not *too* bad, it was only a matter of a few days rest, a little medical attention.

But maybe, Pulcher thought grayly, ignoring the teeming agony of his buckets, maybe the tenant will be something worse.

He had heard queer, smutty stories about female tenants who rented male bodies. It was against the law. But you kept hearing the stories. He had heard of men who wanted to experiment with drugs, with drink, with—with a thousand secret, sordid lusts of the flesh. All of them were unpleasant. And yet in a rented body, where the ultimate price of dissipation would be borne by someone else, who might not try one of them? For there was no physical consequence to the practitioner. If Mrs. Lasser was right, perhaps there was not even a conseqence in the hereafter.

Twenty-four hours had never passed so slowly.

The suction hoses squabbled with the burners. The scoops quarreled with the dynamiters. All the animate submarine mining machines constantly irritably snapped at each other. But the work was getting done.

It seemed to be a lot of work to accomplish in one twenty-four-hour day, Pulcher thought seriously. The pit was down two hundred yards now, and braced. New wet-setting concrete pourers were already laying a floor. Shimmery little spiderlike machines whose limbs held chemical testing equipment were sniffing every load of sludge that came out now for richness of ore. The mine was nearly ready to start producing.

After a time Pulcher began to understand the short tempers of the machines. None of the minds in these machines were able to forget that, up topside, their bodies were going about unknown errands, risking unguessed dangers. At any given moment that concrete pourer's body, for instance, might be dying . . . might be acquiring a disease . . . might be stretched out in narcotic stupor, or might gayly be risking dismemberment in a violent sport. Naturally tempers were touchy.

There was no such thing as rest, as coffee-breaks or sleep for the machines; they kept going. Pulcher, when finally he remembered that he had had a purpose in coming here, it was not merely some punishment that had come blindly to him for a forgotten sin, began to try to analyze his own feelings and to guess at the feelings of the others.

The whole thing seemed unnecessarily *mean*. Pulcher understood quite clearly why anyone who had had the experience of renting would never want to do it again. But why did it have to be so unpleasant? Surely, at least, conditions for the renter-mind in a machine-body could be made more bearable; the tactile sensations could be reduced from pain to some more supportable feeling without enough loss of sensation to jeopardize the desired ends.

He wondered wistfully if Madeleine had once occupied this particular machine.

Then he wondered how many of the dynamiters and diggers were female, how many male. It seemed somehow wrong that their gleaming stainless-steel or phosphor-bronze exteriors should give no hint of age or sex. There ought to be some lighter work for women, he thought idly, and then realized that the thought was nonsense. What difference did it make? You could work your buckets off, and when you got back topside you'd be healthy and rested—

And then he had a quick, dizzying qualm, as he realized that that thought would be the thought in the mind of the tourist now occupying his own body.

Pulcher licked his not-lips and attacked the sand with his buckets more viciously than before.

"All right, Mac."

The familiar steel bug was back beside him. "Come on, back to the barn," it scolded. "You think I want to have to haul you back? Time's up. Get the tracks back in the parking lot."

Never was an order so gladly obeyed.

But the overseer had cut it rather fine. Pulcher had just reached the parking space, had not quite turned his clanking steel frame around when, *rip*, the tearing and the pain hit him. . . .

And he found himself struggling against the enfolded soft shroud that they called "the squeeze."

"Relax, friend," soothed a distant voice. Abruptly the pressure was removed from his face and the voice came nearer. "There you are. Have a nice dream?"

Pulcher kicked the rubbery material off his legs. He sat up.

"Ouch!" he said suddenly, and rubbed his eye.

The man by his head looked down at him and grinned. "Some shiner. Must've been a good party." He was stripping the sections of rubbery gripping material off him as he talked. "You're lucky. I've seen them come back in here with legs broken, teeth out, even bullet holes. Friend, you wouldn't believe me if I told you. 'Specially the girls." He handed Pulcher another bleached towel. "All right, you're through here. Don't worry about the eye, friend. That's easy two, three days old already. Another day or two and you won't even notice it."

"Hey!" Pulcher cried suddenly. "What do you mean, two or three days? How long was I down there?"

The man glanced boredly at the green-tabbed card on Pulcher's wrist. "Let's see, this is Thursday. Six days."

"But I only signed up for twenty-four hours!"

"Sure you did. *Plus* emergency overcalls, naturally. What do you think, friend, the Agency's going to evict some big-spending tourist just because you want your body back in twenty-four hours? Can't do it. You can see that. The Agency'd lose a fortune that way." Unceremoniously Pulcher was hoisted to his feet and escorted to the door. "If only these jokers would read the fine print," the first man was saying mournfully to his helper as Pulcher left. "Oh, well. If they had any brains they wouldn't rent in the first place— then what would me and you do for jobs?"

The closing door swallowed their laughter.

Six days! Pulcher raced through medical check-out, clothes redemption, payoff at the cashier's window. "Hurry, please," he kept saying, "can't you please hurry?" He couldn't wait to get to a phone.

But he had a pretty good idea already what the phone call would tell him. Five extra days! No wonder it had seemed so long down there, while up in the city time had passed along.

He found a phone at last and quickly dialed the private number of Judge Pegrim's office. The judge wouldn't be there, but that was the way Pulcher wanted it. He got Pegrim's secretary. "Miss Kish? This is Milo Pulcher."

Her voice was cold. "So *there* you are. Where have you been? The judge was *furious.*"

"I—" He despaired of explaining it to her; he could hardly explain it to himself. "I'll tell you later, Miss Kish. Please. Where does the kidnap case stand now?"

"Why, the hearing was yesterday. Since we couldn't locate you, the judge had to appoint another attorney. Naturally. After all, Mr. Pulcher, an attorney is supposed to be in court when his clients are—"

"I know that, Miss Kish. What happened?"

"It was open and shut. They all pleaded *non vult*—it was over in twenty minutes. It was the only thing to do on the evidence, you see. They'll be sentenced this afternoon— around three o'clock, I'd say. *If* you're interested."

4

It was snowing again, blue this time.

Pulcher paid the cabdriver and ran up the steps of the courthouse. As he reached for the door he caught sight of three airfish solemnly swimming around the corner of the building toward him. Even in his hurry he paused to glance at them.

It was past three, but the judge had not yet entered the courtroom. There were no spectators, but the six defendants were already in their seats, a bailiff lounging next to them. Counsel's table was occupied by—Pulcher squinted—oh, by Donley. Pulcher knew the other lawyer slightly. He was a youngster, with good political connections—that explained the court's appointing him for the fee when Pulcher didn't show up—but without much to recommend him otherwise.

Madeleine Gaultry looked up as Pulcher approached, then looked away. One of the boys caught sight of him, scowled, whispered to the others. Their collective expressions were enough to sear his spirit.

Pulcher sat at the table beside Donley. "Hello. Mind if I join you?"

Donley twisted his head. "Oh, hello, Charley. Sure. I didn't expect to see you here." He laughed. "Say, that eye's pretty bad. I guess—"

He stopped.

Something happened in Donley's face. The young baby-fat cheeks became harder, older, more worried-looking. Donley clamped his lips shut.

Pulcher was puzzled. "What's the matter? Are you wondering where I was?"

Donley said stiffly, "Well, you can't blame me for that."

"I couldn't help it, Donley. I was renting. I was trying to gather evidence—not that that helps much now. I found one thing out, though. Even a lawyer can goof in reading a contract. Did you know the Tourist Agency has the right to retain a body for up to forty-five days, regardless of the original agreement? It's in their contract. I was lucky, I guess. They only kept me five."

Donley's face did not relax. "That's interesting," he said noncommittally.

The man's attitude was most peculiar. Pulcher could understand being needled by Donley—could even understand this coldness if it had been from someone else—but it wasn't like Donley to take mere negligence so seriously.

But before he could try to pin down exactly what was wrong the other lawyer stood up. "On your feet, Pulcher," he said in a stage whisper. "Here comes the judge!"

Pulcher jumped up.

He could feel Judge Pegrim's eyes rake over him. They scratched like diamond-tipped drills. In an ordinarily political, reasonably corrupt community, Judge Pegrim was one man who took his job seriously and expected the same from those around him. "Mr. Pulcher," he purred. "We're honored to have you with us."

Pulcher began an explanation but the judge waved it away. "Mr. Pulcher, you know that an attorney is an officer of the court? And, as such, is expected to know his duties—and to fulfill them?"

"Well, Your Honor. I thought I was fulfilling them. I—"

"I'll discuss it with you at another time, Mr. Pulcher," the judge said. "Right now we have a rather disagreeable task to get through. Bailiff! Let's get started."

It was all over in ten minutes. Donley made a couple of routine motions, but there was no question about what would happen. It happened. Each of the defendants drew a ten-year sentence. The judge pronounced it distastefully, adjourned the court and left. He did not look at Milo Pulcher.

Pulcher tried for a moment to catch Madeleine's eye. Then he succeeded. Shaken, he turned away, bumping into Donley. "I don't understand it," he mumbled.

"What don't you understand?"

"Well, don't you think that's a pretty stiff sentence?"

Donley shrugged. He wasn't very interested. Pulcher scanned the masklike young face. There was no sympathy there. It was funny, in a way. This was a face of flint; the plight of six young people, doomed to spend a decade each of their lives in prison, did not move him at all. Pulcher said dispiritedly, "I think I'll go see Charley Dickon."

"Do that," said Donley curtly, and turned away.

But Pulcher couldn't find Charley Dickon.

He wasn't at his office, wasn't at the club. "Nope," said the garrulous retired police lieutenant who was the club president—and who used the club headquarters as a checker salon. "I haven't seen Charley in a couple of days. Be at the dinner tonight, though. You'll see him there." It wasn't a question, whether Pulcher would be at the dinner or not; Pop Craig knew he would. After all, Charley had passed the word out. *Everybody* would be there.

Pulcher went back to his apartment.

It was the first time he had surveyed his body since reclaiming it. The bathroom mirror told him that he had a gorgeous shiner indeed. Also certain twinges made him strip and examine his back. It looked, he thought gloomily, staring over his shoulder into the mirror, as though whoever had rented his body had had a perfectly marvelous time. He made a mental note to get a complete checkup someday soon, just in case. Then he showered, shaved, talcumed around the black eye without much success, and dressed.

He sat down, poured himself a drink and promptly forgot it was there. He was thinking. Something was trying to reach the surface of his mind. Something perfectly obvious, which he all the same couldn't quite put his finger on. It was rather annoying.

He found himself drowsily thinking of airfish.

Damn, he thought grouchily, his body's late tenant hadn't even troubled to give it a decent night's sleep! But he didn't want to sleep, not now. It was still only early evening. He supposed the Chester A. Arthur Day Dinner was still a must, but there were hours yet before that. . . .

He got up, poured the untasted drink into the sink and set out. There was one thing he could try to help Madeleine. It probably wouldn't work. But nothing else would either, so that was no reason for not trying it.

The mayor's mansion was ablaze with light; something was going on.

Pulcher trudged up the long, circling driveway in slush that kept splattering his ankles. He tapped gingerly on the door.

The butler took his name doubtfully, and isolated Pulcher in a contagion-free sitting room while he went off to see if the mayor would care to admit such a person. He came back looking incredulous. The mayor would.

Mayor Swinburne was a healthy, lean man of medium height, showing only by his thinning hair that he was in his middle forties. Pulcher said, "Mr. Mayor, I guess you know who I am. I represent the six kids who were accused of kidnaping your son."

"Not accused, Mr. Pulcher. Convicted. And I didn't know you still represented them."

"I see you know the score. All right. Maybe, in a legal sense, I don't represent them anymore. But I'd like to make some representations on their behalf to you tonight— entirely unofficially." He gave the mayor a crisply worded, brief outline of what had happened in the case, how he had rented, what he had found as a renter, why he had missed the hearing. "You see, sir, the Tourist Agency doesn't give its renters even ordinary courtesy. They're just bodies, nothing else. I can't blame those kids. Now that I've rented my-self, I'll have to say that I wouldn't blame anybody who did *anything* to avoid it."

The mayor said dangerously, "Mr. Pulcher, I don't have to remind you that what's left of our economy depends heavily on the Tourist Agency for income. Also that some of our finest citizens are among its shareholders."

"Including yourself, Mr. Mayor. Right." Pulcher nodded. "But the management may not be reflecting your wishes. I'll go farther. I think, sir, that every contract the Tourist Agency holds with a renter ought to be voided as against public policy. Renting out your body for a purpose which well may be in violation of law—which, going by experience, nine times out of ten *does* involve a violation of law—is the same thing as contracting to perform any other illegal act. The contract simply cannot be enforced. The common law gives us a great many precedents on this point, and—"

"Please, Mr. Pulcher. I'm not a judge. If you feel so strongly, why not take it to court?"

Pulcher sank back into his chair, deflated. "There isn't time," he admitted. "And be-sides, it's too late for that to help the six persons I'm interested in. They've already been driven into an even more illegal act, in order to escape renting. I'm only trying to ex-plain it to you, sir, because you are their only hope. You can pardon them."

The mayor's face turned beet red. "Executive clemency, from *me*? For *them*?"

"They didn't hurt your boy."

"No, they did not," the mayor agreed. "And I'm sure that Mrs. Gaultry, at least, would not willingly have done so. But can you say the same of the others? Could she have prevented it?" He stood up. "I'm sorry, Mr. Pulcher. The answer is no. Now you must excuse me."

Pulcher hesitated, then accepted the dismissal. There wasn't anything else to do.

He walked somberly down the hall toward the entrance, hardly noticing that guests were beginning to arrive. Apparently the mayor was offering cocktails to a select few. He recognized some of the faces—Lew Yoder, the County Tax Assessor, for one; probably the mayor was having some of the whiter-collared politicians in for drinks before mak-ing the obligatory appearance at Dickon's fund-raising dinner. Pulcher looked up long enough to nod grayly at Yoder and walked on.

"Charley Dickon! What the devil are you doing here like that?"

Pulcher jerked upright. Dickon here? He looked around.

But Dickon was not in sight. Only Yoder was coming down the corridor toward him; oddly, Yoder was looking straight at him! And it had been Yoder's voice.

Yoder's face froze.

The expression on Yoder's face was an odd one but not unfamiliar to Milo Pulcher. He had seen it once before that day. It was the identical expression he had seen on the face of that young punk who had replaced him in court, Donley.

Yoder said awkwardly, "Oh, Milo, it's you. Hello. I, uh, thought you were Charley Dickon."

Pulcher felt the hairs at the back of his neck tingle. Something was odd here. Very odd. "It's a perfectly natural mistake," he said. "I'm six feet tall and Charley's five feet three. I'm thirty-one years old. He's fifty. I'm dark and he's almost bald. I don't know how anybody ever tells us apart anyway."

"What the devil are you talking about?" Yoder blustered.

Pulcher looked at him thoughtfully for a second.

"You're lucky," he admitted. "I'm not sure I know. But I hope to find out."

5

Some things never change. Across the entrance to The New Metropolitan Cafe & Men's Grille a long scarlet banner carried the words:

VOTE THE STRAIGHT TICKET

Big poster portraits of the mayor and Committeeman Dickon flanked the door itself. A squat little soundtruck parked outside the door blared ancient marches of the sort that political conventions had suffered through for more than two centuries back on Earth. It was an absolutely conventional political fund-raising dinner; it would have the absolutely conventional embalmed roast beef, the one conventionally free watery Manhattan at each place, and the conventionally boring after-dinner speeches. (Except for one.) Milo Pulcher, stamping about in the slush outside the entrance, looked up at the constellations visible from Altair Nine and wondered if those same stars were looking down on just such another thousand dinners all over the Galaxy. Politics went on, wherever you were. The constellations would be different, of course; the Squirrel and the Nut were all local stars and would have no shape at all from any other system. But—

He caught sight of the tall thin figure he was waiting for and stepped out into the stream of small-time political workers, ignoring their greetings. "Judge, I'm glad you came."

Judge Pegrim said frostily, "I gave you my word, Milo. But you've got a lot to answer to me for if this is a false alarm. I don't ordinarily attend partisan political affairs."

"It isn't an ordinary affair, Judge." Pulcher conducted him into the room and sat him at the table he had prepared. Once it had held place cards for four election-board workers from the warehouse district, who now buzzed from table to table angrily; Pulcher had filched their cards. The judge was grumbling:

"It doesn't comport well with the bench to attend this sort of thing, Milo. I don't like it."

"I know, Judge. You're an honest man. That's why I wanted you here."

"Mmm." Pulcher left him before the *Mmm* could develop into a question. He had fended off enough questions since the thoughtful half hour he had spent pacing back and forth in front of the mayor's mansion. He didn't want to fend off any more. As he skirted the tables, heading for the private room where he had left his special guests, Charley Dickon caught his arm.

"Hey, Milo! I see you got the judge out. Good boy! He's just what we needed to make this dinner complete."

"You have no idea how complete," said Pulcher pleasantly, and walked away. He didn't look back. There was another fine potential question-source; and the committeeman's would be even more difficult to answer than the judge's. Besides, he wanted to see Madeleine.

The girl and her five accomplices were where he had left them. The private bar where they were sitting was never used for affairs like this. You couldn't see the floor from it. Still, you could hear well enough, and that was more important.

The boys were showing nervousness in their separate ways. Although they had been convicted hardly more than a day, had been sentenced only a few hours, they had fallen quickly into the convict habit. Being out on bail so abruptly was a surprise. They hadn't expected it. It made them nervous. Young Foltis was jittering about, muttering to himself. The Hopgood boy was slumped despondently in a corner, blowing smoke rings. Jimmy Lasser was making a castle out of sugar cubes.

Only Madeleine was relaxed.

As Pulcher came in she looked up calmly. "Is everything all right?" He crossed his fingers and nodded. "Don't worry," she said. Pulcher blinked. *Don't worry.* It should have been he who was saying that to her, not the other way around. It came to him that there was only one possible reason for her calm confidence.

She trusted him.

But he couldn't stay. The ballroom was full now, and irritable banquet waiters were crashing plates down in front of the loyal Party workers. He had a couple of last-minute things to attend to. He carefully avoided the eye of Judge Pegrim, militantly alone at the table by the speaker's dais, and walked quickly across the room to Jimmy Lasser's father. He said without preamble: "Do you want to help your son?"

Tim Lasser snarled, "You cheap shyster! You wouldn't even show up for the trial! Where do you get the nerve to ask me a question like that?"

"Shut up. I asked you something."

Lasser hesitated, then read something in Pulcher's eyes. "Well, of course I do," he grumbled.

"Then tell me something. It won't sound important. But it is. How many rifles did you sell in the past year?"

Lasser looked puzzled, but he said, "Not many. Maybe half a dozen. Business is lousy all over, you know, since the Icicle Works closed."

"And in a normal year?"

"Oh, three or four hundred. It's a big tourist item. You see, they need cold-shot rifles for hunting the fish. A regular bullet'll set them on fire—touches off the hydrogen. I'm the only sporting-goods merchant in town that carries them, and—say, what does that have to do with Jimmy?"

Pulcher took a deep breath. "Stick around and you'll find out. Meanwhile, think about what you just told me. If rifles are a tourist item, why did closing the Icicle Works hurt your sales?" He left.

But not quickly enough. Charley Dickon scuttled over and clutched his arm, his face furious. "Hey, Milo, what the hell! I just heard from Sam Apfel—the bondsman—that you got that whole bunch out of jail again on bail. How come?"

"They're my clients, Charley."

"Don't give me that! How'd you get them out when they're convicted, anyway?"

"I'm going to appeal the case," Pulcher said gently.

"You don't have a leg to stand on. Why would Pegrim grant bail anyhow?"

Pulcher pointed to Judge Pegrim's solitary table. "Ask him," he invited, and broke away.

He was burning a great many bridges behind him, he knew. It was an exhilarating feeling. Chancy but tingly; he decided he liked it. There was just one job to do. As soon as he was clear of the scowling but stopped committeeman, he walked by a circular route to the dais. Dickon was walking back to his table, turned away from the dais; Pulcher's chance would never be better. "Hello, Pop," he said.

Pop Craig looked up over his glasses. "Oh, Milo. I've been going over the list. You think I got everybody? Charley wanted me to introduce all the block captains and anybody else important. You know anybody important that ain't on this list?"

"That's what I wanted to tell you, Pop. Charley said for you to give me a few minutes. I want to say a few words."

Craig said agitatedly, "Aw, Milo, if you make a speech they're all gonna want to make speeches! What do you want to make a speech for? You're no candidate."

Pulcher winked mysteriously. "What about next year?" he asked archly, with a lying inference.

"Oh. Oh-*ho*." Pop Craig nodded and returned to his list, mumbling. "Well. In *that* case, I guess I can fit you in after the block captains, or maybe after the man from the sheriff's office—" But Pulcher wasn't listening. Pulcher was already on his way back to the little private bar.

Man had conquered all of space within nearly fifty light-years of dull, yellow old Sol, but out in that main ballroom political hacks were talking of long-dead presidents of almost forgotten countries centuries in the past. Pulcher was content to listen—to allow the sounds to vibrate his eardrums, at least, for the words made little sense to him. If, indeed, there was any content of sense to a political speech in the first place. But they were soothing.

Also they kept his six fledglings from bothering him with questions. Madeleine sat quietly by his shoulder, quite relaxed still and smelling faintly, pleasantly, of some floral aroma. It was, all in all, as pleasant a place to be as Pulcher could remember in his recent past. It was too bad that he would have to go out of it soon. . . .

Very soon.

The featured guest had droned through his platitudes. The visiting celebrities had said their few words each. Pop Craig's voluminous old voice took over again. "And now I wanta introduce some of the fine Party workers from our local districts. There's Keith Ciccarelli from the Hillside area. Keith, stand up and take a bow!" Dutiful applause. "And here's Mary Beth Whitehurst, head of the Women's Club from Riverview!" Dutiful applause—and a whistle. Surely the whistle was sardonic; Mary Beth was fat and would never again see fifty. There were more names.

Pulcher felt it coming the moment before Pop Craig reached his own name. He was on his way to the dais even before Craig droned out: "That fine young attorney and loyal Party man—the kind of young fellow our Party needs—Milo Pulcher!"

Dutiful applause again. That was habit, but Pulcher felt the whispering question that fluttered around the room.

He didn't give the question a chance to grow. He glanced once at the five hundred loyal Party faces staring up at him and began to speak. "Mr. President. Mr. Mayor. Justice Pegrim. Honored guests. Ladies and gentlemen." That was protocol. He paused. "What I have to say to you tonight is in the way of a compliment. It's a surprise for an old friend, sitting right here. That old friend is—Charley Dickon." He threw the name at them. It was a special political sort of delivery; a tone of voice that commanded: *Clap now.* They clapped. That was important, because it made it difficult for Charley to think of an excuse to interrupt him—as soon as Charley realized he ought to, which would be shortly.

"Way out here, on the bleak frontier of interstellar space, we live isolated lives, ladies and gentlemen." There were whispers, he could hear them. The words were more or less right, but he didn't have the right political accent; the audience knew there was something wrong. The true politician would have said: *This fine, growing frontier in the midst of interstellar space's greatest constellations.* He couldn't help it; he would have to rely on velocity now to get him through. "How isolated, we sometimes need to reflect. We have trade relations through the Icicle Works—now closed. We have tourists in both directions, through the Tourist Agency. We have ultrawave messages—also through the Tourist Agency. And that's about all.

"That's a very thin link, ladies and gentlemen. *Very* thin. And I'm here to tell you tonight that it would be even thinner if it weren't for my old friend there—yes, Committeeman Charley Dickon!" He punched the name again, and got the applause—but it was puzzled and died away early.

"The fact of the matter, ladies and gentlemen, is that just about every tourist that's come to Altair Nine this past year is the personal responsibility of Charley Dickon. Who have these tourists been? They haven't been businessmen—there's no business. They haven't been hunters. Ask Phil Lasser, over there; he hasn't sold enough fishing equipment to put in your eye. Ask yourselves, for that matter. How many of you have seen airfish right over the city? Do you know why? Because they aren't being hunted anymore! There aren't any tourists to hunt them."

The time had come to give it to them straight. "The fact of the matter, ladies and gentlemen, is that the tourists we've had haven't been tourists at all. They've been natives, from right here on Altair Nine. Some of them are right in this room! I know that, because I rented myself for a few days—and do you know who took my body? Why, Charley did. Charley himself!" He was watching Lew Yoder out of the corner of his eye. The assessor's face turned gray; he seemed to shrink. Pulcher enjoyed the sight, though. After all, he had a certain debt to Lew Yoder; it was Yoder's slip of the tongue that had finally started him thinking on the right track. He went on hastily: "And what it all adds up to, ladies and gentlemen, is that Charley Dickon, and a handful of his friends in high places—most of them right here in this room—have cut off communication between Altair Nine and the rest of the Galaxy!"

That did it.

There were yells, and the loudest yell came from Charley Dickon. "Throw him out! Arrest him! Craig, get the sergeant-at-arms! I say I don't have to sit here and listen to this maniac!"

"*And I say you do,*" boomed the cold courtroom voice of Judge Pegrim. The judge stood up. "Go on, Pulcher!" he ordered. "I came here tonight to hear what you have to say. It may be wrong. It may be right. I propose to hear all of it before I make up my mind."

Thank heaven for the cold old judge! Pulcher cut right in before Dickon could find a new point of attack; there wasn't much left to say anyway. "The story is simple, ladies and gentlemen. The Icicle Works was the most profitable corporation in the Galaxy. We all know that. Probably everybody in this room had a couple of shares of stock. Dickon had plenty.

"But he wanted more. And he didn't want to pay for them. So he used his connection with the Tourist Agency to cut off communication between Nine and the rest of the Galaxy. He spread the word that Altamycin was worthless now because some fictitious character had invented a cheap new substitute. He closed down the Icicle Works. And for the last twelve months he's been picking up stock for a penny on the dollar, while the rest of us starve and the Altamycin the rest of the Galaxy needs stays right here on Altair Nine and—"

He stopped, not because he had run out of words but because no one could hear them any longer. The noises the crowd was making were no longer puzzled; they were ferocious. It figured. Apart from Dickon's immediate gang of manipulators, there was hardly a man in the room who hadn't taken a serious loss in the past year.

It was time for the police to come rushing in, as per the phone call Judge Pegrim had made, protestingly, when Pulcher urged him to the dinner. They did—just barely in time. They weren't needed to arrest Dickon so much; but they were indispensable for keeping him from being lynched.

Hours later, escorting Madeleine home, Milo was still bubbling over. "I was worried about the Mayor! I couldn't make up my mind whether he was in it with Charley or not. I'm glad he wasn't, because he said he owed me a favor, and I told him how he could pay it. Executive clemency. The six of you will be free in the morning."

Madeleine said sleepily, "I'm free enough now."

"And the Tourist Agency won't be able to enforce those contracts anymore. I talked it over with Judge Pegrim. He wouldn't give me an official statement, but he said— Madeleine, you're not listening."

She yawned. "It's been an exhausting day, Milo," she apologized. "Anyway, you can tell me all about that later. We'll have plenty of time."

"Years and years," he promised. "Years and—" They stopped talking. The mechanical cabdriver, sneaking around through backstreets to avoid the resentment of displaced live drivers, glanced over its condenser cells at them and chuckled, making tiny sparks in the night.

SAUCERY

Everyone loves a scoundrel, especially a lovable scoundrel. Everyone has met or seen on television or heard on radio someone like the two gentlemen—we use the term loosely—who are the main characters in 1986's "Saucery," Marchese Boccanegra and Anthony Makepeace Moore. In the nineteenth century they might have sold snake oil or toured the country with exhibits of the most amazing, fantastical—and phony—creatures.

In the twentieth century or the twenty-first, though, these two colorful characters are experts about their respective crackpot theories of alien life on earth or elsewhere.

Unfortunately for them, real, live Martians have been discovered on Mars and are being brought back to Earth. This momentous discovery could ruin their business forever, but these men are nothing if not resourceful. What they will do to survive . . . well, read on and enjoy.

The young talent booker behind the desk was slim, quick, heavily eye-shadowed and, Marchese Boccanegra decided, quite ugly, and he hated her.

He didn't much like her office, either. It was tiny and bare. It didn't do justice to one of the richest television networks in the world, and besides the woman was watching the wrong program. All of this displeased Marchese Boccanegra. Not that he cared that somebody on the NBC payroll was sneaking looks at an offering of CBS, but the program the confounded woman was watching was a pickup from the spaceship *Algonquin,* on its way back from Mars with a bunch of those equally confounded Martians aboard. Nasty-looking things! People said they looked a little bit like seals, but seals at least didn't have spindly legs. No, they were definitely hideous, although it wasn't their looks that made Boccanegra dislike them.

The woman giggled. "They're cute," she said, to Boccanegra or to no one.

Boccanegra sighed—silently. He sat erect in his far from comfortable wooden chair, his hands folded reposefully on his lap, his expression unchanging, and his eyes half-closed. He could see her well enough. Her nose was hardly more than a pug and her teeth, although white enough and bright enough, were unacceptably long. She was at least as unattractive as the Martians, not to mention that she wasn't treating him right. First he had been kept sitting for forty-five minutes in the waiting room outside, with all the jugglers and struggling comics and publicity agents for people who had just written a book. Then when she did let him in most of her attention was on the TV screen, when what she should properly have been doing was deciding exactly when—Boccanegra did not allow himself to say *whether*—he would appear again on the "Today" show.

Boccanegra didn't realize his half-closed eyes had closed all the way until he heard her say irritably, "What's the matter, are you asleep?"

He opened his eyes slowly and gazed at her with the unfathomable look that had always gone so well on television. "I am not asleep," he said austerely.

She was looking less attractive than ever, because she was scowling at him, but at least she had turned off the television set. "I hope you wouldn't fall asleep on the air," she sniffed. "Sorry about that, but I had to watch. Anyway, how do you say yor name?"

"Mar-KAY-say BOH-ka-NAY-gra."

"You can really get screwed up trying to say those foreign names on the air," she said pensively. "What's that first part, a title or a name?"

He allowed himself to twinkle. "It is the name my parents bestowed on me," he said, not truthfully. "It does in fact mean *marquis,* but my family have not used a title for more than a hundred years." That was not untruthful, technically, for they certainly hadn't. Or before then, either, because grape growers hardly ever had one.

"In any case," he went on smoothly, "I don't know if you have had an opportunity to study my sitrep. This latest contact—"

"What in the world is a sitrep?"

"The situation report, that is. It details my latest contact with the Great Galactics, which is actually far more exciting than any I have experienced before. I was meditating before the fireplace in my summer home at Aspen when suddenly the flames of the fire seemed to die away and a great golden presence emerged to—"

"You told me," she said. "They talked to you. What I need to find out is what they said about the Martians."

"Martians? My dear woman, they aren't *Martians.* The Great Galactics come from so far beyond Mars that they are in another universe entirely, which we call the theta band of consciousness—"

"Uh-uh. The people aren't interested in other universes right now, Mr.—" she glanced at her notes and pronounced it, for a wonder, almost correctly"—Boccanegra. I'm booking a particular show. I've got one three-and-a-half-minute spot open, and the show's about Mars. We've already got Sagan, Bradbury, and some woman from NASA and we need a—we need somebody like you, I mean. Now, you've had other experiences with flying saucers, right?"

He said patiently, "*Flying saucers* is a newspaper term. I don't care for it. In my book, *Ultimate Truth: The Amazing Riddle Behind the 'Saucer' Flaps,* I expose the falsity of the so-called flying-saucer stories. On the theta level of reality, what we human beings perceive as 'saucers' are really—"

"No, but, hey, whatever they were, did any of them come from Mars?"

"Of course not!" Then he added hastily, "Naturally, on the other hand, most of the so-called Martian mysteries are explained in my book, as for example the huge stone sculpture of a human face which appears on Mars in—"

"No, no, no face. We've already got the guy who wrote the book doing that on the eight-eighteen spot on Tuesday. Anything else about Mars?" she asked, glancing at her watch.

"No," said Boccanegra, coming to a decision. He had been in the business long enough to know when to cut his losses. She wasn't buying. He would not do the "Today" show on the basis of this interview. All he could do was to try to keep the lines open for the future.

As she was opening her mouth for the don't-call-us-we'll-call-you, he widened his eyes and said quickly, "Oh, just a moment, do you mean *next* week? I am so terribly sorry! My staff must have got the dates wrong, because next week I have to be at a conference in Washington." He gave the woman a meager forbearing smile as he stood up and shrugged apologetically.

As he picked up the gray suede gloves and gold-handled walking stick the woman said, "Well, actually I don't think we could've—"

"No, I insist," Boccanegra cut in. "It's entirely my fault. Good day!" And he was gone, not even pausing to admire his reflection in the full-length mirror on the back of her door. It was just as it ought to be anyway. Tall, spare figure in the severely cut black suit, the moon-white stock gleaming at his throat, and the white carnation in his lapel, he was exactly as striking and vaguely sinister a spectacle as he set out to be. *Color,* the well-meaning experts had said to him. *It's all color on the TV now.* And it was; but for exactly that reason Marchese Boccanegra had stood out in his stark black and white on the talk shows and the panels.

Had once, anyway. There weren't as many of them for him to do anymore. You could put it even more strongly: There were practically none at all, and the reason for that was the Martians. How they had ruined it for everybody!

Passing through the waiting room, Boccanegra gave the receptionist a quick four-fingered wave—it was the benediction and greeting of the Great Galactics, as he had demonstrated it for more than thirty years in the field. But she didn't seem to recognize it. No matter. Boccanegra took the carnation from his buttonhole and laid it caressingly before her (a receptionist who remembered you could make all the difference!) before pacing out to the hall, where he tapped the elevator button with the head of his cane.

Only when the door had opened and he stepped inside did he say in surprise, "Anthony! I didn't expect to see you here!"

The month was June and the day warm, but Anthony Makepeace Moore wore full regalia: fur-collared coat and black slouch hat. His expression was more startled than pleased—so was Boccanegra's own—but the two men greeted each other with the effusion of colleagues and competitors. "Marchese!" Moore cried, wringing his hand. "It's been too long, hasn't it? I suppose you've been granting interviews, too?"

Boccanegra permitted himself a wry smile. "I had intended to appear on the 'Today' show," he said, "but the appearance they wanted me to make is unfortunately out of the question. And you?"

"Oh, nothing as glamorous as the 'Today' show," smiled Moore. "I was just taping a few radio bits for the network news."

"I'll be sure to listen," Boccanegra promised, the generosity of his tone almost completely concealing the envy. The network! It had been at least two years since any network news organization had cared to have Marchese Boccanegra say anything for their listeners—and now that they'd done Moore it would certainly be a while before they wanted anyone else. There was a time—a pretty long-ago time, now—when the two of them had done publicity appearances together. But that was when the alien-encounter business was booming. The fact was, now there just wasn't enough to share.

So Boccanegra was surprised when Moore looked at his watch and said diffidently, "I suppose you're in a great hurry to get to your next engagement?"

"As a matter of fact," Boccanegra began, and then hesitated. He finished, "As a matter of fact, I'm a bit hungry. I was thinking of a sandwich somewhere—would you care to join me?"

Moore courteously bowed him out first as the elevator reached the ground floor. "I'd like that a lot, Marchese," he said warmly. "Anyplace in particular? Something ethnic, perhaps? You know how I like odd foods, and we don't get much of them in Oklahoma."

"I know just the place!" cried Boccanegra.

The very place was the Carnegie Delicatessen, half a dozen blocks from the RCA Building, and both of them had known it well.

As they walked up Seventh Avenue people glanced at them curiously. Where Boccanegra was tall, hawklike, and aloof, Anthony Makepeace Moore was short and round. He wore bushy white sideburns on a head that had no other hair but bushy white eyebrows. He would have been plump even in a bathing suit—so one supposed; no one had ever seen him in one—but his standard costume, winter, spring, and fall, was a bulky coat trimmed with what might well pass for ermine. It made him appear even rounder. As much as anything, Moore resembled a fat leprechaun.

What he wore in the summer was quite different, because in the summer he spent his time on the five hundred acres of his Eudorpan Astral Retreat, just outside of Enid, Oklahoma. There he wore the robes of the Eudorpan Masters. So did everyone else on the premises, though not all in the same colors. Seekers (the paying guests) wore lavender. Adepts (the staff) wore gold. Moore himself, taking a cue from the Pope at Rome, never appeared in anything but spotless and freshly laundered white.

At the delicatessen, Boccanegra stepped courteously aside to let Moore go first through the door. It was midafternoon but there was a short line waiting, and the two men exchanged amused glances. "Fame," whispered Moore, and Boccanegra nodded.

"Your picture used to hang right there, next to the fan," he said.

"And yours over by the door," Moore recalled, "and now they don't even remember who we are." The cashier, overhearing, looked at them curiously, but no identification came before their table was ready.

When Moore took off his coat he revealed a red and white checked sport shirt underneath. "No robes today?" Boccanegra asked. The only answer he got was a frosty look. Then Moore began to pore over the menu and his expression softened.

"That good old pastrami," he said sentimentally. "Remember how they used to send tons of it over to us at WOR? And Long John begging us to take some home because there'd be a new batch the next night?"

"That's where we met, isn't it?" Boccanegra asked, knowing exactly that it was. The all-night "Long John Nebel Show" had, in fact, given both of them their start in the alien-contact industry. "Remember the Mystic Barber, with that tinfoil crown he always wore?"

"And Barney and Betty Hill, and the Two Men in Black, and Will Oursler, and—oh, God, Marco," Moore said, rolling his eyes, "we didn't know when we had it good, did we? We were so young!"

"And no damned Martians to take people's minds off us," Boccanegra grumbled. "Are you ready to order?"

They passed reminiscences back and forth while they were waiting for their food to arrive—Long John and his wonderful scams, the revolving Empire State Building, the bridge off the RCA tower, and all; and not only Long John but every other broadcast medium. They all seemed willing to give air time to talk about intelligences from other worlds, network TV and little local radio stations where you had to crouch between record turntables and hand a single microphone around the guests.

"We were all so young," Moore repeated dreamily, pouring ketchup on his French fries.

"Remember Lonny Zamorra?" Boccanegra asked.

"And the spaceport at Giant Rock?"

"And the mutilated cows? And the car engines that got stopped? And, oh, God, the Bermuda Triangle! Good Lord," said Boccanegra earnestly, "I can think of at least a dozen people that lived for years on just the Bermuda Triangle. You know what they were getting for a single *lecture?* Not counting the books and the workshops and . . ." He trailed off.

"And everything," said Moore somberly. They ate in silence for a moment, thinking of the days when the world had been so eager to hear what they had to say.

In those days everyone wanted to give them a voice. Radio, television, press coverage; there was nothing anyone might say about flying saucers, or men from another planet, or mysterious revelations received in a trance, or astral voyages to other worlds that did not get an audience. A *paying* audience. Both Moore and Boccanegra had had their pick of college lecture dates and handsome honoraria—enough for Boccanegra to start The Press of Ultimate Truth, Inc., to print his books; enough for Moore to buy the tract of played-out Oklahoma grazing land that became the Eudorpan Astral Retreat. Both had flourished wildly. There was no end to the customers for Boccanegra's books, more than fifteen titles in all, or to the Seekers who gladly paid a month's wages to spend a week in their lavender robes, eating lentils and raw onions out of EAR's wooden bowls (and sneaking off to the truck stop just outside the Retreat for hamburgers and sinful beer), and listening worshipfully to Moore's revelations.

When the last of the pastrami and fries was gone, Moore leaned back and signaled for a coffee refill. He looked thoughtfully at Boccanegra and said, "I've been looking forward to your new book. Is it out yet?"

"It's been held up," Boccanegra explained. Actually it was a year overdue, and the new book wasn't going to appear until the bills for the last one were paid, and that didn't seem likely in the near future. "Of course," he added with as near a smile as he ever allowed himself in public, "the timing might be better later on. It's all Martians now, isn't it?"

Moore was startled. "Are you writing a book about the Martians?" he demanded.

"Me? Of course not," Boccanegra said virtuously. "Oh, there are charlatans who'll be doing that, no doubt. I'll bet there are a dozen of the old guard trying to change their stories around to cash in on the Martians."

"Shocking," Moore agreed with a straight face.

"Anyway, I've about decided to take a sort of sabbatical. This fad will run its course. Perhaps in a few months it'll be the right time for my book, which tells how the Great Galactics have provided us with the genetic code that explains all of the mysteries of—"

"Yeah," said Moore, staring into space. His expression did not suggest that he liked what he was seeing.

Boccanegra studied his ancient adversary. It didn't look like a very good time to bring up the sudden inspiration that had come to him in the elevator. Moore sounded depressed.

But there would never be a better time, so Boccanegra plunged in. "I've been think-ing," he said.

Moore focused on him. "Yes?"

Boccanegra waved a deprecating hand. "I'll probably have some free time for awhile. Perhaps the whole summer. So, I wonder—would you be interested in having me as a sort of guest lecturer at the Retreat?" Moore's eyes widened under the bushy eyebrows, but he didn't speak. Boccanegra went on ingratiatingly, "Since I'm at liberty, I mean. Of course, we'd have to make some special arrangement. It wouldn't be appropriate for me to be there just as part of your staff. Some new position? Perhaps I could wear black robes? Naturally the financial arrangements could be worked out—professional courtesy and all that," he finished with a twinkle.

The twinkle dried up. Moore's expression was stony. "No chance," he said.

Boccanegra felt the muscles in his throat begin to tighten. "No chance," he repeated, trying to keep the sudden anger out of his voice. "Well, if it's the robes—"

"It isn't the robes," said Anthony Makepeace Moore.

"No, it wouldn't be that. I suppose, since you and I have been pretty much opponents for so long—"

"Marco," said Moore sadly, "I don't give a shit about that. I can't take you on at the Retreat because there isn't going to be any Retreat this year. I haven't got the customers. By this time I should have had forty or fifty people registered—some years I've had a hundred! You know how many I've got now? Two. And one of those is only a maybe." He shook his head. "The whole thing's down the tube if something good doesn't hap-pen. The bank's been on my back about the mortgage, and they put in that damn inter-state and even the truck stop's losing money every week—"

Boccanegra was startled. "I didn't know you owned the truck stop!"

"Well, this time next month I probably won't. They even took out the Coke ma-chine."

Boccanegra sat in thoughtful silence for a moment. Then he laughed out loud and waved to the grouchy waitress for more coffee.

"You, too," he said. "Well, let's put our heads together and see if we can figure some-thing out."

By the time of the fourth refill the waitress was muttering audibly to herself.

The problem wasn't just the fickle tastes of the public. It was the Martians. There simply was no room for imaginary wonders in the public attention when the real thing was getting a few hundred thousand miles closer to Earth every day. And the unfair part of it was that the Martians were so damned *dull*. They didn't have spiritual counseling for the troubled billions of Earth. They didn't warn of impending disasters, or offer hope of salvation. They just stood there in their stalls on the spaceship *Algonquin 9*, swilling down their scummy soup.

"I guess you've gone over all your books to see if there's anything about Martians in them?" Moore said hopefully.

Boccanegra shook his head. "I mean, yes, I looked. Nothing."

"Me, too," Moore sighed. "I'll tell you the truth, Marco, I never for one minute con-sidered the possibility that when we were visited by creatures from outer space they would be *stupid*. Say!" he cried, sitting up. "What if we say they aren't real? I mean, they're like the household pets of the real Eudorpans?"

"The Great Galactics," Boccanegra corrected eagerly. "Or maybe not pets but, you know, like false clues the superior space beings put there to throw us off the trail?"

"And we can say we've had revelations about it, and—well, hell, Marco," said Moore, suddenly facing reality. "Would anybody believe us?"

"Has that ever made any difference?"

"No, but really, it'd be good if we had some kind of, you know, evidence."

"Evidence," Boccanegra said thoughtfully.

"See, these Martians will actually be here in a few months, right? Next thing you know they'll be landing, and they'll be in a zoo or something, and people can see them for themselves. They don't talk, but they might, you know, communicate something that could blow us right out of the water."

"They really *are* stupid, Tony."

"Yes, but, Marco, if they've got some kind of writings that we don't know about, because all we've ever seen is what they sent on the TV from the spaceship—"

"But maybe they're degenerate," Boccanegra cried, "so they don't know what the stuff *really* means!"

"Well," Moore said doggedly, "there might be a real problem there, all the same. If we wait until they land . . ." Then he shook his head. "Scratch that. We can't wait that long, at least I can't. I could stall the creditors for maybe a month or two, but the spaceship isn't going to land till nearly Christmas."

"And this is only June." Boccanegra puzzled for a moment; there had been, he was almost sure, something good they had come quite close to. But what was it?

"How about," said Moore, "if we found some *other* Martians?"

Boccanegra frowned. "Besides the ones they've found, you mean? Somewhere else on Mars?"

"Not necessarily on Mars. But the same sort of creatures, maybe on Venus, maybe on the Moon—we say they live in caves, see? So nobody's seen them? I mean, they do live in caves on Mars, right? There could even have been some long ago on, what's its name, that moon of Jupiter that's always having volcanic eruptions, only the volcanoes killed them off."

"Um," said Boccanegra. "Yeah, maybe." He was scowling in concentration, because that faint ringing of cash registers was still in his ears, only he couldn't quite tell where it came from. "I don't see where we get any kind of evidence that way, though," he pointed out. "I'd like it if we had something right here on Earth about that."

"Okay, Antarctica! There's a colony of them on Antarctica, or at least there used to be, but they died of cold after the continents migrated."

"There are people all over Antarctica, Tony. Scientific camps. Russians and Americans and everybody."

"Well, could they be at the bottom of the sea?"

"They've got those robot submarines going down there all the time."

"Sure," Moore said, improvising, "but those are all U.S. Navy or something, aren't they? The subs have seen all the proof in the world, but the government's covering up."

"That's good," Boccanegra said thoughtfully. "Let's see if I've got the picture. There were beings like these Martians all over the solar system once. Of course, they're not really 'Martians.' It's just that the first live specimens that turned up were on Mars, all right? They've been on Earth, too, ever since the time the Great Galactics came—the people from Planet Theta, too," he added quickly. "And all these years they've been hiding down there, exerting an influence on what has happened to the human race. It hasn't all been good: wars, depressions—"

"Crazy fads: Narcotics," Moore put in.

"Right! All the things that have gone wrong, it's because these Martians have been willing it; they've degenerated and become evil. We don't call them Martians, of course. We call them something like Emissaries, or Guardians, or—what's a bad kind of guardian?"

"Dead Souls," said Moore triumphantly.

"Sure, they're Dead Souls. Sounds kind of Russian, but that's not bad, either. And they've been in Antarctica under the ice and . . . Aw, no," he said, disappointed. "It won't work. We can't get to Antarctica."

"So?"

"So how do we get evidence that there really are Dead Souls there?"

"I don't really see why you keep harping on evidence," Moore said irritably.

"I don't mean evidence like finding a real, live Dead Soul kind of Martian," Boccanegra explained. "You know. We need some sort of message. Mystic drawings. Carvings. Something like the Nazco lines, or whatever they call them, or the rune stone in Minnesota. Of course," he explained, "they wouldn't be in any Earthly language. We work out translations. *Partial* translations, because we don't give the whole thing at once; we keep translating new sections as we go along."

"We get the key from Planet Theta in a trance," Moore said helpfully.

"Or astral projection," Boccanegra nodded, "from the Great Galactics." He thought for a moment, and then said wistfully, "But it would be better if we had something to take photographs of. I always put photographs in my books; they really make a difference, Tony."

"Maybe we could crack open some rocks, like Richard Shaver? And find mystic drawings in the markings?"

"I don't like to repeat what anybody else has done," Boccanegra said virtuously. "And I don't know where Shaver got the rocks, either. Maybe in a cave, or—"

He stopped in midsentence, the ringing of the cash bells now loud and clear. They stared at each other.

"A cave," Moore whispered.

"Not under the ocean. Under the ground! Tony! Are there any caves under the Retreat?"

"Not a one," Moore said regretfully. "I didn't think of that when I bought the tract. But, listen, there are millions of caves all over. All we have to do is find one big one with a lot of passages no one ever goes into—"

"There are lots right along the Mississippi River," Boccanegra chimed in. "There's even the Mammoth Cave, or Carlsbad—why, there are some in Pennsylvania that haven't even been explored much."

"And then maybe I can say I've seen the carvings while I was in astral projection—"

"And then I can actually go there and discover them and take pictures!" Boccanegra finished triumphantly. "I wouldn't say where they came from at first—"

"—until we got a chance to put the drawings there—"

"—and nobody would argue, because everybody knows you and I have never worked together—"

"—and they'd be kind of like Shaver's Deros—"

"—only not deranged robots; they'll look kind of like the Martians, because they're the same Dead Souls, and they mess everything up for humanity because they're evil—"

"And we'll split the money!" Moore cried. "You do your books. I'll do the Retreats. Maybe along about Labor Day you and I can have a public reconciliation, submerging our old differences because now we've discovered this ultimate reality not even we suspected before—"

"—and I can come to the Retreat—"

"And, sure, you can have black robes," Moore said generously. "Marco, it's doable! The good old days are coming back, for sure!"

The two men smiled at each other, their minds racing. Then Moore said, "What about the 'Today' show? That'd be a great place to start, if you can get in."

Boccanegra pursed his lips. Thank heaven he'd sweetened the receptionist; she'd let him in, probably, and then he could just walk in on the booking woman; then it would just be a matter of how fast he could talk. "At least fifty-fifty," he estimated, "if I get back to NBC before the offices close."

"And I'll go right down to the library and start looking up caves," Moore said. "And we don't want to be seen too much together, so what do you say we just get together for a minute later on tonight, say about seven?"

"Lobby of the Grand Hyatt," Boccanegra agreed. He clapped his hands imperiously at the waitress, sulking by the kitchen door. She came over and dropped the check in front of him.

"I'll get the tip," Moore offered, pulling out a handful of silver. Boccanegra, back in character, merely inclined his head in silent agreement, although inside he was marking up the mental ledger: $9.50 for the pastrami sandwiches, and only five quarters for the tip; next time they would eat in a better place and *he* would take care of the tip. As he waited for the cashier to fill out the slip on the one remaining valid credit card he possessed, Boccanegra said suddenly, "My cane!" He hurried back to the table before the waitress got there and picked up two of the quarters. Then he rejoined Anthony Makepeace Moore at the door and the two prophets went out into the world they were about to conquer.

THE GOLD AT THE STARBOW'S END

Anyone who was old enough to understand the politics that ended NASA's lunar program is quite aware of the constant tug-of-war between those who have a desperate desire to explore the unknown and those who feel that exploring the unknown is a waste of time and money.

"The Gold at the Starbow's End" is about many things. It is at least partly about the conflict between the needs of science and the exigencies of balancing a budget, but that's just the beginning. Here is wild adventure of a most unexpected kind and irony piled upon irony.

A finalist for both the Hugo and Nebula Awards when first published in 1972, this extravagantly original novella remains as remarkable and poignant today as it was when it first appeared.

Constitution One

LOG OF LT.-COL. SHEFFIELD N. JACKMAN, U.S.A.F., commanding U.S. Starship *Constitution*, Day 40.

All's well, friends. Thanks to Mission Control for the batch of personal messages. We enjoyed the concert you beamed us, in fact we recorded most of it so we can play it over again when communication gets hairy.

We are now approaching the six-week point in our expedition to Alpha Centauri, Planet Aleph, and now that we've passed the farthest previous manned distance from Earth we're really beginning to feel as if we're on our way. Our latest navigation check confirms Mission Control's plot, and we estimate we should be crossing the orbit of Pluto at approximately 1631 hours, ship time, of Day 40, which is today. Letski has been keeping track of the time dilation effect, which is beginning to be significant now that we are traveling about some 6 percent of the speed of light, and says this would make it approximately a quarter of two in the morning your time, Mission Control. We voted to consider that the "coastal waters" mark. From then on we will have left the solar system behind and thus will be the first human beings to enter upon the deeps of interstellar space. We plan to have a ceremony. Letski and Ann Becklund have made up an American flag for jettisoning at that point, which we will do through the Number Three survey port, along with the prepared stainless-steel plaque containing the president's commissioning speech. We are also throwing in some private articles for each of us. I am contributing my Air Academy class ring.

Little change since previous reports. We are settling down nicely to our routine. We finished up all our post-launch checks weeks ago, and as Dr. Knefhausen predicted we began to find time hanging heavy on our hands. There won't be much to keep us busy between now and when we arrive at the planet Alpha-Aleph that is really essential to the operating of the spaceship. So we went along with Kneffie's proposed recreational schedule, using the worksheets prepared by the NASA Division of Flight Training and Personnel Management. At first (I think the boys back in Indianapolis are big enough to know this!) it met with what you might call a cool reception. The general consensus was that this business of learning number theory and the calculus of statement, which is what they handed us for openers, was for the birds. We figured we weren't quite desperate enough for that yet, so we fooled around with other things. Ann and Will Becklund played a lot of chess. Dot Letski began writing a verse adaptation of *War and Peace*. The rest of us hacked around with the equipment, and making astronomical observations and gabbing. But all that began to get tiresome pretty fast, just as Kneffie said it would at the briefings. We talked about his idea that the best way to pass time in a spaceship was learning to get interested in mathematical problems—no mass to transport, no competitive element to get tempers up and all that. It began to make sense. So now Letski is in his tenth day of trying to find a formula for primes, and my own dear Flo is trying to prove Goldbach's Conjecture by means of the theory of congruences. (This is the girl who two months ago couldn't add up a laundry list!) It certainly passes the time.

Medically, we are all fit. I will append the detailed data on our blood pressures, pulses, etc., as well as the tape from the rocket and navigating systems readouts. I'll report again as scheduled. Take care of Earth for us—we're looking forward to seeing it again, in a few years!

Washington One

There was a lull in the urban guerrilla war in Washington that week. The chopper was able to float right in to the South Lawn of the White House—no sniper fire, no heat-seeking missiles, not even rock-throwing. Dr. Dieter von Knefhausen stared suspiciously at the knot of weary-looking pickets in their permitted fifty yards of space along the perimeter. They didn't look militant, probably Gay Lib or, who knew what, maybe nature-food or single-tax; at any rate no rocks came from them, only a little disorganized booing as the helicopter landed. Knefhausen bowed to *Herr Omnes* sardonically, hopped nimbly out of the chopper and got out of the way as it took off again, which it did at once. He didn't trouble to run to the White House. He strolled. He did not fear these simple people, even if the helicopter pilot did. Also he was not really eager to keep his appointment with the President.

The ADC who frisked him did not smile. The orderly who conducted him to the West Terrace did not salute. No one relieved him of the dispatch case with his slides and papers, although it was heavy. You could tell right away when you were in the doghouse, he thought, ducking his head from the rotor blast as the pilot circled the White House to gain altitude before venturing back across the spread-out city.

It had been a lot different in the old days, he thought with some nostalgia. He could remember every minute of those old days. It was right here, this portico, where he had stood before the world's press and photographers to tell them about the Alpha Aleph

Project. He had seen his picture next to the president's on all the front pages, watched himself on the TV newscasts, talking about the New Earth that would give America an entire colonizable planet four light-years away. He remembered the launch at the Cape, with a million and a half invited guests from all over the world: foreign statesmen and scientists eating their hearts out with envy, American leaders jovial with pride. The orderlies saluted then, all right. His lecture fees had gone clear out of sight. There was even talk of making him the vice presidential candidate in the next election—and it could have happened, too, if the election had been right then, and if there hadn't been the problem of his being born in another country.

Now it was all different. He was taken up in the service elevator. It wasn't so much that Knefhausen minded for his own sake, he told himself, but how did the word get out that there was trouble? Was it only the newspaper stories? Was there a leak?

The Marine orderly knocked once on the big door of the Cabinet room, and it was opened from inside.

Knefhausen entered.

No "Come in, Dieter, boy, pull up a pew." No vice president jumping up to grab his arm and slap his back. His greeting was thirty silent faces turned toward him, some reserved, some frankly hostile. The full Cabinet was there, along with half a dozen department heads and the president's personal action staff, and the most hostile face around the big oval table was the president's own.

Knefhausen bowed. An atavistic hankering for lyceum-cadet jokes made him think of clicking his heels and adjusting a monocle, but he didn't have a monocle and didn't yield to impulses like that. He merely took his place standing at the foot of the table and, when the president nodded, said, "Good morning, gentlemen, and ladies. I assume you want to see me about the stupid lies the Russians are spreading about the Alpha-Aleph program."

Roobarooba, they muttered to each other. The president said in his sharp tenor, "So you think they are just lies?"

"Lies or mistakes, Mr. President, what's the difference? We are right and they are wrong, that's all."

Roobaroobarooba. The secretary of state looked inquiringly at the president, got a nod and said: "Dr. Knefhausen, you know I've been on your team a long time and I don' want to disagree with any statement you care to make, but are you so sure about that? They's some mighty persuasive figures comin' out of the Russians."

"They are false, Mr. Secretary."

"Ah, well, Dr. Knefhausen. I might be inclined to take your word for it, but they's others might not. Not cranks or malcontents, Dr. Knefhausen, but good, decent people. Do you have any evidence for such as them?"

"With your permission, Mr. President?" The president nodded again, and Knefhausen unlocked his dispatch case and drew out a slim sheaf of slides. He handed them to a major of Marines, who looked to the president for approval and then did what Knefhausen told him. The room lights went down and, after some fiddling with the focus, the first slide was projected over Knefhausen's head. It showed a huge array of Y-shaped metal posts, stretching away into the distance of a bleak, powdery-looking landscape.

"This picture is our radio telescope on Farside, the Moon," he said. "It is never visible from the Earth, because that portion of the Moon's surface is permanently turned away from us, for which reason we selected it for the site of the telescope. There is no electrical interference of any kind. The instrument is made up of thirty-three million separate dipole elements, aligned with an accuracy of one part in several million. Its actual size is an approximate circle eighteen miles across, but by virtue of the careful positioning its performance is effectively equal to a telescope with a diameter of some twenty-six miles. Next slide, please."

Click. The picture of the huge RT display swept away and was replaced by another similar—but visibly smaller and shabbier—construction.

"This is the Russian instrument, gentlemen. And ladies. It is approximately one quarter the size of ours in diameter. It has less than one-tenth as many elements, and our reports—they are classified, but I am informed this gathering is cleared to receive this material? Yes—our reports indicate the alignment is very crude. Even terrible, you could say.

"The difference between the two instruments in information-gathering capacity is roughly a hundred to one, in our favor. Lights, please.

"What this means," he went on smoothly, smiling at each of the persons around the table in turn as he spoke, "is that if the Russians say 'no' and we say 'yes,' bet on 'yes.' Our radio telescope can be trusted. Theirs cannot."

The meeting shifted uneasily in its chairs. They were as anxious to believe Knefhausen as he was to convince them, but they were not sure.

Representative Belden, the chairman of the House Ways and Means Committee, spoke for all of them. "Nobody doubts the quality of your equipment. Especially," he added, "since we still have bruises from the job of paying for it. But the Russians made a flat statement. They said that Alpha Centauri can't have a planet larger than one thousand miles in diameter, or nearer than half a billion miles to the star. I have a copy of the Tass release here. It admits that their equipment is inferior to our own, but they have a statement signed by twenty-two academicians that says their equipment could not miss on any object larger or nearer than what I have said, or on any body of any kind which would be large enough to afford a landing place for our astronauts. Are you familiar with this statement?"

"Yes, of course, I have read it—"

"Then you know that they state positively that the planet you call 'Alpha-Aleph' does not exist."

"Yes, that is what they state."

"Moreover, statements from authorities at the Paris Observatory and the UNESCO Astrophysical Center at Trieste, and from England's Astronomer Royal, all say that they have checked and confirmed their figures."

Knefhausen nodded cheerfully. "That is correct, Representative Belden. They confirm that if the observations are as stated, then the conclusions drawn by the Soviet installation at Novy Brezhnevgrad on Farside naturally follow. I don't question the arithmetic. I only say that the observations are made with inadequate equipment, and thus the Soviet astronomers have come to a false conclusion. But I do not want to burden your patience with an unsupported statement," he added hastily as the congressman opened his mouth to speak again, "so I will tell you all there is to tell. What the Russians say is theory. What I have to counter is not merely better theory, but also objective fact. I know Alpha-Aleph is there because I have seen it! Lights again, Major! And the next slide, if you please."

The screen lit up and showed glaring bare white with a sprinkling of black spots, like dust. A large one appeared in the exact center of the screen, with a dozen lesser ones sprinkled around it. Knefhausen picked up a flash pointer and aimed its little arrowhead of light at the central dot.

"This is a photographic negative," he said, "which is to say that it is black where the actual scene is white and vice versa. Those objects are astronomical. It was taken from our Briareus Twelve satellite near the orbit of Jupiter, on its way out to Neptune fourteen months ago. The central object is the star Alpha Centauri. It was photographed with a special instrument which filters out most of the light from the star itself, electronic in nature and something like the coronascope which is used for photographing prominences on our own Sun. We hoped that by this means we might be able actually to photograph the planet Alpha-Aleph. We were successful, as you can see." The flash pointer laid its little arrow next to the nearest small dot to the central star. "That, gentlemen, and ladies, is Alpha-Aleph. It is precisely where we predicted it from radio-telescope data."

There was another buzz from the table. In the dark it was louder than before. The secretary of state cried sharply, "Mr. President! Can't we release this photograph?"

"We will release it immediately after this meeting," said the president.

Roobarooba. Then the committee chairman: "Mr. President, I'm sure if you say that's the planet we want, then it's the planet. But others outside this country may wonder, for indeed all those dots look about alike to me. I wonder if Knefhausen could satisfy a layman's curiosity. *How* do we know that's Alpha-Aleph?"

"Slide Number Four, please—and keep Number Three in the carriage." The same scene, subtly different. "Note that in this picture, gentlemen, that one object, there, is in a different position. It has moved. You know that the stars show no discernible motion, of course. It has moved because this photograph was taken eight months later, as Briareus Twelve was returning from the Neptune flyby, and the planet Alpha-Aleph had revolved in its orbit. This is not theory, it is evidence; and I add that the original tapes from which the photoprint was made are stored in Goldstone, so there is no question that arises of foolishness."

Roobarooba, but in a higher and excited key. Gratified, Knefhausen nailed down his point. "So, Major, if you will now return to Slide Three, yes— And if you will flip back and forth, between Three and Four, as fast as you can— Thank you." The little black dot called Alpha-Aleph bounced back and forth like a tennis ball, while all the other star points remained motionless. "This is what is called the blink comparator process, you see. I point out that if what you are looking at is not a planet, it is, excuse me, Mr. President, the damnedest funniest star you ever saw. Also it is exactly at the distance and exactly with the orbital period we specified based on the RT data. Now, are there any more questions?"

"No, sir!" "That's great, Kneffie!" "Clear as a cow's ass to the stud bull." "I think that wraps it up." "That'll show the Commies."

The president's voice overrode them all.

"I think we can have the lights on now, Major Merton," he said. "Dr. Knefhausen, thank you. I'd appreciate it if you would remain nearby for a few minutes, so you can join Murray and myself in the study to check over the text of our announcement before we release these pictures." He nodded sober dismissal to his chief science adviser and then, reminded by the happy faces of his cabinet, remembered to smile with pleasure.

Constitution Two

Sheffield Jackman's log. Starship *Constitution*. Day 95.

According to Letski we are now traveling at just about 15 percent of the speed of light, almost 30,000 miles per second. The fusion thrust is operating smoothly and well. Fuel, power, and life-support curves are sticking tight to optimum. No sweat of any kind with the ship, or, actually, with anything else.

Relativistic effects have begun to show up as predicted. Jim Barstow's spectral studies show the stars in front of us are showing a shift to the blue end, and the Sun and the other stars behind us are shifting to the red. Without the spectroscope you can't see much, though. Beta Circini looks a little funny, maybe. As for the Sun, it's still very bright—Jim logged it as minus-six magnitude a few hours ago—and as I've never seen it in quite that way before, I can't tell whether the color looks bright or not. It certainly isn't the golden yellow I associate with type GO, but neither is Alpha Centauri ahead of us, and I don't really see a difference between them. I think the reason is simply that they are so bright that the color impressions are secondary to the brightness impressions, although the spectroscope, as I say, does show the differences. We've all taken turns at looking back. Naturally enough, I guess. We can still make out the Earth and even the Moon in the telescope, but it's chancy. Ski almost got an eyeful of the Sun at full light-gathering amplitude yesterday because the visual separation is only about twelve seconds of arc now. In a few more days they'll be too close to separate.

Let's see, what else?

We've been having a fine time with the recreational-math program. Ann has taken to binary arithmetic like a duck to water. She's involved in what I take to be some sort of statistical experimentation (we don't pry too much into what the others are doing until they're ready to talk about it), and, of all things, she demanded we produce coins to flip. Well, naturally none of us had taken any money with us! Except that it turns out two of us did. Ski had a Russian silver rouble that his mother's uncle had given him for luck, and I found an old Philadelphia transit token in my pocket. Ann rejected my transit token as too light to be reliable, but she now spends happy hours flipping the rouble, heads or tails, and writing down the results as a series of six-place binary numbers, heads for 1 and tails for 0. After about a week my curiosity got too much so I began hinting to find out what she was doing. When I ask she says things like, "By means of the easy and the simple we grasp the laws of the whole world." When I say that's nice but what does she hope to grasp by flipping the coin? she says, "When the laws of the whole world are grasped, therein lies perfection." So, as I say, we don't press each other and I leave it there. But it passes the time.

Kneffie would be proud of himself if he could see how our recreation keeps us busy. None of us has managed to prove Fermat's Last Theorem yet or anything like that, but of course that's the whole point. If we could *solve* the problems, we'd have used them up, and then what would we do for recreation? It does exactly what it was intended to. It keeps us mentally alert on this long and intrinsically rather dull boat-ride.

Personal relationships? Jes' fine, fellows, jes' fine. A lot better than any of us really hoped, back there at the personal-hygiene briefings in Mission Control. The girls take the stripey pills every day until three days before their periods, then they take the green pills for four days, then they lay off pills for four days, then back to the stripes. There was a little embarrassed joking about it at first, but now it's strictly routine, like brushing the teeth. We men take our red pills every day (Ski christened them "stop lights") until our girls tell us they're about to lay off (you know what I mean, each of our individual girls tells her husband), then we take the Blue Devil (that's what we call the antidote) and have a hell of a time until the girls start on the stripes again. None of us thought any of this would work, you know. But it works fine. I don't even think sex until Flo kisses my ear and tells me she's getting ready to, excuse the expression, get in heat, and then like wow. Same with everybody. The aft chamber with the nice wide bunks we call Honeymoon Hotel. It belongs to whoever needs it, and never once have both bunks been used. The rest of the time we just sleep wherever is convenient, and nobody gets uptight about it.

Excuse my getting personal, but you told me you wanted to know everything, and there's not much else to tell. All systems remain optimum. We check them over now and again, but nothing has given any trouble, or even looked as though it might be thinking about giving trouble later on. And there's absolutely nothing worth looking at outside but stars. We've all seen them about as much as we need to by now. The plasma jet thrums right along at our point-seven-five Gee. We don't even hear it anymore.

We've even got used to the recycling system. None of us really thought we'd get with the suction toilet, not to mention what happens to the contents, but it was only a little annoying the first few days. Now it's fine. The treated product goes into the algae tanks, feces and urine together. The sludge from the algae goes into the hydroponic beds, but by then, of course, it's just greeny brown vegetable matter like my father used to get out of his mulch bed. That's all handled semiautomatically anyway, of course, so our first real contact with the system comes in the kitchen. The food we eat comes in the form of nice red tomatoes and nourishing rice pilaf and stuff like that. (We do miss animal protein a little; the frozen stores have to last a long time, so each hamburger is a special feast, and we only have them once a week or so.) The water we drink comes actually out of the air, condensed by the dehumidifiers into the reserve supply, where we get it to drink. It's nicely aerated and chilled and tastes fine. Of course, the way it gets into the air in the first place is by being sweated out of our pores or transpired from the plants (which are irrigated direct from the treated product of the reclamation tanks), and we all know, when we stop to think of it, that every molecule of it has passed through all our kidneys forty times by now. But not directly. That's the point. What we drink is clear sweet dew. And if it once was something else, can't you say the same of Lake Erie?

Well. I think I've gone on long enough. You've probably got the idea by now: We're happy in the service, and we all thank you for giving us this pleasure cruise!

Washington Two

Waiting for his appointment with the president, Dr. Knefhausen reread the communique from the spaceship, chuckling happily to himself. "Happy in the service." "Like wow." "Kneffie would be proud of himself"—indeed Kneffie was. And proud of them, those little wonders, there! So brave. So strong.

He took as much pride in them as if they had been his own sons and daughters, all eight of them. Everybody knew the Alpha-Aleph project was Knefhausen's baby, but he tried to conceal from the world that, in his own mind, he spread his fatherhood to include the crew. They were the pick of the available world, and it was he who had put them where they were. He lifted his head, listening to the distant chanting from the perimeter fence where today's disgusting exhibition of mob violence was doing its best to harass the people who were making the world go. What great lumps they were out there, with their long hair and their dirty morals. The heavens belonged only to angels, and it was Dieter von Knefhausen who had picked the angels. It was he who had established the selection procedures (and if he had done some things that were better left unmentioned to make sure the procedures worked, what of it?). It was he who had conceived and adapted the highly important recreation schedule, and above all he who had conceived the entire project and persuaded the president to make it come true. The hardware was nothing, only money. The basic scientific concepts were known; most of the components were on the shelves, it took only will to put them together. The will would not have existed if it had not been for Knefhausen, who announced the discovery of Alpha-Aleph from his radio-observatory on Farside (and gave it that name, although as everyone realized he could have called it by any name he chose, even his own) and carried on the fight for the project by every means available until the president bought it.

It had been a hard, bitter struggle. He reminded himself with courage that the worst was still ahead. No matter. Whatever it cost, it was done, and it was worthwhile. These reports from *Constitution* proved it. It was going exactly as planned, and—

"Excuse me, Dr. Knefhausen."

He looked up, catapulted back from almost half a light-year away.

"I said the president will see you now, Dr. Knefhausen," repeated the usher.

"Ah," said Knefhausen. "Oh, yes, to be sure. I was deep in thought."

"Yes, sir. This way, sir."

They passed a window and there was a quick glimpse of the turmoil at the gates, picket signs used like battle-axes, a thin blue cloud of tear gas, the sounds of shouting. "King Mob is busy today," said Knefhausen absently.

"There's no danger, sir. Through here, please."

The president was in his private study, but to Knefhausen's surprise he was not alone. There was Murray Amos, his personal secretary, which one could understand; but there were three other men in the room. Knefhausen recognized them as the secretary of state, the Speaker of the House and, of all people, the vice-president. How strange, thought Knefhausen, for what was to have been a confidential briefing for the president alone! But he rallied quickly.

"Excuse me, Mr. President," he said cheerfully. "I must have understood wrong. I thought you were ready for our little talk."

"I am ready, Knefhausen," said the president. The cares of his years in the White House rested heavily on him today, Knefhausen thought critically. He looked very old and very tired. "You will tell these gentlemen what you would have told me."

"Ah, yes, I see," said Knefhausen, trying to conceal the fact that he did not see at all. Surely the president did not mean what his words said; therefore it was necessary to try to see what was his thought. "Yes, to be sure. Here is something, Mr. President. A new report from the *Constitution*! It was received by burst transmission from the Lunar Orbiter at Goldstone just an hour ago, and has just come from the decoding room. Let me read it to you. Our brave astronauts are getting along splendidly, just as we planned. They say—"

"Don't read us that just now," said the president harshly. "We'll hear it, but first there is something else. I want you to tell this group the full story of the Alpha-Aleph project."

"The full story, Mr. President?" Knefhausen hung on gamely. "I see. You wish me to begin with the very beginning, when first we realized at the observatory that we had located a planet—"

"No, Knefhausen. Not the cover story. The truth."

"Mr. President!" cried Knefhausen in sudden agony. "I must inform you that I protest this premature disclosure of vital—"

"The truth, Knefhausen!" shouted the president. It was the first time Knefhausen had ever heard him raise his voice. "It won't go out of this room, but you must tell them everything. Tell them why it is that the Russians were right and we lied! Tell them why we sent the astronauts on a suicide mission, ordered to land on a planet that we knew all along did not exist!"

Constitution Three

Shef Jackman's journal, Day 130.

It's been a long time, hasn't it? I'm sorry for being such a lousy correspondent. I was in the middle of a thirteen-game chess series with Eve Barstow—she was playing the Bobby Fischer games, and I was playing in the style of Reshevsky—and Eve said something that made me think of old Kneffie, and that, of course, reminded me I owed you a transmission. So here it is.

In my own defense, though, it isn't only that we've been busy with other things. It takes a lot of power for these chatty little letters. Some of us aren't so sure they're worthwhile. The farther we get the more power we need to accumulate for a transmission. Right now it's not so bad yet, but, well, I might as well tell you the truth, right? Kneffie made us promise that. Always tell the truth, he said, because you're part of the experiment, and we need to know what you're doing, all of it. Well, the truth in this case is that we were a little short of disposable power for a while because Jim Barstow needed quite a lot for research purposes. You will probably wonder what the research is, but we have a rule that we don't criticize, or even talk about, what anyone else is doing until they're ready, and he isn't ready yet. I take the responsibility for the whole thing, not just the power drain but the damage to the ship. I said he could go ahead with it.

We're going pretty fast now, and to the naked eye the stars fore and aft have blue-shifted and red-shifted nearly out of sight. It's funny, but we haven't been able to observe Alpha-Aleph yet, even with the disc obscuring the star. Now, with the shift to the blue, we probably won't see it at all until we slow down. We can still see the Sun, but I guess what we're seeing is ultraviolet when it's home. Of course the relativistic frequency shifts mean we need extra compensating power in our transmissions, which is another reason why, all in all, I don't think I'll be writing home every Sunday, between breakfast and the baseball game, the way I ought to!

But the mission's going along fine. The "personal relationships" keep on being just great. We've done a little experimental research there too that wasn't on the program, but it's all okay. No problems. Worked out great. I think maybe I'll leave out some of the details, but we found some groovy ways to do things. Oh, hell, I'll give you one hint:

Dot Letski says I should tell you to get the boys at Mission Control to crack open two of the stripey pills and one of the Blue Devils, mix them with a quarter-teaspoon of black pepper and about 2 cc of the conditioner fluid from the recycling system. Serve over orange sherbet, and oh boy. After the first time we had it Flo made a crack about its being "seminal" which I thought was a private joke, but it broke everybody up. Dot figured it out for herself weeks ago. We wondered how she got so far so fast with *War and Peace* until she let us into the secret. Then we found out what it could do for you, both emotionally and intellectually: the creative over the arousing, as they say.

Ann and Jerry Letski used up their own recreational programs early (real early—they were supposed to last the whole voyage!), so they swapped microfiches, on the grounds that each was interested in an aspect of causality and they wanted to see what the other side had to offer. Now Ann is deep into people like Kant and Carnap, and Ski is sore as a boil because there's no *Achillea millefolium* in the hydroponics garden. Needs the stalks for his researches, he says. He is making do with flipping his rouble to generate hexagrams; in fact, we all borrow it now and then, but it's not the right way. Honestly, Mission Control, he's right. Some thought should have been given to our other needs, besides sex and number theory. We can't even use chop bones from the kitchen wastes, because there isn't any kitchen waste. I know you couldn't think of everything, but still— Anyway, we improvise as best we can, and mostly well enough.

Let's see, what else? Did I send you Jim Barstow's proof of Goldbach's Conjecture? Turned out to be very simple once he had devised his multiplex parity analysis idea. Mostly we don't fool with that sort of stuff anymore, though. We got tired of number theory after we'd worked out all the fun parts, and if there is any one thing that we all work on (apart from our private interests) it is probably the calculus of statement. We don't do it systematically, only as time permits from our other activities, but we're all pretty well convinced that a universal grammar is feasible enough, and it's easy enough to see what that leads to. Flo has done more than most of us. She asked me to put in that Boole, Venn and all those old people were on the wrong track, but she thinks there might be something to Leibniz's "calculus ratiocinator" idea. There's a J. W. Swanson suggestion that she likes for multiplexing languages. (Jim took off from it to work out his parity analysis.) The idea is that you devise a double-vocabulary language. One set of meanings is conveyed, say, by phonemes—that is, the shape of the words themselves. Another set is conveyed by pitch. It's like singing a message, half of it conveyed by the words, the other half by the tune. Like rock music. You get both sets of meanings at the same time. She's now working on third, fourth, and nth dimensions so as to convey many kinds of meanings at once, but it's not very fruitful so far (except for using sexual intercourse as one of the communications media). Most of the senses available are too limited to convey much. By the way, we checked out all the existing "artificial languages" as best we could—put Will Becklund under hypnotic regression to recapture the Esperanto he'd learned as a kid, for instance. But they were all blind alleys. Didn't even convey as much as standard English or French.

Medical readouts follow. We're all healthy. Eve Barstow gave us a medical check to make sure. Ann and Ski had little rough spots in a couple of molars so she filled them for the practice more than because they needed it. I don't mean practice in filling teeth; she wanted to try acupuncture instead of procaine. Worked fine.

We all have this writing-to-Daddy-and-Mommy-from-Camp-Tanglewood feeling and we'd like to send you some samples of our home handicrafts. The trouble is there's so much of it. Everybody has something he's personally pretty pleased with, like Barstow's proof of most of the classic math problems and my multimedia adaptation of *Sur le pont d'Avignon*. It's hard to decide what to send you with the limited power available, and we don't want to waste it with junk. So we took a vote and decided the best thing was Ann's verse retelling of *War and Peace*. It runs pretty long. I hope the power holds it. I'll transmit as much of it as I can. . . .

Washington Three

Spring was well advanced in Washington. Along the Potomac the cherry blossoms were beginning to bud, and Rock Creek Park was the pale green of new leaves. Even through the *whap, whap* of the helicopter rotor Knefhausen could hear an occasional rattle of small-arms fire from around Georgetown, and the Molotov cocktails and tear gas from the big Water Gate apartment development at the river's edge were steaming the sky with smoke and fumes. They never stopped, thought Knefhausen irritably. What was the good of trying to save people like this?

It was distracting. He found himself dividing his attention into three parts—the scarred, greening landscape below; the escort fireships that orbited around his own chopper; and the papers on his lap. All of them annoyed him. He couldn't keep his mind on any of them. What he liked least was the report from the *Constitution*. He had had to get expert help in translating what it was all about, and he didn't like the need, and even less liked the results. What had gone wrong? They were his kids, hand-picked. There had been no hint, for instance, of hippiness in any of them, at least not past the age of twenty, and only for Ann Becklund and Florence Jackman even then. How had they got into this *I Ching* foolishness, and this stupid business with the *Achillea mille-folium*, better known as the common yarrow? What "experiments"? Who started the disgustingly antiscientific acupuncture thing? How dared they depart from their programmed power budget for "research purposes," and what were the purposes? Above all, what was the "damage to the ship"?

He scribbled on a pad:

With immediate effect, cut out the nonsense. I have the impression you are all acting like irresponsible children. You are letting down the ideals of our program. Knefhausen

After running the short distance from the chopper pad to the shelter of the guarded White House entrance, he gave the slip to a page from the Message Center for immediate encoding and transmission to the *Constitution* via Goldstone, Lunar Orbiter and Farside Base. All they needed was a reminder, he persuaded himself, then they would settle down. But he was still worried as he peered into a mirror, patted his hair down, smoothed his mustache with the tip of a finger and presented himself to the president's chief secretary.

This time they went down, not up. Knefhausen was going to the basement chamber that had been successively Franklin Roosevelt's swimming pool, the White House press lounge, a TV studio for taping jolly little two-shots of the President with congressmen and senators for the folks back home to see, and, now, the heavily armored bunker in which anyone trapped in the White House in the event of a successful attack from the city outside could hold out for several weeks, during which time the Fourth Armored would surely be able to retake the grounds from its bases in Maryland. It was not a comfortable room, but it was a safe one. Besides being armored against attack, it was as thoroughly soundproof, spyproof and leakproof as any chamber in the world, not excepting the Under-Kremlin or the Colorado NOROM base.

Knefhausen was admitted and seated, while the president and a couple of others were in whispered conversation at one end of the room, and the several dozen other people present craned their necks to stare at Knefhausen.

After a moment the president raised his head. "All right," he said. He drank from a crystal goblet of water, looking wizened and weary, and disappointed at the way a boyhood dream had turned out: the presidency wasn't what it had seemed to be from Muncie, Indiana. "We all know why we're here. The government of the United States has given out information which was untrue. It did so knowingly and wittingly, and we've been caught at it. Now we want you to know the background, and so Dr. Knefhausen is going to explain the Alpha-Aleph project. Go ahead, Knefhausen."

Knefhausen stood up and walked unhurryingly to the little lectern set up for him, off to one side of the president. He opened his papers on the lectern, studied them thoughtfully for a moment with his lips pursed, and said:

"As the president has said, the Alpha-Aleph project is a camouflage. A few of you learned this some months ago, and then you referred to it with other words. 'Fraud.' 'Fake.' Words like that. But if I may say it in French, it is not any of those words, it is a legitimate *ruse de guerre*. Not the *guerre* against our political enemies, or even against the dumb kids in the streets with their Molotov cocktails and bricks. I do not mean those wars, I mean the war against ignorance. For you see, there were certain sings—certain *things* we had to know for the sake of science and progress. Alpha-Aleph was designed to find them out for us.

"I will tell you the worst parts first," he said. "Number one, there is no such planet as Alpha-Aleph. The Russians were right. Number two, we knew this all along. Even the photographs we produced were fakes, and in the long run the rest of the world will find this out and they will know of our *ruse de guerre*. I can only hope that they will not find out too soon, for if we are lucky and keep the secret for a while, then I hope we will be able to produce good results to justify what we have done. Number three, when the *Constitution* reaches Alpha Centauri there will be no place for them to land, no way to leave their spacecraft, no sources of raw materials which they might be able to use to make fuel to return, no nothing but the star and empty space. This fact has certain consequences. The *Constitution* was designed with enough hydrogen fuel capacity for a one-way flight, plus maneuvering reserve. There will not be enough for them to come back, and the source they had hoped to tap, namely the planet Alpha-Aleph, does not exist, so they will not come back. Consequently they will die there. Those are the bad things to which I must admit."

There was a sighing murmur from the audience. The president was frowning absently to himself. Knefhausen waited patiently for the medicine to be swallowed, then went on.

"You ask, then, why have we done this thing? Condemning eight young people to their death? The answer is simple: knowledge. To put it with other words, we must have the basic scientific knowledge we need to protect the free world. You are all familiar, I si—I believe, with the known fact that basic scientific advances have been very few these past ten years and more. Much R&D. Much technology. Much applications. But in the years since Einstein, or better since Weizsäcker, very little basic.

"But without the new basic knowledge, the new technology must soon stop developing. It will run out of steam, you see.

"Now I must tell you a story. It is a true scientific story, not a joke; I know you do not want jokes from me at this time. There was a man named de Bono, a Maltese, who wished to investigate the process of creative thinking. There is not very much known about this process, but he had an idea how he could find something out. So he prepared for an experiment a room that was stripped of all furniture, with two doors, one across from the other. You go into one door, you go through the room, you walk out of the other. He put at the door that was the entrance some material—two flat boards, some ropes. And he got as his subjects some young children. Now he said to the children, 'Now, this is a game we will play. You must go through this room and out of the other door, that is all. If you do that, you win. But there is one rule. You must not touch the floor with your feet or your knees or with any part of your body or your clothing. We had here a boy,' he said, 'who was very athletic and walked across on his hands, but he was disqualified. You must not do that. Now go, and whoever does it fastest will win some chocolates.'

"So he took away all of the children but the first one and, one by one, they tried. There were ten or fifteen of them, and each of them did the same thing. Some it took longer to figure out, some figured it out right away, but it always was the same trick. They sat down on the floor, they took the boards and the ropes, and they tied one board to each foot and they walked across the room like on skis. The fastest one thought of the trick right away and was across in a few seconds. The slowest took many minutes. But it was the same trick for all of them, and that was the first part of the experiment.

"Now this Maltese man, de Bono, performed the second part of the experiment. It was exactly like the first, with one difference. He did not give them two boards. He only gave them one board.

"And in the second part every child worked out the same trick, too, but it was of course a different trick. They tied the rope to the end of the single board and then they stood on it, and jumped up, tugging the rope to pull the board forward, hopping and tugging, moving a little bit at a time, and every one of them succeeded. But in the first experiment the average time to cross was maybe forty-five seconds. And in the second experiment the average time was maybe twenty seconds. With one board they did their job faster than with two.

"Perhaps now some of you see the point. Why did not any of the children in the first group think of this faster method of going across the room? It is simple. They looked at what they were given to use for materials and, they are like all of us, they wanted to use everything. But they did not need everything. They could do better with less, in a different way."

Knefhausen paused and looked around the room, savoring the moment. He had them now, he knew. It was just as it had been with the president himself, three years before. They were beginning to see the necessity of what had been done, and the pale, upturned faces were no longer as hostile, only perplexed and a little afraid.

He went on:

"So that is what Project Alpha-Aleph is about, gentlemen and ladies. We have selected eight of the most intelligent human beings we could find—healthy, young, very adventurous. Very creative. We played on them a nasty trick, to be sure. But we gave them an opportunity no one has ever had. The opportunity to *think*. To think for *ten years*. To think about basic questions. Out there they do not have the extra board to distract them. If they want to know something they cannot run to the library and look it up, and find that somebody has said that what they were thinking could not work. They must think it out for themselves.

"So in order to make this possible we have practiced a deception on them, and it will cost them their lives. All right, that is tragic, yes. But if we take their lives we give them in exchange immortality.

"How do we do this? Trickery again, gentlemen and ladies. I do not say to them. 'Here, you must discover new basic approaches to science and tell them to us.' I camouflage the purpose, so that they will not be distracted even by that. We have told them that this is recreational, to help them pass the time. This too is a *ruse de guerre*. The 'recreation' is not to help them make the trip; it is the whole purpose of the trip.

"So we start them out with the basic tools of science. With numbers: that is, with magnitudes and quantification, with all that scientific observations are about. With grammar. This is not what you learned when you were thirteen years old, it is a technical term; it means with the calculus of statement and the basic rules of communication: that is so they can learn to think clearly by communicating fully and without fuzzy ambiguity. We give them very little else, only the opportunity to mix these two basic ingredients and come up with new forms of knowledge.

"What will come of these things? That is a fair question. Unfortunately there is no answer. Not yet. If we knew the answer in advance, we would not have to perform the experiment. So we do not know what will be the end result of this, but already they have accomplished very much. Old questions that have puzzled the wisest of scientists for hundreds of years they have solved already. I will give you one example. You will say, 'yes, but what does it *mean?*' I will answer, 'I do not know'; I only know that it is so hard a question that no one else has ever been able to answer it. It is a proof of a thing which is called Goldbach's Conjecture. Only a conjecture; you could call it a guess. A guess by an eminent mathematician some many years ago, that every even number can be written as the sum of two prime numbers. This is one of those simple problems in mathematics that everyone can understand and no one can solve. You can say, 'Certainly, sixteen is the sum of eleven and five, both of which are prime numbers, and thirty is the sum of twenty-three and seven, which also are both prime, and I can give you such numbers for any even number you care to name.' Yes, you can; but can you prove that for *every* even number it will *always* be possible to do this? No. You cannot. No one has been able to, but our friends on the *Constitution* have done it, and this was in the first few months. They have yet almost ten years. I cannot say what they will do in that time, but it is foolish to imagine that it will be anything less than very much indeed. A new relativity, a new universal gravitation—I don't know, I am only saying words. But much."

He paused again. No one was making a sound. Even the president was no longer staring straight ahead without expression, but was looking at him.

"It is not yet too late to spoil the experiment, and so it is necessary for us to keep the secret a bit longer. But there you have it, gentlemen and ladies. That is the truth about Alpha-Aleph." He dreaded what would come next, postponed it for a second by consulting his papers, shrugged, faced them and said: "Now, are there any questions?"

Oh, yes there were questions. *Herr Omnes* was stunned a little, took a moment to over-come the spell of the simple and beautiful truths he had heard, but then first one piped up, then another, then two or three shouting at once. There were questions, to be sure. Questions beyond answering. Questions Knefhausen did not have time to hear, much less answer, before the next question was on him. Questions to which he did not know the answers. Questions, worst of all, to which the answers were like pepper in the eyes, enraging, blinding the people to sense. But he had to face them, and he tried to answer them. Even when they shouted so that, outside the thick double doors, the Marine guards looked at each other uneasily and wondered what made the dull rumble that pen-etrated the very good soundproofing of the room. "What I want to know, who put you up to this?" "Mr. Chairman, nobody; it is as I have said." "But see now, Knefhausen, do you mean to tell us you're murderin' these good people for the sake of some Goldbach's theory?" "No, Senator, not for Goldbach's Conjecture, but for what great advances in science will mean in the struggle to keep the free world free." "You're confessing you've dragged the United States into a palpable fraud?" "A legitimate ruse of war, Mr. Secre-tary, because there was no other way." "The photographs, Knefhausen?" "Faked, Gen-eral, as I have told you. I accept full responsibility." And on and on, the words "murder" and "fraud" and even "treason" coming faster and faster.

Until at last the president stood up and raised his hand. Order was a long time com-ing, but at last they quietened down.

"Whether we like it or not, we're in it," he said simply. "There is nothing else to say. You have come to me, many of you, with rumors and asked for the truth. Now you have the truth, and it is classified Top Secret and must not be divulged. You all know what this means. I will only add that I personally propose to see that any breach of this secu-rity is investigated with all the resources of the government, and punished with the full penalty of the law. I declare this a matter of national emergency, and remind you that the penalty includes the death sentence when appropriate—and I say that in this case it is appropriate." He looked very much older than his years, and he moved his lips as though something tasted bad in his mouth. He allowed no further discussion, and dis-missed the meeting.

Half an hour later, in his private office, it was just Knefhausen and the president.

"All right," said the president, "it's all hit the fan. The next thing is: The world will know it. I can postpone that a few weeks, maybe even months. I can't prevent it."

"I am grateful to you, Mr. President, for—"

"Shut up, Knefhausen. I don't want any speeches. There is one thing I want from you, and that is an explanation. What the hell is this about mixing up narcotics and free love and so on?"

"Ah," said Knefhausen, "you refer to the most recent communication from the *Con-stitution*. Yes. I have already dispatched, Mr. President, a strongly worded order. Because of the communications lag it will not be received for some months, but I assure you the matter will be corrected."

The president said bitterly, "I don't want any assurances, either. Do you watch televi-sion? I don't mean *I Love Lucy* and ball games, I mean news. Do you know what sort of shape this country is in? The bonus marches in 1932, the race riots in 1967—they were nothing. Time was when we could call out the National Guard to put down disorder.

Last week I had to call out the Army to use against three companies of the Guard. One more scandal and we're finished, Knefhausen, and this is a big one."

"The purposes are beyond reproach—"

"Your purposes may be. Mine may be, or I try to tell myself it is for the good of science I did this, and not so I will be in the history books as the president who contributed a major breakthrough. But what are the purposes of your friends on the *Constitution*? I agreed to eight martyrs, Knefhausen. I didn't agree to forty billion dollars out of the nation's pockets to give your eight young friends ten years of gang-bangs and dope."

"Mr. President. I assure you this is only a temporary phase. I have instructed them to straighten out."

"And if they don't, what are you going to do about it?" The president, who never smoked, stripped a cigar, bit off the end and lit it. He said, "It's too late for me to say I shouldn't have let you talk me into this. So all I will say is you have to show results from this flim-flam before the lid blows off, or I won't be president anymore, and I doubt that you will be alive."

Constitution Four

This is Shef again and it's, oh, let me see, about Day 250. 300? No, I don't think so. Look, I'm sorry about the ship date, but I honestly don't think much in those terms any more. I've been thinking about other things. Also I'm a little upset. When I tossed the rouble the hexagram was K'an, which is danger, over Li, the Sun. That's a bad mood to be communicating with you in. We aren't vengeful types, but the fact is that some of us were pretty sore when we found out what you'd done. I don't *think* you need to worry, but I wish I'd got a better hexagram.

Let me tell you the good parts first. Our velocity is pushing point four oh C now. The scenery is beginning to get interesting. For several weeks now the stars fore and aft have been drifting out of sight as the ones in front get up into the ultraviolet and the ones behind sink into the infrared. You'd think that as the spectrum shifts the other parts of the EMF bands would come into the visible range. I guess they do, but stars peak in certain frequencies, and most of them seem to do it in the visible frequencies, so the effect is that they disappear. The first thing was that there was a sort of round black spot ahead of us where we couldn't see anything at all, not Alpha Centauri, not Beta Centauri, not even the bright Circini stars. Then we lost the Sun behind us, and a little later we saw the blackout spread to a growing circle of stars there. Then the circle began to widen.

Of course, we know that the stars are really there. We can detect them with phase-shift equipment, just as we can transmit and receive your messages by shifting the frequencies. But we just can't see them anymore. The ones in direct line of flight, where we have a vector velocity of .34c or .37c (depending on whether they are in front of us or behind us) simply aren't radiating in the visible band anymore. The ones farther out to the side have been displaced visually because of the relativistic effects of our speed. But what it looks like is that we're running the hell out of Nothing, in the direction of Nothing, and it is frankly a little scary.

Even the stars off to one side are showing relativistic color shifts. It's almost like a rainbow, one of those full-circle rainbows that you see on the clouds beneath you from an airplane sometimes. Only this circle is all around us. Nearest the black hole in front the stars have frequency-shifted to a dull reddish color. They go through orange and yellow and a sort of leaf green to the band nearest the black hole in back, which are bright blue shading to purple. Jim Barstow has been practicing his farsight on them, and he can relate them to the actual sky map. But I can't. He sees something in the black hole in front of us that I can't see, either. He says he thinks it's a bright radio source, probably Centaurus A, and he claims it is radiating strongly in the whole visible band now. He means strongly for him, with his eyes. I'm not sure I can see it at all. There *may* be a sort of very faint, diffuse glow there, like the *gegenschein,* but I'm not sure. Neither is anyone else.

But the starbow itself is beautiful. It's worth the trip. Flo has been learning oil painting so she can make a picture of it to send you for your wall, although when she found out what you'd been up to she got so sore she was thinking of boobytrapping it with a fusion bomb or something. (But she's over that now. I think.)

So we're not so mad at you anymore, although there was a time when, if I'd been communicating with you at exactly that moment, I would have said some bad things.

. . . I just played this back, and it sounds pretty jumbled and confused. I'm sorry about that. It's hard for me to do this. I don't mean hard like intellectually difficult (the way chess problems and tensor analysis used to be), but hard like shoveling sand with a teaspoon. I'm just not used to constricting my thoughts in this straitjacket anymore. I tried to get one of the others to communicate this time instead of me, but there were no takers. I did get a lot of free advice. Dot says I shouldn't waste my time remembering how we used to talk. She wanted to write an eidetic account in simplified notation for you, which she estimated a crash program could translate for you in reasonable time, a decade or two, and would give you an absolutely full account of everything. I objected that that involved practical difficulties. Not in preparing the account, I don't mean. Shucks, we can all do that now. I don't forget anything, except irrelevant things like the standard-reckoning day that I don't want to remember in the first place, and neither does anyone else. But the length of transmission would be too much. We don't have the power to transmit the necessary number of groups, especially since the accident. Dot said we could Gödelize it. I said you were too dumb to de-Gödelize it. She said it would be good practice for you.

Well, she's right about that, and it's time you all learned how to communicate in a sensible way, so if the power holds out I'll include Dot's eidetic account at the end. In Gödelized form. Lots of luck. I won't honestly be surprised if you miss a digit or something and it all turns into *Rebecca of Sunnybrook Farm* or some missing books of apocrypha or, more likely of course, gibberish. Ski says it won't do you any good in any case, because Henle was right. I pass that on without comment.

Sex. You always want to hear about sex. It's great. Now that we don't have to fool with the pills anymore we've been having some marvelous times. Flo and Jim Barstow began making it as part of a multiplexed communications system that you have to see to believe. Sometimes when they're going to do it we all knock off and just sit around and watch them, cracking jokes and singing and helping with the auxiliary computations. When we had that little bit of minor surgery the other day (now we've got the bones seasoning), Ann and Ski decided to ball instead of using anaesthesia, and they said it was better than acupuncture. It didn't block the sensation. They were aware of their little toes being lopped off, but they didn't perceive it as pain. So then Jim, when it was his turn, tried going through the amputation without anything at all in the expectation that he and Flo would go to bed together a little later, and that worked well too. He was all het up about it; claimed it showed a reverse causality that his theories predicted but that had not been demonstrated before. Said at last he was over the cause-preceding-the-effect hangup. It's like the Red Queen and the White Queen, and quite puzzling until you get the hang of it. (I'm not sure I've got the hang of it yet.) Suppose he hadn't balled Flo? Would his toe have hurt retroactively? I'm a little mixed up on this, Dot says because I simply don't understand phenomenology in general, and I think I'll have to take Ann's advice and work my way through Carnap, although the linguistics are so poor that it's hard to stay with it. Come to think of it, I don't have to. It's all in the Gödelized eidetic statement, after all. So I'll transmit the statement to you, and while I'm doing that it will be a sort of review for me and maybe I'll get my head right on causality.

Listen, let me give you a tip. The statement will also include Ski's trick of containing plasma for up to 500K milliseconds, so when you figure it out you'll know how to build those fusion power reactors you were talking about when we left. That's the carrot before your nose, so get busy on de-Gödelizing. The plasma dodge works fine, although of course we were sorry about what happened when we converted the drive. The explosion killed Will Becklund outright, and it looked hairy for all of us.

Well, anyway. I have to cut this short because the power's running a little low and I don't want to chance messing up the statement. It follows herewith:

$$1973^{354} + 331^{852} + 17^{2008} + 5^{47} + 3^{9606} + 2^{88} \text{ take away } 78.$$

Lots of luck, fellows!

Washington Four

Knefhausen lifted his head from the litter of papers on his desk. He rubbed his eyes, sighing. He had given up smoking the same time as the president, but, like the president, he was thinking of taking it up again. It could kill you, yes. But it was a tension-reducer, and he needed that. And what was wrong with something killing you. There were worse things than being killed, he thought dismally.

Looking at it any way you could, he thought objectively, the past two or three years had been hard on him. They had started so well and had gone so bad. Not as bad as those distant memories of childhood when everybody was so poor and Berlin was so cold and what warm clothes he had came from the *Winterhilfe*. By no means as hard as the end of the war. Nothing like as bad as those first years in South America and then in the Middle East, when even the lucky and famous ones, the Von Brauns and the Ehrickes, were having trouble getting what was due them and a young calf like Knefhausen had to peel potatoes and run elevators to live. But harder and worse than a man at the summit of his career had any reason to expect.

The Alpha-Aleph project, fundamentally, was sound! He ground his teeth, thinking about it. It would work—no, by God, it *was* working, and it would make the world a different place. Future generations would see.

But the future generations were not here yet, and in the present things were going badly.

Reminded, he picked up the phone and buzzed his secretary. "Have you got through to the president yet?" he demanded.

"I'm sorry, Dr. Knefhausen. I've tried every ten minutes, just as you said."

"Ah," he grunted. "No, wait. Let me see. What calls are there?"

Rustle of paper. "The news services, of course, asking about the rumors again. Jack Anderson's office. The man from CBS."

"No, no. I will not talk to the press. Anyone else?"

"Senator Copley called, asking when you were going to answer the list of questions his committee sent you."

"I will give him an answer. I will give him the answer Götz von Berlichingen gave to the Bishop of Bamberg."

"I'm sorry, Dr. Knefhausen, I didn't quite catch—"

"No matter. Anything else?"

"Just a long-distance call, from a Mr. Hauptmann. I have his number."

"Hauptmann?" The name was puzzlingly familiar. After a moment Knefhausen placed it: to be sure, the photo technician who had cooperated in the faked pictures from Briareus Twelve. Well, he had his orders to stay out of sight and shut up. "No, that's not important. None of them are, and I do not wish to be disturbed with such nonsense. Continue as you were, Mrs. Ambrose. If the president is reached you are to put me on at once, but no other calls."

He hung up and returned to his desk.

He looked sadly and fondly at the papers. He had them all out: the reports from the *Constitution,* his own drafts of interpretation and comment, and more than a hundred footnoted items compiled by his staff, to help untangle the meanings and implications of those, ah, so cryptic sometimes, reports from space:

"*Henle.* Apparently refers to Paul Henle (note appended); probably the citation intended is his statement, 'There are certain symbolisms in which certain things cannot be said.' Conjecture that English language is one of those symbolisms."

"*Orange sherbet sundae.* A classified experimental study was made of the material in Document Ref. No. CON-130, Para. 4. Chemical analysis and experimental testing have indicated that the recommended mixture of pharmaceuticals and other ingredients produce a hallucinogen-related substance of considerable strength and not wholly known qualities. One hundred subjects ingested the product or a placebo in a double-blind controlled test. Subjects receiving the actual substance report reactions significantly different from the placebo. Effects reported include feelings of immense competence and deepened understanding. However, data is entirely subjective. Attempts were made to verify claims by standard I.Q., manipulative, and other tests, but the subjects did not cooperate well, and several have since absented themselves without leave from the testing establishment."

"*Gödelized language.* A system of encoding any message of any kind as a single very large number. The message is first written out in clear language and then encoded as bases and exponents. Each letter of the message is represented in order by the natural order of primes—that is, the first letter is represented by the base 2, the second by the base 3, the third by the base 5, then 7, 11, 13, 17, etc. The identity of the letter occupying that position in the message is given by the exponent: simply, the exponent 1 meaning that the letter in that position is an A, the exponent 2 meaning that it is a B, 3 a C, etc. The message as a whole is then rendered as the product of all the bases and exponents. *Example.* The word 'cab' can thus be represented as $2^3 \times 3^1 \times 5^2$, or 600. (= 8×3×25.) The name 'Abe' would be represented by the number 56,250, or $2^1 \times 3^2 \times 5^5$. (= 2×9×3125.) A sentence like

'John lives.' would be represented by the product of the following terms: $2^{10} \times 3^{15} \times 5^8 \times 7^{14} \times 11^0 \times 13^{12} \times 17^9 \times 19^{22} \times 23^5 \times 29^{19} \times 31^{27}$ (in which the exponent '0' has been reserved for a space and the exponent '27' has been arbitrarily assigned to indicate a full stop). As can be seen, the Gödelized form for even a short message involves a very large number, although such numbers may be transmitted quite compactly in the form of a sum of bases and exponents. The example transmitted by the *Constitution* is estimated to equal the contents of a standard unabridged dictionary."

"*Farsight.* The subject James Madison Barstow is known to have suffered from some nearsightedness in his early school years, apparently brought on by excessive reading, which he attempted to cure through eye exercises similar to the 'Bates method' (note appended). His vision at time of testing for Alpha-Aleph project was optimal. Interviews with former associates indicate his continuing interest in increasing visual acuity. *Alternate explanation.* There is some indication that he was also interested in paranormal phenomena such as clairvoyance or prevision, and it is possible, though at present deemed unlikely, that his use of the term refers to 'looking ahead' in time."

And so on, and on.

Knefhausen gazed at the litter of papers lovingly and hopelessly, and passed his hand over his forehead. The kids! They were so marvelous . . . but so unruly . . . and so hard to understand. How unruly of them to have concealed their true accomplishments. The secret of hydrogen fusion! That alone would justify, more than justify, the entire project. But where was it? Locked in that number-jumber gibberish. Knefhausen was not without appreciation of the elegance of the method. He, too, was capable of taking seriously a device of such luminous simplicity. Once the number was written out you had only to start by dividing it by two as many times as possible, and the number of times would give you the first letter. Then divide by the next prime, three, and that number of times would give you the second letter. But the practical difficulties! You could not get even the first letter until you had the whole number, and IBM had refused even to bid on constructing a bank of computers to write that number out unless the development time was stretched to twenty-five years. *Twenty-five years.* And meanwhile in that number was hidden probably the secret of hydrogen fusion, possibly many greater secrets, most certainly the key to Knefhausen's own well-being over the next few weeks. . . .

His phone rang.

He grabbed it and shouted into it at once: "Yes, Mr. President!"

He had been too quick. It was only his secretary. Her voice was shaking but determined.

"It's not the president, Dr. Knefhausen, but Senator Copley is on the wire and he says it is urgent. He says—"

"No!" shouted Knefhausen and banged down the phone. He regretted it even as he was doing it. Copley was very high, chairman of the Armed Forces Committee; he was not a man Knefhausen wished to have as an enemy, and he had been very careful to make him a friend over years of patient fence-building. But he could not speak to him, or to anyone, while the President was not answering his calls. Copley's rank was high, but he was not in the direct hierarchical line over Knefhausen. When the top of that line refused to talk to him, Knefhausen was cut off from the world.

He attempted to calm himself by examining the situation objectively. The pressures on the president just now: They were enormous. There was the continuing trouble in the cities, all the cities. There were the political conventions coming up. There was the need to get elected for a third term, and the need to get the law amended to make that possible. And yes, Knefhausen admitted to himself, the worst pressure of all was the rumors that were floating around about the *Constitution*. He had warned the President. It was unfortunate the President had not listened. He had said that a secret known to two people is compromised and a secret known to more than two is no secret. But the president had insisted on the disclosure to that ever-widening circle of high officials—sworn, of course to secrecy, but what good was that?—and, of course, in spite of everything, there had been leaks. Fewer than one might have feared. More than one could stand.

He touched the reports from *Constitution* caressingly. Those beautiful kids, they could still make everything right, so wonderful. . . .

Because it was he who had made them wonderful, he confessed to himself. He had invented the idea. He had selected them. He had done things which he did not quite even yet reconcile himself to to make sure that it was they and not some others who were on the crew. He had, above all, made assurance doubly sure by insuring their loyalty in every way possible. Training. Discipline. Ties of affection and friendship. More reliable ties: loading their food supplies, their entertainment tapes, their programmed activities with every sort of advertising inducement, M/R compulsion, psychological reinforcement he could invent or find, so that whatever else they did they did not fail to report faithfully back to Earth. Whatever else happened, there was that. The data might be hard to untangle, but it would be there. They could not help themselves; his commandments were stronger than God's: like Martin Luther, they must say *Ich kann nicht anders,* and come Pope or inquisition, they must stand by it. They would learn, and tell what they learned, and thus the investment would be repaid. . . .

The telephone!

He was talking before he had it even to his mouth. "Yes, yes! This is Dr. Knefhausen, yes!" he gabbled. Surely it must be the president now—

It was not.

"Knefhausen!" shouted the man on the other end. "Now, listen, I'll tell you what I told that bitch pig girl of yours, if I don't talk to you on the phone *right now* I'll have Fourth Armored in there to arrest you and bring you to me in twenty minutes. So listen!"

Knefhausen recognized both voice and style. He drew a deep voice and forced himself to be calm. "Very well, Senator Copley," he said, "what is it?"

"The game is blown, boy! That's what it is. That boy of yours in Huntsville, what's his name, the photo technician—"

"*Hauptmann?*"

"That's him! Would you like to know where he is, you dumb Kraut bastard?"

"Why, I suppose—I should think in Huntsville—"

"Wrong, boy! Your Kraut bastard friend claimed he didn't feel good and took some accrued sick time. Intelligence kept an eye on him up to a point, didn't stop him, wanted to see what he'd do. Well, they saw. They saw him leaving Orly Airport an hour ago in an Aeroflot plane. Put your big Kraut brain to work on that one, Knefhausen! He's defected. Now start figuring out what you're going to do about it, and it better be good!"

Knefhausen said something, he did not know what, and hung up the phone, he did not remember when. He stared glassily into space for a time.

Then he flicked the switch for his secretary and said, not listening to her stammering apologies, "That long-distance call that came from Hauptmann before, Mrs. Ambrose. You didn't say where it was from."

"It was an overseas call, Dr. Knefhausen. From Paris. You didn't give me a chance to—"

"Yes, yes. I understand. Thank you. Never mind." He hung up and sat back. He felt almost relieved. If Hauptmann had gone to Russia it could only be to tell them that the picture was faked and not only was there no planet for the astronauts to land on but it was not a mistake, even, actually a total fraud. So now it was all out of his hands. History would judge him now. The die was cast. The Rubicon was crossed.

So many literary allusions, he thought deprecatingly. Actually it was not the judgment of history that was immediately important but the judgment of certain real people now alive and likely to respond badly. And they would judge him not so much by what might be or what should have been, as by what was. He shivered in the cold of that judgment and reached for the telephone to try once more to call the president. But he was quite sure the president would not answer, then or ever again.

Constitution Five

Old reliable peed-off Shef here. Look, we got your message. I don't want to discuss it. You've got a nerve. You're in a bad mood, aren't you? If you can't say anything nice, don't say anything at all. We do the best we can, and that's not bad, and if we don't do exactly what you want us to, maybe it's because we know quite a lot more than you did when you fired us off at that blob of moonshine you call Alpha-Aleph. Well, thanks a lot for nothing.

On the other hand, thanks a little for what little you did do, which at least worked out to get us where we are, and I don't mean spatially. So I'm not going to yell at you. I just don't want to talk to you at all. I'll let the others talk for themselves.

Dot Letski speaking. This is important. Pass it on. I have three things to tell you that I do not want you to forget. *One: Most problems have grammatical solutions.* The problem of transporting people from the Earth to another planet does not get solved by putting pieces of steel together one at a time at random, and happening to find out you've built the *Constitution* by accident. It gets solved by constructing a model (= equation (= grammar)) which describes the necessary circumstances under which the transportation occurs. Once you have the grammatical model, you just put the metal around it and it goes like gangbusters.

When you have understood this you will be ready for: *Two: There is no such thing as causality.* What a waste of time it has been, trying to assign "causes" to "events"! You say things like, "Striking a match causes it to burn." True statement? No, false statement. You find yourself in a whole waffle about whether the "act" of "striking" is "necessary" and/or "sufficient" and you get lost in words. Pragmatically useful grammars are without tenses. In a decent grammar (which this English-language one, of course, is not, but I'll do the best I can) you can make a statement like "There exists a conjunction of forms of matter (specified) which combine with the release of energy at a certain temperature (specified) (which may be the temperature associated with heat of friction)." Where's the causality? "Cause" and "effect" are in the same timeless statement. So, *Three: There are no such things as empirical laws.* When Ski came to understand that, he was able to contain the plasma in our jet indefinitely, not by pushing particles around in brute-force magnetic squeezes but by encouraging them to want to stay together. There are other ways of saying what he does (= "creates an environment in which centripetal exceed centrifugal forces"), but the way I said it is better because it tells something about your characters. Bullies, all of you. Why can't you be nice to things if you want them to be nice to you? Be sure to pass this on to T'in Fa at Tiantsin, Professor Morris at All Soul's, and whoever holds the Carnap chair at UCLA.

Flo's turn. My mother would have loved my garden. I have drumsticks and daffodils growing side by side in the sludgy sand. They do so please us, and we them: I will probably transmit a full horticultural handbook at a future date, but meanwhile it is shameful to eat a radish. Carrots, on the other hand, enjoy it.

A statement of William Becklund, deceased. I emerged into the world between feces and urine, learned, grew, ate, worked, moved and died. Alternatively, I emerged from the hydrogen flare, shrank, disgorged, and reentered the womb one misses so. You may approach it from either end, it makes no difference at all which way you look at it.

Observational datum, Letski. At time *t*, a Dirac number incommensurable with GMT, the following phenomenon is observed:

The radio source Centaurus A is identified as a positionally stable single collective object rather than two intersecting gas clouds and is observed to contract radially toward a center. Analysis and observation reveal it to be a Black Hole of which the fine detail is not detectable as yet. One infers all galaxies develop such central vortices, with implications of interest to astronomers and eschatologists. I, Seymour Letski, propose to take a closer look but the others prefer to continue programmed flight first. Harvard-Smithsonian notification service, please copy.

"Starbow," a preliminary study for a rendering into English of a poem by James Barstow:

> Gaggle of goslings but pick of our race
> We waddle through relativistic space.
> Dilated, discounted, despondent we scan:
> But vacant the Sign of the Horse and the Man.
> Vacant the Sign of the Man and the Horse,
> And now we conjecture the goal of our course.
> Tricked, trapped and cozened, we ruefully run
> After the child of the bachelor sun.
> The trick is revealed and the trap is confessed
> And we are the butts of the dimwitted jest.
> O Gander who made us, O Goose who laid us,
> How lewdly and twistedly you betrayed us!
> We owe you a debt. We won't forget.
> With fortune and firmness we'll pay you yet.
> Give us some luck and we'll timely send
> Your pot of gold from the starbow's end.

Ann Becklund:

I think it was Stanley Weinbaum who said that from three facts a truly superior mind should be able to deduce the whole universe (Ski thinks it is possible with a finite number, but considerably larger than that). We are so very far from being truly superior minds by those standards, or even by our own. Yet we have a much larger number of facts to work with than three, or even three thousand, and so we have deduced a good deal.

This is not as valuable to you as you might have hoped, dear old bastardly Kneffie and all you bastardly others, because one of the things that we have deduced is that we can't tell you everything, because you wouldn't understand. We would help you along, some of you, if you were here, and in time you would be able to do what we do easily enough, but not at remote control.

But all is not lost, folks! Cheer up! You don't deduce like we deduce, but on the other hand you have so very much more to work from. Try. Get smart. You can do it if you want to. Set your person at rest, compose your mind before you speak, make your relations firm before you ask for something. Try not to be loathsome about it. Don't be like the fellow in the Changes. "He brings increase to no one. Indeed, someone even strikes him."

We've all grown our toes back now, even Will, although it was particularly difficult for him since he had been killed, and we've inscribed the bones and used them with very good effect in generating the hexagrams. I hope you see the point of what we did. We could have gone on with tossing coins or throwing the yarrow stalks, or at least with the closest Flo could breed to yarrow stalks. We didn't want to do that because it's not the optimum way.

The person who doesn't keep his heart constantly steady might say, "Well, what's the difference?" That's a poor sort of question to ask. It implies a deterministic answer. A better question is, "Does it make a difference?" and the answer to that is, "Yes, probably, because in order to do something right you must do it right." That is the law of identity, in any language.

Another question you might ask is, "Well, what source of knowledge are you actually tapping when you consult the hexagrams?" That's a better kind of question in that it doesn't *force* a wrong answer, but the answer is, again, indeterminate. You might view the *I Ching* as a sort of Rorschach bundle of squiggles that has no innate meaning but is useful because your own mind interprets it and puts sense into it. Feel free! You might think of it as a sort of memory bank of encoded lore. Why not? You might skip it entirely and come to knowledge in some other tao, any tao you like. ("The superior man understands the transitory in the light of the eternity of the end.") That's fine, too!

But whatever way you do it, you should *do* it that way. We needed inscribed bones to generate hexagrams, because that was the right way, and so it was no particular sacrifice to lop off a toe each for the purpose. It's working out nicely, except for one thing. The big hangup now is that the translations are so degraded, Chinese to German, German to English, and error seeping in at every step, but we're working on that now.

Perhaps I will tell you more at another time. Not now. Not very soon. Eve will tell you about that.

Eve Barstow, the Dummy, comes last and, I'm afraid, least.

When I was a little girl I used to play chess, badly, with very good players, and that's the story of my life. I'm a chronic overachiever. I can't stand people who aren't smarter and better than I am, but the result is that I'm the runt of the litter every time. They are all very nice to me here, even Jim, but they know what the score is and so do I.

So I keep busy and applaud what I can't do. It isn't a bad life. I have everything I need, except pride.

Let me tell you what a typical day is like here between Sol and Centaurus. We wake up (if we have been sleeping, which some of us still do) and eat (if we are still eating, as all but Ski and, of course, Will Becklund do). The food is delicious and Florence has induced it to grow cooked and seasoned where that is desirable, so it's no trouble to go over and pick yourself a nice poached egg or clutch of French fries. (I really prefer brioche in the mornings, but for sentimental reasons she can't manage them.) Sometimes we ball a little or sing old campfire songs. Ski comes down for that, but not for long, and then he goes back to looking at the universe. The starbow is magnificent and appalling. It is now a band about 40° across, completely surrounding us with colored light. One can always look in the other frequencies and see ghost stars before us and behind us, but in the birthright bands the view to the front and rear is now dead black and the only light is that beautiful banded ring of powdery stars.

Sometimes we write plays or have a little music. Shef had deduced four lost Bach piano concerti, very reminiscent of Corelli and Vivaldi, with everything going at once in the tuttis, and we've all adapted them for performance. I did mine on the Moog, but Ann and Shef synthesized whole orchestras. Shef's is particularly cute. You can tell that the flautist has early emphysema and two people in the violin section have been drinking, and he's got Toscanini conducting like a *risorgimento* metronome. Flo's oldest daughter made up words and now she sings a sort of nursery-rhyme adaptation of some Buxtehude chorales; oh, I didn't tell you about the kids. We have eleven of them now. Ann, Dot and I have one apiece, and Florence has eight. (But they're going to let me have quadruplets next week.) They let me take care of them pretty much for the first few weeks, while they're little, and they're *so* darling.

So mostly I spend my time taking care of the kids and working out tensor equations that Ski kindly gives me to do for him, and, I must confess it, feeling a little lonely. I *would* like to watch a TV quiz show over a cup of coffee with a friend! They let me do over the interior of our mobile home now and then. The other day I redid it in Pittsburgh suburban as a joke. Would you believe French windows in interstellar space? We never open them, of course, but they look real pretty with the chintz curtains and lace tiebacks. And we've added several new rooms for the children and their pets (Flo grew them the cutest little bunnies in the hydroponics plot).

Well, I've enjoyed this chance to gossip, so will sign off now. There is one thing I have to mention. The others have decided we don't want to get any more messages from you. They don't like the way you try to work on our subconsciouses and all (not that you succeed, of course, but you can see that it's still a little annoying), and so in future the dial will be set at six-six-oh, all right, but the switch will be in the "off" position. It wasn't my idea, but I was glad to go along. I *would* like some slightly less demanding company from time to time, although not, of course, yours.

Washington Five

Once upon a time the building that was now known as DoD Temp Restraining Quarters 7—you might as well call it with the right word, "jail," Knefhausen thought—had been a luxury hotel in the Hilton chain. The maximum security cells were in the underground levels, in what had been meeting rooms. There were no doors or windows to the outside. If you did get out of your own cell you had a flight of stairs to get up before you were at ground level, and then the guards to break through to get to the open. And then, even if there happened not to be an active siege going on at the moment, you took your chances with the roaming addicts and activists outside.

Knefhausen did not concern himself with these matters. He did not think of escape, or at least didn't after the first few panicky moments, when he realized he was under arrest. He stopped demanding to see the president after the first few days. There was no point in appealing to the White House for help when it was the White House that had put him here. He was still sure that if only he could talk to the president privately for a few moments he could clear everything up. But as a realist he had faced the fact that the president would never talk to him privately again.

So he counted his blessings.

First, it was comfortable here. The bed was good, the rooms were warm. The food still came from the banquet kitchens of the hotel, and it was remarkably good for jailhouse fare.

Second, the kids were still in space and still doing some things, great things, even if they did not report what. His vindication was still a prospect.

Third, the jailers let him have newspapers and writing materials, although they would not bring him his books or give him a television set.

He missed the books, but nothing else. He didn't need TV to tell him what was going on outside. He didn't even need the newspapers, ragged, thin and censored as they were. He could hear for himself. Every day there was the rattle of small-arms fire, mostly far-off and sporadic, but once or twice sustained and heavy and almost overhead, Brownings against AK-47s, it sounded like, and now and then the slap and smash of grenade launchers. Sometimes he heard sirens hooting through the streets, punctuated by clanging bells, and wondered that there was still a civilian fire department left to bother. (Or was it still civilian?) Sometimes he heard the grinding of heavy motors that had to be tanks. The newspapers did little to fill in the details, but Knefhausen was good at reading between the lines. The Administration was holed up somewhere—Key Biscayne or Camp David or Southern California, no one was saying where. The cities were all in red revolt. *Herr Omnes* had taken over.

For these disasters Knefhausen felt unjustly blamed. He composed endless letters to the president, pointing out that the serious troubles of the Administration had nothing to do with Alpha-Aleph; the cities had been in revolt for most of a generation, the dollar had become a laughing stock since the Indochinese wars. Some he destroyed, some he could get no one to take from him, a few he managed to dispatch—and got no answers.

Once or twice a week a man from the Justice Department came to ask him the same thousand pointless questions once again. They were trying to build up a dossier to prove it was all his fault, Knefhausen suspected. Well, let them. He would defend himself when the time came. Or history would defend him. The record was clear. With respect to moral issues, perhaps, not so clear, he conceded. No matter. One could not speak of moral questions in an area so vital to the search for knowledge as this. The dispatches from the *Constitution* had already produced so much!—although, admittedly, some of the most significant parts were hard to understand. The Gödel message had not been unscrambled, and the hints of its contents remained only hints.

Sometimes he dozed and dreamed of projecting himself to the *Constitution*. It had been a year since the last message. He tried to imagine what they had been doing. They would be well past the midpoint now, decelerating. The starbow would be broadening and diffusing every day. The circles of blackness before and behind them would be shrinking. Soon they would see Alpha Centauri as no man had ever seen it. To be sure, they would then see that there was no planet called Aleph circling the primary, but they had guessed that somehow long since. Brave, wonderful kids! Even so they had gone on. This foolishness with drugs and sex, what of it? One opposed such goings-on in the common run of humanity, but it had always been so that those who excelled and stood out from the herd could make their own rules. As a child he had learned that the plump, proud air leader sniffed cocaine, that the great warriors took their sexual pleasure sometimes with each other. An intelligent man did not concern himself with such questions, which was one more indication that the man from the Justice Department, with his constant hinting and prying into Knefhausen's own background, was not really very intelligent.

The good thing about the man from the Justice Department was that one could sometimes deduce things from his questions, and rarely—oh, very rarely—he would sometimes answer a question himself. "Has there been a message from the *Constitution*?" "No, of course not, Dr. Knefhausen; now, tell me again, who suggested this fraudulent scheme to you in the first place?"

Those were the highlights of his days, but mostly the days just passed unmarked.

He did not even scratch them off on the wall of his cell, like the prisoner in the Chateau d'If. It would have been a pity to mar the hardwood paneling. Also, he had other clocks and calendars. There was the ticking of the arriving meals, the turning of the seasons as the man from the Justice Department paid his visits. Each of these was like a holiday—a holy day, not joyous but solemn. First there would be a visit from the captain of the guards, with two armed soldiers standing in the door. They would search his person and his cell on the chance that he had been able to smuggle in a—a what? A nuclear bomb, maybe. Or a pound of pepper to throw in the Justice man's eyes. They would find nothing, because there was nothing to find. And then they would go away, and for a long time there would be nothing. Not even a meal, even if a meal time happened to be due. Nothing at all, until an hour or three hours later the Justice man would come in with his own guard at the door, equally vigilant inside and out, and his engineer manning the tape recorders, and his questions.

And then there was the day when the man from the Justice Department came and he was not alone. With him was the president's secretary, Murray Amos.

How treacherous is the human heart! When it has given up hope, how little it takes to make it hope again!

"Murray!" cried Knefhausen, almost weeping, "it's so good to see you again! The president, is he well? What can I do for you? Have there been developments?"

Murray Amos paused in the doorway. He looked at Dieter von Knefhausen and said bitterly, "Oh, yes, there have been developments. Plenty of them. The Fourth Armored has just changed sides, so we are evacuating Washington. And the president wants you out of here at once."

"No, no! I mean—oh, yes, it is good that the president is concerned about my welfare, although it is bad about the Fourth Armored. But what I mean, Murray, is this: Has there been a message from the *Constitution*?"

Amos and the Justice Department man looked at each other. "Tell me, Dr. Knefhausen," said Amos silkily, "how did you manage to find that out?"

"Find it out? How could I find it out? No, I only asked because I hoped. There has been a message, yes? In spite of what they said? They have spoken again?"

"As a matter of fact, there has been," said Amos thoughtfully. The Justice Department man whispered piercingly in his ear, but Amos shook his head. "Don't worry, we'll be coming in a second. The convoy won't go without us. . . . Yes, Knefhausen, the message came through to Goldstone two hours ago. They have it at the decoding room now."

"Good, very good!" cried Knefhausen. "You will see, they will justify all. But what do they say? Have you good scientific men to interpret it? Can you understand the contents?"

"Not exactly," said Amos, "because there's one little problem the code room hadn't expected and wasn't prepared for. The message wasn't coded. It came in clear, but the language was Chinese."

Constitution Six

Ref.: CONSIX T51/11055/*7

CLASSIFIED MOST SECRET

Subject: Transmission from U.S. Starship *Constitution*.

The following message was received and processed by the decrypt section according to standing directives. Because of its special nature, an investigation was carried out to determine its provenance. Radio-direction data received from Farside Base indicate its origin along a line of sight consistent with the present predicted location of the *Constitution*. Strength of signal was high but within appropriate limits, and degradation of frequency separation was consistent with relativistic shifts and scattering due to impact with particle and gas clouds.

Although available data do not prove beyond doubt that this transmission originated with the starship, no contraindications were found.

On examination, the text proved to be a phonetic transcription of what appears to be a dialect of Middle Kingdom Mandarin. Only a partial translation has been completed. (See note appended to text.) The translation presented unusual difficulties for two reasons: One, the difficulty of finding a translator of sufficient skill who could be granted appropriate security status; two, because (conjecturally) the language used may not correspond exactly to any dialect but may be an artifact of the *Constitution*'s personnel. (See PARA EIGHT, Lines 43–49 below, in this connection.)

This text is PROVISIONAL AND NOT AUTHENTICATED and is furnished only as a first attempt to translate the contents of the message into English. Efforts are being continued to translate the full message, and to produce a less corrupt text for the section herewith. Later versions and emendations will be forwarded when available.

TEXT FOLLOWS:

1 PARA ONE. The one who speaks for all [*Lt.-Col. Sheffield*
2 *H. Jackman?*] rests. With righteous action comes surcease
3 from care. I [*identity not certain, but probably*
4 *Mrs. Annette Marin Becklund, less probably one of*
5 *the other three female personnel aboard, or one of*
6 *their descendants*] come in his place, moved by charity
7 and love.

8 PARA TWO. It is not enough to study or to do
9 deeds which make the people frown and bow their
10 heads. It is not enough to comprehend the
11 nature of the sky or the sea. Only through
12 the understanding of all can one approach
13 wisdom, and only through wisdom can one act
14 rightly.

15 PARA THREE. These are the precepts as it is given us to
16 see them.

17 PARA FOUR. The one who imposes his will by force
18 lacks justice. Let him be thrust from a cliff.

19 PARA FIVE. The one who causes another to lust for a
20 trifle of carved wood or a sweetmeat lacks courtesy.
21 Let him be restrained from the carrying out of wrong
22 practices.

23 PARA SIX. The one who ties a knot and says, "I do
24 not care who must untie it," lacks foresight. Let him
25 wash the ulcers of the poor and carry nightsoil for all
26 until he learns to see the day to come as brother to the
27 day that is.

28 PARA SEVEN. We who are in this here should not impose
29 our wills on you who are in that here by force.
30 Understanding comes late. We regret the incident of
31 next week, for it was done in haste and in error. The
32 one who speaks for all acted without thinking. We
33 who are in this here were sorry for it afterward.

34 PARA EIGHT. You may wonder [*literally: ask thoughtless*
35 *questions of the hexagrams*] why we are communicating
36 in this language. The reason is in part recreational,
37 in part heuristic [*literally: because on the staff*
38 *hand one becomes able to strike a blow more ably*
39 *when blows are struck repeatedly*], but the nature
40 of the process is such that you must go through it before
41 you can be told what it is. Our steps have trodden

42 this path. In order to reconstruct the Chinese of the
43 *I Ching* it was first necessary to reconstruct the German
44 of the translation from which the English was
45 made. Error lurks at every turn. [*Literally: false apparitions*
46 *shout at one each time the path winds.*] Many
47 flaws mark our carving. Observe it in silence for hours
48 and days until the flaws become part of the work.
49 PARA NINE. It is said that you have eight days before
50 the heavier particles arrive. The dead and broken
51 will be few. It will be better if all airborne nuclear reactors
52 are grounded until the incident is over.
53 PARA TEN. When you have completed rebuilding send
54 us a message, directed to the planet Alpha-Aleph. Our
55 home should be prepared by then. We will send a
56 ferry to help colonists cross the stream when we are
57 ready.

The above text comprises the first 851 groups of the transmission. The remainder of the text, comprising approximately 7,500 groups, has not been satisfactorily translated. In the opinion of a consultant from the Oriental Languages Department at Johns Hopkins it may be a poem.

/s/ Durward S. RICHTER

Durward S. RICHTER
Maj. Gen. U.S.M.C.
Chief Cryptographer
Commanding

Distribution: X X X BY HAND ONLY

Washington Six

The president of the United States (Washington) opened the storm window of his study and leaned out to yell at his Chief Science Adviser. "Harry, get the lead out! We're waiting for you!"

Harry looked up and waved, then continued doggedly plowing through the dripping jungle that was the North Lawn. Between the overgrown weeds and the rain and the mud it was slow going, but the president had little sympathy. He slammed down the window and said, "Damn that man, he just goes out of his way to aggravate me. How long am I supposed to wait for him so I can decide if we're gonna have to move the capital or not?"

The vice president looked up from her knitting. "Jimbo, honey, why do you fuss yourself like that? Why don't we just move and get it over with?"

"Well, it looks so lousy." He threw himself into a chair despondently. "I was really looking forward to the Tenth Anniversary parade," he complained. "Ten years, that's really worth bragging about! I don't want to hold it the hell out in the sticks, I want it right down Constitution Avenue, just like the old days, with the people cheering and the reporters and the cameras all over and everything. Then let that son of a bitch in Omaha say I'm not the real president."

His wife said placidly, "Don't fuss yourself about him, honey. You know what I've been thinking, though? The parade might look a little skimpy on Constitution Avenue anyway. It would be real nice on a kind of littler street."

"Oh, what do you know? Anyway, where would we go? If Washington's under water, what makes you think Bethesda would be any better?"

His secretary of state put down his solitaire cards and looked interested. "Doesn't have to be Bethesda," he said. "I got some real nice land up near Dulles we could use. It's high there."

"Why, sure. Lots of nice land over to Virginia," the vice president confirmed. "Remember when we went out on that picnic after your second inaugural? That was at Fairfax Station. There was hills there all around. Just beautiful."

The president slammed his fist on the coffee table and yelled, "I'm not the president of Fairfax Station, I'm the president of the U. S. of A.! What's the capital of the U. S. of A.? Washington! My God, don't you see how those jokers in Houston and Omaha and Salt Lake and all would laugh if they heard I had to move out of my own capital?"

He broke off, because his chief science adviser was coming in the door, shaking himself, dripping mud as he got out of his oilskin slicker. "Well?" demanded the president. "What did they say?"

Harry sat down. "It's terrible out there. Anybody got a dry cigarette?"

The president threw him a pack. Harry dried his fingers on his shirt front before he drew one out. "Well," he said, "I went to every boat captain I could find. They all said the same. Ships they talked to, places they'd been. All the same. Tides rising all up and down the coast."

He looked around for a match. The president's wife handed him a gold cigarette lighter with the Great Seal of the United States on it, which, after some effort, he managed to ignite. "It don't look good, Jimmy. Right now it's low tide and that's all right, but it's coming in. And tomorrow it'll come in a little higher. And there's going to be storms, not just rain like this, I mean, but you got to figure on a tropical depression coming up from the Bahamas now and then."

"We're not in the tropics," said the secretary of state suspiciously.

"It doesn't mean that," said the science adviser, who had once given the weather reports over the local ABC television station, when there was such a thing as a television network. "It means storms. Hurricanes. But they're not the worst things; it's the tides. If the ice is melting then they're going to keep getting higher regardless."

The president drummed his fingers on the coffee table. Suddenly he shouted, "I don't *want* to move my capital!"

No one answered. His temper outbursts were famous. The vice president became absorbed in her knitting, the secretary of state picked up his cards and began to shuffle, the science adviser picked up his slicker and carefully hung it on the back of a door.

The president said, "You got to figure it this way. If we move out, then all those local yokels that claim to be the president of the United States are going to be just that much better off, and the eventual reunification of our country is going to be just that much more delayed." He moved his lips for a moment, then burst out, "I don't ask nothing for myself! I never have. I only want to play the part I have to play in what's good for all of us, and that means keeping up my position as the *real* president, according to the U. S. of A. Constitution as amended. And that means I got to stay right here in the real White House, no matter what."

His wife said hesitantly, "Honey, how about this? The other presidents had like a Summer White House, and Camp David and like that. Nobody fussed about it. Why couldn't you do the same as they did? There's the nicest old farm house out near Fairfax Station that we could fix up to be real pretty."

The president looked at her with surprise. "Now, that's good thinking," he declared. "Only we can't move permanently, and we have to keep this place garrisoned so nobody else will take it away from us, and we have to come back here once in a while. How about that, Harry?"

His science adviser said thoughtfully, "We could rent some boats, I guess. Depends. I don't know how high the water might get."

"No 'guess'! No 'depends'! That's a national priority. We have to do it that way to keep that bastard in Omaha paying attention to the real president."

"Well, Jimbo, honey," said the vice president after a moment, emboldened by his recent praise. "You have to admit they don't pay a lot of attention to us right now. When was the last time they paid their taxes?"

The president looked at her foxily over his glasses. "Talking about that," he said, "I might have a little surprise for them anyway. What you might call a secret weapon."

"I hope it does better than we did in the last war," said his wife, "because if you remember, when we started to put down the uprising in Frederick, Maryland, we got the pee kicked out of us."

The president stood up, indicating the Cabinet meeting was over.

"Never mind," he said sunnily. "You go on out again, Harry, and see if you can find any good maps in the Library of Congress where they got the fires put out. Find us a nice high place within, um, twenty miles if you can. Then we'll get the Army to condemn us a Summer White House like Mae says, and maybe I can sleep in a bed that isn't moldy for a change."

His wife looked worried, alerted by his tone. "What are you going to do, Jim?"

He chuckled. "I'm going to check out my secret weapon."

He shooed them out of his study and, when they were gone, went to the kitchen and got himself a bottle of Fresca from the six-pack in the open refrigerator. It was warm, of course. The Marine guard company was still trying to get the gas generator back in operation, but they were having little success. The president didn't mind. They were his personal Praetorians and, if they lacked a little as appliance repairmen, they had proved their worth when the chips were down. The president was always aware that during the Troubles he had been no more than any other congressman—appointed to fill a vacancy, at that—and his rapid rise to Speaker of the House and Heir Apparent, finally to the presidency itself, was due not only to his political skills and knowhow, but also to the fact that he was the only remotely legitimate heir to the presidency who also happened to have a brother-in-law commanding the Marine garrison in Washington.

The president was, in fact, quite satisfied with the way the world was going. If he envied presidents of the past (missiles, fleets of nuclear bombers, billions of dollars to play with), he certainly saw nothing, when he looked at the world around him, to compare with his own stature in the real world he lived in.

He finished the soda, opened his study door a crack and peered out. No one was nearby. He slipped out and down the back stairs. In what had once been the public parts of the White House you could see the extent of the damage more clearly. After the riots and the trashings and the burnings and coups, the will to repair and fix up had gradually dwindled away. The president didn't mind. He didn't even notice the charred walls and the fallen plaster. He was listening to the sound of a distant gasoline pump chugging away, and smiling to himself as he approached the underground level where his secret weapon was locked up.

The secret weapon, whose name was Dieter von Knefhausen, was trying to complete the total defense of every act of his life that he called his memoirs.

He was less satisfied with the world than the president. He could have wished for many changes. Better health, for one thing; he was well aware that his essential hypertension, his bronchitis, and his gout were fighting the last stages of a total war to see which would have the honor of destroying their mutal battleground, which was himself. He did not much mind his lack of freedom, but he did mind the senseless destruction of so many of his papers.

The original typescript of his autobiography was long lost, but he had wheedled the president—the pretender, that is, who called himself the president—into sending someone to find what could be found of them. A few tattered and incomplete carbon copies had turned up. He had restored some of the gaps as best his memory and available data permitted, telling again the story of how he had planned Project Alpha-Aleph and meticulously itemizing the details of how he had lied, forged and falsified to bring it about.

He was as honest as he could be. He spared himself nothing. He admitted his complicity in the "accidental" death of Ann Barstow's first husband in a car crash, thus leaving her free to marry the man he had chosen to go with the crew to Alpha Centauri. He had confessed he had known that the secret would not last out the duration of the trip, thus betraying the trust of the president who made it possible. He put it all in, all he could remember, and boasted of his success.

For it was clear to him that his success was already proved. What could be surer evidence of it than what had happened ten years ago? The "incident of next week" was as dramatic and complete as anyone could wish. If its details were still indecipherable, largely because of the demolition of the existing technology structure it had brought about, its main features were obvious. The shower of heavy particles—baryon? perhaps even quarks?—had drenched the Earth. The source had been traced to a point in the heavens identical with that plotted for the *Constitution*.

Also there were the messages received, and, take them together, there was no doubt that the astronauts had developed knowledge so far in advance of anything on Earth that, from two light-years out, they could impose their will on the human race. They had done it. In one downpour of particles, the entire military-industrial complex of the planet was put out of action.

How? How? Ah, thought Knefhausen, with envy and pride, that was the question. One could not know. All that was known was that every nuclear device—bomb, power-plant, hospital radiation source or stockpile—had simultaneously soaked up the stream of particles and at that moment ceased to exist as a source of nuclear energy. It was not rapid and catastrophic, like a bomb. It was slow and long-lasting. The uranium and the plutonium simply melted in the long, continuous reaction that was still bubbling away in the seething lava lakes where the silos had stood and the nuclear power plants had generated electricity. Little radiation was released, but a good deal of heat.

Knefhausen had long since stopped regretting what could not be helped, but wistfully he still wished he had the opportunity to measure the total heat flux properly. Not less than 10^{16} watt-years, he was sure, just to judge by the effects on the Earth's atmosphere, the storms, the gradual raising of temperature all over, above all by the rumors about the upward trend of sea level that bespoke the melting of the polar ice caps. There was no longer even a good weather net, but the fragmentary information he was able to piece together suggested a world increase of four, maybe as many as six or seven degrees Celsian already, and the reactions still seething away in Czechoslovakia, the Congo, Colorado, and a hundred lesser infernos.

Rumors about the sea level?

Not rumors, no, he corrected himself, lifting his head and staring at the snake of hard rubber hose that began under the duckboards at the far end of the room and ended outside the barred window, where the gasoline pump outside did its best to keep the water level inside his cell low enough to keep the water below the boards. Judging by the inflow, the grounds of the White House must be nearly awash.

The door opened. The president of the United States (Washington) walked in, patting the shoulder of the thin, scared, hungry-looking kid who was guarding the door.

"How's it going, Knefhausen?" the president began sunnily. "You ready to listen to a little reason yet?"

"I'll do whatever you say, Mr. President, but as I have told you there are certain limits. Also I am not a young man, and my health—"

"Screw your health and your limits," shouted the president. "Don't start up with me, Knefhausen!"

"I am sorry, Mr. President," whispered Knefhausen.

"Don't be sorry! What I got to judge by is results. You know what it takes to keep that pump going just so you won't drown? Gas is rationed, Knefhausen! Takes a high national priority to get it! I don't know how long I'm gonna be able to justify this continuous drain on our resources if you don't cooperate."

Sadly, but stubbornly, Knefhausen said: "As far as I am able, Mr. President, I cooperate."

"Yeah. Sure." But the president was in an unusually good mood today, Knefhausen observed with the prisoner's paranoid attention to detail, and in a moment he said: "Listen, let's not get uptight about this. I'm making you an offer. Say the word and I'll fire that dumb son-of-a-bitch Harry Stokes and make you my Chief Science Adviser. How would that be? Right up at the top again. An apartment of your own. Electric lights! Servants—you can pick 'em out yourself, and there's some nice-looking little girls in the pool. The best food you ever dreamed of. A chance to perform a real service for the U. S. of A., helping to reunify this great country to become once again the great power it should and must be!"

"Mr. President," Knefhausen said, "naturally, I wish to help in any way I can. But we have been all over this before. I'll do anything you like, but I don't know how to make the bombs work again. You saw what happened Mr. President. They're gone."

"I didn't say bombs, did I? Look, Kneffie, I'm a reasonable man. How about this. You promise to use your best scientific efforts *in any way you can.* You say you can't make bombs; all right. But there will be other things."

"What other things, Mr. President?"

"Don't push me, Knefhausen. Anything at all. Anything where you can perform a service for your country. You give me that promise and you're out of here today. Or would you rather I just turned off the pump?"

Knefhausen shook his head, not in negation but in despair. "You do not know what you are asking. What can a scientist do for you today? Ten years ago, yes. Even five years ago. We could have worked something out maybe; I could have done something. But now the preconditions do not exist. When all the nuclear plants went out— When the factories that depended on them ran out of power— When the fertilizer plants couldn't fix nitrogen and the insecticide plants couldn't deliver— When the people began to die of hunger and the pestilences started—"

"I know all that, Knefhausen. Yes or not?"

The scientist hesitated, looking thoughtfully at his adversary. A gleam of the old shrewdness appeared in his eyes.

"Mr. President," he said slowly. "You know something. Something has happened."

"Right," crowed the president. "You're smart. Now tell me, what is it I know?"

Knefhausen shook his head. After seven decades of vigorous life, and another decade of slowly dying, it was hard to hope again. This terrible little man, this upstart, this lump—he was not without a certain animal cunning, and he seemed very sure. "Please, Mr. President. Tell me."

The president put a finger to his lips, and then an ear to the door. When he was convinced no one could be listening, he came closer to Knefhausen and said softly:

"You know that I have trade representatives all over, Knefhausen. Some in Houston, some in Salt Lake, some even in Montreal. They are not always there just for trade. Sometimes they find things out, and tell me. Would you like to know what my man in Anaheim has just told me?"

Knefhausen did not answer, but his watery old eyes were imploring.

"A message," whispered the president.

"From the *Constitution?*" cried Knefhausen. "But, no, it is not possible! Farside is gone, Goldstone is destroyed, the orbiting satellites are running down—"

"It wasn't a radio message," said the president. "It came from Mount Palomar. Not the big telescope, because that got ripped off too, but what they call a Schmidt. Whatever that is. It still works. And they still have some old fogies who look through it now and then, for old times' sake. And they got a message, in laser light. Plain Morse code. From what they said was Alpha Centauri. From your little friends, Knefhausen."

He took a sheaf of paper from his pocket and held it up.

Knefhausen was racked by a fit of coughing, but he managed to croak: "Give it to me!"

The president held it away. "A deal, Knefhausen?"

"Yes, yes! Anything you say, but give me the message!"

"Why, certainly," smiled the president and passed over the much-creased sheet of paper. It said:

PLEASE BE ADVISED. WE HAVE CREATED THE PLANET ALPHA-ALEPH, IT IS BEAUTIFUL AND GRAND. WE WILL SEND OUR FERRIES TO BRING SUITABLE PERSONS AND OTHERS TO STOCK IT AND TO COMPLETE CERTAIN OTHER BUSINESS. OUR SPECIAL REGARDS

TO DR. DIETER VON KNEFHAUSEN, WHOM WE WANT TO TALK TO VERY MUCH. EX-
PECT US WITHIN THREE WEEKS OF THIS MESSAGE.

Knefhausen read it over twice, stared at the president and read it again. "I—I am very glad," he said inadequately.

The president snatched it back, folded it and put it in his pocket, as though the message itself was the key to power. "So you see," he said, "it's simple. You help me, I help you."

"Yes. Yes, of course," said Knefhausen, staring past him.

"They're your friends. They'll do what you say. All those things you told me that they can do—"

"Yes, the particles, the ability to reproduce, the ability, God save us, to build a planet—" Knefhausen might have gone on cataloguing the skills of the spacemen indefinitely, but the president was impatient:

"So it's only a matter of days now, and they'll be here. You can imagine what they'll have! Guns, tools, everything—and all you have to do is get them to join me in restoring the United States of America to its proper place. I'll make it worth their while, Knefhausen! And yours, too. They—"

The president stopped, observing the scientist carefully. Then he cried "Knefhausen!" and leaped forward to catch him.

He was too late. The scientist had fallen limply to the duck-boards. The guard, when ordered, ran for the White House doctor, who limped as rapidly to the scene as his bad legs and brain soaked with beer would let him, but he was too late too. Everything was too late for Knefhausen, whose old heart had failed him . . . as it proved a few days later (when the great golden ships from Alpha-Aleph landed and disgorged their bright, terrible crewmen to clean up the Earth), just in time.

GROWING UP IN EDGE CITY

Chandlie is a bright young fellow and he has a healthy curiosity. His world, Edge City, is a very orderly place. Everything about it, with very few exceptions, is regulated. The temperature is constant, the proctors who monitor his progress have all the devices they need to make sure that Chandlie and everyone else in Edge City does what he or she is supposed to do. Life is hermetically sealed off from the outside, from the sun, the wind, the rain . . . from the unexpected. One day, Chandlie's curiosity makes him go exploring—not to a dangerous or forbidden place, but to a place where his personal transponder stops transmitting. He discovers the Outside, an unregulated, dirty, confusing place. The natural world.

Such a place as the City doesn't exist today, but others have written about similar social experiments. George Orwell's *1984* comes to mind. "Growing Up in Edge City," which was a Nebula Award finalist when first published in 1975, is a cautionary tale, lest we forget that we are not the world, but merely part of it. . . .

In the evenings after school Chandlie played private games. He was permitted to do so. His overall index of gregariousness was high enough to allow him to choose his own companions, or no companion at all but a Pal, when he wanted it that way. On Tuesday and Fourthday he generally spent his time with a seven-year-old female named Marda, quick and bright, with a chiseled, demure little face that would have beseemed a pretty woman of twenty, apt at mathematical intuitions and the stringing of beads. The proctors logged in their private games under the heading of "sensuality sensitivity training," but they called them "You Show Me Yours and I'll Show You Mine." The proctors, in their abstract and deterministic way, approved of what Chandlie did. Even then he was marked for special challenge, having been evaluated as Councilman potential, and when on most other evenings Chandlie went down to the machine rooms and checked out a Pal, no objections were raised, no questions were asked, and no follow-up warnings were flagged in the magnetic cores of his record-fiche. He went off freely and openly, wherever he chose. This was so even though there was a repeating anomaly in his log. Almost every evening for an hour or two, Chandlie's personal transponder stopped broadcasting his location fix. They could not tell where he was in Edge City. They accepted this because of their own limitations. It was recorded in the proctors' basic memory file that there were certain areas of the City in which old electromagnetic effects interfered with the radio direction-finding signals. They were not strategically important areas. The records showed nothing dangerous or forbidden there. The proctors noted the gap in the log but attached no importance to it. As a matter of routine they opened up the Pal's chrome-steel tamper-proof course-plot tapes from time to time, but it was only spot-checking. They did the same for everyone's Pal. They never found anything significantly wrong in Chandlie's. If they had been less limited, they might have inquired further. A truly good program would have cross-referenced Chandlie's personality profile, learned from it that he was gifted in man-machine interactions, and deduced from this the possibility that he had bugged the Pal. If they had then checked the Pal's permanent record of instructions, they would have learned that it was so. They did not do that. The proctors were not particularly sophisticated computer programs. They saw in their inputs no reason to be suspicious. Chandlie's father and mother could have told the programs all about him, but they had been Dropouts since he was three.

At the edge of Edge City, past the school sections, near the hospital and body-disposal units, there was a dark and odorous place. Ancient steel beams showed scarred and discolored. They bore lingering radioactivity, souvenir of an old direct hit from a scrambler missile. It was no longer a dangerous place, but it was not an attractive one, either, and on the master location charts it was designated for storage. It was neither very useful nor very much used. What could be stored there was only what was not very much valued, and there were few such things kept in Edge City. If they were remembered. The air was dank. Spots of mildew and rust appeared and swelled on whatever was there. However often the Handys came in to scrub and burn and polish, the surfaces were never clean. It was environmentally interesting, in a city where there was no such thing as environment, for at times it was pervaded by a sound like a distant grumbling roar, and at times it grew quite cold or quite hot. These were the things that had first interested Chandlie in it. What capped his interest was discovering by accident, one evening when he had just returned from wandering in the strange smells and sounds, that the proctors had not known where he was. He determined to spend more time there. The thought of doing something the proctors did not know all about was both scary and irresistible. His personal independence index had always been very high, almost to the point of remedial action. On his second visit, or third, he discovered the interesting fact that some of the closed doors were not locked on a need-to-enter basis. They were merely closed and snapped. Turning a knob would open them. Anyone could do it. He opened every door he passed. Most of them led only to empty rooms, or to chambers that might as well be empty for all he could make of the gray metal cylinders or yellowed fiber cartons that were stacked forgotten inside them. Some of the doors, however, led to other places, and some of the places were not even marked on the city charts. With his Pal romping and humming its shrill electronic note by his side, Chandlie penetrated the passages and stairways he found right up to the point at which he became certain he was not permitted to be there. A buckled guide rail that gouged at his flesh told him that. These areas were dangerous. Having reached that conclusion, he returned to his studies and spent a week learning how to reprogram the Pal to go into sleep mode on voice command from himself. He then returned to the dangerous area, left the Pal curled up inside one of the uninteresting doors, and went on into the unknown, down a broad and dusty flight of stairs.

In the pits under Edge City the air was damper and danker even than in the deserted places above. It was not at all cold. Chandlie was astonished to discover that he was sweating. He had never known what it was like to sweat before in his life, except as a natural consequence of exercise or, once or twice, while experiencing an illness surrogate. It took some time for him to realize that the reason for this was that the air about him was quite warm, perhaps as much as ten degrees over the 28°C at which he had spent his life. Also, the grumbling roaring noise was sharper and nearer, although not as loud as he had sometimes heard it before. He looked about himself wonderingly and uncertainly. There were many things here that were strange, unfamiliar, and, although he had not had enough of a background of experience to be sure of correctly identifying the sensation, frightening. For example, this part of the City was not very well lighted. Every other public place he had ever seen had been identically illuminated with the changing skeins of soft brilliance from their liquid crystal walls. Here it was not like that. Light came from discrete points. There was a bright spot enclosed in a glass sphere here, another there, another five meters away. Objects cast shadows. Chandlie spent some time experimenting with making shadows. Sometimes there were considerable gaps between the points of light, with identical glass spheres that looked like the others but contained no central glowing core, as though they had stopped working and for some reason the Handy machines had not made them work again. Where this happened the shadows merged to produce what he recognized as darkness. Sometimes as a little boy during the times when his room light was sleep-reduced he had pulled the coverlid over his head to see what darkness was like. Warm and cozy. This was not cozy. Also, there were distant thumping, creaking sounds. Also, he remembered that not far above him and beyond him was the corpse-disposal area, and while he had no unhealthy fear of cadavers, he did not like them. Chandlie felt to some degree ill at ease. To some degree he wished that he had not countercommanded his Pal to stay behind. It was exciting to be all on his own, but it was also worrisome. It would have been a comfort to have the Pal gamboling and humming beside him, to see its bright milky-blue eyes following him, to know that in the event of any unprogrammed event it would automatically relay a data pulse to the proctors for evaluation and, if need be, action. What action? he thought. Like rescuing a little boy from goblins, he joked to himself, remembering a story from his preprimary anthropology talk-times. Joking to himself helped him put aside the cobwebby fears. He still felt them, but he did not feel any of them strongly enough to turn back. His index of curiosity, also, was very high.

All of this was taking place on a Wonday, after scheduled hours, which meant that Chandlie had received his weekly therapies that day and was chockful of hormones, vitamins, and confidence. Perhaps it was that which made him so bold. On such accidents of timing so many things depend. But he went on. After a time he discovered that the new world he was exploring was no longer getting darker. It was getting lighter. Simultaneously it was becoming even more hot. Sweat streamed from his unpracticed pores. Salty moisture drenched the long hair at his temples, dampened his chest, rolled in beads from his armpits and down his back. He became aware that he himself had an odor. The light was brighter before him than it was behind, and rounding a corner, he saw a yellow radiance that made him squint. He stopped. Reinventing the Eskimo glare-reducer on the spot, he stared through his half-spread fingers. Then, heedless, he ran down a flight of ancient steps, almost falling as one slid loosely away beneath him but righting himself and running on. He stopped on an uneven surface of grayish yellowish gritty grains that he recognized, from Earth Sciences, as sand. The great distant noise was close now, grave and impersonal rather than threatening; he saw what it came from. Rolling hillocks of water humped themselves slowly up out of a flat blue that receded into infinity before him. They grew, peaked, bent forward, and crashed in white wet spray, and the noise was their serial collision with themselves and with the sand. The heat was unbearable, but Chandlie bore it. He was entranced, thrilled, consternated, delighted almost out of his skull. This was a "beach!" That was "sea!" He was "outdoors!" No such things had ever happened to any young person he had ever known or heard of. No such things happened to anyone but Dropouts. He had never expected any such thing to happen to him. It was not that he was unaware that there were places not in the Cities. Earth Sciences had taught him all that, as they taught him about the sluggishly molten iron core at the Earth's heart and the swinging distant bodies that were called "Moon" and "planets" and "stars." He had even known, by implication and omission rather than by ever hearing it stated as a fact, that somewhere in the world between the Cities were places like the places where people had lived generations and, oh, ages ago, when people were dull and cruel, and that it was at least in theory possible for a person from a city to stand in such a place and not at once become transformed into a Dropout, or physically changed, or killed. But he had never known that such places could be found near Edge City.

All that very painful brightness came from one central brightness which, as Chandlie knew, was the "Sun." It cost him some pain and several minutes of near blindness to learn that it could not be looked at directly without penalty. Its height, he recalled, meant "midday," which was puzzling until he deduced and remembered enough to understand that City time was world time. He had known that solar time differed as one went east or west, but it had never mattered before. As he became able to see again he looked about him. When he looked before him, he saw the rolling sweep of the ocean, dizzyingly big. When he looked behind him, he saw the skirted and stilted bulk of Edge City rising away like the Egyptian tetrahedral tombs for the royal dead. To his right was a stretch of irregular sand and sea that curved around out of sight under a corner of the city. But to his left, to his left, there was something quite strange. There were buildings. Buildings, plural. Not one great polystructure like a proper City, buildings. People moved among them. He breathed deeply to generate courage and walked toward them. Plodding through the sand was new to him, difficult, like walking with five-kilogram anklets on a surface that slid and slipped and caved irregularly away under his footgloves. The people saw him long before he was close enough to speak or hear, even a shout, over the wind and the breaking waves. They spoke to each other, and then gestured toward him. He could see that they were smiling. He knew at once that they were Dropouts. As he came closer to them, and a few of them walked toward him, he could see that some of them were not very clean, and all of them were straggly-haired, the women just on their scalps, the men wherever men could grow hair, beards, sideburns, mustaches, one barrel of a man thatched front and back with a bear's pelt. They all seemed quite old. Surely not one was under twenty. Physically they were deviant in accidental and unwholesome ways. On school trips to the corpse-disposal areas Chandlie had been struck by the unkemptness of the dead, but these people were living and unkempt. Some were gray and balding. Some women's breasts hung like sucked-dry fruits. Some wore glass disks in frames before their eyes. The faces of some were seamed and darkened. Some stood stooped, or bent, or walked limping. The clothes they wore did not hug and constrain them as right clothing should. The things they wore were smocks or shorts or sweaters. Or anything at all. As Chandlie had never seen an ugly person, he did not recognize what he felt as revulsion; and as he did not recognize it, it was not that, it was only disquiet. He looked at them curiously and seekingly. It occurred to him that his father and his mother might be among these people. He did not recognize them, but then he had very little memory of what his father and mother looked like.

As a very little boy Chandlie had experienced a programming malfunction in one of his proctors. It had taken the form of giving him incomplete answers and sometimes incomplete questions. The parts it left out were often the direct statements. The parts it gave him were then only the supplementary detail: "Proctor, what is the shape of the Earth?" "—which is why your transparency buildups show a ship disappearing from the bottom up as it reaches the horizon." He had required remedial confidence building after that. And may have had an overdose. It was a little like that with the Dropouts. They made him welcome, speaking to him from very close up so that he turned his head to avoid their breaths. They offered him disgusting sorts of food, which he ate anyway, raw fruits and cooked meats. Some of them actually touched him or tried to kiss him. "What we want to give you," they said, "is love." This troubled him. He did not want to conceive a child with any of them, and some of the speakers, also, were male. They said things like, "You are so young to come to us, and so pretty. We welcome you." They showed him everything they did and offered him their pleasures. On a walkway made of wood with the beach below them and surf spraying up onto his face they took him into a round building with a round turntable. Some of the younger, stronger men pushed at poles and stanchions and got it revolving slowly and wobblingly. It bore animal figures that moved as it turned, and they invited him to ride them. "It is a merry-go-round," they cried. To oblige them he sat on one of the horses for a revolution or two, but it was nothing compared to a Sleeter or Jumping Pillows. "We live freely and without constraint," they said. "We take what the world gives us and harm no one. We have joys the City has forgotten." Causing him to detach the lower part of his day garment so that his feet and legs were naked to the codpiece, they walked with him along the edge of the water. Waves came up and bathed his ankles and receded again. Grit lodged between his toes. His thighs itched from drying salt. They said to him: "See over here, where the walls have corroded away." They led him under the skirt of the City to an in-port. Great cargo carriers were rolling in from the agrocommunes, pouring grain and frozen foods into the hoppers, from which three of the youngest Dropouts were scooping the next day's meals into canvas pouches. "The City does not need all of this," they said, "but if they knew we took it, they would drive us away." They warmed berries between their grimy palms and gave them to Chandlie until he could eat no more. "Stay with us," they pleaded. "You are a human being, or you would not have come here alone! The City is not a life for human beings." He began to feel quite ill. He was conscious, too, of the passage of time. As the sun disappeared behind the gray pyramid and the wind from the sea became cold, they said: "If you must go back, go back. But come again. We do not have many children here ever. We like you. We want to love you." He allowed some of them to touch him, then turned and retraced his steps. He did not like the way he felt and did not understand the way he smelled. It was the first time in his life that Chandlie had been dirty.

When he reactivated his Pal, the machine immediately went into receiving mode. It then turned to Chandlie with its milky-blue eyes gleaming and spoke: "Chandlie, you must report at once to the proctors." "All right," he said. He had been expecting it. Although he was good at reprogramming machines, he had not expected to be gone so long and had not prepared for it.

The proctors received him in the smallest of the Interview Halls. He entered through a door that closed behind him and immediately became only one more square in a checkerboard of mirrors and gray metal panels. Behind some of the mirrors the proctors were scanning him. Behind others there might be members of the council, or apprentices, or interested citizens, anyone. He could not see, he could only see himself reflected into infinity wherever he looked. He stood under the heatless bright lights, blinking stubbornly. The proctors did not ask him any questions. They did not make any threats, either. They merely made a series of statements as follows: "Chandlie. First, you have interfered with the operation of your Pal. Second, you have absented yourself without authorization. Third, you have visited an area of the City where you have no occasion to go. Fourth, you have failed to report your activities in the proper form." They were then silent for a time. It was at this time that he was permitted to offer any corrections or supplementary information if he wished to do so. He did not. He stood mute, and after the appropriate time had passed, the proctors instructed him to withdraw. One square of mirror swung forward and became a door again, and he left the room. He returned to his dormitory. His peers were all in their own rooms and presumably asleep; it was very late. Chandlie bathed carefully, attempted to vomit, failed, rinsed his mouth carefully, and put on a sleeping blouse. The food the Dropouts had given him did not satisfy him, but he was afraid to eat until it had gone through his system. All that night he tossed and turned, waking up enough to know where he was and remember where he had been and then falling back to sleep again, unsatisfied and unresolved.

For some days Chandlie continued his normal life, but he was aware that the matter would not stop there. Prudence suggested to him that he should behave at least normally, if possible exemplarily. Curiosity overrode prudence. In free-study times he dialed for old books that were known to be of interest to Dropouts, *Das Kapital* and *Walden* and silly, sexy satires by people like Voltaire and Swift. He played old ballads by people like Dylan Thomas and Joan Baez. He read poetry: Wordsworth, Browning, Ginsberg. He studied old documents that, so said his books, had once been electrically important, and was baffled by contextual ignorance ("A well-regulated militia being necessary to the security of a free State, the right of the people to keep and bear arms shall not be infringed." "Militia"? "State"? "Bear"—in the sense of bearing a child, perhaps? But only the arm parts?), until he reached the decision to ask for clarification from the preceptors for Social Studies. Then he was baffled to understand why these things were important. They were gritty days for Chandlie. His age-peers detected that something was wrong almost at once, deduced that he was in trouble with the proctors and, naturally enough, anticipated the punishment of the proctors with punishments of their own. In Living Chess he was played only as a pawn, though usually he had been a bishop and once a rook. His Tai Chi movements were voted grotesque, and he was not invited to exercise with the rest of his group. They did not speak of his situation to him directly, except for Marda. She sat down next to him in free time and said, "I'll miss you if you go away, Chandlie." He pored mulishly over a series of layover transparency prints. "Why do you look at them when I'm here?" she cried. He said crushingly, "Your genitalia are juvenile. These are adult, much more interesting." She grew angry. "I don't think I want to conceive with you ever," she said. He put down the cassette of transparencies, stood up, and rapped on the door of an older girl. It was the first time he had ever seen tears. The second time was the following Fiveday, when he was called before the council of decision-making persons and saw his own.

The council, which was charged with the responsibility for making decisions in all cases not covered by standing instructions to the proctors, met when it needed to, where it chose to. Chandlie was of some interest to them, for whatever personal reasons each of them had for concerning him-herself, and so there were nearly twenty-five persons present when he was admitted. The room they chose to use this time was rather like the drawing room of a gentlemen's club. There were small tables with inlaid chessboards, sideboards with coffee, candies, refreshments of all kinds, stereopaints of notables of the City's history squirming on the walls. The head of the council, as of that hour, indicated a comfortable seat for Chandlie and gave him a cup of chilly sweet foam that was flavored with fruits and mint. He was a man. He looked about thirty, with neat bangs, wide-spaced tawny eyes, diffraction-grating rings on his fingers that moved hypnotically as he gestured. "Chandlie," he said, "we have a full file of reports. Beach sand, bits of weathered wood and caked salt have been found on your garments and on your skin, after evaporating wash water. Stool analysis shows consumption of nearly raw vegetable foods. We then ordered a spectral study of your skin and found compensatory pigmentation of your arms, face, neck, and lower body compatible with exposure to unfiltered sunlight. There is no point in wasting our time, Chandlie. It is clear that you have been outside the City." The boy nodded and said, "Yes, I have been outside the City." He had thought carefully of what he should say when he was asked questions, for he was aware of the risks involved. Risks to himself, to some extent. His ambitions were not fully formed at that time, but they excluded being downgraded as a potential Dropout. Risks to the Dropouts themselves in a much more immediate way, of course. "What did you see outside?" asked the head of the council in a friendly and curious way, and all of the twenty-five, or almost all, stopped talking or reading to listen. "I saw a beach," cried Chandlie. "It was very strange. The Sun was so hot, the wind so strong. There were waves a meter and a half high that came in and crashed on the sand. I walked in the water, I found berries. They did not taste very good, but I ate them. There were buildings made of wood and, I think, plaster?" He was asked to describe the buildings; he did so. He was asked why he was there; he told them it was curiosity. Finally he was asked, very gently. "And did you see any people?" At once he replied: "Of course, there were some women in the corpse-disposal area. I think someone they knew had died. And a man adjusting some Handys." "No," said the head of the council, "we mean outside. Did you see anyone there?" Chandlie looked astonished. "How could anyone live there?" he asked. "No. I didn't see anyone." The head of the council, after a while, looked around at the others. He held up seven fingers inquiringly. Most of them nodded, some shrugged, a few were paying no attention at all. "You have seven demerits, Chandlie," he said, "and you will work them off as the proctors direct." At once Chandlie was enraged. "Seven!" he cried. "How unfair!" It was maddening that they should have believed him and still awarded so harsh a punishment, seven days without free time, or seven weeks with no optional-foods privileges, or seven of whatever the proctors judged would be most punitive, and therefore most likely to discourage repetition of the infractions, for him. Before he left he was in tears, which only resulted in two additional demerits. He was then returned to his peer group, who gradually accepted him again as before.

For more than twenty years Chandlie kept the secret of the Dropout colony outside Edge City. He did not return there in all that time. But he did not speak of it, not even to Marda, by whom he did indeed conceive a child at the appropriate time. As a child he accumulated very few further demerits, and as a young adult none. His conduct was a model to the entire city and particularly, almost offensively, to his peer group, who reluctantly but inevitably elected him their age representative when he was almost thirty. It was then, with a seat on the council, that he achieved his intention. He disclosed the full truth of his expedition outside the City. He denounced the former councilpersons for their failure to recognize when a little boy was lying. He accused them of suspecting that there was indeed a Dropout colony at the edge of Edge City, and proposed that he himself be given the authority to deal with it. Angrily the ones he had denounced left, refusing to vote. Resentfully the ones who remained gave him the authority. He then in person, in person, he himself, went outside, himself directing the armed Pals with their lasers and serrated steel fangs. The weathered buildings burned sullenly but surely as the heat of the lasers drove out the long accumulation of brine. The Dropouts screamed and ran before the Pals snapping at them. Some escaped, but not very many. A crew of Handys was set to repairing and strengthening the walls around the food input areas, so that in the event any Dropouts returned they would be unable to continue their pilferage. When Chandlie reentered the City, there was nothing left outside that was alive, or useful. The following year he was elected head of the council years before his turn, and several times again. This had been his intention. He knew that he could not have achieved this so soon if it had not been for the Dropouts. In a sense he remained forever grateful to them. Sometimes he wondered if any of them were still alive in whatever part of the scarred and guarded Earth they had fled to. In a way he hoped some were. It would have been useful to know of another Dropout colony, although he really had no particular interest in harrying them, unless, of course, he could see a way in which it would benefit his career.

THE KNIGHTS OF ARTHUR

The threat of nuclear war became real to the American public after World War II, but it wasn't until the Cold War, the nonshooting hostilities between the U.S. and the U.S.S.R. in the 1950s, that the real fear of nuclear war became palpable. In 1958, when "The Knights of Arthur" was published, both superpowers had already tested bombs equal in power to megatons of dynamite, but with, of course, far greater effects than mere explosive.

In this story of survival amidst the ruins, the nuclear war hasn't been over for terribly long, and the only people who survived are those who were lucky enough to have been either deep underwater or otherwise shielded from the effects of a nuclear blast and its immediate aftermath.

The eponymous Arthur is an unusual character, to be sure. And his knights—well, maybe not knights, but very good friends—follow that most basic human instinct: survival. But this is about far more than survival. There are other pursuits that are important to people, and, as you'll discover in this lively, irrepressible story, as long as people are able, not even nuclear war will stop them from pursuing them.

There was three of us—I mean if you count Arthur. We split up to avoid attracting attention. Engdahl just came in over the big bridge, but I had Arthur with me so I had to come the long way around.

When I registered at the desk, I said I was from Chicago. You know how it is. If you say you're from Philadelphia, it's like saying you're from St. Louis or Detroit—I mean *nobody* lives in Philadelphia anymore. Shows how things change. A couple years ago, Philadelphia was all the fashion. But not now, and I wanted to make a good impression.

I even tipped the bellboy a hundred and fifty dollars. I said: "Do me a favor. I've got my baggage booby-trapped—"

"Natch," he said, only mildly impressed by the bill and a half, even less impressed by me.

"I mean *really* booby-trapped. Not just a burglar alarm. Besides the alarm, there's a little surprise on a short fuse. So what I want you to do, if you hear the alarm go off, is come running. Right?"

"And get my head blown off?" He slammed my bags onto the floor. "Mister, you can take your damn money and—"

"Wait a minute, friend." I passed over another hundred. "Please? It's only a shaped charge. It won't hurt anything except anybody who messes around, see? But I don't want it to go off. So you come running when you hear the alarm and scare him away and—"

"No!" But he was less positive. I gave him two hundred more and he said grudgingly: "All right. If I hear it. Say, what's in there that's worth all that trouble?"

"Papers," I lied.

He leered. "Sure."

"No fooling, it's just personal stuff. Not worth a penny to anybody but me, understand? So don't get any ideas—"

He said in an injured tone: "Mister, naturally the *staff* won't bother your stuff. What kind of a hotel do you think this is?"

"Of course, of course," I said. But I knew he was lying, because I knew what kind of hotel it was. The staff was there only because being there gave them a chance to knock down more money than they could make any other way. What other kind of hotel was there?

Anyway, the way to keep the staff on my side was by bribery, and when he left I figured I had him at least temporarily bought. He promised to keep an eye on the room and he would be on duty for four more hours—which gave me plenty of time for my errands.

I made sure Arthur was plugged in and cleaned myself up. They had water running— New York's very good that way; they always have water running. It was even hot, or nearly hot. I let the shower splash over me for a while, because there was a lot of dust and dirt from the Bronx that I had to get off me. The way it looked, hardly anybody had been up that way since it happened.

I dried myself, got dressed and looked out the window. We were fairly high up— fifteenth floor. I could see the Hudson and the big bridge up north of us. There was a huge cloud of smoke coming from somewhere near the bridge on the other side of the river, but outside of that everything looked normal. You would have thought there were people in all those houses. Even the streets looked pretty good, until you noticed that hardly any of the cars were moving.

I opened the little bag and loaded my pockets with enough money to run my errands. At the door, I stopped and called over my shoulder to Arthur: "Don't worry if I'm gone an hour or so. I'll be back."

I didn't wait for an answer. That would have been pointless under the circumstances.

After Philadelphia, this place seemed to be bustling with activity. There were four or five people in the lobby and a couple of dozen more out in the street.

I tarried at the desk for several reasons. In the first place, I was expecting Vern Engdahl to try to contact me and I didn't want him messing with the luggage—not while Arthur might get nervous. So I told the desk clerk that in case anybody came inquiring for Mr. Schlaepfer, which was the name I was using—my real name being Sam Dunlap—he was to be told that on no account was he to go to my room but to wait in the lobby; and in any case I would be back in an hour.

"Sure," said the desk clerk, holding out his hand.

I crossed it with paper. "One other thing," I said. "I need to buy an electric typewriter and some other stuff. Where can I get them?"

"PX," he said promptly.

"PX?"

"What used to be Macy's," he explained. "You go out that door and turn right. It's only about a block. You'll see the sign."

"Thanks." That cost me a hundred more, but it was worth it. After all, money wasn't a problem—not when we had just come from Philadelphia.

The big sign read px, but it wasn't big enough to hide an older sign underneath that said macy's. I looked it over from across the street.

Somebody had organized it pretty well. I had to admire them. I mean I don't like New York—wouldn't live there if you gave me the place—but it showed a sort of go-getting spirit. It was no easy job getting a full staff together to run a department store operation, when any city the size of New York must have a couple thousand stores. You know what I mean? It's like running a hotel or anything else—how are you going to get people to work for you when they can just as easily walk down the street, find a vacant store and set up their own operation?

But Macy's was fully manned. There was a guard at every door and a walking patrol along the block-front between the entrances to make sure nobody broke in through the windows. They all wore green armbands and uniforms—well, lots of people wore uniforms.

I walked over.

"Afternoon," I said affably to the guard. "I want to pick up some stuff. Typewriter, maybe a gun, you know. How do you work it here? Flat rate for all you can carry, prices marked on everything, or what is it?"

He starred at me suspiciously. He was a monster; six inches taller than I, he must have weighed two hundred and fifty pounds. He didn't look very smart, which might explain why he was working for somebody else these days. But he was smart enough for what he had to do.

He demanded: "You new in town?"

I nodded.

He thought for a minute. "All right, buddy. Go on in. You pick out what you want, see? We'll straighten out the price when you come out."

"Fair enough." I started past him.

He grabbed me by the arm. "No tricks," he ordered. "You come out the same door you went in, understand?"

"Sure," I said, "if that's the way you want it."

That figured—one way or another: either they got a commission, or, like everybody else, they lived on what they could knock down. I filed that for further consideration.

Inside, the store smelled pretty bad. It wasn't just rot, though there was plenty of that; it was musty and stale and old. It was dark, or nearly. About one light in twenty was turned on, in order to conserve power. Naturally the escalators and so on weren't running at all.

I passed a counter with pencils and ballpoint pens in a case. Most of them were gone—somebody hadn't bothered to go around in back and had simply knocked the glass out—but I found one that worked and an old order pad to write on. Over by the elevators there was a store directory, so I went over and checked it, making a list of the departments worth visiting.

Office Supplies would be the typewriter. Garden & Home was a good bet—maybe I could find a little wheelbarrow to save carrying the typewriter in my arms. What I wanted was one of the big ones where all the keys are solenoid-operated instead of the cam-and-roller arrangement—that was all Arthur could operate. And those things were heavy, as I knew. That was why we had ditched the old one in the Bronx.

Sporting Goods—that would be for a gun, if there were any left. Naturally, they were about the first to go after it happened, when *everybody* wanted a gun. I mean everybody who lived through it. I thought about clothes—it was pretty hot in New York—and decided I might as well take a look.

Typewriter, clothes, gun, wheelbarrow. I made one more note on the pad—try the tobacco counter, but I didn't have much hope for that. They had used cigarettes for currency around this area for a while, until they got enough bank vaults open to supply big bills. It made cigarettes scarce.

I turned away and noticed for the first time that one of the elevators was stopped on the main floor. The doors were closed, but they were glass doors, and although there wasn't any light inside, I could see the elevator was full. There must have been thirty or forty people in the car when it happened.

I'd been thinking that, if nothing else, these New Yorkers were pretty neat—I mean if you don't count the Bronx. But here were thirty or forty skeletons that nobody had even bothered to clear away.

You call that neat? Right in plain view on the ground floor, where everybody who came into the place would be sure to go—I mean if it had been on one of the upper floors, what difference would it have made?

I began to wish we were out of the city. But naturally that would have to wait until we finished what we came here to do—otherwise, what was the point of coming all the way here in the first place?

The tobacco counter was bare. I got the wheelbarrow easily enough—there were plenty of those, all sizes; I picked out a nice light red-and-yellow one with rubber-tired wheel. I rolled it over to Sporting Goods on the same floor, but that didn't work out too well. I found a 30-30 with telescopic sights, only there weren't any cartridges to fit it—or anything else. I took the gun anyway; Engdahl would probably have some extra ammunition.

Men's Clothing was a waste of time, too—I guess these New Yorkers were too lazy to do laundry. But I found the typewriter I wanted.

I put the whole load into the wheelbarrow, along with a couple of odds and ends that caught my eye as I passed through Housewares, and I bumped as gently as I could down the shallow steps of the motionless escalator to the ground floor.

I came down the back way, and that was a mistake. It led me right past the food department. Well, I don't have to tell you what *that* was like, with all the exploded cans and the rats as big as poodles. But I found some cologne and soaked a handkerchief in it, and with that over my nose, and some fast footwork for the rats, I managed to get to one of the doors.

It wasn't the one I had come in, but that was all right. I sized up the guard. He looked smart enough for a little bargaining, but not too smart; and if I didn't like his price, I could always remember that I was supposed to go out the other door.

I said: "Psst!"

When he turned around, I said rapidly: "Listen, this isn't the way I came in, but if you want to do business, it'll be the way I come out."

He thought for a second, and then he smiled craftily and said: "All right, come on."

Well, we haggled. The gun was the big thing—he wanted five thousand for that and he wouldn't come down. The wheelbarrow he was willing to let go for five hundred. And the typewriter—he scowled at the typewriter as though it were contagious.

"What you want that for?" he asked suspiciously. I shrugged.

"Well—" he scratched his head—"a thousand?"

I shook my head.

"Five hundred?"

I kept on shaking.

"All right, all right," he grumbled. "Look, you take the other things for six thousand—including what you got in your pockets that you don't think I know about, see? And I'll throw this in. How about it?"

That was fine as far as I was concerned, but just on principle I pushed him a little further. "Forget it," I said. "I'll give you fifty bills for the lot, take it or leave it. Otherwise I'll walk right down the street to Gimbel's and—"

He guffawed.

"What's the matter?" I demanded.

"Pal," he said, "you kill me. Stranger in town, hey? You can't go anyplace but here."

"Why not?"

"Account of there *ain't* anyplace else. See, the chief here don't like competition. So we don't have to worry about anybody taking their trade elsewhere, like—we burned all the other places down."

That explained a couple of things. I counted out the money, loaded the stuff back in the wheelbarrow and headed for the Statler; but all the time I was counting and loading, I was talking to Big Brainless; and by the time I was actually on the way, I knew a little more about this "chief."

And that was kind of important, because he was the man we were going to have to know very well.

I locked the door of the hotel room. Arthur was peeping out of the suitcase at me.

I said: "I'm back. I got your typewriter." He waved his eye at me.

I took out the little kit of electricians' tools I carried, tipped the typewriter on its back and began sorting out leads. I cut them free from the keyboard, soldered on a ground wire, and began taping the leads to the strands of a yard of forty-ply multiplex cable.

It was a slow and dull job. I didn't have to worry about which solenoid lead went to which strand—Arthur could sort them out. But all the same it took an hour, pretty near, and I was getting hungry by the time I got the last connection taped. I shifted the typewriter so that both Arthur and I could see it, rolled in a sheet of paper and hooked the cable to Arthur's receptors.

Nothing happened.

"Oh," I said. "Excuse me, Arthur. I forgot to plug it in."

I found a wall socket. The typewriter began to hum and then it started to rattle and type:

DURA AUK UKOO RQK MWS AQB

It stopped.

"Come on, Arthur," I ordered impatiently. "Sort them out, will you?"

Laboriously it typed:

! ! !

Then, for a time, there was a clacking and thumping as he typed random letters, peeping out of the suitcase to see what he had typed, until the sheet I had put in was used up.

I replaced it and waited, as patiently as I could, smoking one of the last of my cigarettes. After fifteen minutes or so, he had the hang of it pretty well. He typed:

YOU DAMQXXX DAMN FOOL WHUXXX WHY DID YOU LEAQNXXX LEAVE ME ALONE Q Q

"Aw, Arthur," I said. "Use your head, will you? I couldn't carry that old typewriter of yours all the way down through the Bronx. It was getting pretty beat-up. Anyway, I've only got two hands—"

YOU LOUSE, it rattled, ARE YOU TRYONXXX TRYING TO INSULT ME BECAUSE I DONT HAVE ANY QQ

"Arthur!" I said, shocked. "You know better than that!"

The typewriter slammed its carriage back and forth ferociously a couple of times. Then he said: ALL RIGHT SAM YOU KNOW YOUVE GOT ME BY THE THROAT SO YOU CAN DO ANYTHING YOU WANT TO WITH ME WHO CARES ABOUT MY FEELINGS ANYHOW

"Please don't take that attitude," I coaxed.

WELL

"Please?"

He capitulated. ALL RIGHT SAY HEARD ANYTHING FROM ENGDAHL Q Q

"No."

ISNT THAT JUST LIKE HIM Q Q CANT DEPEND ON THAT MAN HE WAS THE LOUSIEST ELECTRICIANS MATE ON THE SEA SPRITE AND HE ISNT MUCH BETTER NOW SAY SAM REMEMBER WHEN WE HAD TO GET HIM OUT OF THE JUG IN NEWPORT NEWS BECAUSE

I settled back and relaxed. I might as well. That was the trouble with getting Arthur a new typewriter after a couple of days without one—he had so much garrulity stored up in his little brain, and the only person to spill it on was me.

Apparently I fell asleep. Well, I mean I must have, because I woke up. I had been dreaming I was on guard post outside the Yard at Portsmouth, and it was night, and I looked up and there was something up there, all silvery and bad. It was a missile—and that was silly, because you never *see* a missile. But this was a dream.

And the thing burst, like a Roman candle flaring out, all sorts of comet trails of light, and then the whole sky was full of bright and colored snow. Little tiny flakes of light coming down, a mist of light, radiation dropping like dew; and it was so pretty, and I took a deep breath. And my lungs burned out like slow fire, and I coughed myself to death with the explosions of the missile banging against my flaming ears . . .

Well, it was a dream. It probably wasn't like that at all—and if it had been, I wasn't there to see it, because I was tucked away safe under a hundred and twenty fathoms of Atlantic water. All of us were on the *Sea Sprite*.

But it was a bad dream and it bothered me, even when I woke up and found that the banging explosions of the missile were the noise of Arthur's typewriter carriage crashing furiously back and forth.

He peeped out of the suitcase and saw that I was awake. He demanded: HOW CAN YOU FALL ASLEEP WHEN WERE IN A PLACE LIKE THIS Q Q ANYTHING COULD HAPPEN SAM I KNOW YOU DONT CARE WHAT HAPPENS TO ME BUT FOR YOUR OWN SAKE YOU SHOULDNT

"Oh, dry up," I said.

Being awake, I remembered that I was hungry. There was still no sign of Engdahl or the others, but that wasn't too surprising—they hadn't known exactly when we would arrive. I wished I had thought to bring some food back to the room. It looked like long waiting and I wouldn't want to leave Arthur alone again—after all, he was partly right.

I thought of the telephone.

On the off-chance that it might work, I picked it up. Amazing, a voice from the desk answered.

I crossed my fingers and said: "Room service?"

And the voice answered amiably enough: "Hold on, buddy. I'll see if they answer."

Clicking and a good long wait. Then a new voice said: "Whaddya want?"

There was no sense pressing my luck by asking for anything like a complete meal. I would be lucky if I got a sandwich.

I said: "Please, may I have a Spam sandwich on Rye Krisp and some coffee for Room Fifteen Forty-one?"

"Please, you go to hell!" the voice snarled. "What do you think this is, some damn delicatessen? You want liquor, we'll get you liquor. That's what room service is for!"

I hung up. What was the use of arguing? Arthur was clacking peevishly:

WHATS THE MATTER SAM YOU THINKING OF YOUR BELLY AGAIN Q Q

"You would be if you—" I started, and then I stopped. Arthur's feelings were delicate enough already. I mean suppose that all you had left of what you were born with was a brain in a kind of sardine can, wouldn't you be sensitive? Well, Arthur was more sensitive than you would be, believe me. Of course, it was his own foolish fault—I mean you don't get a prosthetic tank unless you die by accident, or something like that, because if it's disease they usually can't save even the brain.

The phone rang again.

It was the desk clerk. "Say, did you get what you wanted?" he asked chummily.

"No."

"Oh. Too bad," he said, but cheerfully. "Listen, buddy, I forgot to tell you before. That Miss Engdahl you were expecting, she's on her way up."

I dropped the phone onto the cradle.

"Arthur!" I yelled. "Keep quiet for a while—trouble!"

He clacked once, and the typewriter shut itself off. I jumped for the door of the bathroom, cursing the fact that I didn't have cartridges for the gun. Still, empty or not, it would have to do.

I ducked behind the bathroom door, in the shadows, covering the hall door. Because there were two things wrong with what the desk clerk had told me. Vern Engdahl wasn't a "miss," to begin with; and whatever name he used when he came to call on me, it wouldn't be Vern Engdahl.

There was a knock on the door. I called: "Come in!"

The door opened and the girl who called herself Vern Engdahl came in slowly, looking around. I stayed quiet and out of sight until she was all the way in. She didn't seem to be armed; there wasn't anyone with her.

I stepped out, holding the gun on her. Her eyes opened wide and she seemed about to turn.

"Hold it! Come on in, you. Close the door!"

She did. She looked as though she were expecting me. I looked her over—medium pretty, not very tall, not very plump, not very old. I'd have guessed twenty or so, but that's not my line of work; she could have been almost any age from seventeen on.

The typewriter switched itself on and began to pound agitatedly. I crossed over toward her and paused to peer at what Arthur was yacking about: SEARCH HER YOU DAMN FOOL MAYBE SHES GOT A GUN

I ordered: "Shut up, Arthur. I'm *going* to search her. You! Turn around!"

She shrugged and turned around, her hands in the air. Over her shoulder, she said: "You're taking this all wrong, Sam. I came here to make a deal with you."

"Sure you did."

But her knowing my name was a blow, too. I mean what was the use of all that sneaking around if people in New York were going to know we were here?

I walked up close behind her and patted what there was to pat. There didn't seem to be a gun.

"You tickle," she complained.

I took her pocketbook away from her and went through it. No gun. A lot of money—an *awful* lot of money. I mean there must have been two or three hundred thousand dollars. There was nothing with a name on it in the pocketbook.

She said: "Can I put my hands down, Sam?"

"In a minute." I thought for a second and then decided to do it—you know, I just couldn't afford to take chances. I cleared my throat and ordered: "Take off your clothes."

Her head jerked around and she stared at me. *"What?"*

"Take them off. You heard me."

"Now wait a minute—" she began dangerously.

I said: "Do what I tell you, hear? How do I know you haven't got a knife tucked away?"

She clenched her teeth. "Why, you dirty little man! What do you think—" Then she shrugged. She looked at me with contempt and said: "All right. What's the difference?"

Well, there was a considerable difference. She began to unzip and unbutton and wriggle, and pretty soon she was standing there in her underwear, looking at me as though I were a two-headed worm. It was interesting, but kind of embarrassing. I could see Arthur's eye-stalk waving excitedly out of the opened suitcase.

I picked up her skirt and blouse and shook them. I could feel myself blushing, and there didn't seem to be anything in them.

I growled: "Okay, I guess that's enough. You can put your clothes back on now."

"Gee, thanks," she said.

She looked at me thoughtfully and then shook her head as if she'd never seen anything like me before and never hoped to again. Without another word, she began to get back into her clothes. I had to admire her poise. I mean she was perfectly calm about the whole thing. You'd have thought she was used to taking her clothes off in front of strange men.

Well, for that matter, maybe she was; but it wasn't any of my business.

Arthur was clacking distractedly, but I didn't pay any attention to him. I demanded: "All right, now who are you and what do you want?"

She pulled up a stocking and said: "You couldn't have asked me that in the first place, could you? I'm Vern Eng—"

"Cut it out!"

She stared at me. "I was only going to say I'm Vern Engdahl's partner. We've got a little business deal cooking and I wanted to talk to you about this proposition."

Arthur squawked: WHATS ENGDAHL UP TO NOW Q Q SAM IM WARNING YOU I DONT LIKE THE LOOK OF THIS THIS WOMAN AND ENGDAHL ARE PROBABLY DOUBLECROSSING US

I said: "All right, Arthur, relax. I'm taking care of things. Now start over, you. What's your name?"

She finished putting on her shoe and stood up. "Amy."

"Last name?"

She shrugged and fished in her purse for a cigarette. "What does it matter? Mind if I sit down?"

"Go ahead," I rumbled. "But don't stop talking!"

"Oh," she said, "we've got plenty of time to straighten things out." She lit the cigarette and walked over to the chair by the window. On the way, she gave the luggage a good long look.

Arthur's eyestalk cowered back into the suitcase as she came close. She winked at me, grinned, bent down and peered inside.

"My," she said, "he's a nice shiny one, isn't he?"

The typewriter began to clatter frantically. I didn't even bother to look; I told him: "Arthur, if you can't keep quiet, you have to expect people to know you're there."

She sat down and crossed her legs. "Now then," she said. "Frankly, he's what I came to see you about. Vern told me you had a pross. I want to buy it."

The typewriter thrashed its carriage back and forth furiously.

"Arthur isn't for sale."

"No?" She leaned back. "Vern's already sold me his interest, you know. And you don't really have any choice. You see, I'm in charge of materiel procurement for the Major. If you want to sell your share, fine. If you don't, why, we requisition it anyhow. Do you follow?"

I was getting irritated—at Vern Engdahl, for whatever the hell he thought he was doing; but at her because she was handy. I shook my head.

"Fifty thousand dollars? I mean for your interest?"

"No."

"Seventy-five?"

"No!"

"Oh, come on now. A hundred thousand?"

It wasn't going to make any impression on her, but I tried to explain: "Arthur's a friend of mine. He isn't for sale."

She shook her head. "What's the matter with you? Engdahl wasn't like this. He sold his interest for forty thousand and was glad to get it."

Clatter-clatter-clatter from Arthur. I didn't blame him for having hurt feelings that time.

Amy said in a discouraged tone: "Why can't people be reasonable? The Major doesn't like it when people aren't reasonable."

I lowered the gun and cleared my throat. "He doesn't?" I asked, cuing her. I wanted to hear more about this Major, who seemed to have the city pretty well under his thumb.

"No, he doesn't." She shook her head sorrowfully. She said in an accusing voice: "You out-of-towners don't know what it's like to try to run a city the size of New York. There are fifteen thousand people here, do you know that? It isn't one of your hick towns. And it's worry, worry, worry all the time, trying to keep things going."

"I bet," I said sympathetically. "You're, uh, pretty close to the Major?"

She said stiffly: "I'm not married to him, if that's what you mean. Though I've had my chances . . . But you see how it is. Fifteen thousand people to run a place the size of New York! It's forty men to operate the power station, and twenty-five on the PX, and thirty on the hotel here. And then there are the local groceries, and the Army, and the Coast Guard, and the Air Force—though, really, that's only two men—and—Well, you get the picture."

"I certainly do. Look, what kind of a guy *is* the Major?"

She shrugged. "A guy."

"I mean what does he like?"

"Women, mostly," she said, her expression clouded. "Come on now. What about it?"

I stalled. "What do you want Arthur for?"

She gave me a disgusted look. "What do you think? To relieve the manpower shortage, naturally. There's more work than there are men. Now if the Major could just get hold of a couple of prosthetics, like this thing here, why, he could put them in the big installations. This one used to be an engineer or something, Vern said."

"Well . . . *like* an engineer."

Amy shrugged. "So why couldn't we connect him up with the power station? It's been done. The Major knows that—he was in the Pentagon when they switched all the aircraft warning net over from computer to prosthetic control. So why couldn't we do the same thing with our power station and release forty men for other assignments? This thing could work day, night, Sundays—what's the difference when you're just a brain in a sardine can?"

Clatter-rattle-*bang*.

She looked startled. "Oh. I forgot he was listening."

"No deal," I said.

She said: "A hundred and fifty thousand?"

A hundred and fifty thousand dollars. I considered that for a while. Arthur clattered warningly.

"Well," I temporized, "I'd have to be sure he was getting into good hands—"

The typewriter thrashed wildly. The sheet of paper fluttered out of the carriage. He'd used it up. Automatically I picked it up—it was covered with imprecations, self-pity and threats—and started to put a new one in.

"No," I said, bending over the typewriter, "I guess I couldn't sell him. It just wouldn't be right—"

That was my mistake; it was the wrong time for me to say that, because I had taken my eyes off her.

The room bent over and clouted me.

I half turned, not more than a fraction conscious, and I saw this Amy girl, behind me, with the shoe still in her hand, raised to give me another blackjacking on the skull.

The shoe came down, and it must have weighed more than it looked, and even the fractional bit of consciousness went crashing away.

I have to tell you about Vern Engdahl. We were all from the *Sea Sprite*, of course—me and Vern and even Arthur. The thing about Vern is that he was the lowest-ranking one of us all—only an electricians' mate third, I mean when anybody paid any attention to things like that—and yet he was pretty much doing the thinking for the rest of us. Coming to New York was his idea—he told us that was the only place we could get what we wanted.

Well, as long as we were carrying Arthur along with us, we pretty much needed Vern, because he was the one who knew how to keep the lash-up going. You've got no idea what kind of pumps and plumbing go into a prosthetic tank until you've seen one opened up. And, naturally, Arthur didn't want any breakdowns without somebody around to fix things up.

The *Sea Sprite*, maybe you know, was one of the old liquid-sodium-reactor subs—too slow for combat duty, but as big as a barn, so they made it a hospital ship. We were cruising deep when the missiles hit, and, of course, when we came up, there wasn't much for a hospital ship to do. I mean there isn't any sense fooling around with anybody who's taken a good deep breath of fallout.

So we went back to Newport News to see what had happened. And we found out what had happened. And there wasn't anything much to do except pay off the crew and let them go. But us three stuck together. Why not? It wasn't as if we had any families to go back to any more.

Vern just loved all this stuff—he'd been an Eagle Scout; maybe that had something to do with it—and he showed us how to boil drinking water and forage in the woods and all like that, because nobody in his right mind wanted to go near any kind of a town, until the cold weather set in, anyway. And it was always Vern, Vern, telling us what to do, ironing out our troubles.

It worked out, except that there was this one thing. Vern had bright ideas. But he didn't always tell us what they were.

So I wasn't so very surprised when I came to. I mean there I was, tied up, with this girl Amy standing over me, holding the gun like a club. Evidently she'd found out that there weren't any cartridges. And in a couple of minutes there was a knock on the door, and she yelled, "Come in," and in came Vern. And the man who was with him had to be somebody important, because there were eight or ten other men crowding in close behind.

I didn't need to look at the oak leaves on his shoulders to realize that here was the chief, the fellow who ran this town, the Major.

It was just the kind of thing Vern *would* do.

Vern said, with the look on his face that made strange officers wonder why this poor persecuted man had been forced to spend so much time in the brig: "Now, Major, I'm sure we can straighten all this out. Would you mind leaving me alone with my friend here for a moment?"

The Major teetered on his heels, thinking. He was a tall, youngish-bald type, with a long, worried, horselike face. He said, "Ah, do you think we should?"

"I guarantee there'll be no trouble, Major," Vern promised.

The Major pulled at his little mustache. "Very well," he said. "Amy, you come along."

"We'll be right here, Major," Vern said reassuringly, escorting him to the door.

"You bet you will," said the Major, and tittered. "Ah, bring that gun along with you, Amy. And be sure this man knows that we have bullets."

They closed the door. Arthur had been cowering in his suitcase, but now his eyestalk peeped out and the rattling and clattering from that typewriter sounded like the Battle of the Bulge.

I demanded: "Come on, Vern. What's this all about?"

Vern said: "How much did they offer you?"

Clatter-bang-BANG. I peeked, and Arthur was saying: WARNED YOU SAM THAT ENGDAHL WAS UP TO TRICKS PLEASE SAM PLEASE PLEASE PLEASE HIT HIM ON THE HEAD KNOCK HIM OUT HE MUST HAVE A GUN SO GET IT AND SHOOT OUR WAY OUT OF HERE

"A hundred and fifty thousand dollars," I said.

Vern looked outraged. "I only got forty!"

Arthur clattered: VERN I APPEAL TO YOUR COMMON DECENCY WERE OLD SHIPMATES VERN REMEMBER ALL THE TIMES I

"Still," Vern mused, "it's all common funds anyway, right? Arthur belongs to both of us."

I DONT DONT DONT REPEAT DONT BELONG TO ANYBODY BUT ME

"That's true," I said grudgingly. "But I carried him, remember."

SAM WHATS THE MATTER WITH YOU Q Q I DONT LIKE THE EXPRESSION ON YOUR FACE LISTEN SAM YOU ARENT

Vern said, "A hundred and fifty thousand, remember."

THINKING OF SELLING

"And of course we couldn't get out of here," Vern pointed out. "They've got us surrounded."

ME TO THESE RATS Q Q SAM VERN PLEASE DONT SCARE ME

I said, pointing to the fluttering paper in the rattling machine: "You're worrying our friend."

Vern shrugged impatiently.

I KNEW I SHOULDNT HAVE TRUSTED YOU, Arthur wept. THAT ALL I MEAN TO YOU EH

Vern said: "Well, Sam? Let's take the cash and get this thing over with. After all, he *will* have the best of treatment."

It was a little like selling your sister into white slavery, but what else was there to do? Besides, I kind of trusted Vern.

"All right," I said.

What Arthur said nearly scorched the paper.

Vern helped pack Arthur up for moving. I mean it was just a matter of pulling the plugs out and making sure he had a fresh battery, but Vern wanted to supervise it himself. Because one of the little things Vern had up his sleeve was that he had found a spot for himself on the Major's payroll. He was now the official Prosthetic (Human) Maintenance Department Chief.

The Major said to me: "Ah, Dunlap. What sort of experience have you had?"

"Experience?"

"In the Navy. Your friend Engdahl suggested you might want to join us here."

"Oh. I see what you mean." I shook my head. "Nothing that would do you any good, I'm afraid. I was a yeoman."

"Yeoman?"

"Like a company clerk," I explained. "I mean I kept records and cut orders and made out reports and all like that."

"Company clerk!" The eyes in the long horsy face gleamed. "Ah, you're mistaken, Dunlap! Why, that's *just* what we need. Our morning reports are in foul shape. Foul! Come over to HQ. Lieutenant Bankhead will give you a lift."

"Lieutenant Bankhead?"

I got an elbow in my ribs for that. It was that girl Amy, standing alongside me. "I," she said, "am Lieutenant Bankhead."

Well, I went along with her, leaving Engdahl and Arthur behind. But I must admit I wasn't sure of my reception.

Out in front of the hotel was a whole fleet of cars—three or four of them, at least. There was a big old Cadillac that looked like a gangsters' car—thick glass in the windows, tires that looked like they belonged on a truck. I was willing to bet it was bulletproof and also that it belonged to the Major. I was right both times. There was a little MG with the top down, and a couple of light trucks. Every one of them was painted bright orange, and every one of them had the star-and-bar of the good old United States Army on its side.

It took me back to old times—all but the unmilitary color. Amy led me to the MG and pointed.

"Sit," she said.

I sat. She got in the other side and we were off.

It was a little uncomfortable on account of I wasn't just sure whether I ought to apologize for making her take her clothes off. And then she tramped on the gas of that little car and I didn't think much about being embarrassed or about her black lace lingerie. I was only thinking about one thing—how to stay alive long enough to get out of that car.

See, what we really wanted was an ocean liner.

The rest of us probably would have been happy enough to stay in Lehigh County, but Arthur was getting restless.

He was a terrible responsibility, in a way. I suppose there were a hundred thousand people or so left in the country, and not more than forty or fifty of them were like Arthur—I mean if you want to call a man in a prosthetic tank a "person." But we all did. We'd got pretty used to him. We'd shipped together in the war—and survived together, as a few of the actual fighters did, those who were lucky enough to be underwater or high in the air when the ICBMs landed—and as few civilians did.

I mean there wasn't much chance for surviving, for anybody who happened to be breathing the open air when it happened. I mean you can do just so much about making a "clean" H-bomb, and if you cut out the long-life fission products, the short-life ones get pretty deadly.

Anyway, there wasn't much damage, except of course that everybody was dead. All the surface vessels lost their crews. All the population of the cities were gone. And so then, when Arthur slipped on the gangplank coming into Newport News and broke his fool neck, why, we had the whole staff of the *Sea Sprite* to work on him. I mean what else did the surgeons have to do?

Of course, that was a long time ago.

But we'd stayed together. We headed for the farm country around Allentown, Pennsylvania, because Arthur and Vern Engdahl claimed to know it pretty well. I think maybe they had some hope of finding family or friends, but naturally there wasn't any of that. And when you got into the inland towns, there hadn't been much of an attempt to clean them up. At least the big cities and the ports had been gone over, in some spots anyway, by burial squads. Although when we finally decided to move out and went to Philadelphia—

Well, let's be fair; there had been fighting around there after the big fight. Anyway, that wasn't so very uncommon. That was one of the reasons that for a long time—four or five years, at any rate—we stayed away from big cities.

We holed up in a big farmhouse in Lehigh County. It had its own generator from a little stream, and that took care of Arthur's power needs; and the previous occupants had been just crazy about stashing away food. There was enough to last a century, and that took care of the two of us. We appreciated that. We even took the old folks out and gave them a decent burial. I mean they'd all been in the family car, so we just had to tow it to a gravel pit and push it in.

The place had its own well, with an electric pump and a hot-water system—oh, it was nice. I was sorry to leave but, frankly, Arthur was driving us nuts.

We never could make the television work—maybe there weren't any stations near enough. But we pulled in a couple of radio stations pretty well and Arthur got a big charge out of listening to them—see, he could hear four or five at a time and I suppose that made him feel better than the rest of us.

He heard that the big cities were cleaned up and every one of them seemed to want immigrants—they were pleading, pleading all the time, like the TV-set and vacuum-cleaner people used to in the old days; they guaranteed we'd like it if we only came to live in Philly, or Richmond, or Baltimore, or wherever. And I guess Arthur kind of hoped we might find another pross. And then—well, Engdahl came up with this idea of an ocean liner.

It figured. I mean you get out in the middle of the ocean and what's the difference what it's like on land? And it especially appealed to Arthur because he wanted to do some surface sailing. He never had when he was real—I mean when he had arms and legs like anybody else. He'd gone right into the undersea service the minute he got out of school.

And—well, sailing was what Arthur knew something about and I suppose even a prosthetic man wants to feel useful. It was like Amy said: He could be hooked up to an automated factory—

Or to a ship.

HQ FOR THE MAJOR'S TEMPORARY MILITARY GOVERNMENT—that's what the sign said— was on the ninety-first floor of the Empire State Building, and right there that tells you something about the man. I mean you know how much power it takes to run those elevators all the way up to the top? But the Major must have liked being able to look down on everybody else.

Amy Bankhead conducted me to his office and sat me down to wait for His Military Excellency to arrive. She filled me in on him, to some degree. He'd been an absolute nothing before the war; but he had a reserve commission in the Air Force, and when things began to look sticky, they'd called him up and put him in a Missile Master control point, underground somewhere up around Ossining.

He was the duty officer when it happened, and naturally he hadn't noticed anything like an enemy aircraft, and naturally the anti-missile missiles were still rusting in their racks all around the city; but since the place had been operating on sealed ventilation, the duty complement could stay there until the short half-life radioisotopes wore themselves out.

And then the Major found out that he was not only in charge of the fourteen men and women of his division at the center—he was ranking United States Military Establishment officer farther than the eye could see. So he beat it, as fast as he could, for New York, because what Army officer doesn't dream about being stationed in New York? And he set up his Temporary Military Government—and that was nine years ago.

If there hadn't been plenty to go around, I don't suppose he would have lasted a week—none of these city chiefs would have. But as things were, he was in on the ground floor, and as newcomers trickled into the city, his boys already had things nicely organized.

It was a soft touch.

Well, we were about a week getting settled in New York and things were looking pretty good. Vern calmed me down by pointing out that, after all, we had to sell Arthur, and hadn't we come out of it plenty okay?

And we had. There was no doubt about it. Not only did we have a fat price for Arthur, which was useful because there were a lot of things we would have to buy, but we both had jobs working for the Major.

Vern was his specialist in the care and feeding of Arthur and I was his chief of office routine—and, as such, I delighted his fussy little soul, because by adding what I remembered of Navy protocol to what he was able to teach me of Army routine, we came up with as snarled a mass of red tape as any field-grade officer in the whole history of all armed forces had been able to accumulate. Oh, I tell you, nobody sneezed in New York without a report being made out in triplicate, with eight endorsements.

Of course there wasn't anybody to send them to, but that didn't stop the Major. He said with determination: "Nobody's ever going to chew *me* out for noncompliance with regulations—even if I have to invent the regulations myself!"

We set up in a bachelor apartment on Central Park South—the Major had the penthouse; the whole building had been converted to barracks—and the first chance we got, Vern snaffled some transportation and we set out to find an ocean liner.

See, the thing was that an ocean liner isn't easy to steal. I mean we'd scouted out the lay of the land before we ever entered the city itself, and there were plenty of liners, but there wasn't one that looked like we could just jump in and sail it away. For that we needed an organization. Since we didn't have one, the best thing to do was borrow the Major's.

Vern turned up with Amy Bankhead's MG, and he also turned up with Amy. I can't say I was displeased, because I was beginning to like the girl; but did you ever try to ride three people in the seats of an MG? Well, the way to do it is by having one passenger sit in the other passenger's lap, which would have been all right except that Amy insisted on driving.

We headed downtown and over to the West Side. The Major's Topographical Section—one former billboard artist—had prepared road maps with little red-ink *X*s marking the streets that were blocked, which was most of the streets; but we charted a course that would take us where we wanted to go. Thirty-fourth Street was open, and so was Fifth Avenue all of its length, so we scooted down Fifth, crossed over, got under the Elevated Highway and whined along uptown toward the Fifties.

"There's one," cried Amy, pointing.

I was on Vern's lap, so I was making the notes. It was a Fruit Company combination freighter-passenger vessel. I looked at Vern, and Vern shrugged as best he could, so I wrote it down; but it wasn't exactly what we wanted. No, not by a long shot.

Still, the thing to do was to survey our resources, and then we could pick the one we liked best. We went all the way up to the end of the big-ship docks, and then turned and came back down, all the way to the Battery. It wasn't pleasure driving, exactly—half a dozen times we had to get out the map and detour around impenetrable jams of stalled and empty cars—or anyway, if they weren't exactly empty, the people in them were no longer in shape to get out of our way. But we made it.

We counted sixteen ships in dock that looked as though they might do for our purposes. We had to rule out the newer ones and the reconverted jobs. I mean, after all, U-235 just lasts so long, and you can steam around the world on a walnut-shell of it, or whatever it is, but you can't store it. So we had to stick with the ships that were powered with conventional fuel—and, on consideration, only oil at that.

But that left sixteen, as I say. Some of them, though, had suffered visibly from being left untended for nearly a decade, so that for our purposes they might as well have been abandoned in the middle of the Atlantic; we didn't have the equipment or ambition to do any great amount of salvage work.

The *Empress of Britain* would have been a pretty good bet, for instance, except that it was lying at pretty nearly a forty-five-degree angle in its berth. So was the *United States,* and so was the *Caronia.* The *Stockholm* was straight enough, but I took a good look, and only one tier of portholes was showing above the water—evidently it had settled nice and even, but it was on the bottom all the same. Well, that mud sucks with a fine tight grip, and we weren't going to try to loosen it.

All in all, eleven of the sixteen ships were out of commission just from what we could see driving by.

Vern and I looked at each other. We stood by the MG, while Amy sprawled her legs over the side and waited for us to make up our minds.

"Not good, Sam," said Vern, looking worried.

I said: "Well, that still leaves five. There's the *Vulcania,* the *Cristobal*—"

"Too small."

"All right. The *Manhattan,* the *Liberté* and the *Queen Elizabeth.*"

Amy looked up, her eyes gleaming. "Where's the question?" she demanded. "Naturally, it's the *Queen.*"

I tried to explain. "Please, Amy. Leave these things to us, will you?"

"But the Major won't settle for anything but the best!"

"The *Major?*"

I glanced at Vern, who wouldn't meet my eyes. "Well," I said, "look at the problems, Amy. First we have to check it over. Maybe it's been burned out—how do we know? Maybe the channel isn't even deep enough to float it any more—how do we know? Where are we going to get the oil for it?"

"We'll get the oil," Amy said cheerfully.

"And what if the channel isn't deep enough?"

"She'll float," Amy promised. "At high tide, anyway. Even if the channel hasn't been dredged in ten years."

I shrugged and gave up. What was the use of arguing?

We drove back to the *Queen Elizabeth* and I had to admit that there was a certain attraction about that big old dowager. We all got out and strolled down the pier, looking over as much as we could see.

The pier had never been cleaned out. It bothered me a little—I mean I don't like skeletons much—but Amy didn't seem to mind. The *Queen* must have just docked when it happened, because you could still see bony queues, as though they were waiting for customs inspection.

Some of the bags had been opened and the contents scattered around—naturally, somebody was bound to think of looting the *Queen*. But there were as many that hadn't been touched as that had been opened, and the whole thing had the look of an amateur attempt. And that was all to the good, because the fewer persons who had boarded the *Queen* in the decade since it happened, the more chance of our finding it in usable shape.

Amy saw a gangplank still up, and with cries of girlish glee ran aboard.

I plucked at Vern's sleeve. "You," I said. "What's this about what the *Major* won't settle for less than?"

He said: "Aw, Sam, I had to tell her something, didn't I?"

"But what about the Major—"

He said patiently: "You don't understand. It's all part of my plan, see? The Major is the big thing here and he's got a birthday coming up next month. Well, the way I put it to Amy, we'll fix him up with a yacht as a birthday present, see? And, of course, when it's all fixed up and ready to lift anchor—"

I said doubtfully: "That's the hard way, Vern. Why couldn't we just sort of get steam up and take off?"

He shook his head. "*That* is the hard way. This way we get all the help and supplies we need, understand?"

I shrugged. That was the way it was, so what was the use of arguing?

But there was one thing more on my mind. I said: "How come Amy's so interested in making the Major happy?"

Vern chortled. "Jealous, eh?"

"I asked a question!"

"Calm down, boy. It's just that he's in charge of things here so naturally she wants to keep in good with him."

I scowled. "I keep hearing stories about how the Major's chief interest in life is women. You sure she isn't ambitious to be one of them?"

He said: "The reason she wants to keep him happy is so she *won't* be one of them."

The name of the place was Bayonne.

Vern said: "One of them's *got* to have oil, Sam. It *has* to."

"Sure," I said.

"There's no question about it. Look, this is where the tankers came to discharge oil. They'd come in here, pump the oil into the refinery tanks and—"

"Vern," I said. "Let's look, shall we?"

He shrugged, and we hopped off the little outboard motorboat onto a landing stage. The tankers towered over us, rusty and screeching as the waves rubbed them against each other.

There were fifty of them there at least, and we poked around them for hours. The hatches were rusted shut and unmanageable, but you could tell a lot by sniffing. Gasoline odor was out; smell of seaweed and dead fish was out; but the heavy, rank smell of fuel oil, that was what we were sniffing for. Crews had been aboard these ships when the missiles came, and crews were still aboard.

Beyond the two-part superstructures of the tankers, the sky-line of New York was visible. I looked up, sweating, and saw the Empire State Building and imagined Amy up there, looking out toward us.

She knew we were here. It was her idea. She had scrounged up a naval engineer, or what she called a naval engineer—he had once been a stoker on a ferryboat. But he claimed he knew what he was talking about when he said the only thing the *Queen* needed to make 'er go was oil. And so we left him aboard to tinker and polish, with a couple of helpers Amy detached from the police force, and we tackled the oil problem.

Which meant Bayonne. Which was where we were.

It had to be a tanker with at least a fair portion of its cargo intact, because the *Queen* was a thirsty creature, drinking fuel not by the shot or gallon but by the ton.

"Saaam! Sam *Dunlap!*"

I looked up, startled. Five ships away, across the U of the mooring, Vern Engdahl was bellowing at me through cupped hands.

"I found it!" he shouted. "Oil, lots of oil! Come look!"

I clasped my hands over my head and looked around. It was a long way around to the tanker Vern was on, hopping from deck to deck, detouring around open stretches.

I shouted: "I'll get the boat!"

He waved and climbed up on the rail of the ship, his feet dangling over, looking supremely happy and pleased with himself. He lit a cigarette, leaned back against the upward sweep of the rail and waited.

It took me a little time to get back to the boat and a little more time than that to get the damn motor started. Vern! "Let's not take that lousy little twelve horsepower, Sam," he'd said reasonably. "The twenty-five's more what we need!" And maybe it was, but none of the motors had been started in most of a decade, and the twenty-five was just that much harder to start now.

I struggled over it, swearing, for twenty minutes or more.

The tanker by whose side we had tied up began to swing toward me as the tide changed to outgoing.

For a moment there, I was counting seconds, expecting to have to make a jump for it before the big red steel flank squeezed the little outboard flat against the piles.

But I got it started—just about in time. I squeezed out of the trap with not much more than a yard to spare and threaded my way into open water.

There was a large, threatening sound, like an enormous slow cough.

I rounded the stern of the last tanker between me and open water, and looked into the eye of a fire-breathing dragon.

Vern and his cigarettes! The tanker was loose and ablaze, bearing down on me with the slow drift of the ebbing tide. From the hatches on the forward deck, two fountains of fire spurted up and out, like enormous nostrils spouting flame. The hawsers had been burned through, the ship was adrift, I was in its path—

And so was the frantically splashing figure of Vern Engdahl, trying desperately to swim out of the way in the water before it.

What kept it from blowing up in our faces I will never know, unless it was the pressure in the tanks forcing the flame out; but it didn't. Not just then. Not until I had Engdahl aboard and we were out in the middle of the Hudson, staring back; and then it went up all right, all at once, like a missile or a volcano; and there had been fifty tankers in that one mooring, but there weren't any more, or not in shape for us to use.

I looked at Engdahl.

He said defensively: "Honest, Sam, I thought it was oil. It *smelled* like oil. How was I to know—"

"Shut up," I said.

He shrugged, injured. "But it's all right, Sam. No fooling. There are plenty of other tankers around. Plenty. Down toward the Amboys, maybe moored out in the channel. There must be. We'll find them."

"No," I said. "*You* will."

And that was all I said, because I am forgiving by nature; but I thought a great deal more.

Surprisingly, though, he did find a tanker with a full load, the very next day.

It became a question of getting the tanker to the *Queen.* I left that part up to Vern, since he claimed to be able to handle it.

It took him two weeks. First it was finding the tanker, then it was locating a tug in shape to move, then it was finding someone to pilot the tug. Then it was waiting for a clear and windless day—because the pilot he found had got all his experience sailing Star boats on Long Island Sound—and then it was easing the tanker out of Newark Bay, into the channel, down to the pier in the North River—

Oh, it was work and no fooling. I enjoyed it very much, because I didn't have to do it.

But I had enough to keep me busy at that. I found a man who claimed he used to be a radio engineer. And if he was an engineer, I was Albert Einstein's mother, but at least he knew which end of a soldering iron was hot. There was no need for any great skill, since there weren't going to be very many vessels to communicate with.

Things began to move.

The advantage of a ship like the *Queen,* for our purposes, was that the thing was pretty well automated to start out with. I mean never mind what the seafaring unions required in the way of flesh-and-blood personnel. What it came down to was that one man in the bridge or wheelhouse could pretty well make any part of the ship go or not go.

The engine-room telegraph wasn't hooked up to control the engines, no. But the wiring diagram needed only a few little changes to get the same effect, because where in the original concept a human being would take a look at the repeater down in the engine room, nod wisely, and push a button that would make the engines stop, start, or whatever—why, all we had to do was cut out the middleman, so to speak.

Our genius of the soldering iron replaced flesh and blood with some wiring and, presto, we had centralized engine control.

The steering was even easier. Steering was a matter of electronic control and servo-motors to begin with. Windjammers in the old movies might have a man lashed to the wheel whose muscle power turned the rudder, but, believe me, a big superliner doesn't. The rudders weigh as much as any old windjammer ever did from stem to stern; you have to have motors to turn them; and it was only a matter of getting out the old soldering iron again.

By the time we were through, we had every operational facility of the *Queen* hooked up to a single panel on the bridge.

Engdahl showed up with the oil tanker just about the time we got the wiring complete. We rigged up a pump and filled the bunkers till they were topped off full. We guessed, out of hope and ignorance, that there was enough in there to take us half a dozen times around the world at normal cruising speed, and maybe there was. Anyway, it didn't matter, for surely we had enough to take us anywhere we wanted to go, and then there would be more.

We crossed our fingers, turned our ex–ferry stoker loose, pushed a button—

Smoke came out of the stacks.

The antique screws began to turn over. Astern, a sort of hump of muddy water appeared. The *Queen* quivered underfoot. The mooring hawsers creaked and sang.

"Turn her off!" screamed Engdahl. "She's headed for Times Square!"

Well, that was an exaggeration, but not much of one; and there wasn't any sense in stirring up the bottom mud. I pushed buttons and the screws stopped. I pushed another button, and the big engines quietly shut themselves off, and in a few moments the stacks stopped puffing their black smoke.

The ship was alive.

Solemnly Engdahl and I shook hands. We had the thing licked. All, that is, except for the one small problem of Arthur.

The thing about Arthur was they had put him to work.

It was in the power station, just as Amy had said, and Arthur didn't like it. The fact that he didn't like it was a splendid reason for staying away from there, but I let my kind heart overrule my good sense and paid him a visit.

It was way over on the East Side, miles and miles from any civilized area. I borrowed Amy's MG, and borrowed Amy to go with it, and the two of us packed a picnic lunch and set out. There were reports of deer on Avenue A, so I brought a rifle, but we never saw one; and if you want my opinion, those reports were nothing but wishful thinking. I mean if people couldn't survive, how could deer?

We finally threaded our way through the clogged streets and parked in front of the power station.

"There's supposed to be a guard," Amy said doubtfully.

I looked. I looked pretty carefully, because if there was a guard, I wanted to see him. The Major's orders were that vital defense installations—such as the power station, the PX and his own barracks building—were to be guarded against trespassers on a shoot-on-sight basis and I wanted to make sure that the guard knew we were privileged persons, with passes signed by the Major's own hand. But we couldn't find him. So we walked in through the big door, peered around, listened for the sounds of machinery and walked in that direction.

And then we found him; he was sound asleep. Amy, looking indignant, shook him awake.

"Is that how you guard military property?" she scolded. "Don't you know the penalty for sleeping at your post?"

The guard said something irritable and unhappy. I got her off his back with some difficulty, and we located Arthur.

Picture a shiny four-gallon tomato can, with the label stripped off, hanging by wire from the flashing-light panels of an electric computer. That was Arthur. The shiny metal cylinder was his prosthetic tank; the wires were the leads that served him for fingers, ears and mouth; the glittering panel was the control center for the Consolidated Edison Eastside Power Plant No. 1.

"Hi, Arthur," I said, and a sudden ear-splitting thunderous hiss was his way of telling me that he knew I was there.

I didn't know exactly what it was he was trying to say and I didn't want to; fortune spares me few painful moments, and I accept with gratitude the ones it does. The Major's boys hadn't bothered to bring Arthur's typewriter along—I mean who cares what a generator-governor had to offer in the way of conversation?—so all he could do was blow off steam from the distant boilers.

Well, not quite all. Light flashed; a bucket conveyor began crashingly to dump loads of coal; and an alarm gong began to pound.

"Please, Arthur," I begged. "Shut up a minute and listen, will you?"

More lights. The gong rapped half a dozen times sharply, and stopped.

I said: "Arthur, you've got to trust Vern and me. We have this thing figured out now. We've got the *Queen Elizabeth*—"

A shattering hiss of steam—meaning delight this time, I thought. Or anyway hoped.

"—and it's only a question of time until we can carry out the plan. Vern says to apologize for not looking in on you—" *hiss*—"but he's been busy. And after all, you know it's more important to get everything ready so you can get out of this place, right?"

"Psst," said Amy.

She nodded briefly past my shoulder. I looked, and there was the guard, looking sleepy and surly and definitely suspicious.

I said heartily: "So as soon as I fix it up with the Major, we'll arrange for something better for you. Meanwhile, Arthur, you're doing a capital job and I want you to know that all of us loyal New York citizens and public servants deeply appreciate—"

Thundering crashes, bangs, gongs, hisses, and the scream of a steam whistle he'd found somewhere.

Arthur was mad.

"So long, Arthur," I said, and we got out of there—just barely in time. At the door, we found that Arthur had reversed the coal scoops and a growing mound of it was pouring into the street where we'd left the MG parked. We got the car started just as the heap was beginning to reach the bumpers, and at that the paint would never again be the same.

Oh, yes, he was mad. I could only hope that in the long run he would forgive us, since we were acting for his best interests, after all.

Anyway, I *thought* we were.

Still, things worked out pretty well—especially between Amy and me. Engdahl had the theory that she had been dodging the Major so long that *anybody* looked good to her, which was hardly flattering. But she and I were getting along right well.

She said worriedly: "The only thing, Sam, is that, frankly, the Major has just about made up his mind that he wants to marry me—"

"He *is* married!" I yelped.

"Naturally he's married. He's married to—so far—one hundred and nine women. He's been hitting off a marriage a month for a good many years now and, to tell you the truth, I think he's got the habit. Anyway, he's got his eye on me."

I demanded jealously: "Has he said anything?"

She picked a sheet of onionskin paper out of her bag and handed it to me. It was marked *Top Secret,* and it really was, because it hadn't gone through his regular office— I knew that because I *was* his regular office. It was only two lines of text and sloppily typed at that:

Lt. Amy Bankhead will report to HQ at 1700 hours
1 July to carry out orders of the Commanding Officer.

The first of July was only a week away. I handed the orders back to her.

"And the orders of the Commanding Officer will be—" I wanted to know.

She nodded. "You guessed it."

I said: "We'll have to work fast."

On the thirtieth of June, we invited the Major to come aboard his palatial new yacht.

"Ah, thank you," he said gratefully. "A surprise? For my birthday? Ah, you loyal members of my command make up for all that I've lost—all of it!" He nearly wept.

I said: "Sir, the pleasure is all ours," and backed out of his presence. What's more, I meant every word.

It was a select party of slightly over a hundred. All of the wives were there, barring twenty or thirty who were in disfavor—still, that left over eighty. The Major brought half a dozen of his favorite officers. His bodyguard and our crew added up to a total of thirty men.

We were set up to feed a hundred and fifty, and to provide liquor for twice that many, so it looked like a nice friendly brawl. I mean we had our radio operator handing out highballs as the guests stepped on board. The Major was touched and delighted; it was exactly the kind of party he liked.

He came up the gangplank with his face one great beaming smile. "Eat! Drink!" he cried. "Ah, and be merry!" He stretched out his hands to Amy, standing by behind the radio op. "For tomorrow we wed," he added, and sentimentally kissed his proposed bride.

I cleared my throat. "How about inspecting the ship, Major?" I interrupted.

"Plenty of time for that, my boy," he said. "Plenty of time for that." But he let go of

Amy and looked around him. Well, it was worth looking at. These Englishmen really knew how to build a luxury liner. God rest them.

The girls began roaming around.

It was a hot day and late afternoon, and the girls began discarding jackets and boleros, and that began to annoy the Major.

"Ah, cover up there!" he ordered one of his wives. "You too there, what's-your-name. Put that blouse back on!"

It gave him something to think about. He was a very jealous man, Amy had said, and when you stop to think about it, a jealous man with a hundred and nine wives to be jealous of really has a job. Anyway, he was busy watching his wives and keeping his military cabinet and his bodyguard busy too, and that made him too busy to notice when I tipped the high sign to Vern and took off.

In Consolidated Edison's big power plant, the guard was friendly. "I hear the Major's over on your boat, pal. Big doings. Got a lot of the girls there, hey?"

He bent, sniggering, to look at my pass.

"That's right, pal," I said, and slugged him.

Arthur screamed at me with a shrill blast of steam as I came in. But only once. I wasn't there for conversation. I began ripping apart his comfy little home of steel braces and copper wires, and it didn't take much more than a minute before I had him free. And that was very fortunate because, although I had tied up the guard, I hadn't done it very well, and it was just about the time I had Arthur's steel case tucked under my arm that I heard a yelling and bellowing from down the stairs.

The guard had got free.

"Keep calm, Arthur!" I ordered sharply. "We'll get out of this, don't you worry!"

But he wasn't worried, or anyway didn't show it, since he couldn't. I was the one who was worried. I was up on the second floor of the plant, in the control center, with only one stairway going down that I knew about, and that one thoroughly guarded by a man with a grudge against me. Me, I had Arthur, and no weapon, and I hadn't a doubt in the world that there were other guards around and that my friend would have them after me before long.

Problem. I took a deep breath and swallowed and considered jumping out the window. But it wasn't far enough to the ground.

Feet pounded up the stairs, more than two of them. With Arthur dragging me down on one side, I hurried, fast as I could, along the steel galleries that surrounded the biggest boiler. It was a nice choice of alternatives—if I stayed quiet, they would find me; if I ran, they would hear me, and then find me.

But ahead there was—what? Something. A flight of stairs, it looked like, going out and, yes, *up*. Up? But I was already on the second floor.

"Hey, you!" somebody bellowed from behind me.

I didn't stop to consider. I ran. It wasn't steps, not exactly; it was a chain of coal scoops on a long derrick arm, a moving bucket arrangement for unloading fuel from barges. It did go up, though, and more important it went *out*. The bucket arm was stretched across the clogged roadway below to a loading tower that hung over the water.

If I could get there, I might be able to get down. If I could get down—yes, I could see it; there were three or four mahogany motor launches tied to the foot of the tower.

And nobody around.

I looked over my shoulder, and didn't like what I saw, and scuttled up that chain of enormous buckets like a roach on a washboard, one hand for me and one hand for Arthur.

Thank heaven, I had a good lead on my pursuers—I needed it. I was on the bucket chain while they were still almost a city block behind me, along the galleries. I was halfway across the roadway, afraid to look down, before they reached the butt end of the chain.

Clash-clatter. *Clank!* The bucket under me jerked and clattered and nearly threw me into the street. One of those jokers had turned on the conveyor! It was a good trick, all right, but not quite in time. I made a flying jump and I was on the tower.

I didn't stop to thumb my nose at them, but I thought of it.

I was down those steel steps, breathing like a spouting whale, in a minute flat, and jumping out across the concrete, coal-smeared yard toward the moored launches. Quickly enough, I guess, but with nothing at all to spare, because although I hadn't seen anyone there, there was a guard.

He popped out of a doorway, blinking foolishly; and overhead the guards at the conveyor belt were screaming at him. It took him a second to figure out what was going on, and by that time I was in a launch, cast off the rope, kicked it free, and fumbled for the starting button.

It took me several seconds to realize that a rope was required, that in fact there was no button; and by then I was floating yards away, but the pudgy pop-eyed guard was also in a launch, and he didn't have to fumble. He knew. He got his motor started a fraction of a second before me, and there he was, coming at me, set to ram. Or so it looked.

I wrenched at the wheel and brought the boat hard over; but he swerved too, at the last moment, and brought up something that looked a little like a spear and a little like a sickle and turned out to be a boathook. I ducked, just in time. It sizzled over my head as he swung and crashed against the windshield. Hunks of safety glass splashed out over the forward deck, but better that than my head.

Boathooks, hey? I had a boathook too! If he didn't have another weapon, I was perfectly willing to play; I'd been sitting and taking it long enough and I was very much attracted by the idea of fighting back. The guard recovered his balance, swore at me, fought the wheel around and came back.

We both curved out toward the center of the East River in intersecting arcs. We closed. He swung first. I ducked—

And from a crouch, while he was off balance, I caught him in the shoulder with the hook.

He made a mighty splash.

I throttled down the motor long enough to see that he was still conscious.

"*Touché,* buster," I said, and set course for the return trip down around the foot of Manhattan, back toward the *Queen.*

It took awhile, but that was all right; it gave everybody a nice long time to get plastered. I sneaked aboard, carrying Arthur, and turned him over to Vern. Then I rejoined the Major. He was making an inspection tour of the ship—what he called an inspection, after his fashion.

He peered into the engine rooms and said: "Ah, fine."

He stared at the generators that were turning over and nodded when I explained we needed them for power for lights and everything and said: "Ah, of course."

He opened a couple of stateroom doors at random and said: "Ah, nice."

And he went up on the flying bridge with me and such of his officers as still could walk and said: "Ah."

Then he said in a totally different tone: "What the devil's the matter over there?"

He was staring east through the muggy haze. I saw right away what it was that was bothering him—easy, because I knew where to look. The power plant way over on the East Side was billowing smoke.

"Where's Vern Engdahl? That gadget of his isn't working right!"

"You mean Arthur?"

"I mean that brain in a bottle. It's Engdahl's responsibility, you know!"

Vern came up out of the wheelhouse and cleared his throat. "Major," he said earnestly, "I think there's some trouble over there. Maybe you ought to go look for yourself."

"Trouble?"

"I, uh, hear there've been power failures," Vern said lamely. "Don't you think you ought to inspect it? I mean just in case there's something serious?"

The Major stared at him frostily, and then his mood changed. He took a drink from the glass in his hand, quickly finishing it off.

"Ah," he said, "hell with it. Why spoil a good party? If there are going to be power failures, why, let them be. That's my motto!"

Vern and I looked at each other. He shrugged slightly, meaning, well, we tried. And I shrugged slightly, meaning, what did you expect? And then he glanced upward, meaning, take a look at what's there.

But I didn't really have to look because I heard what it was. In fact, I'd been hearing it for some time. It was the Major's entire air force—two helicopters, swirling around us at an average altitude of a hundred feet or so. They showed up bright against the gathering clouds overhead, and I looked at them with considerable interest—partly because I considered it an even-money bet that one of them would be playing crumple-fender with our stacks, partly because I had an idea that they were not there solely for show.

I said to the Major: "Chief, aren't they coming a little close? I mean it's *your* ship and all, but what if one of them takes a spill into the bridge while you're here?"

He grinned. "They know better," he bragged. "Ah, besides, I want them close. I mean if anything went wrong."

I said, in a tone that showed as much deep hurt as I could manage: "Sir, what could go wrong?"

"Oh, you know." He patted my shoulder limply. "Ah, no offense?" he asked.

I shook my head. "Well," I said, "let's go below."

All of it was done carefully, carefully as could be. The only thing was, we forgot about the typewriters. We got everybody, or as near as we could, into the Grand Salon where the food was, and right there on a table at the end of the hall was one of the typewriters clacking away. Vern had rigged them up with rolls of paper instead of sheets, and maybe that was ingenious, but it was also a headache just then. Because the typewriter was banging out:

LEFT FOUR THIRTEEN FOURTEEN AND TWENTY-ONE BOILERS

WITH A FULL HEAD OF STEAM AND THE SAFETY VALVES LOCKED BOY I TELL YOU WHEN THOSE THINGS LET GO YOURE GOING TO HEAR A NOISE THATLL KNOCK YOUR HAT OFF

The Major inquired politely: "Something to do with the ship?"

"Oh, *that*," said Vern. "Yeah. Just a little, uh, something to do with the ship. Say, Major, here's the bar. Real scotch, see? Look at the label!"

The Major glanced at him with faint contempt—well, he'd had the pick of the greatest collection of high-priced liquor stores in the world for ten years, so no wonder. But he allowed Vern to press a drink on him.

And the typewriter kept rattling:

LOOKS LIKE RAIN ANY MINUTE NOW HOO BOY IM GLAD I WONT BE IN THOSE WHIRLYBIRDS WHEN THE STORM STARTS SAY VERN WHY DONT YOU EVER ANSWER ME QQ ISNT IT ABOUT TIME TO TAKE OFF XXX I MEAN GET UNDER WEIGHT QQ

Some of the "clerks, typists, domestic personnel and others"—that was the way they were listed on the T/O; it was only coincidence that the Major had married them all—were staring at the typewriter.

"Drinks!" Vern called nervously. "Come on, girls! Drinks!"

The Major poured himself a stiff shot and asked: "What *is* that thing? A teletype or something?"

"That's right," Vern said, trailing after him as the Major wandered over to inspect it.

I GIVE THOSE BOILERS ABOUT TEN MORE MINUTES SAM WELL WHAT ABOUT IT Q Q READY TO SHOVE OFF Q Q

The Major said, frowning faintly: "Ah, that reminds me of something. Now what is it?"

"More scotch?" Vern cried. "Major, a little more scotch?"

The Major ignored him, scowling. One of the "clerks, typists" said: "Honey, you know what it is? It's like that pross you had, remember? It was on our wedding night, and you'd just got it, and you kept asking it to tell you limericks."

The Major snapped his fingers. "Knew I'd get it," he glowed. Then abruptly he scowled again and turned to face Vern and me. "Say—" he began.

I said weakly: "The boilers."

The Major stared at me, then glanced out the window. "What boilers?" he demanded. "It's just a thunderstorm. Been building up all day. Now what about this? Is that thing—"

But Vern was paying him no attention. "Thunderstorm?" he yelled. "Arthur, you listening? Are the helicopters gone?"

YESYESYES

"Then shove off, Arthur! Shove off!"

The typewriter rattled and slammed madly.

The Major yelled angrily: "Now listen to me, you! I'm asking you a question!"

But we didn't have to answer, because there was a thrumming and a throbbing underfoot, and then one of the "clerks, typists" screamed: "The dock!" She pointed at a porthole. "It's moving!"

Well, we got out of there—barely in time. And then it was up to Arthur. We had the whole ship to roam around in and there were plenty of places to hide. They had the whole ship to search. And Arthur *was* the whole ship.

Because it was Arthur, all right, brought in and hooked up by Vern, attained to his greatest dream and ambition. He was skipper of a superliner, and more than any skipper had ever been—the ship was his body, as the prosthetic tank had never been; the keel his belly, the screws his feet, the engines his heart and lungs, and every moving part that could be hooked into central control his many, many hands.

Search for us? They were lucky they could move at all! Fire Control washed them with salt water hoses, directed by Arthur's brain. Watertight doors, proof against sinking, locked them away from us at Arthur's whim.

The big bull whistle overhead brayed like a clamoring Gabriel, and the ship's bells tinkled and clanged. Arthur backed that enormous ship out of its berth like a racing scull on the Schuylkill. The four giant screws lashed the water into white foam, and then the thin mud they sucked up into tan; and the ship backed, swerved, lashed the water, stopped, and staggered crazily forward.

Arthur brayed at the Statue of Liberty, tooted good-bye to Staten Island, feinted a charge at Sandy Hook and really laid back his ears and raced once he got to deep water past the moored lightship.

We were off!

Well, from there on, it was easy. We let Arthur have his fun with the Major and the bodyguards—and by the sodden, whimpering shape they were in when they came out, it must really have been fun for him. There were just the three of us and only Vern and I had guns—but Arthur had the *Queen Elizabeth*, and that put the odds on our side.

We gave the Major a choice: row back to Coney Island—we offered him a boat, free of charge—or come along with us as cabin boy. He cast one dim-eyed look at the hundred and nine "clerks, typists" and at Amy, who would never be the hundred and tenth.

And then he shrugged and, game loser, said: "Ah, why not? I'll come along."

And why not, when you come to think of it? I mean ruling a city is nice and all that, but a sea voyage is a refreshing change. And while a hundred and nine to one is a respectable female-male ratio, still it must be wearing; and eighty to thirty isn't so bad, either. At least, I guess that was what was in the Major's mind. I know it was what was in mine.

And I discovered that it was in Amy's, for the first thing she did was to march me over to the typewriter and say: "You've had it, Sam. We'll dispose with the wedding march—just get your friend Arthur here to marry us."

"Arthur?"

"The captain," she said. "We're on the high seas and he's empowered to perform marriages."

Vern looked at me and shrugged, meaning, you asked for this one, boy. And I looked at him and shrugged, meaning, it could be worse.

And indeed it could. We'd got our ship; we'd got our ship's company—because, naturally, there wasn't any use stealing a big ship for just a couple of us. We'd had to manage to get a sizable colony aboard. That was the whole idea.

The world, in fact, was ours. It could have been very much worse indeed, even though Arthur was laughing so hard as he performed the ceremony that he jammed up all his keys.

CREATION MYTHS OF THE
RECENTLY EXTINCT

"Why," Bill Moyers asked recently, when he was presented the fourth annual Global Environment Citizen Award by the Center for Health and the Global Environment at Harvard Medical School, "are we stealing our children's and grandchildren's future? Betraying their trust? Despoiling their world?" He was referring to the systematic destruction of our environment by pollution, by destruction of natural habitats, and by other means.

He had several reasons, none of them very cheerful. They included greed and blind self-interest.

It is difficult to fathom the logic of those who would ignore the evidence of their eyes (and noses, in some cases) and pollute the cradle of humanity knowing that their children and grandchildren will inherit their mess.

Then again, one good war could do the trick much more quickly. This 1994 tale offers a brief, pungent view by an outsider.

When the check team for the Great Galactics got within sensor range of their new colony site the captain summoned them to the ship's centrum. They came reluctantly. Although they had each spent as much time as possible in their own quarters—sleeping, sulking, working on their own projects or merely hiding from the rest—the interminable flight had made them thoroughly sick of each other's presence.

Still, at first, they were delighted with what the sensors revealed. The little blue planet was right where the original surveyors had reported it, sixty-odd million years before . . . but then details began to emerge.

"Oh, yuck," cried the captain, writhing in revulsion. "We're in trouble here! The place is *infested*. It's got *living things* all over it again."

That was the worst of news. The Great Galactics didn't care to share the planets they inhabited with any kind of living things but themselves. The deputy moaned, "What are we going to do now?"

The captain gave him a brief stare of contempt. "Think it through," he ordered. "As I see it, we have two options. We can go back to Galactic Central and report failure. Or we can clean it up some way or another. Which would you prefer?" The collective shudder was answer enough. "Right, then. How do we go about the cleanup?"

There was silence for a moment, until the political representative offered, "We could tickle the star until it went nova and burned the planet clean."

"With our budget? Get real."

"Or we could dump a big asteroid on it and kill everything off that way," the deputy captain said hopefully.

"The survey team tried that sixty-five million years ago, and all they did was get rid of the big scaly things with the sharp teeth. No, we need something *thorough* and *cheap*. Anybody else got any ideas?"

There was silence for a moment, and then the most junior member of the expedition raised his feeler. "You know I've been working in my shop to pass the time," he said diffidently. "Well, I've come up with a little invention that might help us out here. I call it a 'Black Monolith.'"

"We don't have time for your silly contraptions," the captain said menacingly.

The junior shivered, but stuck to his guns. "I think it might do the trick," he insisted. "This Black Monolith thing of mine is an intelligence stimulator. What we do with it, we set it down among those little furry things down there—" he meant the australopithecines, but that word had not been invented—"and it will teach them to use sticks and bones and things to hit other things. That's to say, they'll learn to use *tools*. And then that would mean that they'd need to use their 'hands,' as I call them, in more complicated and subtle ways, which would mean that before long they'd develop a more complex nervous system in their 'hands' and 'arms'—and, ultimately, even a more elaborate *central* nervous system in their 'brains.' Do you see what that means? Those little animals could evolve toward intelligence."

"By the Great Blast," the captain swore, "what's got into you? Vermin are bad enough, but do you think the Great Galactics will sit still for *intelligent* vermin?"

"No, I think it would really work out," the junior said, growing braver. "See, once the Monolith taught them to use tools in the first place they wouldn't stop there. They'd go right on inventing more tools, of all different kinds—simple things like wheels and levers at first, but then they'd go on to much more complicated ones. Before you know it they'd start making machines, and discovering chemistry, and inventing vehicles; why, in a million revolutions of this planet or so—long before the first colony gets here from Galactic Central—there'd be billions of them."

"And then?"

"Well, then, what comes with all that kind of primitive industrialization? You know the answer to that as well as I do: Pollution! Ecological destruction! Trust me, Captain. All we have to do is get them started, and those little creatures'll have the planet scorched sterile in no time!"

THE MEETING

(with C. M. Kornbluth)

Frederik Pohl has collaborated with many other writers. When he was just starting out, he wrote many stories with other aspiring science fiction writers; since then he's written not just stories, but novels, too, with Jack Williamson, Lester del Rey, and C. M. Kornbluth. And there are probably others.

His collaborations with Kornbluth were perhaps the most fruitful. Their novel *The Space Merchants* was, and remains, a huge success, one of the classic SF novels of the 1950s. Pohl and Kornbluth collaborated on other very good novels, and on a number of terrific stories. Unfortunately, C. M. Kornbluth died way too young, in 1964, or there's no doubt they would have collaborated successfully for a long time.

"The Meeting," which won the Hugo Award in 1973 for best short story, is one of their finer collaborations. Completed after Kornbluth's death, it is a thoughtful, challenging story about a modern dilemma with no easy answers.

Harry Vladek was too large a man for his Volkswagen, but he was too poor a man to trade it in, and as things were going he was going to stay that way a long time. He applied the brakes carefully ("Master cylinder's leaking like a sieve, Mr. Vladek; what's the use of just fixing up the linings?"—but the estimate was a hundred and twenty-eight dollars, and where was it going to come from?) and parked in the neatly graveled lot. He squeezed out of the door, the upsetting telephone call from Dr. Nicholson on his mind, locked the car up and went into the school building.

The Parent-Teachers Association of the Bingham County School for Exceptional Children was holding its first meeting of the term. Of the twenty people already there, Vladek knew only Mrs. Adler, the principal, or headmistress, or owner of the school. She was the one he needed to talk to most, he thought. Would there be any chance to see her privately? Right now she sat across the room at her scuffed golden oak desk in a posture chair, talking in low, rapid tones with a gray-haired woman in a tan suit. A teacher? She seemed too old to be a parent, although his wife had told him some of the kids seemed to be twenty or more.

It was 8:30 A.M. and the parents were still driving up to the school, a converted building that had once been a big country house—almost a mansion. The living room was full of elegant reminders of that. *Two* chandeliers. Intricate vine-leaf molding on the plaster above the dropped ceiling. The pink-veined white marble fireplace, unfortunately prominent because of the unsuitable andirons, too cheap and too small, that now stood in it. Golden oak sliding double doors to the hall. And visible through them a grim, fireproof staircase of concrete and steel. They must, Vladek thought, have had to rip out a beautiful wooden thing to install the fireproof stairs for compliance with the state school laws.

People kept coming in, single men, single women, and occasionally a couple. He wondered how the couples managed their baby-sitting problem. The subtitle on the school's letterhead was "an institution for emotionally disturbed and cerebrally damaged children capable of education." Harry's nine-year-old Thomas was one of the emotionally disturbed ones. With a taste of envy he wondered if cerebrally damaged children could be baby-sat by any reasonably competent grownup. Thomas could not. The Vladeks had not had an evening out together since he was two, so that tonight Margaret was holding the fort at home, no doubt worrying herself sick about the call from Dr. Nicholson, while Harry was representing the family at the PTA.

As the room filled up, chairs were getting scarce. A young couple was standing at the end of the row near him, looking around for a pair of empty seats. "Here," he said to them. "I'll move over." The woman smiled politely and the man said thanks. Emboldened by an ashtray on the empty seat in front of him, Harry pulled out his pack of cigarettes and offered it to them, but it turned out they were nonsmokers. Harry lit up anyway, listening to what was going on around him.

Everybody was talking. One woman asked another, "How's the gall bladder? Are they going to take it out after all?" A heavy, balding man said to a short man with bushy sideburns, "Well, my accountant says the tuition's medically deductible if the school is for pyscho*somatic*, not just for psycho. That we've got to clear up." The short man told him positively, "Right, but all you need is a doctor's letter; he recommends the school, refers the child to the school." And a very young woman said intensely, "Dr. Shields was very optimistic, Mrs. Clerman. He says without a doubt the thyroid will make Georgie accessible. And then—" A light-coffee-colored black man in an aloha shirt told a plump woman, "He really pulled a wing-ding over the weekend, two stitches in his face, busted my fishing pole in three places." And the woman said. "They get so bored. My little girl has this thing about crayons, so that rules out coloring books altogether. You wonder what you can do."

Harry finally said to the young man next to him, "My name's Vladek. I'm Tommy's father; he's in the beginners group."

"That's where ours is," said the young man. "He's Vern. Six years old. Blond like me. Maybe you've seen him."

Harry did not try very hard to remember. The two or three times he had picked Tommy up after class he had not been able to tell one child from another in the great bustle of departure. Coats, handkerchiefs, hats, one little girl who always hid in the supply closet and a little boy who never wanted to go home and hung onto the teacher. "Oh, yes," he said politely.

The young man introduced himself and his wife; they were named Murray and Celia Logan. Harry leaned over the man to shake the wife's hand, and she said, "Aren't you new here?"

"Yes. Tommy's been in the school a month. We moved in from Elmira to be near it." He hesitated, then added, "Tommy's nine, but the reason he's in the beginners group is that Mrs. Adler thought it would make the adjustment easier."

Logan pointed to a suntanned man in the first row. "See that fellow with the glasses? He moved here from *Texas*. Of course, he's got money."

"It must be a good place," Harry said questioningly.

Logan grinned, his expression a little nervous.

"How's your son?" Harry asked.

"That little rascal," said Logan. "Last week I got him another copy of the *My Fair Lady* album, I guess he's used up four or five of them, and he goes around singing 'luv-er-ly, luv-er-ly.' But *look* at you? No."

"Mine doesn't talk," said Harry.

Mrs. Logan said judiciously, "Ours talks. Not *to* anybody, though. It's like a wall."

"I know," said Harry, and pressed. "Has, ah, has Vern shown much improvement with the school?"

Murray Logan pursed his lips. "I would say, yes. The bedwetting's not too good, but life's a great deal smoother in some ways. You know, you don't hope for a dramatic breakthrough. But in little things, day by day, it goes smoother. Mostly smoother. Of course there are setbacks."

Harry nodded, thinking of seven years of setbacks, and two years of growing worry and puzzlement before that. He said, "Mrs. Adler told me that, for instance, a special outbreak of destructiveness might mean something like a plateau in speech therapy. So the child fights it and breaks out in some other direction."

"That too," said Logan, "but what I meant was, you know, the ones you don't expect." He brooded silently a moment, then said with relief, "Oh, they're starting."

Vladek nodded, stubbing out his cigarette and absent-mindedly lighting another. His stomach was knotting up again. He wondered at these other parents, who seemed so safe and, well, untouched. Wasn't it the same with them as with Margaret and himself? And it had been a long time since either of them had felt the world comfortable around them, even without Dr. Nicholson pressing for a decision. He forced himself to lean back and look as tranquil as the others.

Mrs. Adler was tapping her desk with a ruler. "I think everybody who is coming is here," she said. She leaned against the desk and waited for the room to quiet down. She was short, dark, plump and surprisingly pretty. She did not look at all like a competent professional. She looked so unlike her role that, in fact, Harry's heart had sunk three months ago when their correspondence about admitting Tommy had been climaxed by the long trip from Elmira for the interview. He had expected a steel-gray lady with rimless glasses . . . a Valkyrie in a white smock like the nurse who had held wriggling, screaming Tommy while waiting for the suppository to quiet him down for his first EEG . . . a disheveled old fraud . . . he didn't know what. Anything except this pretty young woman. Another blind alley, he had thought in despair. Another, after a hundred too many already. First, "Wait for him to outgrow it." He doesn't. Then, "We must reconcile ourselves to God's will." But you don't want to. Then give him the prescription three times a day for three months. And it doesn't work. Then chase around for six months with the Child Guidance Clinic to find out it's only letterheads and one circuit-riding doctor who doesn't have time for anything. Then, after four dreary, weepy weeks of soul-searching, the State Training School, and find out it has an eight-year waiting list. Then the private custodial school, and find they're fifty-five hundred dollars a year—without medical treatment! —and where do you get fifty-five hundred dollars a year? And all the time everybody warns you, as if you didn't know it: "Hurry! Do something! Catch it early! This is the critical stage! Delay is fatal!" And then this soft-looking little woman; how could she do anything?

She had rapidly shown him how. She had questioned Margaret and Harry incisively, turned to Tommy, rampaging through that same room like a rogue bull, and turned his rampage into a game. In three minutes he was happily experimenting with an indestructible old windup cabinet Victrola, and Mrs. Adler was saying to the Vladeks, "Don't count on a miracle cure. There isn't any. But improvements, yes, and I think we can help Tommy."

Perhaps she had, thought Vladek bleakly. Perhaps she was helping as much as anyone ever could.

Meanwhile Mrs. Adler had quickly and pleasantly welcomed the parents, suggested they remain for coffee and get to know each other, and introduced the PTA president, a Mrs. Rose, tall, prematurely gray and very executive. "This being the first meeting of the term," she said, "there are no minutes to be read; so we'll get to the committee work reports. What about the transportation problem, Mr. Baer?"

The man who got up was old. More than sixty; Harry wondered what it was like to have your life crowned with a late retarded child. He wore all the trappings of success— a four-hundred-dollar suit, an electronic wristwatch, a large gold fraternal ring. In a slight German accent he said, "I was to the district school board and they are not cooperating. My lawyer looked it up and the trouble is all one word. What the law says, the school board may, that is the word, may reimburse parents of handicapped children for transportation to private schools. Not shall, you understand, but may. They were very frank with me. They said they just didn't want to spend the money. They had the impression we're all rich people here."

Slight sour laughter around the room.

"So my lawyer made an appointment, and we appeared before the full board and presented the case—we don't care, reimbursement, a school bus, anything so we can relieve the transportation burden a little. The answer was no." He shrugged and remained standing, looking at Mrs. Rose, who said:

"Thank you, Mr. Baer. Does anybody have any suggestions?"

A woman said angrily, "Put some heat on them. We're all voters!"

A man said, "Publicity, that's right. The principle is perfectly clear in the law, one taxpayer's child is supposed to get the same service as another taxpayer's child. We should write letters to the papers."

Mr. Baer said, "Wait a minute. Letters I don't think mean anything, but I've got a public relations firm; I'll tell them to take a little time off my food specialties and use it for the school. They can use their own know-how, how to do it; they're the experts."

This was moved, seconded and passed, while Murray Logan whispered to Vladek, "He's Marijane Garlic Mayonnaise. He had a twelve-year-old girl in very bad shape that Mrs. Adler helped in her old private class. He bought this building for her, along with a couple of other parents."

Harry Vladek was musing over how it felt to be a parent who could buy a building for a school that would help your child, while the committee reports continued. Some time later, to Harry's dismay, the business turned to financing, and there was a vote to hold a fund-raising theater party for which each couple with a child in the school would have to sell "at least" five pairs of orchestra seats at sixty dollars a pair. Let's get this straightened out now, he thought, and put up his hand.

"My name is Harry Vladek," he said when he was recognized, "and I'm brand-new here. In the school and in the county. I work for a big insurance company, and I was lucky enough to get a transfer here so my boy can go to the school. But I just don't know anybody yet that I can sell tickets to for sixty dollars. That's an awful lot of money for my kind of people."

Mrs. Rose said, "It's an awful lot of money for most of us. You can get rid of your tickets, though. We've got to. It doesn't matter if you try a hundred people and ninety-five say no just as long as the others say yes."

He sat down, already calculating. Well, Mr. Crine at the office. He was a bachelor and he did go to the theater. Maybe work up an office raffle for another pair. Or two pairs. Then there was, let's see, the real estate dealer who had sold them the house, the lawyer they'd used for the closing—

Well. It had been explained to him that the tuition, while decidedly not nominal, eighteen hundred dollars a year in fact, did not cover the cost per child. Somebody had to pay for the speech therapist, the dance therapist, the full-time psychologist and the part-time psychiatrist, and all the others and it might as well be Mr. Crine at the office. And the lawyer.

And half an hour later Mrs. Rose looked at the agenda, checked off an item and said, "That seems to be all for tonight. Mr. and Mrs. Perry brought us some very nice cook-ies, and we all know that Mrs. Howe's coffee is out of this world. They're in the begin-ners' room, and we hope you'll all stay to get acquainted. The meeting is adjourned."

Harry and the Logans joined the polite surge to the beginners room, where Tommy spent his mornings. "There's Miss Hackett," said Celia Logan. That was the beginners' teacher. She saw them and came over, smiling. Harry had seen her only in a tentlike smock, her armor against chocolate milk, finger paints and sudden jets from the "water play" corner of the room. Without it she was handsomely middle-aged in a green pants suit.

"I'm glad you parents have met," she said. "I wanted to tell you that your little boys are getting along nicely. They're forming a sort of conspiracy against the others in the class. Vern swipes their toys and gives them to Tommy."

"He *does?*" cried Logan.

"Yes, indeed. I think he's beginning to relate. And, Mr. Vladek, Tommy's taken his thumb out of his mouth for minutes at a time. At least half a dozen times this morning, without my saying a word."

Harry said excitedly, "You know, I thought I noticed he was tapering off. I couldn't be sure. You're positive about that?"

"Absolutely," she said. "And I bluffed him into drawing a face. He gave me that glare of his when the others were drawing; so I started to take the paper away. He grabbed it back and scribbled a kind of Picasso-ish face in one second flat. I wanted to save it for Mrs. Vladek and you, but Tommy got it and shredded it in that methodical way he has."

"I wish I could have seen it," said Vladek.

"There'll be others. I can see the prospect of real improvement in your boys," she said, including the Logans in her smile. "I have a private case afternoons that's really tricky. A nine-year-old boy, like Tommy. He's not bad except for one thing. He thinks Donald Duck is out to get him. His parents somehow managed to convince themselves for two years that he was kidding them, in spite of three broken TV picture tubes. Then they went to a psychiatrist and learned the score. Excuse me, I want to talk to Mrs. Adler."

Logan shook his head and said, "I guess we could be worse off, Vladek. Vern giving something to another boy! How do you like that?"

"I like it," his wife said radiantly.

"And did you hear about that other boy? Poor kid. When I hear about something like that— And then there was the Baer girl. I always think it's worse when it's a little girl because, you know, you worry with little girls that somebody will take advantage; but our boys'll make out, Vladek. You heard what Miss Hackett said."

Harry was suddenly impatient to get home to his wife. "I don't think I'll stay for coffee, or do they expect you to?"

"No, no, leave when you like."

"I have a half-hour drive," he said apologetically and went through the golden oak doors, past the ugly but fireproof staircase, out onto the graveled parking lot. His real reason was that he wanted very much to get home before Margaret fell asleep so he could tell her about the thumb-sucking. Things were happening, definite things, after only a month. And Tommy drew a face. And Miss Hackett said—

He stopped in the middle of the lot. He had remembered about Dr. Nicholson, and besides what was it, exactly, that Miss Hackett had said? Anything about a normal life? Not anything about a cure? "Real improvement," she said, but improvement how far?

He lit a cigarette, turned and plowed his way back through the parents to Mrs. Adler. "Mrs. Adler," he said, "may I see you just for a moment?"

She came with him immediately out of earshot of the others. "Did you enjoy the meeting, Mr. Vladek?"

"Oh, sure. What I wanted to see you about is that I have to make a decision. I don't know what to do. I don't know who to go to. It would help a lot if you could tell me, well, what are Tommy's chances?"

She waited a moment before she responded. "Are you considering committing him, Mr. Vladek?" she demanded.

"No, it's not exactly that. It's—well, what can you tell me, Mrs. Adler? I know a month isn't much. But is he ever going to be like everybody else?"

He could see from her face that she had done this before and had hated it. She said patiently, " 'Everybody else,' Mr. Vladek, includes some terrible people who just don't happen, technically, to be handicapped. Our objective isn't to make Tommy like 'everybody else.' It's just to help him to become the best and most rewarding Tommy Vladek he can."

"Yes, but what's going to happen later on? I mean, if Margaret and I—if anything happens to us?"

She was suffering. "There is simply no way to know, Mr. Vladek," she said gently. "I wouldn't give up hope. But I can't tell you to expect miracles."

Margaret wasn't asleep; she was waiting up for him, in the small living room of the small new house. "How was he?" Vladek asked, as each of them had asked the other on returning home for seven years.

She looked as though she had been crying, but she was calm enough. "Not too bad. I had to lie down with him to get him to go to bed. He took his gland-gunk well, though. He licked the spoon."

"That's good," he said and told her about the drawing of the face, about the conspiracy with little Vern Logan, about the thumb-sucking. He could see how pleased she was, but she only said: "Dr. Nicholson called again."

"I told him not to bother you!"

"He didn't bother me, Harry. He was very nice. I promised him you'd call him back."

"It's eleven o'clock, Margaret. I'll call him in the morning."

"No, I said tonight, no matter what time. He's waiting, and he said to be sure and reverse the charges."

"I wish I'd never answered the son of a bitch's letter," he burst out and then, apologetically: "Is there any coffee? I didn't stay for it at the school."

She had put the water on to boil when she heard the car whine into the driveway, and the instant coffee was already in the cup. She poured it and said, "You have to talk to him, Harry. He has to know tonight."

"Know tonight! Know tonight," he mimicked savagely. He scalded his lips on the coffee cup and said, "What do you want me to do, Margaret? How do I make a decision like this? Today I picked up the phone and called the company psychologist, and when his secretary answered, I said I had the wrong number. I didn't know what to say to him."

"I'm not trying to pressure you, Harry. But he has to know."

Vladek put down the cup and lit his fiftieth cigarette of the day. The little dining room—it wasn't that, it was a half breakfast alcove off the tiny kitchen, but they called it a dining room to each other—was full of Tommy. The new paint on the wall where Tommy had peeled off the cups-and-spoons wallpaper. The Tommy-proof latch on the stove. The one odd aqua seat that didn't match the others on the kitchen chairs, where Tommy had methodically gouged it with the handle of his spoon. He said, "I know what my mother would tell me, talk to the priest. Maybe I should. But we've never even been to Mass here."

Margaret sat down and helped herself to one of his cigarettes. She was still a good-looking woman. She hadn't gained a pound since Tommy was born, although she usually looked tired. She said, carefully and straightforwardly, "We agreed, Harry. You said you would talk to Mrs. Adler, and you've done that. We said if she didn't think Tommy would ever straighten out we'd talk to Dr. Nicholson. I know it's hard on you, and I know I'm not much help. But I don't know what to do, and I have to let you decide."

Harry looked at his wife, lovingly and hopelessly, and at that moment the phone rang. It was, of course, Dr. Nicholson.

"I haven't made a decision," said Harry Vladek at once. "You're rushing me, Dr. Nicholson."

The distant voice was calm and assured. "No, Mr. Vladek, it's not me that's rushing you. The other little boy's heart gave out an hour ago. That's what's rushing you."

"You mean he's dead?" cried Vladek.

"He's on the heart-lung machine, Mr. Vladek. We can hold him for at least eighteen hours, maybe twenty-four. The brain is all right. We're getting very good waves on the oscilloscope. The tissue match with your boy is satisfactory. Better than satisfactory. There's a flight out of JFK at six fifteen in the morning, and I've reserved space for yourself, your wife and Tommy. You'll be met at the airport. You can be here by noon; so we have time. Only just time, Mr. Vladek. It's up to you now."

Vladek said furiously, "I can't decide that! Don't you understand? I don't know how."

"I do understand, Mr. Vladek," said the distant voice and, strangely, Vladek thought, it seemed he did. "I have a suggestion. Would you like to come down anyhow? I think it might help you to see the other boy, and you can talk to his parents. They feel they owe you something even for going this far, and they want to thank you."

"Oh, no!" cried Vladek.

The doctor went on: "All they want is for their boy to have a life. They don't expect anything but that. They'll give you custody of that child—your child, yours and theirs. He's a very fine little boy, Mr. Vladek. Eight years old. Reads beautifully. Makes model airplanes. They let him ride his bike because he was so sensible and reliable, and the accident wasn't his fault. The truck came right up on the sidewalk and hit him."

Harry was trembling. "That's like giving me a bribe," he said harshly. "That's telling me I can trade Tommy in for somebody smarter and nicer."

"I didn't mean it that way, Mr. Vladek. I only wanted you to know the kind of boy you can save."

"You don't even know the operation's going to work!"

"No," agreed the doctor. "Not positively. I can tell you that we've transplanted animals, including primates, and human cadavers, and one pair of terminal cases; but you're right, we've never had a transplant into a well body. I've shown you all the records, Mr. Vladek. We went over them with your own doctor when we first talked about this possibility, five months ago. This is the first case since then when the match was close and there was a real hope for success, but you're right, it's still unproved. Unless you help us prove it. For what it's worth, I think it will work. But no one can be sure."

Margaret had left the kitchen, but Vladek knew where she was from the scratchy click in the earpiece: in the bedroom, listening on the extension phone. He said at last, "I can't say now, Dr. Nicholson. I'll call you back—in half an hour. I can't do any more than that right now."

"That's a great deal, Mr. Vladek. I'll be waiting right here for your call."

Harry sat down and drank the rest of his coffee. You had to be an expert in a lot of things to get along, he was thinking. What did he know about brain transplants? In one way, a lot. He knew that the surgery part was supposed to be straightforward, but the tissue rejection was the problem, but Dr. Nicholson thought he had that licked. He knew that every doctor he had talked to, and he had now talked to seven of them, had agreed that medically it was probably sound enough, and that every one of them had carefully clammed up when he got the conversation around to whether it was right. It was his decision, not theirs, they all said, sometimes just by their silence. But who was he to decide?

Margaret appeared in the doorway. "Harry. Let's go upstairs and look at Tommy."

He said harshly, "Is that supposed to make it easier for me to murder my son?"

She said, "We talked that out, Harry, and we agreed it isn't murder. Whatever it is. I only think that Tommy ought to be with us when we decide, even if he doesn't know what we're deciding."

The two of them stood next to the outsize crib that held their son, looking in the night light at the long fair lashes against the chubby cheeks and the pouted lips around the thumb. Reading. Model airplanes. Riding a bike. Against a quick sketch of a face and the occasional, cherished, tempestuous, bruising flurry of kisses.

Vladek stayed there the full half hour and then, as he had promised, went back to the kitchen, picked up the phone and began to dial.

LET THE ANTS TRY

This may seem like another story about nuclear war, and it is set in the future (1960), just after such a war. But this tale, penned in 1949, is quite different, because there's a time machine involved.

We are a hopeful people, and a time machine is a perfect vehicle for second chances—at least that's what Salva Gordy thought before he stepped into the breach. But Frederik Pohl's stories are seldom that simple, and this is no exception.

He credited a friend, George R. Spoerer, for the idea behind this story. Pohl and Spoerer worked together in Midtown Manhattan and lived only four blocks apart. In decent weather they would walk home together. As Pohl wrote in an introduction to a previous reprinting of it, "One night Spoerer said, 'Over the weekend I thought up a science fiction story,' and proceeded to tell me the story as we walked. 'Good story,' I said. 'Why don't you write it?' 'No,' he said, 'I want you to write it.' After about six such exchanges I said I would, and I went home and that evening I did."

Gordy survived the Three-Hour War, even though Detroit didn't; he was on his way to Washington, with his blueprints and models in his bag, when the bombs struck.

He had left his wife behind in the city, and not even a trace of her body was ever found. The children, of course, weren't as lucky as that. Their summer camp was less than twenty miles away, and unfortunately in the direction of the prevailing wind. But they were not in any pain until the last few days of the month they had left to live. Gordy managed to fight his way back through the snarled, frantic airline controls to them. Even though he knew they would certainly die of radiation sickness, and they suspected it, there was still a whole blessed week of companionship before the pain got too bad.

That was about all the companionship Gordy had for the whole year of 1960.

He came back to Detroit, as soon as the radioactivity had died down; he had nowhere else to go. He found a house on the outskirts of the city, and tried to locate someone to buy it from. But the Emergency Administration laughed at him. "Move in, if you're crazy enough to stay."

When Gordy thought about it all, it occurred to him that he was in a sort of state of shock. His fine, trained mind almost stopped functioning. He ate and slept, and when it grew cold he shivered and built fires, and that was all. The War Department wrote him two or three times, and finally a government man came around to ask what had happened to the things that Gordy had promised to bring to Washington. But he looked queerly at the pink, hairless mice that fed unmolested in the filthy kitchen, and he stood a careful distance away from Gordy's hairy face and torn clothes.

He said, "The Secretary sent me here, Mr. Gordy. He takes a personal interest in your discovery."

Gordy shook his head. "The secretary is dead," he said. "They were all killed when Washington went."

"There's a new secretary," the man explained. He puffed on his cigarette and tossed it into the patch Gordy was scrabbling into a truck garden. "Arnold Cavanagh. He knows a great deal about you, and he told me, 'If Salva Gordy has a weapon, we must have it. Our strength has been shattered. Tell Gordy we need his help.' "

Gordy crossed his hands like a lean Buddha.

"I haven't got a weapon," he said.

"You have something that can be used as a weapon. You wrote to Washington, before the war came, and said—"

"The war is over," said Salva Gordy. The government man sighed, and tried again, but in the end he went away. He never came back. The thing, Gordy thought, was undoubtedly written off as a crackpot idea after the man made his report; it was exactly that kind of a discovery, anyhow.

It was May when John de Terry appeared. Gordy was spading his garden. "Give me something to eat," said the voice behind Gordy's back.

Salva Gordy turned around and saw the small, dirty man who spoke. He rubbed his mouth with the back of his hand. "You'll have to work for it," he said.

"All right." The newcomer set down his pack. "My name is John de Terry. I used to live here in Detroit."

Salva Gordy said, "So did I."

Gordy fed the man, and accepted a cigarette from him after they had eaten. The first puffs made him light-headed—it had been that long since he'd smoked—and through the smoke he looked at John de Terry amiably enough. Company would be all right, he thought. The pink mice had been company, of a sort; but it turned out that the mutation that made them hairless had also given them an appetite for meat. And after the morning when he had awakened to find tiny tooth marks in his leg, he'd had to destroy them. And there had been no other animal since, nothing but the ants.

"Are you going to stay?" Gordy asked.

De Terry said, "If I can. What's your name?" When Gordy told him, some of the animal look went out of his eyes, and wonder took its place. "*Doctor* Salva Gordy?" he asked. "Mathematics and physics in Pasadena?"

"Yes, I used to teach at Pasadena."

"And I studied there." John de Terry rubbed absently at his ruined clothes. "That was a long time ago. You didn't know me; I majored in biology. But I knew you."

Gordy stood up and carefully put out the stub of his cigarette. "It was too long ago," he said. "I hardly remember. Shall we work in the garden now?"

Together they sweated in the spring sunlight that afternoon, and Gordy discovered that what had been hard work for one man went quickly enough for two. They worked clear to the edge of the plot before the sun reached the horizon. John de Terry stopped and leaned on his spade, panting.

He gestured to the rank growth beyond Gordy's patch. "We can make a bigger garden," he said. "Clear out that truck, and plant more food. We might even—" He stopped. Gordy was shaking his head.

"You can't clear it out," said Gordy. "It's rank stuff, a sort of crabgrass with a particularly tough root. I can't even cut it. It's all around here, and it's spreading."

De Terry grimaced. "Mutation?"

"I think so. And look." Gordy beckoned to the other man and led him to the very edge of the cleared area. He bent down, picked up something red and wriggling between his thumb and forefinger.

De Terry took it from his hand. "Another mutation?" He brought the thing close to his eyes. "It's almost like an ant," he said. "Except—well, the thorax is all wrong. And it's soft-bodied." He fell silent, examining the thing.

He said something under his breath, and threw the insect from him. "You wouldn't have a microscope, I suppose? No—and yet, that thing is hard to believe. It's an ant, but it doesn't seem to have a tracheal breathing system at all. It's something different."

"Everything's different," Gordy said. He pointed to a couple of abandoned rows. "I had carrots there. At least, I thought they were carrots; when I tried to eat them they made me sick." He sighed heavily. "Humanity has had its chance, John," he said. "The atomic bomb wasn't enough; we had to turn everything into a weapon. Even I, I made a weapon out of something that had nothing to do with war. And our weapons have blown up in our faces."

De Terry grinned. "Maybe the ants will do better. It's their turn now."

"I wish it were." Gordy stirred earth over the boiling entrance to an anthole and watched the insects in their consternation. "They're too small, I'm afraid."

"Why, no. These ants are different, Dr. Gordy. Insects have always been small because their breathing system is so poor. But these are mutated. I think—I think they actually have lungs. They could grow, Dr. Gordy. And if ants were the size of men . . . they'd rule the world."

"Lunged ants!" Gordy's eyes gleamed. "Perhaps they will rule the world, John. Perhaps when the human race finally blows itself up once and for all . . ."

De Terry shook his head, and looked down again at his tattered, filthy clothes. "The next blowup is the last blowup," he said. "The ants come too late, by millions and millions of years."

He picked up his spade. "I'm hungry again, Dr. Gordy," he said.

They went back to the house and, without conversation, they ate. Gordy was preoccupied, and de Terry was too new in the household to force him to talk.

It was sundown when they had finished, and Gordy moved slowly to light a lamp. Then he stopped.

"It's your first night, John," he said. "Come down-cellar. We'll start the generator and have real electric lights in your honor."

De Terry followed the older man down a flight of stairs, groping in the dark. By candlelight they worked over a gasoline generator; it was stiff from disuse, but once it started it ran cleanly. "I salvaged it from my own house," Gordy explained. "The generator—and that."

He swept an arm toward a corner of the basement. "I told you I invented a weapon," he added. "That's it."

De Terry looked. It was as much like a cage as anything, he thought—the height of a man and almost cubical. "What does it do?" he asked.

For the first time in months, Salva Gordy smiled. "I can't tell you in English," he said. "And I doubt that you speak mathematics. The closest I can come is to say that it displaces temporal coordinates. Is that gibberish?"

"It is," said de Terry. "What does it do?"

"Well, the War Department had a name for it—a name they borrowed from H. G. Wells. They called it a Time Machine." He met de Terry's shocked, bewildered stare calmly. "A time machine," he repeated. "You see, John, we can give the ants a chance after all, if you like."

Fourteen hours later they stepped into the cage, its batteries charged again and its strange motor whining . . .

And, forty million years earlier, they stepped out onto quaking, humid soil.

Gordy felt himself trembling, and with an effort managed to stop. "No dinosaurs or saber-toothed tigers in sight," he reported.

"Not for a long time yet," de Terry agreed. Then, "My Lord!"

He looked around him with his mouth open wide. There was no wind, and the air was warm and wet. Large trees were clustered quite thickly around them—or what looked like trees; de Terry decided they were rather some sort of soft-stemmed ferns or fungi. Overhead was deep cloud.

Gordy shivered. "Give me the ants," he ordered.

Silently de Terry handed them over. Gordy poked a hole in the soft earth with his finger and carefully tilted the flask, dropped one of the ant queens he had unearthed in the backyard. From her belly hung a slimy mass of eggs. A few yards away—it should have been farther, he thought, but he was afraid to get too far from de Terry and the machine—he made another hole and repeated the process.

There were eight queens. When the eighth was buried he flung the bottle away and came back to de Terry.

"That's it," he said.

De Terry exhaled. His solemn face cracked in a sudden, embarrassed smile. "I—I guess I feel like God," he said. "Good Lord, Dr. Gordy! Talk about your great moments in history—this is all of them! I've been thinking about it, and the only event I can remember that measures up is the Flood. Not even that. We've created a race!"

"If they survive, we have." Gordy wiped a drop of condensed moisture off the side of his time machine and puffed. "I wonder how they'll get along with mankind," he said.

They were silent for a moment, considering. From somewhere in the fern jungle came a raucous animal cry. Both men looked up in quick apprehension, but moments passed and the animal did not appear.

Finally de Terry said, "Maybe we'd better go back."

"All right." Stiffly they climbed into the closet-sized interior of the time machine.

Gordy stood with his hand on the control wheel, thinking about the ants. Assuming that they survived—assuming that in forty million years they grew larger and developed brains—what would happen? Would men be able to live in peace with them? Would it—might it not make men brothers, joined against an alien race?

Might this thing prevent human war, and—his thoughts took an insane leap—could it have prevented the war that destroyed Gordy's family!

Beside him, de Terry stirred restlessly. Gordy jumped, and turned the wheel, and was in the dark mathematical vortex which might have been a fourth dimension.

They stopped the machine in the middle of a city, but the city was not Detroit. It was not a human city at all.

The machine was at rest in a narrow street, half blocking it. Around them towered conical metal structures, some of them a hundred feet high. There were vehicles moving in the street, one coming toward them and stopping.

"Dr. Gordy!" de Terry whispered. "Do you see them?"

Salva Gordy swallowed. "I see them," he said.

He stepped out of the time machine and stood waiting to greet the race to which he had given life.

For these were the children of ants in the three-wheeled vehicle. Behind a transparent windshield he could see them clearly.

De Terry was standing close behind him now, and Gordy could feel the younger man's body shaking. "They're ugly things," Gordy said mildly.

"Ugly! They're filthy!"

The antlike creatures were as big as a man, but hard-looking and as obnoxious as black beetles. Their eyes, Gordy saw with surprise, had mutated more than their bodies. For, instead of faceted insect eyes, they possessed iris, cornea and pupil—not round, or vertical like a cat's eyes, or horizontal like a horse's eyes, but irregular and blotchy. But they seemed like vertebrate's eyes, and they were strange and unnatural in the parchment blackness of an ant's bulged head.

Gordy stepped forward, and simultaneously the ants came out of their vehicle. For a moment they faced each other, the humans and the ants, silently.

"What do I do now?" Gordy asked de Terry over his shoulder.

De Terry laughed—or gasped. Gordy wasn't sure. "Talk to them," he said. "What else is there to do?"

Gordy swallowed. He resolutely did not attempt to speak in English to these creatures, knowing as surely as he knew his name that English—and probably any other language involving sound—would be incomprehensible to them. But he found himself smiling pacifically to them, and that was of course as bad . . . the things had no expressions of their own, that he could see, and certainly they would have no precedent to help interpret a human smile.

Gordy raised his hand in the semantically sound gesture of peace, and waited to see what the insects would do.

They did nothing.

Gordy bit his lip and, feeling idiotic, bowed stiffly to the ants.

The ants did nothing. De Terry said from behind, "Try talking to them, Dr. Gordy."

"That's silly," Gordy said. "They can't hear." But it was no sillier than anything else. Irritably, but making the words very clear, he said, "We . . . are . . . friends."

The ants did nothing. They just stood there, with the unwinking pupiled eyes fixed on Gordy. They didn't shift from foot to foot as a human might, or scratch themselves, or even show the small movement of human breathing. They just stood there.

"Oh, for heaven's sake," said de Terry. "Here, let me try."

He stepped in front of Gordy and faced the ant-things. He pointed to himself. "I am human," he said. "Mammalian." He pointed to the ants. "You are insects. That—" He pointed to the time machine—"took us to the past, where we made it possible for you to exist." He waited for reaction, but there wasn't any. De Terry clicked his tongue and began again. He pointed to the tapering metal structures. "This is your city," he said.

Gordy, listening to him, felt the hopelessness of the effort. Something disturbed the thin hairs at the back of his skull, and he reached absently to smooth them down. His hand encountered something hard and inanimate—not cold, but, like spongy wood, without temperature at all. He turned around. Behind them were half a dozen larger ants. Drones, he thought—or did ants have drones? "John," he said softly . . . and the inefficient, fragile-looking pincer that had touched him clamped his shoulder. There was no strength to it, he thought at once. Until he moved, instinctively, to get away, and then a thousand sharp serrations slipped through the cloth of his coat and into the skin. It was like catching oneself on a cluster of tiny fishhooks. He shouted, "John! Watch out!"

De Terry, bending low for the purpose of pointing at the caterpillar treads of the ant vehicle, straightened up, startled. He turned to run, and was caught in a step. Gordy heard him yell, but Gordy had troubles of his own and could spare no further attention for de Terry.

When two of the ants had him, Gordy stopped struggling. He felt warm blood roll down his arm, and the pain was like being flayed. From where he hung between the ants, he could see the first two, still standing before their vehicle, still motionless.

There was a sour reek in his nostrils, and he traced it to the ants that held him, and wondered if he smelled as bad to them. The two smaller ants abruptly stirred and moved forward rapidly on eight thin legs to the time machine. Gordy's captors turned and followed them, and for the first time since the scuffle he saw de Terry. The younger man was hanging limp from the lifted forelegs of a single ant, with two more standing guard beside. There was pulsing blood from a wound on de Terry's neck. Unconscious, Gordy thought mechanically, and turned his head to watch the ants at the machine.

It was a disappointing sight. They merely stood there, and no one moved. Then Gordy heard de Terry grunt and swear weakly. "How are you, John?" he called.

De Terry grimaced. "Not very good. What happened?"

Gordy shook his head, and sought for words to answer. But the two ants turned in unison from the time machine and glided toward de Terry, and Gordy's words died in his throat. Delicately one of them extended a foreleg to touch de Terry's chest.

Gordy saw it coming. "John!" he shrieked—and then it was all over, and de Terry's scream was harsh in his ear and he turned his head away. Dimly from the corner of his eye he could see the sawlike claws moving up and down, but there was no life left in de Terry to protest.

Salva Gordy sat against a wall and looked at the ants who were looking at him. If it hadn't been for that which was done to de Terry, he thought, there would really be nothing to complain about.

It was true that the ants had given him none of the comforts that humanity lavishes on even its criminals . . . but they had fed him, and allowed him to sleep—when it suited their convenience, of course—and there were small signs that they were interested in his comfort, in their fashion. When the pulpy mush they first offered him came up thirty minutes later, his multilegged hosts brought him a variety of foods, of which he was able to swallow some fairly palatable fruits. He was housed in a warm room, and, if it had neither chairs nor windows, Gordy thought, that was only because ants had no use for these themselves. And he couldn't ask for them.

That was the big drawback, he thought. That . . . and the memory of John de Terry.

He squirmed on the hard floor until his shoulderblades found a new spot to prop themselves against, and stared again at the committee of ants who had come to see him.

They were working an angular thing that looked like a camera—at least, it had a glittering something that might be a lens. Gordy stared into it sullenly. The sour reek was in his nostrils again . . .

Gordy admitted to himself that things hadn't worked out just as he had planned. Deep under the surface of his mind—just now beginning to come out where he could see it—there had been a furtive hope. He had hoped that the rise of the ants, with the help he had given them, would aid and speed the rise of mankind. For hatred, Gordy knew, started in the recoil from things that were different. A man's first enemy is his family—for he sees them first—but he sides with them against the families across the way. And still his neighbors are allies against the ghettos and Harlems of his town—and his town to him is the heart of the nation—and his nation commands life and death in war.

For Gordy, there had been a buried hope that a separate race would make a whipping-boy for the passions of humanity. And that, if there were struggle, it would not be between man and man, but between the humans . . . and the ants.

There had been this buried hope, but the hope was denied. For the ants simply had not allowed man to rise.

The ants put up their cameralike machine, and Gordy looked up in expectation. Half a dozen of them left, and two stayed on. One was the smallish creature with a bangle on the foreleg which seemed to be his personal jailer; the other a stranger to Gordy, as far as he could tell.

The two ants stood motionless for a period of time that Gordy found tedious. He changed his position, and lay on the floor, and thought of sleeping. But sleep would not come. There was no evading the knowledge that he had wiped out his own race—annihilated them by preventing them from birth, forty million years before his own time. He was like no other murderer since Cain, Gordy thought, and wondered that he felt no blood on his hands.

There was a signal that he could not perceive, and his guardian ant came forward to him, nudged him outward from the wall. He moved as he was directed—out the low exit-hole (he had to navigate it on hands and knees) and down a corridor to the bright day outside.

The light set Gordy blinking. Half blind, he followed the bangled ant across a square to a conical shed. More ants were waiting there, circled around a litter of metal parts. Gordy recognized them at once. It was his time machine, stripped piece by piece.

After a moment the ant nudged him again, impatiently, and Gordy understood what they wanted. They had taken the machine apart for study, and they wanted it put together again.

Pleased with the prospect of something to do with his fingers and his brain, Gordy grinned and reached for the curious ant-made tools . . .

He ate four times, and slept once, never moving from the neighborhood of the cone-shaped shed. And then he was finished.

Gordy stepped back. "It's all yours," he said proudly. "It'll take you anywhere. A present from humanity to you."

The ants were very silent. Gordy looked at them and saw drone-ants in the group, all still as statues.

"Hey!" he said in startlement, unthinking. And then the needle-jawed ant claw took him from behind.

Gordy had a moment of nausea—and then terror and hatred swept it away.

Heedless of the needles that laced his skin, he struggled and kicked against the creatures that held him. One arm came free, leaving gobbets of flesh behind, and his heavy-shod foot plunged into a pulpy eye. The ant made a whistling, gasping sound and stood erect on four hairy legs.

Gordy felt himself jerked a dozen feet into the air, then flung free in the wild, silent agony of the ant. He crashed into the ground, cowering away from the staggering monster. Sobbing, he pushed himself to his feet; the machine was behind him; he turned and blundered into it a step ahead of the other ants, and spun the wheel.

A hollow insect leg, detached from the ant that had been closest to him, was flopping about on the floor of the machine; it had been that close.

Gordy stopped the machine where it had started, on the same quivering, primordial bog, and lay crouched over the controls for a long time before he moved.

He had made a mistake, he and de Terry; there weren't any doubts left at all. And there was . . . there *might* be a way to right it.

He looked out at the Coal Measure forest. The fern trees were not the fern trees he had seen before; the machine had been moved in space. But the time, he knew, was identically the same; trust the machine for that. He thought: I gave the world to the ants, right here. I can take it back. I can find the ants I buried and crush them underfoot . . . or intercept myself before I bury them . . .

He got out of the machine, suddenly panicky. Urgency squinted his eyes as he peered around him.

Death had been very close in the ant city; the reaction still left Gordy limp. And was he safe here? He remembered the violent animal scream he had heard before, and shuddered at the thought of furnishing a casual meal to some dinosaur . . . while the ant queens lived safely to produce their horrid young.

A gleam of metal through the fern trees made his heart leap. Burnished metal here could mean but one thing—the machine!

Around a clump of fern trees, their bases covered with thick club mosses, he ran, and saw the machine ahead. He raced toward it—then came to a sudden stop, slipping on the damp ground. For there were *two* machines in sight.

The farther machine was his own, and through the screening mosses he could see two figures standing in it, his own and de Terry's.

But the nearer was a larger machine, and a strange design.

And from it came a hastening mob—not a mob of men, but of black insect shapes racing toward him.

Of course, thought Gordy, as he turned hopelessly to run—of course, the ants had infinite time to work in. Time enough to build a machine after the pattern of his own—and time to realize what they had to do to him, to insure their own race safety.

Gordy stumbled, and the first of the black things was upon him.

As his panicky lungs filled with air for the last time, Gordy knew what animal had screamed in the depths of the Coal Measure forest.

SPEED TRAP

Systems. Almost anything can be thought of as part of a system. Chaos theory is based on that idea; we don't always see the system at work because we're looking at it from within the system itself or because we don't have the tools to see the entirety of the system.

Dr. Grew, the protagonist of "Speed Trap," isn't a systems man, but because he attends many conferences and meets a lot of scientists in other fields, he's had occasion to think about how systems—better systems—can make him and everyone function much more efficiently, get more done.

The other side of systems: conspiracy theory. The world is full of people who see conspiracies everywhere. Often those who see conspiracies where there are none are very systematic—one might say "obsessive," even "paranoid."

Then again, there are times when paranoia isn't anything but a sane response to a real threat.

Dr. Grew's dilemma—and yours—is to decide what is really going on in this rather tantalizing little puzzler from 1967.

My reservation was for a window seat, up front, because on this particular flight they serve from the front back; but on the seat next to mine, I saw a reservation tag for Gordie MacKenzie. I kept right on going until the hostess hailed me. "Why, Dr. Grew, nice to have you with us again . . ."

I stood blocking the aisle. "Can I switch to a seat back here somewhere, Clara?"

"Why, I think—let me see . . ."

"How about that one?" I didn't see a tag on it.

"Well, it's not a window seat . . ."

"But it's free?"

"Well, let's look." She flipped the seating chart out of her clipboard. "Certainly. May I take your bag?"

"Uh-uh. Work to do." And I did have work to do, too; that was why I didn't want to sit next to MacKenzie. I slouched down in the seat, scowling at the man next to me to indicate that I didn't want to strike up a conversation; he scowled back to show that that suited him fine. I saw MacKenzie come aboard, but he didn't see me.

Just before we took off, I saw Clara bend over him to check his seat belt; and in the same motion, she palmed the reservation card with my name on it. Smart girl. I decided to buy her a drink the next time I found myself in the motel where her crew stayed between flights.

I don't want to give you the idea that I'm a jet-set type who's on first-name terms with every airline stewardess around. The only ones I see enough of at all are a couple on the New York–L.A. run, and a few operating out of O'Hare, and maybe a couple that I see now and then between Huntsville and the Cape—oh, and one Air France girl I've flown with once or twice out of Orly, but only because she gave me a lift in her Citroën one time when there was a *métro* strike and no cabs to be found. Still, come to think of it, well—all right—yes, I guess I do get around a lot. Those are the hazards of the trade. Although my degree's in atmospheric physics, my specialty is signatures—you know, the instrument readings or optical observations that we interpret to mean such-and-such pressure, temperature, chemical composition and so on—and that's a pretty sexy field right now, and I get invited to a lot of conferences. I said "invited." I don't mean in the sense that I can say no. Not if I want to keep enough status in the department to have freedom to do my work. And it's all plushy and kind of fun, at least when I have time to have fun; and really, I've got pretty good at locating a decent restaurant in Cleveland or Albuquerque (try the Mexican food at the airport) and vetoing an inferior wine.

That's funny, too, because I didn't expect it to be this way—not when I was a kid reading Willy Ley's articles and going out to hunt ginseng in the woods around Potsdam (I mean the New York one) so I could earn money and go to MIT and build spaceships. I thought I would be a lean, hungry-eyed scientist in shabby clothes. I thought probably I would never get out of the laboratory (I guess I thought spaceships were designed in laboratories) and I'd waste my health on long night hours over the slide rule. And, as it turns out, what I'm wasting my health on is *truite amandine* and time-zone disorientation.

But I think I know what to do about that.

That's why I didn't want to spend the four and a half hours yakking with Gordie MacKenzie, because, by God, I maybe *do* know what to do about that.

It's not really my field, but I've talked it over with some systems people and they didn't get that polite look people get when you're trying to tell them about their own subject. I'll see if I can explain it. See, there are like twenty conferences and symposia and colloquia a month in any decent-sized field, and you're out of it unless you make a few of them. Not counting workshops and planning sessions and get-the-hell-down-here-Charley-or-we-lose-the-grant meetings. And they do have a way of being all over the place. I haven't slept in my own home all seven nights of any week since Christmas before last, when I had the flu.

Now, question is, what do all the meetings accomplish? I had a theory once that the whole *Gestalt* was planned—I mean, global scatter, jet travel and all. A sort of psychic energizer, designed to keep us all pumped up all the time—after all, if you're going somewhere in a jet at six hundred miles an hour, you know you've got to be doing something important, or else you wouldn't be doing it so fast. But who would plan something like that?

So I gave up that idea and concentrated on ways of doing it better. You know, there really is no more stupid way of communicating information than flying three thousand miles to sit on a gilt chair in a hotel ballroom and listen to twenty-five people read papers at you. Twenty-three of the papers you don't care about anyway, and the twenty-fourth you can't understand because the speaker has a bad accent and, anyway, he's rushing it because he's under time pressure to catch his plane to the next conference, and that one single twenty-fifth paper has cost you four days, including travel time, when you could have read it in your own office in fifteen minutes. And got more out of it, too. Of course, there's the interplay when you find yourself sitting in the coffee shop next to somebody who can explain the latest instrumentation to you because his company's doing the telemetry; you can't get that from reading. But I've noticed there's less and less time for that. And less and less interest, too, maybe, because you get pretty tired of making new friends after about the three hundredth; and you begin to think about what's waiting for you on your desk when you get back, and you remember the time when you got stuck with that damn loudmouthed Egyptian at the I.A.U. in Brussels and had to fight the Suez war for an hour and a half.

All right, you can see what I mean. Waste of time and valuable kerosene jet fuel, right?

Because the pity of it is that electronic information handling is so cheap and easy. I don't know if you've ever seen the Bell Labs' demo of their picture phone—they had it at a couple of meetings—but it's *nearly* like face-to-face. Better than the telephone. You get all the signatures, except maybe the smell of whiskey on the breath or something like that. And that's only one gadget: there's facsimile, telemetry, remote-access computation, teletype—well, there it is, we've got them, why don't we use them? And go farther, too. You know about how they can strip down a taped voice message—leave out the unnecessary parts of speech, edit out the pauses, even drop some of the useless syllables? And you can still understand it perfectly, only at about four hundred words a minute instead of maybe sixty or seventy. (And about half of them repetitions or "What I mean to say.")

Well, that's the systems part; and, as I say, it's not my field. But it's there for the taking—expert opinion, not mine. A couple of the fellows were real hot, and we're going to get together on it as soon as we can find the time.

Maybe you wonder what I have to contribute. I do have something, I think. For example, how about problem-solving approaches to discussions? I've seen some papers that suggest a way of simplifying and pointing up a conference so you could really *confer*. I've even got a pet idea of my own. I call it the Quantum of Debate, the irreducible minimum of argument which each participant in a discussion can use to make one single point and get that understood (or argued or refuted) before he goes on to the next.

Why, if half of what I think is so, then people like me can get things done in—oh, be conservative—a quarter of the time we spend now.

Leaving three quarters of our time for—what? Why, for work! For doing the things that we know we ought to do but can't find the time for. I mean this literally and really and seriously. I honestly think that we can do four times as much work as we do. And I honestly think that this means we can land on Mars in five years instead of twenty, cure leukemia in twelve years instead of fifty, and so on.

Well, that's the picture, and that's why I didn't want to waste the time talking with Gordie MacKenzie. I'd brought all my notes in my briefcase, and four and a half hours was just about enough time to try to pull them all together and make some sort of presentation to show my systems friends and a few others who were interested.

So as soon as we were airborne, I had the little table down and I was sorting out little stacks of paper.

Only it didn't work out.

It's funny how often it doesn't work out—I mean, when you've got something you want to do and you look ahead and see where the time's going to be to do it, and then, all of a sudden, the time's gone and you didn't do it. What it was was that Clara worked her way back with the cocktails—she knew mine, an extra-dry martini with a twist of lemon—and I moved the papers out of her way out of politeness, and then she showed up with the hors d'oeuvres and I put them back in my bag out of hunger, and then I had to decide how I wanted my *tournedos,* and it took almost two hours for dinner, including the wine and the B & B; and although I didn't really want to watch the movie, there's something about seeing all those screens ahead of you, with the hero just making his bombing run on your own screen but shot up and falling in flames on the ones you can see out of the corner of your eye in the forward seats—and back in the briefing room, or even in the pub the night before on the screens in the other row that the film gets to after it gets to yours—all sort of like a cross section of instants of time, a plural "now." Disconcerting. It polarized my attention; of course, the liquor helped; and, anyway, by the time the movie was over, it was time for the second round of coffee and mints, and then the seat-belt sign was on and we were over the big aluminum dome on Mount Wilson, coming in, and I never had found the time to do my sorting. Well, I was used to that. I'd never found any ginseng back in Potsdam, either. I had to get through school on a scholarship.

I checked in, washed my face and went down to the meeting room just in time for a very dull tutorial on clear-air turbulence in planetary atmospheres. There was quite a good turnout, maybe seventy or eighty people in the room; but what they thought they were getting out of it, I cannot imagine, so I picked up a program and ducked out.

Somebody by the coffee machine called to me. "Hi, Chip."

I went over and shook his hand, a young fellow named Resnik from the little college where I'd got my bachelor's, looking bored and angry. He was with someone I didn't know, tall and gray-haired and bankerish. "Dr. Ramos, this is Chesley Grew. Chip, Dr. Ramos. He's with NASA—I think it's NASA?"

"No, I'm with a foundation," he said. "It's a pleasure to meet you, Dr. Grew. I've followed your work."

"Thank you. Thank you very much." I would have liked a cup of coffee, but I didn't particularly want to stand there talking to them while I drank it, so I said, "Well, I'd better get checked in, so if you'll excuse me . . ."

"Come off it, Chip," said Larry Resnik. "I saw you check in half an hour ago. You just want to go up to your room and work."

That was embarrassing, a little. I didn't mind it with Resnik, but I didn't know the other fellow. He grinned and said, "Larry tells me you're like that. Matter of fact, when you went by, he said you'd be back out in thirty seconds, and you were."

"Well. Clear-air turbulence isn't my subject, really . . ."

"Oh, nobody's blaming you. God knows not. Care for some coffee?"

The only thing to do was to be gracious about it, so I said, "Yes, please. Thanks." I watched him take a cup and fill it from the big silver urn. He looked vaguely familiar, but I couldn't place him. "Did we meet at the Dallas Double-A S sessions?"

"I'm afraid not. Sugar? No, I've actually been to very few of these meetings, but I've read some of your papers."

I stirred my coffee. "Thank you, Dr. Ramos." One of the things I've learned to do is repeat a name as often as I can so I won't forget it. About half the time I forget it anyway, of course. "I'll be speaking tomorrow morning, Dr. Ramos. 'A Photometric Technique for Deriving Slopes from Planetary Fly-bys.' Nothing much that doesn't follow from what they've done at Langley, I'm afraid."

"Yes, I saw the abstract."

"But you'll get your brownie points for reading it, eh?" said Larry. He was breathing heavily. "How many does that make this year?"

"Well, a lot." I tried to drink my coffee both rapidly and inconspicuously. Larry seemed in an unhappy mood.

"That's what we were talking about when you came in," he said. "Thirty papers a year and committee reports between times. When was the last time you spent a solid month at your desk? I know, in my own department . . ."

I could feel myself growing interested and I didn't want to be, I wanted to get back to my notes. I took another gulp of my coffee.

"You know what Fred Hoyle said?"

"I don't think so, Larry."

"He said the minute a man does anything, anything at all, the whole world enters into a conspiracy to keep him from ever doing it again. Program chairmen invite him to read papers. Trustees put him onto committees. Newspaper reporters call him up to interview him. Television shows ask him to appear with a comic, a bandleader and a girl singer, to talk about whether there's life on Mars."

"And people who sympathize with him buttonhole him on his way out of meetings," said Dr. Ramos. He chuckled. "Really, Dr. Grew. We'll understand if you just keep on going."

"I'm not even sure it's this world," said Larry.

He was not only irritable, he was hardly making sense. "For that matter," he added, "I haven't even really done anything yet. Not like you, Chip. But I can, someday."

"Don't be modest," said Dr. Ramos. "And look, we're making a lot of noise here. Why don't we find some place to sit down and talk—unless you really do want to get back to your work, Dr. Grew?"

But you see, I was already more than half convinced that this *was* my work, to talk to Larry and Dr. Ramos; and what we finally did was go up to my room and then up to Larry's where he had a Rand Corporation report in his bag with some notes I'd sent him once, and we never did get back to the meeting room. Along about ten we had dinner sent up, and that was where we stayed, drinking cold coffee off the set-up table and sparingly drinking bourbon out of a bottle Larry had brought along, and I told them everything I'd ever thought about a systems approach to the transmission of technological information. And what it implied. And Dr. Ramos was with it at every step, the best listener either of us had ever had, though most of what he said was, "Yes, of course," and "I see." There really was a lot in it. I'd believed it, sitting by myself and computing, like a child anticipating Christmas, how much *work* I could get done for a couple K a year in amortization of systems and overhead. And with the two of them, I was sure of it. It was a giddy kind of evening. Toward the end, we even began to figure out how quickly we could colonize Mars and launch a fleet of interstellar space liners, with all the working time of the existing people spent *working;* and then there was a pause and Larry got up and threw back the glass French window and we looked out on his balcony. Twenty stories up, and Los Angeles out in front of us and a thunderstorm brewing over the southern hills. The fresh air cleared my head for a moment and then made me realize, first, that I was sleepy and, second, that I had to read that damned paper in about seven hours.

"We'd better call it a day," said Dr. Ramos.

Larry started to object, then grinned. "All right for you old fellows," he said. "Anyway, I want to look at those notes of yours by myself, Chip, if you don't mind."

"Just so you don't lose them," I said, and turned to go back to my room and get into my bed and lie with my eyes wide open, smiling to myself, before I fell asleep to dream about fifty weeks a year working at my trade.

Even so, I woke easily the moment the hotel clock buzzed by my head. We'd fixed it to have breakfast in Larry's room so I could reclaim my notes and maybe chat for a moment before the morning session began; and when I got to his floor, I saw Dr. Ramos padding toward me. "Morning," he said. "I just woke up two honeymooners who didn't appreciate it. Wasn't Larry's room 2051?"

"It's 2052. The other way." He grinned and fell into step and told me a fast and quite funny honeymooner joke, timing the punch line just as we reached Larry's door.

He didn't answer my knock. Still laughing, I said, "You try." But there was no answer to Dr. Ramos's knock, either.

I stopped laughing. "He couldn't have forgotten we were coming, could he?"

"Try the door, why don't you?"

And I did and it opened easily.

But Larry wasn't in the room. The door to the bath was standing open and so was the balcony window, and no Larry. His bed was rumpled but empty.

"I don't think he's gone out," said Dr. Ramos. "Look, his shoes are still there."

The balcony wasn't big enough to hide on, but I walked over and looked at it. Rain-slick and narrow, all that was on it were a couple of soaked deck chairs and some cigarette butts.

"Looks like he was out here," I said; and then, feeling melodramatic, I leaned over the rail and looked down; and it wasn't actually melodramatic after all, because there in the curve of the hotel's sweeping front, on the rim of a fountain, something was sprawled, and a man was standing by it, shouting at the doorman. It was too early for much noise, and I could hear his voice faintly coming up the two hundred vertical feet between us and what was left of Larry.

They canceled the morning session but decided to go ahead in the afternoon, and I got into a long, bruising fight with Gordie MacKenzie because he wanted to give his paper when it was scheduled, at three in the afternoon, and I'd been reshuffled into that time and I just wasn't feeling cheerful enough to let him get away with anything. Not after spending two hours with the coroner's men and the hotel staff, trying to help them figure out why Larry would have jumped or slipped off the balcony, and especially not after finding out that he had had all my notes in his hand when he jumped and they were now in sticky, sloppy clusters all over Los Angeles County.

So I was about fed up. I once heard Krafft Ehricke give what I would figure to be a twelve-minute paper in three minutes and forty-five seconds, and I tried to beat his record and pretty nearly made it. Then I threw everything I owned into my suitcase and checked out, figuring to head right out to the airport and get on the first plane going home.

But the clerk said, "I have a message for you, Mr. Grew. Dr. Ramos asked you not to leave without seeing him."

"Thanks," I said, after a moment of debating whether to do anything about it or not; but as it turned out, I didn't have to make the decision. Ramos came hurrying toward me across the lobby, his friendly face concerned.

"I thought you'd be leaving," he said. "Give me twenty minutes of your time first."

I hesitated and he snapped a finger at a bellboy. "Here. Let him take care of your bag and let's go down and have a cup of coffee." So I let him lead me to the outdoor patio by the coffee shop, warm and clean now after the rain. I wondered if he recognized the place where Larry had hit, but I'm not sensitive about that sort of thing and apparently neither was he. He really had a commanding presence when he wanted to. He had a waitress beside us before we had quite slid our chairs closer to the table, sent her after coffee and sandwiches without consulting me and started in on me without a pause. "Chip," he said, "don't blow it. I'm sorry about your notes. But I don't want to see you give up."

I leaned back in my chair, feeling very weary. "Oh, that I won't do, Dr. Ramos . . ."

"Call me Laszlo."

"That I won't do, Laszlo. As a matter of fact, I've been thinking about it already."

"I knew you would be."

"I figure that by cutting out a couple of meetings next week—I can use Larry's death as an excuse, some way; I'll use anything, actually—I can reconstruct most of them from memory. Well, maybe not in a week, come to think of it. I'll have to send for copies of some of the reports. But sooner or later . . ."

"Right. That's what I want to talk to you about." The girl brought the coffee and sandwiches and he waved her away briskly as soon as she'd set them down. "You see, you're the man I came here to see."

I looked at him. "You're interested in photometry?"

"No. Not your paper—your idea. What we were talking about all night, for God's sake. I didn't know it was you I wanted until Resnik mentioned you yesterday. But after last night, I was sure."

"I already have a job, Dr.—Laszlo."

"And I'm not offering you a job."

"Then, what . . ."

"I'm offering you a chance to make your idea work. I've got money, Chip, foundation money looking for something to be spent on. Not space research or cancer research or higher mathematics—they're funded well enough now. My foundation is looking for projects that don't fit into the usual patterns. Big ones. Like yours."

Well, of course I was excited. It was so good to be taken that seriously.

"I called the board secretary in Washington first thing—I mean, as soon as they were open there. Of course, I couldn't give him enough over the phone for a formal commitment. But he's on the hook, Chip. And the board will go along. There's a meeting next week and I want you there."

"In Washington? I suppose . . ."

"Well, no. The foundation's international, Chip, and this meeting's at Lake Como. But we'll pick up the tab, of course, and you can get a lot more done there, where your office isn't going to call you . . ."

"But, I mean, I'm not sure . . ."

"We'll back you. Everything you need. A staff. A headquarters. We've got the beginnings of a facility in Ames, Iowa; you'll have to go out there, of course. But it shouldn't be more than, oh, say, a couple days a month. And"—he grinned, a little apologetically—"I know it won't mean anything to you. After you've got one medal on your chest, the rest aren't too exciting. But it'll look nice in your *Who's Who* entry; and, anyway, the secretary has already authorized me to tell you that you're invited to accept appointment to a trusteeship."

I began to need the coffee and I took a long swallow. "You're moving too fast for me, Laszlo," I said.

"The trustees meet in Flagstaff; they've got a country-club deal there. You'll like it. Of course, it's only six times a year. But it's worth it, Chip. I mean, we have our politics like everything else; and if you're a trustee, you swing a lot of weight."

And he prattled on, and I sat there listening, and it was all coming true, everything I'd hoped for; and the next week in Italy, in a great shiny room with an enormous window looking out over Lake Como, I found myself a full-fledged project director, with status as a trustee, honorary membership on the priorities committee and a staff of forty-one.

Next week we dedicate the Lawrence Resnik Memorial Building in Ames—the name was my idea, but everybody agreed—and although it's been a hell of a year, I can see where we'll really make progress now. It still seems a little incongruous that I should be putting in so much time on managerial work and conferences. But when I mentioned it to Laszlo the other day in Montreal, he gave me the grin and an approving look. "I wondered how long it would take you to think of that," he chuckled. "But it's best to make haste slowly, and you can see for yourself it's paying off. Have I told you what a good impression your lecture tour made?"

"Thanks. Yes, as a matter of fact, you did. Anyway, once we get the Resnik installation going, there'll be a little more time."

"Damn right! And don't say I told you"—he winked—"but remember what I told you about a possible appointment to the President's Commission on Interdisciplinary Affairs? Well, it's not official. But it's definite. We've already taken a suite at the Shoreham for you. You'll be using it a lot. We've even fitted up a room as an office; you can keep your notes and things there between trips."

Well, I told him, of course, that if he meant the notes I had been trying to reconstruct, they didn't require all that much room. Not by quite a lot, since I haven't in all truth got very far.

I think I would have, somehow or other, with a little luck. But I haven't actually been very lucky. Poor Honeyman, for instance—I'd already written him for another copy of the report he'd made up for me when I heard that his yawl had capsized in a storm. They didn't even find his body for a week. And nobody seems to know where he kept his copy of the report, if he ever made one. And . . .

Well, there was that funny thing Resnik said the day he died, about how the world conspired against anybody who'd ever done anything. And then he said, "I'm not even sure it's this world."

I figured out what the joke was—that is, if it was a joke. I mean, just for a hypothesis, suppose Somebody didn't want us to get ahead as fast as we could, Somebody from another world . . .

That's silly. That is, I think it's silly.

But if that line of thinking isn't silly, then it must be something quite the opposite of silly; by which I mean it must be dangerous. Just recently, I've almost been run over twice by crazy drivers in front of my own house. And then there's the air taxi I missed and saw crash on take-off before my eyes.

Just for the fun of it, there are two things I'd like to know. One is where the foundation gets its money and why. The other—and I just might see if I can get an answer to this one, next time I'm in L.A.—is whether there really were a pair of honeymooners in room 2051 that morning, to be accidentally awakened by Laszlo Ramos just about the time that Larry was on his way down twenty flights.

THE DAY THE MARTIANS CAME

First published in Harlan Ellison's huge, groundbreaking anthology of original stories, *Dangerous Visions,* in 1967, this is not, on the surface, a groundbreaking story. However, as many have observed before now, the devil—or God, if you prefer—is in the details.

The occasion of the arrival of beings from another planet—what a grand idea. What a momentous occasion. Indeed, Frederik Pohl wrote a whole book about what might happen in many spheres of life on Earth if and when that should happen. It was titled *The Day the Martians Came.*

It's an outstanding book, and you should read it. This is the final chapter of the book, but it stands entirely alone as a short story. When a work of science fiction—or *any* fiction—is judged, the validity of that work rests largely on whether the author has made the people believable. Because the people are our touchstone. How would *we* react in the situation of the story?

In those terms, this is a real gem.

There were two cots in every room of the motel, besides the usual number of beds, and Mr. Mandala, the manager, had converted the rear section of the lobby into a men's dormitory. Nevertheless he was not satisfied and was trying to persuade his colored bellmen to clean out the trunk room and put cots in that too. "Now, please, Mr. Mandala," the bell captain said, speaking loudly over the noise in the lounge, "you know we'd do it for you if we could. But it cannot be, because first we don't have any other place to put those old TV sets you want to save and because second we don't *have* any more cots."

"You're arguing with me, Ernest. I told you to quit arguing with me," said Mr. Mandala. He drummed his fingers on the registration desk and looked angrily around the lobby. There were at least forty people in it, talking, playing cards and dozing. The television set was mumbling away in a recap of the NASA releases, and on the screen Mr. Mandala could see a picture of one of the Martians, gazing into the camera and weeping large, gelatinous tears.

"Quit that," ordered Mr. Mandala, turning in time to catch his bellman looking at the screen. "I don't pay you to watch TV. Go see if you can help out in the kitchen."

"We been in the kitchen, Mr. Mandala. They don't need us."

"Go when I tell you to go, Ernest! You too, Berzie." He watched them go through the service hall and wished he could get rid of some of the crowd in the lounge as easily. They filled every seat and the overflow sat on the arms of the chairs, leaned against the walls and filled the booths in the bar, which had been closed for the past two hours because of the law. According to the registration slips they were nearly all from newspapers, wire services, radio and television networks and so on, waiting to go to the morning briefing at Cape Kennedy. Mr. Mandala wished morning would come. He didn't like so many of them cluttering up his lounge, especially since he was pretty sure a lot of them were not even registered guests.

On the television screen a hastily edited tape was now showing the return of the *Algonquin Nine* space probe to Mars but no one was watching it. It was the third time that particular tape had been repeated since midnight and everybody had seen it at least once; but when it changed to another shot of one of the Martians, looking like a sad dachshund with elongated seal-flippers for limbs, one of the poker players stirred and cried: "I got a Martian joke! Why doesn't a Martian swim in the Atlantic Ocean?"

"It's your bet," said the dealer.

"Because he'd leave a ring around it," said the reporter, folding his cards. No one laughed, not even Mr. Mandala, although some of the jokes had been pretty good. Everybody was beginning to get tired of them, or perhaps just tired.

Mr. Mandala had missed the first excitement about the Martians, because he had been asleep. When the day manager phoned him, waking him up, Mr. Mandala had thought, first, that it was a joke and, second, that the day man was out of his mind; after all, who would care if the Mars probe had come back with some kind of animals? Or even if they weren't animals, exactly. When he found out how many reservations were coming in over the teletype he realized that some people did in fact care. However, Mr. Mandala didn't take much interest in things like that. It was nice the Martians had come, since they had filled his motel, and every other motel within a hundred miles of Cape Kennedy, but when you had said that you had said everything about the Martians that mattered to Mr. Mandala.

On the television screen the picture went to black and was replaced by the legend *Bulletin from NBC News*. The poker game paused momentarily.

The lounge was almost quiet as an invisible announcer read a new release from NASA: "Dr. Hugo Bache, the Fort Worth, Texas, veterinarian who arrived late this evening to examine the Martians at the Patrick Air Force Base reception center, has issued a preliminary report which has just been released by Colonel Eric T. 'Happy' Wingerter, speaking for the National Aeronautics and Space Administration."

A wire-service man yelled, "Turn it up!" There was a convulsive movement around the set. The sound vanished entirely for a moment, then blasted out:

". . . Martians are vertebrate, warm-blooded and apparently mammalian. A superficial examination indicates a generally low level of metabolism, although Dr. Bache states that it is possible that this is in some measure the result of their difficult and confined voyage through 137,000,000 miles of space in the specimen chamber of the *Algonquin Nine* spacecraft. There is no, repeat no, evidence of communicable disease, although standing sterilization precautions are . . ."

"Hell he says," cried somebody, probably a stringer from CBS. "Walter Cronkite had an interview with the Mayo Clinic that . . ."

"Shut up!" bellowed a dozen voices, and the TV became audible again:

". . . completes the full text of the report from Dr. Hugo Bache as released at this hour by Colonel 'Happy' Wingerter." There was a pause; then the announcer's voice, weary but game, found its place and went on with a recap of the previous half-dozen stories. The poker game began again as the announcer was describing the news conference with Dr. Sam Sullivan of the Linguistic Institute of the University of Indiana, and his conclusions that the sounds made by the Martians were indeed some sort of a language.

What nonsense, thought Mr. Mandala, drugged and drowsy. He pulled a stool over and sat down, half asleep.

Then the noise of laughter woke him and he straightened up belligerently. He tapped his call bell for attention. "Gentlemen! Ladies! Please!" he cried. "It's four o'clock in the morning. Our other guests are trying to sleep."

"Yeah, sure," said the CBS man, holding up one hand impatiently, "but wait a minute. I got one. What's a Martian high-rise? You give up?"

"Go ahead," said a red-haired girl, a staffer from *Life*.

"Twenty-seven floors of basement apartments!"

The girl said, "All right, I got one too. What is a Martian female's religious injunction requiring her to keep her eyes closed during intercourse?" She waited a beat. "God forbid she should see her husband having a good time!"

"Are we playing poker or not?" groaned one of the players, but they were too many for him. "Who won the Martian beauty contest? . . . Nobody won!" "How do you get a Martian female to give up sex? . . . Marry her!" Mr. Mandala laughed out loud at that one, and when one of the reporters came to him and asked for a book of matches he gave it to him. "Ta," said the man, puffing his pipe alight. "Long night, eh?"

"You bet," said Mr. Mandala genially. On the television screen the tape was running again, for the fourth time. Mr. Mandala yawned, staring vacantly at it; it was not much to see but, really, it was all that anyone had seen or was likely to see of the Martians. All these reporters and cameramen and columnists and sound men, thought Mr. Mandala with pleasure, all of them waiting here for the ten A.M. briefing at the Cape would have a forty-mile drive through the palmetto swamps for nothing. Because what they would see when they got there would be just about what they were seeing now.

One of the poker players was telling a long, involved joke about Martians wearing fur coats at Miami Beach. Mr. Mandala looked at them with dislike. If only some of them would go to their rooms and go to sleep he might try asking the others if they were registered in the motel. Although actually he couldn't squeeze anyone else in anyway, with all the rooms doubly occupied already. He gave up the thought and stared vacantly at the Martians on the screen, trying to imagine people all over the world looking at that picture on their television sets, reading about them in their newspapers, *caring* about them. They did not look worth caring about as they sluggishly crawled about on their long, weak limbs, like a stretched seal's flippers, gasping heavily in the drag of Earth's gravity, their great long eyes dull.

"Stupid-looking little bastards," one of the reporters said to the pipe smoker. "You know what I heard? I heard the reason the astronauts kept them locked in the back was the stink."

"They probably don't notice it on Mars," said the pipe smoker judiciously. "Thin air."

"Notice it? They love it." He dropped a dollar bill on the desk in front of Mr. Mandala. "Can I have change for the Coke machine?" Mr. Mandala counted out dimes silently. It had not occurred to him that the Martians would smell, but that was only because he hadn't given it much of a thought. If he had thought about it at all, that was what he would have thought.

436 | PLATINUM POHL

Mr. Mandala fished out a dime for himself and followed the two men over to the Coke machine. The picture on the TV changed to some rather poorly photographed shots brought back by the astronauts, of low, irregular sand-colored buildings on a bright sand floor. These were what NASA was calling "the largest Martian city," altogether about a hundred of the flat, windowless structures. "I dunno," said the second reporter at last, tilting his Coke bottle. "You think they're what you'd call intelligent?"

"Difficult to say, exactly," said the pipe smoker. He was from Reuter's and looked it, with a red, broad English squire's face. "They do build houses," he pointed out.

"So does a bull gorilla."

"No doubt. No doubt." The Reuter's man brightened. "Oh, just a moment. That makes me think of one. There once was—let me see, at home we tell it about the Irish— yes, I have it. The next spaceship goes to Mars, you see, and they find that some dread Terrestrial disease has wiped out the whole race, all but one female. These fellows too, gone. All gone except this one she. Well, they're terribly upset, and they debate it at the UN and start an anti-genocide pact and America votes two hundred million dollars for reparations and, well, the long and short of it is, in order to keep the race from dying out entirely they decide to breed a non-human man to this one surviving Martian female."

"Cripes!"

"Yes, exactly. Well, then they find Paddy O'Shaughnessy, down on his luck and they say to him, 'See here, just go in that cage there, Paddy, and you'll find this female. And all you've got to do is render her pregnant, do you see?' And O'Shaughnessy says, 'What's in it for me?' and they offer him, oh, thousands of pounds. And of course he agrees. But then he opens the door of the cage and he sees what the female looks like. And he backs out." The Reuter's man replaced his empty Coke bottle in the rack and grimaced, showing Paddy's expression of revulsion. "'Holy saints,' he says, 'I never counted on anything like this.' 'Thousands of pounds, Paddy!' they say to him, urging him on. 'Oh, very well, then,' he says, 'but on one condition.' 'And what may that be?' they ask him. 'You've got to promise me,' he says, 'that the children'll be raised in the Church.'"

"Yeah, I heard that," said the other reporter. And he moved to put his bottle back, and as he did his foot caught in the rack and four cases of empty Coke bottles bounced and clattered across the floor.

Well, that was just about more than Mr. Mandala could stand and he gasped, stuttered, dinged his bell and shouted, "Ernest! Berzie! On the double!" And when Ernest showed up, poking his dark plum-colored head out of the service door with an expression that revealed an anticipation of disaster, Mr. Mandala shouted: "Oh, curse your thick heads, I told you a hundred times, keep those racks cleaned out." And he stood over the two bellmen, fuming, as they bent to the litter of whole bottles and broken glass, their faces glancing up at him sidewise, worried, dark plum and Arabian sand. He knew that all the reporters were looking at him and that they disapproved.

And then he went out into the late night to cool off, because he was sorry and knew he might make himself still sorrier.

The grass was wet. Condensing dew was dripping from the fittings of the diving board into the pool. The motel was not as quiet as it should be so close to dawn, but it was quiet enough. There was only an occasional distant laugh, and the noise from the lounge. To Mr. Mandala it was reassuring. He replenished his soul by walking all the galleries around the rooms, checking the ice makers and the cigarette machines, and finding that all was well.

A military jet from McCoy was screaming overhead. Beyond it the stars were still bright, in spite of the beginnings of dawn in the east. Mr. Mandala yawned, glanced mildly up and wondered which of them was Mars, and returned to his desk; and shortly he was too busy with the long, exhausting round of room calls and checkouts to think about Martians. Then, when most of the guests were getting noisily into their cars and limo-buses and the day men were coming on, Mr. Mandala uncapped two cold Cokes and carried one back through the service door to Ernest.

"Rough night," he said, and Ernest, accepting both the Coke and the intention, nodded and drank it down. They leaned against the wall that screened the pool from the access road and watched the newsmen and newsgirls taking off down the road toward the highway and the ten o'clock briefing. Most of them had had no sleep. Mr. Mandala shook his head, disapproving so much commotion for so little cause.

And Ernest snapped his fingers, grinned and said, "I got a Martian joke, Mr. Mandala. What do you call a seven-foot Martian when he's comin' at you with a spear?"

"Oh, hell, Ernest," said Mr. Mandala, "you call him sir. Everybody knows that one." He yawned and stretched and said reflectively, "You'd think there'd be some new jokes. All I heard was the old ones, only instead of picking on the Jews and the Catholics and—and everybody, they were telling them about the Martians."

"Yeah, I noticed that, Mr. Mandala," said Ernest.

Mr. Mandala stood up. "Better get some sleep," he advised, "because they might all be back again tonight. I don't know what for. . . . Know what I think, Ernest? Outside of the jokes, I don't think that six months from now anybody's going to remember there ever were such things as Martians. I don't believe their coming here is going to make a nickel's worth of difference to anybody."

"Hate to disagree with you, Mr. Mandala," said Ernest mildly, "but I don't think so. Going to make a difference to some people. Going to make a *damn* big difference to me."

DAY MILLION

Who knows what people will be like on Day Million? That's a long time from now, and when Frederik Pohl spun out his story of "boy meets girl" in the far future, he pulled out all the stops.

The kind of speculation that fuels the story of "Day Million" is freewheeling, unrestrained, pretty cool stuff. John Varley, in his "Eight Worlds" stories in the late 1970s, impressed people with his creative notions of what people would be like in the future.

Varley's stories have nothing on "Day Million."

This story is from 1966 and first saw publication in *Rogue* magazine. I'm not sure whether *Rogue*'s readers liked it, but it really doesn't matter. "Day Million" stands quite well on its own.

On this day I want to tell you about, which will be about a thousand years from now, there were a boy, a girl and a love story.

Now although I haven't said much so far, none of it is true. The boy was not what you and I would normally think of as a boy, because he was a hundred and eighty-seven years old. Nor was the girl a girl, for other reasons; and the love story did not entail that sublimation of the urge to rape and concurrent postponement of the instinct to submit which we at present understand in such matters. You won't care much for this story if you don't grasp these facts at once. If, however, you will make the effort, you'll likely enough find it jam-packed, chock-full and tiptop-crammed with laughter, tears and poignant sentiment which may, or may not, be worthwhile. The reason the girl was not a girl was that she was a boy.

How angrily you recoil from the page! You say, who the hell wants to read about a pair of queers? Calm yourself. Here are no hot-breathing secrets of perversion for the coterie trade. In fact, if you were to see this girl, you would not guess that she was in any sense a boy. Breasts, two; vagina, one. Hips, callipygean; face, hairless; supra-orbital lobes, nonexistent. You would term her female at once, although it is true that you might wonder just what species she was a female of, being confused by the tail, the silky pelt or the gill slits behind each ear.

Now you recoil again. Cripes, man, take my word for it. This is a sweet kid, and if you, as a normal male, spent as much as an hour in a room with her, you would bend heaven and earth to get her in the sack. Dora (we will call her that; her "name" was omicron-Dibase seven-group-totter-oot S Doradus 5314, the last part of which is a color specification corresponding to a shade of green)—Dora, I say, was feminine, charming and cute. I admit she doesn't sound that way. She was, as you might put it, a dancer. Her art involved qualities of intellection and expertise of a very high order, requiring both tremendous natural capacities and endless practice; it was performed in null-gravity and I can best describe it by saying that it was something like the performance of a contortionist and something like classical ballet, maybe resembling Danilova's dying swan. It was also pretty damned sexy. In a symbolic way, to be sure; but face it, most of the things we call "sexy" are symbolic, you know, except perhaps an exhibitionist's open fly. On Day Million when Dora danced, the people who saw her panted; and you would too.

About this business of her being a boy. It didn't matter to her audiences that genetically she was male. It wouldn't matter to you, if you were among them, because you wouldn't know it—not unless you took a biopsy cutting of her flesh and put it under an electron-microscope to find the XY chromosome—and it didn't matter to them because they didn't care. Through techniques which are not only complex but haven't yet been discovered, these people were able to determine a great deal about the aptitudes and easements of babies quite a long time before they were born—at about the second horizon of cell division, to be exact, when the segmenting egg is becoming a free blastocyst—and then they naturally helped those aptitudes along. Wouldn't we? If we find a child with an aptitude for music we give him a scholarship to Juilliard. If they found a child whose aptitudes were for being a woman, they made him one. As sex had long been dissociated from reproduction this was relatively easy to do and caused no trouble and no, or at least very little, comment.

How much is "very little"? Oh, about as much as would be caused by our own tampering with Divine Will by filling a tooth. Less than would be caused by wearing a hearing aid. Does it still sound awful? Then look closely at the next busty babe you meet and reflect that she may be a Dora, for adults who are genetically male but somatically female are far from unknown even in our own time. An accident of environment in the womb overwhelms the blueprints of heredity. The difference is that with us it happens only by accident and we don't know about it except rarely, after close study; whereas the people of Day Million did it often, on purpose, because they wanted to.

Well, that's enough to tell you about Dora. It would only confuse you to add that she was seven feet tall and smelled of peanut butter. Let us begin our story.

On Day Million Dora swam out of her house, entered a transportation tube, was sucked briskly to the surface in its flow of water and ejected in its plume of spray to an elastic platform in front of her—ah—call it her rehearsal hall. "Oh, shit!" she cried in pretty confusion, reaching out to catch her balance and find herself tumbled against a total stranger, whom we will call Don.

They met cute. Don was on his way to have his legs renewed. Love was the farthest thing from his mind; but when, absentmindedly taking a shortcut across the landing platform for submarinites and finding himself drenched, he discovered his arms full of the loveliest girl he had ever seen, he knew at once they were meant for each other. "Will you marry me?" he asked. She said softly, "Wednesday," and the promise was like a caress.

Don was tall, muscular, bronze and exciting. His name was no more Don than Dora's was Dora, but the personal part of it was Adonis in tribute to his vibrant maleness, and so we will call him Don for short. His personality color-code, in Angstrom units, was 5290, or only a few degrees bluer than Dora's 5314, a measure of what they had intuitively discovered at first sight, that they possessed many affinities of taste and interest.

I despair of telling you exactly what it was that Don did for a living—I don't mean for the sake of making money, I mean for the sake of giving purpose and meaning to his life, to keep him from going off his nut with boredom—except to say that it involved a lot of traveling. He traveled in interstellar spaceships. In order to make a spaceship go really fast about thirty-one male and seven genetically female human beings had to do certain things, and Don was one of the thirty-one. Actually he contemplated options. This involved a lot of exposure to radiation flux—not so much from his own station in the propulsive system as in the spillover from the next stage, where a genetic female preferred selections and the subnuclear particles making the selections she preferred demolished themselves in a shower of quanta. Well, you don't give a rat's ass for that, but it meant that Don had to be clad at all times in a skin of light, resilient, extremely strong copper-colored metal. I have already mentioned this, but you probably thought I meant he was sunburned.

More than that, he was a cybernetic man. Most of his ruder parts had been long since replaced with mechanisms of vastly more permanence and use. A cadmium centrifuge, not a heart, pumped his blood. His lungs moved only when he wanted to speak out loud, for a cascade of osmotic filters rebreathed oxygen out of his own wastes. In a way, he probably would have looked peculiar to a man from the twentieth century, with his glowing eyes and seven-fingered hands; but to himself, and of course to Dora, he looked mighty manly and grand. In the course of his voyages Don had circled Proxima Centauri, Procyon and the puzzling worlds of Mira Ceti; he had carried agricultural templates to the planets of Canopus and brought back warm, witty pets from the pale companion of Aldebaran. Blue-hot or red-cool, he had seen a thousand stars and their ten thousand planets. He had, in fact, been traveling the starlanes with only brief leaves on Earth for pushing two centuries. But you don't care about that, either. It is people that make stories, not the circumstances they find themselves in, and you want to hear about these two people. Well, they made it. The great thing they had for each other grew and flowered and burst into fruition on Wednesday, just as Dora had promised. They met at the encoding room, with a couple of well-wishing friends apiece to cheer them on, and while their identities were being taped and stored they smiled and whispered to each other and bore the jokes of their friends with blushing repartee. Then they exchanged their mathematical analogs and went away, Dora to her dwelling beneath the surface of the sea and Don to his ship.

It was an idyll, really. They lived happily ever after—or anyway, until they decided not to bother anymore and died.

Of course, they never set eyes on each other again.

Oh, I can see you now, you eaters of charcoal-broiled steak, scratching an incipient bunion with one hand and holding this story with the other, while the stereo plays d'Indy or Monk. You don't believe a word of it, do you? Not for one minute. People wouldn't live like that, you say with an irritated and not amused grunt as you get up to put fresh ice in a stale drink.

And yet there's Dora, hurrying back through the flushing commuter pipes toward her underwater home (she prefers it there; has had herself somatically altered to breathe the stuff). If I tell you with what sweet fulfillment she fits the recorded analog of Don into the symbol manipulator, hooks herself in and turns herself on . . . if I try to tell you any of that you will simply stare. Or glare; and grumble, what the hell kind of love-making is this? And yet I assure you, friend, I really do assure you that Dora's ecstasies are as creamy and passionate as any of James Bond's lady spies, and one hell of a lot more so than anything you are going to find in "real life." Go ahead, glare and grumble. Dora doesn't care. If she thinks of you at all, her thirty-times-great-great-grandfather, she thinks you're a pretty primordial sort of brute. You are. Why, Dora is farther removed from you than you are from the australopithecines of five thousand centuries ago. You could not swim a second in the strong currents of her life. You don't think progress goes in a straight line, do you? Do you recognize that it is an ascending, accelerating, maybe even exponential curve? It takes hell's own time to get started, but when it goes it goes like a bomb. And you, you Scotch-drinking steak-eater in your Relaxacizer chair, you've just barely lighted the primacord of the fuse. What is it now, the six or seven hundred thousandth day after Christ? Dora lives in Day Million. A thousand years from now. Her body fats are polyunsaturated, like Crisco. Her wastes are hemodialyzed out of her bloodstream while she sleeps—that means she doesn't have to go to the bathroom. On whim, to pass a slow half-hour, she can command more energy than the entire nation of Portugal can spend today, and use it to launch a weekend satellite or remold a crater on the Moon. She loves Don very much. She keeps his every gesture, mannerism, nuance, touch of hand, thrill of intercourse, passion of kiss stored in symbolic-mathematical form. And when she wants him, all she has to do is turn the machine on and she has him.

And Don, of course, has Dora. Adrift on a sponson city a few hundred yards over her head or orbiting Arcturus, fifty light-years away, Don has only to command his own symbol-manipulator to rescue Dora from the ferrite files and bring her to life for him, and there she is; and rapturously, tirelessly they ball all night. Not in the flesh, of course; but then his flesh has been extensively altered and it wouldn't really be much fun. He doesn't need the flesh for pleasure. Genital organs feel nothing. Neither do hands, nor breasts, nor lips; they are only receptors, accepting and transmitting impulses. It is the brain that feels, it is the interpretation of those impulses that makes agony or orgasm; and Don's symbol-manipulator gives him the analog of cuddling, the analog of kissing, the analog of wildest, most ardent hours with the eternal, exquisite and incorruptible analog of Dora. Or Diane. Or sweet Rose, or laughing Alicia; for to be sure, they have each of them exchanged analogs before, and will again.

Balls, you say, it looks crazy to me. And you—with your aftershave lotion and your little red car, pushing papers across a desk all day and chasing tail all night—tell me, just how the hell do you think you would look to Tiglath-Pileser, say, or Attila the Hun?

THE MAYOR OF MARE TRANQ

As mentioned more than once earlier in this collection, Frederik Pohl has written as a partner-in-crime with a number of other writers. One of the writers with whom he has collaborated most successfully is Jack Williamson, the venerable dean of science fiction. With more than a half-dozen novel cowritten works, including the Starchild trilogy, Pohl and Williamson have proven to be a marvelously creative and productive team.

In 1996, Tor Books published *The Williamson Effect*, an anthology of stories written especially for that volume, a festschrift in honor of Williamson. Some of the stories took place in the settings of memorable Williamson works such as *Darker Than You Think* or *The Legion of Space*. Others were about Williamson himself.

"The Mayor of Mare Tranq" is alternate history in which Jack Williamson becomes an astronaut. How he got to do this is part of the charm of the story. A seamlessly entertaining tale of human striving in the face of daunting odds, "Mayor . . ." will have special meaning for anyone who has ever had lunar dreams.

The incident that changed young Johnny Williamson's life took place in Arizona, in the year of 1916. If it had just rained a little more in that bad, dry year, Johnny's father, Sam Williamson, might have made a go of the farm. But it didn't. The soil dried. The seedlings withered. The crop would not be made. Sam let the dust flow through his fingers and made his decision: dryland farming was too chancy to feed a family; something had to be done.

His first thought was to move on to some more hospitable area, Texas or maybe even Old Mexico, where it did sometimes rain. But he didn't have to. His neighbor, the Republican party boss of the county, made him an offer: he would give Sam a job in his general store if only Sam would put his name in as a candidate for the Congress of the United States. That wasn't meant as a serious prospect for a career in government. The boss only wanted a name to put before the voters in order to complete the ticket, with no real chance of being elected. Big Bill Bronck, the Democratic incumbent, was well known to be unbeatable in any election. However, Fate intervened. The day before the election Big Bill Bronck was shot to death in the parlor of a county-seat brothel, and when the votes were counted Sam Williamson, with his wife and children, was on his way to the capital.

The city of Washington, D.C., was a marvel to Sam's boys, young Johnny and his brother Jim. They had never been in a big city before. The storefront moving-picture shows, the clanging trolley cars in the streets, the hordes of people rushing about on their business—the boys blossomed there. It wasn't all to their good. The city was a lot more fun than school, and, sadly, they both developed a talent for playing hookey in order to explore the wonders of the metropolis. Happily, that didn't much matter, because they were both bright enough to breeze through their classes in grammar and high school. When Johnny was eighteen years old he graduated from high school as valedictorian of his class . . . the week before his father died.

That was a terrible blow to the family. They were left with no reason to stay in Washington, and only a Congressman's pension to feed the young family. Johnny's mother decided their best bet was to head west for Texas, where cousins had land outside of Dallas and ranch living was cheap. That didn't solve Johnny's problem. He was ready for college, but where was the tuition money to come from? However, in the event that problem was no problem. Representative Bob Blakeless of Ohio, formerly Sam Williamson's closest associate on the Fish, Game and Poultry Subcommittee, was ready and willing to give his late colleague's boy a Congressional appointment to any service school he chose, and young Johnny selected the U.S. Military Academy at West Point.

At the Academy Johnny stopped playing hookey. He thrived at the Point. He paid attention to his studies, lived by the cadet code, and walked off his demerits until he stopped getting them. He turned out to be a first-rate cadet. When he graduated, fifth in his class, he was privileged to pick his own branch of Army service, and what he chose was the fledgling Army Air Corps.

Those were bad years economically. The stock market had collapsed and the country was groaning under the weight of the Great Depression. Money was scarce everywhere, even for the military, and the equipment of the Army Air Corps showed it. The slow, cranky biplanes the Corps was flying belonged to another, obsolete generation; every airman knew that the sleek new planes the Germans and the English were practicing with across the Atlantic could outfly and outfight any of them. Accidents were frequent and often terminal, but Second Lieutenant Williamson was lucky . . . and skilled, too. He took to flying like a duck to water. He became an instructor, then a check pilot for the new P-36s that were coming in, and then war broke out in Europe. Pearl Harbor changed everything—for Williamson as well as for everyone else. He was one of the first fighter pilots sent to North Africa and quickly showed he was one of the best. The ten-year lieutenant became a captain, then a major commanding a squadron. He had four clusters to his Air Medal and his confirmed kills amounted to eleven by the time of V-J Day. He was one of the few urged to stay on when most of the Army, Navy and Marine Corps were demobbing. By the time he reached his twenty-year retirement he was a full colonel . . . and possessed by a new ambition.

John had been in London at the time of the V-2s. He had sneaked across the Channel to Peenemunde to see the place where those rockets came from, and he had been struck by the thought that those same rockets could take something—maybe even someone—into space, and he wished with all his heart for that to happen. To *him*. So, now a civilian, he went to work for an aerospace company in Texas, doing his best to make sure that if ever someone tried to make that great leap into the unknown there would be machines available to make it work.

He thrilled when the new President, John Fitzgerald Kennedy, made his speech about putting men on the Moon. It was his chance. Slim, yes, but a lot better than no chance at all, and so Williamson instantly began calling in old favors. His former seconds-in-command were now colonels and generals; he begged them to help get him into the space program. And they tried. They really tried. They pulled all the strings they could for their old boss, but time was against them. Col. John Stewart Williamson (Retd.) was fifty-three on the day when Kennedy made his historic speech . . . and that was simply Too Old.

His dream was over. His prospects of getting into space were exactly zero . . . that is, they were until the events of November 1963.

What brought John Williamson into the city that day was his brother's little son, Gary. The boy was as dedicated to the idea of space travel as his uncle, and a devoted admirer of the President who was going to make it real. What Gary Williamson wanted, more than anything else, was to see his hero and maybe even take some pictures of him with his new movie camera.

By the time they got to a point where the Presidential procession was going to pass all the good places were taken, but John Williamson was up to that challenge. There was a kind of a warehouse building by the side of the road, apparently unoccupied at the moment. Williamson tried doors until he found one that would open, and he and the boy climbed stairs to look out on the street. They found a good window at once, but there was a tree that seemed to be in the way. Williamson left the boy there and scouted some of the other rooms . . . and, in the third one, was startled to see a scruffy man with a rifle glaring angrily down at the street.

It could have been something innocent. It could even have been (Williamson thought later) a Dallas detective in plain clothes, guarding the route of the procession. He didn't stop to think of any of those possibilities. Reflexes took over. He charged the man, knocked the rifle out the window, overpowered the would-be assassin and was sitting on his chest when a pair of actual Dallas cops, alerted by the sight of the rifle falling out of the window, came pounding up the stairs to take charge.

That night Williamson and his nephew were called to see the President on Air Force One. Mrs. Kennedy was there, looking sweet and appealing in her pink suit and pink pillbox hat; so were Texas Governor John Connally and his wife; so were a couple of Secret Service men, amiably but carefully watching every move Williamson and the boy made. The President got up from his overstuffed chair, grimacing with some sort of pain in his back, and extended a hand to Williamson. "Colonel Williamson," he said, "they tell me you're the one who took out this fellow—"

"Oswald," his wife supplied. "His name is Lee Harvey Oswald."

"Yes, Oswald. I don't know what kind of a shot he was. My Secret Service friends here tell me that we would have been a pretty tough target to hit—"

"A damn impossible target," Governor Connally grumbled, and the First Lady said sweetly:

"Oh, not *impossible*. I'm glad we didn't have to find out."

"But anyway," the President said, "it looks like you just might have saved my life and maybe Jackie's, too. I owe you, Colonel. Is there something I can do for you?"

"I want to go to the Moon," Williamson said promptly.

Kennedy grinned. "Can't blame you there; so do I. Well, put in your application and we'll—"

"I did," Williamson interrupted. "They turned me down. They said I was too old. But I have eighteen hundred hours, mostly in P-38s and P-51s but some jets, too. I believe I can handle a spacecraft whenever there's one to handle, and I know I can pass any physical they can give me."

The President looked at him thoughtfully. "I bet you could, at that. All right. Put in your application again . . . and this time, write on the bottom that you have an age waiver officially granted by the President of the United States."

Williamson did pass the physical. Williamson did excel in astronaut training. Williamson was the second one of the Mercury Eight to make a suborbital flight, and when the Apollo program reached the point of actually doing what President Kennedy had promised and putting a man on the surface of the Moon, Colonel John Stewart Williamson was one of the three men strapped into the capsule as the giant Saturn-V lifted off from Cape Canaveral.

He was not, however, one of the landers. Williamson's job was to remain in the orbiter while Armstrong and Aldrin rode the lunar landing capsule down to the surface. It wasn't perfect. He would have preferred to be in on the actual descent. But it was one hell of a lot better than anything else around, and he accepted the assignment with grace and pleasure . . . until the moment when the capsule was scheduled to take off again for orbital rendezvous.

For all those hours of waiting in the orbiter while Armstrong and Aldrin capered around the lunar surface in their ungainly suits, John Williamson had worn around his neck a leather strap that held a small volume with complete, preplanned instructions for actions he should take in every possible emergency. *Almost* every possible emergency, anyway. There was one exception.

At the planned moment of liftoff Williamson was over the horizon in his orbit, out of sight of the landing area in Mare Tranquilitatis. He could neither see the capsule nor hear their transmissions to Mike Collins at Earth Control at that second. He didn't know what had happened until he rounded the curve of the Moon, and by the time he could pick up their messages the situation had become critical. "—tipping too far," said Buzz Aldrin's voice from the surface. "Try again!" urged the voice from Earth Control. "Can't," said Aldrin despairingly. "Looks like the soil's a little soft under that leg. We're tipping already from the vibration. If we go to full burn we'll just tip this beast over on its side."

That was when Williamson cut in. "You can't get lift?" he demanded unbelievingly.

" 'Fraid not, Johnny," said Aldrin. "We're stuck. Say good-bye to everybody for us when you get back."

And that was the one contingency for which Williamson had no instructions. In the event that the lunar module was unable to lift off there was no way for the orbiter to come down to their rescue. And so the book did not say what to do, because in that case there was simply nothing to be done.

Or at least nothing that the people who wrote the book had been able to foresee.

Colonel John Stewart Williamson, on the other hand, was not in the habit of doing nothing. He was a pilot. Stuff happened, but no matter how bad things looked there was always something you could try—right up to the moment when you crashed or died, and that was all she wrote. But until that moment came you never gave up.

So he did three more lunar orbits, keeping his camera on the landing module in its drunken, half-toppled posture every minute he was above the horizon, knowing that all around the world there were two billion people—now two and a half billion—now maybe three, as new ones heard what was going on and tuned in—billions of Earth's people, all watching the terrible scene on the lunar surface. Williamson's heart was heavy, but his mind was still racing. And when at last he started the burn that would lift him out of lunar orbit and start him on the long, slow fall toward reentry he got on the radio again. "Earth Control, Earth Control," he said into his microphone, "Earth Control, don't stand around with your thumbs up your asses, start figuring out what you're going to do for these guys."

The time it took for an answer was longer than the normal couple of seconds transit-time delay. Then Mike Collins, the Boston controller, said, "Hey, Johnny, cut that out! The whole world's listening to you. Don't get their hopes up when you know we can't do a thing."

"I say again, Earth Control," Williamson snapped, "you don't want to waste any more time talking about what you can't do. You *have* to do something. You don't want to let them die there!"

The next pause was longer, and when the voice came on it wasn't Mike Collins, it was the Director himself, and savage. "Colonel Williamson, have you gone out of your tree? We can't rescue them! They're well and truly stuck!"

"Who said rescue? Just keep them *alive!* There are two more lunar modules and three Apollos at the Cape right now, and enough Saturn Fives to lift them. All right, you can't send another crew down until you figure out what went wrong. But you can send a god-dam *capsule* down—crewless, on automatic—and load it with air and water—lots of it, because you don't have to bother filling the tank with return fuel—and keep them going for a couple of weeks—until you send another one down—and another, and another until you figure out how to get them home. You can do that, all right. The only thing you *can't* do is let them die there!"

Would NASA have listened to what Williamson was saying if half the world hadn't heard it at the same time? Perhaps it would have. But also, perhaps not. Perhaps organization and precedent would have carried the day, and the proposal been turned over to an assessment committee. And only then, a week or month later, would a decision have been made—to abandon the pair on the Moon to preserve the project's orderly schedule, or perhaps even to do what Williamson urged . . . though by then Armstrong and Aldrin would, of course, be dead.

That didn't happen. Neither the controllers in Boston nor their masters in Washington had the choice. Within minutes the phone lines to NASA were hot with loud-talking citizens demanding that the space agency send immediate help to the stranded astronauts—and so were the lines to the White House, and to both houses of Congress, and to every newspaper and broadcasting station, too, and not just in the United States. The whole world was crying out to save the astronauts, and within the hour the order went out to start preflighting the next Moon-bound Apollo.

And, of course, the rest is history. On any clear night when the Moon is at quarter everyone in the world can see the diamond-dust lights of the community in Mare Tranq, and everyone knows how it got there. How twelve separate missions brought air, food and water down to Mare Tranquilitatis. How on the seventh mission Colonel Williamson himself piloted the module down to the surface to become the third man on the Moon . . . and to stay. How by the time all the design flaws in the landing struts had been identified and fixed there was such a wealth of matériel clustered around the original landing site—"The Earthlight Trailer Park," one astronaut dubbed it—that it had become a de facto lunar outpost, and before long a priceless resource. The next step in space travel was clearly the stars. The way to get there was clearly by nuclear-fusion propulsion, fueled by helium-4 . . . and where else in the solar system was there a richer store of He-4 than the masses the solar wind had sown into the lunar soil, atom by atom, over the four-and-a-half-billion-year life of the Sun?

And then there was no question of who was the right person to head it . . . and so John Stewart Williamson became the first, and so far the only, loved and honored Mayor of Mare Tranq.

FERMI AND FROST

In 1986, "Fermi and Frost" won the Hugo Award for best short story.

Several other stories in this collection dealt with nuclear war. This is the only one that gives an account of how such a war might happen and what results would ensue.

War, death, the threat of extinction—these are powerful themes. Facing these prospects with humanity and down-to-earth practicality is the only response that might ennoble mankind in such a situation.

Here, then, is the final story in this collection. Like the best of Frederik Pohl's short fiction, it is deceptively simple, elegant in its execution.

They say you should save the best for last. I couldn't agree more.

On Timothy Clary's ninth birthday he got no cake. He spent all of it in a bay of the TWA terminal at John F. Kennedy Airport in New York, sleeping fitfully, crying now and then from exhaustion or fear. All he had to eat was stale Danish pastries from the buffet wagon and not many of them, and he was fearfully embarrassed because he had wet his pants. Three times. Getting to the toilets over the packed refugee bodies was just about impossible. There were twenty-eight hundred people in a space designed for a fraction that many, and all of them with the same idea. Get away! Climb the highest mountain! Drop yourself splat, spang, right in the middle of the widest desert! Run! Hide!—

And pray. Pray as hard as you can, because even the occasional planeload of refugees that managed to fight their way aboard and even take off had no sure hope of refuge when they got wherever the plane was going. Families parted. Mothers pushed their screaming children aboard a jet and melted back into the crowd before screaming, more quietly, themselves.

Because there had been no launch order yet, or none that the public had heard about anyway, there might still be time for escape. A little time. Time enough for the TWA terminal, and every other airport terminal everywhere, to jam up with terrified lemmings. There was no doubt that the missiles were poised to fly. The attempted Cuban coup had escalated wildly, and one nuclear sub had attacked another with a nuclear charge. That, everyone agreed, was the signal. The next event would be the final one.

Timothy knew little of this, but there would have been nothing he could have done about it—except perhaps cry, or have nightmares, or wet himself, and young Timothy was doing all of those anyway. He did not know where his father was. He didn't know where his mother was, either, except that she had gone somewhere to try to call his father; but then there had been a surge that could not be resisted when three 747s at once had announced boarding, and Timothy had been carried far from where he had been left. Worse than that. Wet as he was, with a cold already, he was beginning to be very sick. The young woman who had brought him the Danish pastries put a worried hand to his forehead and drew it away helplessly. The boy needed a doctor. But so did a hundred others, elderly heart patients and hungry babies and at least two women close to childbirth.

If the terror had passed and the frantic negotiations had succeeded, Timothy might have found his parents again in time to grow up and marry and give them grandchildren. If one side or the other had been able to preempt, and destroy the other, and save itself, Timothy forty years later might have been a graying, cynical colonel in the American military government of Leningrad. (Or body servant to a Russian one in Detroit). Or if his mother had pushed just a little harder earlier on, he might have wound up in the plane of refugees that reached Pittsburgh just in time to become plasma. Or if the girl who was watching him had become just a little more scared, and a little more brave, and somehow managed to get him through the throng to the improvised clinics in the main terminal, he might have been given medicine, and found somebody to protect him, and take him to a refuge, and live. . . .

But that is in fact what did happen!

Because Harry Malibert was on his way to a British Interplanetary Society seminar in Portsmouth, he was already sipping Beefeater martinis in the terminal's Ambassador Club when the unnoticed TV at the bar suddenly made everybody notice it.

Those silly nuclear-attack communications systems that the radio stations tested out every now and then, and nobody paid any attention to anymore—why, this time it was real! They were serious! Because it was winter and snowing heavily Malibert's flight had been delayed anyway. Before its rescheduled departure time came, all flights had been embargoed. Nothing would leave Kennedy until some official somewhere decided to let them go.

Almost at once the terminal began to fill with would-be refugees. The Ambassador Club did not fill at once. For three hours the ground-crew stew at the desk resolutely turned away everyone who rang the bell who could not produce the little red card of admission; but when the food and drink in the main terminals began to run out the Chief of Operations summarily opened the club to everyone. It didn't help relieve the congestion outside, it only added to what was within. Almost at once a volunteer doctors' committee seized most of the club to treat the ill and injured from the thickening crowds, and people like Harry Malibert found themselves pushed into the bar area. It was one of the Operations staff, commandeering a gin and tonic at the bar for the sake of the calories more than the booze, who recognized him. "You're Harry Malibert. I heard you lecture once, at Northwestern."

Malibert nodded. Usually when someone said that to him he answered politely, "I hope you enjoyed it," but this time it did not seem appropriate to be normally polite. Or normal at all.

"You showed slides of Arecibo," the man said dreamily. "You said that radio telescope could send a message as far as the Great Nebula in Andromeda, two million light-years away—if only there was another radio telescope as good as that one there to receive it."

"You remember very well," said Malibert, surprised.

"You made a big impression, Dr. Malibert." The man glanced at his watch, debated, took another sip of his drink. "It really sounded wonderful, using the big telescopes to listen for messages from alien civilizations somewhere in space—maybe hearing some, maybe making contact, maybe not being alone in the universe anymore. You made me wonder why we hadn't seen some of these people already, or anyway heard from them— but maybe," he finished, glancing bitterly at the ranked and guarded aircraft outside, "maybe now we know why."

Malibert watched him go, and his heart was leaden. The thing he had given his professional career to—SETI, the Search for Extra-Terrestrial Intelligence—no longer seemed to matter. If the bombs went off, as everyone said they must, then that was ended for a good long time, at least—

Gabble of voices at the end of the bar; Malibert turned, leaned over the mahogany, peered. The *Please Stand By* slide had vanished, and a young black woman with pomaded hair, voice trembling, was delivering a news bulletin:

"—the president has confirmed that a nuclear attack has begun against the United States. Missiles have been detected over the Arctic, and they are incoming. Everyone is ordered to seek shelter and remain there pending instructions—"

Yes. It was ended, thought Malibert, at least for a good long time.

The surprising thing was that the news that it had begun changed nothing. There were no screams, no hysteria. The order to seek shelter meant nothing at John F. Kennedy Airport, where there was no shelter any better than the building they were in. And that, no doubt, was not too good. Malibert remembered clearly the strange aerodynamic shape of the terminal's roof. Any blast anywhere nearby would tear that off and send it sailing over the bay to the Rockaways, and probably a lot of the people inside with it.

But there was nowhere else to go.

There were still camera crews at work, heaven knew why. The television set was showing crowds in Times Square and Newark, a clot of automobiles stagnating on the George Washington Bridge, their drivers abandoning them and running for the Jersey shore. A hundred people were peering around each other's heads to catch glimpses of the screen, but all that anyone said was to call out when he recognized a building or a street.

Orders rang out: "You people will have to move back! We need the room! Look, some of you, give us a hand with these patients." Well, that seemed useful, at least Malibert volunteered at once and was given the care of a young boy, teeth chattering, hot with fever. "He's had tetracyclin," said the doctor who turned the boy over to him. "Clean him up if you can, will you? He ought to be all right if—"

If any of them were, thought Malibert, not requiring her to finish the sentence. How did you clean a young boy up? The question answered itself when Malibert found the boy's trousers soggy and the smell told him what the moisture was. Carefully he laid the child on a leather love seat and removed the pants and sopping undershorts. Naturally the boy had not come with a change of clothes. Malibert solved that with a pair of his own jockey shorts out of his briefcase—far too big for the child, of course, but since they were meant to fit tightly and elastically they stayed in place when Malibert pulled them up to the waist. Then he found paper towels and pressed the blue jeans as dry as he could. It was not very dry. He grimaced, laid them over a bar stool and sat on them for a while, drying them with body heat. They were only faintly wet ten minutes later when he put them back on the child—

San Francisco, the television said, had ceased to transmit.

Malibert saw the Operations man working his way toward him and shook his head. "It's begun," Malibert said, and the man looked around. He put his face close to Malibert's.

"I can get you out of here," he whispered. "There's an Icelandic DC-8 loading right now. No announcement. They'd be rushed if they did. There's room for you, Dr. Malibert."

It was like an electric shock. Malibert trembled. Without knowing why he did it, he said, "Can I put the boy on instead?"

The Operations man looked annoyed. "Take him with you, of course," he said. "I didn't know you had a son."

"I don't," said Malibert. But not out loud. And when they were in the jet he held the boy in his lap as tenderly as though he were his own.

If there was no panic in the Ambassador Club at Kennedy there was plenty of it everywhere else in the world. What everyone in the superpower cities knew was that their lives were at stake. Whatever they did might be in vain, and yet they had to do something. Anything! Run, hide, dig, brace, stow . . . pray. The city people tried to desert the metropolises for the open safety of the country, and the farmers and the exurbanites sought the stronger, safer buildings of the cities.

And the missiles fell.

The bombs that had seared Hiroshima and Nagasaki were struck matches compared to the hydrogen-fusion flares that ended eighty million lives in those first hours. Firestorms fountained above a hundred cities. Winds of three hundred kilometers an hour pulled in cars and debris and people, and they all became ash that rose to the sky. Splatters of melted rock and dust sprayed into the air.

The sky darkened.

Then it grew darker still.

When the Icelandic jet landed at Keflavik Airport Malibert carried the boy down the passage to the little stand marked *Immigration*. The line was long, for most of the passengers had no passports at all, and the immigration woman was very tired of making out temporary entrance permits by the time Malibert reached her. "He's my son," Malibert lied. "My wife has his passport, but I don't know where my wife is."

She nodded wearily. She pursed her lips, looked toward the door beyond which her superior sat sweating and initialing reports, then shrugged and let them through. Malibert took the boy to a door marked *Snirting*, which seemed to be the Icelandic word for toilets, and was relieved to see that at least Timothy was able to stand by himself while he urinated, although his eyes stayed half closed. His head was very hot. Malibert prayed for a doctor in Reykjavik.

In the bus the English-speaking tour guide in charge of them—she had nothing else to do, for her tour would never arrive—sat on the arm of a first-row seat with a microphone in her hand and chattered vivaciously to the refugees. "Chicago? Ya, is gone, Chicago. And Detroit and Pittsburrug—is bad. New York? Certainly New York too!" she said severely, and the big tears rolling down her cheek made Timothy cry too.

Malibert hugged him. "Don't worry, Timmy," he said. "No one would bother bombing Reykjavik." And no one would have. But when the bus was ten miles farther along there was a sudden glow in the clouds ahead of them that made them squint. Someone in the USSR had decided that it was time for neatening up loose threads. That someone, whoever remained in whatever remained of their central missile control, had realized that no one had taken out that supremely, insultingly dangerous bastion of imperialist American interests in the North Atlantic, the United States airbase at Keflavik.

Unfortunately, by then EMP and attrition had compromised the accuracy of their aim. Malibert had been right. No one would have bothered bombing Reykjavik—on purpose—but a forty-mile miss did the job anyway, and Reykjavik ceased to exist.

They had to make a wide detour inland to avoid the fires and the radiation. And as the sun rose on their first day in Iceland, Malibert, drowsing over the boy's bed after the Icelandic nurse had shot him full of antibiotics, saw the daybreak in awful, sky-drenching red.

It was worth seeing, for in the days to come there was no daybreak at all.

The worst was the darkness, but at first that did not seem urgent. What was urgent was rain. A trillion trillion dust particles nucleated water vapor. Drops formed. Rain fell; torrents of rain; sheets and cascades of rain. The rivers swelled. The Mississippi overflowed, and the Ganges, and the Yellow. The High Dam at Aswan spilled water over its lip, then crumbled. The rains came where rains came never. The Sahara knew flash floods. The Flaming Mountains at the edge of the Gobi flamed no more; a ten-year supply of rain came down in a week and rinsed the dusty slopes bare.

And the darkness stayed.

The human race lives always eighty days from starvation. That is the sum of stored food, globe wide. It met the nuclear winter with no more and no less.

The missiles went off on the eleventh of June. If the world's larders had been equally distributed, on the thirtieth of August the last mouthful would have been eaten. The starvation deaths would have begun and ended in the next six weeks; exit the human race.

The larders were not equally distributed. The Northern Hemisphere was caught on one foot, fields sown, crops not yet grown. Nothing did grow there. The seedlings poked up through the dark earth for sunlight, found none, died. Sunlight was shaded out by the dense clouds of dust exploded out of the ground by the H-bombs. It was the Cretaceous repeated; extinction was in the air.

There were mountains of stored food in the rich countries of North America and Europe, of course, but they melted swiftly. The rich countries had much stored wealth in the form of their livestock. Every steer was a million calories of protein and fat. When it was slaughtered, it saved thousands of other calories of grain and roughage for every day lopped off its life in feed. The cattle and pigs and sheep—even the goats and horses; even the pet bunnies and the chicks; even the very kittens and hamsters—they all died quickly and were eaten, to eke out the stores of canned foods and root vegetables and grain. There was no rationing of the slaughtered meat. It had to be eaten before it spoiled.

Of course, even in the rich countries the supplies were not equally distributed. The herds and the grain elevators were not located on Times Square or in the Loop. It took troops to convey corn from Iowa to Boston and Dallas and Philadelphia. Before long, it took killing. Then it could not be done at all.

So the cities starved first. As the convoys of soldiers made the changeover from seizing food for the cities to seizing food for themselves, the riots began, and the next wave of mass death. These casualties didn't usually die of hunger. They died of someone else's.

It didn't take long. By the end of "summer" the frozen remnants of the cities were all the same. A few thousand skinny, freezing desperadoes survived in each, sitting guard over their troves of canned and dried and frozen foodstuffs.

Every river in the world was running sludgy with mud to its mouth, as the last of the trees and grasses died and relaxed their grip on the soil. Every rain washed dirt away. As the winter dark deepened the rains turned to snow. The Flaming Mountains were sheeted in ice now, ghostly, glassy fingers uplifted to the gloom. Men could walk across the Thames at London now, the few men who were left. And across the Hudson, across the Whangpoo, across the Missouri between the two Kansas Cities. Avalanches rumbled down on what was left of Denver. In the stands of dead timber grubs flourished. The starved predators scratched them out and devoured them. Some of the predators were human. The last of the Hawaiians were finally grateful for their termites.

A Western human being—comfortably pudgy on a diet of twenty-eight hundred calories a day, resolutely jogging to keep the flab away or mournfully conscience-stricken at the thickening thighs and the waistbands that won't quite close—can survive for forty-five days without food. By then the fat is gone. Protein reabsorptions of the muscles is well along. The plump housewife or businessman is a starving scarecrow. Still, even then care and nursing can still restore health.

Then it gets worse.

Dissolution attacks the nervous system. Blindness begins. The flesh of the gums recedes, and the teeth fall out. Apathy becomes pain, then agony, then coma.

Then death. Death for almost every person on Earth. . . .

For forty days and forty nights the rain fell, and so did the temperature. Iceland froze over.

To Harry Malibert's astonishment and dawning relief, Iceland was well equipped to do that. It was one of the few places on Earth that could be submerged in snow and ice and still survive.

There is a ridge of volcanoes that goes almost around the Earth. The part that lies between America and Europe is called the Mid-Atlantic Ridge, and most of it is under water. Here and there, like boils erupting along a forearm, volcanic islands poke up above the surface. Iceland is one of them. It was because Iceland was volcanic that it could survive when most places died of freezing, but it was also because it had been cold in the first place.

The survival authorities put Malibert to work as soon as they found out who he was. There was no job opening for a radio astronomer interested in contacting far-off (and very likely nonexistent) alien races. There was, however, plenty of work for persons with scientific training, especially if they had the engineering skills of a man who had run Arecibo for two years. When Malibert was not nursing Timothy Clary through the slow and silent convalescence from his pneumonia, he was calculating heat losses and pumping rates for the piped geothermal water.

Iceland filled itself with enclosed space. It heated the spaces with water from the boiling underground springs.

Of heat it had plenty. Getting the heat from the geyser fields to the enclosed spaces was harder. The hot water was as hot as ever, since it did not depend at all on sunlight for its calories, but it took a lot more of it to keep out a − 30°C chill than a + 5°C one. It wasn't just to keep the surviving people warm that they needed energy. It was to grow food.

Iceland had always had a lot of geothermal greenhouses. The flowering ornamentals were ripped out and food plants put in their place. There was no sunlight to make the vegetables and grains grow, so the geothermal power-generating plants were put on max output. Solar-spectrum incandescents flooded the trays with photons. Not just in the old greenhouses. Gymnasia, churches, schools—they all began to grow food under the glaring lights. There was other food, too, metric tons of protein baaing and starving in the hills. The herds of sheep were captured and slaughtered and dressed—and put outside again, to freeze until needed. The animals that froze to death on the slopes were bulldozed into heaps of a hundred, and left where they were. Geodetic maps were carefully marked to show the locations of each heap.

It was, after all, a blessing that Reykjavik had been nuked. That meant half a million fewer people for the island's resources to feed.

When Malibert was not calculating load factors, he was out in the desperate cold, urging on the workers. Sweating navvies tried to muscle shrunken fittings together in icy foxholes that their body heat kept filling with icewater. They listened patiently as Malibert tried to give orders—his few words of Icelandic was almost useless, but even the navvies sometimes spoke tourist-English. They checked their radiation monitors, looked up at the storms overhead, returned to their work and prayed. Even Malibert almost prayed when one day, trying to locate the course of the buried coastal road, he looked out on the sea ice and saw a gray-white ice hummock that was not an ice hummock. It was just at the limits of visibility, dim on the fringe of the road crew's work lights, and it moved. "A polar bear!" he whispered to the head of the work crew, and everyone stopped while the beast shambled out of sight.

From then on they carried rifles.

When Malibert was not (incompetent) technical adviser to the task of keeping Iceland warm or (almost incompetent, but learning) substitute father to Timothy Clary, he was trying desperately to calculate survival chances. Not just for them; for the entire human race. With all the desperate flurry of survival work, the Icelanders spared time to think of the future. A study team was created, physicists from the University of Reykjavik, the surviving Supply officer from the Keflavik airbase, a meteorologist on work-study from the University of Leyden to learn about North Atlantic air masses. They met in the gasthuis where Malibert lived with the boy, and usually Timmy sat silent next to Malibert while they talked. What they wanted was to know how long the dust cloud would persist. Some day the particles would finish dropping from the sky, and then the world could be reborn—if enough survived to parent a new race, anyway. But when? They could not tell. They did not know how long, how cold, how killing the nuclear winter would be. "We don't know the megatonnage," said Malibert, "we don't know what atmospheric changes have taken place, we don't know the rate of isolation. We only know it will be bad."

"It is already bad," grumbled Thorsid Magnesson, Director of Public Safety. (Once that office had had something to do with catching criminals, when the major threat to safety was crime.)

"It will get worse," said Malibert, and it did. The cold deepened. The reports from the rest of the world dwindled. They plotted maps to show what they knew to show. One set of missile maps, to show where the strikes had been—within a week that no longer mattered, because the deaths from cold already began to outweigh those from blast. They plotted isotherm maps, based on the scattered weather reports that came in—maps that had to be changed every day, as the freezing line marched toward the Equator. Finally the maps were irrelevant. The whole world was cold then. They plotted fatality maps—the percentages of deaths in each area, as they could infer them from the reports they received, but those maps soon became too frightening to plot.

The British Isles died first, not because they were nuked but because they were not. There were too many people alive there. Britain never owned more than a four-day supply of food. When the ships stopped coming they starved. So did Japan. A little later, so did Bermuda and Hawaii and Canada's offshore provinces; and then it was continents' turn.

And Timmy Clary listened to every word.

The boy didn't talk much. He never asked after his parents, not after the first few days. He did not hope for good news, and did not want bad. The boy's infection was cured, but the boy himself was not. He ate half of what a hungry child should devour. He ate that only when Malibert coaxed him.

The only thing that made Timothy look alive was the rare times when Malibert could talk to him about space. There were many in Iceland who knew about Harry Malibert and SETI, and a few who cared about it almost as much as Malibert himself. When time permitted they would get together, Malibert and his groupies. There was Lars the postman (now pick-and-shovel ice excavator, since there was no mail), Ingar the waitress from the Loftleider Hotel (now stitching heavy drapes to help insulate dwelling walls), Elda the English teacher (now practical nurse, frostbite cases a specialty). There were others, but those three were always there when they could get away. They were Harry Malibert fans who had read his books and dreamed with him of radio messages from weird aliens from Aldebaran, or worldships that could carry million-person populations across the galaxy, on voyages of a hundred thousand years. Timmy listened, and drew sketches of the worldships. Malibert supplied him with dimensions. "I talked to Gerry Webb," he said, "and he'd worked it out in detail. It is a matter of rotation rates and strength of materials. To provide the proper simulated gravity for the people in the ships, the shape has to be a cylinder and it has to spin—sixteen kilometers is what the diameter must be. Then the cylinder must be long enough to provide space, but not so long that the dynamics of spin cause it to wobble or bend—perhaps sixty kilometers long. One part to live in. One part to store fuel. And at the end, a reaction chamber where hydrogen fusion thrusts the ship across the Galaxy."

"Hydrogen bombs," said the boy. "Harry? Why don't the bombs wreck the worldship?"

"It's engineering," said Malibert honestly, "and I don't know the details. Gerry was going to give his paper at the Portsmouth meeting; it was one reason I was going." But, of course, there would never be a British Interplanetary Society meeting in Portsmouth now, ever again.

Elda said uneasily, "It is time for lunch soon. Timmy? Will you eat some soup if I make it?" And did make it, whether the boy promised or not. Elda's husband had worked at Keflavik in the PX, an accountant; unfortunately he had been putting in overtime there when the follow-up missile did what the miss had failed to do, and so Elda had no husband left, not enough even to bury.

Even with the earth's hot water pumped full velocity through the straining pipes it was not warm in the gasthuis. She wrapped the boy in blankets and sat near him while he dutifully spooned up the soup. Lars and Ingar sat holding hands and watching the boy eat. "To hear a voice from another star," Lars said suddenly, "that would have been fine."

"There are no voices," said Ingar bitterly. "Not even ours now. We have the answer to the Fermi paradox."

And when the boy paused in his eating to ask what that was, Harry Malibert explained it as carefully as he could:

"It is named after Enrico Fermi, a scientist. He said, 'We know that there are many billions of stars like our sun. Our sun has planets, therefore it is reasonable to assume that some of the other stars do also. One of our planets has living things on it. Us, for instance, as well as trees and germs and horses. Since there are so many stars, it seems almost certain that some of them, at least, have also living things. People. People as smart as we are—or smarter. People who can build spaceships, or send radio messages to other stars, as we can.' Do you understand so far, Timmy?" The boy nodded, frowning, but— Malibert was delighted to see—kept on eating his soup. "Then, the question Fermi asked was, 'Why haven't some of them come to see us?' "

"Like in the movies," the boy nodded. "The flying saucers."

"All those movies are made-up stories, Timmy. Like Jack and the Beanstalk, or Oz. Perhaps some creatures from space have come to see us sometime, but there is no good evidence that this is so. I feel sure there would be evidence if it had happened. There would have to be. If there were many such visits, ever, then at least one would have dropped the Martian equivalent of a McDonald's Big Mac box, or a used Sirian flash cube, and it would have been found and shown to be from somewhere other than the Earth. None ever has. So there are only three possible answers to Dr. Fermi's question. One, there is no other life. Two, there is, but they want to leave us alone. They don't want to contact us, perhaps because we frighten them with our violence, or for some reason we can't even guess it. And the third reason—" Elda made a quick gesture, but Malibert shook his head—"is that perhaps as soon as any people get smart enough to do all those things that get them into space—when they have all the technology we do—they also have such terrible bombs and weapons that they can't control them anymore. So a war breaks out. And they kill themselves off before they are fully grown up."

"Like now," Timothy said, nodding seriously to show he understood. He had finished his soup, but instead of taking the plate away Elda hugged him in her arms and tried not to weep.

The world was totally dark now. There was no day or night, and would not be again for no one could say how long. The rains and snows had stopped. Without sunlight to suck water up out of the oceans there was no moisture left in the atmosphere to fall. Floods had been replaced by freezing droughts. Two meters down the soil of Iceland was steel hard, and the navvies could no longer dig. There was no hope of laying additional pipes. When more heat was needed all that could be done was to close off buildings and turn off their heating pipes. Elda's patients now were less likely to be frostbite and more to be the listlessness of radiation sickness as volunteers raced in and out of the Reykjavik ruins to find medicine and food. No one was spared that job. When Elda came back on a snowmobile from a foraging trip to the Loftleider Hotel she brought back a present for the boy. Candy bars and postcards from the gift shop; the candy bars had to be shared, but the postcards were all for him. "Do you know what these are?" she asked. The cards showed huge, squat, ugly men and women in the costumes of a thousand years ago. "They're trolls. We have myths in Iceland that the trolls lived here. They're still here, Timmy, or so they say; the mountains are trolls that just got too old and tired to move anymore."

"They're made-up stories, right?" the boy asked seriously, and did not grin until she assured him they were. Then he made a joke. "I guess the trolls won," he said.

"Ach, Timmy!" Elda was shocked. But at least the boy was capable of joking, she told herself, and even graveyard humor was better than none. Life had become a little easier for her with the new patients—easier because for the radiation-sick there was very little that could be done—and she bestirred herself to think of ways to entertain the boy.

And found a wonderful one.

Since fuel was precious there were no excursions to see the sights of Iceland-under-the-ice. There was no way to see them anyway in the eternal dark. But when a hospital chopper was called up to travel empty to Stokksnes on the eastern shore to bring back a child with a broken back, she begged space for Malibert and Timmy. Elda's own ride was automatic, as duty nurse for the wounded child. "An avalanche crushed his house," she explained. "It is right under the mountains, Stokksnes, and landing there will be a little tricky, I think. But we can come in from the sea and make it safe. At least in the landing lights of the helicopter something can be seen."

They were luckier than that. There was more light. Nothing came through the clouds, where the billions of particles that had once been Elda's husband added to the trillions of trillions that had been Detroit and Marseilles and Shanghai to shut out the sky. But in the clouds and under them were snakes and sheets of dim color, sprays full of dull red, fans of pale green. The aurora borealis did not give much light. But there was no other light at all except for the faint glow from the pilot's instrument panel. As their eyes widened they could see the dark shapes of the Vatnajökull slipping by below them. "*Big* trolls," cried the boy happily, and Elda smiled too as she hugged him.

The pilot did as Elda had predicted, down the slopes of the eastern range, out over the sea, and cautiously back in to the little fishing village. As they landed, red-tipped flashlights guiding them, the copter's landing lights picked out a white lump, vaguely saucer-shaped. "Radar dish," said Malibert to the boy, pointing.

Timmy pressed his nose to the freezing window. "Is it one of them, Daddy Harry? The things that could talk to the stars?"

The pilot answered: "Ach, no, Timmy—military, it is." And Malibert said:

"They wouldn't put one of those here, Timothy. It's too far north. You wanted a place for a big radio telescope that could search the whole sky, not just the little piece of it you can see from Iceland."

And while they helped slide the stretcher with the broken child into the helicopter, gently, kindly as they could be, Malibert was thinking about those places, Arecibo and Woomara and Socorro and all the others. Every one of them was now dead and certainly broken with a weight of ice and shredded by the mean winds. Crushed, rusted, washed away, all those eyes on space were blinded now; and the thought saddened Harry Malibert, but not for long. More gladdening than anything sad was the fact that, for the first time, Timothy had called him "Daddy."

In one ending to the story, when at last the sun came back it was too late. Iceland had been the last place where human beings survived, and Iceland had finally starved. There was nothing alive anywhere on Earth that spoke, or invented machines, or read books. Fermi's terrible third answer was the right one after all.

But there exists another ending. In this one the sun came back in time. Perhaps it was just barely in time, but the food had not yet run out when daylight brought the first touches of green in some parts of the world, and plants began to grow again from frozen or hoarded seed. In this ending Timothy lived to grow up. When he was old enough, and after Malibert and Elda had got around to marrying, he married one of their daughters. And of their descendants—two generations or a dozen generations later—one was alive on the day when Fermi's paradox became a quaintly amusing old worry, as irrelevant and comical as a fifteenth-century mariner's fear of falling off the edge of the flat Earth. On that day the skies spoke, and those who lived in them came to call.

Perhaps that is the true ending of the story, and in it the human race chose not to squabble and struggle within itself, and so extinguish itself finally into the dark. In this ending human beings survived, and saved all the science and beauty of life, and greeted their star-born visitors with joy. . . .

But that is in fact what did happen!

At least, one would like to think so.

AFTERWORD
FIFTY YEARS AND COUNTING

I DON'T KNOW IF Johnny Appleseed ever went back, after dropping all those seeds over all those years, to see how the trees had grown. I think I know how he would have felt if he had, though. In much the same way, what we have here is a big slice of my life—half a century's worth of those of my short stories and novelettes that best pleased my estimable editor, James Frenkel. Some of these stories were written while I was in my twenties, some when I was well into my—well, never mind exactly which decade we're talking about. Many were written in whatever home I was living in at the time—the big old New Jersey house, where I could look from my third-floor office across the river at the town of Red Bank, or my present office in my almost as big (but never big enough) home in Palatine, Illinois. Many were written wherever I happened to be at the time—sitting on a wharf in the East River on sunny summer days, or in an airplane, in a hotel, on a ship or (in at least one case) in the pro station of the Air Force Base of Chanute Field, Illinois, the only place where I could use my typewriter late on a Saturday night.

Apart from the sites of their generation many of these stories have special personal associations for me. "The Celebrated No-Hit Inning" came about when Horace Gold told me I couldn't write a science fiction story about baseball. If you've ever heard the 1970s British rock group that called themselves The Icicle Works, my story "The Day the Icicle Works Closed" will tell you where they got their name. "Day Million" is special to me because it wrote itself so quickly and easily, one night between midnight and dawn—and (I should admit) because the piece works so well when I do a reading. "The Gold at the Starbow's End" was in two ways a first: the first story all my own that appeared in *Analog* (although John Campbell had published a number of my collaborations he never took a solo job), as well as being the very first story Ben Bova bought when he took over after John's death. (The readers, used to thirty-seven years of John Campbell's G-rated editing, didn't quite know what to make of my story's somewhat sexual content. In that month's poll 50 percent of the readers voted it in first place, the other 50 percent in last.) "The Meeting" gave me the first Hugo I had ever won as a writer (I'd picked up a couple as editor of the magazine *If*)—and the only one ever given to my vastly underappreciated collaborator, Cyril Kornbluth. "Shaffery Among the Immortals" sticks out in my memory because of two things Isaac Asimov said to me about it—first, that he hadn't known I was capable of writing that sort of story; second, that he wished he had done it himself. "Let the Ants Try" was the first short story of mine that I remained pleased with after I saw it in print (which makes all the more humbling the fact that the idea was given to me by my friend and boss at *Popular Science*, George Spoerer, who would not accept a share in either the payment or the byline.)

"Growing Up in Edge City" stays with me because I didn't know I was going to write it until it happened; I was visiting friends in Cape May, New Jersey; they had to go out on family business, leaving me alone in an otherwise empty house with a coffee pot and a typewriter, and the story came out. "To See Another Mountain" is in my mind inextricably linked to my favorite of all violin concerti, Mendelssohn's E-minor, because I played the record of it over and over while I was writing the story. . . .

Well, enough of that; the stories really must speak for themselves. I should only add that, as every writer knows, writing is hard and sometimes painful work, while having written, on the other hand, is pure joy. So producing these stories has, on balance, been fun for me . . . and I hope reading them has been pleasurable for you as well.

—Frederik Pohl
Palatine, Illinois
March 2005

ABOUT THE AUTHOR

FREDERIK POHL has written science fiction for more than fifty years. His novel *Gateway* won the Hugo, Nebula, and John W. Campbell Memorial Awards for best SF novel. *Man Plus* won the Nebula Award, and altogether he has won four Hugo Awards and two Nebula Awards, among his many awards. His most recent novel is *The Boy Who Would Live Forever*.

In addition to his solo fiction, Pohl has collaborated with other writers, including C. M. Kornbluth, Lester del Rey, and Jack Williamson. One Pohl-Kornbluth collaboration, *The Space Merchants,* is a bestselling classic of satiric science fiction. *The Starchild Trilogy* with Williamson is one of the more notable collaborations in the field.

Pohl became a magazine editor when still a teenager. In the 1960s he piloted *Worlds of If* to three successive Hugos for best magazine. He has edited original-story anthologies, notably the seminal *Star* series of the early 1950s. Among his other activities in the field, he has been a literary agent, has edited lines of science fiction books, and has been president of the Science Fiction Writers of America. He and his wife, Elizabeth Anne Hull, an academic active in the Science Fiction Research Association, live in Palatine, Illinois.

CPSIA information can be obtained at www.ICGtesting.com
Printed in the USA
LVOW10s1910260914

406078LV00001B/74/P